KILLER TRILOGY

THE COMPLETE SERIES

ALEXIS ABBOTT

PATHFORGERS PUBLISHING

Get an EXCLUSIVE book, **FREE** just as a thank you for signing up for my newsletter! Plus you'll never miss a new release, cover reveal, or promotion!

http://alexisabbott.com/newsletter

KILLER FOR HIRE

LUCA

I'm not doing this for me.

Drops of rain patter on the crumpled piece of paper I'm holding in my hand as I squint at the running ink on it. It's the only piece of evidence for what I'm going to do tonight. Written on it is nothing but the address and room number Claudio gave me. Leaning on the back of my car, cigarette in my mouth, my lips curls into a frown at the thought of that smug bastard.

The scrape of my lighter is the only sound beside the rain in the alley where I've parked, and once I light my cigarette, I flick the tongue of flame on again to hold up to the scrap of paper, watching the red glow eat away at it and the words on it before there's nothing but a blank scrap left. I let the little cinder fall to the ground and watch it die out in the raindrops on the asphalt.

I put out the cigarette and stick it in my pocket. I'm not leaving any evidence, even this far from what's about to take place. It would be a rookie mistake. I'm young, but I'm not that stupid.

And with so much on the line, I will not take any chances.

I set off through the alleyways, staying off the main roads as much as I can as I wind through the streets of the Bronx. I've lived here long enough to know my way around, and I know that I need to keep a low profile tonight.

Not that it's going to matter after I do what I'm about to. The Bronx is big, but my community is small. We're tight-knit. Word will spread. It'll be on everyone's mind when they see me.

Mafioso.

I feel anger boiling up inside me as I walk, my footsteps nearly silent. That word cast a darkness over my child-hood. I could sense it in every shadow. Now, that's the very same inky blackness I walk in.

But for her, I'd walk through the fires of hell.

I don't have far to go. I turn yet another corner, and a cat perched on a dumpster slinks off silently, a freshly-killed rat in its mouth. As I approach the corner, I glance out to make sure the way is clear.

I hold my place and keep still in the cover of the brick wall as a pair of drunk men stumble by, arm-in-arm. As they laugh their worries away, I go unnoticed. I wait for their voices to fade away around another corner before I slip around leaving the sidewalk and stepping onto the filthy, grassy space below an overpass. I can see my goal ahead of me.

It's a hotel, and not the kind business travelers reserve for ritzy trips or vacations. I'm looking at it from the back under a worn-down overpass, and I know from experience it isn't much prettier in front. It's attached to a storage facility with a rusted sign.

I'm tall, standing at least a head over most men, and I have the broad shoulders to match. My clothes hide the muscular build under them, bulked up and toned from years of manual labor. You can see a hint of that life in my rough, powerful hands when I let them slip from my front pocket. I'm clean-shaven, so I have my hood up and a pair of sunglasses covering my eyes. Intimidating as I am, this hotel would let me walk through the front door up to the rooms if I wanted.

But if I'm going to sink into the shadows. I'll do it with finesse.

I make my way to one of the pillars that support the overpass, and there I wait. I know time is passing, and I don't have much of it. I glance to the service door impatiently. My window of opportunity is only open so long.

My job tonight is straightforward. A man must die. But like many men who've earned the mafia's crosshairs, he's skittish. Afraid. Always looking over his shoulder. A man like that could run at a moment's notice. A man like that could fight viciously. So a man like that needs to be taken by surprise.

That takes bait.

Tonight, that bait is a woman. It's a pretty common tactic for the mafia. They'll set up a call girl to meet with the mark as if he's going out for a good time, usually at a hotel like this. Usually at nicer ones, but this guy is apparently a real lowlife, an old loan shark they found out was taking a little more than his weekly cut.

They're all monsters tearing each other apart.

Except the girls. I know what the mafia can be like with women. And all Claudio told me was that this girl is new, and that she's not to be harmed, just dropped off somewhere on her way to her next job. I've got a bad feeling in my gut. I'm not just worrying about whether this girl will botch the whole job tonight. I'm worried I'll be driving her to something worse, and that I'll just be another set of hands sending someone innocent further in over her head.

And if I'm going to be working for the mafia, I'd better

get used to it. There's more at stake than my conscience, in my case.

But I don't have any more time to think about this woman I've never even met.

I hear the click of the door, and I hear footsteps traveling out, along with the loud clinking of a garbage cart full of trash bags.

I waste no time. The second the janitor has his back to the door, I dart behind him and into the building. I've stepped inside a small utility room with a cleaner's cart sitting unattended. Without wasting a moment, I grab a pair of latex gloves from it and move on. A moment later, I step out into the hallway. My hood up, and my heart is racing.

Maybe I was meant to be a hunter after all.

I know I'm going to be caught on camera. Maybe the mob wants me to take the fall for this. But if I'm fast enough and have luck on my side, the only thing the camera will catch is a tall hooded man with unclear features.

Room 232, I recite in my head. I head up the nearest set of stairs I can find, seeing nobody in the hallways. It's late enough that most are asleep for the night. I glance at the room numbers on my way through the hall, and I feel a pulse race through my veins as I see the number I'm after.

I pass it by, heading to the bathrooms just a few doors down. One more stop, and the timing has to be perfect.

I enter the bathroom and head for the second stall down, entering and closing the door behind me. As soon as I'm in, I stoop down onto the cool tile floor and slip the latex gloves on. Carefully, I reach around the back of the toilet. My fingers brush against something small and plastic.

A janitor's master keycard. It was planted earlier by a

friend of the mafia. At least, that's what they call the men and women that are either paid off or under threat.

As I take the card in hand, I check my watch, standing and turning around. Right on time. Now I have to wait for the mark to get in place.

But that thought's interrupted as the bathroom door swings open, and footsteps echo in the ugly little room.

I freeze. My mind races with possibilities in an instant. Did the staff see me come in? Have the police been tipped off? Is it some random joe coming to waste my time? None of the options are good, and every muscle in my body is tense. Nothing can go wrong here.

One wrong move, and everything could go to hell.

Then my eye catches a glimpse of the man in the bathroom mirror when he walks past my stall. Skinny, white, wispy mustache, ropey muscles, graying brown hair, and green eyes.

It's my mark.

He turns a faucet on and starts to run cold water, splashing some in his face and rubbing it as he lets out a groan followed by an ugly shiver. I hear the rattle of a pill bottle, and he pops something into his mouth. As if there were any shadow of a doubt this is my man, he's taking a pill to keep him stiff.

My jaw is set. My hand is burning to go to the gun tucked behind me. All it would take would be one swift motion, and I could be out there. He hasn't noticed me watching. If a man as tall as me were to step out, dressed like I am, he'd bolt. Could I take him down before then? It could be quick, clean, and there would be no risk to the girl in the room.

I see him staring in the mirror, and his eyes flit to the closed door of my stall. I'm bent enough that my head doesn't stick out the top, but just how skittish is this man?

He peers at the door silently for a moment. Does he

suspect something? Will he run? In that instant, I know what it means for the wolf to stare at a deer from the shadows.

The man crooks his arm and lets out a hacking cough, spitting something vile into the sink before washing his mouth off and popping a mint. I feel my muscles start to relax as he turns and makes his way out the door, no more alert than a moment ago. He doesn't suspect a thing. I know the walk of someone who's hiding something.

As easy as it would have been to take him, I had to restrain myself. There would be a cleaner coming after me to cover my tracks. They're specialists who make sure the crime scene was scrubbed clean of any evidence. It's grizzly work, but necessary for the people who do this kind of business.

People like me, I remind myself.

I check my watch, each second ticking by as if it were a minute. I have to give the mark time to get into the room and feel safe. If I burst out of the bathroom and barrel after him, he'll run. If I kick down the door the moment he goes in, he might try something stupid. The deer is most exposed when its head is down to graze.

I shudder. It's a disgusting thought.

But I take deep, slow breaths and let my body focus itself as I count to fifty, visualizing the man's movements in my head. I imagine him walking down the stained carpet of the hallway to Room 232...his cardkey slipping in...the door swinging open...the terrified sight of the girl on the bed...and he steps forward, closing the door behind him as he slips his jacket off. I can see his yellowed, grinning teeth in my mind's eye when I can't keep focus any longer.

The mafia wants to treat girls like disposable things to throw away when they're used up. But when I think of a young girl being used to lure such human slime in, my gut turns, and even though I have no idea who the woman behind that door is, all I can picture is one girl.

The one girl in the world I'd kill for.

I can't take it any longer. I slide open the latch of my door as quietly as I can, and I let my legs carry me out of the bathroom, cardkey in hand.

The walk to Room 232 is like pushing through a dream. There's no going back after this. It isn't like fighting behind the workshop with the other Italians I call my brothers, my friends. It isn't like hunting a deer, either. My uncle's teaching is in my head like a ringing in my ears.

To kill a man is to cross a line there's no coming back from.

I hold the cardkey up to the slot and listen. The doors are heavy. I can hardly hear a thing through there. That's good, but…

The sound of a woman's voice on the other side of the door reaches me, and my blood runs cold. I know that voice.

No. It can't be.

Without another moment's wait, I slide the cardkey and push through the door, vanishing from the hallway like a shadow.

"The fuck?!" is the shout that greets me.

Then a girl's cry of fear, and my eyes fall on the both of them.

His belt and pants are already undone, and there's the unmistakable look of lust written on his face. But my eyes are only on her.

She's half-sitting on the bed, one hand up at the beautiful dress that he's already started taking off her. Her face is turned away, and she's raising her other arm to shield herself from what she knows is coming. Everything about her body language says she's terrified.

Instinct takes over.

I forget about the gun I brought. I won't need it. I lunge forward as the man dives for his jacket, no doubt reaching for his own weapon. Before he can reach it, I'm on him.

I seize his wrist and thrust my palm into his outstretched arm at the elbow. With a sickening crack, it snaps, and he lets out a croaking gasp of pain.

Without thought, pure, raw adrenaline coursing through my body and awakening what I was built to do, I easily wrap my arm around his mouth, muffling his scream as he thrashes in my arms. But he's nothing compared to me. All the strength in his frail bones amounts to an ounce of mine.

He struggles in my grip, and his good hand grasps at my leg, pounding, doing anything he can, and finally, he finds his wits and reaches for something in his pant leg. I see the flash of a blade.

CRACK.

The man's knife falls from his hand as his grip slackens, and slowly, I feel his body go limp in my arms. His neck is broken, eyes going glassy as he stares up at the ceiling. All it took was one quick motion, and it was over.

Gently, I lower the body to the ground before standing up over it, looking down at my kill.

My first kill.

I'm still as I look at him. I expected my hands to be shaking, my body to be trembling, but my massive frame doesn't shudder. I'm poised. Ready for more. I'm not stupid, I know what my body is capable of. But it's something different to look down at a corpse and realize your body is ready to do it again.

"Oh...oh my God!" The shuddering cry snaps me out of my thoughts, and my heart comes alive again as I look at the woman on the bed. She isn't looking down at the body in horror. She's looking at me.

Our eyes meet. And even through the hood and the

glasses, I know she recognizes me. How couldn't she? Her hazel eyes are staring up at me, as expressive and deep as the first time I'd seen them.

And they're full of fear. Fear of *me*.

How can it be her? How can she be the girl they got for this? Claudio never mentioned her. Of course he didn't. He knew it would be the one thing that would make me turn down this job. That putting her in danger would be the one thing that would keep me from acting.

I start to reach for her with the gloved hand that just took a life, and for the first time, I watch her recoil from me, clutching her clothes close to her as her lips part, quivering.

"...Luca?"

SEVERAL YEARS LATER...

*I*t's early.

God, it's too early.

With a heavy sigh, I poke my arm out from underneath the comforter to swat the alarm clock, accidentally knocking it off the night stand in the process. The loud clatter of plastic on tile immediately sends my brain into full-on wake-up mode.

Well, that's one way to kickstart another grueling Monday grind.

I sit up in bed and push the hair out of my eyes, tucking it behind my ears as I blink blearily in the dim light of dawn. The sunlight streaking in through the cracks in the blinds tells me that I've probably snoozed the alarm at least four times before finally turning it off. I have never been a natural morning person, and if it were totally up to me, I wouldn't get out of bed until at least eleven. But I'm not one of those girls lucky enough to play to my own whims. I don't get to sleep in. I've got serious responsibilities, and if I don't get up now and get the day started, the delicate balance that keeps all the balls rolling in my life will be seriously disrupted. There is a lot to juggle, and it all starts right now. Every weekday at six in the morning.

So I launch myself out of bed, wiggling my feet into my worn-down slippers, and pad my way across the bedroom to the little en suite bathroom to start the shower. While I wait for the water to warm up, I yawn and lean over the sink to look at myself in the mirror. Sleepy hazel eyes with purplish bags below them blink back at me. I try to force myself to smile. It's something my dad used to always tell me: "Smile, even when it's the last thing you feel like doing, and you'll be amazed at how your outlook can brighten just a little bit."

But my smile in the mirror just looks lopsided and forced, and I quickly look away. I wish it were easier to follow my dad's advice, but these days, everything seems a lot harder than it was when he was still alive.

As the mirror begins to fog up, I shed my nightgown and slippers and slip under the hot stream of water. A pleasurable shiver runs down my spine while steam gathers around me. It's a bad habit, I know, taking such hot showers. "One of these days you're going to boil yourself alive in there," my mom has told me on numerous occasions. But I can't help it. I love the feeling of scrubbing all my worries away, feeling the hot water cleanse my skin and make me feel brand new again. Shower time is one of the few moments I get to purely be myself and give into my own needs throughout the day. There was a time, long ago before things got so hectic and crazy, when I used to sink into a hot bubble bath and stay there for hours reading or just daydreaming about the future. About pretty things and handsome boys and faraway places I would someday visit.

Nowadays, I've had to settle for a steamy shower in the morning.

Still, I can't help but wonder if my love for a good scrub is part of what fuels me to keep plugging away at the struggling family business. I manage a luxury bath goods shop called Bathing Beauty, and even though it's been a long, long time since I was last blessed with the opportunity to partake in any of my sweet-smelling bath bombs or shower gels, I still feel pretty passionate about going into work every day. Sure, it's a lot of effort for not a lot of pay-off, but it's close to my heart just the same. And it's lucky that I feel that way, because my passion almost makes up for the fact that I don't have much hands-on business experience. Nor do I have the kind of financial backing most people need to keep such a frivolous business afloat. But I can't give up. I refuse to.

As I shampoo my hair, I run through the list of things to do today. First of all, I need to remind mom to drop off the power bill. Of course, it would make my life much easier to have all the bills set up to pay automatically online each month. But my mother is old-fashioned, and she likes the ritual of writing a check and handing it to a living, breathing associate. And she's held onto this almost vintage-level quirk for years, even though it's no longer her name on the check anymore. It's mine.

If it were up to her, she would still be signing off on everything. God knows how difficult it is for a woman of her bearing to give up control and lose face like that. I've tried a million times to convince her that it's no big deal, that I don't mind being the breadwinner. But even though these days she's finally given in and allowed me to take control of the finances— purely because the alternative was much worse— she's still quite bitter about the whole thing.

You see, my mother comes from serious money. She's a born-and-raised mafia princess, and she's had the best of everything since the day she was born. So, naturally, our fall from power and money in recent years has hit her pretty hard. Sometimes I find her just poring over old photographs, her finger tracing over the fancy fur-lined coats, Prada handbags, and Hermes scarves she used to wear all the time. She's had to sell a lot of her old wardrobe classics, which to me doesn't seem like a huge loss, since I've never been quite as much of a clotheshorse as my mom, but to her I think it really does feel like she's lost a chunk of her identity.

Someday, though, I'm gonna put her back into the pearls and perfumes she's used to. I know good things are coming. I can feel it. After all, I've often heard that bad luck can only go on for so long until there's a bounce in the opposite direction. As far as I'm concerned, we hit rock bottom years ago, and everything has been on the up-and-up ever since.

But God, is it a long, slow ride back up to the top. And I've had to put aside my own pain to help my mom through hers. Losing my dad... well, it ruined her entire life. It just almost ruined mine.

I turn off the water and start towel-drying my hair, then move on to applying the kind of low-key makeup I tend to live in these days. When I was a teenager, I used to wear the raciest red lipstick and the most outlandishly vivid colors imaginable. Back then, I was never afraid of standing out from the crowd. It wasn't that I was starved for attention, either. Daddy spoiled the hell out of me, and like my mom, I walked around with the kind of self-assured cheekiness you get when you come from money. But I wanted to make a statement. I wanted everything. I wanted to wring every last drop of excitement out of life that I could manage.

Nowadays, I settle for some lightly tinted chapstick, a splash of mascara, and a ponytail. Just enough to make me look professional, yet approachable. God, I wanted to be approachable. Anything to draw a customer into my shop. I was a hard worker, and I had passion out the wazoo, but none of that could matter if I didn't make a sale.

I dress in a simple pair of dark jeans and a summery pink floral blouse, paired with a navy blue blazer and some kitten heels, and then I'm on my way. As I pass my mother's bedroom, I knock gently on the door and say, "Hey, Mom, don't forget to take that power bill downtown, okay? It's in an envelope on the table."

There's the faint sound of the bed creaking and then I hear her footsteps trudging across the room. The door opens just a crack to reveal my mother's face, older and sadder but still beautiful. There is a regal air about her, still, no matter how drastically our circumstances have changed over time. She gives me a nod and runs her hand back over her raven-black hair.

"Of course, dear. I'll see to it this afternoon. Will you be home for dinner?" she asks, stifling a yawn.

I bite my lip.

"Um, maybe. Not sure yet. I have a lot of inventory to do today, and I would hate to keep you waiting on me," I reply, giving her an apologetic half-smile.

"Right, yes. Well, do let me know. I can always call for some pizza or something if you're going to be late. I can wait up for you," she says, and it's hard not to giggle at the way she says pizza, as though it's some bizarre exotic food. I suppose when you've spent most of your life eating caviar, a pepperoni pie delivery might feel a little pedestrian.

"Okay, Mom. Sounds good. I'll text you later," I tell her, blowing her a kiss as I hurry off down the stairs. I hear her door click closed as I rush out the front entry and into my car. I took a little too long in the shower this morning, and I don't want to be late for opening hours at the shop. After all, I am the only employee. If I'm not there to open the store, and a customer just so happens to wander up at 7:30

to find it closed, I'll probably lose that customer for life. One thing I have learned both in studying business and by running one myself, is that every single tiny human interaction counts. If I make one miniscule mistake, I might lose a potential patron. And every one I lose is another sale I lose. Or more.

I really hate math, but even I know that it all adds up quickly.

I make the long drive from our house in Riverdale down to Morris Park, thinking over the work I have to do today. Once I'm inside the shop, I turn on the little radio I keep behind the counter (I can't yet afford to install a real speaker system for background music) and get started. I turn on the coffee maker and start going through my inventory checklist, wiping down counters and making note of what labels need reprinting as I go. That's the cruel beauty of being the one and only employee: you learn how to multitask. Sometimes I think that I've gotten so used to being three people at once, I can hardly remember how to just be myself.

As I sip my coffee, I hear the telltale jingle of the front door being opened. My heart immediately skips a beat and I glance up eagerly, expecting to see a customer. And so early in the day, too! However, my excitement dims slightly when I notice that my customer is just a rough-looking guy, rather than the typical girly-girl the shop usually attracts. For a moment I wonder if maybe he might be lost, having wandered into the wrong business by accident.

Still, I have a role to play. With a big smile, I greet him, "Good morning! Welcome to Bathing Beauty, how can I help you?"

The man looks at me with two cold eyes that make my heart freeze momentarily.

Something about him feels... off. I can't quite put my finger on it, but something about him makes me incredibly uneasy. He's dressed in jeans and a beat-up leather jacket, and it's obvious that he hasn't shaved in several days, judging by the scruff along his jaw. He gives me a wry smirk and strolls up to the counter. Even as I feel myself bristling with nervousness, I don't let the smile fade from my face. *Maybe he's here to buy his sister a birthday gift*, I tell myself, trying to calm my nerves.

"Is there anything in particular you're looking for today?" I ask, trying to keep my tone even and chipper as he stands in front of me, squinting as though he's sizing me up. He chuckles, then gives me an exaggerated once-over. I instantly feel stripped and exposed — a feeling that I despise. My mind immediately flashes back to another time when I felt degraded, and how I felt just like this before getting into that car.

But I force myself to stay strong. I can't think about the past right now. It's just paranoia, getting the better of me. My natural instincts trying to keep me safe, but they're being too over-protective. That's all. That's all.

"I think I found exactly what I'm lookin' for already," he replies, giving me a wink. His voice is gruff, like he's been smoking heavily for years. He does have an admittedly handsome face, and I might have found him attractive when I was a reckless teenager, but these days, guys like him just make me nervous.

"Oh," I answer awkwardly. He leans on the counter, peering toward me.

"This is a pretty nice setup you've got here, ma'am," he says, gesturing broadly.

"Th-thank you," I stutter, damning myself inwardly for being so weak.

"You know," he begins, rubbing his palms together, "I'm a discerning entrepreneur, and I really think you've got somethin' good goin' here. Is business good lately? How's your profit margin?"

"Uh, well, it's… um," I struggle, taken aback by this change in topic. Who the hell is this guy?

Without letting me answer, he continues.

"I've been watching this shop for a while now, and my people think it might be a good place to, uh, make our mark. It's a good thing you're doin' here, bringin' an upstanding business like this to Morris Park. I've got an interest in cleanin' up the neighborhood, so to speak, and it's nice to see a local girl like you set up shop."

"Oh. Well, thank you," I reply, surprised again. This is definitely not the way I thought this conversation was headed a moment ago, but I guess it could be worse.

"Yeah, yeah, so we're thinkin' you could benefit from our services. You know, as a part of the local community here and all," he adds, locking eyes with me.

"I'm sorry, I don't understand," I admit, frowning. If this guy is trying to sell me insurance or something, he's certainly got a weird way of making his pitch.

He takes a phone out of his jacket pocket and quickly sends a text before looking back up at me with a dangerous grin. Suddenly, my whole body is on high alert. Something is definitely wrong here. *Never ignore your instincts, Serena,* the back of my mind nags at me. *It's what'll keep you safe.* But what good is that? I can't exactly dart out of the store like a maniac. My hand reaches out for my phone, but it's too far away to do it discretely.

"Me and my guys, we're all about tackling risk management head-on. Just lookin' out for the neighborhood to maintain the integrity of our little community. I'm sure you understand, right? You're a business-minded girl, I can tell. So, listen up," he says, just as the front door jingles again.

Two hulking, musclebound men dressed in similar clothes have entered the shop. They each flank the first guy, walking around the store with menacing glares on their ugly faces.

Shit. I may be fresh, but I'm not totally naive. This is a shakedown.

As the two goons have a grand old time knocking expensive soaps and displays off the shelves, making me wince, the first guy introduces himself to me.

"I'm Lorenzo. Nice to make your acquaintance, Miss De Laurentis." As soon as he says my last name, I feel my knees buckle. This is bad. This is very bad.

"Now, I like a nice, fragrant bath from time to time, but let's be real here. I'm a lot less interested in the shit you sell here than I am in your profits. And your rent for this lovely space. I know exactly who the hell you are, and I know you're not stupid," he says, lowering his voice to a growl. He comes around to stand behind the counter, effectively boxing me in. My stomach churns and I feel sick.

"Now, look here, I'm a generous man, and I would hate for our little partnership to start out on the wrong foot, so I'm gonna grant you a little more time. I'm not even gonna penalize you for your late payment, see? I've got a heart, you know," Lorenzo says, grinning. The two goons laugh.

"Please don't hurt me," I manage to murmur, the small of my back pressed hard against the countertop while Lorenzo towers over me.

"Oh, I would never. Unless you make me. But I see no reason why we can't have a feel-good agreement. I think you'd rather keep this civil, right?" he answers, narrowing his eyes at me.

My breath is lodged in my throat, my words totally fallen silent. I give him a vigorous nod.

"Atta girl," Lorenzo sneers, patting me on the shoulder. I flinch slightly and he chuckles again before turning and gesturing for the two other guys to follow him out of the store. As he steps out the door, he glances back over his shoulder and says, "Nice doin' business with you, sweetheart. We'll be seein' each other again real soon."

As soon as the door closes and the men disappear from sight, I collapse to the floor behind the counter, pulling my knees in close to my chest. My heartbeat slowly starts to calm again, and I close my eyes, forcing myself to take deep breaths. I should have known this day would come. They just couldn't leave me well enough alone, could they?

I know better than to try and fight them. It's pointless. I'm just one girl against a whole bunch of guys. This isn't my first rodeo. I know how quickly shit goes south when gangbangers are involved.

Still, I find myself asking the question: if Bathing Beauty is barely breaking even right now, then how the hell am I gonna be able to pay protection fees to the mafia? And what's the cost when I can't pay up?

The orange afternoon sun is on my back when I bring my car to a stop about a block away from the well-to-do little store on the corner of the street. When I turn my ignition off, I lean back and just stare at it, letting out a deep breath.

How long has it been?

The light playing off the glass window panes make it impossible to see inside the shop, but the sign outside is clear as ever: Bathing Beauty. I feel a smile on my face. As many mixed memories as it stirs up in me, there's something comforting about knowing it's still there, unchanged as ever. Maybe even a little nicer.

All thanks to her.

I catch a glimpse of myself in the car mirror. I've changed so much over the years. It feels like a lifetime ago that I was just a teenager, freshly landed in America. I kept my hair cut short back then, and my face was clean-shaven. I run a hand through the long locks that hang nearly to my shoulders now. It's grown out thick and wavy. Even I have to admit it's unkempt, and the short, coarse black beard on my face matches.

My voice sounds different, too. I think back to the thick accent I had in those years that I was still learning English, fresh from the old country. I'm so used to it now that English almost sounds as natural as my native Italian on my tongue. I might as well be a different person.

Better that way, I think. When I look into that mirror, I'm not sure I even see myself anymore. What I do see is the face of a man who's done terrible things. A "made man," they call us in this country. *Mafioso.*

What are you really doing here, Luca?

My mind flashes back to her face, that gorgeous face that's kept me going all this time. A bright candle in the darkness.

That face doesn't need to know fear ever again. It doesn't need to know me.

So why am I here, coming to risk dragging the past back? I don't dare turn the ignition and drive off. I've made my decision, and I'm a man of my word.

After all, I remind myself, I'm not here just to see her, to remind myself that she's alive and living happily, that what I did for her was all worth it. I'm here to make sure she's safe.

The Cleaners.

Their name makes my lip curl. They are a gang that sprung up almost overnight, and they've gone from being a nuisance to a threat in just as little time.

A few years ago, they were nobodies in East Harlem. But times changed, East Harlem started to get cleaned up, and that meant the gangs had to move around. Soon, the Bronx found itself with new faces hitting warehouses on the south side. And goddamn, they're vicious.

The Cleaners fight like men who have nothing to lose. I learned that the first week they hit our streets, and hit it hard.

I hit back, harder.

Those days left me with scars and them with worse ones, but the Cleaners have dug their heels in. They've been shaking down business left and right, and one of my boss's associates gave us a tip that some of them might be skulking around here, Morris Park.

This is a nicer part of the Bronx. Places like Bathing Beauty can do pretty well for themselves, if they play their cards right. It would be a gamble to go after businesses this deep into our territory.

But if experience has taught me anything, it's that the Cleaners are gambling men.

I pop on a pair of aviators in case there could be any chance of her still recognizing me—well, that, and a good pair of aviators can do a man some favors—and I step out of the car and cross the street. It's a walk I've thought about taking a long time, but I never wanted to make her see this face again.

I've never wanted Serena to go through that pain again.

But I won't stand by and let a rival gang get to her, either. My associates know that this store in particular is off-limits.

If Serena knew the reason why, it would kill her. All the more reason I must stay a stranger to her.

And the fact that we can't touch Bathing Beauty makes it a prime target for the Cleaners. That's something I can't tolerate.

I reach the simple door and push it open.

There's a rush of fragrant air from inside as a little bell jingles. I nearly have to stoop to step inside. If I felt out of place just being in the nicer side of town, I feel *really* out of place in this quaint little shop. But even so, the place so clearly has her personal touch to it that I can't keep the faintest smile off my bearded face.

At least, until my eyes fall to the floor.

There's broken glass all over, freshly fallen from some

of the shelves and ornate displays lined up all around the shop. Expensive liquid soaps pool on the floor in puddles, some of the sparkling colors swirling together and changing color as they mix. In one corner, one of those fancy chalky balls you throw into a bath has fallen over, and it fizzes and pops in the liquid soap spill.

There's something almost beautiful to the big mess, I have to admit.

I can see brightly-colored footprints leading back and forth from the door to the back of the shop. The space near the checkout counter seems to have been recently cleaned up.

And no sooner has the front door closed behind me than the back door swings open, and the afternoon light filtering in behind me falls on her.

Serena.

I have to keep my jaw from dropping.

Her dark blonde hair shines like gold in the sunlight, playing against her shoulders as if she were posing for a painting. It's grown out a little since we were younger, and it suits her beautifully. Her hazel eyes could be jewels, gazing at me, taking in my form in that first split-second. Her olive-toned skin gives away the Italian blood running strong in her. And as the years passed and the sun kissed her skin, time has been very, very good to her. The Serena I knew as a teenager was a beautiful work-in-progress, and what I'm looking at now is a masterpiece that takes my breath away.

But then I see fear flash through her eyes. An old, familiar fear I'd hoped never to see again. Does she recognize me?

I then realize the sun is behind me, half-blinding her. I must look like little more than a 6'2" silhouette, clad in jeans, a tight-fitting white shirt, and a worn leather jacket that's seen better days.

"Are you...closed?" I say slowly, trying to keep my Italian accent buried.

"Oh, oh no," she says, and I can see the worry melting away from her face. An anxious smile replaces it, and she brushes a strand of hair from her face. I notice she's carrying a large bucket of cleaning supplies in her other arm, and she sets it down on the counter. "Just, um, taking care of a little mess, nothing to close early for!"

"What happened?" my deep voice rumbles as I carefully step into the shop, trying not to step in the bright blue and violet rivers of moisturizer creeping along the tile.

"Well, you know," she laughs nervously, tearing off a few paper towels to gingerly step over to the colorful chalk-ball and pick up the remnants of it. "It's kind of a messy business!"

"I...see." I arch an eyebrow, watching her drop the fizzy thing into a garbage bag. "There are worse things to spill everywhere."

"Yes," she says, as much to herself as to me, visibly trying to keep calm as she looks around at the damage surrounding her. "Yes, there definitely is. Yeah. I've got this. No problem." As if remembering she has a customer, her eyes flutter back toward me, and she bites her lip apologetically. "I'm so sorry, just give me a minute or two and I'll have all this cleaned up!"

She starts to dig through her bucket, but I've already made my way across the shop to the mop leaning against the wall and picked it up. A look of horror crosses her face when she sees me start to drag the thing through the mess.

"Oh- no, you don't have to do that! Really, it won't be long."

I want to glance up at her and silence her with a wink, but I keep my head down as I get some of the fragrant slop pushed into a more manageable puddle. "I came in here to try some soap, didn't I? This can be a test run. What's this one called?" I ask as I dip the mop into a puddle of bright blue.

She's stunned to silence for a few moments, but she finally says absently, "...that's *Blue-bury the Hatchet*."

"Good one," I say, suppressing a grin on my face, and I can feel hers from across the room.

"Thanks."

Not even a minute with her, and I already feel like we've never been apart. But I can't let her feel too comfortable around her. I'm a stranger, after all. I have to play the part.

"Don't you have any other help around here?" I ask, glancing at the back. "It can't be just you running this place alone."

"Just me," she says, emptying the bucket of supplies onto the counter and carrying the bucket to a sink to fill with water. "I've usually got a handle on everything—I promise I'm not *that* much of a mess," she laughs off, and as her back is turned, I can't help but look up at her.

Her ass looks even better than I remember. I feel myself thickening between my legs, and I look back down to the mess as she brings the bucket over to set next to me.

"Usually isn't this bad, I just...had a *really* bad spill this time," she says, raising her eyebrows as she hesitates. I know what she looks like when she's holding something back. She always was a proud girl, and now she's a proud woman.

The years haven't taken her spirit. Nothing could do that.

I dip the tip of my mop into the water and wring it out. I feel her watching me, and it makes me want to work all the harder. But I didn't come here just to clean up.

"Just think of it as free advertising," I say as my strong forearms work the handle. "People will be smelling this from a block away."

I hear her gentle laugh, so full of life and quick wit, and

it makes my heart just a little lighter to be able to draw that out of her so easily.

"It certainly helps draw in burly strangers to work for free," she quips, and I grin as she breaks out some paper towels and spray to start scrubbing the floors in detail where I've already passed by. But I still have my suspicions to chase down.

"From the looks of this place, I'd say burly strangers are the last thing this shop needs—let me guess, did a football team come through here and get a little rowdy?" I'm probing to see how much she's willing to tell me about what happened, because I have a feeling this isn't the kind of mess that happens on accident.

"No, no," she says with that slight flippant scoff that tells me she's lying. Even after all these years, I can read her like a book. Thankfully my new look, the bright light and the rough voice cigarettes gave me keep her from recognizing me. "Just...you know, someone bumps into one of the displays, things start falling, and it's one big chain reaction."

"This is a big chain reaction," I say, glancing at the various bits of broken glass across the shop.

"Tell me about it," she says under her breath.

I'm not convinced for a second, but I let it go as we work together. It goes fast, both of us working as a team— it happened almost wordlessly, but it feels so natural. She still works quickly, thinking I'm a new customer and not wanting to embarrass herself, but I take my time to make sure the job is done well.

"Oh my god," she says as she checks the clock when I stand up from detailing the floors, wiping my hands on a towel, "we've been at this for half an hour!"

"Making good time," I say, looking around the shop proudly. It's cleaned up pretty nicely.

"No, I mean, you spent all this time!" she says, letting

out an incredulous laugh as she washes her hands off and dries them.

"Don't mention it," I say, setting the mop against the wall where I'd found it.

"I think I should," she says, hands on her hips as she smiles at me. "Seriously, though, I really appreciate it. After everything that's happened today, I never expected a stranger to take that kind of time."

"What's happened today?" I ask, quirking a brow, and I see her cheeks tinge with a bit of color.

"Wh- oh, nothing. The guy who caused the accident just kind of ran off, is all," she lies, averting her eyes to the setting sun outside.

"Dirty move," I say, crossing my arms. "Good thing you run a soap store."

She just stares at me in disbelief for a beat before she bursts into a laugh at my awful pun, covering her face for a moment. "Oh...wow," she says, starting to take a few steps toward me. "Who *are* you?"

"Someone who can tell you've had too much on your plate for one day," I say. Every muscle in my body wants to take a step toward her as well, to play the game between us that she's slipping into already. I want to flirt with her, charm her all over again, even as a stranger, take her out for a good time. If I'm *really* honest, I want to bend her over that counter and take her right here and now.

But for her safety, I have to keep my distance. I'm just checking in to make sure she's okay, and then I can disappear from her life all over again. With any luck, she'll never even realize I was back into it.

"Oh, who am I kidding," she says, running a hand through her hair and looking out the door. "You're right. Today's been a nightmare." She looks back to me, eyes flitting up and down my form. "Thank you, though. Really. God, I feel so silly, you didn't come here to--"

"Get some rest," I say, her name on the tip of my tongue before I reel it back in. "I'll come back by tomorrow. Maybe I can take care of any other messes that come up," I say, a boyish smile on my face.

I see the color flush into her cheeks, and she loses her words for a moment before she says, "I'll be here!"

She was a spoiled brat when I knew her, but even then, it was the easiest thing in the world to get her off her guard and swooning. But I liked that about her. She didn't feel shame for her feelings. She felt everything intensely. It was good to see that hadn't changed.

There's so much more I want to say, but I step out into the cool air without another word to her as I hear her voice calling, "Wait, I didn't get your name!"

I pretend not to hear.

Seeing how happy she is now, I can't let our tangled past flood into her life and upset everything she has. She's running her own business, for God's sake.

How would she feel about me if she knew I was an enforcer for the mafia?

I don't even know how I feel about myself.

No, the boy she once knew is gone. And now, there's just me.

I shake that thought off me as I start to walk away from the building. I have to keep my mind clear and focused for business. In truth, I had no plans to leave her for the night. A wrecked shop and a nervous business owner are telltale signs of extortionists coming through. Have the Cleaners gotten to her already? Whatever the case, I was planning to post up in my car and stake the place out for a night until I could watch Serena leave the shop and get to her car without incident. I'd even tail her home to make sure she gets there safely. I'm good enough at this kind of thing that I don't worry about getting caught by her. Hell, I'm good enough at it that I make myself uneasy.

And my fears are validated as I approach my car in time to see a black sedan roll down the street.

I slow my pace, eyes watching it, and I can feel eyes inside it watching me. My hand itches to go to the gun under my jacket. But just after what feels like an eternity, the car picks up speed again and takes off. My lip curls into a grimace.

Serena's being watched.

"Have you been doing those morning affirmations I taught you?" chirps my best friend Rafaela through the speakerphone.

I roll my eyes, relieved that she can't see me do it. It's midday, and the store has been dead-empty for two hours. At this rate, I'm half-tempted to call it a day and just go home, but that ravenous, desperate hunger for a sale keeps me riveted to my usual haunt behind the counter. Besides, my mind is distracted. It's hard to think about work when all my thoughts seem to center around that handsome, rugged guy who came into the shop a few days ago. Last night, I even dreamed about him, only I couldn't quite see his face.

Something about him is so shockingly familiar, but he kept looking away from me, speaking in a low voice. He definitely fit the bill of tall, dark and mysterious. I can't imagine where I would know him from. At first, I thought maybe he was a guy from my classes or something, but I don't remember seeing anyone looking so rough and unkempt on campus. Everything about him seemed to exude mystery, from the way he dodged my gaze and wore his hood up to the way he seemed to appear and disappear without giving me a chance to even ask his name.

My brain has been working overtime to try and figure him out. Why did my body have such a strange, visceral reaction to his presence? It felt almost like deja vu, like we have met before sometime, maybe once upon a dream. It's like he's just on the tip of my tongue, and I can't help but feel like if maybe I had seen his face properly, I would know who he is.

It's enough to drive me mad, especially when work is so boring and there's nothing to distract me from my thoughts. Luckily, Rafaela is between classes right now, so it's the perfect time to chat.

I lean over the phone lying on the counter and reply, "Yeah, yeah. Breathe in, breathe out, I'm a powerful goddess woman who can handle whatever life throws my way, blah blah blah."

"Hey!" she laughs, failing to sound indignant. "You know, that kind of thing really does help a lot of people with their self-confidence. It's not *all* just psycho-babble, I swear."

"I know, I know," I answer, resting my chin on my hands as I watch the rain streak down the front window of the shop. "Maybe that's why it's so slow today," I murmur aloud.

"What?" Rafaela asks, confused.

"Oh, God, sorry. I just zoned out for a minute. It's raining cats and dogs over here. I think maybe that's why nobody is coming into the shop today. You know how New Yorkers are— they're all too comfy in their apartments to go outside unless it's nice out."

Rafaela chuckles. "Yeah, like you wouldn't be snuggled up under a blanket back in Riverdale right now if you had the option."

"True," I admit, sighing. "I wish I was home right now.

Watching TV, painting my nails, sipping some tea… ugh, now you've just killed the last measly dregs of my willpower today. If I can manage to get through the afternoon without calling it quits, it'll be a miracle."

"I feel you there, girl. I literally almost fell asleep on the subway this morning."

I burst out laughing, picturing my friend with her long, curly black hair and signature scarlet lipstick nodding off on the train, falling over into the lap of some scruffy homeless guy. Then I can't help but picture the guy who came into the shop a few days ago. My mystery man. He'd looked pretty scruffy, himself. What is his story? Who is he?

I shake the thought away and reply, "Yeah, that would've been pretty bad."

"I swear, between classes and the bar and studying and trying to still be a good girlfriend to Nico, the grind is about to put me out of commission for good," she laments. "And yeah, I know it's all good for my future or whatever, but really, I'm just tired. You know?"

"Oh, trust me, I know," I agree. "You and me both. We haven't even had a proper girls' night in, like, months. I miss being roommates with you. Are you sure you don't want to move into my empty old house with me and my mom? I'm only half-joking here," I add with a laugh.

"Hmm, tempting offer, but I don't think Mama De Laurentis would be too pleased to have me and Nico move into that old manor. She's a little old for our antics, I think."

I try to visualize what our household would look like—and it is not a pretty picture. My mom is a very private person these days, having retreated into a quiet loneliness to lick her wounds after losing everything years ago when Dad died. Vivacious, quick-talking Rafaela would be the opposite of a calming presence for my mom, even though for me, she's been a lifesaver in the past couple of years. Rafaela and I met in college, when I was studying business and she was a psychology Master's student. Somehow, we ended up having lunch together in the courtyard almost every week, and our friendship blossomed from there. I'm done with school after earning my Bachelor's, but Rafaela is still chiseling away at a PhD. She's six years older than me, but every bit as determined and ambitious, and for a while we even lived together. It was never a permanent situation, as I was still paying for the mortgage on my family home in Riverdale, but during exam times it just made more sense to crash at Rafaela and Nico's apartment rather than wasting time going back and forth all the time.

Living with Rafaela gave me a taste of freedom and independence I still crave, but my duty to keep the family home running and afloat, as well as take care of my mom, keeps me where I am. Sure, it's frustrating sometimes, but my dad taught me that family is the most important thing in the world. And I know he would want me to look after mom and the old house, so I do it for him.

"I'm working at the bar tonight if you want to come by!" Rafaela says brightly. She runs a bar called *Room With A View* alongside her boyfriend Nico, and when I was a student I spent a lot of time there. In fact, I wrote most of my reports and term papers sitting at the corner table of the bar. It was a cozy, homey atmosphere, and I missed it.

"I'll see what I can do. So, is your next class the one with the hot professor?" I ask, quickly changing the subject. But before I can hear Rafaela's response, my attention is distracted by the flash of a shiny black car pulling up to the street parking outside the shop. My heart sinks, my instincts going on high alert. Something feels off, and I realize it's because that car looks like a mobster's ride.

"Nah, unfortunately this is the class with that weird lady who looks like Danny Devito's cousin or something,"

Rafaela is saying through the speakerphone. With a shaking hand, I quickly snatch up the phone and turn off the speaker, pressing the receiver to my face.

"Rafaela, um, I gotta go, babe. I-I'll talk to you later, okay?" I manage to mumble, staring at the front door with my heart hammering away in my chest.

"Wait, what? What's wrong? You sound weird. Is everything okay, Serena?"

"Uh, y-yeah. It's fine. I'm fine. I just—I gotta go. Love you. Bye," I reply quickly, ending the call before she can even respond. I glance down at the phone and shakily type in 9-1-1 before tucking the phone into my pocket. I want to have that number ready to go just in case things go sour. Of course, I realize with a sinking feeling, involving the police would probably only make the situation worse when it comes to the mafia. They've got cops on the take. I know what it's like. I learned just enough from eavesdropping on my dad's conversations years ago to know that I have to tread carefully here. One misstep, and I could lose everything. Hell, I could lose my life.

Just as expected, three skulking figures come through the front door a moment later, led by the same asshole who threatened me before: Lorenzo. And this time, there's no attempt at disarming me with charm or subtlety. The three of them come marching toward me with glowering expressions. I look around quickly, wondering if there's any way I can get out of this, any escape route I can take. But I know it's pointless. These guys are smarter than they look, I'm sure, and they're faster and stronger by far. No. The only thing I can do is stand my ground and take my beating.

I gulp back my fear and try not to let my eyes fill with tears as I face the wrath of the mob.

"Miss De Laurentis, you've been warned," Lorenzo snarls, cornering me behind the counter just like he did the other day. This time, he doesn't mince words. "Maybe I didn't make myself clear enough the last time we spoke, but you better cough up the money. Now. This isn't a negotiation, sweetheart, this is a shakedown. Do you wanna fuckin' die?"

"I-I'm sorry," I murmur. "Business has been slow. I'm barely breaking even as it is."

Lorenzo's eyebrows perk upward and he glances back over his shoulder at the two goons behind him. "You hear that, boys? Hmm, sounds like an excuse to me. And a shitty one, too. Don't you lie to me, you little bitch. We know what kinda money is sunk into this place. Your daddy bankrolled you good, didn't he? You think you can hide that shit from us?"

"No, I swear. That money—it's all run out. I'm not lying. If I-I had the money I would pay you, I promise. It's just… it's not there anymore," I blurt out, feeling my whole body shake. Lorenzo glares at me so hard I wonder if he might be able to bore a hole in my face.

"Nice try," he scoffs. "But the thing is, I don't give a shit what your sob story is. Hard times, whatever. Everybody's gotta pay the rent somehow, and if you're not makin' ends meet sellin' soap to rich bitches, then it looks like you're gonna have to make up the deficit some other way."

He looks me up and down, stepping closer. The smell of his cheap cologne is so overbearing it almost makes my eyes water. I know what he's implying, and that's all it takes to send my thoughts hurtling back in time.

I'm shivering. It's not even cold, but my body won't stop convulsing. I feel sick to my stomach, but I know if I throw up they'll just hurt me more. What am I going to do? How am I going to survive…?

"Listen, you spoiled little brat. I know Daddy's not around to spank you anymore, but if you need someone else to step in and whip your sweet little ass into shape, I'm your man," Lorenzo growls, the faint hint of a lascivious smile playing on his filthy lips.

Just then, there's the jingle from the front door, and all four of us whip around at the sound to see another man in the doorway. My stomach does a somersault. It's the guy from a few days ago! My mystery man. But what the hell is he doing here? I feel guilty instantly, knowing that now this man is in danger, too, because he's unwittingly interrupted mafia business. He's a witness now. And it's all my fault. I want to call out to him, tell him to leave, but my voice is caught in my throat.

"Who's this?" Lorenzo growls under his breath. Then, he shouts, "Who the fuck are you? Get out of here. This is private. Shop's closed."

The mystery guy pushes back the hood of his jacket to reveal a scruffy, handsome face with a coarse black beard, framed by long, gently curling black hair. There's a wildness to his face that thrills me, even in the tense danger of the moment.

"Shit, that's one of the Costa boys," says one of Lorenzo's goons.

Costa? My heart skips a beat. Another mafia guy. I should have known.

"Leave. Now. Before anyone has to get hurt," commands the mystery guy. His voice is like crushed velvet, deep and rumbling. It thrums through my body down to my core, and I shiver.

Lorenzo lets out a cruel laugh. "Yeah, you'd like that, wouldn't you? Have us just walk outta here before we get a chance to break that pretty-boy face of yours. You think that beard can hide you? I know who the hell you are. And this is no business of yours. Get out."

The Costa guy approaches slowly, shaking his head. "You really don't wanna mess with me."

All three of the others guffaw at his threat. "Right, sure,

there are three of us and one of you. I'm sure we should all be scared right now, huh? You don't fuckin' scare me, man. But if you wanna go, we'll go. No sweat off my back. In fact, my boys have been itchin' for some target practice, right, boys?"

The two goons nod, grinning as they saunter toward Mystery Guy, squaring up for a fight.

"No," I breathe, terrified. But within the next few seconds, a flash of violent movement breaks out right in front of me, as the two goons move to swing at my Mystery Guy.

To my surprise, he manages to dodge them both, and there's a series of sickening crunches as his fist collides with one face and the other hand strikes a neck. They both swivel around, lumbering clumsily like two enraged bulls, only to be manhandled to the ground as Mystery Guy uses their own weight against him. He takes out a pistol, and with a flash of fluorescent light on silver metal, bashes them both upside the head. I scream at the sight of the gun, instinctively ducking down behind the counter. Lorenzo abandons me to take on the Mystery Guy, and even though I can't see what's going on, I can hear them.

"You wanna take me on, too?" growls Mystery Guy.

"You little fuckin' bitch!" yelps Lorenzo. There is a brief tussle and then I hear the telltale slam of knuckles against jawbone, and there's a stomach-turning cracking noise as Lorenzo cries out in agony. *Fuck, fuck, fuck.* Shit is getting real!

I hear the scramble of heavy, faltering footsteps and the jingle of the front door. Lorenzo sneers, "I'll remember this, you Costa piece of shit! This is just the beginning, motherfucker. You're gonna regret interfering with the Cleaners!"

"Yeah, you'll remember me when I mail your teeth back to you, asshole!" shouts back Mystery Guy, and the door slams shut. I stay cowering behind the counter, my knees pulled to my chest, while my heart races along at a stammering rhythm.

I hear footsteps approaching and I steel myself for whatever harm is due to come my way. After all, three mafia guys may be gone, but there's still one more left: Mystery Guy. He might hail from a different gang, but he's still a dangerous man, and I have no reason to believe that he's really here to help me. For all I know, that could have just been a tussle over territory, over who gets to terrorize me next.

So when Mystery Guy comes around behind the counter and offers me a hand to help me up, I hesitate for a long moment before taking it. I slowly look up at him to meet his gaze. I take in his dark clothing, the sleeves pushed to his elbows to reveal blood smeared along his hands and forearms, remnants of the battle. I stare at his face, that strangely familiar expression hidden behind a tangle of scraggly hair and beard. As soon as my eyes lock with his, it's like I'm hypnotized. His eyes peer down into my very being, to stroke the depths of my wounded soul.

It's almost overwhelming, that stare. Too much to take in.

But why? And how?

"I won't hurt you," he says softly, and that familiar thrum shakes through me. Stiffly, as though in a trance, I hold out my hand and take his. He pulls me to my feet, then places both hands on my shoulders, his eyes peering into my face with genuine concern.

"Are you okay? Did they hurt you before I got here?" he asks. I manage to shake my head. I somehow tear my eyes away from his and notice that some of the blood on his hands and arms seems to be his own, and that he's injured.

"I-I'm okay," I murmur, "but you're hurt."

He takes his hands off of me and curls them into fists

hanging at his sides. "No, I'm alright. It's nothing at all. As long as you're okay… I'll go."

As he turns to leave, some kind of strange impulse takes hold of my body and I reach out to stop him, my hands falling at his chest. He stops and looks down at me, eyes flashing. For a moment, I'm almost frightened by the wildness of that expression, but then he softens.

"Let me clean you up before you go, at least," I offer, biting my lip. "I mean, you can't go out all bloody and injured like that. It's unsanitary. And if there's one thing I do have here in abundance, it's soap. Just let me clean your wounds. Please. It's the least I can do."

He hesitates, clearly fighting some kind of internal battle as he looks at me, considering my strange request. Finally, he gives in, and I gently lead him to a sink, pulling up a stool for him to sit on while I grab the least-feminine-scented soap I can find and start lathering up his fists and forearms. Even as he sits on the stool, he's nearly eye-to-eye with me, he's so tall. And I consider myself to be relatively tall for a woman, too, at five-foot-seven, so it's unusual for a man to tower over me in such a way.

He doesn't even wince at the sting of soap on his cut-up, bruised knuckles, and from the number of scars I feel underneath my fingers as I wash them, he seems to have seen his fair share of fights. I wonder what kind of life he leads, how many times he has done this. Is this his job? Really? To go around protecting women he doesn't even know?

But Lorenzo and his goons called him a Costa guy. If he's a mafia associate, then why did he help me? Sure, when I was young and Dad was still alive, things were good. My folks and the mafia were more than just simpatico, they were family. But things have changed drastically since then, and as far as I know, the Costa family certainly don't make my safety and wellbeing a priority these days. I'm nothing to them. In fact, they probably hate me after everything that happened.

So why in the world did this rough-and-tough Costa enforcer come to my rescue?

As I make my way up his arm, scrubbing gently at the bloody lacerations and dark bruises, I come across a familiar sight. A tattoo. One I have not seen with my own two eyes in many years. The sight of it instantly throws me back, and a tidal wave of confused emotions overtake me. I freeze up, staring at the intricate lines of the tattoo, suddenly remembering all the things I have tried so hard to forget, dark things that time has buried.

And with it, an overwhelming sense of urgency to ask, to know for certain that this man is who my heart wills him to be. By chance, by fate, by magic. By whatever means necessary for him to have walked back into my world again, albeit beaten down and roughened up and subdued.

I look up from the tattoo to meet his gaze, and the answer to my question is there in his pale green eyes long before the words even leave my lips. It's him. I know it is. But I still can't stop myself from asking, just to be sure.

"Luca? Is… is that you?"

For a few long, sweet moments, we stare into each other's eyes, frozen. Her hands are still holding my forearm, her soft fingers on my rough, hardened hands warm even as the water starts to get cold. Her touch is one of the things I've missed most from my old life. I never want it to end.

But as strong as my arm is, as powerful as the body sitting before her in the little shop may be, those eyes of hers hold me still. Her gaze searches mine. Those eyes are feasting themselves, staring right into my soul, making me want to let her know everything they want to know even as my own eyes hold her paralyzed.

Finally, I let myself give her the smile I've been waiting years to give her.

"*Ciao, bella.*"

And just like that, we're teenagers again.

Tears swell up like springwater in those endless eyes, and her lip quivers for half a second as a tidal wave of emotion crashes through her system.

"*Luca!*" she squeals, and before I can open my mouth, she flings herself at me, little arms wrapping around my torso as she buries her face in my chest. My chest is rippling with muscle, but even I can feel how tight she's trying to squeeze me, and I couldn't keep the grin off my face if my life depended on it.

My thick arms wrap around her, practically covering her in me as I hold her warmth against my body, and I hear her start to sob before I can put my lips to the top of her golden head. My large hand strokes her back, and I feel my own heart swelling as I give her a gentle squeeze back.

"Serena," I say, and it feels so good, so free to feel her name roll of my tongue. I've held myself back from this moment for so long. I still don't know if it was the right choice. But right now, in this moment, I let myself just *be* with her as we hold each other tight.

I'm a hardened man, but I can still feel. And Serena is the sweetest feeling in the world.

After what feels like forever, she turns her head up to look at me. Those wet, reddened eyes don't dampen the smile on her face. "Oh my god, it really is you! I...I can't..."

"Shush, shush, you've been through a lot today," I say, giving her a reassuring squeeze, my huge arms holding her protectively. I feel her take a breath and let it out slowly.

She bites her lip, trying desperately to bring her emotions back in line, but it's useless. And I can't believe the joy I feel in my own heart—the relief.

She isn't afraid of me? After everything. After how we parted ways last time?

Not only that, she's overjoyed to see me. To be with me.

"I just...I never thought I'd see you again," she confesses, half-laughing, half-sobbing. She sniffs, wiggling an arm free to wipe her eyes and laugh at herself all over again. "Oh my god, I'm such a mess, don't look at me!"

It's my turn to laugh as I hug her tight to me as she tries to get away, and she gives a little squeal of delight as I give her a bear hug that lifts her feet off the ground for a moment. It's like no time has passed between us at all.

I set her down and release her. She immediately grabs a paper towel from the counter and dabs her eyes, checking in the mirror to see what the damage is. She could have raccoon eyes streaming down her whole face, and she'd still be irresistible to me.

After another sniff, she takes a step back and looks at me with a gaze that really see *me* for the first time. "Oh my god, and you were in here yesterday! I... I can't believe I didn't recognize you!"

I give a cocky smile. "That was the plan. Besides the glasses, though, I've changed a lot, Serena."

"No you haven't," she says in a laughing sob, looking over my face as more and more recognition crashes through her. "If it weren't for that beard... but I'd know those eyes anywhere," she says, dreamily, and I can tell she only half-realizes the words are coming from her mouth. Catching herself, she blushes and runs her fingers through her hair, getting a stray lock out of her face. Another sniff.

"You're one to talk," I say, a warm smile on my face as I take her in, looking her up and down. Her face reddens at my gaze, but she doesn't turn away, either. She always was like that—she liked to play shy, but my gaze excited her. It always had, and it still does, I see. "Serena, you look... incredible."

A moment passes between us in silence as we just stare at each other, smiling stupidly. Teenagers all over again.

But her smile fades, and I see concern on her face. "Luca... my god, where have you been all these years? Have you been safe? Do... do you know those guys that were here earlier? How are you even still in town, I--"

"Serena," I cut her off gently, putting two hands on her shoulders. I feel her instinctively melt in my hands, shoulders relaxing immediately. I never believed her when she told me I have a calming presence, but it's true for her, at least. "Serena, you've had a terrible day thanks to some terrible men. You don't need more things to trouble yourself. Not today, at least." I return her smile as those doe-eyes look up at me. "But I do think you could stand to get out of here and get a drink. Why don't we go get something?"

A smile slowly creeps back over her pretty face. After a moment's hesitation, she says, "I think I'd like that. Yeah."

~

"*N*ice ride," she says as she climbs into the passenger's seat of my black company sedan. "Nicer than that beat-up old pickup I remember."

I smile as she shuts the door and I pull out onto the road.

A lot of baggage comes with this car, Serena.

Still, it feels good to make her happy. I shift up through the gears and start tearing down the roads we've both grown up around.

"So," she says after a moment, "got anywhere in mind?"

"Well," I half-laugh, "the places I usually go, I don't think you'd find the most relaxing."

She smiles. "Still running with the old crowd, huh?"

"Something like that," I say. The only place that comes to mind is a dive that some of the rougher Italian crowd haunts. It's dingy, falling apart, and doesn't have anything you could call service, but it's been my place for a while. It's got a homey feel to it. But just because it's homey doesn't mean it's the place I'd take someone shaken-up to calm down.

"I've got somewhere you'd like, though," I say, remembering somewhere... cozy. It's a mob-run place, and while it's a little closer to work than I'd like to bring her, it's somewhere I know is safe.

I follow the roads to a place that I'm not sure I'd call a hotel, exactly, judging by the outside. It's an older building, but people have taken care of it over the years. Good people. As good as you find in this business.

"Room With A View?" I hear Serena say as we pull up on the side of the road and climb out of the car.

"I haven't been here in a long time, but I remember it being a good place. I'm sure it doesn't look like much from the outside, but-"

"Are you kidding?" she laughs, a bright smile on her face, crossing the street with me and looking at me as if I'm unreal. "I totally know this place, come on!"

I blink in surprise as she runs ahead of me to the door, but I follow. She's really been getting around, hasn't she?

The interior is all wood—and good wood, at that. It's an old building. A few candles are burning on the tables, and the windows are just dark enough to make the whole place feel cozy. Past the tables and the bar, I see a set of stairs leading up to the next floor, to what I assume are a few rooms. It can't be many. The place is tiny, and it looks like most of the people here are here for the drinks.

There's a woman with light brown skin and dark, curly hair behind the bar, and her eyes light up at the sight of Serena.

"Hey girl, you didn't tell me you were coming over!" she says, coming around to cross the floor and hug Serena around the neck. Even as she does though, she gives me a suspicious look, eyeing me like a judge. "Who's your tall friend?"

I crack a smile at the protective edge in her voice.

"It was kind of a last minute thing," she says, breaking the hug and turning to me. "I'll explain later. Rafaela, this is Luca. He's... an old friend," she introduces me with an anxious smile, and I watch Rafaela's eyebrows go up in understanding as she glances at me. "Luca, this is Rafaela. She runs this place," she adds with a wink. Rafaela rolls her eyes.

"Co-owns. Nico's around here somewhere. I'll have him come get your orders. I'm... guessing you two want a table?" she asks, giving Serena a curious look. Serena rolls her eyes, holding back a grin.

"That'd be great," Serena says, "thanks." Rafaela watches us as we head to a quaint little table by the window, surprise written all over her face. Serena must not bring guys through here very much.

I have to be careful as I slide into the tiny seat. The table's a little low, so I put my legs out to the side as I awkwardly fit my way in. Serena giggles as she watches me, and I grin back.

"Rafaela and I go way back," she says once we're situated. "She's like, my best friend. I wouldn't have survived college without her."

"Sounds like she keeps an eye out for you," I say.

"Yeah, she can be like that. Kind of like a big sister, too. She likes putting that Psych degree to use."

A man with his sleeves rolled up approaches the table, looking at both of us with a warm smile. This one, I recognize, and we give each other a knowing nod.

His name is Nico Tosetti, and he's what we call an associate. One of us. He must be the boyfriend Rafaela mentioned. I've crossed paths with him once or twice, but he's small potatoes—which is a good thing to be, in this business. He's a tall, goofy-looking guy, and he's got a good heart. He doesn't need to be tangled up in this business too deep.

"Luca," he says with a smile, "didn't think I'd see you around here."

"You know each other?" Serena asks, looking surprised.

"Yeah, we've met," I say, clapping hands with the guy. "Didn't know this was your place."

"Me and Rafaela," he says with a nod back to the bartender. "They said running a bar would be a nightmare, but between the two of us, it's the dream," he says with a boyish smile.

Probably a hell of a lot better than enforcement on the south side of town, I think, and I give him a nod.

"So, what can I get you two?" he asks, putting his hands on his hips. I make eye contact with Serena before I speak.

"Got any Campari back there?"

"Of course."

"How about a couple Americanos, then? Hold the Vermouth."

"So...just Campari and soda water?"

"That's right."

Nico nods with a smile before darting off, and I catch Serena grinning at me across the table.

"Bastard Americanos, huh?" she asks, and I feel a grin spread across my face. An Americano in this case isn't the coffee—it's a cocktail with Campari, a little Vermouth, and soda water. Back in the day, when we were younger, I'd find ways to sneak a bottle of Campari every now and then, but I never bothered with the Vermouth. So, I called them 'bastard' Americanos.

That was also because I was a teenager still learning English, and I'd just learned the word 'bastard.'

"I'm surprised you remembered," I say.

"'An Americano for my Americana?' How could I forget that?" she says, and I cover my face with a massive hand.

"Oh god, I forgot about that," I laugh, remembering that cheesy line, and soon I can hear her laughter too.

"It was cute!" she says, and as our laughter fades, her face gets a little more pensive. "Feels like a lifetime ago. Sitting on the back of that old pickup you and the other boys worked out of. Sneaking drinks from some Italian place I couldn't pronounce."

I look at her, sitting there, the picture of beauty. The dim lighting in here just makes her all the more alluring, and I want to just take her right now, as if years hadn't passed between us.

But we're moving fast. Too fast. We need to talk, and I know it. And yet... why spoil the moment while it lasts? As if on cue, Nico sets our drinks down in front of us and heads off.

"It's been too long, Serena," I say, watching her as she takes her drink and stirs it pensively.

"I know," she nearly whispers. "I still can't believe it's real. You, here, I mean." She looks up at me and hesitates a moment. "Those guys, back there at the shop..."

"The Cleaners," I say in a low tone, glancing around the bar. I don't want to stir up commotion here, and talking about a rival crime syndicate is a good way to do that.

"How did you know they were gonna be there?" she asks.

"Things are getting rough, Serena," I say before taking a swig of my drink. "I was worried someone might come causing trouble around your place. I was right." She's watching me with wide eyes. "I have to be my own eyes and ears. It's how it always is, with these people."

"So it's true," she says softly, looking into my eyes. "You're working with..."

The words *the mafia* hang between us. I nod.

"It's been a long few years, Serena," I say. Even low, my voice is gruff, and the beard and long hair don't help the image. I reach over and cover one of her small hands in my large, warm one. "For now, just know that I'm not going to let anything happen to you. And you don't need to worry yourself about all that right now, okay?"

She looks at me with that glint in her eye I know so

well. Serena doesn't like things being held back from her, and I know she'll come back to this soon enough. She's a precocious girl like that. So it's all the more surprising to me when I hear her say, "Alright, sure." She tilts her head to the side, narrowing her eyes at me. "Just tell me one thing, if you're gonna be all secretive... what's with the beard?"

I'm left speechless for a moment, then burst out laughing, putting a hand to my face. "I don't know, really. What, you don't like it?"

"Do you?"

I frown. "I've had it since..." *Since life tore us apart.* "For a while."

"I think I miss your face," she decides.

"I've been missing yours, *passerotta mia.*"

She blushes before hiding her face with her drink, which she finishes with a tinkling of ice cubes. "Woo, I forgot how strong that stuff is!"

"Careful now," I say after finishing my own. "I know how much of a lightweight you are."

"I'll have you know I've gotten *lots* better," she says playfully. Before I can reply, the sound of music floods the bar as someone turns on the speakers, and I flash a glance at the little open space between the tables—a wooden floor perfect for dancing.

Anyone who passes up the chance to dance with a pretty lady is no man at all.

"Alright, let's see it then," I say, standing up, and Serena flutters her eyes in confusion as I reach down to take her hands.

"Wait, what?"

"Rafaela, two more!" I call to the bartender, and she winks at Serena as I drag her out to the dance floor.

"Luca, what are you doing?" she laughs as some of the patrons give us amused looks.

"If you're so good at holding your liquor, let's see it! What good are a few drinks if they don't help you dance?"

She yelps as I swing her onto the clearing between tables that passes for a dance floor, and the next moment, I'm drawing her by the hand all around me. It's lively music, the kind you jump into to shake off your embarrassment and get into the heat of it. Serena is laughing already. After the first few awkward seconds of jerking around, we're dancing. I'm normally not a man who expresses himself much. Especially not the past few years. But the way Serena dances around me, the way I can lead her so easily, it kindles an old fire in me.

That, and well, dancing is in my blood.

A song goes by, and by the time the one after that is done, a few people around the bar have joined us. Our blood is racing, and after Serena and I grab another drink, we dive right back in. It's like there's nothing else in the world but the two of us.

We don't need words. All that gets shed by our body language. And as I'm watching her body move with mine, leading her on effortlessly, I realize how much I've missed her.

More dangerously, I realize how much I want her.

I need her.

Her soft hands brush against my muscular forearms, my strong hands on her hips, her ass against my crotch, the energy between us draws us closer and closer.

She turns, and our eyes meet for just a second, and it's like lightning flashes between us. Primal desire is bursting through, even though both of us have been trying to ignore it this whole time, but its message is plain as day.

We want each other. Now.

My heart is racing and I can feel every pulse of blood in my veins. Despite the three cocktails I've had, my brain doesn't feel fuzzy or out of focus. In fact, everything around me seems intensified, my senses all heightened, the colors in the bar seem brighter and more garish than ever before. It's like someone has turned up the contrast on the photo lens of the world around us. I feel exhilarated. I feel alive. I know exactly what I want.

And he's standing right in front of me. I look up at him with a dizzy smile on my face, drinking in the vivid green-peridot of his eyes, the fullness of his lips, the gentle slope of his nose. Even with that thick beard and scraggly hair, he's painfully attractive. He's grown up a lot since I last saw him, and I suppose that I have, too.

The scrappy young man I fell head over heels for as a teenager has transformed into a towering, musclebound, scarred, and stoic lumberjack type. If someone had told me years and years ago that we would meet again this way, I would never have believed it. After everything we went through, I assumed I would never see Luca again.

And even if we did, I thought he would turn away from

me. I'm a reminder to him of dark times, just as he is to me. I can't pretend that running into him, resparking that old fire hasn't knocked me off my feet. Those memories, the ones I have worked so hard to put in the ground, float around me like the remains of some tragic shipwreck. Every now and then I wade too close to a piece of shrapnel, and the warning sirens go off in my head. As we talked and caught up with each other tonight, I had to remind myself that things are different now. That old danger is in the past.

Of course, there are new dangers now. Lorenzo and the Cleaners. The shop barely making a profit. Trying to keep my old, expensive, and empty family house up and running. And now there's a new, added fear to the mix: losing Luca again.

It's like a dream, a surreality, an impossible twist of fate that we should find each other again years after the horrors that broke us apart. Throughout the evening, I've been occasionally tempted to pinch myself, to shake myself awake. This has to be a dream.

But when I reach up to brush my hand along the wiry hair on Luca's jaw and feel him lean into my touch, closing those beautiful eyes as though he's losing himself in the ecstasy of the moment... I know for certain that this is real. This is actually happening. And I can't lose him again. Not now. Not yet. There are still so many things I need to ask him, need to find out. I want to know him again the way I used to. We just need time—the one thing there never seems to be enough of.

Luca turns his face slightly to kiss the soft skin of my palm, sending a curious thrill down through my body, burning down to my very core. I can feel that vibration way down in my toes. His warm, whiskey-tinged breath is like a jolt of electricity to my soul.

"Luca…" I murmur, my voice trailing off and getting lost in the raucous thrum of competing conversations all around us in the bar. The counter is packed with patrons, and every table is full. Luca and I have been standing against the far wall for… god only knows how long. Just talking. Reminiscing gently, both of us too afraid to really push too far and split open old wounds. I can tell, without even having to ask, that he's not ready to talk about what happened yet. Not fully. I don't blame him. I wish I could push those terrible thoughts of my mind, make room for better things hopefully to come.

Like right now.

I'm more than ready to make a new memory with Luca. A much better one.

And it appears that he feels the same, leaning toward me, talking close. All evening he's been pressed right up against me, that glorious, powerful body moving rhythmically with mine. It's delicious, it's intoxicating, and I can't believe I've managed to survive all this time without it. Sometimes, someone can enter your life and remind you just how much you've been missing out on. Luca was mine once, and nothing in the world has ever compared to the thrill of belonging to him.

I want him to claim me again. Tonight. As the two struggling grown-ups we are now.

"*Passerotta mia*," he whispers, brushing his lips along the shell of my ear. A tingling warmth spreads through my body and I shiver, feeling goosebumps rise across my skin. I turn to catch his face mere centimeters from mine, the tips of our noses barely touching. We lock eyes for a tense, clenching moment, and then he glances down ever so quickly at my lips and I know.

He wants to kiss me. He's feeling the same fire that I feel.

But he pulls back before giving in, lifting a calloused,

powerful carpenter's hand to stroke the hair back out of my face. "Where can we go?" he asks softly.

It's a bigger question in my mind than he probably intends for it to be. Where can we go? In what world does our relationship belong? Where are we safe, the two of us? Right now, right here, I have an idea for a temporary safe haven.

"Stay here. I'll be right back," I tell him. Then, as I'm turning to walk away, I add, "Please… don't leave."

Luca gives me a brilliant, warming smile. "I'm not going anywhere without you, Serena."

It's hard to tear myself away from him, even for a moment, but I have to. I rush through the crowd, squeezing past various groups of bachelorette parties and post-grind investment bankers tossing back a few beers, finally reaching the bar counter. I wiggle in between two women giggling with umbrella drinks and locate Rafaela, who is engaged in a battle with one of her old nemeses: the daiquiri blender. At any other time, I might have burst out laughing at the sight— god knows we've talked about that evil blender a million times. She's even confessed to me on one occasion that she's pretty sure it's possessed by a demon. It's that bad.

But not as dire as my current situation.

I finally catch her eye, giving her an urgent expression. We know each other well enough to pick up on unspoken cues, and she immediately abandons the evil blender to hurry over to me.

"What's up, babe?" she asks, her voice miraculously cutting through the din of high-pitched laughter and yells coming from all directions here at the center of the activity.

"I need a room," I tell her plainly. I'm too determined to be coy about this. There's no time to waste. Every moment

I'm here instead of standing in front of Luca is a moment I can hardly bear.

To her infinite credit and grace, she doesn't razz me at all. Rafaela simply nods, swivels around, bends down to unlock a little gray safe behind the counter, and take out a room key. She places it in my hand and gives me a wink.

"Room 6. King-sized bed, en suite bathroom, window overlooking the community garden next door. Go get 'im, tiger," she says, grinning.

"Do I need to—?"

She shakes her head. "Don't worry about paying. It's an empty room, you need it, and you're my best friend. Consider this an early wedding present," she adds, laughing. Blushing, I reach out and squeeze her hand gratefully.

"Thank you. Seriously."

I turn away and start maneuvering back through the crowd again, my eyes peeled for Luca. Finally, I arrive at the same spot where we were standing just minutes ago and he isn't there.

My heart sinks down into my stomach and the room starts to go dizzy.

Where is he? Did he leave? How could this have happened? Maybe I spooked him somehow. Maybe he thought better of this and decided to make a break for it before things got too heavy. Maybe I only imagined the magic sparking between us. Maybe... it wasn't meant to be.

Just as I'm about to give up and go back to the bar to return the key to Rafaela, I feel an arm snake around my waist. I look down, then back up, and to my uncontrollable joy I see Luca beaming down at me, a fire in his eyes.

"I'm here, Serena. I told you I wasn't going anywhere."

Wordlessly, I hold up the key. His expression changes instantly, that affable smile melting into a white-hot smoulder. He nods and takes me by the hand, leading me to the staircase down the hall, tucked away just out of the hubbub of the bar crowd. Before we can even make it all the way up the stairs, Luca pushes me against the wall, leaning in close over me. His chest is heaving and I can tell that he's working as hard as he can to control himself, to stay level-headed. It's a thrill to think that he's as intoxicated by me as I am by him.

The noise at the bar fades into nothing as he takes my face gently in both of his rough, strong hands. Luca peers into my face as though he's searching for something, some answer hidden in the shape of my features that he's desperate to decode. And then, with only a split-second's hesitation, he closes the space between us and captures my lips in a passionate kiss.

Immediately, I feel my entire body going limp and pliable, the sensation of his full lips moving against mine like a shot of Everclear straight to my brain. He's like a drug, like the most addictive dream, and I need more. His tongue gently pushes into my mouth as his hands slide down to my shoulders, then down to grip my waist possessively. I am riveted to the spot, afraid to move for fear that this magical dream will fade away and leave me standing alone in the stairwell.

I feel his hands roving back over my hips to cup my ass, feeling his fingers digging into the soft flesh of my upper thighs. He wedges a leg between my thighs and presses the full length of his body against me. I'm warm between my legs and the sensation of his thigh rubbing against me is delicious. I moan into his mouth as he takes my wrists in his hands and pins them up above my head, making me feel both vulnerable and powerful at the same time.

He breaks our kiss for a moment, nudging me to turn my head to one side so he can kiss a line down my jaw to breathe softly in my ear. I tremble and arch toward him as his lips press into the ticklish skin of my neck, sucking and nipping gently in a way that makes my whole body shake.

He remembers me so well, perfectly mapping out each of the places on my body that are sensitive. He knows me better than anyone else in the world, and after I lost him so many years ago, I never thought I would feel this good again.

How can this be real? Am I dreaming?

Suddenly, the echoing clack-clack of high-heeled shoes interrupts us and I glance around Luca's shoulder to see the shadows of some women approaching. Quickly, Luca hoists me up and I wrap my legs around his waist as he carries me up the rest of the stairs.

"Which room?" he asks, his voice rough and gravelly with desire.

"Six," I whisper. We find the door at the end of the hallway and he bends his knees so that I can fish out the key and fit it into the keyhole with a laugh. Once the door is open, he takes the key, shoves it in his pocket, and pushes through into the room.

Rafaela really, truly came through for me on this one. I've seen some of the rooms here, and while all of them are decent, standard-issue lodging, this particular room stands out. It's designed with a kind of 1960s vintage charm, and there is a king-sized canopy bed by the massive bay window.

"Wow, she really hooked us up," I murmur as Luca sets me down on my feet. But before I can say anything else, he pulls me close into another kiss, stealing the breath right from my lungs. I close my eyes and fold into his arms easily, letting him lean me backward onto the bed.

"I've thought about you so many times," Luca growls, bending to kiss me again. His hands reach down to peel my blouse up and over my arms, leaving me bare-chested except for my bra. He cups my breasts while his leg wedges between my thighs again, and I let out a groan of frustration. I need more, more, more. He's got me craving him like an addict.

"Please, don't take your time," I beg him. "I-I can't wait, Luca."

He groans and stands up to strip off his jacket, shirt, and then unzip his jeans. He pushes them down to stand in his boxers and I can't help but sit up and lean toward him, my fingers roving across the massive bulge in the fabric. He's much bigger than I even remember.

"Take off your clothes," he commands softly. Without a word, I obey, unclasping my bra, then pulling off my shoes, skirt, and panties to sit totally naked in front of him.

"Can I...?" I ask meekly, almost licking my lips at the sight of his cock straining to break free of his underwear. Luca nods and I hungrily tug his boxers down so he can step out of them. His cock springs free, bouncing in front of my face. I reach up to stroke him with both hands, feeling his enormous size and warmth. I can't resist. I need to taste him.

Adjusting to kneel on the bed, I lower my head down to take his cock into my mouth, stretching my lips to accommodate his size. As I slowly begin to work his shaft with my mouth and both hands, Luca groans appreciatively. His hand comes down to press lightly against the back of my head, pushing me down on his cock further until I'm almost choking on it. I wish desperately I could take his full length into my mouth, feel him swelling and pulsing against the back of my throat. I bob up and down, sucking him hard and fast until his hips are moving in rhythm with me. I can feel myself getting wetter by the second, just from the intoxicating taste of Luca's cock in my mouth.

But then he stops me suddenly, gently pushing me back away from him. I don't get a moment to feel sad, though, because he lifts and tosses me further back on the bed before climbing on top to straddle me. Once again, he takes hold of my wrists and pins my arms down, this time on either side of me. Then he leans to kiss his way down to my breasts, his lips nipping and suckling at my nipples until I'm crying out with need. Every kiss and bite sends a thrum of heady desire down to that secret place deep inside me, and before long I'm nearly teary-eyed with frustration.

"Please, Luca. I need you inside me. I'm so wet… I've waited so long for you," I murmur, hardly even aware of what I'm saying.

"Are you sure?" he asks gruffly, and I know it's taking every ounce of his self-control to resist.

"Yes! God, yes. Please! Fuck me, Luca," I plead desperately, yelping when he lets out an animalistic growl and bites harder. I'm arching my hips toward him, my body lifting up off the bed.

Finally, he pulls back and readies the head of his cock at my slick opening, and just this gentle touch is enough to make me tremble. For a few moments, he swirls the tip of his beautiful cock against my clit, making me groan and grip the sheets. My pussy is aching, swelling with desire.

"Fuck me," I mumble. "I want you so bad! Don't make me wait any longer."

And with that, Luca shoves the entire massive length of his cock inside of me in one smooth motion, until the tip brushes against that sweet spot deep within me and I wrap my legs around his waist, pulling him down to me. I need him close. I need to be flush with his body, to feel every part of him at once all around me.

"Oh my god," I whimper as he starts to thrust, pulling almost all the way out to slam back into me again and again and again. He groans and kisses my neck, his teeth grazing my skin. I can tell he wants to let go, to use my body like a fuck toy. But he's too gentle, too careful with me to do so.

But I want him to let go.

"You don't have to be gentle, Luca," I whisper, my breath tousling his hair softly. "You can fuck me however you want to."

And that's all it takes. Permission granted.

His teeth sink into my skin while his hands grope at my breasts, squeezing my nipples between his fingers while his cock slides in and out of me faster and faster. "Fuck, I've thought about this so many times, *mia passerotta*," he hisses through gritted teeth. "I've thought about how badly I wanted to touch you, fill you up with my cock."

"Harder," I breathe, scarcely able to form coherent thoughts as I lose myself in the swift rhythm of his thrusts. My pussy clenches with every movement, tightening around his cock. Luca reaches down between my legs to massage my clit with two fingers, making me scream in pleasure. His other hand comes up to cup over my mouth while he fucks me mercilessly, making my pussy ache with every powerful push. Finally, I feel my pleasure mounting to a climax and I cry out, orgasming against him. He moves faster and his fingers don't relent, even as I try to pull away from the overstimulation. He isn't going to give me a break. Not at all.

I come again and again, tears burning in my eyes as I toss my head back and twist the sheets in my fists. "Oh god, it feels so fucking good," I pant.

"I want to fill you up with my come, baby," Luca growls. "I want to pump you full."

"Do it," I reply, with a daring tone. "Please. I want your come inside me!"

With a few short, rapid thrusts, Luca comes. "Fuck, Serena!" he shouts. His cock pulses with jet after jet of thick, hot come, filling me up while I orgasm again. He fucks into me a few more times and then collapses next to me, peppering my face with kisses.

We lie there breathing heavily for a few minutes, just soaking in the magical afterglow. He pulls me into his arms and holds me there, both of us totally silent and content. If this is a dream, then I never, ever want to wake up again. This is perfect. This is… paradise.

Finally, I make the suggestion that we should shower off. I slip out of his arms and prance across the room, feeling his hot seed slipping down my thighs mingled with my own juices. "Come on," I beckon flirtatiously. "Let's get wet again."

Luca sits up and smiles at me, lighting a fire inside my heart yet again. "I'll be there in a minute. I promise." But just then, there's the buzz of a cell phone going off. I wait in the doorway of the en suite bathroom while Luca gets up to check it. His face pales slightly, and his smile fades away.

"What… what is it?" I ask, a little worried.

Luca looks up at me, a pained expression on his handsome face. "I was summoned by the *Capo*." My heart drops into my stomach. Is Luca in trouble with the Mafia?

And if so… was it my fault?

The scent of her is still on me when I get into the car. It's something that's going to be on me all day, I know, and I'll remember it even longer. And when I see her next, what's to stop me from getting her on me all over again?

My eyes flick down to my phone before I stuff it into my pocket and check behind me to pull out into the road.

When I first saw the message, I wanted to crush the phone in my bare hand and throw the remains out the window. My instinct was to tear down anything that would dare step in and interrupt what I was having with Serena. And under any other circumstance, that's just what I would have done. But this message came from the very thing that forced us to be apart. It was one thing that I hated more than anything, but I knew it was also the only thing that would make sure she could be safe.

My bosses. The mafia.

This message came from Diego Milani, to be precise, a capo. The capos are the guys who manage enforcers and associates like me in our business. I've known Diego as long as I've been involved with these men. A message from someone like him means either something very good or very bad.

And considering what happened back at Serena's shop, I have a feeling I'm about to get chewed out. I don't care. I did what I had to for Serena's protection, and that's all my whole career has been about. That's all I acted for.

Is it, though?

I grip the steering wheel as I move through traffic, trying not to let my thoughts distract me. My mind flashes back to Serena on that bed, me tearing her clothes away, the feeling of her bare skin in my hands, the way my bare cock felt sinking into her to the hilt…

My manhood starts to swell between my legs. Just the thought of her stirs up a beast within me I can hardly control. And that's the problem. Everything I'm doing with these thugs is to give her a chance at life. I've done terrible things to make sure she'll be kept safe, out of all this ugly business.

I gave up my life to protect her, but I can't protect her from myself.

When I was a teenager, I let the fire in my soul rule me. I did what I felt was right, what I wanted. Serena makes me feel like that all over again, no matter how much the short years tried to snuff that fire out. It's dangerous. She makes me dangerous.

I feel a smile tug at my stony face as I pull up on the side of the road. I've beaten men down with my bare hands, fought off seasoned enforcers in knife-fights, and rained gunfire on rivals, but this woman who barely stands to my chest makes me more dangerous than any of them.

I climb out of the car and head around the side of the building to step into the room we "rent" at the back of this liquor store. It's been a place we use for last-minute meetings for a while, and the owner is an associate of ours. It's not a bad deal for him. He gets a break from protection money in exchange for letting a few musclebound Italians meet in the back of his store. I have my gun on me. I know it'll get taken, but it's a formality to show that I'm never unready.

In my business, you could come out of a meeting with your boss with a promotion or in a body bag.

When I get up to the door, there's a man outside it waiting for me. I've seen him before, but I don't know his name. He just nods to me and opens the door to usher me in. My eyes regard him carefully as I step inside, but he's relaxed. When a man's about to fight, he has tells, like a gambler about to lie. I've gotten good at recognizing them. A twitch of the finger, legs poised a certain way. You can even see it in the eyes.

But as I walk through the door, he just closes it behind me and gestures for me to hold my arms out. I smile.

"Diego's not that jumpy, is he?" I ask as he takes the gun from me and pats me down for any other weapons.

"Apparently I need to be," a voice calls from further in the room, past shelves of stacked liquor and beer, "if my men are gonna start jumping the gun like you. Get your ass in here, Luca."

That's Diego's voice, no doubt about it. I snort as the doorman finishes checking me over, and I stride down the aisles of stock to the cleared-out space where he takes care of business. I've been in here only once before, and it wasn't on the best terms.

When I step forward, I start to rethink whether I'm about to be killed.

Diego isn't a man who likes a lot of ceremony, but this looks like a miniature courtroom. Diego himself is looking over a stacked box of expensive Scotch, and in a semicircle around him are men I recognize. Some, I know by name. Most are enforcers like me, but one man sitting on a crate next to Diego takes me by surprise.

It's a consigliere. In every business like ours, there's usually only one man like him, maybe two. Consiglieri don't stick to our hierarchy.

He's the Don's own advisor, which makes him the most important man I've been in the same room as for a long time. It also means that this meeting is serious. I feel his hawkish gray eyes watching me carefully as he sits there. Diego turns to look me up and down before I can say anything.

"Luca," he says, crossing his arms, "I'm sure you're familiar with our consigliere, Antonio Tomasi."

I give the man a nod with a tight but respectful smile. He doesn't react.

"Mr. Tomasi thought it would be wise to sit in on this little business meeting," Diego goes on, his formality starting to relax into his usual self. "Because when our men make waves as big as you did out of line earlier today, he likes to hear the *very good reason* I'm sure you have firsthand."

"News travels fast," I say, keeping my eyes on Diego evenly.

"That it does," he says, pacing in a slow circle around me, "especially when a soldier like you takes it upon himself to pick a fight with the likes of Lorenzo Abruzzi."

That last name gets my attention. But I don't show the slightest hint of emotion. I'm being grilled, and Diego can smell a crack in someone's defenses from a mile away.

"Didn't get his name while I was knocking his teeth out," I say, and I watch Diego's jaw set. "He was in our territory, boss. Deep in our territory."

"Don't pretend that's what this is about, I know where the fight went down," Diego says, coming to a stop and resting his hands on his hips as he glares at me. "I know you got your reasons to go stalking that girl, and before today, I didn't give two shits."

My fists clench instinctively at what Diego is hinting, and Diego steps forward as I say, "It was still our territory, Diego. I caught some Cleaners starting to start shit deep in our territory, and I was taking care of business. I was doing my job."

"Your job is to do what the family needs," Diego says, restraining the anger in his voice as much as I'm holding back mine. "And the family did *not* need to spark a turf war with the goddamn Cleaners!"

There's a silence in the room for a few moments that everyone can *taste*.

The Cleaners have been like a bad word the past few months, a curse you don't say out loud. They've been trying to cut in on our territory like nothing our family has ever faced before. Our family—the Costa family—has its heels dug into the Bronx deep, but everyone's feeling the tension with the Cleaners.

That nickname, "Cleaners," that's stuck with them since day one. They're fast, they're good at what they do, and by the time they're gone, the cops have lost their trail before they've even started on it.

But as much as us Costas don't want to admit it, the Cleaners are a rival family of Italians—the Abruzzi family. The family Lorenzo belongs to.

"We've butted heads with Cleaners all over town," I say, not giving an inch on this, "don't pretend *I'm* the one out to start a turf war here."

"This is different, Luca," Diego nearly growls. "Lorenzo Abruzzi isn't some nobody cleaning up the streets-"

"Like me," I interrupt with a smile, and Diego gives a cruel smile back.

"Yeah, like you, a walking death-wish. No, Lorenzo is Abruzzi blood. You didn't wonder why he thought he could waltz into our territory like that and push that girl around? He's a spoiled little daddy's boy, Luca—Lorenzo Abruzzi is their boss's *son*."

Shit.

"That asshole calling himself 'Don Abruzzi'? He's letting his snot-nosed brat run loose?" I ask with a grimace.

"Yeah, *that* asshole," Diego says, striding back to the stacked bottles of beer, looking like he wants to pull one out, bad.

I let out a chuckle that makes Diego raise an eyebrow at me. "You think this shit's funny?" he says incredulously.

"Kind of," I admit. "I like seeing 'royalty' knocked down a peg."

Diego shakes his head with a smile of disbelief. "Been trying to send your ass on jobs to get you killed for years, and you keep comin' back with this shit. You're something else, you know that?"

He's only half-joking, and I know by the look in his eyes he'd like to try to beat that smile off my face if he weren't in front of the consigliere, whose face hasn't changed this whole time.

"Listen, you son of a bitch," Diego says, stepping toward me slowly, "I don't care if you're the best man I've got on the ground out here, you were out of line. You were out somewhere you weren't supposed to be, doing shit you weren't supposed to be doing, and you beat the shit outta some guy you weren't supposed to touch with a thirty-foot pole."

"So you dragged me out here to tighten my leash?" I say, raising my eyebrows. I hold my arms out, exposing my torso to him and the enforcers in the room. "Well then, take your shots. I can take a beating, I know how this goes."

Diego gives a cruel laugh, glaring daggers at me. I'm embarrassing him in front of his superior, and he knows it. The man could put a bullet in my head if he wanted to, though, so I know better than to push it. My temper is flaring, but in the back of my mind, Serena's safety is still my number one priority. If I get myself killed, she won't be safe. I lower my arms.

"Nah, if this was about that, you'd be feeling it already, and we wouldn't be getting the floor of this fine establishment dirty," he says. He then moves back to stand beside the consigliere, and both of them look at me like judges.

"The Cleaners are going to take Lorenzo's smashed-up face as an act of war," Diego says, "and if there's one thing I know about the Abruzzis, it's that they take insults like that very personally." Diego pauses to take out a cigarette and light it, and the smell of tobacco fills the space between us. He stares me down. "You got us in some real hot fuckin' water, Luca, you know that? Things are tense with the Cleaners as it is—I've had people calling me to tell me I oughta have your ass killed to smooth things over with them."

"Don't give me that shit," I snarl, and even some of the enforcers in the room looks surprised at my talking to my boss like that. Diego just watches me, burning cigarette in hand.

"I gave my life to this family, you all know that," I say, looking around at the gathered people, even making eye contact with the consigliere. "I haven't forgotten that, and I'll take as many bullets as you have me dish out to those *stronzi*. But you know Serena's safety means more than anything to me, and it has from the very start," I say, looking back to Diego.

"Think about the past few months," I say, knowing it's time to show my bargaining chips if I want to get out of here unscathed. "The fight at the warehouse down by the river? I had that gunfight on lockdown. The Cleaners would have put all our men in the grave that night if I hadn't been there, ask any one of them. Just last week, when that fucking rat Gabe tried to catch a bus out of state to cozy up to the Russians, I'm the one who put a bullet in his head coming out of his hotel room. When you need a job done right, Diego, you've come to me," I say, "I'm the best you've got, and you know it."

I can tell by the look in Diego's eye he's ready to start a fight with me right then and there. Some of the enforcers look to be of the same mind. Diego opens his mouth to speak, but to everyone's surprise...the consigliere raises a hand.

It's a simple move, but it silences Diego.

"You're right, Luca," his calm voice says simply. He sounds older than he looks. "Diego, Luca's a big boy. He does good work for our family, and he's proven more than capable. Which is why he's going to take care of his own mess here."

Diego and I both look at the consigliere blankly.

"Luca, part of your 'agreement' with us means that we don't touch Serena De Laurentis or her business. We respect that. But you've crossed the line here and dragged her into our business, whether she likes it or not."

I feel heat wash over my body. Damn him, I know he's right. I should have been protecting Serena, not getting involved with her like this. I've endangered us both just by coming near her. That's the one accusation I can't fight off.

"But you're a man who takes responsibility," he goes on, folding his hands in front of him as he watches me carefully. "So I have a solution that should make us both happy. I'm assigning you to her and her business. You'll be her personal guard, and I expect you to handle the situation with all the stubbornness I've seen tonight."

So that's how it is. That's why he's here. He saw a chance to get the family to protect Serena's business, and he took it. He's good. And he's right—because I'd take a bullet to the heart before I let anything happen to Serena.

"Lorenzo Abruzzi takes these kinds of things very personally," the consigliere says. "If it makes you feel better about watching over Miss De Laurentis's place, chances are good he'll see this as between the two of you above all."

"So what, should I expect a hit squad to come shoot up my place sometime soon?" I say.

"I wouldn't rule that out," Diego speaks up, "but Lorenzo has a reputation... with women."

I raise an eyebrow.

"He's not good to his girls, and the Abruzzis don't shy away from the sex trade. Kid's got an ego so fragile even someone like Serena can shake it. Hell, *especially* someone like her. He won't like the fact that you showed his ass up in front of her. That shop of hers is going to be on his mind, Luca—and so is she. The Cleaners know who she is. That and this new history the three of you have makes her a high-value target."

They're goading me into anger, but as much as the heat is boiling up inside me, I won't show it. "What are you saying?"

"I'm saying," the consigliere says, standing up and locking eyes with me, "that going after you isn't enough for a man like Lorenzo. We got a tip. Lorenzo has his eyes set on Serena. If he gets his hands on her, he's going to make her disappear into the sex trade. Or worse."

*L*ast night was a whirlwind.

I was still reeling from the rush of it all when I finally made it back home last night around two in the morning. Thankfully, Mom was already in her bedroom with the lights off by then, instead of waiting up for me to come home like she often did. I wonder what time she gave up waiting for me, and the thought is almost enough to deflate my high spirits. In the back of my mind there's a small voice telling me I should feel guilty for leaving her here all alone for so long when I know good and well that she's prone to worrying about me. But then again, I do spend all my time working and doing everything in my power to look after Mom and the house. Don't I deserve a break every now and then?

Besides, there's no way in hell I could have resisted a reunion with Luca, even if I wanted to.

He's the one who got away, the knight in shining armor who has finally returned from a long, arduous eternity at war. From the very second it clicked in my brain who he was, it's been totally clear to me that I have been waiting for him all this time, without even realizing it. Even though I thought I was over it, over all the awful stuff that went down several years ago between and around us, there's always been a little part of me who kept looking for him everywhere I went.

And now he's back. He's back! It's almost impossible to fathom, that we could find our way back to each other again after all this time. He's changed, that's for damn sure. No longer the scrappy, rebellious teenager who first captured my heart. No, he's a man now.

Standing in the shower after waking up late — I somehow managed to sleep through my alarm again — I think about how much he's changed. That face of his, always handsome, has gained a more serious, world-weary expression. Like he's seen and done things that the teenage version of him could never imagine. It hurts my heart to think of him in pain.

And then there are the more physical changes: his height, his rippling muscles, the scruffy beard obscuring his strong jawline and making him look like some rugged mountain man in the very best way imaginable. I shiver involuntarily, feeling myself getting wet between my thighs just at the thought of him. If I thought I was subconsciously longing for him before, there was no hiding the fact that I *very* consciously wanted him now. Especially after last night, when I found myself wrapped up in the most explosively fantastic sex of my life.

Until the evening was cut short by that phone call.

I still have no idea what that was really about, but right now is not the right time to think about it, since staying up late last night made me oversleep, and now I'm late for opening the shop! I've never allowed a man or my emotions to override my intense desire to maintain my responsibilities. I'm a hard worker, and I know that the future of my little, broken family is in my hands.

So I hurry through my shower and the rest of my

morning routine, get dressed and dash out the door. It's not until I'm already driving to work that I realize I forgot to even say good morning to my mother. That familiar, heavy feeling of guilt settles down over me and when I pull into a gas station to fill up my tank, I take out my phone and send her a text message.

Good morning! Sorry I had to rush. Slept thru my alarm.

Barely ten seconds pass before I get a reply: **You were very late coming home last night.**

My heart sinks. So she was awake for that. I type out, **I'm sorry, did I wake you up? Time got away from me.** As I put the gas cap back on and slide into the driver's seat to start my car, the phone buzzes again.

No, I was already awake. Just waiting for you to come home. I do worry when you're out so late, Serena. You're young and you should be enjoying life. I know how hard you work, dear. But things aren't the way they were when I was your age. Not anymore. It's dangerous out there.

I sigh, wondering how to respond. I decide that because I'm already late for work, I don't have time to write out a long reply. I simply answer, **I know, Mom. I'll be more careful. I love you.** Then I start the car and make my way downtown to work. Even my mother's worrying can't totally puncture my giddiness as I dreamily relive the events of last night, playing it over and over in my head.

However, when I walk up to the shop front, my good mood instantly melts away and my heart begins to race. Right there, on each of the two wide windows that I keep so spotlessly clean, is bright red graffiti. Both windows have a massive skull with three legs coming out of it. The symbol looks vaguely familiar, and then it hits me. In one of my introductory college history classes, I remember seeing a symbol similar to this one in a list of various national flags from around the world.

If I recall correctly, this particular one belongs to Sicily, only with a normal human face in the center instead of a gruesome skull. It dawns on me that this must be used as some kind of gang or mafia insignia around here. Probably the same guys who threatened me for protection money. I swallow hard, almost afraid to even go inside my own shop, the beloved store I call home for the majority of my waking hours. The one asset left of my father's former dynasty.

Tears burn in my eyes as passersby cross the street to avoid having to walk close to my shop. I can feel them all whispering, averting their eyes, making mental notes to never set foot in Bathing Beauty, because it's now tainted with mob activity. I can just hear them gossiping at the office water cooler with their stuffy, white-collar coworkers, talking about how my shop has been marked. Discussing the inevitable failure of my business. Hedging bets on how long it'll be before Bathing Beauty shuts down forever. The thought makes me feel dizzy and weak in the knees.

"What am I doing just standing here?" I murmur to myself angrily. I shake myself out of my stunned, tragic state and go inside to grab some rags and window cleaner, then set to work trying to scrub away the graffiti. I'll be damned if all my hard work gets undone by some arrogant hooligans. I may be just one young woman, but I'm also my Dad's daughter, and he would be disappointed to see me fall apart so easily. I'm better than that.

However, the window cleaner doesn't seem to be affecting the graffiti at all, and after about an hour of fruitless scrubbing, my arms are aching and I decide to just leave it for now. After all, there's inventory to do and shelves to clean and stock. So I go inside and get to work, turning on some upbeat radio station and trying my best to pretend everything is okay.

A couple hours pass before there's the jingle of the front door and I glance over eagerly, hoping that maybe some brave customer has decided to look past the graffiti and come in anyway. But it's actually even better than that: Luca is walking in!

Despite everything, my mouth immediately upturns into a smile as I take in his freshly-shaven face, the sexy button-up shirt he's wearing rolled to his elbows, and the giant bouquet of exotic-looking red flowers in his hands. He grins at me and it's almost like the beauty of his smile knocks me back a step. God, he's handsome.

"Good morning, *mia passerotta*," he says, his voice a delicious deep thrum.

"Luca, I wasn't expecting to see you," I say, feeling as bashful as a preteen girl with a schoolyard crush. I nervously tuck my hair behind my ears as he steps up to the counter and offers me the bouquet. "What are these? They're beautiful!" I ask.

"Nearly as beautiful as you," Luca adds. "In fact, you're the most beautiful thing I have ever seen since I last saw these flowers growing wild back home in Italy. It just so happened this morning that I noticed the neighborhood florist had some in the window and I had to get them for you. It's fate."

His words immediately warm my soul and help me relax a little. Luca has always had a calming presence about him, and it's intoxicating to be around. But then his expression darkens a little.

"I can't help but notice the new artwork on your front windows there," he points out, those green eyes locked with mine. There's a deep sympathy there. I look away.

"Yeah, it was there when I got here this morning," I

answer, fiddling with the bouquet. "I tried washing it off but I couldn't get it to even smudge."

"It's the special kind of paint they use. I'll have to get you some heavy-duty industrial-grade cleaner to get rid of it," Luca tells me. "In fact, I'll go get it now. I know just where to find it. I'll be back in twenty minutes."

He nods and turns to leave, clearing the space to the door with several long strides.

"Luca, you don't have to—"

He glances back and gives me a consoling smile. "I want to."

Then he walks out and gets into his car to drive off, leaving me standing here slack-jawed and stunned, still holding the beautiful flowers. I quickly find a vase in the back room, fill it with water, and by the time I'm finished trimming and arranging the flowers into the vase, the door jingles again and in walks Luca with a giant white bottle of cleaner in his hand. It can't have even been fifteen minutes, much less twenty!

At my shocked expression, Luca laughs and says, "I know a guy. Now, just give me a few minutes and I'll have this shit come right off."

I stand inside, watching through the window as Luca easily scrubs away the red graffiti until the glass sparkles and shines again. It's like magic. Luca is like magic. When he comes back in, he goes to wash his hands and I follow, thanking him profusely.

"It's no big deal," he assures me. "I can't have you trying to run a shop with that ugly shit on the windows. Problem solved. The nightmare's behind you now, sweetheart. However," he adds with a grin brightening his face, "you're all shaken up. Too shaken up to try and keep the shop running today. You need a break."

I blink a few times, confused. "No, no. I-I'm fine, really. I have a lot of work to do."

Luca glances around. "Looks spic-and-span in here, Serena. Not much to do."

I shifted uncomfortably, biting my lip. "Well, it's just…I can't leave. What if I have a customer? I need to meet my daily sales quota or the profit margin gets totally skewed, and I'm already barely breaking even, as it is, and—"

"Hey," Luca interrupts, his hands landing gently on my shoulders as he peers into my face. I feel my body heating up just from this light touch. "If it's a quota you're after, just let me know how much it is and I'll make it happen."

I raise an eyebrow skeptically. "What, do you 'know a guy' who needs a few hundred dollars' worth of bath bombs and soaps?"

Luca chuckles. "Yeah. Me."

I stare at him blankly. "You. You want three-hundred-dollars of bath goods."

He shrugs and walks over to pick up a wicker shopping basket. "Sure. Load me up."

"Luca, that's ridiculous, you can't just—"

"Why not? You're really going to turn away a paying customer?" he asks earnestly, with a mischievous glint in his gorgeous eyes. Against my better judgement, I have to laugh.

"Okay. Fine. If you're totally sure."

"Oh, I definitely am. Now, do you have any manly-scented stuff or am I just gonna go full floral with this deal?" he asks, picking up and peering quizzically at a lavender-scented bubble bath gel.

I giggle and direct him toward the corner of the shop dedicated to slightly more masculine scents like sandal-wood, cedar, and evergreen. I realize I'm not quite sure how to proceed. Usually I have to make some kind of eloquent sales pitch, going through the motions of giving free samples, gingerly soaping and rinsing a customer's hands while describing the various benefits and quirks of our homemade products.

"So, do you want to just kind of take some of everything or...?" I question.

"No, no. I want the full spiel. I want some testers and samples. Let's do this," Luca says brightly. I can't help but grin. He seems like such a serious guy, it's amazing to see how relaxed and whimsical he can actually be.

So we spend the next forty-five minutes testing out a ton of different scents and products in the sink while I explain how, every month, I spend a whole weekend in the back kitchen creating all these soaps, bath bombs, and everything else. It's a long, back-breaking process, but it's also really fun and relaxing in some ways. I get to zone out and listen to my favorite music while I play mad scientist, mixing essential oils and playing with new combinations. My mom taught me everything, which she learned from a summer of soap-making classes over a decade ago, back when life was easy and she was just a bored housewife looking for a new hobby. Long before this became the one business endeavor keeping us afloat. Barely.

And it's fun today, too, washing Luca's strong, scarred hands in the sink, the two of us leaning close together, so close I can feel the masculine heat coming from his powerful body. We flirt shamelessly throughout the whole process, and by the time we're done, we've moved from the men's section and outward, so that his basket is also filled with rose- and lavender-scented products, too.

"So, you're really gonna use this stuff? You're gonna squeeze your massive body into a little bathtub and take a sugar-cookie-scented bubble bath?" I ask him, giggling.

He gives me a wink. "Maybe I will. Or maybe I'll just save all that stuff so that you can use it when you stay over at my place. Gotta make my bathroom more lady-friendly, of course."

I can feel myself blushing, and I look away. But Luca takes me gently by the chin and turns me back to face him before leaning down and kissing me softly. A tingling warmth shoots all the way down my body and I melt into the kiss. Luca sets all three of his heaping-full shopping baskets down on the counter and pulls me in close, deepening the kiss. I lose myself in the moment, our tongues gently pushing against each other while his hands stroke the hair back from my face.

When we break apart, he says, "Well, I guess I'm ready to check out."

As I ring him up, the total reaches well over the daily sales quota and my stomach flip-flops.

"Luca, are you sure? This is...really expensive. You don't have to buy all this stuff."

He shakes his head. "Nope. You can't talk me out of it. Your sales pitch was just too convincing, and yes, I *do* need three baskets of bath products. It's final."

After he pays— in cash— I help him load all his purchases into the trunk of his car, and then he turns to me and says, "Well, now that that's over, I think it's time you take the rest of the day off. After all, you have officially met your daily quota. What else could there be for you to do?"

At first I open my mouth to protest, to tell him that it would be irresponsible for me to abandon my duties even now. What would my mother think? What would my *father* think? But instead, I realize that I have no way of resisting Luca's offer, and even if I did...well, I really do want to go with him and see whatever he has in store for me.

So I give in easily and decide to lock up the shop for the day. It's thrilling, like the feeling of ditching class for the first time as a teenager, that delicious, forbidden sense of freedom and danger. I have no idea what to expect from a day out with Luca. It's been so long since we last spent time together this way, and even though I know him, he's definitely changed since then. But I am so willing and excited to find out.

"So, where are we headed on this day of rebellious truancy?" I pipe up as I slide into the passenger seat of his sleek car. Luca revs the engine into gear and glances over at me with a smile.

"Have you ever been to the aquarium?" he asks.

"The aquarium?" I repeat incredulously. "Really? No, I-I haven't been there, actually."

"Well, today's the day then," Luca declares, reaching over to gently squeeze my thigh through the thin fabric of my dress. That telltale heatwave vibrates through me again.

But after a few minutes of driving, I realize we're not going in the direction of the New York Aquarium. In fact, I have no idea where we're actually headed.

I don't let myself glance at the rear-view mirror more than once every few minutes. I've learned to act natural in situations like this, to almost convince *myself* that nothing is out of the ordinary as I carefully weave through traffic. It's important to stay relaxed, not to show the slightest hint that you know anything is out of the ordinary.

Because we're being tailed.

I noticed it several blocks back, and it took a lot of strength not to swear. The black sedan that's been keeping up with us isn't one that I recognize. It's the Cleaners, I have no doubt in my mind about that.

And I want to unload every chamber in my gun at them.

Normally, I wouldn't feel so furious about getting tailed. Over the years, I've come to recognize it as part of business. An inconvenient part that meant things were soon to get very fast and very exciting, but still just another part.

But the thought that they would have the audacity to tail me right now fills me with fury that I have to force myself to hold back from my face. The reason is sitting right next to me. With Serena in the car, I feel a protective instinct rear its head inside me. It's not a new feeling. I knew it well when we were teenagers. I forgot how powerful it made me feel.

These men dare put Serena at risk, and if it comes to it, I won't hesitate to kill for that. But for now, I carefully plan out a path in my head that will take us through traffic where I know I can lose them. All it will take is a little patience.

I'm so caught up thinking of Serena's safety that I almost forget we're heading out on a date. That just makes me all the more furious at the bastards behind us for intruding on a moment with Serena.

"So," Serena's voice snaps me out of my concentration a moment, "I've gotta admit, you don't strike me as an aquarium kinda guy."

I raise my eyebrow at her. "No?"

"No, something about the rippling muscle and guns don't scream 'I love dolphins'."

"Dolphins are alright," I say simply. My face is still, but I can see her cracking a smile out of the corner of my eye as if she can't tell if I'm joking or not.

"But you've been here before, right?" she says, glancing at the road.

"Once." I take a turn, hand on the gear shift, and I'm at the other end of the road taking another turn by the time I see our pursuers come into sight. I'm gaining ground.

"Oh. Did some starfish owe you money or something?" she asks with a smile, and I can't help but feel a grin tug at my lips.

"Seal, actually," I say, and she giggles. It's nice to hear her joking, feeling at ease with me. But every time we share something lighthearted together, I can't help but feel that nagging voice at the back of my mind. It reminds me that I the closer I get to her, the more I could put her in danger.

I can't let that happen. But I can't abandon her, either. We've opened the Pandora's Box, and I'm not prepared to lose her again.

To let her go again, I correct myself.

"Really, though, who convinced you to go check out the fish?"

"My uncle," I say, my smile fading into a more wistful one as I think back to him. Along with Serena, my uncle is one of the few people I can think of in this country and feel happy.

"Carlo?"

"You remember him?" I say with a smile, glancing over at her before glancing back to the rear-view. Damn it, they're back on us again.

"You talked about him a lot," she says, "seems like a really nice guy."

I give a half-smile, thinking back to my teenage years. "Yeah, yeah he is."

"So what, you take your old uncle to the aquarium for his birthday or something?"

"Opposite," I say, leaning back in the seat. "When I first got here—to America, I mean—my uncle wanted to show me the sights, and for some reason he thought the aquarium was a good place to start. I think I was...thirteen? Fourteen?"

"Ohhh my god," she says, grinning broadly, and I know she's picturing my punk-ass getting dragged around New York by the old man.

"I was a little shit," I say with a laugh, thinking back to myself fresh off the 'boat.' "I think he didn't realize what age I was at, and he kept trying to get me interested in all the sharks and jellyfish and all the dangerous ones. All I did was grouch around the place. Every time he tried to show me something, I'd fuck off somewhere else or swear at him with some of the English words I learned."

"Wow, you were bad," she giggles, and I shake my head, chuckling.

"He got back at me, though. When he started teaching me his carpentry, he drilled me, constantly."

"Wait-"

"No, not literally," I say, "it was just intense. He wouldn't accept anything less than perfection. He's a poor man, but I've never seen carpentry better than what he'd make, and he expected me to be able to do the same. I was getting there, too."

That wasn't the only thing Uncle Carlo taught me, either. There were other skills I got from him, skills that made me so good at what I do now. Uncle Carlo has a lot of secrets Serena doesn't need to hear about. Not now, at least.

"Wow," she says, and I notice she's looking down at my hand on the stick-shift. "I always wondered what made your hands like that."

"Like what?"

A little color comes to her cheeks. "Hm? Oh. I dunno. Rough. It's...kinda nice."

I smile, feeling quiet pride swelling in my chest, and she twirls a lock of hair around her finger for a few moments of silence between us before speaking up again.

"Are you *sure* you've been to the aquarium before?" I hear her ask. Despite the situation, I smile. I was wondering when she'd notice. She's sharp. She always has been.

"I am."

"...are you sure this is the right way?"

"Yes."

She just stares at me blankly for a few moments, and I realize that I can't hide anything from her. It's better that she know, anyway—easier to keep her safe when she knows what I'm watching out for. "Look up at the mirror and tell me if you see a black sedan three cars behind us. Be subtle."

Her body tenses up immediately, but she manages to look up at the mirror without jerking around. "Yeah."

"It's been following us since about five blocks from where we left."

"Shit, really?" she hisses, and before she can say anything else, I reach over and take one of her small, slender hands in my rough fingers. I give it a squeeze, glancing over at her to smile.

"Let me worry about him," I say calmly. "I might not have been born here, but I know the Bronx better than these *stronzi* from over the river."

She nods, and I shift gears and pull out of traffic through a side-road when I have the chance. It's a quick move, and I soon have us out onto another road that lets me weave through traffic a little more freely.

"I know a way Dad used to take us when things were...kinda heated," she says suddenly, and I'm so surprised I look over at her with a raised eyebrow. She looks a little unsure of herself, but she nods to the road up ahead. "About five blocks down, take a right. I think I remember it pretty well."

"Serena..."

"I'm sure about it," she says with a little more confidence, and I crack a smile.

Following Serena's direction, I take us on a winding path through the city, but I'm impressed by how Serena handles herself. I glance over at her now and then, and I can see she's scared, but she keeps herself calm on the surface. Her eyes go to the mirror periodically, but she knows better than to be obvious. She's strong. She's had to be strong for so long. She shouldn't have to be.

It takes us about half an hour out of the way, but around the third time I check the mirror and see nothing there, I hear Serena say cautiously, "I think you lost them."

"Yes," I say, turning onto a road to take us back toward where I still plan on taking her. "You shouldn't have to worry about all that."

"You seem pretty used to it," she says, and I watch her eyes move up and down me swiftly.

"Yes," I say, letting the matter rest there as I speed us toward the aquarium.

Sometime later, we come to a halt in the crowded parking lot.

Even as I get out of the car, my eyes are scanning the lot to see if we've been followed despite my efforts. The thought of work intruding on my time with Serena is infuriating, but not as infuriating as the thought of her getting hurt.

My glance around the lot is subtle, but as I walk around the car to Serena, I feel her meaningful squeeze on my arm, and I look down at her. She's smiling up and me, and I know she's telling me silently not to worry.

I give a smile back, but that won't make my demons go away so easily.

Inside the aquarium, oddly, the sights and sounds of a big and happy crowd puts me a little more at ease, and I can enjoy the feeling of the temperature-controlled rooms with slightly dimmed lighting.

It's a beautiful place. After stopping by the ticket booth, it's Serena who takes the lead, dragging me to the nearest exhibits that catch her eye, growing more excited with each minute that goes by. While soft, happy music plays all around us, we make our way around some of the big and small glass tanks.

"Luca Luca Luca oh my God!" she squeals, her arm half-submerged in one of the open touch pools. I step up beside her to see her gently touching a brightly-colored starfish that's lazing on the bottom.

"What's the matter?" I chuckle, raising an eyebrow at her.

"It feels weeeeird," she half-whispers, as if not wanting to offend the aquarium worker hovering around.

"You never felt a starfish before?" I say, a grin spreading across my face.

"You have?!" she shoots back.

I roll up my sleeve and sink my thick arm into the water, and I notice the worker glancing at me uneasily. I guess I look more likely to break something than Serena's small hand. I give the man a wink and turn my attention back to Serena.

"I grew up on the coast. We used to go swimming and find sea urchins and other things. You can let them crawl on your hand, if you're careful."

"Wow," she says, "I only ever went swimming in a public pool. You uh, really don't want to pick up anything you find at the bottom of those."

I chuckle, and we soon move on, drying our hands with cheap little paper towels.

As we walk, Serena slips her arm through mine, sighing gently as we stroll past the exhibits, and her eyes are wide as we walk through the glass tunnel that lets sea life float lazily all around us. I stand a head taller than most of the people around us, and I have a look about me that makes most people give us all the space we need.

I find myself watching her more than any of the fish, though. I didn't think an aquarium was all that special, but she seems really swept up in the atmosphere of the place. As her eyes travel around the half-cylinder of the tunnel, they fall on me, and she blushes as she realizes I'm looking at her. "Stop! Look at the fish," she playfully whines, and I give her hand a squeeze as we move on.

When I'm not looking at Serena, though, I'm glancing over my shoulder, at every corner, half-expecting to see someone following us. It would be beyond stupid for anyone to follow us in here, but I can't help but look.

Our walk soon takes us into a wide, very dark room, the only illumination coming from the soft blue glow of the tanks around us. The ceiling is low, and the only sound is the gentle droning of the machinery that keeps the place running. Only a handful of people wander around here—I suspect there's a show going on somewhere drawing most of the day-crowd.

As we walk, Serena's eyes are drawn to the beautiful displays of sea life floating around in view, but I catch her glancing at me from time to time. She's a perceptive girl. I know she can sense my tension, as much as I try to hide it. We walk across the soft carpet to one of the windows, peering out into the blue, fuzzy space beyond, and I feel her squeeze my arm.

"Hey," she says.

"Hey."

"Is something up? You seem kind of…"

I give her a tight smile. "I don't like being tailed, Serena."

"Not just that," she says, shaking her head, and I can see those round eyes looking straight through me. She can read me like an open book, as closed as I try to keep myself. "You've been tense all day. Did something happen at that meeting you had to run off to?"

"Serena, I don't want to worry you with business."

"Don't say that," she says softly, those beautiful eyes watching a shark glide around the bottom of its tank, "that's what Dad used to say all the time."

I'm silent for a few moments, but then she turns her head to look at me, a smile on her lips. "If you can trust me to lose someone tailing us, you can trust me with anything else that's going on, I think."

If you only knew the half of it.

I give her a sad smile, looking down at her, watching the wavy light reflecting off the water dance across her face, her hair, those eyes. "It isn't that I don't want to talk business because I don't trust you, Serena," I say, enveloping her hand in mine. I turn and take her small chin in my free hand, stroking her jaw with my thumb as she smiles up at me. "You thrive even though everything is stacked against you. You own a business. You're a survivor. And you're better than all this—that's why I don't want you getting wrapped up in anything dangerous."

She sets her hand on my hip, feeling the strong muscles under my tight-fitting shirt. "I've got you here, though," she says, her eyes playful, lidded, a smile creeping over those lips. "As long as you're with me, Luca, it's kinda hard to feel like anything could hurt me. I saw what you did in the shop. I feel...well, *safe* when you're around."

I feel warmth spreading through my chest, and I can't help but smile in pride. I wrap my arms around her waist, holding her protectively as the scent of her hair fills my nostrils. "You know how naive that sounds, *passerotta mia*," I say, only half-seriously, and she looks up at me with a challenging smile.

"Don't give me that," she says, her Italian blood showing, "you and I both know how well we work together."

I feel a chuckle escaping me, and I bring my face close to hers as I rumble, "All too well, Serena."

Our lips meet.

All the world seems to melt away as I hold her there. We're not standing in a public place, we're off in our own world, far away from all our troubles, all our danger. A place we've visited before when things got too heated. A place we went when we both *were* young and naive. Things haven't changed so much after all.

Just the world around us has.

But I eventually feel her soft lips leaving mine, and she looks up at me, her smiling eyes proud of the thickening shaft growing between my legs. But I can't let everything go unspoken between us. Looking at her evenly, our eyes locked, I level with her.

"You're in danger, Serena," I say softly yet firmly. "I won't lie to you." I watch the ghost of fear wash over her face briefly, but she swallows.

"You mean...those guys you fought with."

"The Cleaners."

She gives me a puzzled look, and I turn back to the aquarium tank with her in my arm, hugged to my side. "There have always been a lot of gangs fighting for dominance down in Spanish Harlem. There's always been a small Italian presence, but they've kept to themselves for a long time. Now, Spanish Harlem is changing, and they got pushed out with nowhere else to go. A group of them calling themselves the Abruzzi family showed up in the south side of the Bronx a while back. They earned a reputation, and the nickname stuck. They've been pushing into our territory.

"That's who was at my shop?" she says, her eyes widening. I squeeze her side. "Is that why they were there? Why would anyone bother with my shop if-"

"The Cleaners don't play by any rules, Serena," I say. My voice is low, both to keep our conversation quiet and keep her calm. "The man harassing you, Lorenzo—he's the so-called Don's son. He's a spoiled man in a family of upstarts," I say, not hiding the edge of disgust in my voice. I don't like mafia politics on a good day, and the Cleaners are the worst of the worst. I've been...tactful in how I describe the situation, though. The last thing I want is to scare her too much.

"Oh God," she breathes, leaning into me. "The mark on the window today...this isn't going to go away, is it?"

"I've been assigned to protect you, Serena," I say, looking down at her, and I can practically feel her heart flutter as she looks up at me. "I don't want the rest of my associates getting involved unless I'm the one calling the shots. I'm going to keep you safe *and* out of all that business."

I know old memories are getting dredged up, and I see the shining hint of tears welling up in her eyes. I squeeze her, and she opens her mouth silently before saying, "Do you think that's going to be a problem? That the m- that your associates are going to start caring about my shop?"

"No," I say firmly, squeezing her hand. "I've made sure of that. And if that changes, Serena," I say, leaning in to whisper into her ear, "then the mafia can go fuck themselves. You and I are the only ones I care about, *carina*. I'll be right here, at your side, watching over you. As long as this heart of mine is beating, I swear, nothing will touch you unless you want it to."

Her lip is quivering, and I meet her embrace as she hugs me, sinking into my arms, and I feel a tear stain the shoulder of my shirt.

Growing up with families like ours, you don't escape the shadow of the mafia. But maybe together, we can keep just one light aflame to see us through the dark.

Sometime later, I walk her through the rest of the aquarium to ease her mind off of such heavy things. She's spacey at first, but soon, the play of the dolphins and the gentle, hypnotic floating of the jellyfish we pass help her smile, and by the time we get a bite to eat, she's chatting about some biology class she took in college as if she didn't have a care in the world.

It's the little things that give me some hope for the future. But even so, as the day winds down and we make our way out to the parking lot and look up at the dark sky, I know we can't escape our troubles that easily. I hold her tight to me as we make our way down the parking lot that's not lit up by nothing but street lights.

While Serena has a spring to her step, I'm already expecting what makes her freeze in her tracks when my car comes into view.

"Luca-"

"I know," I say, my eyes darting around the lot as my gun hand twitches.

Parked next to my car is the black sedan that was tailing us earlier today.

"*B*e casual, follow my lead," I say as I guide her to the side, walking away from my parked car.

"Where are we going?"

"Just stay close to me," I say as softly as if I were teaching her how to drive a car. "Do what I say, and be ready to run if I tell you to."

"You know I won't," she says, tenacious even in a tense situation, and I can't help but smile. *That's my girl.*

"Then just be ready," I say, my hand on the small of her back as I guide her.

There's going to be trouble tonight. That much is unavoidable. I know we have eyes on us now, and it won't be long before they close in. But if we're going to have a fight, I will pick the battleground. We'll do things on my terms.

The boardwalk is next to the aquarium. It's still only as well-lit as the street lights will let it be, but there are less surprises in an open space than in a parking lot. I guide us onto the wooden planks, empty for a long way on either side by this time of the evening. Most people are either heading home or know better than to hang around the waterfront at night.

It's *mostly* empty, anyway. My eyes have been scanning the area as I guide Serena out, and by the time we step onto the boardwalk, I've spotted the men following us out there. There are three of them. I size them up. They're big, one of them almost as big as me.

"Luca?" Serena whispers.

"Remember what I said," I assure her as I guide her to the nearest light, watching the shadowy figures present themselves about ten paces away from us. The looks on their faces tell me they're about as ready to drop the pretense as I am. Riegelmann Boardwalk is basically a straight line—two of them are up ahead of us, and the big guy is behind us.

"You boys lost?" I say to them, looking between both of them. "This area can be a little dangerous at night."

"Shut the fuck up, Lomaglio," the big one addresses me by my last name, his deep voice rumbling from a mouth with a missing front tooth. "You know what this is about."

"Oh, Lorenzo wants his teeth back? Sorry, didn't bring 'em with me," I say, rolling my shoulders back as they take steps forward. "Tell him to meet me himself if he wants 'em. I'd say you could bring back some of your own and tell him they're his, but it looks like you tried that already."

As he makes a snarling face, I notice his hand twitch as if for a gun, but he stops himself. The NYPD station is just a block away. I have no doubt the cops have been paid off to turn a blind eye to the area for the next hour or so. That kind of thing happens all the time, even by my own associates. But even so, I'm guessing they didn't give a bribe big enough to ignore gunshots in the police's back yard.

Instead, I see the big guy's fist glimmer in the lamplight with a pair of brass knuckles.

"Fuck him up, boys, and take the girl," he orders, and he moves forward while the two in front charge.

I turn in time to see the two of them, the flash of a knife in the hand of each. Serena hunches down on instinct, and I step forward to put myself between her and them.

One lunges, but I turn with his strike and simply grab his wrist to pull him along, using his own momentum to throw him off-balance while I deal with the other guy.

The second knife swings from below, but I can see it coming from a mile away, and I simply catch him by the fist and squeeze. The muscles of my thick forearms ripple as he throws a wild punch with his other hand, but by the time it strikes my jaw, he's already screaming in agony as his wrist crunches with a sickening noise in my grip.

I hear Serena gasp from behind me. It makes me all the more furious that these fuckers are spoiling our date.

I answer his weak punch by seizing his other wrist, leaving him totally open, and my knee shoots up to the dead-center of his diaphragm, knocking the wind out of him. His knife falls to the ground as he doubles over and crumples to the ground. I kick the knife far away.

It might be useful, but it's not worth bending over to pick up.

Especially not as I hear a grunt from behind me, and the squirrelly man I threw off-balance a moment ago throws his arms around my neck. I catch his fist just in time to see the point of the blade aimed at my throat.

My jaw clenches as I hold the man's weapon away from me, both of us twisting as we struggle against each other. He's stronger than he looks, but not strong enough to overcome me.

"Turn him around!" the big guy commands, and I hear Serena's yelp with the sound of flesh striking flesh.

My anger burns in me like a flame, and I see red.

Adrenaline surges through every corner of my body. I

twist the man's knife away and crouch down to hurl him over my shoulder, hearing him *thump* solidly on the ground before my fist comes down on his face. There's the sound of cracking bone, and I know I've broken more than his nose when the force turns his head and puts him out cold.

An angry roar behind me makes me jump up to face the big guy, but what I see surprises me. He has Serena by the wrist, trying to hold her up and keep her off-guard—him grabbing her must have been the sound I heard. But in Serena's right hand is a little black cylinder.

She turns her head and shuts her eyes as the little can of pepper spray unleashes on him, and the man shouts out in pain and drops Serena, who scurries back while he wipes his eyes.

"Fucking brat! I'll kill you both!" he shouts, opening bloodshot eyes that fall squarely on me. His heavy foot-steps carry him toward me, giving me enough time to square up and anticipate the jab he comes in with.

By his build and the way he carries himself, even with eyes full of pepper spray, I can tell this guy must be a boxer. A lot of them trickle down into the mob's ranks, and I know what to expect when this gorilla of a man comes swinging.

A jab and a cross first, brass knuckles humming through the air as if they were blades. A basic combo. With simple, quick movements, I dodge the blows, just like when I play-fought with the guys behind Uncle Carlo's shop. But instead of the hook I'm expecting, he surprises me with a left uppercut. I move fast, and it glances off the side of my face, leaving my ears ringing for a moment.

I see him getting ready for another onslaught—it's going to be hard to get this guy close enough to grapple. He lunges in for another jab, but I'm faster this time and catch him on the nose. He blinks in confusion, and then I see his face contort in pain after the sound of a thud from behind him. He reaches over his shoulder with his teeth gritted…

And I see Serena backing away from him in shock at what she's done, moments before the big guy turns enough for me to see the switchblade she just sunk into his back.

I take the opening. In half a second, I side-step him to get behind him, and in the instant that he rips Serena's blade out, I wrap my arms around him in a sleeper hold. He snarls—it's astounding he's even still standing—and he starts stabbing blindly behind him with the switchblade, trying to sink it into my leg. I hold my grip, an expert at controlling my foes this close up, and I feel the man's bulk start to get heavier as his strength leaves him.

Finally, the sound of the switchblade hitting the ground tells me it's over. I let the man collapse to the pavement awkwardly, and I step back, surveying our work. But I only do so long enough to make sure nobody's moving.

As soon as I have, I turn and embrace Serena, who's shaking in my arms as I hug her close to me, tears staining my shirt.

"O-o-oh my God, did I kill him?!" she stammers in a panic, and I can't help but smile as I rock her gently, stroking her hair to calm her down.

"No, no, Serena, everything's okay. You're okay. I've got you."

"Luca, I-I've never used that knife before, I just had it and thought-"

"You were wonderful," I say, holding her shoulders and pulling her back enough to look her in those shining eyes, beaming at her.

And with adrenaline still pumping through my body, she's never looked more attractive to me. Her slender frame feels so *right* in these hands of mine, fresh from protecting her without a weapon on hand. And as her panicked form stops shaking while she looks up at me, I see a glint of the same in her eyes.

As if we had the same thought, we dive at each other in a deep kiss, and my hand goes to her ass when I feel my manhood growing between my legs.

But after a second that felt like an eternity, I break the kiss and whisper, "Come on, we need to get out of here."

~

"I'm staying the night," I say firmly once we're through the front door of her place and I lock it. I used one of the men's knives to slash their car tires before I drove us off. After that beating, those men would be lucky if they were awake by morning, much less able to track us down with their battered bodies.

Still, I'm not going anywhere. For more than one reason.

"Are you sure they didn't follow us?" Serena gasps, almost forgetting to take off her jacket when she steps inside, hand starting to shake again. She's gotten jittery in waves between then and the ride to her home.

"Yes."

"Oh my god, Luca, they were trying to kill you!"

"Yes."

"A-are you sure you're okay?" she says, rushing up to me and looking me over, "I-"

I silence her by putting a hand to her soft lips, looking at her steadily in the eyes. "Yes."

Without another word, I pull her into me and bring my lips to hers. I feel and hear a soft, surprised gasp from her before she starts to melt into me. We both have so much pent-up energy left over from the rush of the fight, and we desperately need somewhere to put it.

"You did well tonight," I say as she tugs my hand, beckoning me to be quiet as she leads me to her bedroom. It's on the far corner of the house, and she relaxes once the door clasps shut.

"I was so scared," she breathes as she tilts her head back, exposing her neck to me now that we're in private. I take the bait and attack her neck, kisses running up and down the sensitive skin, teeth grazing it and making her gasp. "Luca, if you hadn't been there-"

"You made me proud," I say, quieting her with a squeeze of her ass. "You've become a strong woman, *passerotta mia*." We kick our shoes off in a hurry, and I haven't even gotten her top off before my hand gropes her chest, cupping a breast and savoring the feel of it through the thin fabric. She shivers at my touch. My other hand goes to her ass as I work her back toward the bed.

Finally, I sit her down on it, and I kneel over her, sliding my hand up to her back as we stare into each other's eyes, seeing the passion in each other's gaze. "*I've gotten strong? What even was that?*"

I run my fingers into her hair, letting the silky feel of it run over my hand like water. "My work isn't something to be proud of, Serena."

"It does have its perks," she says, her eyes roving over the rippling muscle of my body, and I see her bite her lip as she runs her hands down my sides before reaching the hem of my shirt. She tugs at it, looking up at me with a pout to her lip.

It's a look I've seen before, and it still teases the same fire in me.

"You *are* a brat, you know that?" I tease, and a smile tugs her lips into a curl.

"Just for you."

I tear her top off up over her head, tossing it to the side. I glower down at her exposed form, nothing but a bra left on her chest, and with one hand, I unhook it and let it slide off her arms before easing her down onto the soft cushions.

Her breasts free, I descend on them. I let my hot breath wash over her nipple, panting over it like I'm about to devour it, and she arches her back, gasping as I play with the sensitive nub of her nipple relentlessly. My teeth toy with it, grazing against its sides ever so gently. Feeling the nipple harden under my tongue sends fire through me. My hand moves to her other nipple, and I run my thumb over it to excite it as well.

The taste of her is delicious. My tongue lashes back and forth over her nipple, darting out to play between my teeth before I toy with her stiff nipple and cover the area with my mouth.

My other hand gropes her breast, possessing her, letting her know she is *mine*. I push my thumb against the bottom of her nipple and flick it and rub it gently with my index finger. I can make my thick hands handle delicate things, when I want them to.

Her nipples stiffen, and her breathing is quick under me. I can feel her legs squirming, and I know just how much she's getting bothered between her thighs. It brings a smile to me, even as my mouth moves across her breast playfully, teasingly.

I shouldn't be doing this. This is dangerous for both of us. But if we're going to face danger anyway, I want to us to face it together.

I turn my eyes up as I nip her breasts, and I see a mess of blonde hair spilling around her neck and shoulders, mouth hanging open as she whimpers for me. I raise my head away from her breasts, replacing my teeth with my hand on her right breast. I have to look down on Serena.

On my woman.

Her limbs are sprawled out across the bed, long and willowy. She looks like some dancer exhausted from practice, but I'm just getting her started. She turns her eyes to me as she feels the change, and color rushes to her cheeks at the sight of me looming over her, thumbs roving possessively over her nipples.

She bites her lip, and I take my hands away to pull my shirt off over my head and toss it to the floor, displaying my body over her.

Even though she's seen it bare before, even recently, the light I see spark up in her eyes is like she's never seen anything like me before. I feel pride swell up in my chest as I roll my shoulders back, and her gaze meets mine.

To be able to get such a stir from a woman as beautiful as Serena is a thrill. And it should be—she deserves nothing but the very best.

I descend upon her again, this time cupping my hand under her neck and bringing my mouth to it. I kiss her, my other hand holding her by the wrist and splaying out her body as I start to rock my pelvis into her. Even through our pants, I know she can feel my hardness. I've been with women, sure, but nobody has ever made me as ready for love as Serena makes me. Every cell in my body cries out for her when I'm near her.

I run my hands down her body to her hips, and I bring my mouth to her lips. She lifts her head up with a whimper to meet me, and I smile into the kiss as I pull her hips up into me, rocking into her gently while her arms slip around my neck to hold on. Her lips are soft, and I let out a low groan into them before her tongue starts trying to tease mine out. I hold nothing back from her. My tongue dives into her mouth, and we play with each other while I feel a pulse go through my hard body.

I want her. I need her. We don't even need to speak to know how badly we desire each other. My rough hands run up and down her body, feeling every inch of smooth, olive skin. It's the easiest thing in the world to pick her up and turn her however I please, and when I slide her up the couch, she giggles at being held by me, squirming in the cushions, looking up at me with playful eyes.

"You're playing with fire, princess," I say with a low rumble to my voice, but I know Serena and the look in her eyes well enough to know that she likes playing with fire.

In a swift motion, I tear the buttons of her jeans apart, and she gasps when I tug her pants down over her thighs. She tries to kick them the rest of the way off, but I don't want to wait. I yank them the rest of the way off, panties and all, before I slide my hand under the small of her back and lift her legs up.

I run my mouth over her inner thigh, fingers squeezing her soft flesh as I let my breath wash over her, face tickling her as I rove over it.

"God, Luca," she whines, trying in vain, "God, I need you in me, don't keep me waiting!"

I deliver a quick slap to her bare ass, feeling the taut skin quiver under my touch, and she gives a yelp of delight as I squeeze her. "I'm going to take my time devouring you," I growl, "you're too sweet not to savor."

She opens her mouth to respond, but I silence her by lowering my head and dragging my tongue across her slit.

A long, hissing gasp escapes her, and I listen to it hang in the air like a musical note as I look at her lower lips. They're swollen with need like my cock is, and the darker, endlessly sensitive skin folds in on itself, just begging for attention. Her whole body is crying out for me. Just the thought that I have the power to bother her figure so much makes me swell so hard I think my shaft is going to burst from my pants.

I bring my face closer again, breathing heavily on the smooth surface of her pussy. I breathe in, and the heady scent of her makes me want to turn her over and thrust inside of her until neither of us can move anymore.

And I will. But not yet.

I let my tongue forth again, letting it slide through her lips and taste just how ready she is, savoring the flavor of the hot entry the tip of my tongue dances across. I slide my tongue deep into her, as deep as I can, probing and exploring like I own this sanctuary of hers. As the taste of her drives me wild, I reach up and grab her breast with one hand while the other cradles her ass.

Her honey is like wine to me. My tongue dives in, again and again, and I feel her pushing her hips up at me with each stroke. Her breathing is shallow, and each time I reach some new part of her that I haven't touched yet, I hear a gasp to reward me. She's coaxing me further.

She's my brat, and she knows how to get me to dig into her. She likes getting more than she bargained for.

My tongue delves deep into her, drawing up more honey with each sweep. The inside of her vagina is hot, tense, endlessly needy. The more I enter her, the more she wants. I lose track of where my tongue has gone as it slides across the landscape within her.

All I know is that my face is soaked, and so are her lips. A few moments ago, they were puffy with need, and now, a gorgeous sheen glistens on them.

Her legs wrap around my sides as best they can—her legs are long, but my chest is thick with muscle. I can't help but smile at her efforts. I decide to reward her by driving her home.

I draw my tongue up to her clit, and the tip of my tongue darts onto her swollen nub to the sound of a sharp gasp. Fuck, she's close already.

I start to torment her, swirling just beyond her clit, edging nearer with each stroke as she claws at my back and the couch desperately. I think about all the years her poor clit has gone without my touch. I have a lot of time to make up for.

I drive my tongue in and lavish her nub with attention, pushing and flicking around it freely. It's a matter of seconds before her steady gasping becomes a high-pitched squeal, and she tries to close her legs as her honey flows onto my tongue, but I use my hands to keep her thighs apart. "You're not getting free so easy," I growl, and I attack her again.

My lips close around the area of her cunt as I savor her taste. My tongue dives deep into her, and I bring it up slowly, painfully slowly, to her clit, where I torment her until she's squirming relentlessly in my hands.

I raise my eyes enough to look at her, and there's a smile of absolute bliss on her face as I take her with my mouth. Her first orgasm left her glowing, and I know she's tingling head to toe, but even so, she wants more.

She's panting by the time I decide I've had my fill of her heady wine. Slowly, I push myself to my knees, looming over her like a statue. She bats her eyelashes at me, worrying her lip as her eyes stare up at me in a haze.

"Fuck, look at you" I say, running my hands up and down her thighs gently, wetting my lips at the sight of her. I dive back down to her nipples, my hands grasping her wrists as she gasps, but I feel them tug away.

"Wait," she breathes, and I stop, lifting my head to meet her gaze. As her eyes lock with mine, she loses her words for a moment, but I follow her gaze down to the bulge outlined in my pants. "I...I want to taste you," she says, the thirst in her voice so thick I can hear it in every syllable.

I give her a challenging smile. "You think you can do to me what I did to you?" I say, moving further up to her to hold her chin in my fingers. I lower my come-soaked lips to her mouth, and we kiss, a moan between us as I feel her hips push up into me. "Don't you know you already ruin me?" I growl when our lips part. "Or are you just a greedy little girl?"

"All of the above?" she says with a shy edge to her voice, and I sit back, taking my belt off and setting it on the floor. I see the hunger in her eyes as she pulls her legs back and folds them under her, and I take my time. My thick hands move to the button of my pants, undoing them one by one. The tight muscles of my stomach make a V leading down below the waist of my pants, promising what's below.

She waits, as if waiting for a word from me, but she fidgets impatiently as she watches my hands start to slide my pants down. She starts to move forward when she can see the thick base of the shaft. I want to tease her a little longer, but the sight of her so hungry for me, her lips so needy—I'm not so cruel as to keep her waiting any longer.

I pull my pants down and let my mast free, standing stiff and swollen. She reaches out for it carefully, as if touching something valuable, and when her soft fingers finally stroke up its length, I feel a shiver of pleasure run up me.

She's going to make me eat my words now that I've eaten her out.

She wraps her hand around the girth of my shaft, feeling its weight, and her other hand strokes it up to the bulging crown. It stands even stiffer at her touch. It wants to be inside her as much as she wants it. As much as *I* want it.

I lean back with her gently before she parts her lips and puts them to my crown, and warmth washes over me when I feel her tongue on the tip of my cock. She lets out a gentle moan into it as her thumbs slide down the sides of it, feeling every detail, every vein, and I see her hips squirm. She's imagining it inside her, and that only spurs her on as she opens her mouth a little more to take more of me in.

My neck leans my head back to the arm of the couch as my whole crown gets bathed in her tongue, and one of her hands takes my balls in her hand. She's soft and warm, innocently playing with the weight of my heavy, needy balls, not realizing how much tension she's playing with.

Or maybe she does. My woman likes playing with fire.

As her tongue starts to rove further down the soft underside of my shaft, I look down at her to see her eyes glittering at me. She slides more of my shaft into her mouth, and I can feel her whole tongue moving under me, sending wave after wave of pleasure up me. I let out a deep groan as she runs the tip of her tongue from the bottom to the tip of my cock, then again and again.

"Fuck, Serena," I groan, reaching out and taking a fistful of her hair—I don't hold her back, I just hold her, letting her know I can tug her around and steer her however I like. "You're the same brat I was sneaking around with when we were teenagers," I say, my voice gravelly.

She arches her back instinctively at my words, the warmth of her mouth utterly engulfing my cock. I'm impressed by how much of it she can take in, and her soft moans of pleasure spur me on, growing stiffer, more swollen, more ready for her than ever.

Her fingers play with my balls while her other hand feels the base of my shaft that her lips can't quite reach. My cock is so far in her that I worry she'll choke, but I'm keeping a close watch on her, ready to pull her back if she gets too greedy.

She lavishes my cock with attention like I tortured her pussy with my mouth, her face telling me how much she loves the feel of my cock sitting on her tongue, the taste of me, the feel of my shaft pulsing when she finds a way to stroke it that makes it twitch just right for her.

Dangerously so. She finds a way to move her tongue along the base of my crown to the head of my cock that makes my whole crotch tighten, and she can feel it in my balls. Excited by what she's discovered, she starts to stroke it more, her tongue lashing over it as her playful eyes flutter up at me.

My jaw hangs open, and I feel the tension building up in my whole body. It's so great that my balls ache with need, and I can tell just how badly she wants to release the pearly reward for her efforts.

It's tempting to give her what she wants—knowing that she takes so much pleasure from knowing how to unlock the best secrets of this massive, musclebound body of mine gives me so much pleasure. But as she starts unconsciously moving her hips when my body nears the point of no return, I know there are other parts of her that need attention.

Before that mouth of her makes me spill over the edge, I tighten my grip on her hair just enough to tug her back. She fights me a moment, but my hand is strong, and she reluctantly lets go of my cock.

When her mouth comes off it, it's more swollen than ever, now glistening with her. She sticks a lip out at me as I sit up and take her chin in my hand, brushing my thumb over that pouty lip.

"Do you think I'd let you drive me there when that pussy of yours is still so needy?"

She wets her lips at that, and her hands rove up my hips to feel my sides.

"You know I'm yours," she breathes, a blush in her cheeks as she says the words. "I just get greedy sometimes."

"I know," I say, reaching down to the floor. She follows my hand as it grasps the belt on the floor, and her eyes widen. "That's why I'm going to make sure you behave for me."

I stand up, nodding for her to turn around. She looks at me curiously, wonder in her face, but I reassure her, running my fingers through her hair. "Don't worry," I husk lowly, "I've got you. Tell me if you want me to stop. The safeword is Crimson."

"Crimson," she nods, licking her lips, and she doesn't resist when I gently take her hands and cross her wrists behind her back. I use the belt to tie them together, and she shivers as she realizes what I've done, testing her restraints. "What are you going to do to me?" she asks, her voice heavy with desire.

I take my shirt and rip it, making her gasp, and I do it again until I've got a black strip of cloth in my hands that I bring to her. "Show you that you're mine," I growl before I put the black cloth over her eyes and tie it behind her hair.

My Serena starts to squirm around on the bed, but I chuckle at her softly before I scoop her up in my arms. She yelps, and I carry her over to the wall. The way she feels in my arms never gets old.

"I could hold you forever," I whisper into her ear, and I feel her shiver, a smile playing across her lips.

"Where are you taking me?" she asks.

"No farther," I say.

Before she can speak again, I shift her in my hands so I'm holding her by the ass, and I let her back fall gently against the wall. My girl, my prisoner, sits there in my hands, wrapping her legs around my waist as best she can as she realizes what's about to happen. It looks rough, with her hands tied behind her back and her eyes blindfolded, but I'm careful with her. I wouldn't do this if I didn't know what I was doing.

When I look down at her exposed, vulnerable, tormented pussy, my cock stiffens as much as it had when it was a prisoner of Serena's lips.

"Remember," I say in a husky voice as I lower her just enough to perch her lower lips on the tip of my cock. The moment it touches, my cock swells to attention, and her mouth falls open. Every time I prepare to enter her, it seems she forgets just how big I am for her. "The moment you need me to stop, say Crimson. Until then...you're mine."

With those words, I let her sink onto my shaft, and she lets out a cry of pleasure as we lock into each other like my cock and her pussy were made for each other. Immediately, I start bucking into her, and she's utterly paralyzed by me, mouth wide open as her toes curl and her hips thrust forward.

"Oh, oh God, fuck!" she cries. We're both so slick that we grind into each other effortlessly, moving so fast, so wonderfully that I can already feel her tightening. "Luca, I'm gonna-"

She loses her voice to a silent scream, biting down on her lower lip to muffle it. I feel her whole body pulse around me, heels digging into my hips as I thrust myself up into her to the hilt. Her honey floods me, and I can hear it with each new thrust. I don't let up. I ride her pleasure like a wave that's about to break. Holding her effortlessly in my hands, I pull back and angle her back just so that I can hit the top of her inner depths better.

When the tip of my cock grinds against her g-spot, her silent scream becomes a real one. Just for a beautiful moment, she loses control of herself as I buck into her like a machine. My hips are a piston, moving with such precision and regular force, taming the wildfire that her body has become. Her mouth hangs open and her cheeks are blushing furiously. Every now and then, I see her trying to tilt her head back to look at my body past the blindfold, but another orgasm seizes her.

I can feel every inch of her, from the depths that my cock is thrusting into to the outermost lips kissing my base with every thrust. I feel her quick heartbeat through my cock, and I know she can feel my own powerful pulse.

That isn't the only pulse she's getting, either.

She's like a doll in my hands as I fuck her, but this is Serena. She tightens her pussy around me, thrusting as much as her spasming body will let her. Her golden hair spills over her shoulder as her head leans this way and that. She's totally in my power. And seeing that excite her so much fills me with pride.

I lean back to impale her on my cock, and now I'm doing most of the work, fucking her rough and hard while I move her. My pace never lets up. I'm hard as a rock, and I don't think I could get any harder or more needy. My balls are in such urgent need of emptying into her that they're sore.

The more I explore within her, the hotter my love for her burns. "You're my girl, Serena," I whisper huskily as I pump into her, "just as much now as you were before."

"Fuck, Luca," she whimpers, "fuck, I need you so bad!"

I let her sink onto my cock, letting more of her weight onto it, but my cock still holds her up as strong as ever. When I buck up into her, it's like I'm bouncing her on it alone, and a sharp cry from her lets me know she's come yet again.

I've lost count by now. She's trying to make me come, I can feel it, but I've won this time—I've got the control over her.

She clenches her pussy as tight as she can as she thrusts, struggling against her restraints like a little prisoner, and I wrap a hand around the back of her neck. "I'll fuck you until I'm good and done with you, Serena," I growl, and she lets out a desperate sigh, a pouting gasp as I buck up into her fiercely.

Her back is grinding against the wall, but she hasn't shown a single sign of letting up, no hint of saying that simple word that will make me stop. Crimson. She's a brave girl, that's for sure. My girl.

I feel another orgasm pulse through her body, but she's

on the verge of going limp. "Luca," she gasps, "Luca, I-I don't know how much more I can--oh God!" She whimpers the last words, and I groan into her as she writhes on my cock.

I slide my hand down from her neck to hold her back, and now, I'm holding her as much as she's leaning on the wall. She's utterly wrapped around me, calves tight against my rock-hard sides. She thrusts up against me with her chest out, and I feel my body revolt against me—it wants to *have* her, and it wants her *now*.

I let out a sharp groan as I feel myself crashing into those first few seconds before the orgasm, and I start pounding into her g-spot so that she lets out a cry of absolute bliss.

Just as I feel her honey wash over my red-hot cock, my balls tighten, and a stronger pulse of release than I've felt in a very, very long time shocks my whole frame. My jaw falls open, and my whole body goes paralyzed as a shot of hot come releases itself into her.

The first pulse hasn't even ended before the second one follows, and it's even stronger than the last. My knees feel weak, and a lesser man might have buckled. The second shot spills into her hot and fast, and Serena sighs in ecstasy, letting her head fall back to the wall as she pushes her hips up, drinking me in with each pulse.

It lasts for what feels like an eternity, my body tightening and relaxing in a flurry of feeling that makes me want to stay buried in her forever. Finally, when the pulsing starts to let up, I stay rock-hard inside her, gently thrusting up and teasing a surprised little gasp from her.

My heart pounds in my chest as I feel such incredible relief. The look in Serena's blushing face tells me she's feeling what I'm feeling even more.

"*Cazzo*," I breathe, my whole body feeling like it could

sleep for a hundred years. She's basically pudding in my hands, utterly limp as my thrusting slows to a stop.

"Luca, that was...I don't think I've ever felt like that," she says, genuine wonder in her voice. I give her a loving squeeze on the ass as I slowly step back. She gasps as I start to slide my cock out. It's a strange feeling, the cool air on my cock again as it glistens in the light. Some of my seed spills out of her with the cock, and I feel a strange pride at the sight of her.

I've marked her.

With my cock out, I gently take her in my arms and walk her to the bed, where I lay her on her side before slipping my pants off the rest of the way and getting into bed after her. She's a melted mess, chest rising and falling. I move my hands to her wrists gently, and I take care in undoing the restraints I made for her.

The moment her hands are free, she brings them to her front again as I slip into the big spoon position behind her. My cock is still stiff, and she draws in a sharp, shivering breath as it slides against her. She lets the breath out with a pleased moan.

I take her tiny wrists in my hands and rub them with my thumbs. I bring one to my lips and breathe on it, kissing the light pink marks. "Are you hurt?"

"No," she says, smiling, "it's a little rough, but I like it. I just hope my mom didn't hear."

I smile and gently take off her blindfold. Her warm brown eyes flutter open, and she looks back at me. The heart I've worked so hard to harden over the years melts at the sight of those eyes. I wrap my arms around her and hug her to me, and she snuggles in with a contented sigh.

"God, I could fall asleep right now," she says, and I can practically feel the relaxation in her voice, the utter satisfaction that drips from every word.

"That's the adrenaline coming down," I say, rubbing her

arm. I walk on my knees over to her and gently turn her onto her stomach. I straddle her, and before she can speak, I start running my hands up and down her back slowly, firmly enough for her to really feel it. Instantly, I hear a soft sigh of pleasure from her.

"Oh my God," she whispers, eyes half-shutting as I feel her relaxed muscles melt to my touch. "Are you like, a real person?"

I give her a light slap on the asscheek, and she squeals then giggles, wiggling her ass up into me as I rub her back.

"You did so well today, Serena," I say, "I mean that. Both the fight and... everything else," I say, my voice taking a husky undertone. "And you went through a lot more excitement than you're used to. You need to come down slow from that."

"I've never done anything with like, bondage and stuff," she muses into the blanket. "Is this uh, aftercare?"

"Something like that, if that's how you wish to think about it," I say, finding myself grinning at her innocence as my hands rub the spot on her back where she was against the wall. "Aftercare usually doesn't come after a knife-fight with a bunch of thugs, though."

"Doesn't it?" she laughs, but it soon relaxes into a sleepy sigh. "I think...I think I like it, though," she says. "I wish we could get some more alone-time that doesn't come with life-threatening danger every now and then."

I flip her onto her back and put my fists on either side of her, looming over her and smiling warmly down at her form, then up to her face. Her golden hair spills all around her like the sun. I bend down and press my lips to hers.

When we part, I move my mouth to her ear and whisper, "If that's what you want, maybe you're with the wrong guy, *dolcezza*." Her face turns serious, contemplating my words so direly.

God, he looks good.

It's just shy of noon, and all morning Luca has been subtly keeping guard right outside Bathing Beauty while I tend to regular business inside. Well, he's about as subtle as someone who looks like him could ever possibly be. At first, I worried that his imposing figure might scare off potential customers. Especially considering his leather jacket and crossed-arm stance. But it turns out, it's not just me who feels a calming aura from him. All morning, he's been smiling and giving courteous nods to passersby, occasionally even striking up conversation. Many of those who stop to talk to him also come into the shop to browse, and by this time of day, I don't normally have this many sales in the bag. Luca has been less like an intimidating bouncer and more like an engaging shop attendant.

Only, you know, unbelievably rugged and sexy.

"Excuse me, do you happen to have anything that smells like lemon or lime? My grandmother's eightieth birthday is coming up, and she loves citrus-y scents," asks a young woman to my right. I manage to tear my eyes away from Luca and give her a helpful nod.

"Of course!" I tell her, taking in her appearance. She looks to be no older than fifteen, with her hair in a flouncy ponytail. She has a sweet, round face, and she reminds me of how I looked and acted at her age. Fifteen. Back when everything was so simple. Before my entire world shattered into tiny, razor-sharp pieces all around me.

I guide the young customer over to a shelf of lemon- and grapefruit-scented products, explaining to her how our soaps and lotions are made. I'm so used to doing the sales spiel that I can almost zone out entirely while my body goes on autopilot. As I'm talking, my mind can't help but drift idly back in time, to when I first met Luca so long ago.

He was so handsome, even back then, even when we were both in our awkward teenage years. He was never gawky or skinny. Never a jerk like so many guys that age are. God knows he had all the reason in the world to be an arrogant ass, with those good looks and smooth-talking style. But he wasn't. Sure, there was a hint of snarkiness in his tone sometimes, and he certainly was confident, but never cocky. He was just...perfect. From day one that he stepped into my life.

Bringing myself back to the present moment, I successfully persuade the young girl to buy a whole line of lemon soap, bubble bath, and a candle. I tell her I hope her grandmother has a fantastic birthday, and she leaves.

I look around the shop with a warm, fuzzy feeling washing over me. There are more customers here than usual, and so far it seems like almost everyone has bought something. I can't help but smile. Things might finally be turning up for me, despite all the mess with the mafia activity lately. If not for Luca, I would probably still be falling to pieces, losing my mind stressing over what to do and whether I should go to the cops. But with Luca around, it's hard to even let those negative thoughts into my head for a second. I just feel so safe with him, and no matter how many years have passed us by, I still feel like I can trust him with my life. In fact, I *know* I can.

After all, he's saved me once, and I have a pretty strong feeling he would do it again in a heartbeat. I don't quite see why he cares about me as much as he does, but I know I must be the luckiest girl in the world. Danger will always follow him, but so will I. Besides, I doubt there's much of anything he can't handle.

I ring up the rest of the customers and, just in time for lunch, the door jingles and in walks Rafaela. She gives me a little wave and holds up a paper bag which I dearly hope contains some kind of burrito or burger. I've been so busy all morning here that I've definitely worked up an appetite.

Once everyone else has cleared out, Rafaela walks up to the counter, sets down the paper bags, and gives me a quick hug. "Class was canceled today so I figured I would surprise you!" she says, grinning her bright white smile.

"Oh, it's so good to see you. I'm glad class was canceled because I've missed your face," I reply happily, glancing down at the paper bag hungrily. "Please tell me one of those bags is for me. I'm starving, Raf."

"Yup! I went to that food truck around the corner from campus. Chicken burrito, no sour cream, extra pico. That's your order, right?" she asks, pushing the bag toward me.

I nod ravenously. "Oh yes. That's my order exactly. You have a damn good memory, wow."

She shrugs, smiling. "Well, yeah. Years of bartending will do that."

We both dig into our food, and I make sure to save half my burrito and chips for Luca, just in case he's hungry, too. It's the least I can do to thank him for hanging around all day keeping the shop safe and in business. Rafaela and I chat about her classes, how the bar is doing, how my shop is doing, and soon the conversation turns to more serious topics.

"So, like, what is your life plan?" she asks suddenly, shielding her mouth full of food. I lift an eyebrow and give her a quizzical look.

"Uh, what do you mean? And where did that come from?" I laugh.

She swallows and sighs. "It's just that I've been thinking a lot about how busy we both are and wondering if maybe we're, like, missing out on stuff. Life. Our youth."

"Okay, Miss *Eat-Pray-Love*, I guess I just try not to think about stuff like that," I answer, wrapping up the half of my burrito left over. "This is so not the way I thought my life would ever pan out. If you told teenage-me how my life would turn out, I don't think she would believe you. But you know, that's how it goes. I'm a planner, and I like to know what's coming, but if there's anything I've learned over the years, it's that some things just happen whether you plan for them or not."

Rafaela nods, a thoughtful expression on her pretty face. She crunches into a chip dipped in extra-spicy salsa. "You're right. I know you're right. It's just frustrating sometimes. Like, I'm so used to just being stuck in that daily grind of class, work, sleep, rinse, repeat that when I get a rare break like today, it really hits me how nice it would be to just slow down a little bit."

"You know what they say: youth is wasted on the young," I tell her, sighing. "And you and I are hard workers. I know what keeps me going is thinking about what my dad would say to me. He'd be so proud of me for taking on the family business and doing everything I can to take care of the house and Mom. I know he would want me to be happy, though, too."

"Yeah, whenever I get a chance to send some money

home to my great-grandmother in Venezuela, I do feel pretty damn good about myself. You should see the letters she writes me, Serena. You'd think I was President of the United States from the way she talks. It's nice to know that she's proud of me. I'll try to focus on that," Rafaela decides, a dreamy look in her eyes. I know she's had a hard life, growing up very poor in Spanish Harlem. Her grandparents immigrated here to give her family a better life, and while Rafaela was born and raised in America, she still has close ties to Venezuela.

I, on the other hand, grew up in the lap of luxury, only to have it all taken away in one fell swoop years ago with my father's death. Rafaela and I couldn't have come from more different backgrounds, but we've always been able to find plenty of common ground. Suddenly, I feel the burning need to confide in my best friend.

"So, lately I've been having some trouble here at the shop," I begin, launching into an explanation of the mafia activity threatening my barely-afloat business. I describe the 'rough types' who have been hanging around causing trouble, telling her all about the bright red graffiti.

"Holy cow," she says, shaking her head. "That's crazy, *chica*. How are you getting by? Have you gone to the cops? And, uh, is that guy standing outside the shop one of those 'rough types' you mentioned? Because he definitely looks a little intimidating."

I snort. "Oh, Luca? No, he's actually...been helping me, believe it or not. He's an old friend."

"Wait," she says, squinting as she stares at him through the window. "Oh my God, is that the same guy you came to the bar with the other night?"

I start to blush, my cheeks burning. "Yep. That's the guy."

"Nice catch," she says, giving me a cheesy wink. "He's a stud."

"Oh my God, stop," I laugh, rolling my eyes.

And almost as though he knew were talking about him, Luca walks into the shop, shrugging off his jacket and folding it over his arm as he walks by, giving us both a nod. Rafaela wiggles her fingers in a faux-flirtatious wave.

"Luca," I say, "this is Rafaela. We met in college. She's my best friend."

Luca shakes her hand and smiles. "Nice to meet you."

"*Encantada*," she responds, grinning.

"Oh! And she came bearing the very best of gifts: food. I saved half my burrito for you if you want it," I offer, handing the bag to Luca.

"Thanks," he says, taking a massive bite before heading into the back room to give Rafaela and I more privacy to keep chatting. He's still within earshot, but I know he doesn't want to hover.

He's so cute, Rafaela mouths silently at me. I nod emphatically.

"I know, right?" I whisper back.

Rafaela clears her throat. "So, anyway, wanna hear something weird?"

"Of course. You know I do," I laugh.

"Well, I mean, I guess it's not really funny. It's sad, actually. But it is definitely super weird, too. So, you know how my cousin Alejandro is a vet tech? Well, yesterday he told me that his office has been getting, like, an abnormal amount of injured dogs. Like, way more than they usually get. Everyone in his office thinks there might be some kind of dog-fighting ring going down somewhere in the city. Isn't that horrible?" she says, shaking her head as she eats another chip.

"Oh, wow. That *is* awful. Is there anyone looking into it? Cops? ASPCA?" I ask, concerned. I'm a huge animal lover despite the fact that my mom has never allowed pets in our household, and the idea of all these hurt dogs breaks my heart.

Rafaela shrugs. "I have no idea. I don't know if they would even know how to help, honestly. The cops probably don't care, and the ASPCA is so overworked already. They might not have the resources to do much of anything about it."

"Well, Alejandro's office probably has all the dogs' information on file, right? That's got to be a good start," I suggest.

Before long, the topic moves away from this tragedy and we spend the next hour just catching up and talking about when we should meet up for a girls' night out. We're both so busy that we rarely get the chance to just relax and hang out like we did in college. I hope that when Rafaela graduates we'll have more opportunities.

"Oh shit, I gotta head to the bar," she says suddenly, looking at the digital time on her cell phone screen. "That shady dude Nico hired to help out on weekday afternoons has been really flaky about showing up for shifts lately. Nico's too forgiving to fire him just yet, so take a wild guess who's been picking up the slack?" She gestures toward herself with a sigh.

I giggle and give her a hug. "Tell Nico I said hi. It was really, really good to see you, Raf. I'll come by the bar sometime this week to hang out. Text me."

"I will, I will. Have a good day, *chica. Hasta luego.*"

"*Hasta luego,*" I call as she walks out the door.

Moments later, Luca comes out of the back room with a stormy expression on his handsome face, and I know he's heard our conversation. Something is bothering him, and I have a feeling I know what it is.

"The dog fights," I murmur, biting my lip. He nods.

"Yes. It's pretty damn low, even for the Cleaners. Must be those East Harlem boys."

"I wonder what to do. I wish I could help somehow. I hate to think of those innocent dogs being abused for sport like that. Just horrible."

"It's inexcusable," Luca agrees, his voice low and gruff. There's a flash of terrifying anger in his gorgeous green eyes. He puts his leather jacket back on and adds, "I'm going out. Can you hold down the fort today? You've made enough sales already, I'm sure, that you could close up shop and head home if you need to."

I shake my head and reach out to take his hand. "I'll be fine. But...will *you* be okay?"

He lifts my hand and kisses the back of it softly, sending a pleasurable shiver down my spine.

"Don't worry about me. I've just got some business to take care of. I'll come back to you when the smoke has cleared," Luca assures me.

"Be careful," I tell him, a pleading note in my voice.

He gives me a devilish smirk. "I can't promise that, but I promise I will come back to you."

LUCA

Tony's driving. I'm in the passenger seat. Mike and Paul are in the back. I'm loading the last of the 9mm pistols I have on my person. I can hear the two in the back doing the same, but there's an uneasy feeling in the car.

"Not much farther now," says Tony, keeping his eyes on the road, windshield wipers pushing aside the gentle rain that's been falling. It's not nearly enough to flush out an outside event like the one we're going to, but it's enough to give us the cover of darkness.

We couldn't ask for better conditions.

I put out feelers when I heard about the dogfighting rumors, calling a few friends of friends who owed me favors. And in this business, a good tip is as good as money.

My hunch was right. There's a junkyard on the southeast side of town, right on the border of the territory the Cleaners are trying to make their own. If the word from my contact is good—and this guy doesn't disappoint—there's something going down there tonight.

We won't tolerate it. Not on our turf.

At least, that's what the bosses said. When I told them what I'd found out, I expected to be going in hot with a half-dozen men and a lot more firepower.

The bosses decided I could handle it with these two. Tony stays in the car, we'll need a quick getaway. I'd almost rather go in on my own.

"So, remind me what we know about these guys besides that we're gonna go fuck up anything they got goin' on," Mike says as he straps the gun to his side. They're are packed like sardines back there, but we're all used to getting ready in tight conditions.

"Not as much as I'd like," Paul grumbles.

"Shit, you're tellin' me," Mike says, his hand reaching for a cigarette he doesn't have. "Ever get the impression your boss is tryin' to kill you?"

Tony doesn't say anything. He never does.

"It's a low-stakes job," says Paul. "All the bosses need is to make a statement with a few good mooks and a lotta bullets—that's us. Not like we got bright futures ahead of us or nothin'."

Mike gives a rueful laugh. "What, Paulie, you don't think I'm a model citizen? Look at me, I take a few more bullets for the family and I'll have a pension, just you watch."

"You take a few more bullets and the lead will be worth more than your pension," Paul chuckles.

The boys rib each other, laughing. Even I crack a smile. Joking about it helps, because the reality of everyday life for us is pretty goddamn grim.

"Nah, if the capo cared that much, we'd have a lot more people out here to take on Cleaners," says Mike.

"Luca's fought with 'em before, and he's here," Paul says. "Besides, Luca, you've got all that special-whatever training your crazy uncle gave you. You call the shots tonight, how 'bout that?"

"Think I'd leave you high and dry?" I say, raising an eyebrow into the mirror. "Don't bother thinking about the big men in the cushy chairs back home, we rely on each other while we're out here. But don't go saying stupid shit like that, either," I add with a warning glance. "We're soldiers. We're all on equal ground."

"One more block and I'm stopping," Tony says, giving us a heads-up. I nod before I look back to the two men. I feel like I'm obligated to give some kind of pep talk. These are good men, but they know as well as I do when we've been given a shit hand.

"Should be a small crowd tonight betting on a few dogs. We're coming in about ten minutes early, so I want us to be in there before the fuckers take the dogs out of their cages. Paul, you've got a pit bull, I don't have to tell you to watch your shot."

Paul nods with a hardened face. He's got a special hatred for fights like these. There's nothing about them that isn't monstrous.

"Cleaners don't have numbers on their side, but they're vicious," I say. "They don't pull punches, and neither should you. We've all been to this junkyard before, so no surprises. Hit them hard and fast, don't give them a second to organize. The gamblers are going to scatter, but unless one of them pulls a gun, let 'em go—the more people hear about tonight, the better." I glance between the two of them. "If I didn't trust the two of you, I wouldn't be bothering with this shit, alright? Let's show these assholes who runs the Bronx."

The men give me resolute nods just as we come to a stop on the outside of a fence with barbed wire running along the top. Tony turned the headlights off a while ago. All four of us climb out of the sedan, and Tony moves around to the trunk to take out a big, thick carpet.

As we make our way to the fence, Tony hands me the

rug. I open my mouth to tell him we'd see him later, but he says, "Let me come with. Got a bad feeling about tonight."

I'm surprised, but after a quick glance to Mike and Paul, I give Tony a curt nod. "Lock the car. You carrying?"

Tony pulls his jacket to the side to show off a pair of glocks strapped to his chest. I smile. Tony's from the old country, like me. We don't fuck around with business like this.

I take the lead, climbing the fence up to the wire. With a quick motion, I toss the thick rug over it and use that as padding to climb over. This isn't exactly a high-security lot. They might as well have left out a welcome mat for anyone wanting to do what the Cleaners are doing tonight.

Once inside, the four of us start making our way through the shadows of the junkyard. Rain patters on crumpled, rusted metal all around us. The half-smashed, ruined cars and machines piled up all around us are like ridges of a mountain. I hear a rat scuttle away every thirty paces or so.

It doesn't take long for us to start hearing voices. I glance back at my men to make sure everyone's still good. I draw my weapon, and they do the same, triple-checking that they're loaded and ready to go.

As we get closer to the sounds, it's clear where the group is set up. There's an encircled dirt clearing not far from the center of the junkyard that's protected by a ring of stacked cars and warped metal. Perfect for things like this. Only a few ways out, but plenty of cover. You can't hear anything going on in there from outside the junkyard.

I know, because I killed a man here a year ago. He was a loan shark who'd crossed the wrong people—I don't regret it.

I look back to nod to Paul and Tony, gesturing for them to circle around to another entryway. There's one almost directly across from the one I'm taking Mike toward. We should be able to see each other with no problem.

"What's the signal?" Paul asks in a low whisper.

"You'll know," I say simply. Paul gives me a look, but he knows better than to question me. He nods, and the two of them disappear, hugging the shadow of a semi-truck as they slide around to their position.

Me and Mike make it to a small outcropping made of what looks like the remains of a Volvo and a stack of tires, where we crouch down. Through the smashed-out window, we have a clear sight of the scene.

There's a makeshift ring set up in the middle of the clearing, set up from rebar, heavy metal barrels, and a few other odds and ends the ringleaders must have thrown together. A few people are leaning on the edges, beers in hand, while others crowd around a man standing on top of a small platform, taking bets. Next to him is a big burly guy with a scar across his face, bulging arms crossed.

That's one guard. I spot a second one walk by the opening between two stacks of metal, a third and a fourth by the ring. I always assume there's at least one more that I can't see.

"Something look off to you, Mike?" I murmur, narrowing my eyes at the scene.

"Yeah," he replies. "Where's the dogs?"

I notice the man taking bets checking his watch periodically. His brow is knit, and he's looking red-faced. He shouts at the guard every now and then, who looks unmoved.

"Must be running late," I say. "All the better. No risk of hurting anyone who doesn't have it coming." I reach into my coat pocket and pull out the little glass bottle I stashed in there on the ride over.

It's filled with alcohol and a little rag. The Americans call it a Molotov cocktail.

"That's your signal, huh?" Mike says through a smirk.

"Told you I was going in hot," I say with a wink before I see the patrol disappear behind the cars again and dart to the edge of the entrance. Crouching low, Mike follows behind me. I glance around the corner long enough to see Paul's face in the shadows on the other side.

I take out a lighter and set the tip of my Molotov ablaze. I give myself a half-second to take aim at the edge of the ring where two of the guards are standing, and I hurl it.

Chaos erupts.

The firebomb goes off with a crash, and the two men scream as they stagger back, flames on their clothes keeping them from fumbling for their weapons. Like clockwork, I see Paul pop out of cover and fire at the big guy with the scar, who takes two to the chest and goes down. Immediately, the crowd scatters. Cursing fills the air as the gambling men run for the exitways, and a few people who spot us just start crawling out over the piles of cars.

The man taking bets pulls out a pistol and fires back at Paul, but I come out of cover with mine raised and put a bullet in his head before he can get off more than a couple shots that ricochet off the metal.

The two guards by the ring are burned badly, but they're getting to their feet and getting their weapons out, so Mike and I move in.

Mike fires at them, but I haven't forgotten the other guard just beyond the entryway. I blind-fire around the corner and hear a curse, and the first guard lunges at me from behind cover, closing the distance before I can aim a shot at him. But I'm ready.

I crouch down and brace for his impact, throwing him over my shoulder when he rushes in. Almost as soon as he's on the ground, I'm on top of him. I drop my knee down onto his throat with all my weight, crushing his neck instantly.

"Shit!" I hear Mike curse, and I look back to see him taking cover, holding his arm. He's been hit.

"Get down!" I shout, and I provide covering fire for him, hitting one of the two burned guards in the stomach. He crumples, and I see Paul and Tony moving in from behind the other side, guns out.

That's when I hear the sound of an engine.

I watch Paul and Tony's attention turn to their right from across the ring, and Tony cries out, pushing Paul out of the way as a truck comes barreling out of nowhere. It pulls a hard right as it flies toward the two, and I shout as Tony gets slammed by the side of the truck going God-knows-how fast.

His body goes rolling to the side as Paul scrambles to cover, and bullets are already flying from the truck. The truck flips its brights on, blinding me and Mike, and we're forced to cover, firing at it from behind the ruins of a car.

My adrenaline is racing, because I caught a glimpse of what's in the bed of that truck: about four more men, and the sound of those bullets told me they've got automatic weapons. Uzis, if I were a betting man.

"*It's a fucking trap!*" I shout, "Paul, get out of there!"

But there are already gunshots ringing out, and I can't see Paul. I grab Mike and pull him close to me. "I'll draw their fire, get Paul and get the fuck out of here!"

"What?!" he hisses, "I'm not leaving you, Luca!"

We both duck on reflex as bullets pelt the car, and I know I have to move fast. Then I hear his voice.

"Luca, you still alive?" calls Lorenzo from the truck, a mocking edge to his voice. "Think we have some unsettled business! My boys here have been dying to meet you, why don't you come say hi?"

"Fuck," I mutter. "Mike, I'm not fucking around, when I

move, you move opposite me." I don't give him a moment to respond. Blind-firing to cover myself, I dart out from behind the car, crossing through plain sight. Bullets start peppering the ground around me, but adrenaline is pumping through my body now. I don't look back to see whether Mike listened to me, but in what feels like a second, I'm back into the labyrinth of shadows and cars, away from the ring.

If I want to survive tonight, I need to draw them into my territory.

I get low and reload my gun, making a wide circle to their position. I know they'll either be tailing me, trying to head me off, or both, depending on their numbers. I need to be ready for that.

"Your pal here left a dent in my truck, Luca," Lorenzo calls. "Don't worry, I'll try to keep your death nice and clean. Cleaner than this shmuck, anyway." His words come with the sound of a single shot as he puts Tony down for good.

I grit my teeth.

They'll pay for tonight.

I hear footsteps up ahead of me. They're moving quietly, but my ears are sharper. Without having to think, I move to the wall of cars and climb into the nearest gap I can find, pressing myself flat against it. I can hear my heart pounding. I never liked skulking through the shadows, but they'll be my ally tonight. Pistol still in one hand, I draw my knife.

In the blink of an eye, I watch two figures pass by me. I seize my chance. Like a specter, I lunge out from the darkness. My gun-hand wraps around the mouth of one while I drive the knife into the base of his skull with all the force I need.

His body hasn't hit the ground twitching before his comrade turns, wide-eyed, and fires blindly at me as I dive for him too. I feel the sting of at least two bullets in my shoulder, but that doesn't stop me from driving the knife into his throat.

Shit. I used the knife because I wanted to keep from making too much sound, but the man has given me away. As he crumples to the ground, I stow my knife and pistol to collect the Uzis from the men. Their blood is sticky on the handles.

The others must have been close, because no sooner have I picked up the guns than I hear the rush of running footsteps behind me. I whirl around in time to see another two of the thugs running my way, but they stagger to a halt as they see me and my guns.

On reflex, they fire off at me, and I dive for cover as I shoot back. There's a sting in my thigh, and I know I'm hit, but I see one of them hit the ground, dead, and the other groans. I think I hit him in the gut.

I can hear Uncle Carlo in the back of my mind, chiding me for being so imprecise. *You're the one who taught me how to defend myself in the first place, you crazy bastard.*

To my right, I see light filtering through the cars. I realize the light is coming from the headlights—there's a crack in the rusted machines just big enough to slip through and get back into the clearing where the ring is. And I wouldn't care to do so, except that I see a familiar figure walking nearby in that light.

Lorenzo.

There's a guard with him, though. I have to make this count. I draw my pistol again. I need to be precise. I move up carefully, as silently as I can be. My heart sinks as I see Paul on the ground, across from them, not moving. I get up just close enough to where I can make the shot, and Lorenzo's back is to me.

Broken glass crunches under my boot. The guard's gaze darts to me. I have to act *now*.

As he raises his gun to fill me with lead, I lunge forward and seize Lorenzo from behind, arm around his neck and pistol to his head. The guard has his gun trained on me, his face twisted into a grimace, but he freezes, and Lorenzo tenses up.

"You're a ballsy cock-sucker, you know that?" Lorenzo growls, struggling a moment against my grip. Our faces are so close I can hear his breathing. It's closer than I'd like to be to this piece of shit, but if my head isn't close enough to Lorenzo's to be a risk, I know that guard will take the shot.

"You're one to talk," I hiss back, "you've got guts, coming out here to die in a junkyard."

"I wouldn't be so sure," Lorenzo says as I keep my eyes locked with his guard, standing off with me uneasily. "I can feel the blood spilling out your wounds. My boys got you good."

"If you think this is bad, you're more spoiled than I thought," I chuckle.

"Tough talk. Serena's made you soft, Luca," he says in a taunting, almost singsong voice, "but she can get me hard, if you know what I mean."

I'm about ready to throw caution to the wind and pull the trigger when a hint of movement catches my eye.

Paul.

His firing-arm lifts up and aims at the guard from behind. I see it at the same time as Lorenzo. But just as Paul fires, Lorenzo throws his elbow into my side and twists away. He tries to get a hold of my wrist and take that with him. I wrench myself free, but I have to let my weapon fall out of my hands to do so. It falls to the dust as Lorenzo pulls himself away and turns to flee.

I hear the guard cry out in pain and fall to his knees, but I'm already chasing after Lorenzo, who's racing for the truck. My body is a better-tuned machine, though, and I catch up to him, diving into a tackle that brings him to the ground with a hard thud. The next moment, we're locked in each other's arms.

My legs twist to try to get a hold of him, but he's more careful than to let me have that. He throws a punch that catches me in the eye, but I push through the ringing in my ears to return the blow, then work my way around him to try to get him in a sleeper hold.

But before I can do that, he rolls away and pushes himself up onto his feet. I do the same, and he draws a knife, a trickle of blood running down his nose and out his mouth. His eyes are wide.

I smile. That's fear in his eyes. "Let's settle this like men, *codardo!*"

Lorenzo's eyes dart to his guard...but the man is dead, breathing his last on the ground. My jaw tightens as I realize Paul is gone, too. He used the last of his strength to give me a chance. My grip on my knife tightens as I ready to lunge at Lorenzo.

But as I move my leg, I feel a sharp pain shoot through my body, and I suppress a grunt of pain. I look down at my leg and realize that the entire side of my pants are soaked in red. My dizziness is catching up to my adrenaline.

For a moment, Lorenzo looks as if he's going to take me on, but he proves himself even more of a coward than I thought. He takes his chance and runs, hopping into his truck.

I run for my gun on the ground and pick it up to shoot at the vehicle, but he's already turned the ignition on and started roaring away. I fire my weapon and watch the sparks as it hits the back, but it just blazes on, tearing out of the junkyard.

I swear under my breath in my mother tongue. I have to go after him. I look around, and my gaze falls on Tony's broken body. Cursing, I stoop down beside him, fighting off the fuzziness of my vision. I say a quick prayer I remember from my youth as I reach into my dead friend's jacket to get the keys.

I start running toward where we parked the car. I have to go after Lorenzo. I have to end this tonight, dammit. I have to make sure he'll never lay another hand on Serena. As I move through the junkyard, I pass the bodies of the men I've slain tonight. It looks like a wild animal has been turned loose on them.

That's what this life has made me, I think in my delirious state. A wild animal. *Un diavolo.*

When I reach the fence, I realize that I don't remember running through the rest of the junkyard. My leg feels cold. I look behind me and see spots of blood I've left as tracks. Shit.

Tony and Paul, gone. Did Mike make it out? Did the stupid fucking idiot listen to me and save his hide? They set a trap for us. They cost me two damn fine men. I'll kill him with my own two hands. I'll…

I shout out in pain that jolts me awake, and I realize I'm sitting in the car already. "Luca, you son of a bitch," I talk to myself in Italian, using the sound of my voice and the pain to keep me awake, "you're not done yet. You're not done yet."

I fight off the blurriness one more time as my bloodied hand turns the key in the ignition.

"Seriously, you need to chill out, *chica*. This is supposed to be our one night to relax, right? You've checked your phone, like, thirty times in the past five minutes," Rafaela says, interrupting the dark train of thought I've been riding along in silence. I blink a few times and hastily put my phone in my back pocket, then look across the kitchen and give her an apologetic smile. I can feel just how unconvincing a smile it is, though. That nagging ball of worry in my gut just won't leave me alone.

"Yeah. Yeah, sorry," I murmur, swiping a hand back through my hair and sighing. Rafaela walks to the fridge and takes out a pre-cut lime section, then starts squeezing it over the green bowl of guacamole. She glances over at me as she mixes the contents of the bowl.

"You're really into him, huh?" she asks gently. The genuine understanding in her voice almost makes me lose my cool—I've been fighting to keep myself composed the past day or so since Luca stormed out of Bathing Beauty with some vague, probably dangerous mission on his horizon. So I nod.

"I am. I know it's probably so stupid of me. I don't have

time in my life right now for some torrid romance or whatever, but ugh, Raf. I just like him a lot. He and I go way back and it's just...I guess I was prepared to just never see him again. In fact, I'm starting to think that's partly why I've been so willing to just throw myself into work and give up on dating and all that. Whether I knew it or not, I think I've subconsciously been kind of, you know, saving myself for him," I finish, shrugging.

Raf raises an eyebrow and narrows her eyes suspiciously. "You don't mean, like...sexually. Right? I mean, I did go to college with you. I remember that one party where you made out with that frat guy on a couch at the club for, like, an hour."

Suddenly, the tension in my body breaks and I burst out laughing. "No, oh my god. I don't mean that I'm, like, a born-again virgin or anything like that. It's just that I haven't let myself fall in love since— well, since Luca stepped out of my life the first time."

"Ah, okay. So it's more like your heart is a born-again virgin. Saving your heart for him. Got it," Rafaela says jokingly, but there's a twinge of kindness to her sarcasm. I know she understands. After all, she and Nico have been together for as long as I've known Rafaela. It used to make my heart ache the way Nico and Rafaela look at each other, like each of them thinks the other put the stars in the night sky. I used to think I would never have that again. That I would just have to settle for finding the little pieces of happiness in my career, my broken family, my friendships.

And all of those things are well and good on their own. But now that Luca has come back into my world and tinted everything a rosy pink, well, I don't know if I could stand to lose that kind of endless, all-encompassing sunshine again. Even if it means that I'll be living on the edge of serious danger for the rest of my life. He's worth it. That much I know for sure.

"*Bueno*. Guacamole is done, we got the tortilla chips and the salsa, and Ryan Gosling is waiting for us in the DVD player. Let's get this girly night started!" Rafaela says brightly, gesturing with one hand for me to follow her into the living room while she grasps the bowl of guacamole in the other. I grab the bag of chips and the bowl of salsa and follow her to the big comfy couch.

As soon as we both settle into the couch and turn on the movie, Rafaela jumps back up. "Oh! I almost forgot the most important thing: tequila! Okay, I'll be right back. Just gonna make two very strong tequila sunrises."

"Should I pause it?" I call after her as she jogs back to the kitchen.

"Nah, I've seen this movie, like, seven billion times. Nico's starting to think Ryan Gosling is my second boyfriend at this point," she answers, amid the clinking of glasses. "He's my celebrity freebie, just in case."

I grin and turn back to the movie, trying to force myself to focus on the TV screen instead of letting my mind wander to the phone in my pocket. I distract myself with a few chips laden with guac. I try my best to focus on how cute Ryan Gosling is, how comfy the couch is, how happy I'll be to have a cocktail in my hand with my best friend beside me. God knows I need this.

Girls' night. We only managed to make it work tonight at the last minute, when Nico's new employee took Raf's shift at the bar in apology for all his missed shifts. Still, when Rafaela called to let me know she was free, my immediate reflex was to turn her down, to stay cooped up at home in my bedroom waiting for my phone to go off. I planned to sip tea and stare at my cell phone screen for as many hours as it took for Luca to finally get back in touch with me and let me know he was okay.

My stomach churns at the thought. What if he *isn't* okay? What if he's hurt and bleeding somewhere out there in the night, silently suffering while I sit here all warm and cozy at Raf's apartment. I bite my lip nervously and give into temptation, pulling my phone out of my pocket and lighting up the screen for the hundredth time. Still nothing. No text messages, no missed calls.

"I see you," says Rafaela, causing me to jump a little. I look up at her with what must be a panic-stricken expression, because she instantly hands me a tequila sunrise and adds, "Geez, are you okay? You look like you've seen a ghost or something."

I shake my head. "God, I'm sorry I'm such a mess tonight. I just can't stop worrying."

"Why? Just worried he's not gonna call you or worried because he's doing something dangerous and you don't know if he's okay?" she asks sagely. I take a sip of my drink, feeling the warmth spread down my body.

"Wow, how did you…?"

Rafaela rolls her eyes good-naturedly. "*Chica*, I could tell from the second I saw that boy that he's living some kind of crazy life. Those muscles and scars? Trust me, where I grew up, that's a neon sign for rough stuff."

"Okay," I begin, staring down into the gold-and-peachy colors swirling in my glass. "So, you know how you were telling me about the dogs coming into your cousin's vet office lately?"

"Yeah," she says warily. "What about?"

"Well, I think Luca is, um, looking into that."

Raf's eyes go big and round. "What, in like a cop kind of way?"

I shrug, giving a wishy-washy gesture. "Uh, not so much a cop. More like, well, I'm not really sure what he would consider himself, to be honest. But he's a good guy. That much I'm sure of."

"I could tell that, too. *Immediatamente*. He's a good one," Rafaela agreed, nodding.

"And so I haven't heard from him since he went off to look into the dog-fighting thing, and now I'm really worried that he got himself into big trouble and he's hurt somewhere and— I just don't know what to do," I blurt out, heaving out a breath I've been subconsciously holding in my chest all evening.

Rafaela reaches out to put a hand on my shoulder, looking into my eyes meaningfully. "*Chica.* Finish that drink. We're gonna go find him, okay?"

She turns off the movie, downs her tequila sunrise in a few short gulps, then snaps her fingers as she gets to her feet. "*Vámonos,*" she adds emphatically. So I toss back the cocktail, letting the alcohol numb my nerves just a little bit, then I hop to my feet. Rafaela tucks the guacamole away in the fridge— always keeping her priorities straight— and then the two of us head out into the night.

"Where should we check first?" she asks. I think about it for a minute.

"Well, let's go to his apartment first. And if he's not there— then I guess I'll just have to go track down a dog-fighting ring myself," I tell her honestly. Rafaela links her arm with mine.

"You're *loca*, you know that? But I get it. That's your man. You gotta do what you gotta do. But you're an idiot if you think I'm gonna let you do any of that by yourself," she adds with a conspiratorial smile.

So we set off for Luca's apartment, the address of which I have entered into my phone. He lives across town from Rafaela's place, so we take a taxi. The whole ride over, my stomach is twisting in knots, my heart hammering away like a tribal drum.

When we finally arrive, I'm surprised to see that it's a relatively modest, well-kept apartment building. It looks far too humble and innocent to house a guy like Luca, but I'm already learning once again that he is a man of many

surprises. Rafaela and I exchange looks of nervous anticipation, and then we walk into the lobby. It's dimly lit
inside, and there's no one around. We muddle our way
through to an elevator, then take it up to the fourth floor.
All the while, my mind is racing in a million directions,
terrified that he'll either not be home or, possibly even
worse, he *will* be home but in bad shape. The thought of
seeing him hurt is enough to send my thoughts into a
frenzy.

We get to his door and I hesitate a moment before
knocking. There's a long silence, and then I knock again,
leaning forward to try and peer through the peephole. I
look at Rafaela, who shrugs.

"Maybe he isn't home," I whisper, feeling crushed. But I
look through the peephole once more and nearly fall over
with shock to see an eye looking back at me. A green eye.

Luca's eye.

There's the sound of several locks clinking open and
then the door opens just a fraction. Luca's face peers
through the crack, looking confused and almost angry. My
heart skips a beat.

"Serena?" he asks, his voice low and broken.

"It's me. And— and Rafaela. She's here, too."

"Hi," she squeaks from behind my shoulder.

Luca sighs and opens the door wider to reveal his white
t-shirt and loose flannel pants— and a few patches of deep
red blood staining through the fabric. One on his left
thigh, one near his shoulder, and the third— most worry-
ingly— slightly below his ribs.

"*Mierda,*" Rafaela breathes, letting out a low whistle.

"Oh my god, Luca, what the hell happened?" I ask, my
voice higher-pitched than usual, as it often does when I'm
panicked. Luca leans out the doorway, looking up and
down the hall with a slightly suspicious air, then nods for
us to come in.

"Come inside before someone sees," he growls. "You, too, Rafaela."

We both rush into the apartment, which is exactly as spartan and neat as I would expect from a guy of Luca's self-discipline. But I'm a little too distracted by the massive bloodstains peppering his body to pay too much attention to the details of his residence.

He walks gingerly to a stool pulled to the center of his little kitchen area, with an open box of bandage wraps, a bottle of rubbing alcohol, and a needle and thread sitting on the otherwise pristine granite countertop. My stomach turns when I catch sight of the drops of blood on the white tile floor.

"I was hoping you wouldn't see me like this," Luca says, sounding genuinely downtrodden. "I remember you being squeamish about this kind of thing."

I can't even protest. It's true. I've never been good with blood and guts. Hell, I have trouble watching some TV shows involving hospitals because they all make me queasy. Rafaela, however, immediately jumps into medic mode.

"Okay. I know I'm just a head doctor, but I took enough med courses to help," she says, a look of determination on her face. While I'm feeling woozy, Raf is already scrubbing her hands in the kitchen sink, preparing to do God knows what.

"Neither of you should be getting involved with this," Luca protests softly, staring at me with those hard, green eyes. Rafaela is going through the cupboards, looking for something.

"Well, tough luck. Because she's involved with you, and she's my best friend, so I'm automatically involved. Plus, it's like a Hippocratic Oath kind of thing. I may not be a real doctor yet, but I'm still not gonna turn away a guy bleeding out in his kitchen from what looks to be three separate gunshot wounds. Now, where the hell do you keep your rubber gloves? This apartment is spic and span, so I know you've got some hidden away somewhere," Rafaela says matter-of-factly.

A smile twitches momentarily at the corner of Luca's mouth. "Hallway closet. Second shelf."

"Thanks," she replies, and walks off to find them. When she returns, she tells Luca to take off his shirt, which he does obediently. Against my better judgement, I take a few steps closer, the breath hitching in my throat as I take in the gore of the situation. Dried blood. Bruising. Nicks and scratches.

The world spins for a moment and I carefully sit down on the tile floor while Rafaela tends to Luca's wounds. She gently dabs them clean, then begins the painstaking work of stitching him up. Thankfully, she's as professional and focused as a true doctor, even under these strange circumstances, and before long she has him as patched up as well as could be expected for this kind of serious injury.

"You're lucky," Rafaela says, tossing the rubber gloves into a garbage can. Turning to me, she continues, "It looks really bad, I know. The rib shot and the thigh shot were just really bad grazes. The shoulder wound is the worst, but your guy here managed to wiggle the bullet out on his own before I got here. It'll all heal. As long as he takes care of himself."

"Thank you," I murmur, feeling overwhelmed.

"I could have done this myself," Luca says, "but probably not as neatly. So, thank you."

Rafaela waves off his gratitude. "Just doin' my job. Now, you really, really do need to take it easy. I'm serious. No crazy acrobatics or bad boy moves or whatever it is you do. Just chill out for awhile. Spend some quality time with your lady. She's been worried out of her mind all night about you, ya know?"

A flicker of pain crosses Luca's face and he locks eyes with me. "I'm sorry, Serena," he says softly. "I didn't want to worry you. This—all of this—you shouldn't have to deal with it. This is my bloody, filthy world. Not yours."

I stand up and walk over to him, taking his hands in mine. "And you are *my* world. So, like it or not, I'm here to stay. Don't push me out again. Please. I'd rather know what's going on."

Luca lifts his good arm to stroke my face. I close my eyes, leaning into his touch.

"I promise. And I will do everything in my power to keep you safe, *mia passerotta*. But you have to trust me," he replies. I nod, turning his hand to kiss his open palm.

"Okay! And that's my cue to leave, I think," Rafaela says suddenly, reminding us both that she's still here. My cheeks burn with embarrassment, having gotten caught up in the moment with Luca.

"Thank you so much again," I tell her earnestly, walking over to give her a tight hug. I whisper in her ear, "You have no idea how much this means to me."

"It's all good, *amiga*. Now, I assume you wanna stay and look after your boy. I'm gonna head home and go to town on that guacamole until Nico gets off work. Just me and Ryan Gosling for a few hours," she says, winking.

"Sorry our girls' night got ruined," I tell her.

"Eh, it's okay. More guac for me. But you do owe me. Just buy me a drink next time we're out, and we're square," she says good-heartedly. I give her a big grin.

"You got it. Text me when you get home."

Luca carefully gets to his feet, fishes a wad of money out of a wallet on the countertop, and hands it to Rafaela. At first, she shakes her head, refusing it.

"Take it. You've done me a huge service here. Not to mention taxi fare. It's the very least I can do," Luca insists, and she gives in.

"Okay," she says. "I'm leaving now. Take it easy. Seriously. I'm pretty good at stitches but you still don't want to risk them reopening or something."

I flinch at the thought. Once Rafaela is gone, I rush into Luca's arms, laying my head against his powerful chest, careful not to touch his wounds. I look up at him, overwhelmed with feeling.

"How did this happen? What did you do? Who did this to you? Did you go to the cops? Where did this all go down? Are you safe now? Is someone looking for you?" I ask, the words stumbling over themselves in a rush to get out.

Luca gently strokes my hair, calming me down. "It's okay. It's over for now. There's no need to rehash all this mess—it's *my* mess. And besides, you heard Rafaela: we have to relax, right?"

I want to protest, but I think better of it. "Fine. You've got to be exhausted."

Luca yawns. "I actually am. Nothing like a firefight to knock you right out."

"I'm staying here tonight," I insist.

He doesn't fight me on it, and the two of us carefully make our way to his bedroom, both of us curling up under the sheets and falling asleep pressed up against each other. We both sleep like the dead, probably because of all the stress of recent events, and when I wake up in the morning, it's to the glorious smell of coffee. *Good* coffee.

I roll out of bed, the events of last night returning to my foggy brain as I stretch and make my way into the kitchen. There, I find Luca shirtless, using his one uninjured side to pour coffee and arrange fresh fruit and pastries on two plates.

"What's all this?" I ask, sidling up next to him.

"Proper Italian breakfast. It's light, but it's something."

"You're supposed to be taking it easy, aren't you?" I chide him gently. He chuckles.

"It's not like I'm an invalid, Serena. I can handle putting fruit and *sfoglie* on plates."

"Still," I interject, running my hands up his chest. I stand on tiptoe to kiss him. Even though he's wounded, I can feel that powerful strength rippling through his body, and it thrills me to my core.

"Careful, *mia passerotta*," he growls, pressing against me so that I'm pinned into the counter. "Touch me like that and I might change my mind about what I want for breakfast."

A shiver runs down my legs. Suddenly, I can't resist egging him on. "Oh? What are you hungry for this morning, Luca?"

He leans down to kiss me, gently at first, and then more passionately. I can feel myself growing wet between the thighs. I become acutely aware of his cock pressing hard against my leg as his arms come down around me, pulling me tight to him. "We have to take it easy," I murmur between kisses.

"I'll do my best," he says, and immediately hoists me up with his one uninjured arm, setting me on the counter. Within thirty seconds, he whips off my panties, pulling me forward so that my ass rests on the edge of the counter. He bends down and wrenches my thighs open, parting me to get easy access to my flower. Glancing up at me with a devilish glint in his gorgeous eyes, he begins to swirl his tongue around my clit, making me cry out.

"Oh my god," I mumble, my head falling back as I close my eyes.

Luca gently nips and sucks at my clit, his tongue exploring my wet folds as my body shudders around him. It's like he knows me instinctively, knows exactly how to unlock and unravel me with the flick of his tongue and the softness of his lips. Before long, I'm writhing on the counter, trying not to move too much and risk knocking our breakfast to the floor.

"Luca," I gasp, feeling my pleasure mounting ever higher. "Feels so...fucking...good."

Without warning, he slides a finger inside of me, hooking it to stroke my g-spot just right. Combined with the expert lashing of his tongue, I fall apart instantly, my orgasm exploding in his mouth.

"Fuck!" I whimper, bucking my hips. Luca holds me still, never letting up even though it almost hurts—but it hurts so fucking good. A moment later, a second climax shakes my body and my hands wander down to tangle my fingers in Luca's dark hair, gently pushing his face into my pussy.

He fingers me harder and faster while his tongue rhythmically laps at my clit, sending me into ecstasy again and again. Finally, when I'm totally spent, he kisses his way up my body to gently kiss my breasts, my neck, my lips. He strokes the hair out of my face while I slowly return to my senses.

And when I do, I immediately slide off the counter, dropping to my knees without a word, to return the favor. I'm aching to feel his cock in my hands, in my mouth. I need to make him feel as good as I do. And he doesn't stop me.

I pull down his flannel pants and boxers, letting his massive length spring free. I'm careful not to touch the wound on his thigh, kissing my way to his cock. His hand strokes the back of my head, gently guiding me to his shaft, and I have to smile. I love the way he can't resist, the way he wants so badly for me to touch him, to suck him. The fact that I can have such an effect on a guy like Luca is intoxicating.

But I want to take my time. I gently begin to stroke his

cock with one hand at first, my thumb slowly sliding up and down along the underside of his shaft, making soft circles around the sensitive head. I adore the feeling of him in my hands—hard, hot, and smooth. My mouth is nearly watering for it. I add my other hand, applying a little more pressure as I work his shaft, letting his enormous length slide through my fingers as I lean forward and give the head a tantalizing kiss. Luca groans, his hand pushing a little harder against the back of my head. I peer up at him, smiling sweetly. I know what he wants, and I want it, too.

I want it so bad.

I open my mouth and take the tip of his cock between my lips, letting my tongue gently swirl around the end while my hands continue to pump his shaft— faster now, a little tighter.

"Yes, sweetheart, that's it," Luca growls, and I feel myself getting even wetter at the sound of his voice, the neediness in his tone. I can't stand it anymore. I need him.

I open my mouth and take him in as deeply as I can in one movement, feeling Luca tighten up as I envelop him. He begins to move his hips, and I can tell it's taking all his willpower not to just let go and fuck my mouth mercilessly. He needs this as badly as I do, and that knowledge makes me all the more determined to make him feel amazing. I start to bob my head up and down along his shaft, my hands working his cock in tandem with my mouth. I suck him harder, moaning a little to send vibrations through his body.

"Fuck, baby, that's so fucking good," he groans, pushing me down on his cock so that I can feel the tip gently grazing the back of my throat. Before I start to choke, he relents. I can tell he's trying so hard to maintain control, to be gentle. But I want him to fuck my mouth. I want him to use me. I want him to let go completely.

I move faster, reveling in the sensation of his hard,

smooth cock in my mouth as I gently work his balls before wrapping my arms around his thighs, deep throating him again and again. He pushes me down on his cock, bucking his hips as I move faster and faster.

"Gonna make me come, baby," he murmurs roughly. "Swallow for me, sweetheart."

With a few rapid, deep thrusts, I feel him seize up and then shoot his sweet, hot honey down my throat. I swallow it back hungrily, not wanting to waste a single drop. "Fuck, Serena!" Luca snarls through gritted teeth. I work his cock until he's totally spent, pushing me off.

He pulls me to my feet and kisses me deeply, not giving a damn about the taste of his own come in my mouth. "I think I'm awake now," he says, holding me close.

"Good," I reply, wiping my mouth. "Because I'm starving."

"Still?" he asks wryly.

I laugh. "Yes. For real food. Breakfast."

We both clean up and sit down to finally eat, both of us glowing and happy. It's as if the events of the past twenty-four hours have all been power-washed away. But no sooner has the peace arrived than it gets broken.

Luca's phone buzzes. I pick it up to hand to him, catching a glimpse of the text message on the screen. It says simply, **Don't go home.**

We both look at each other, sharing a dark expression.

We're already home. And only God knows why we shouldn't be.

LUCA

"You made one hell of a splash last night, Luca" says Antonio. I'm not sitting in the back of any liquor store today. I'm in a proper office, standing in the middle of a room that's packed with shelves of thick books. The consigliere lives pretty well. I've heard he was a lawyer a while back, or maybe he still is.

We got the hell out of the house after I got that message, and I took Serena to Rafaela's bar to lay low for the day. The guy who sent the message was one of ours. He must have assumed I'd go straight to one of our medics, because word of what happened at the junkyard spread fast.

It wasn't long after I'd gotten Serena to safety that I'd been summoned here, to the consigliere's own house.

This isn't a grilling, though, not like last time. I'm not surrounded by other soldiers this time. There are only three people in this room, and all of them are way over my pay grade. Two of them are familiar faces: the consigliere and Diego, my capo. The third is a man even I've never met and only seen once.

Giacomo "Jackie" Pisano, the underboss. Where he goes, business is serious.

The consigliere is sitting in a leather armchair, but not behind the big desk in the room. Jackie is leaning on that, while Diego sulks by the window.

Jackie scrolls through his phone, his face hard to read. He's a massive, meaty guy with thick, heavy features, and he always looks vaguely pissed-off. "Haven't seen a body count like this in a while."

"Neither have the Cleaners," I say, and Jackie's small eyes look me up and down, appraising me. I don't let it faze me. "Have we heard from Mike?"

"Mike's fine," Jackie says, putting his phone down. "Got himself patched up with one of our guys. We've already had a word with him."

"So you know how things went down," I say.

"We know," says Jackie, crossing his arms and pacing around the room, "that things were going fine until Lorenzo Abruzzi pulled up with a truck full of fuckers packin' military-grade weapons. We know our intel was bad, and the guy who gave you that tip is being dealt with right now. We know that you told Mike to get the fuck out of there, and we know he assumed you'd be hauling ass too, like any reasonable goddamn person would." Jackie stops to turn and look at the bandages visible on me. "But judging by the way you look and the fact that the Cleaners are out for blood, I'm guessing that didn't happen."

I clench my teeth for a moment before I force myself to relax and speak. "Lorenzo knew I was going to be there. He was after me. It was business between the two of us. He killed Paul and Tony, I wasn't about to let him get away with that. So I hunted his men down, and I almost killed him, too. But he fled. He's a coward."

"Mike told me what he saw," Jackie says. "He saw the

guns those maniacs got a hold of. How the fuck are you alive?"

There's a pause between us as we hold each other's gaze. "My uncle," I say after a moment, "he taught me, when I was young. Taught me how to defend myself. He was in the army." That's a lie. Uncle Carlo was part of a Special Forces unit. I don't want to tell them too much detail, though, or they'll have me doing hits for them with Diego. I gesture to my body with a nonchalant expression. "The rest? Good genes, I guess. Luck?"

Jackie's ugly mug twists into a smile, and he chuckles. "You're a stupid son of a bitch, you know that?"

"I'm alive, aren't I?"

Jackie stops chuckling, but he holds his smile for a moment before it fades. "You weren't the only target last night."

My brow knits. "What?"

Jackie scrolls through his phone to pull up a few messages. "That dive bar we run, Pete's? They got hit hard right before last call."

"Fuck," I breathe, running my hand over my face and clenching my fist. Bad enough that I couldn't keep a hold on the situation with Lorenzo, but another place too? "What happened?"

"Driveby," Jackie explains, and he holds out his phone to me. It's a picture of the bar in question, an old place I've gone to before. The front is riddled with bullets, all the windows are shot out, and I recognize bloodstains on the walls. "Pete made it out with a bullet in his side, but he'll pull through. The bar's done for, though."

"So, two places in one night and more bodies than the city's seen in a long time. Do we know who they've got on the take?" I ask. We have our own cops on our payroll, but if they're turning a blind eye to this much...

"Our boys in blue suddenly don't know a thing," Diego

speaks up ruefully. "I don't know who they've got to, but it's someone who can pull some major strings."

"This has become a war," the consigliere says calmly. "They're making moves fast and hard, and if we don't act now, they'll have their heels dug into our territory even deeper. That's why I'm promoting you, Luca."

That hits me like a bolt of lightning. I stare at him, and I realize both Jackie and Diego are eyeing me expectantly. So this is why I got dragged out here.

"A promotion?"

"That's right," says Jackie, making no show of pomp or circumstance. "What happened last night would have gotten all four of you killed under most circumstances. Nobody could have been ready for that. But you and Mike got out of there because you can think on your feet, and god knows how many bullets it takes to put your ass down."

"That's the kind of initiative we need calling shots on the frontlines," the consigliere says, finally turning to look up at me. "Luca, I'm putting you in charge of the block the de Laurentis girl's shop is on."

Serena's block.

"So what, you're using her as a front line now?" I say, and the look Diego shoots me tells me I'm out of line, but I don't care. I'm sick of her getting endangered, dragged back into this life.

And I admit that the guilt in my gut is wearing me down. If I'd just avoided her...

I shake the thought away. No, I didn't bring this heat down on her. Lorenzo was shaking down her shop before I ever got there, and there's no way Bathing Beauty could've paid the protection fees. Besides, her father was the one that put the target on her back. I was just the one that made Lorenzo take it more personally.

But Serena would've been in danger, with or without

me. At least now, I'll have the power and authority to keep her safe. And once I kill Lorenzo…

"No," the consigliere says, putting out a hand, shaking me from my thoughts. He must have anticipated my reaction. "This is a sign of trust, Luca. I'm giving you more control over something that's very close to the heart all this violence."

"In other words, it's you that Lorenzo's got a beef with," says Jackie. "And you're one of us. If he wants a war, it's you he'll come after first. We're giving you the means to defend yourself."

"So we let them come to me," I say, and the men nod in agreement.

"I'll send you a list of the men who'll be under your command," says Jackie. "They'll be headed your way ASAP, because the Cleaners aren't gonna wait around long before they try to strike again."

"Good," I say. Not because I'm proud of the responsibility—I don't forget for a second that these mobsters are only interested in covering their own asses through me. "There are two alleys that run through that block that'll be to our advantage, and there's an office building on the opposite corner that will be useful for keeping an eye on the area. I'll give the men the rundown personally."

"You've got promise, Luca," says Jackie, nodding at me. "That's good. Show your men you're in control, and don't let 'em see weakness."

I crack a smile. "How could they see something that isn't there?'

~

*H*ours later, I'm back out to the only place I care to be—with Serena.

We're in Belmont, another little Italian corner of the

Bronx. It's a nice little place, perfect for a peaceful moment away from everything else that's been going on.

"Are you sure you're okay?" Serena says as we walk down the sidewalk, glancing up and down at my body. I've got a slight limp, but with each step I get better at hiding it.

"Don't worry about me," I say, "you'll know when I'm feeling it. This is nothing."

"I can't *not* worry about you," she says with a smile, and I squeeze her hand.

She's wearing a sundress and a wide-brimmed hat today, and compared to me in my rough leather jacket and t-shirt, I feel like the bodyguard to some celebrity. I might as well be. Every time I glance over at Serena, it's like looking at someone out of a movie or a fairy tale.

Colorful streamers are strung up between buildings over the street, and the red brick buildings look warm in the afternoon sun as we stroll down the sidewalk. Serena keeps smiling, and I have a hard time tearing my eyes off her. She catches me once or twice and blushes, and the third time, she bumps her hip into mine and says "Quit it!" as we laugh.

After a moment, she looks over at me with those warm eyes glittering in the sun. "It feels weird to have a breather with everything that's going on."

"Weird?"

"Nice-weird," she says, and I take a hold of her hand as we turn into a fresh produce store.

It's a quiet little place with a few fans lazily running overhead, and there's that familiar scent all produce stores seem to have. A few flies are buzzing around the place, and the floors are just plain brown concrete. It's nothing fancy, but we're not looking for anything fancy today. Just a little time together.

"This is probably the most Italian place in the neighborhood," I say, looking around the place with raised eyebrows.

"Oh yeah?"

"All it's missing is a few people smoking outside," I say with a smile, and she giggles as we start to look around at some of the assorted stuff.

"You know, you don't talk about it very much, come to think of it."

"Italy?"

She nods her head as we pick out a couple of apples to eat on the way out. I pay for the food and look pensively up at the little Italian flag hanging from the window of one of the shops. "No, I guess I don't. It's a complicated place, where I'm from."

"Where is it?"

"Taranto," I say, a faint smile crossing my face. Taranto brings up a lot of mixed feelings. It's a far cry from the picture of Italy most Americans think about.

"That sounds familiar," she says thoughtfully.

"Probably because it sounds like Toronto," I say playfully, and she slaps me on the shoulder. "Don't laugh, that's where most people thought I was from when I first got here."

"Seriously, though."

"Seriously, okay," I say, looking up at the sky, trying to think of the best way to describe my hometown as I can. We're soon strolling through a park in the Bronx, but my memories take me back nearly ten years.

"It's in the far south. If you think of Italy like a boot, it's on the heel, facing the gulf. The land is very sunny. It's like the whole place is bathed in gold sometimes, and we don't get winters as harsh as the rest of the country up north. Taranto itself is very old. It was a Greek settlement, a long time ago."

"Woah," Serena says, raising her eyebrows. "The house I

grew up in was built in the forties, and I thought *that* was old."

"All the buildings are sun-baked, for the most part. Imagine if you turned gold into stone, they'd look kind of like that. Only not as pristine. There's a lot of black soot on everything because of the factory nearby."

"Sounds romantic," she says with playful sarcasm.

"It's an acquired taste," I say with a chuckle. "The old town looks a something like the Little Italy up in Manhattan. Lots of clustered apartments, clothes lines strung up over narrow alleyways that *motorini*—er, scooters—zip down, big churches here and there...and the old military fort looms over everything on the water. Something about the palm trees and shining sea puts you at peace, though. It's hard to describe if you haven't seen it."

Serena is quiet for a moment before saying, "And you're from the old town?"

"No," I say, tossing the cores of our now-eaten apples into a trash can as our shoes click on the paved walkways. "My family lives a little ways out of the city. In the country. It looks like..." I frown, trying to draw a comparison. "Have you ever seen those old Western movies?"

Serena blinks, then bursts out laughing. "Wait, what?"

"No, seriously," I say. "They filmed some of those down in southern Italy. It's like a desert, but...more trees," I say, realizing I've never been to an American desert to compare to. I shake my head, laughing at myself. "My dad used to take me on drives around some of the villages in the area. They're really beautiful. They use a lot of smooth white stone that never goes dark like the ones in Taranto do. And some of them are up on mountains where you can see for miles in any direction."

"Wow," she says softly.

"When I was...very small," I say, holding my hand down to my knee to show how tall I was, "my dad would carry me on his shoulders and point out some of the other villages from this park up on a mountain ridge. Then we'd go get gelato from the little shops close by, and he'd tell me about the places he went when he was growing up."

I feel Serena's steady gaze on me, and the look on her face reminds me that I'm starting to get a little misty-eyed. I blink it away, and shake my head. "That was a long time ago, though."

There's silence between us as we walk slowly, and finally she says, "Your dad sounds like a good guy."

I nod.

"The place reminds me a little of what my dad used to describe," she says, and she wraps her arms around my bicep to lean her head on me as we walk. "He was just a teenager when they left Sicily, but it sounds like they're a lot alike."

"Sicily and the mainland? They have everything and nothing in common," I say. "But they're both beautiful places. We ought to go sometime."

"Just up and go to Italy?" she says, a slight laugh to her voice, but I smile at her perfectly sincere.

"Why not? I'll make sure you get time off from work to close the shop for a few days."

"Oh god, I could never!"

"When customers come in, I'll 'encourage' them to make a few purchases," I say, playing up my best menacing accent and cracking my knuckles. Serena giggles and slaps my chest in protest, but I surprise her by scooping her up off the ground and spinning in a circle with her, then planting a kiss on her lips as she throws her arms around my neck. It was painful in my condition, but worth it.

We look at each other for a long moment, smiling, and I know we're both losing ourselves in the fantasy for a little bit.

"It's starting to get dark," I finally say, gently setting her down. "I ought to get you back."

We make our way back toward the car and climb in, but once we're driving, I can't help but feel like something's lacking from our little date. After a moment, I look over to Serena.

"Feel like going for a drive?"

"A drive?"

"I know someplace nice," I say. "It's too nice a night to waste inside.

A few minutes later, I turn off to head toward Orchard Beach, an idea forming in my mind. When Serena realizes where we're headed, a confused smile plays across her lips. "Luca, it's like, eight at night!"

"I want to show you something," I say simply, parking the car. "It's on the far end of the beach, this way."

As we approach the sand, Serena gasps at the sight, and immediately, I start looking around for danger, but then I hear her voice.

"Oh my god, Luca, look at the water!"

My concern melts away as I look up at it. The full moon is low on the water, casting a carpet-like stream of white reflective light on the gentle waves. There's not a cloud in the sky, and it couldn't be more beautiful.

I feel Serena looking at me, and I turn to see the most pleading eyes I've ever seen. "Do you want to go for a walk on the beach?" I ask with an arched eyebrow and a wide smile.

"How'd you guess?" she says, laughing before she darts over to the sand, kicking off her shoes and picking them up. I shake my head as I catch up to her and do the same.

We make our way out onto the beach proper. We're not the only ones out here tonight—I can see a few people further down here and there—but we're the only ones in this area. No other sounds but our feet crunching in the sand and the gentle sounds of the waves kissing the shore.

Serena goes almost to where the icy waters touch, and I start leading her to where I have in mind. The beach is pretty flat and open, and we're technically not supposed to be out here this late, but nothing's going to bother us while I'm around.

Before long, we come up to a little outcropping of rocks, and I lead Serena around it. "What's this?" she asks, and I crouch down to squint at the rock, looking it up and down. After a moment, I smile and point to something.

The words *VOGLIO TORNARE* are carved in a crude hand, a little weathered but still there. Serena blinks at it blankly.

"When I first got here, to America," I say, "well, I told you about how I was kind of a shit. I ran away from home once, the first few weeks. I *really* didn't want to be here. So I ran all the way out here to this beach and hid out for...I don't know, a few hours." I grin. "I was a rebel, but I got bored easy."

Serena reaches out and brushes her hand over the words. "Did you write this?"

"It means 'I want to go back,'" I explain, nodding. Serena is quiet for a few moments.

"It must have been hard, getting used to somewhere this new," she says. I'm thoughtful for a moment, but then I reach up and pull her down with me, rolling onto the sand, and she yelps as I hug her close to me.

"I might have settled down if I'd had you to distract me sooner," I whisper into her ear, and she wiggles in protest, giggling. Soon, though we find ourselves sitting up, Serena between my legs as we watch the bright, moonlit water.

"Think it's dangerous out here?" Serena asks, leaning her head back against my shoulder. Wisps of her hair flutter as I breathe in and out.

"Could be," I say, reaching to my pocket, "I've never had to worry about that kind of thing." I pull out a switchblade, opening it and letting it gleam in the moonlight as Serena looks down at it.

"Are you kidding? Giant, musclebound Italian guy with a knife?" she teases, but I squeeze her to me, chuckling as I plant a kiss on her neck. She squirms away from it with a smile, and I pepper her neck with kisses until she starts turning her neck up and scooting her butt into my crotch, her playful giggling melting away to short breaths.

"Why, are you afraid of something?" I ask, lowering my voice, and I bring my knife up to her collarbone. She hold still as I let the blade glide across her skin, and it gives her goosebumps.

"...Maybe I like a little danger," she says, and I feel her shiver wonderfully against my hardening manhood. I smile, and my throat rumbles as I bring the blade up to her chin and whisper into her ear.

"Little lady like you should be careful, coming out so far with a dangerous man."

Even in the moonlight, I can see her cheeks start to flush with color. Her eyes flash to the rest of the beach. "We're pretty exposed out here," she breathes.

"I don't care," I growl, my hand reaching up to her breast and squeezing it. She suppresses a yelp, and she bites her lip. "I don't care if someone sees, I want to take you, Serena."

"God, I want you, Luca," she whimpers. She gives the shore one last worried look, but the same energy within her I've always known she has overtakes her. "Are you sure it's safe?"

"Trust me," I say, and I slip my jacket off to lay on the sand before I pull her onto it carefully. Her chest is rising and falling, hair spilling over her shoulders as she looks up at me and the knife, terrified yet full of need.

I take my shirt off and toss it aside, letting my whole torso gleam in the moonlight, and her eyes devour me. She reaches up to run her hands over my muscled body, and I put the knife in my teeth to rip her shirt up over her arms. Her bra comes the next moment, and I feast my eyes on her exposed body.

I take her wrists in my hand and hold them up over her head, planting a knee on either side of her as I draw the blade slowly across my tongue.

"Be still," I caution her, slowly bringing the cool metal down to her torso. Her breathing is quick, but she nods softly and relaxes a bit at my deep, reassuring voice. "No sudden movements. I need all your trust, Serena."

"I want this," she says, red cheeks beautiful under stray locks of hair. "I want you, Luca."

I bring the knife down to her left breast and trace a circle around her nipple. She draws in breath at its cool touch, but I'm careful not to make more than the faintest contact. I've practiced this on myself before trying it with anyone, much less my Serena.

The blade slides around her breast, and I bring it to the other, playing dangerously close to her areola. My hand brings the knife to the nape of her neck, where I draw it across slowly, so slowly, wetting my lips as I watch its progress.

I pause to look up into her eyes, and they're wide with excitement, and she's breathing through her mouth. I smile and look back to the knife to bring it up to her chin, then to her lip, where I let it linger for a moment before gently using it to nudge her mouth open.

When that's done, I close the blade and toss it aside. The next moment, I attack her mouth. Our lips lock, and my bulge is growing rock-hard.

Our tongues explore each other's mouths, and my

hands slide down to her hips, squeezing them greedily, possessively.

We don't even talk. The heady drive of our lust is too strong for that tonight. I bring my mouth down to her nipple where I'd had the knife just a few moments ago, and my teeth do what the knife was too shy to do. I hear her gasp as my tongue washes over it, and meanwhile, I use my hands to start working her pants down. I have no patience tonight. I'm going to claim her, hard and fast.

As soon as her pants are down, I put my fingers to my mouth to wet them, but when I put those fingers to her lower lips, I find her already soaking-wet.

"That's my girl," I groan between kisses. I let my teeth graze her nipples one last time before I undo my own pants and let my shaft out, eager to meet her needy pussy.

His cock spears deeply inside of me as I cry out and arch my back, my hands grasping at either side of me, only to grab fistfuls of sifting sand. I close my eyes and feel my whole body tense up. The coarseness of the sand brushing against my back is just ever so slightly painful, adding a sharp edge to the pleasurable sensations between my legs.

Luca pauses for a moment, letting his massive length and girth fill me, the head of his shaft pressed squarely against that lovely, forbidden spot. I open my eyes again, slowly, to blink up at Luca with anticipation. He's looking down at me with an almost peaceful smile, but there's that fiery spark in his green eyes that tells me I'm in for the ride of my life.

I can't believe that the seed that was planted between us so long ago still blooms so strongly. The trust, the love, the lust I have for him... He makes me feel like a love-struck teenager all over again. He's awakened things in me that I didn't even know were there.

And somehow, his presence in my life... it's soothed those old pains instead of inflaming them. When he first came back in my life, the memories I'd repressed came rushing back, and I had to face the demons in my past. The darkness that was lurking in the corner of my psyche.

But when I'm with him... I feel such love. Such trust. I knew he'd never hurt me, not even by accident, as that cool blade had run up and down my body. So instead of frightening me, it simply thrilled me, and made me feel so... alive.

He runs his hands down my body, from my neck all the way down to squeeze my thighs, prying them open wider as he gradually slides his cock back out of me. I want to wrap my legs around him tightly, keep him inside me as much as possible. It's like an instinctive, almost animalistic need. To keep him. To hold him here. As though if I were to let him go, he might disappear into the fog rolling down across the beach. But I remember his words the other night at the bar: *I'm not going anywhere.*

Without warning, Luca suddenly slams into me, his cock hammering into my pussy. I let out a shriek of surprise and pleasure, and Luca claps a hand over my mouth as he begins to thrust harder and faster. A thrill runs through my body at the newness of this; I've never had anybody cover my mouth during sex before. After what I went through as a teenager, with anybody else I might be scared. But I trust Luca completely, without question. I know he would never, ever hurt me. And the joy of feeling so safe coupled with the hint of danger makes everything that much sexier.

"Shh," he whispers, passing his thumb delicately over my lips. "Someone might hear you."

"I'm sorry," I gasp, feeling my body tingle with ecstasy as he pumps into me again and again. "I'm trying to be quiet but— oh fuck— it feels so good."

I can barely get the words out, as wave after wave of pleasure rushes over me. Luca gives me a devilish grin and leans down to kiss me just as I open my mouth to let out another involuntary cry. He slips a hand down between my legs, his fingers finding my clit easily. I inhale sharply as he works my clit while his cock slams into me incessantly. His breath is hot on my neck, teasing me, until he finally kisses the ticklish skin there and starts to nip and suck. I'm overwhelmed with the competing sensations all over my body, my eyes rolling back and closing. I lift my hips again and again to meet his thrusts, moaning words without meaning.

"So good for me, baby," he purrs, the words dancing tantalizingly across my neck. I tremble with anticipation of looking in the mirror later to see the mark he's leaving there.

It might be juvenile, but I have always loved seeing those pink and purple love bites on my skin, a reminder of intense pleasure that lasts for days. It's a symbol, a trademark, telling the world that I belong to someone. And the thought of belonging to someone like Luca... well, it doesn't get any better than that.

"You're mine," he growls, almost as though he can read my thoughts. I groan, dragging my hands down his back and wrapping my legs around his waist, pulling him in close to me. I need to be closer, always closer to him. I can never get enough.

"I love it when you say that," I murmur. I can feel my pussy clenching around him, preparing for an inevitable climax. "I am yours. I belong to you. I always have."

"Gonna make sure everybody knows it. I'm going to claim you, mia passerotta. You're mine."

And with that, he lunges forward to suck a biting kiss into the flesh just above my collarbone and I yelp as my body trembles through an orgasm. I'm whimpering now, nearly incoherent with the overwhelming symphony of sensations.

"Good girl, very good," Luca whispers, stroking the hair back from my face and planting a soft kiss on my lips. "I want you to ride me, sweetheart."

With one swift, fluid movement, he grabs hold of me and spins around so that his back is on the sand and I'm straddling him. I'm still swaying in the throes of pleasure, but I start working my hips, leaning forward to let my clit rub against him as I ride his cock. Luca reaches up to caress my breasts, rolling my nipples between his thumbs and forefingers, sending shockwaves of pleasure down to my core. I start to lose control, bouncing up and down on his cock with abandon, needing to feel him slam deep inside of me even though it almost hurts. I'm greedy for it now, all coyness and shyness completely faded away by my desire.

"Oh my god," I groan, leaning backward and arching my back as I ride him. Luca pulls up to a sitting position, tugging my legs around him so that we're straddling each other now, facing each other. He gently strokes my face before aggressively taking a fistful of my hair and holding me in place. I never thought I would love being manhandled like this, but everything Luca does is delicious. Perfect. With him, I can completely let go of my insecurities and anxieties and just *be*. At any moment, someone could come walking down the beach and find us here in the most vulnerable position. We could be discovered. A cop could show up. We could get in trouble for this.

But I don't care. It's worth the risk. Luca is worth every risk.

Even though I'm technically on top, Luca seizes control, thrusting into me while he holds me in place with both of his powerful hands firm on my hips. My second orgasm shatters over me and I start to scream, but Luca lets go of my hip to cover my mouth with his hand again.

"Such a good girl for me. I love feeling you come all

over my cock, Serena. I want to make you feel so good," he snarls, never relenting in his fast, hard rhythm. I'm losing myself to the shivers of intense pleasure, the world melting away around me. All that matters is this: Luca and me. Together.

He picks up the pace while one of his hands slides around to cup my ass, giving it a hard slap as I bounce on his cock. "Oh, fuck," I moan. "Do that again. Please."

He spanks me harder, his other hand sliding down from my mouth to my throat, applying gentle, careful pressure. It's just enough to make me feel that edge of thrilling danger again, but never enough to scare or hurt me. He knows exactly what to do without even asking. He knows me.

"I knew you were a dirty girl underneath that sweet smile," he whispers, his breath warm against the shell of my ear. I shiver and lean into him as he gives my ass another hard slap. He's thrusting into me harder and harder, and I know I'm going to be aching later, but it doesn't matter. Nothing matters except for this. I couldn't stop even if I wanted to.

"You make me dirty," I respond breathlessly. "You make me feel like I've never felt before."

"And I'm going to keep you on your toes forever, *mia passerotta*. My sweet sparrow. I want to show you everything. Give you everything," he answers, giving my throat a momentary squeeze. The sensation fills me with adrenaline and spurs me to ride his cock faster, rolling my hips.

"I want you to come, Luca. Please," I beg, wrapping my arms around him.

"Anything for you, baby," he whispers.

And with that, he lets out a growl of pleasure, pumping his hot, sweet seed deep inside of me while I continue to bounce up and down on his cock, milking every last drop from him. He groans and leans in to kiss me hard, his tongue pushing into my mouth while my pussy fills with his cream. He thrusts a few more times and then stops, his hands roving down my back and up to my face, cupping my cheeks as we kiss. There's a passion, a desperation in his kisses, as though he's just as afraid of losing me as I am of losing him. We cling to each other this way for what has to be several minutes, just soaking up the glow of being together, the perfection of the moment.

Finally, we both start laughing softly, resting our foreheads against one another's while the ocean waves crash behind us in the fading light. "Now, time to take you home," Luca says.

My heart sinks for a moment until he adds, "I'm gonna cook you dinner. I think we've both earned that, don't you?"

I nod vigorously, overjoyed to spend more time with him. I never want to be out of his sight. I would follow him anywhere, and that thought doesn't scare me at all. Being vulnerable with Luca doesn't feel scary or forced—it feels *real*.

We gingerly get dressed, trying and probably failing to get all the sand off of our bodies and clothing as we make our way back to the car. On the drive home, we listen to a radio station playing old Sinatra and Elvis songs, the windows rolled down to let the evening air blow through our hair. Luca reaches across the console to take my hand, and I feel my heart swell. This is everything I've ever wanted. I never thought I could find this kind of bliss.

When we get to his apartment building and step out of the elevator onto his floor, there's a fluffy, fat cat meowing at us just as the doors open. Luca chuckles, shifting the groceries from the market to one arm and bending down to pick the cat up with his other arm, to my surprise. "*Ciao*, Grasso," he says, stroking the cat's head as it closes its yellow eyes and purrs.

"Whose cat is that?" I ask bemusedly.

"My neighbor, Mrs. Rodriguez— he's always sneaking out on her. Little bastard," he says, cooing fondly at the cat as he carries it toward the door next to his and knocks.

There's a pause, and then the tell-tale shuffle of slippered feet on carpet. The door rattles open to reveal a tiny, stooped older woman with snowy-white hair and big brown eyes. Her lipstick is slightly smudged, as though she'd wiped her mouth after forgetting she was wearing it. She's wearing a bathrobe over her floral-patterned pajamas, and when she realizes who's at the door, her wrinkled face splits into a genuine smile.

"Oh! Luca, you found Grasso!" she exclaims, reaching out to take the massive cat into her arms. It purrs happily, curling its tail around its body. "*Pobrecito*, he just gets so bored cooped up in here with me sometimes, he wants to go on an adventure. But when he gets out there, he's afraid. Thank you for bringing him back. I was just about to watch Jeopardy and go to bed without him!"

"No problem, Mrs. Rodriguez," Luca says, smiling. "I've brought you some groceries, too."

The woman's eyes light up. "Oh *gracias, mi querido*. You are too good to me."

"Just looking out for my favorite neighbor," Luca replies, handing her one of the bags. I can feel my heart swelling with pride and warmth. Luca puts an arm around me. "By the way, this is Serena. She's my—"

"*Tu novia! Que linda! Much gusto*," Mrs. Rodriguez gushes, pushing through the doorway to give me a hug, the cat still curled up in the crook of her arm.

"Oh, nice to meet you, too!" I reply, hugging her back. I give Luca a look over her shoulder and he grins, shrugging.

"I always tell Mister Luca, I say to him, 'Mister Luca! You need a woman to look after you! A handsome young man like you should not be spending so much time alone!'"

she says, holding up one finger with mock sternness. "I am so happy for you, Mister Luca! You be sweet to Serena. I like her. And so does Grasso."

"I promise I'll be sweet," Luca says, nodding dutifully. He gives me a wink when she's not looking. Mrs. Rodriguez gives each of us a peck on the cheek, with Luca having to bend nearly perpendicular for her to reach, then she wishes us goodnight and retreats back into her apartment, still cooing to the cat.

Luca and I exchange expressions of amusement and then he takes me by the hand and leads me into his apartment. Once the door is shut, I burst out laughing.

"That was the cutest thing that's ever happened to me," I say genuinely. Luca chuckles and heads into the kitchen.

"She's a sweetheart. A little batty and forgetful sometimes, but she's a good neighbor. She bakes me a cake every April," Luca answers. I follow him into the kitchen, watching him take out ingredients for what looks to be a very impressive dinner.

"April? Why?" I ask, confused.

He shrugs and takes out a knife and cutting board to start chopping onions and tomatoes. "She thinks my birthday is in April. It's in September, but I don't have the heart to keep reminding her, so I just let it go."

"Aww," I reply, smiling. "You know, you've got to be one of the most surprising people I've ever met, Luca. Every time I think I have you all figured out, you go the other way entirely."

"Is that a bad thing?" he asks, glancing sidelong at me as I lean against the counter.

I grin and shake my head, walking over to kiss him on the cheek. "No. It's the best thing."

The rest of the evening I spend looking through his apartment, finally taking the time to look at the minimalist decor and little quirks that speak to his character and personality. He lives simply, without frills or opulence, but he lives well. Cleanly. I can see his appreciation for the nicer things, but he doesn't go over the top. There's a refurbished vintage record player in the corner of the living room, a set of dumbbells tucked into an alcove, a colorful blanket folded over the back of the couch.

I ask him about the blanket and he explains that it's a traditional pattern from the area of Italy he hails from. I run my fingers over it lovingly, as though I can get a glimpse of that version of Luca just from touching the vibrant threads. I want to know everything about him, but I know it's better to let him show me slowly, at his own pace. After all, I don't plan on ever losing him again, so we have all the time in the world to learn all those little things about each other. Sure enough, he explains that the blanket is one of the few things he was able to bring with him when he first came to the States to work as a carpenter under his uncle's tutelage. He's kept it all these years as a memento of home, reminding him where he comes from and who he is.

Dinner is, of course, another surprise. It's course after course of delicious, authentic Italian food. At first he tells me to just relax and let him do all the work, but I sidle up next to him in the kitchen and ask how I can help. As he goes along, he teaches me how to prepare everything, how to plate it.

"It's funny, my family is Italian but I never learned to cook," I tell him, slightly embarrassed. "When I was growing up, we always had a chef who came to the house to prepare most of our meals. Mom knew how to cook, but my dad didn't want her to have to lift a finger. She was spoiled, you know? And he wanted to keep spoiling her as much as he could. And then after my dad died...well, I just didn't get the chance to learn. We've had a lot of takeout over the years. Mom cooks sometimes, but I think it makes her kind of sad. A lot has had to change since Dad died, and I try to make it as easy on her as I can."

"You're a good daughter," Luca says, putting an arm around me and kissing the top of my head. "I know your father would be proud of you. Anybody would."

After an hour or so of working side-by-side in the kitchen, Luca shoos me away to the table so he can serve me. It's a parade of ridiculously rich, amazing food. Wine, prosciutto, fresh mozzarella, perfectly cooked pasta, massive shrimp cooked in a spicy red sauce, a tray of expertly cut and arranged fruit. By the second course I'm already stuffed, but I keep eating, unable to resist anything Luca brings to the table.

Over dinner, we talk about the old days, reminiscing about how young and stupid we used to be before the world knocked us off our feet.

We don't talk about that horrible thing that happened, and I'm more than okay with that. I don't want to think about it. Everything is so good right now, and I want it to stay this way as long as possible. I'm happy, truly happy, for the first time in a long, long while.

After dinner, we take our time cleaning up all the dishes together, just chatting and listening to the music playing from the record player. As I'm putting the wine bottle back into the rack, I notice a bottle of liquor in his cabinet that looks interesting. "Is that Campari?" I ask, pointing it out.

Luca walks over and takes it out, along with a bottle of Prosecco. "Ah, good eye. Here, let me make you our drink."

It's even better with the prosecco than the soda water, and immediately I feel lighter and happier than ever. "I feel like I should pinch myself," I laugh.

"I can assure you that the drink in your hand is real," Luca says coyly.

"I know that," I say, leaning into him and resting my

cheek on his chest. "I just can't believe that you're real. That any of this is happening. It's too good to be true."

Luca tips my chin upward with his finger. He kisses me softly. "It's all real. I promise."

Finally, we both finish our drinks and sleepily make our way to his bed, where we curl up in each other's arms. I feel safe and wanted, like this is exactly where I'm supposed to be. Like I've been waiting my whole life for a moment this perfect. I've been dreaming about this, and now it's here.

And it's happening again—I'm falling for him. I've fallen for him.

For better or for worse, there's no denying it: I've fallen in love with a mafioso. Just like my mother. I'm the disgraced mafia princess, following in my mother's footsteps.

Yet a pit in my stomach won't go away, it knows something has to go wrong. Something painfully soon.

"*Buongiorno.*"

I open my eyes at the sound of Luca's velvety voice sending warm shivers down my body. His lips press against the back of my neck, making me twinge away from the ticklish sensation. His powerful arms are wrapped around me, with my head resting comfortably in the crook of his right elbow on the pillow. I have no idea what time it is, but I'm finding it really hard to care when there's a beautiful man pressed up against my back. I yawn and pull his left arm over me tighter, wiggling backward into him so that my ass is pushed against his crotch. He's so warm, radiating enough heat that I probably don't even need a blanket. He kisses my neck again and I giggle, shrugging my shoulders playfully.

"Good morning to you, too," I murmur, my throat feeling scratchy as it always does when I first wake up. Despite the fact that I routinely get up early to go into Bathing Beauty, I am really, definitely not a morning person. Left to my own devices, I would gladly lie in bed until noon. I know today is a work day, and I'm dreading looking at the alarm clock on Luca's nightstand. I don't want to know. I want more time here in this warm, cozy heaven with the man I adore. The idea of getting out of this bed is completely repugnant to me right now.

"I should get up," I groan. "Gotta go to work."

"Mmm, that sounds terrible. Don't do that," Luca replies in a growly voice, pulling me closer and breathing hotly against the back of my neck. Goosebumps rise up along my arms and legs.

"You're making this very hard for me," I chide him, grinning. He rocks his hips forward and I can feel his massive shaft stiff against my ass.

"Oh, I think you're the one making it hard," he answers coyly.

"Who, me? I haven't done anything," I reply, with mock indignation. "I'm totally innocent."

Luca chuckles and sits up a little, leaning over to kiss the side of my neck and up to my cheek. He turns my face gently to kiss my lips, his cock still rock-hard against me.

"Oh no, I have morning breath," I protest weakly.

"You taste wonderful," he replies, kissing me again. "I don't care."

"You're going to make me late for work," I add, feeling myself start to give in. It's impossible to resist him, and every part of me wants desperately to stay in this bed.

"Well, we'd better get started then," he replies mischievously. Before I can even respond, he dives under the comforter, pushing it back out of the way as he exposes my body bit by bit. He sleeps naked, unsurprisingly, but I'm wearing one of his t-shirts, which is comically huge on me, and a pair of decidedly-unsexy black panties. Nothing special. I mean, they're not granny panties, but they're definitely not lingerie either. I feel my face flushing pink at the realization that Luca, the most blisteringly hot man I have ever been intimate with, is seeing this underwear on me.

"Sorry for the ugly undies," I mumble.

Luca, tugging them down my thighs to take them off, looks up at me with a wry smile. "First of all, you look fantastic in everything. Second of all, it doesn't matter anyway because they're about to come off. Lingerie is nice, but I think we both know I prefer you without anything on at all. You're the gift. I don't care about the wrapping paper."

I can't stop the grin that plasters itself on my face. I've never met anyone so good at putting my mind at ease. It's like magic. He just melts away all my anxiety, all those years of stress and fear. He cuts away all that bullshit to get to me— the real me. The version of myself I never thought I could find again. And it's liberating.

Luca drops the offending panties over the side of the bed and pushes my thighs wide open, kneeling down between my legs. I inhale sharply in anticipation as he leans in and gently begins to suck at my clit, his tongue flicking over it while one of his fingers slides inside of me. Fuck, I'm already wet. All it takes is Luca's presence to make me give in. I can't resist.

"Oh my God," I murmur, my eyes closing and my head falling backward onto the pillow. My hands instinctively reach down to comb through Luca's hair, and before long my hips are rolling, bucking up to meet him. He knows just how to work my clit, just how to angle the tip of his finger inside me to reach that little bundle of nerves that makes me weak. He's an expert, like he's been studying my body for years or something. I don't know how he knows, but he does. He just *knows*.

He groans, his finger sliding in and out up against that special spot faster and faster. I fling my arms outward to grasp at the bedsheets, gritting my teeth as my pleasure mounts to a climax.

Just before my orgasm hits, Luca backs off, grabs me by the hips, and flips me onto my stomach. Then he pulls me to my knees and rubs the head of his thick shaft against my slick opening, sliding over my sensitive clit. I back into him, desperate for that delicious friction, but he grabs my hips and holds me in place.

"Please, Luca," I whimper. "I want to come."

He lets out a growly kind of chuckle and says, "Oh, you're going to come, sweetheart. But only when I'm good and ready for it."

A shiver runs down my spine and I feel myself getting even wetter. I never expected to be the kind of woman who likes to be bossed around and dominated in bed, especially after what I went through years ago. But with Luca, it's different. I want him to tell me what to do. I want him to use me however he wants to, because I know he would never hurt me. I can trust him to push me right to the very edge and then bring me back over and over again, making it feel so good every time.

"So wet for me, Serena," he says softly, his voice gravelly and rough. I can tell this is taking all of his self-restraint, too. And the thought that he's struggling to keep it together, that he wants me just as badly as I want him, makes me feel powerful and desired.

"I want you inside me," I beg him, twisting to peer back at him. He's a formidable sight, all muscle and smooth skin, with that impossibly handsome face. Those flashing green eyes. And then, he smiles at me. A devilish grin. He knows just how badly I need this, and he's going to give it to me.

He slides the full length of his cock along my wet slit, making me tremble. I'm so sensitive right now, all my nerves on fire, just hovering over the edge. Then he gives my ass a hard slap. I cry out, shuddering with the mingled pain and pleasure.

"Good girl," he says quietly, now circling the tip of his cock around my wet opening, teasing me.

"Please, I need you to fill me up, Luca," I plead. I'm aching for his cock.

"Oh, I'm going to, *mia passerotta*. I'm going to fill you up and fuck you hard. But I don't want you to come until I say so, *si*?" he explains, keeping his tone even-keeled even though I can hear that husky need in his voice.

"Whatever you say," I answer, grinding back against him. I'm a little scared that I won't be able to hold on— I'm already so close. He has me dangling over the edge, and I just know that the second his cock is inside of me, I'll be a goner.

And then, it happens. He grabs my hips and pushes his cock deep inside me, penetrating me to the hilt. I can feel my pussy clenching around him and I cry out, grabbing for the pillow to hold myself steady. I'm trying so hard to keep myself from coming. I want to do what he told me to do.

"Don't come yet, baby," he says, even as his hips start to move and his cock slides in and out of me while he reaches around my thigh to gently rub my clit with his finger. By now, I'm an incoherent mess. Every last thread of my focus is centered on not giving in, not climaxing. But it's so hard.

"Oh God," I groan as he starts to fuck me deeper, but slower. "Luca, I-I'm gonna come, I can't take it. It feels so fucking good!"

"Yeah? You want to come for me, sweetheart? You want to come all over my cock?" he teases me, circling my clit with his finger and sending shockwaves of unbearable pleasure through me.

"Please, oh fuck," I whimper. He slaps my ass again, hard.

"You want me to fuck you harder, Serena?" he asks.

"I need it, I need you," I answer breathlessly. I'm hanging on by a mere thread. "Please!"

And with that, he starts to thrust harder, his cock hammering at my g-spot while his finger works my clit, fucking me hard and fast. "Are you ready? I know you want to come."

"Oh God! Please, I need it!" I cry out, my fingers twisting in the sheets.

"Come for me, baby. Come all over my cock. Now."

Instantly, my body seizes up in an overwhelming rush of pleasure. Wave after wave of electric bliss rolls over me and I let out an involuntary shriek, feeling my pussy pulsing intensely around his cock. Luca doesn't let up for even a second, fucking me harder and faster until I'm coming again and again, lost in a sea of extreme pleasure.

"Good girl, very good," he groans, and I can tell he's gritting his teeth, trying so hard to keep his own climax in check. I decide to take business into my own hands. He's not the only one who can play at this game. I begin to roll my hips back, impaling myself on his cock hard and fast, clenching as tightly as I can.

"It's. Your. Turn," I manage to mumble, and I can tell by his increasingly erratic thrusts that he's about to blow. He's almost there. The fact that I have this power to make this beautiful, amazing man feel so good is intoxicating.

"Fuck, Serena," Luca groans. "Just like that."

He thrusts a few more times quickly and sharply and then holds me still, his fingertips digging into my hips as he shoots his thick honey deep inside me. His deep voice thrums through my body as he cries out, and he shudders through his orgasm.

We're both still panting as I feel him lean forward to kiss a gentle line up the arch of my back before withdrawing. We fall on our backs side by side, and his hand finds mine underneath the tangle of sheets. I look over at him, beaming uncontrollably, to see an identical look of bliss on his face. Warmth. Everything about Luca is comfortable. Everything about him feels like home.

"Well, that was definitely worth being late to work for,"

I laugh, turning over to get my phone from the nightstand. The battery is nearly dead, as I forgot to bring my charger last night, but it can still show me the time. Nine-thirty-eight, and then my phone dies.

"Shit," I mumble, wriggling out of bed and whipping Luca's huge t-shirt off. I hop into the bathroom, pulling on my socks which I'm pretty sure are inside out, but that's a problem for future me to sort out. "I don't have clean clothes!" I call out, staring around the bathroom in a mild panic.

Luca comes shuffling in behind me, totally naked and unreserved. He wraps his arms around me and presses a kiss to my cheek. "You can borrow one of my shirts again."

"Uh-huh, and it'll look like I'm a grifter who just wandered into the shop one day," I giggle, rolling my eyes. Then, I get an idea. "Actually, could you bring me your biggest, longest, most stretched-out shirt?"

Luca gives me a skeptical smirk but nods. "I feel like that's the opposite of what you'd want, but your wish is my command." He steps into the walk-in closet attached to the bathroom suite and starts poring through his surprisingly meticulous wardrobe.

"Any luck?" I ask, reluctantly slipping back into yesterday's bra, panties, and leggings. I can't just walk into the shop wearing the same dress as yesterday. Too obvious. Even if nobody else notices, I would still feel icky all day.

"Uhh, how do you feel about, um, vintage?" Luca says, making me laugh.

"How vintage?"

"Let's just say I had to dig back through my sort of nostalgic section of clothing for this one," he explains, giving me an apologetic shrug. "All my clothing from recent years has been tailored. I have a guy. So there's not a lot of wildly oversized stuff in here anymore."

I hold my hand out. "Alright. Just give it to me. Let's see."

He hesitantly hands over a faded, well-worn gray t-shirt with some kind of brand logo that has nearly been washed blank by the years. It's a little threadbare, but it will do. I tug it on, then knot the hem at one hip so that it falls almost like a stretched-out, slightly off-kilter shift dress.

Luca laughs. "Wow. That is real ingenuity."

"Shut up," I giggle, swatting at him playfully. "Well, no time to really do my makeup now."

"Can you do it in the car?"

I raise an eyebrow. "While driving? No, I value my life just a *little* more than that."

"As a passenger, of course. I'm driving you to work," he says, matter-of-factly.

"You sure? I could always get a cab."

"I'm going to work with you anyway, so we might as well carpool. Save the earth and all that," he adds, emerging from the walk-in closet again, this time fully dressed and looking like a million bucks. He's only wearing a white button-down, black pants, and gray blazer, but he looks like some kind of secret agent about to crack a case or steal a diamond or something.

"Wow, way to show me up," I comment, crossing my arms and eyeing him up and down.

"Well, I do have the advantage of my entire personal wardrobe here," he says, walking over to envelop me in his arms. He smells wonderful, like a mix of fancy cologne and his own particular, musky, delicious scent. "And besides, you make everyone in every room you walk into look terrible by comparison. Anyway, let's get you to work. Bath emergencies wait for no man."

We pile into his car and head out, with the mid-morning sun beaming joyfully overhead. Everything is so bright and crystal-clear today, with the kind of bright blue skies and puffy cotton-ball clouds that seem better suited for a painting than real life. It's hard to determine whether the beauty of the world is actually intensified today, or if I'm just seeing it this way because of the gorgeous man beside me in the driver's seat.

"This is gonna be a good day," I say softly. "I can feel it."

"Every day with you is a good day," Luca adds, squeezing my thigh gently.

As soon as the words leave his mouth, there is a sudden flash of gray across the windshield and Luca hits the brakes. I look out my window to see that there is a pillar of smoke blowing down from an alleyway next to us at the stop light. "What the hell?" I murmur, rolling down my window to look.

"Smoke," Luca says.

"From where?" I ask, squinting into the occasional clear spots. Then it hits me.

I know where we are.

Before the car can start rolling again, I unlock and hop out the door, taking off down the alleyway. Luca somehow manages to pull over and park, halfway on the sidewalk, and run after me. I burst through the alleyway and across the street to stand in front of the source of the fire.

Room With A View is in flames, a clamoring crowd gathering in a messy semicircle out into the road. There's a fire truck out front, its siren wailing while the firefighters run in and out of the burning building. I dart around, looking for Nico or Rafaela, my heart pounding in my chest. Luca catches up to me and takes my hand, pointing to an area closer to the front line. Police are blocking the crowd from getting much closer, and luckily Luca can see better over the crowd from his height than I can.

"Up there!" he says, pulling me along behind him as we push through the crowd.

I shove past lots of angry spectators, caring only about locating my friends. If they were inside when the place caught on fire...

"Rafaela!" I shout, catching sight of my best friend and wiggling past a couple of cops to reach her. There's ash on her skin and she's crying, but there's a hardened expression on her face. Rafaela is not the kind of girl to cry over just anything. She's incredibly tough, and even with the tears clearing a path down her sooty cheeks, she looks about ready to fight someone.

She turns to pull me into a hug, and I can tell she's been needing this. As strong as she is, I know that she can be vulnerable, too, with people she trusts. Like me.

"Oh, Serena, it's fucking horrible. Everything we have— had—it's all gone. This bar was our everything. I-I don't know how this happened. But I have an idea *who*," she says, her eyes flashing with anger.

"Are you okay? Where's Nico? Is there anybody inside?" I ask, panicked.

She shakes her head. "Not anymore. The firefighters got everyone out, but two of our boarders are already en route to the hospital. It—it doesn't look good," she adds, looking horrified. "But Nico is over there. The cops keep trying to talk to him but he doesn't want to say anything to them yet."

I glance around her to see Nico and Luca huddled together, several feet away from the line of policemen. Nico looks unscathed, and I silently thank the heavens that both of my friends are okay. I link arms with Rafaela and walk her away from the cops, trying to look unobtrusive.

"So, what do you think happened?" I ask quietly. She shakes her head, blinking back tears.

"I think it was one of those fucking gangs, *chica*. Probably the same shitheads who graffitied your shop and hurt those dogs," she says bitterly. "I just feel like this is my fault.

I should've been here more. I've just been so distracted with school lately and leaving Nico to look after the Room by himself. I should've done something ages ago. *Mierda.* I fucked up."

I give her another tight hug. "No. No. You can't blame yourself for this, Raf. You're not a superhero. Nobody could've prevented this."

She sighs heavily and tucks her hair behind her ears like she does when she's nervous. She fixes me with a sorrowful look. "I just know there's something else going on here. *No sé.* I think—I think I'm a little out of my pay grade, you know? Like, maybe I should've just stayed in Harlem. Maybe I'm reaching too far trying to make it in this neighborhood."

I squeeze her hand supportively. "Hey, don't say that. You've achieved so much. Seriously, you know what I said a minute ago about you not being a superhero? I was wrong about that. You *are* a superhero, Raf. And you're gonna get through this just fine. Like you always do. Just don't blame yourself, okay? It's not like you set the fire."

"How do you know I didn't burn it down for insurance money or whatever?" she pipes up, a flicker of that old attitude flaring through.

I grin.

"There's my girl. Just, not so loud, the cops might hear. Now, let's go find Luca and Nico and regroup, okay?"

We weave through the crowd, gingerly avoiding eye contact with the cops. Rafaela is right. I may not know the details, but I'm pretty sure this fire is no accident. Somebody did this, and I have a feeling things are about to get worse before they get better. When we reach the guys, Nico puts his arms around Rafaela and points out a man in slightly nicer clothing than the rest of the crowd.

"Babe, that's a detective. We're gonna have to make a statement to him. No big deal. Just tell the truth, and nothing else. Everything is gonna be fine," he tells her. Then, looking at Luca and me, he gives a quick nod. "Thanks for being here."

"Of course," I say.

The two of them make their way down the street to the detective and Luca turns to me, giving me a quick kiss before staring into my eyes emphatically. "We need to get away from here. Now."

"What?"

"We're being watched. I'm sure of that. Let's go. Back to the car."

We quietly sneak back through the masses and down the alleyway to the car. Once we're inside and driving away, Luca continues. "The two men who were injured are mafiosi. They're in critical care. I do not expect that they will live through this."

"Oh my God," I murmur, my head starting to spin. "So, this is a *gang* thing."

"Essentially," he agrees. "The Cleaners are responsible for this, no doubt. I don't know if you were aware of this, but your friends have been running a kind of halfway house there. Mafia guys in hiding, a place for newcomers to blend into the city, a place to lay low when things get heated. Well, they just got too hot."

"How in the world... are you serious? Room With A View. A mafia den," I mutter, raking my fingers back through my hair. I never would have expected it. Rafaela can't possibly be involved with this stuff. But Nico—well, I don't know as much about him as I probably should.

"Nico is one of our guys. A casual. Low profile. But he does what he can," Luca explains. "This is a hit by the Cleaners. Everything up until now has just been a test run, trying out our limits, making plans. Now, the war is started. There's no telling how long the bar has been compromised. They could've had eyes on us for months, just waiting for the right time to strike."

I think about our night together in one of the boarding rooms and my stomach turns. All this time, they could've been watching us. Even that night, maybe.

"So, what the hell are we gonna do?" I ask, feeling like my entire world has been turned upside down. Luca glances over at me, those green eyes lighting up in the sunshine.

"We're going to bite back, of course."

"You're sure?" I say into my cellphone, a frown on my face. I'm standing in front of a counter in the back of Bathing Beauty, looking at a row of about four small TVs with camera feeds hooked up to them.

All is clear on the video feed, but as I listen to Diego over the phone, my frown only deepens. He's been helpful in giving me updates as they come in. The heat might be turning up with the Cleaners, but at least I can rely on my own allies to keep me informed. But the news isn't good.

"I see. I'll update the men. Keep your ass safe out there," I end the call while running a hand through my hair. The piece of news I just got is the worst yet. Just as I'm about to make a call to the men I have patrolling the block, I hear the door to the back room open, and Serena's face appears in the crack.

"Hey, you alive back here?" she asks, glancing at the flickering screens. I smile warmly at her. She's been incredibly strong through all this. Her store has practically become the front lines of a battleground she never wanted to set foot on, but she still manages to keep the doors of the shop open as if nothing's the matter.

"As far as I know," I say, and I stride over to her to pull her the rest of the way into the room and wrap my hands around her hips. "How's business?"

"It's going," she says, tilting her head to the side. "I'm not exactly advertising that there are mobsters patrolling the streets, so it's business as usual."

"Maybe you should try that," I say with a playful smile. "Think about it: 'Bathing Beauty, so fresh it's a crime.'"

She bites her lip and stares at me lovingly. "I...think we should leave the marketing to me."

"Probably," I say, and I plant a kiss on her forehead. She giggles and hugs me after a quick glance to make sure the front of the store is quiet, then looks back up at me with a slightly more serious look.

"Really though, you look kind of uneasy. Is everything alright? The streets have been quiet all day."

I pause, glancing down at my phone, and I decide it's best to be totally upfront with her. It's never done her any favors to leave her in the dark about what's happening in her own life.

"That was Diego on the phone," I say. "We knew the Cleaners had cops in their pocket—that's not unusual for any organization." Serena nods slowly, and I go on. I squeeze her hips gently and give her the most reassuring look I can. "It goes deeper than I thought. They have someone on the take who's higher up than I thought—a detective."

Serena's eyes widen. "A detective?"

"Detective Will Price. He's a piece of shit," I say, and that's something I can say sincerely. "He's been crooked from the start, but he deals with drug runners and traffickers—the kind of man that helps scum like the Cleaners thrive."

"Is he going to be a problem for us?" Serena asks, but the look in her eyes tells me she already knows the answer. I run my hand through her hair, letting my strong fingers play gently with her golden locks.

"We don't know yet," I say. "Diego knows he's in the area, and he's making it easier for the Cleaners to do what they want, but none of our men have been in touch with him."

Serena nods, and I hug her close to me, kissing her on the top of the head. "I'd take on the whole NYPD before I let any danger come too close to you, Serena. We'll cross this bridge when we come to it. For now, we have enough on our plate."

Serena looks up at me, pink lips smiling, and the sight of her smiling softly at me is enough to give me all the strength in the world. "I'm glad you're here, whatever happens," she says, and then she steps away from me, heading back into the front. "It's about closing time, so I'm gonna start wrapping things up out front."

"I've got an eye on you," I say with a wink and a nod back to the CCTV feeds, and she blushes before heading back to the front.

Half an hour later, Serena is closing the blinds on the windows of the shop, and soon there's nothing but the lights keeping the shop bright inside. I step into the front of the shop as she closes up some of the displays and finishes cleaning a few surfaces off, and she turns to quirk an eyebrow at the two long objects in my hand.

"What are those?"

I hold up the two sheaths, then set them on the front counter. "Remember the tussle on the boardwalk the other night?"

"Sure."

"I wasn't kidding when I said you handled yourself well," I say, unbuttoning the sheaths and taking out the objects inside. I pull out two rubber knives, holding them up to show them to her. She cocks her head to the side.

"Are those…?"

"Not real," I say with a grin, "they're rubber. Training knives. Me and my boys are going to keep you safe, but if things get too hot," I say, stepping closer to her and looking down at her, "I won't let my *passerotta* be caught defenseless."

She looks up at me silently for a few moments, then down at the hilt of the rubber knife I'm offering her. She takes it and feels its weight, getting a firm grip on it. The way she holds it tells me she'll be a natural.

"I got lucky on the boardwalk," she says, brandishing the knife around a little experimentally. "I don't think I could go toe-to-toe with someone like that guy you took down."

"It shouldn't come to that," I say, stepping around behind her and adjusting her stance, bending her elbow just so and turning her hips. "But just in case, a little extra luck doesn't hurt," I say with a smile down at her.

"By 'luck' you mean a few inches of steel, right?" she says with a coy smile, and I grin.

"That helps, too."

"Okay," she says, taking a deep breath to relax as she tosses the knife up and down in her hand a few times and catching it. "I'm game. No problem. Soap shop owner and knife-fighter. I can make that work. Where do you want to practice?"

"This will do," I say, looking around the front of the shop. She raises her eyebrows at me, and I carefully slide some of the tables in the center out of the way to give us a little more room.

"Are you sure? Going out back might be a little more convenient."

"You don't get convenient space in a fight," I say, "and

besides, unless you changed your mind about branding this place as a mob front, I don't think a knife-fight out back will be the best public image."

"Fair enough," she says, and she sinks back into the stance that I showed her. As I finish moving the tables, I look at her and smile. Her body is good at remembering the posture.

"That's good," I say, "managing your own center of gravity is half the fight. You're light, you'll need to use that to your advantage a lot."

"How do I do that?"

I square up with her, holding my own knife at the ready. "I'll show you step by step. I'll move in, and I'll show you how to move yourself so you can use my weight against me. You might not be able to push me around, but I can't lift myself. Like this…"

I start showing her the basics of knife-fighting, the sounds of our feet scuffling around the shop the only noise besides my instruction.

Serena proves to be a good student. She seems naturally able to move where I tell her, and half the time, she anticipates what I'm going to tell her. I can see her athletic youth shining through, and her muscles serve her well.

I show her the basic moves, how to keep an enemy from using his height to his advantage, how to move quickly and effortlessly to match an enemy's better reach. I have to be careful not to run into the displays in the shop, but it's good practice in using the limited space.

While I teach her how to use her body, it isn't long before she starts making use of the knife to fight back with the movements. "That's good," I tell her as I parry one of her quick jabs, "let the movement come first, and the attacks can follow. That's the trick—they'll see you coming from a mile away if you come in to attack. Let him come to you and make him regret it."

She nods and slips around me to make a stab at my kidney, and I roll around to pull her arm behind her back, gently. I tap her on the collar with the knife, and she huffs, getting back into position. "Again."

She gets into the swing of things fast, and soon, we're going back and forth at a steady rhythm, our pace only getting more regular. I move in, she moves around me, and I catch her.

After a few minutes of practicing a set of about five maneuvers, I finally feel a tap of the rubber on my kidney, and she gives a triumphant little laugh, skipping back and smiling brightly. "Ha!"

"Not bad," I admit, grinning proudly at her. "Now do it again."

Soon, the sound of our heavy breathing is in the air as we run through the routines until I feel that they're coming almost unconsciously to her. She moves in like a viper, and she's starting to learn my openings. I don't fight people as small as her, so she soon finds openings in my defenses even I didn't know were there. She's impressive.

And I know that the guys she'd potentially be fighting are no different than me. They don't fight women like her. They simply…

I shake my mind of the thought. I can't go back to that night. I can't let myself think of what would happen if I didn't show up.

I parry another stab, but Serena gets too bold soon, and when she tries to dart under my arms and bring the knife up to my throat, I catch her by the wrist and whirl her around, holding the knife to her own throat with her back pressed against my front.

We freeze there for a moment, our heavy breathing filling the air, and I let the rubber blade brush against her skin.

"Playing with fire, *carina*," I whisper into her ear. She

smiles and twists away from my grip, twirling the blade in her hand a moment before darting in again. This time, she gets up under me, and I catch her before she can draw her knife across my thigh, but she shifts her weight the way I showed her, and I go down to one knee to keep her from getting out of my grasp.

I bring my knife down to her throat, but at the same moment that my rubber touches her neck, I feel a prod at my gut from her knife.

We look into each other's faces a moment, both of us 'dead' by the other's hand.

"You learn fast," I say in a low tone, between breaths.

She's panting as well, her skin glistening in the light of the shop. "Have to, with a big brute like you coming after me."

"It'll take more than that to keep me from coming after you," I say, my voice lowering into a husk, and before she can respond, I descend upon her and press my lips to hers.

Surprised, she moans into the kiss, her heart still beating fast from the exercise, and I soon drop my knife and use one hand to lower myself over her while the other slides up under her neck to lift it ever so slightly into my kiss. She squirms under me, and I hear her rubber hit the ground too as her hands slide up to my shirt, feeling the tight muscles under the thin fabric.

I let her explore me, her fingers going from my swollen pecs down to my abs. She feels my wounds, but the dull twinge of pain is nothing to me with Serena in my hands. The pleasure she gives me is worth a fresh gunshot wound. She wraps her arms around me, and I feel her ankles go around my waist as she clings to me tight, our lips still locked.

I stand up with her wrapped around me, and with no patience left in my body, I take her to the front counter and set her down on it. My hands run down her sides before they reach her leggings, and I roughly jerk them down as she wiggles to help them slide off.

"Spread your legs," I order her, and she puts her hands back to lean on as she obeys, color flushing into her cheeks. The fabric reveals her lips, looking as swollen as needy as ever, and I feel my hunger for them overwhelm me.

I kneel down and run my hands over her smooth thighs, gripping the sensitive skin. She seems so delicate, even though we've just spent nearly an hour teaching her how to be all the more deadly.

She's deadlier to others, at least. To me, Serena is already my fatal poison.

I lean forward and breathe in her scent, letting my breath wash over her pussy, and I hear her gasp as she grips the table, knuckles white already. I breathe along her slit, taunting her by coming so close, so very close to touching her, and when my stubble finally grazes her skin, she whimpers, trying to close her legs.

My strong, gentle grip holds them apart, though, and she pushes her hips in a little, begging for me, needing me.

"Do you think you've earned this?" I ask, teasing her with a smile curling on my lips.

"Fuck, Luca, don't do this to me!" she whines. Her face smiles, but as I let another quick breath roll over her lips, it fades into desperate need.

"Am I torturing you, *carina*?" I ask, using my thumbs to tease her inner thighs before I run my mouth along them, teeth grazing them, five o'clock shadow teasing them.

"I've been thinking about this all day," Serena whimpers, "fuck, I wanted you to bend me over the counter since you walked in this morning."

"That's not very professional," I growl, and I wait for her to open her mouth to reply before I let my tongue out over her cunt.

She tenses immediately, and I feel the beginnings of her honey on the tip of my tongue as it travels from the bottom of her slit, deep into her lips, then up to the tip of that sensitive nub that's so very desperate for attention. I've teased her, but she's done well tonight—she deserves a proper reward.

I let loose, my tongue attacking her clit relentlessly. Its tip rolls back and forth over it, up and down, rhythmically, slowly at first. But as I build up a little speed, her jaw hangs open, and I feel her hands go to my head to get a grip. My hair pokes through her tight fingers as she holds onto me, and I feel her honey start to flood my face freely. Her body is uninhibited—it knows what it wants, and what it wants is my mouth.

I let my teeth graze her as I lavish her clit with attention, and each time they touch, I feel her tighten her grip, hear another gasp escape her pretty mouth.

My tongue moves back and forth, darting in and out to kiss her swollen nub, and I feel her start to buck her hips ever so slightly, rhythmically, needfully. I hear her gasps start to get more regular, more like a steady pace of whining breaths, and her fingers start to tighten on my head.

"Oh, oh, oh Luca, Luca, fuck!" she gasps, breathing in sharply as my name dances across her tongue, and I feel her whole body convulse and tighten as she comes for me, hard. Exercise always makes your body more ready for release, more needy to get rid of all that tension. I feel my face getting so wet as she lets out a wonderfully satisfied sigh, head falling back as she struggles to keep herself up, the poor thing.

I don't give her a moment to breathe, though. I keep lavishing her clit, and soon, I let my tongue roll over the rest of her pussy, too. It runs deep, drawing out as much honey as she serves up to me. I'm devouring her, and it isn't long before she tenses up again, orgasm crashing through her frame.

Her beauty might be my weakness, but the things I can make her body do is my secret weapon against her.

I rise up to face her panting expression, and her hazy eyes meet mine, full of so much need that I haven't tapped yet. I smile and let out a rumbling groan from my chest as I wrap my hand around the back of her neck and pull her into a kiss. Her wetness gets all over her face as we messily embrace each other, and she brings her hips forward to push against my black pants.

"Baby, you're so wet," I groan between sloppy kisses. "You weren't kidding."

"We're making such a goddamn mess," she half-laughs as I bring my mouth down to her neck to tickle her with kisses, getting more aggressive and nipping her, nearly biting her as the scent of her drives me wild.

"You make me a mess, baby," I whisper, my accent coming out more thick as I get almost dizzy in the heady scent of her lust. "Now I'm going to give you what you want."

Without further warning, I seize her hips and slide her forward, smiling wickedly as I loom over her. I pick her up with ease and flip her around so that her ass is facing me, and I bend her over. She gasps as I press on her back, and I let my hands run down to her ass. I squeeze her, a low growl escaping me as I look on her body. We aren't naked, we're still in the clothes we've gone through the day in. It makes it feel so sudden, so wanton, and my cock grows at the sight of her with her pants pulled down, exposed and vulnerable before me.

While her ass taunts me, I unbutton my pants and let my thick shaft spring free. I stroke it, letting my fingers play across the veiny girth and up to the bulging crown. It's so stiff and ready for her that I could explode at any moment. But I want to savor her. I pick her hips up to help her get to just the right angle, and I slide my cock to caress her soaking-wet lips.

She whimpers and pushes her hips back, desperate for me to fill her. I bring my crown to her lips and just barely penetrate her, letting the stiff tip wander around her lips like my tongue did just moments ago.

"Oh, fuck you," she whimpers, "God, I need you in me so bad, Luca!"

"Every night I don't have you sheathed on my cock, Serena," I whisper in a husk, "I feel like something's missing."

"Glad it's not just me," she gasps, looking back at me with heavily lidded eyes, her mouth hanging open and her cheeks blushing.

"Better make up for lost time, then," I say, and seizing her hips, I enter her from behind.

The gasp that escapes her lips is a sound I could never get tired of. I feel her inner walls tight against my cock. My shaft pulses within her, as if roaring in triumph at being united with the depths it was meant to be in.

I thrust forward, and she arches her back for me, even as I hold her up. Her golden hair spills over her shoulders and hangs down as she grips the other end of the counter. This place is her livelihood, and I'm fucking her hard within it. I feel a ripple of pleasure run up my body as I thrust further up into her, rocking back and forth and caressing her ass with each thrust.

Serena never asked for any of this to fall into her lap. She never asked to get attacked by a mob, dragged back into a life she came so close to escaping. I still know in the back of my mind that this is wrong, that it's irresponsible to be with her like this...

But the one thing she did ask for is me. And I can't deny my girl anything.

I hear her gasp as I thrust hard against her upper walls, sliding against the slick, wonderfully hot sheath that is her pussy. My cock swells within her, and I grunt as I pound her fiercer, harder, faster.

Her gasping is getting louder, and she's letting whimpers and cries of pleasure flow more freely. I know if she's much louder, someone outside might hear, but I don't care. I'm taking her, *now*, and that's what she wants—that's all that matters right now.

She clenches her pussy, and I slap her on the ass with a sound that rings through the whole room. My heavy balls swing under her, and the sounds of our flesh slapping and grinding keeps me red-hot, harder than ever, and my whole body feels poised.

She gets a rhythm going, tightening each time I slide in, making it all the sweeter when I touch that sweet spot far within her, and she lets out an exasperated gasp. As the orgasm floods my cock, her strength gives out, and I have to hold her hips up entirely on my own as she loses her grip on the counter for a moment.

"I've got you, *dolcezza*," I growl, hoisting her up into me, and the way I bring her to sink onto my cock sends a shiver up her back that even I can feel. She stifles a yelp that sounds almost like a musical note, and the next moment, she's back on her hands, pushing her pert ass back onto me, and I do not hold back.

I feel tension building up within me, but I'm not ready to let it go just yet. There's a monster within me that wants me to give into my instincts, to let loose hard and fast with abandon. But I'm no beast—I'm a man who will please his woman well, and I'll finish when I'm good and done fucking her.

I start bucking into her like a piston, my rhythm unstoppable like a machine, and her shoulders freeze as her cunt clenches. She starts to look back at me, but her eyes are shut tight and her mouth hangs open. I can feel pressure in her body winding up like a spring. I don't let up, every muscle in my body driving forward with unstoppable heat.

And just before her spring uncoils, I withdraw from her.

The whimper she lets out his heartbreaking, and her eyes open wide, begging me for mercy. "Fuck, Luca, I'm so close!"

"And I'm going to take you there," I growl, slapping her on the ass before I pull her leggings the rest of the way down until they're off her legs, leaving her bare from the waist down in her own shop, but for the oversized shirt. I take a handful of her hair and gently tug her back until she's standing up in front of me. "Hold on tight."

Without warning, I sit up on the counter, my cock standing upright like a mast. Serena looks at it hungrily for a moment before I seize her by the waist and lift her up. She makes a surprised squeak as I lift her up high, but when she sees the waiting cock below her, a bead of precum glistening above the sheen of her honey she spreads her legs and starts to wrap them around me.

"I want to look into your eyes when we come," I say thickly, and I let her sink to the hilt onto my hot, throbbing cock. My precum mixes with her wetness. The sound of her loving sigh as our sexes are united again is like honey to my ears.

She rests her hands on my shoulders and looks down at me, but I'm supporting her hips with my hands. She's safe in my grasp, and I can see in her eyes just how much she trusts me.

When I start rocking my hips, it takes her no time to join right in with the rhythm again, as if we hadn't paused at all. Serena bites her lip and knits her brow, and her flushed face tells me she's using the last of her strength to work with me as I rock forward, my cock harder and stronger than ever.

My Serena feels like nothing I've ever felt in my lap, my cock perfectly sheathed deep inside her. Every time I help her rock forward and her hips dig deeper for more, we're both finding parts of her that we've never felt, feeling sensations only we can unlock in each other.

In a bold move, she reaches to the hem of her shirt, letting go of the support of my shoulders for a moment. She pulls it up over her head, but she manages to keep balance on my cock, even though I don't stop rocking and bucking up into her. It takes her a few moments, but she gets it off and shakes her gorgeous locks of golden hair out before tossing it to the side. Instinct kicks in, and I reach up to unhook her bra, which comes off next.

She exposes her breasts to me and rests her arms around my shoulders again. It brings her close enough that I reach behind her with one hand and put my teeth to her breast. She leans her chin against my head as I lick her nipple until it's soaked, then suck it between my teeth and toy with it more. I give both her breasts attention, never breaking pace for a moment, and her whole body begins to coil up in ecstatic tension once again.

"Luca...oh, Luca," she murmurs, almost chanting as I rock her into a trance-like pace, pumping up and rocking with her, my cock getting stiffer as pressure mounts in me, too. I feel her nails dig into my back, and I know it's time.

I pick up the pace, pounding up into her, any hope of finesse or precision getting thrown to the wind. My pounding gets savage, relentless, and I hold one hand in her hair in a fist while the other grips her hips, pulling her into me.

She breathes in sharply, and she starts losing control of her body as the pleasure wells up into an unstoppable flood. Just as she reaches the peak of the cliff, I let myself go. The incredible tension in my cock unlocks, floodgates opening as my seed bursts up into her at the same time as she lets out a scream of ecstasy, her whole pussy tightening and pulsing around me as I throb into her.

It isn't until the second pulse of hot seed that I realize a loud groan is escaping my lips too, and as we finish together, we melt into each other, soaking-wet sexes locked into each other, and the tide of bliss rocks us into a daze as I bring the rocking rhythm slower, slower, until we're just sitting there, sweating on the counter of her shop, seed spilling out her pussy onto my balls.

It's a mess, but god, I wouldn't trade that moment for the world.

Finally, she pushes herself up, shivering as my still-stiff cock twitches inside her, and her glowing face looks down at me like an angel. We're both at a loss for words. Smiles play across our faces, and we finally start laughing, bringing our foreheads together to rest on each other until we settle down and kiss playfully.

"So, do all knife-fights end like this?" she asks.

"Of course," I joke, grinning. "At least, the ones with us will."

"I might have to get more serious about this, then," she says, and I brush a lock of hair out of her eyes as I smile up at her before picking her up off my cock and setting her down gently. She wobbles a moment, but keeps her balance, putting her hands on her hips proudly.

I wet my lips as I button my pants back up. "You'd better get your clothes back on unless you want round two to be sooner than you think."

She raises her eyebrows and tilts her head to the side. "Oh yeah? Maybe we should take it back to my place."

I smile wickedly, but I put up a hand for her to wait as I move to the back room. "Hold that thought. I have something for you."

She blinks, confused, and calls after me, "Uh, seriously though, if gun practice is next then I might need a breather."

"Later," I say as I pull out my bag and dig through it to get two little black boxes. One is a long rectangle, the other is a square. I carry them back into the main room to find Serena pulling her leggings back on. She peers at the little boxes curiously.

"What are those?"

"A couple of things I want you to have," I say, setting them down on the counter. "You know, gifts. One of them I didn't want to give you until later, but I think you're ready."

Serena's eyes are wide with surprise, and she's even more surprised when I pick her up to set her on the edge of the counter and hold out the rectangular box first. In my massive palms, it looks a lot smaller than it actually is.

"Oh! Is there an occasion?" she asks. She looks at the box shyly, but I know my girl—she likes presents, and I like to spoil her.

"You want me to say something cheesy like 'every day is an occasion with you?' I mean, it is, but…"

"Stop!" she giggles, kicking playfully at my leg before she bites her lip. "Kinda." She takes the thing and sets it on her lap to open it carefully, sliding an inner compartment out, and her eyes shine at what she sees inside. "Oh my god, Luca, is this-"

"Yours," I say proudly. Inside the box in a foam casing is an ornate switchblade, its handle jet-black. "Be careful, it's brand-new and sharper than just about anything *I've* handled."

Her careful fingers reach in and take it out, holding it up to the light with round, wondrous eyes. "Woah, it's…a step up from the one I had. Luca, I don't know what to say!"

"Open it," I urge her, and she points the blade away from us to push its switch. With a click, the blade pops out.

"It *looks* sharp," she says, experimentally holding the thing in her hand, and that's when she notices something on the base of the blade. She brings it closer to her eyes to squint at and read. When she reads it, I see tears start to well up in her eyes.

I start to say, "It says-"

"*Passerotta,*" she finishes, smiling and looking up at me.

"A *passerotta* for my *passerotta,*" I say, taking the blade from her hand and sheathing it again. "My sparrow. I had it made specially for you."

She throws her arms around me, and I chuckle as I hug her tightly. "That's the most dangerous and romantic gift I've ever gotten, Luca."

"I thought it was fitting," I say, kissing her on the forehead, "but that's not all."

"Oh, the square box!" she says, reaching over and taking it as I stow the switchblade. She opens the next box, and her face lights up—this one needs no explanation.

"Oh my *God*, Luca!"

She reaches in and draws out a necklace, silver glittering in the lights above us down to the set topaz pendant. "It's beautiful," she breathes.

"Serena, you deserve nothing but the best in life," I say, reaching out and sliding my hand around the back of her neck. She looks up at me, tears still welled up in her eyes, and when she blinks, they roll down her cheeks as she smiles, still glowing. "We're going through hell, but I wouldn't want to go through it with anyone but you. And if we're going through hell, I'll treat you like we're going to die tomorrow. And if we pull through this, I'll treat you like the princess you are, every day of our lives."

"Luca, I-I don't know what to say," she says softly. She

sniffs, and I wipe away a tear, which makes her smile. "Thank you. For everything."

"Come on," I say, nodding to the door. "Let's get out of here."

"Let's? Are we going back to my place?" she asks, hopping down from the counter and finishing getting her shirt on.

"As much as I'd love to, not tonight," I say. "Rafaela agreed to let you stay at her place tonight. I messaged her earlier. Things are a little hot right now, and I don't want to make us easy to find until we can get a better grip on the situation."

"I'll text my mom and let her know. And… maybe suggest she stay in a hotel for the evening. Treat herself."

I'm about to say something when I hear my phone buzzing in the other room. I stride over to it and pick it up. Nico.

"What's up?" I answer the phone, my brow knit.

"Luca, where are you tonight?" he asks, sounding urgent.

"Why? What's the matter?" Serena is looking over at me with concern on her face.

"We got a tip, Luca."

"I'm not walking into another trap, Nico," I say.

"If we got any more bad informants on our radar, you can take my kidneys," Nico says. "This one's good, so good most of the Cleaners don't even know about it. Comes from someone we got among the Irish."

"The Irish? What the fuck do they want?" We've had a long history with the Irish—a lot of ups and downs, but things have been quiet from their end for a long time. The last thing we need is another front in this war.

"There's a meeting going down tonight, Luca," Nico says. "The Cleaners are reaching out to some of the higher-up Paddies. Probably want to sweet-talk them into an alliance if they can persuade them we're weak enough to take a shot at."

"Fucking hell," I hiss, pacing around the back room, and Serena comes to lean on the side of the door, biting her lip. "Tell me you've got something else."

"I do, and you're gonna owe me for this one," Nico says.

"Not if you keep me waiting, Nico."

"I got where the meeting's happening," Nico says in a low voice, and my eyes widen. "Some of the biggest names from both sides showing up to parley. Probably a drug handoff, as a show of good faith. Something that shows the Irish that the Cleaners are worth their time."

"You're shitting me."

"There's more, Luca," Nico says. "The Cleaners aren't even telling a lot of their own men—Luca, Lorenzo's gonna be there to oversee the handoff personally."

From the expression darkening Luca's face, I can tell he's reading bad news on his phone screen. He heaves a sigh, slips the phone into his back pocket, and looks over at Giovanni, who is clearly waiting for some kind of order. He shakes his head and Giovanni's face settles into a stony look of resignation, his eyes narrowing. This wordless exchange is enough to throw my anxiety into high gear. I may not be in tune with how the mafia operates these days, but I am certainly in tune with Luca's body language, and I know this is not good.

He strides over to me and gently takes my face in his huge hands, staring into my eyes for a moment before kissing me. There's a sort of quiet desperation in his kiss, the way his fingers press against my cheeks as he leans close to me. I can tell something is wrong. Very wrong, from the way things feel right now. A knot of worry balls up in my stomach.

"I have to go," Luca tells me softly, those bright green eyes burning into mine. Somehow, I knew exactly what he was going to say before he even opened his mouth. But there's no use in fighting it. Luca is a mafioso and he does exactly what he has to do, whether I like it or not.

So I give him a quick nod. "You have to promise me that you'll come back safe, okay? I-I don't have a good feeling about any of this, Luca. I can't— I *won't* lose you again."

"*Mia passerotta*," he says, tracing his thumb over my chin fondly, "I will never leave you for long. You can trust in that. I will be careful. I have something very important to live for."

It's almost as if there's a silent *now* missing at the end of his sentence, and it breaks my heart to think that before he found me again, he didn't think he had any real reason to keep going. I vow to myself to make his life beautiful again, to bring him the kind of joy that will make him happy to be alive. I want to give him everything.

But he has to survive this first. We both do.

Luca kisses me one more time and then slips out of the apartment, leaving me here with Rafaela and Giovanni, the two most unlikely companions for this situation. Rafaela comes up behind me and takes my arm, giving it an encouraging squeeze.

"Come on, *chica*. Let's have some of that cocoa and try to just relax," she suggests, holding up the box of fancy dark chocolate cocoa I brought as a sort of weak apology for getting Rafaela tangled up in this mess. Though, to be honest, her involvement with Nico probably would have made her a target at one point or another anyway. For such a big metropolitan city, New York is starting to feel like a claustrophobic little town. And we're all snagged in the same dangerous web.

"Giovanni, you want some?" Rafaela asks. He looks stoically amused for a moment, and then gives a shrug.

"Sure," he answers flatly.

"*Claro*," she replies, a smile tugging at the corner of her mouth as we go into the kitchen. She heats up some milk on the stove while I stare blankly at the tile floor, trying to remain as calm as possible despite the nervous energy bubbling in my veins.

"Ugh, I wish I could just turn my brain off for a while," I murmur, closing my eyes.

"I know what you mean," she says. "It's hard not to think of the worst-case scenario. But jumping to conclusions when you don't know anything for sure only adds unnecessary stress."

"Are you counseling me right now?" I ask, narrowing my eyes.

She smiles. "If that's what you need. But if I were your real therapist, I wouldn't do this."

She reaches up to take down a bottle of whiskey from a cabinet, pouring about half a shot into the cocoa mug before mixing in the hot milk and cocoa mix. Then she hands it to me.

"Wow, if I could get boozy cocoa at the therapist I might actually go," I tease, blowing gently on the mug to cool it down.

"Well, whatever it takes, I guess," Rafaela says. Then she calls out, "Giovanni, do you want some super special deluxe cocoa?"

Giovanni walks into the kitchen with a curious look on his face, having to tilt his head slightly walking through the doorway because he's so tall. When he sees the bottle of whiskey on the counter his face breaks into a surprisingly pleasant smile. He nods. "*Si*, a little bit."

"You got it," she answers, pouring his concoction and handing it over. She turns to me and says, "Okay. So, let's play therapist. Tell me what you're feeling right now."

I roll my eyes. "Oh, I don't know, Raf. I don't think I want to talk right now."

She shakes her head and puts a hand on her hip. "*Dale, ahora*. It'll help, I promise."

"Fine," I sigh, gently swirling the contents of my mug. "Well, first of all, I'm terrified that something bad is going to happen to Luca. I know this is some deep shit we're all in, and I'm afraid that it's at least partly my fault."

"Mhm, and why is that?"

"Well, because of the stuff with my dad. And the shop. And now Luca is back and we found each other but once again I'm in trouble and he has to save me and— ugh, I really hate this," I confess.

"And you're feeling worried about him, why?"

"Geez, you're relentless, you know that?" I groan. Rafaela shrugs, waiting patiently for me to keep going. "Okay. I'm upset because I care about him. A lot. In fact, I think I might be falling in love with him all over again. And you know me—that's totally not normal for me. I don't just fall head over heels and lose my mind like this. I'm ambitious. I have a lot of responsibilities to take care of and I don't usually let my feelings get in the way. But with Luca, it's impossible. I can't just ignore how I feel. It's too real and at the same time it feels like a dream, and now with everything going on, I'm just so afraid that I'll lose it all."

"I feel the same way about Nico," Rafaela agrees, taking a sip of her cocoa. "Here I was, fresh out of Harlem and ready to make something of myself. I'm gonna be a doctor. I'm gonna help people. I have to get perfect grades and work so hard and I can't lose focus but there he is: the man I can't help but fall in love with. And he's a distraction. He takes up all the space in my mind where I should be keeping information for my exams and my dissertation and stuff. Instead of just dreaming about having my own clinic and my own fancy office with a skyscraper view, I'm thinking about how cool it'll be to grow old with him. I'm thinking about marriage and babies and seeing the world together. I want all of it, my career and my love, and it looked like I was gonna make it happen. But now… I don't know anything. I'm scared, too, Serena."

"It is impossible to turn away from love when it burns so brightly and beautifully that it nearly hurts to look with your own eyes upon it. We are eternally trying to get as close to the fire as we can in the hopes of warming our hearts, but the closer we step, the more dangerous the flames become. Love will always be a dance between too close and not close enough, but it is a dance that makes life worth living. *'If good, why this effect: bitter, mortal? If bad, then why is every suffering sweet?'*" Giovanni says suddenly, his deep voice thick with emotion.

Rafaela and I stare at him wide-eyed, surprised at such a lyrical outburst from the most unsuspecting of speakers. "Whoa," she murmurs.

Giovanni shrugs and downs the rest of his spiked cocoa in one go. "I read a lot of Petrarch. These security jobs get very boring sometimes. The mind needs stimulation."

"You're going to make some girl very happy someday," I comment, shaking my head in awe.

Giovanni grins, almost looking bashful for a moment. "Someday maybe, but for now my heart belongs to the most beautiful one of all: Italia."

"Speaking of Italy, I could really go for some pasta right now," Rafaela says, patting her stomach with a pitiful expression. "Serena, you want to help me get some dinner started? We may be on lockdown here but we still gotta eat."

"Sure," I answer, and the two of us start taking out ingredients for spaghetti while Giovanni pulls a small book from his jacket pocket and sits on a bar stool reading silently. "Raf, do you have a pasta strainer anywhere?" I ask.

"Oh yeah, we got a new one the other day. It's still in the foyer in a shopping bag if you want to go grab it," she says, chopping tomatoes at the counter.

I walk into the entranceway of the apartment to look for the bag, glancing at the door to make triple-sure it's locked and deadbolted while I'm at it. Just as I look over at the door, something dark passes by the peephole and my blood runs cold.

Surely it's just one of Raf's neighbors coming home from work or something. Or just a trick of the eye. Nothing to worry about. But just in case, I step closer and look through the peephole. There's another flash of black and then the door rattles with a loud thump from the other side. I fall backward with a cry, and Giovanni comes running.

"What is it?" Rafaela calls out from the kitchen.

"*Cazzo*," Giovanni says under his breath. He reaches out and yanks me to my feet, pushing me behind him and gesturing for me to get out of the way. "Run! Hide!" he hisses.

I take off for the kitchen, grab Rafaela around the waist, and the two of us bolt for her bedroom. "I think they've found us," I whisper, hastily locking the bedroom door before we run into the en suite bathroom and lock ourselves in there.

"*Mierda*," she mumbles, her face going ashen gray. "What are we gonna do?"

"Be quiet and hide and hope Giovanni can keep them out, I guess," I reply, feeling totally helpless. Out of the corner of my eye I see my jacket lying on the bathroom counter and I reach for it to take the knife out of its pocket. Rafaela looks at it wide-eyed.

"What the fuck are you planning to do with that?" she mutters, clearly terrified.

"Whatever's necessary," I answer shortly. "Now hush."

We climb into the tub and pull the shower curtain closed, sitting in the dark, waiting for the inevitable battle to ensue. There's a short silence, and then several earsplitting bangs. Rafaela starts to scream and I clap a hand over her mouth, shielding her with my arms as we huddle in the bathtub. There's the unmistakable crack of the front door being kicked in, and the shouts of angry male voices out in the apartment. Next we hear the sound of breaking glass, the grunts and thumps of men fighting, and my heart aches for Giovanni, worrying that he might already be dead by now. From the sound of it, he's definitely outnumbered, and it's only a matter of time.

Suddenly, more silence.

All I can hear is Rafaela's shallow, panicked breathing beside me in the darkness. And then a horrible voice cracking across the apartment, a familiar one I hoped to never hear again.

"Miss De Laurentis!" Lorenzo calls out, his heavy footsteps thumping the floor as he approaches the bedroom. I can hear him clearly, even through the two locked entrances. "I did tell you I'd be back to see you again, didn't I? I have to admit, it hurts to see that you're shacking up with other men, having a real party here tonight. Maybe my invitation got lost in the mail. I'll give you the benefit of the doubt one more time, *bella*. But my patience is wearing very, very thin. Come out and see me."

Tears pulse down Rafaela's cheeks as she struggles to keep quiet. My heart sinks. This can't be how this goes down. It can't happen like this. Where is Luca? What happened to Giovanni?

"Knock, knock!" Lorenzo shouts, banging on the bedroom door. "Come out and play!"

He tries the lock for a moment and then I hear him bark an order in Italian. A moment later, there's a resounding crash and I just know they've kicked the bedroom door down.

Lorenzo laughs, a terrible, nasally sound. "Oh, these cheap apartments in the city are so shoddily made. Just fall apart all over the place. Now, those houses out in Riverdale are much better quality, aren't they, Serena? Your daddy kept you up there in that damn mansion of his, guarding you just like all the good fortune that didn't rightly belong to him."

There's a sharp rap at the bathroom door and Rafaela squeals in fear, burrowing into my side and sobbing. Lorenzo laughs again. "I wonder what your daddy would think now, hmm? His precious virginal little daughter caught up in the same shit that killed him. I doubt he'd be very proud."

I grit my teeth, closing my eyes and tightening my grip on the knife. He's wrong. Maybe I have made some big mistakes, but I'll be damned if I go down without a battle. My father would've wanted me to fight for my life. I've always had to fight, ever since the day he died, and I won't stop now.

"Last chance," Lorenzo continues, his voice sharp and low. "Open the door and we won't kill your Costa side piece here. We're not after him or your little friend in there. I want you. I think we both know it's in everybody's best interest if you just come quietly."

I sit there for a moment, soaking in his words. On the one hand, I don't want to give up. It goes against my nature entirely to just surrender now. It's what Lorenzo wants, and I would hate to ever give him the satisfaction of beating me down. And I don't trust him to just completely let Rafaela and Giovanni go free. Lorenzo is a lying, scamming, treacherous piece of shit. I can't take his word.

On the other hand, maybe if I give myself up without a fight he'll take pity on me. I don't want to risk pissing him off further and putting Rafaela and Giovanni in any more danger than they're already in. My heart thumps away in my chest as my mind races in every direction. What the hell can I do? I'm caged here, cornered like a wild animal.

"I'm giving you a chance here, Miss De Laurentis. Give yourself up and save your friends. Or my associate here can kick the door down and kill both of them. It's up to you. Will you sell out your friends to benefit yourself? Like your good-for-nothing daddy did?" Lorenzo snarls.

Sneering, I sit up and pull the shower curtain to one side.

"No," Rafaela breathes. "Don't."

"I have to. If it gives you any chance of survival, I have to," I reply simply, climbing out of the tub to unlock the door and deliver myself to the devil. I turn the lock and open the door, letting the light stream into the darkened bathroom. Lorenzo takes me by my knife arm and pulls me close, looking me up and down with rakish glee. One of his henchmen runs into the bathroom and grabs hold of Rafaela. Giovanni is slumped over the combined shoulders of two henchmen, looking void of life.

"You said you wouldn't hurt them!" I shout, slapping Lorenzo across the face. He grabs my hand and wrenches it behind my back, his eyes flashing with fury.

"No, I said I would not kill them. Your guard dog here will catch a nice ransom from the Costa family. And as for you and your pretty friend, I have my own plans," he says, smirking cruelly. Remembering my training, I manage to quickly wiggle free of Lorenzo's grasp, using his own weight against him to pin him in the doorway with my knife pressed against his throat. I can tell the only reason I'm able to get the upper hand is by the element of surprise, but regardless I'm grateful. Two henchmen come barreling toward us to presumably free Lorenzo from me, but he shakes his head ever so slightly.

He raises an eyebrow and says, "No, no, boys. Leave us be. Miss Serena, if you kill me it will be your friend's blood on your hands."

I glance over to see a man holding the barrel of a gun to Rafaela's head and my stomach turns.

Shit.

There's nothing I can do.

"Now, let's all just calm down and walk out of here like nothing is wrong," Lorenzo orders.

Reluctantly, I lower my knife and allow one of the henchmen to wrest my arms behind my back, confiscating my blade in the process. Lorenzo rubs at his neck gingerly and gestures for everyone to leave, leading the way through Rafaela's ravaged apartment. Then he falls back to walk beside me, the henchman handing me over. Lorenzo holds my wrists tightly at the small of my back, leaning in to perversely sniff at my neck.

"Smells like a glorious addition to my collection," he says quietly as we file out of the apartment and down the hallway. "Don't worry, there's room enough for you and your Spanish friend in my bedroom. I think you'll be very happy there."

"How many do you see?" I ask into the burner phone, my other wrist resting on the wheel of the car as I sit back and let my shoulders relax. I wonder if I'll ever be immune to that tension I feel in my back that wells up when I know I'm about to take a life.

Tonight, it will be many lives.

"At least eight," says Nico through the phone, his voice so hushed I wouldn't be able to hear him if I weren't in the privacy of the car. "The intel was good. Irish are here. I've seen a couple of them before. Nobody too important. They must be cautious."

"Smart," I say, putting my phone between my shoulder and jaw to free up my hands and let me check over the weapons I have strapped to me.

Nico is about a block away, perched up on a rooftop and watching the meeting site through the scope of a sniper rifle. I'm sitting in my car around the block, out of sight until I'm ready to move.

He's being my eyes for now, but he's a damn good shot, too. A weapon like the one he has isn't one you use lightly, so this needs to count. He offered it to me, but I'm more of a hands-on man.

I want to look Lorenzo in the eyes when I kill him.

"Five Cleaners, three Irish," Nico confirms.

"And Lorenzo?" I ask.

"No sight of him..." Nico says, trailing off. "Wait. There's a car pulling up. Tinted windows, but the Irish are watching it."

"There he is," I say, smiling.

"Window's coming down," Nico whispers. "Someone inside is saying something. I think it's Lorenzo in there, but it's hard to tell. Shit, I can't line up a good shot, the people outside keep moving too much. One miss and that car will tear out of here."

"I'll take care of that," I say casually, rolling my shoulders back and putting my car into gear.

"What?"

"Be ready."

"Luca, what are y-" but I end the call before Nico can finish. Headlights off, I pull out, my jaw set.

I'm not giving Lorenzo half a chance to slip away again.

My engine tears down the narrow road as I near the meeting site. They've heard me by now, and in a few moments, they'll realize I'm coming their way. No time for hesitation now, I have to strike fast.

I come up on the corner fast, and I use the handbrake to pull a hard, screeching turn to point the front of my car right down the alley. As soon as I do, I flip my brights on, and I'm treated to the sight of exactly what Nico described: one black sedan and eight men looking at me, wide-eyed and stunned.

I throw the car back into gear and barrel down the alley.

A couple of the men are sharp and quick enough to dive

for cover, but the car doesn't have the blessing of being able to get moving so fast.

I can hear curses and shouts from the group and I tear forward, and I brace myself for impact.

Metal groans with a loud crash and glass shatters as my car rams the black sedan, my whole body lurching forward with the momentum. I had time to see the driver's door crumple and the driver throw his arms up in defense before I covered my eyes with my arm, and I feel the sting of glass in my own skin.

In the next moment, a stunned silence like the calm before the storm, I roll out of the car and draw my weapons.

"*Lorenzo!*" I shout, and the word has hardly left my mouth before I hear bullets start flying.

A pistol in each hand, I open fire on the car while I run for cover. The driver is slumped over his wheel and a man in the back isn't moving, but the rest are scrambling to spill out the other side.

In front of the car, two Cleaners are already firing at me, and with a quiet *thud* I see one of them jolt, a bullet wound in his head, and he slumps to the ground.

Nico is giving me cover with his rifle.

"A fucking sniper!" the other man calls, a moment before another bullet silences him too.

Three Cleaners are still standing, not counting the three more from the car who I can now see clearly. I feel rage boil up within me as I see each of their faces.

Lorenzo isn't among them.

As the three remaining Cleaners open fire, I dive behind a battered dumpster. I hear the sound of hurried footsteps, and I turn to see the three Irish making a run for it. I let them go—someone will need to spread the word tonight.

Bullets spray my cover, and as I blindfire back at them,

I hear another dull *thud*, and the firing stops as the men shout at each other to take cover from the sniper. It's a chance I have to seize.

I leap out from cover and charge after the three from the car who are trying to dig their heels in behind its ruins. I leap over my own car and rain bullets down on them, catching one in the heart and putting him to the ground while the others scramble to react.

They weren't expecting such a flagrant attack, and if I'm honest, neither was I—but I'm seeing red, and these men will pay for their deception.

At close range, one man tries to swing at me. I dodge his blow and catch his wrist, pulling him around my front with the sickening sound of his elbow getting broken. I use his shoulder as a rest to fire at the third man, who takes a bullet to the shoulder and staggers back, diving around the front of their car.

I curse and put my gun to my captive's head, executing him swiftly. I have just half a second to take cover before the injured man starts blind-firing at me.

He's got me pinned down, and I know Nico can't get a good shot at him while he's crouching behind the front of the car. I'm crouching by the driver's door—we're so close I can hear him breathing, but neither of us can pop out of cover without getting shot, and with the other three Cleaners still alive and trying to get a shot at me, my time is running out.

Then a steady rumbling sound catches my attention— the Cleaners' car is still running. Without a second thought, I pull the car door open, pull the dead man out, climb in, and keep my head down before flooring the acceleration.

I hear a surprised scream from the man as the car plows over him, and I roll back out the moment he's down to finish him off with a quick shot. A loud clang tells me the force of the impact knocked the already-loose car door off its hinges, and it now lies flat on the ground nearby.

I feel the sting of a bullet hit my arm, and I draw in a sharp breath through my teeth—the three remaining Cleaners are getting bolder, and I turn to see they've found cover behind the dumpster.

My adrenaline is pumping, I'm exposed, and I don't have time to think. In a fluid motion, I seize the car door and lift it up like a shield to cover my body. I hardly feel its weight with the rush of the fight coursing through my veins. It's by no means good protection, but it's better than nothing.

Nothing else to lose, I charge them.

I see one of them peek around the corner, and his face goes white at the sight of me, battered, half-covered in blood, furiously rushing them with a car door for a shield. I must look like some lunatic barbarian warrior, out of time and place in reality.

Bullets start raining in on my barrier, and some ricochet off to the brick walls around us, while some make it through, and I feel the hot sting pierce my other arm and my shoulders as bullets graze them.

But by the time I make it to them, two of them stagger back when I hurl the thing at them. One man gets the full force of it, and the others stagger back for fear that I'm going to charge through the lot of them.

I put a bullet in one of the two while Nico picks off the other.

Before he can struggle for his gun, I put my foot on top of the car door, pinning the man under it with a pained grunt as I point my pistol at him. I don't know when I dropped my other one, but at this point, I don't care.

"Lorenzo," I bark, bloodthirsty eyes boring into his pained face. "Where is he?"

"*Vaffanculo*," he spits, and I have no patience to twist him for information.

I pull the trigger, leaving his brains on the asphalt.

I hold my weapon pointed at the body for a few moments before I realize I can hear the ringing in my ears, feel my chest rising and falling, the tension in my gritted teeth. I lower my gun, looking around at the scene.

Eight bodies, two wrecked cars, walls and ground riddled with bullet holes, and more blood than I've seen in a long time. The Cleaners' car is devastated, but somehow, mine looks...well, it's serviceable. I hear the engine still running, at least, and there are only a few bullet holes in it.

For a moment, everything around me feels like it's dulled by the ringing in my ears, but that soon fades as I realize I can hear the buzz of my phone from my car. I stride toward it, broken glass crunching underfoot. I calmly pull the car door open and reach to the floorboard to pick up the phone.

It's Nico.

I put the phone to my ear and look up to his location. "Still with me up there?"

"Luca, what in the everloving fuck was that?!" he snaps, but I just grin up at him and wink.

"Come on, dinner with Rafaela's parents can't be much worse than this," I say. There's a solid five seconds of silence from the other end of the call. "What, did I cross the line?"

"Hold still, I'm deciding whether to shoot you now or later," Nico says. "Christ, Luca, warn me before you pull that cowboy bullshit next time. You alright? You're covered in blood."

I look down at myself. I can't feel much of the pain yet, thanks to the rush of adrenaline still surging through me. "Most of it's not mine. Glass cuts, a few grazing shots, and

I'd say they got two good shots in," I say, checking out the bloody mess of my shoulder.

"There's a saint watching over you somewhere, I swear," Nico says.

"Lorenzo wasn't here, Nico," I say. I'm oddly calm. "Was this another trap?"

"I don't know," Nico admits, "I'll go take care of my informant. Luca, do you-"

"You do that," I say, striding back to my car and stowing my weapons, picking up the one I'd dropped. I'm going to need every bullet I've got left. "Save yourself some time and put a bullet in him for me."

"Luca, what are you doing?"

I get into my car, putting it into reverse and moving my battered car back out of the wreckage, a grim look on my face.

"I have a bad feeling. I need to get to Serena. *Now*."

"Where are you taking us?" I ask, sitting blindfolded in the back seat of what feels like a rickety old van. Every time we go over a speed bump the whole vehicle rattles ominously, like it's just seconds away from falling apart completely. It feels like quite a departure from the usual sleek, shiny black company cars the mafia uses.

"Somewhere very nice," Lorenzo answers smugly from somewhere ahead of me. I assume he's in the front passenger seat, with one of his henchmen driving. I'm seated next to Rafaela, whose hand is clutched in mine. Her fingers are clammy and cold and every now and then I give her a squeeze of reassurance, even though I'm desperately in need of reassurance myself. The guilt I feel for getting her involved in this mess is overwhelming. After my mother and Luca, Rafaela is the most important person in my life, and I can't believe I've allowed my own mess to infect her life, too.

I just wish I knew where we were going. Again and again the urge to rip off my blindfold and take a look comes over me, but I know that would only put us in danger. I've dealt with the mafia and seen enough crime television to know that it's best to just go along with their plans. They're like wild animals—you can't make any sudden movements or they'll be on you with their claws.

"What's going to happen to Giovanni?" I press on. I'm not being disobedient by asking questions, at least. They can kidnap me and blind me but they haven't made me shut up yet, so I'm going to keep talking until they do, just in case Lorenzo lets some important tidbit of information slip.

"Why are you so concerned about him? Here I thought the Lomaglio boy was your beau. Or is that too old-fashioned of me? Maybe you're fucking both of them. After all, your mother was a Gaspari slut, and the apple doesn't fall far from the tree," Lorenzo sneers. There's a thick layer of bitterness in his voice, jealousy even.

The dig at my mother is almost laughable. I know her reputation— long before she met my father, when she was just a teenager, she was notoriously known to be an ice queen. My father once joked that he had managed to melt her icy heart and charm the *untouchable Luisa Gaspari* even though all his friends said it was impossible. It was a story my father liked to tell when he'd had a little too much to drink, and even though my mother would roll her eyes in typical ice-queen fashion, there was always just a hint of a smile on her face. Even though they seemed like total opposites, and despite all the trickiness of dealing with their combined mafia ties, my parents were truly in love. That much I know for certain. Nothing can tarnish the memories I have of them dancing together to old Sinatra vinyls in the living room, holding hands at the dinner table, my father doing the most outlandish things to make Mom laugh even though she fought so hard to maintain that cool composure.

In spite of everything, I smile.

Of course, I quickly remember the direness of my current situation and the smile melts away. But thinking about my parents and their love for each other and for me has warmed me up a little bit, and I feel a little less afraid.

Their love was truly one for the books, and now that I have Luca, I know what that feels like.

True love within the mafia was always a little bit dangerous. And maybe that makes it just a little bit sweeter. With the threat of death never far from you, you learn to appreciate those you love and trust so much more.

I just hope he's okay.

"Are--are you going to hurt us?" Rafaela pipes up, her voice thin and quaking. It's obvious without even having to see her face that she's crying. I give her hand another light squeeze.

"Only if that's what you're into," Lorenzo replies flippantly. My heart sinks. What the hell does he have planned for us? He mentioned having enough space in his bed for both of us...

Suddenly, those horrible memories come flashing back. The ones I so desperately forgot. The ones that even Luca's reappearance in my life couldn't bring back.

A dark room. Goosebumps prickling across my skin. Feeling exposed. Violated. Terrified. Cold.

No!

"You'll have to pass inspection first, of course," Lorenzo adds, breaking me out of my thoughts. "The Don will want to look you over, make sure you're in mint condition. I know he'll be pleased that I've brought him two different flavors of slut: Italian *and* Spanish," Lorenzo laughs.

"*Soy venezolana, pajizo,*" Rafaela quips indignantly, a surprising note of strength in her tone. There's the fiery woman I call my best friend.

"Mexican, Cuban, Venezuelan, doesn't matter. You're all the same to me. Either way, you'll be a treat for the boys.

Maybe I'll let them taste my sloppy seconds when I'm done with you," he replies.

Rafaela lets out a tiny whimper and I lean into her, nudging her shoulder with mine. I wish I could hug her or tell her it will all be okay, but I don't want to do anything that might provoke the henchmen to tie my hands.

We ride along in silence for a while longer. I have no idea how much time passes. It could be five minutes, it could be five hours. I just try to focus on keeping cool. At the moment, our lives don't seem to be in immediate danger, and Lorenzo's threats seem to be lewd rather than murderous, not that it's much better this way.

Especially with the trauma of what happened to me years ago still hovering in the back of my mind like a storm cloud. I can't let him get into my head, though. For my sake and Rafaela's, I have to keep calm as much as possible. There's nothing else I can do right now.

I push down the memories, back into the dark corner of my psyche where they've lived for so long. I don't have the luxury of having Rafaela play psychologist for me right now. No, I have to stay strong for the both of us.

I've survived the mafia's wrath before. I'll survive it again.

There's the rattle of wheels on gravel, perhaps even on dirt, for what seems to be a few minutes. This frightens me because it signals to me that we're not in the city anymore. When the car stops, my stomach starts to twist, fear settling into my bones. I don't know where we are, but we've evidently reached our destination.

"Take off the blindfolds. They'll have no fucking clue where we are anyway. Grab them and don't let them go," Lorenzo says. "We're going to march into the building."

The henchmen take off our blindfolds and we both blink uncomfortably in the onslaught of light. We've apparently been driving all through the night, because the sun is peeking out over the horizon in a splash of gorgeous pink and orange. It's a strange sight, seeing something so lovely when we're in such an awful situation. We're hauled out of the van with our arms twisted behind our backs.

Up ahead of us is a massive, classical-style villa surrounded by countryside. There are thick white pillars and balconies, wide windows with shining glass panes, and immaculately-maintained hedges leading up to the pearly front door. It looks like some sort of ancient pleasure palace. The henchmen drag us away, up the front steps and through the entrance, which opens into an impressive foyer with a vaulted ceiling and a grand staircase.

"*Coño*, what the hell is this?" Rafaela murmurs quietly.

Lorenzo steps up to us and bids the henchmen to move away. Lorenzo looks us up and down and then barks at one of the henchmen, "Get the Don. They're ready. No time like the present."

One of the men goes upstairs and we wait nervously for a few minutes while Lorenzo stands back and gazes at us, his arms crossed and a sly grin on his stupid face. There's the click-clack of dress shoes on marble and we all turn to see an older man, with steel-gray hair and a stern expression. He's wearing an exquisitely-tailored suit with a tie nearly the same color as his hair. Even though he's considerably shorter than the massive henchman walking behind him, there's a disquieting, commanding presence about the man. Lorenzo steps out of his way with an ingratiating gesture of deference, and the man walks up to stand in front of Rafaela and me.

His expression stays exactly the same as he looks us up and down, his eyes critical and his mouth set in a hard line. He reaches out to take Raf's chin in his fingers, turning her face side to side. He grabs a handful of her thick, curly hair and tugs it gently. Rafaela is frozen in place, her brown eyes wide and fearful.

The man says, "Turn around slowly." His voice is deep and flat.

Rafaela hesitates for a moment before giving in and doing a slow spin. The man pauses, then snaps his fingers, and another man comes up to take Rafaela by the arm and drag her away down the hall. She starts to cry again, wordlessly pleading with her eyes for me to help her.

"No! No! Don't take her," I burst out, making a move forward. But the Don reaches out and stops me with one hand, giving me a stern look. He holds me by my shoulders, keeping me still while he surveys my body, like I'm some prize cow about to be sold for slaughter. He turns my head side to side, running his thumb over my bottom lip and opening my mouth to check my teeth. Then he cups my breasts with both hands, and I gasp sharply.

Like a reflex, I knock his hands away and stumble backward. Two men hurriedly grab hold of me and to my horror the Don is now grinning, as though this is the reaction he was hoping for. I want to spit at him, slap him across the face, kick him in the balls. Anything. Something. But there is nothing I can do. I'm helpless again, just like I was all those years before.

"So this is the bitch my nephew has been so worked up about," says the Don coolly. "The other girl is a fine toy for my men, but this one… well, she will make a fantastic trophy. Might even bear a few of his children before we're finished with the takeover. Good work, boys."

"Thank you, sir," Lorenzo says. The fucking brown-noser.

"Well, I have business to attend to upstate," the Don continues, dusting off his immaculate suit. "Enjoy yourselves while I'm away, but try not to get killed in my absence. You're all expendable, but I hardly have the time for new recruits."

The Don snaps his fingers and I, too, get dragged away

down the hall, with Lorenzo's eyes following me hungrily. The men push me into a darkened room and lock the door. A moment later, someone is wrapping their arms around me and I let out a shriek of fear.

"Serena! *Chica*, it's me," Raf says tearfully. I relax and turn around to hug her. "What the hell is going on? What are they gonna do to us? Who the fuck was that guy?"

"I think that was the Don," I answer, sighing. "The head honcho."

"*El jefe*," she breathes, her shoulders sagging. "I'm so scared, Serena. I don't know what to do. I-I'm really worried about Nico. And I know it's stupid but I'm supposed to be in class right now, you know? I have a life out there that isn't gonna wait for me and now I don't even know if I'm ever gonna make it out of this place alive."

"Hey. Hey. It's gonna be alright. I promise. We're gonna get through this. We just have to stick together as much as we can, okay?" I tell her, petting her hair. She nods, and as my eyes readjust to the low light, I can see tears shining on her face.

"Breathe in. Breathe out. You're a powerful goddess woman who can handle whatever life throws her way," I say to her, repeating the daily affirmations she's so fond of repeating to me. She gives me an incredulous look that makes me smile despite myself. Now she knows how I feel when she says it to me.

There's a knock at the door and we both jump in fear, clinging to each other as the door opens just a fraction. A few skimpy items of what looks like lacy lingerie are thrown into the room. Lorenzo's awful voice hisses, "Fix yourselves up nice for me. I'll be waiting in the bedroom. While the Don is away, Lorenzo will play. My men will come to get you soon. I'm going to blow your fucking minds, you little sluts. Don Abruzzi won't mind if I break you in, get that filthy Costa scent off of you before we hand you over to his nephew."

The door closes and we're both left staring down at the little pile of lingerie. A sense of heavy despair has fallen over the room. We know what we have to do. Feeling utterly helpless, we silently strip out of our clothes and dress ourselves in our new digs. There doesn't seem to be any point in fighting this. I'm going into survival mode now. Dignity isn't important anymore. We just have to keep living, keep fighting to stay alive despite whatever these disgusting pieces of shit do to us.

"I-I'm scared of what Nico will think," Rafaela whispers sadly.

I hug her.

"He'll understand. You and I have to do whatever it takes to survive, okay? You and me— we're going to live through this to see the other side. I don't know how long we'll be here, but don't give up. Just… try not to think too hard about it. I know that sounds impossible, but you have to just pretend none of this is happening. I'm here with you. You are not alone."

I hesitate for a moment, letting those long-buried memories start to wash back over me. I swallow hard and continue, "Look, Rafaela. I've been through something like this before. I—"

Before I can go on, the door swings open. One of the henchmen gives us a wry smile, looking at our exposed bodies, and then says, "Lorenzo is ready for you."

LUCA

My car tears down the road as if it's on fire like my heart. I weave in and out of traffic, handling the battered remains of this sedan with more finesse than it should be able to pull off. This is going to be the car's last ride, and for all I know, it could be mine as well.

I don't care anymore. There's only one life on my mind, and that's Serena.

I arrived at Rafaela's house barely five minutes earlier. There was a single black sedan parked out front, and I knew that she wasn't alone in the house. When I made my way inside through a window, silent as a shadow, the first man I found never heard me when I caught him from behind and broke his neck.

Moving silently through the house, I found the second man in Rafaela's bedroom, picking through some of her things in a drawer. He looked like he was going to shit himself when he looked up and saw me aiming a gun at him.

The gun should have been the least of his fears. I got the

information I wanted from him. He and his comrade were Abruzzi soldiers, looting the house after they'd been taken.

Once I had the information I needed from him, and I put him down with a single shot to the head. I'd deal with cleanup later.

Serena was in the dragon's lair.

He told me that Lorenzo had her and Rafaela taken into the Abruzzi compound, and he told me where it was. He was a tough man, but a little pressure went a long way. Men who put on a tough face are always the weakest, just under the surface.

I take a corner hard, and I hear the sounds of car horns around me as I speed by. I give the clutch a squeeze. *Come on, just a little further now...!*

In the back of my mind, I hear a voice reminding me that what I'm doing is insane. A family compound is just that—a fortress housing the most important members of a crime family. As I see the estate come into view in the distance, I glance down at my arsenal. After that fight in the alley, I haven't even stopped to take stock of everything I have. Time is too pressing.

I'm armed with two guns, a few spare cases of bullets, and two knives. My clothes are torn and bloody, and the best I can say about my injuries is that they've stopped bleeding. Taking a moment to wrap some duct tape around them did the trick.

But love makes you push your limits.

I grip the steering wheel as I fly down the road toward the entrance of the compound. It's a beautiful place, with dark red ivy spilling down its walls, and the driveway leading up to the place is nicely taken care of.

Almost a shame to spill so much blood in a place that shows off this city's beauty so well.

The man posted at the entrance steps out of his guardhouse at the sight of me, his face growing alarmed, and he has time to raise what looks like a cellphone to his ear before I blow past him, pulling my handbrake as I screech into the courtyard of the estate.

I keep my head down since I'm coming in hot. The screams and couple of *thumps* I feel against the car as it screeches over the cobblestone tells me there were a few guards on their way to investigate when I peeled in.

Immediately, I throw the car door open and dive out, keeping low and whipping my guns out.

The courtyard is a small square decorated with simple hedges, a fountain, and the bodies of the three men I ran over on my way in, sprawled on the ground. Up by the door, there are two stunned men watching me get out, and they waste no time in raising their own guns.

Bullets start flying.

I dive behind the fountain as a bullet chips the concrete to the right of my head, and I hear them cursing and calling for backup in Italian. Getting on my stomach, I use the fountain for cover and crawl along the side until they come into view, firing on where I'd been a moment ago. Two quick shots, and one of the men drops.

The other swears and fires at me to cover himself as he throws the door open and heads inside, on his way to raise the alarm, I assume.

If I wanted secrecy, I wouldn't have hurdled into the place at 50mph.

A bullet grazes my leg from behind, and I curse and whip around to fire on the gate guard, who takes the shot to the gut and drops his weapon, doubling over on the ground. Stowing my weapons, I race over to him and tackle him to his back, resting my knee on his neck.

"Keys, *stronzo*," I growl as he groans in pain. "Get me into this place."

"You're a dead man, Lomaglio," he gurgles with a

pained grin on his face. With a grunt, I slam his head back into the ground and put him out.

I have to move fast. In a matter of seconds, this court-yard will become a killzone with as many Cleaners as there are windows in the manor popping out to gun me down. No time to strategize, I have to make an entrance. If I have any chance at surviving this, it'll be in a lightning fast rampage that's all bravado and luck. It's way too late for stopping and planning.

I race around to the side of the building, and I can hear scuffling and shouting inside from behind the walls. The walls aren't exactly made for climbing, but there's enough stonework between the windows that it will have to do. A tall cypress tree grows by the wall as part of a row, and I leap up onto it and start climbing.

By the time I near the second story of the building, I can hear the sounds of footsteps in the courtyard. Someone must have figured out I'm not in sight, and they're sending men to look for me. I can't be exposed any longer than I have to be.

I look to the nearest window. It has a balconette, just what I need to get a grip. But the window is shut, of course. Wrapping my legs around the tree, I slip my jacket off and toss it to the balconette. It hangs there, and clad in nothing more on my torso than a white shirt stained with blood, I leap after it.

I catch the railing and haul myself up, getting a sturdy foothold. I take my jacket and ball it up over my fist like a glove, and without hesitating, I throw my fist into the window by the handle inside.

The panel smashes to pieces, and I let my glass-ridden jacket fall to the ground as I unlock the window and push it open, climbing inside. I've made a lot of noise, and I need to get to cover fast.

"East wing guest room, move!" I hear from down the

hall, and the sound of feet approaching tells me I have only a few seconds. It's a lavish room, decorated in true Sicilian style with lavish rugs and exposed stonework. I don't bother gathering my jacket. I make my way to the door and press myself against the wall to the side and wait, drawing my knife.

I let the first man rush in unharmed, but when the second follows, I turn my knife downward and drive it into the base of his skull. Before his comrade can so much as turn around, I shove the dying man's body into him, throwing him off-balance.

The two of them topple to the ground, and I dive onto the living man and put the knife to his throat, a finger to my lips as he glares up at me with pure hatred in his eyes.

"Will you be as stubborn as the corpses outside?" I ask in a hushed tone.

"I don't talk to dead men," he hisses back. "That's what you and your whole family are."

"To hell with the Costa," I say, "this is personal business. Tell me where Serena is and I'll let you get out of here."

"Probably moaning through Lorenzo's co-" he tries to say, but I silence him with my blade, and I cover his mouth as he convulses under me.

I stand to my feet over the two dead men. The soldiers in this compound aren't going to fess up—these must be the men who made the Cleaners a force to be feared. Still, there aren't as many as I would have expected.

That's a shame. If they had more men, the odds might be more even. That's cockiness speaking, but it's all I have left at this point. That, my knives and some bullets.

I stow my knife and draw a gun out, holding it at the ready as I move out into the hallway.

The manor is lavish, but I can tell it's new. There's no soul to this place yet, and everything looks too clean to be authentic. Whether the Abruzzis are new or old money doesn't matter to me, but the place reeks of lavish spending and bad taste.

I make my way down a long hallway toward what I can see to be a set of marble stairs. I'm about halfway down when I hear the sounds of footsteps coming up fast. Cursing, I kick open the door to a room on the side and take cover.

As soon as I do, a terrified woman inside screams and covers her mouth as she staggers back. I don't bother trying to hush her—my kicking down the door already let them know I'm here. Judging by how she's dressed, I'd guess she's a cleaning lady. I gesture for her to get down, and she nods, moving further back into the room and crouching down.

I use the doorframe to stabilize my arm as I wait for the men to come into sight. Three of them come up the stairway, and I wait for all three to show themselves before I start firing. My first shot catches one in the heart, and as he falls back down the stairs with a cry of pain, the others move for cover in side-rooms of their own. I get a shot into one of their shoulders before they dig themselves in safely, but when they start shooting from cover, I know this is a useless battle. I'll just waste bullets while reinforcements have time to get here.

My jaw set, I'm thinking of my options when I hear a voice from behind me.

"Sir!" the domestic whispers loudly. I fire off a couple shots down the hall before I glance back at her. She's standing beside a panel in the wall that I would have missed, but she finds a subtle handle on it and pulls it aside, revealing a small staircase leading up and down. My eyes widen.

"This is a laundry room," she hisses, "stairs go up and down to other servants' quarters. Take it up, these men won't find you."

Hardly able to believe my eyes, I fire off another shot down the hall before I move over and look down on her. "Why are you helping me?"

"These men are monsters," she says, "whatever you're here for, it can't be worse than them. I'll take the stairs down, they won't catch me."

I give a curt nod. "Lorenzo's room, where is it?"

"Three floors up from here," she says, "it won't take you to his room, but close."

I glance at the door, then nod. "Thank you," I grunt before squeezing my body into the narrow opening. True to her word, while shots ring out in the hallway, she heads down the stairs and closes the panel behind us. I draw my knife and start my climb.

The stairs are surprisingly quiet. They have to be, if service workers are supposed to be seen and not heard, I would guess.

I climb past several panels that look like doorways, counting them as I go. When I reach the third, I put my ear to it before carefully sliding it open. Sure enough, I find myself in what looks like a utility room, and the door at the far end of the little space is closed, but I can hear the sounds of walking footsteps and voices outside it.

I move carefully up to it, swapping my knife for my gun, and I put my ear close to the door.

"I don't care if the second floor looks clear, sweep it again, he didn't vanish into thin goddamn air," a scruffy voice says. I don't hear a response, so I gather that he's on a cellphone. "No, you'll get him to the doctor after we have this God damned ordeal dealt with. I want this fucker's head on a plate before Don Abruzzi gets wind of anything that goes on here, understand? Because if word gets out, he'll have *my* head after I get *yours*." I hear the beep of the call ending.

I take that as my cue, and I simply push the door open, gun raised at the man now about three feet from me.

He's a middle-aged man with a tired face and graying hair. Despite his age, the muscles under the rolled-up sleeves of his shirt tell me this guy can pull his weight. A capo, no doubt. These Cleaners were just shaping up to be a real crime family.

"Son of a bitch," he mutters, letting his phone fall to the ground as he raises his hands.

"Let's make this easy," I say in a low tone in Italian.

"You went past 'easy' when you drove a fuckin' sedan into our front yard, you cock-sucker," he says in a grizzled voice, speaking in the same language. He has a tired look in his eyes, but they're still the eyes of a killer. "I knew Lorenzo was in over his head going after the De Laurentis girl, but shit, kid, I gotta hand it to you, you know how to make waves."

I frown at him and set my jaw. "And what do you think you know about Serena?"

He gives a scoffing laugh. "Look at me, you think I'm one of these bloodthirsty young fucks? I know who she is. *She's mafia royalty.* I know who her dad was—he was the guy who used to run the Costas you work for. I know there was a power struggle, and her daddy got taken out by the guys who are your bosses now. And I heard she was next on the chopping block, until *someone* intervened."

My eyes narrow. The old guy is looking at me meaningfully. As much as I've tried to bury the past, it can't stay hidden forever. But it's strange to hear it spoke out loud again after so long.

"And I'm willing to bet that someone was you," he says. "You think you can bring down the whole Abruzzi family over some spoiled mafia princess? You're sticking your neck out under a big sword, kid."

"Enough," I growl, raising my gun.

"Not so fast," he says quickly, holding his hands up higher. "Lorenzo's room is right down this hall. One gunshot, and they'll know something's up too close for comfort. That door's locked and I've got the key. You really think you got time to make it down there and unlock the door before Lorenzo puts a bullet in your girl's pretty head?"

"You look like an old-school kind of guy. Is it a duel you want?"

"Fuck that," he half-laughs, "look at you, you look like Rambo just crawled fresh out of 'Nam." He stretches his arms out to the side. "Look, you got lucky, kid. Disarm me, and I'll unlock that door and disappear. Even if Lorenzo kills your ass, I'm a dead man to Don Abruzzi."

I don't like it, but I don't have time to bargain. I give a sharp nod and approach him with my gun trained on his head. He turns around and lets me remove the guns from his person, and he walks forward toward the door.

My eyes follow his hand to his coat pocket as he pulls out a cardkey and hands it to me. I take it, and he whirls around to face me as he steps backward. He gives Lorenzo's door a final glance, then nods to me before walking backward to the stairs and moving down them, out of sight.

As I hold the key near the door, knife in my other hand, I take a breath and say a quick prayer in my head to whoever might be listening. The door lock clicks, and a little green light flashes. I drop the key and throw the door open.

"The fuck do you think you're-" comes Lorenzo's voice as he turns around, and the scene I walk in on freezes in place for half a second in time. At the far end of the room, Lorenzo stands with his shirt off, half-kneeling on the bed where I see Serena and Rafaela laying, eyes widening at the sight of me, Serena's mouth falling open and tears coming to her eyes. On either side of the door I just burst through are two guards, each holding guns.

But I've burst in on enough meetings to be ready for that, and I move before they can gather themselves.

I go to the right first, one hand grabbing the wrist of the hand that holds his gun and pointing it down. The gun goes off just before I slash his throat with one quick motion and roll around his body, just in time for the man on the left to shoot. The guard's body takes the shot for me, and I have enough time to flip the blade around and throw it at him. The blade sinks into his eye, and his hand squeezes as his body convulses, another shot ringing through the room before he falls to the ground.

I draw my spare knife and point it at Lorenzo, standing there covered in blood, chest breathing heavily, and all the fury I've ever known burning in my eyes at the sight of what he was about to do to my girl and to Rafaela.

"Get away from them, Lorenzo," I snarl, "I've got the blood of half this compound on my hands, and I'm not leaving without yours."

Lorenzo moves fast, diving for the dresser and seizing a long hunting knife mounted on it, and he turns to face me. His eyes are wild, and there's a smile on his face.

"I was wondering if you'd make it," he says, readying himself in a stance. "I love a good fight before I take a woman."

I have no more patience for words, and I lunge forward at him. He moves faster than I thought he could, and he dodges me and thrusts up toward my gut. I roll with the attack, and it only grazes my side. I bring my fist around and feel it connect with his jaw in payback, and he staggers back.

Lorenzo spits blood, and he charges me again. This time, I'm ready for him. I feign like I'm going to move in to tackle him, and when he brings his knife in to catch me from above, I move to the side and bring my knee up into his gut.

He groans, but he keeps his momentum and wraps his arms around my waist to bring me to the ground. We hit the wooden floor together, and I immediately try to get on top of him, wary of the thrusting knife. We're evenly matched as we struggle. One moment, I'm about to get on top of him and bring my knife to his throat, and the next, he's got his elbow in my gut and is worming his way away before I get my hands on him again, trading blows and grappling with each other.

Out of the corner of my eye, I notice something—Serena. She's crawling out of bed and is moving toward what I recognize as Lorenzo's coat on the ground, and she starts digging through it hastily.

But I can't focus on it too long—whatever Serena's doing, I don't want Lorenzo to put his attention on it. I pull him up to his knees with me and bring my head down on his, hard, dazing both of us before I stagger back and he tries to jump up, shaky on his feet.

"Is that how you learned to fight in the Bronx?" he laughs, spitting blood to the side as he tries to refocus his eyes. "If that's the best you've got then- *AAAAGHHHH!*"

Lorenzo shrieks in pain and falls to his knee as Serena scrambles away from his legs, blood pouring from the Achilles tendon she just cut. In her right hand, her knife *Passerotta* glistens with its first ruby-red blood. I see the telltale look of an adrenaline rush in her eyes, and when he opens his eyes in a rage to slash behind him at her, she skillfully dodges out of the way, just like I taught her.

He struggles to his good leg to come at her again, but in the millisecond he turns his back on me, I fly at him, and I catch him from behind, putting my knife to his throat.

"Tell the devil there's more where you came from," I growl before my knife rips through his throat, opening his neck to let hot blood run over my arms as Serena watches the life fade from Lorenzo Abruzzi.

I release him, and his body crumples to the ground, blood pooling around him.

For a moment, we just stand there. My eyes move from Lorenzo, then up to Serena standing before me and Rafaela looking stunned on the bed. The next moment I step forward and Serena is already halfway to meeting me, our arms locking as I hug her tight to me.

"You're alive!" Serena says through a sob, "Luca, I thought you were dead!"

"Hell wouldn't keep me away from you, *passerotta mia*," I say, my heart soaring as we're reunited, breathing the same air and feeling each other's warmth once again. Just as it should be.

But we don't have time for a proper reunion. I look between Rafaela and Serena. "Are either of you hurt?"

"No," Rafaela says, her smile of relief fading as she stands up from the bed, looking at the door as if making sure nobody was coming. "Our egos are a little bruised, but seeing these bastards on the ground makes up for it, I think."

"Luca, he was going to-" Serena starts, but she's unable to finish as I hug her to me. I know just what kinds of memories this dragged back up for her.

"It's over now," I say reassuringly, holding her close. "It's all over. I told you, Serena, as long as I'm alive, nobody will hold you against your will."

Serena smiles warmly up at me, but I can tell she's shaken badly. These aren't the kinds of scars that heal overnight.

"We need to get out of here," I say, nodding to the door. "There's still a compound full of soldiers who don't know their boss is dead."

"I got Lorenzo's keys," Rafaela says, holding up Lorenzo's jacket. "Any ideas how to get out of here?"

"A worker showed me a way up here," I say, remembering the cleaning lady heading downstairs. "And I have a feeling we can take it down to somewhere that won't be crawling with gunmen. Stay close to me and move as quietly as you can."

$\sim$

It's nearly twenty minutes later that we've peeled out of the compound in Lorenzo's own car, out the back road and to civilization where it's too crowded to chase us. Besides, with Lorenzo dead and his capo gone, the organization in the compound is shot to hell.

We make it out without trouble, and before we know it, it's like we're in a totally different world.

I'm driving, my bloodstained shirt drying in the sunlight as the luxury sports car rolls down the roads just outside New York City proper. Serena sits in the passenger's seat, her legs close together as she holds her arms, looking out the window with a dreamy look in her eyes. Rafaela is in the back seat, looking up at the ceiling with a look of disbelief on her face.

Back in the city, the abrupt change in scenery feels jarring. It's like moving from a warzone to civilization in the blink of an eye, like waking up from a nightmare.

"I just can't believe it," Serena finally says softly, turning her head to look at the road in front of us."

"What?" I'm starting to feel twinges of pain as my adrenaline starts to fade, letting my wounds take their toll, but I'm not about to show pain right now.

"That we made it out of there," says Serena. "I know this is like, a regular Saturday for you, Luca, but it just doesn't feel real."

"Maybe a slightly more exciting Saturday than usual," I say with a smile.

That earns a smile from her, but she shakes her head. "I don't know why, but I just had this sense of things coming to an end when we got taken. Rafaela, if you hadn't been there with me…"

"You'd have been alright, give yourself some credit," Rafaela says with the kind of smile only a good friend can give. "You're the one who cut that fucker's legs out from under him."

"You two handled yourselves well," I say, and I mean it. "Not many people could keep it together under so much pressure."

Serena is quiet for a moment, but there's a soft smile on her face. After about a minute, she speaks again. "So, what happens now?"

"Now," I say, getting off the highway, "I'm taking you to a safehouse. Both of you. You're going to need to vanish for a few weeks while we figure out where things stand with the Abruzzi. Best case scenario, they're willing to call a truce while the Don buries Lorenzo and mourns. I never bet on the best case, but this is a blow the Cleaners won't recover from anytime soon."

"No," Rafaela says, raising her eyebrows. "It's a hell of a blow to their spirits, too. You might have stopped a much longer, bloodier war here, Luca."

"No offense, Rafaela," I say honestly, "but the only family I'm interested in protecting is my own, not the mobsters we work for." I smile at Serena, who returns it, and Rafaela grins.

"You won't hear me arguing. Maybe it's time I convince Nico to move upstate and get out of all this noise."

"So, where is this safehouse?" Serena asks.

"Just around this corner," I say, pointing to the turn I'm

about to make. "It's a cozy little place we don't use much, and…"

The thought trails off as I turn the corner. The apartment complex the safehouse is in has no less than four police cars parked out front, and nearly a dozen officers standing outside.

"Luca, what-" Serena starts to say, and without a moment to lose, I try to take a turn down a side-road and slip out of sight before we're noticed.

But the moment I do, a fifth car pulls up to block my path, coming to a screeching halt while the beat cops start running up to the car, guns coming out.

"What the fuck is this?!" Rafaela hisses.

"*No,*" I whisper through gritted teeth, and from the fifth car, I watch a tall man with a thin face and short dark hair step out of the car, pulling a shining badge out of his trench coat in one hand while he moves to the car and uses his other hand to pull the door open.

"Luca Lomaglio," the man says in a tone that tells me exactly what's coming next. I put my hands up as another cop pulls me out of the car, and Serena and Rafaela are take out from the other side.

"What the fuck are you doing?" I say in a gravelly, warning tone, glaring at the man as he takes out a pair of handcuffs.

"Detective William Price," he barks, gesturing for me to turn around. "You're under arrest for racketeering, assault with a deadly weapon, possession of unlicensed firearms…" His voice trails off to me as my ears start ringing, and I feel another cop pulling my hands down and trying to shove me against the front of my car.

"Serena!" I shout, watching the girls getting pulled away by the cops. Her terrified face looks to me desperately.

"Luca! Luca, what-"

"Stay calm!" I shout as I try to pull away from the officers to stay in sight of her. Immediately, I feel two officers wrestling me back, shoving me into the back of a police car, "I love you, baby!"

"I love you, Luca!" she calls, tears streaking down her face.

And that's the last sight I see before the police car door slams shut.

KILLER DESIRE

"*D*rop me off up at that corner, please," I tell the cab driver, leaning forward to point at the crossing of two residential streets. I tuck my hair behind my ear before it has a chance to fall across my eyes as I settle back into the plush leather seat. I'm flanked on either side by glossy shopping bags in various shades of pink, white, and green, and when the hazy late afternoon sun glares through the tinted windows, I tip my designer shades down over my eyes.

The taxi pulls to a stop and I pay him, giving a hefty tip, as I always do. My mother rolls her eyes at how easily I spend money, particularly when I spend it on other people, but Dad is always sure to remind me that there's no use in having money if you keep it all to yourself. And what can I say? I'm a daddy's girl.

I carefully hook my arms through the handles of my shopping bags and climb out of the cab, giving the driver a little wave as he drives off. I had the cabbie let me out at the corner because our driveway and the street in front of our new house are both crammed with construction trucks and piles of building materials. It's just easier to walk through that obstacle course than have some poor taxi driver try and maneuver through it.

I make my way down the street to the construction site, gingerly stepping over the upturned, muddy bits of lawn and stacks of perfectly-sawed dark lumber. I just know the bottoms of my Manolo Blahniks are going to be caked with reddish mud by the time I make it across the yard to the front door. Luckily, I think to myself with a smile, there's a brand new pair from this season in one of the bags I'm holding right now anyway.

The only part of the house which is even remotely livable at the moment is the first floor den, which is currently serving as a sort of operations base for the construction job. My father spends most of his free time here, having set up a makeshift office in order to keep tabs on how things are going. He's a hands-on kind of guy, and I think there's a part of him that really wishes he was out there helping build the house himself. He's more of a numbers guy, I think, though. I've never been one-hundred-percent certain as to what his work consists of, but I know he makes good money and he goes to a lot of private meetings. He keeps secrets sometimes, and he does everything in his power to keep his work separate from my mom and me.

Occasionally I do worry about him. Despite his attempts to keep it all under lock and key, sometimes I can see the stress of his job bleeding through into his interactions with Mom and me. He tries to be a jokey, good-natured guy and most of the time that's exactly what he is. But now and then I can see something else going on underneath the surface, like maybe things aren't quite as rosy as he makes them out to be. Still, I can't complain. Our life — my life — is amazing. I have never wanted for anything in all my years, and I know at the end of the day my dad can take care of absolutely anything the world throws his way. He's a strong man, that much I do know.

And besides, this whole construction thing has definitely made him happier. I catch him still awake late at night in his study, poring over blueprints and running numbers on his calculator, a look of feverish joy on his face. I think he must have been an architect in another life or something. It's always fun to come with him to the new house and watch him boss the construction guys around. He's never cruel about it, but I can tell he means business. Everyone can tell. He has a booming voice and his checkbook always in his hand, ready to write out another big number and hand it off to whomever he thinks he can trust to get shit done. My mom says he's too showy with his money, but I think he's just honest. Why hide it? Everybody knows we're rich. Everybody knows my dad. I don't know for sure what his reputation is, but I do know that he has one.

I push open the front door and slip inside, my arms starting to ache with the weight of my shopping bags. I squeeze through the skeletal wooden archway and into the den, where a cheap plastic desk and office chair sit in the center of the room. My dad is sitting on a couch on the other side of the room, his cell phone pressed to his ear. His face lights up at the sight of me and he gives me a wink.

"Hi pumpkin," he mouths at me. I wave back before carefully setting my shopping bags down on the desk, covering the mish-mash of blueprints and contracts. I grimace at the state of my expensive shoes, debating whether to try and wash them off in the one barely-functioning sink or just wait until I can ask our maid, Janet, how to take care of them.

"*Si. Bene. Parliamo più tardi,*" my dad says quickly into the receiver, then promptly hangs up and sets the phone down on his lap. His expression turns from vaguely grim to bright and joyous as he grins at me, holding his arms wide open for me to come hug him. I smile and walk over to embrace him, then settle into the couch beside him.

"How is *mia principessa?*" he asks me warmly. "I see you did a little light shopping," he adds with good-natured sarcasm.

"Fifth Avenue was full of tourists today," I lament with a sigh. "I mean, it always is, but today was especially annoying. I think a couple of people even snapped photos of Katie and me while we were walking down the street. I mean, that's got to be illegal or something, right?"

It happens more often than I would like. Sadly, when you're an immaculately-manicured, fairly attractive young woman wearing flashy designer clothing walking around with your equally well-dressed and pretty friend, people are bound to stare. It's not something I would consider a point of pride. It's just the way it is. There are always photographers out on the street in the city, trying to snap a new, magical iconic photo that might propel their portfolio to stardom. My best friend Katie and I are both exactly the kind of fashion mag street-style editorial muses your everyday Joe Schmoe with a high-definition lens go looking for. And today the lighting is beautiful. It's June, warm, and just the right amount of clouds in the sky to filter the sunlight. All the girls like me, with money and means, are dressed in our best summer dresses, heels, and sparkly jewelry.

I guess I should have expected the attention I got today. It's nothing new. And if I'm being totally honest, it doesn't even really bother me all that much. It's flattering to think that some people find my look photo-worthy, even if it's kind of superficial.

"Don't let some low-life photog rain on your parade,"

my father says, giving my shoulders a squeeze. "I hope you had a good afternoon anyway."

"I did," I answer truthfully.

"Good. Well, I'm probably going to finish up here in about an hour if you want to just sit tight for a little while, pumpkin. Just got to go talk shop with the crew and set some things straight and then we can go home. Sound okay?" he asks, standing up.

"Mmhm. Sounds fine," I answer absent-mindedly, already trying to figure out what to do to pass the time until we leave.

"Just make sure you stay out of the guys' way, alright? Wouldn't want you to get hurt."

"Okay, Dad."

"Good girl. Won't take long, I promise."

I like hanging out with my father, and going to visit the construction site is always exciting. I enjoy seeing what changes have progressed since the last time I saw the house. Riverdale is a ritzy neighborhood, full of old money and high-class reputations, and I know rebuilding a house in a place like this is a huge deal for my dad. He's always looking for that next step up the ladder, clawing his way to fortune. He wants my mom and me to have comfortable lives and give us the very best, and I know this new house means a lot to him.

As soon as my dad disappears, I get up, too antsy to just sit here in silence for the next hour waiting on him to finish up. I know he wants me to stay out of the way, but I'm sure there's something interesting happening.

Besides, my shoes are already mud-stained. What's a little more dirt going to do?

I creep out of the den and back out the front door, taking note of my dad standing at the end of the long driveway talking to the foreman sitting in his big white utility truck. I sneak around the corner to the back of the house, where the guys are working on building a luxurious, massive back porch and sunroom. The sun is sinking a little closer to the horizon, making its slow, long descent across the sky. I know the sun won't actually go down until much later, because it's summer and the days seem to last forever. But the sun hovers in that orange, lazy space overhead, sinking the world into magical light. The bugs are starting to buzz around a bit more now that the unbearable noon heat has relented. In a couple hours, it'll be evening, and the residential neighborhoods will start to smell like barbecue smoke and domestic bliss.

I'm sixteen, and the world is full of potential at every turn, like I'm standing in a room with a hundred unlocked doors. Behind every door is another world waiting for me, mine for the taking, if I can only choose which door to open first. It's almost overwhelming how easy life is, how smoothly everything flows along from one season to the next.

Sometimes, though, I do wonder if it'll end eventually. Everyone tells me these are the best years of my life, and I'm scared that maybe I'll waste them by being too good, by staying too on-track. After all, I've always made perfect grades and followed the rules to the letter, staying away from drugs and partying and all those dark temptations my parents have warned me about. Katie and some of my other friends go to those crazy rager parties in Brooklyn every other weekend, and even though I'm always invited, I don't go.

I always tell myself it's just not the right time, that next time I'll feel up to it. But deep down I know I'm kidding myself. I'm just not cut out for that kind of thing. I like to shop and hang out with my friends and sometimes I'll go to parties, but I don't get wasted and black out like everyone else seems to. I don't know if I'm just too afraid or if I'm just of really strong moral caliber or whatever.

Either way, I'm fully aware that I'm curating a stick-in-the-mud reputation for myself by abstaining from all that crazy stuff. I don't want to be known as the good girl, but as the same time, I don't think I have what it takes to be a bad girl, either.

Most of the time when I do go to the party, I end up pretending to laugh at people's dumb jokes and taking sips of my water while telling everyone who asks that it's vodka and Sprite. In the back of my mind, I'm always just tallying up how many books I could have devoured instead of awkwardly loitering around the kitchen in some stranger's loft in Midtown. According to my mom, my curfew is midnight, but my dad says as long as I keep in touch and look after myself I can come home later than that.

I rarely stay out past my mom's assigned curfew, though. I just get bored and take a cab home before the party even starts to really warm up. There's nothing like the feeling of coming home, changing out of my form-fitting party dress and into soft pajamas, then eating cereal in bed while reading a book and listening to my dad's old vinyl collection until I conk out and go to sleep.

But this summer, I'm starting to feel different. I'm starting to get restless. I want something more to do, something new to try out. It's like I'm outgrowing this version of myself and I'm ready to be somebody else for a change.

I'm so lost in thought that I'm not even paying attention to where I'm going, and as I start idly turning around to walk back to the front of the house I nearly walk smack into a stack of wood coming my way. I jump backward, startled, and realize that there's a man standing in front of me with a half-amused, half-concerned look on his face.

His extremely *handsome* face.

"Whoa," he says, shifting the wood planks on his

shoulder and giving me a roguish grin. "Damn near took your head off just then."

"Sorry, I kind of zoned out for a minute," I apologize quickly, feeling my face start to flush pink. The guy seems to immediately take notice, but to his credit, he doesn't say anything. For a moment, time seems to slow to stop all around me as all of my attention zeroes in on the hot guy in front of me. His biceps bulge through the thin fabric of his white t-shirt as he balances the wooden planks on his shoulder effortlessly. His skin is a golden, ruddy tan and he's clearly no stranger to working hard outdoors. He has dark hair and an intoxicating smile as he towers a head taller than me.

And his eyes. Bright, vibrant green eyes piercing right through me, like he can see into my thoughts, into my heart, see it pumping furiously in my chest as I try to get ahold of myself. It's not like I've never seen a gorgeous guy before. Hell, I live in New York City. There are actors, underwear models, musicians of all flavors walking the streets every day. I've been hit on by so many attractive boys at school, and sometimes older men flirt with me when I'm out and about because my makeup and my high heels make me look more mature than I am.

But god, there is just something about this guy that's throwing me for a loop.

"You alright?" he asks, puncturing my thoughts and bringing me back to the present.

I nod vigorously, letting out a nervous laugh as I tuck my hair back behind my ears. "Yeah, yeah, sorry. It's—it's the summer heat, I guess. Making me a little dizzy," I lie quickly.

"Oh, it's definitely getting hot out here," he replies, just a twinge of double meaning in the flash of his smile. "Let me set this down over there and I'll get you something cool to drink."

"Oh no, you don't have to do that," I interject, but it's too late. The guy has run across the yard to deliver the gigantic wood planks to the crew, taken a bottle of water out of a red cooler on the ground, and is now jogging back to me, all rippling muscle and boyish charm.

I try to regain my composure, reminding myself who the hell I am. I'm Serena De Laurentis, new money princess who's moved on up from the Bronx to Manhattan and soon to the affluent neighborhood of Riverdale. I wear this season's designer clothes and I have friends in high places. My dad is a powerful man and my mom is a notoriously snobby socialite.

I should absolutely be able to keep my cool around this construction guy.

But as soon as he gets back and hands me the bottle of water, I nearly forget my own name. It's like he's putting out some kind of dumbing fog which turns me into a speechless, star struck little girl. *Be cool*, I tell myself firmly.

"Thank you, that's so sweet," I comment, taking a sip of the water.

"It'll cool off a bit when the sun finally goes down," he replies, standing with his hands on his hips as he looks me over. Now that I'm starting to chill out a little bit, I can detect an accent bleeding through his words, a faint one, like he's trying his best to suppress it. "So, is this gonna be your house?" he adds.

I nod. "Yea. My father's talking to the foreman right now. This house is kind of like his passion project or something. His baby."

"And how do you feel about it?" the guy asks, surprising me. I didn't expect such a weird question. It's my future house, but it has nothing to do with me. I just go where I'm told.

"Um, I mean, it seems very nice," I answer haltingly. Then, when the guy's green eyes stay locked on me, clearly expecting a longer answer, I go on. "I don't know. I like our apartment in Manhattan. It's close to my school and all my friends and stuff. So moving out here is going to be… different, I guess. I'm a little worried that I might get lonely sometimes. But it is what it is."

I'm shocked at myself for sharing so much with this complete stranger. I'm usually better about keeping my cards close to my chest. I don't let just anyone in, and I'm always careful not to overshare with anybody, even with my close friends. But there's something about him that just makes me feel secure, like anything I say is safe with him. Besides, who is he going to tell? He's not from the same side of the tracks as I am, and I know for a fact he runs in very different circles. Hell, I'll probably never see him again after today.

Weirdly enough, that thought sends a slight pang of sadness through my heart, which is just ridiculous. I don't know him. He doesn't know me. I don't even know his name.

"I'm Luca, by the way," he says, almost like he can read my mind. He holds out his hand for me to shake and I reluctantly take it, feeling his warm, calloused palm against mine. I hope to god my hands aren't clammy.

"I'm Serena," I reply, unable to suppress a smile.

"Well, Serena, I'm going to do everything within my power to make sure this house is perfect for you. Hopefully that will make the move a little less painful," Luca says, without a single note of sarcasm. He's earnest, one-hundred-percent.

"Thank you," I answer quietly, feeling very small and silly all of a sudden. Changing the subject, I ask, "So, what is this back porch monstrosity going to look like when it's finished?"

Without missing a beat, Luca launches into an in-depth explanation of the dimensions, materials, and projected design for the back of the house, using terms I can't even begin to understand as he rapidly paints me a picture I can only half-imagine. Either way, I'm impressed. I expected that he was just kind of a grunt worker following orders since he looks to be about my age and I don't know any guys my age who could even build a birdhouse, much less a house for a person to live in. But he seems to genuinely understand the process of craftsmanship, and even though I can't quite follow what he's saying, I can tell that he feels passionate about what he's doing. Passion. I don't know any guys my age who show the least amount of enthusiasm for anything, much less a job.

But everything about him tells me Luca is different. He's not the kind of guy I'm used to, the kind of dude who sits next to me in chemistry class and tries to throw tiny paper balls down my cleavage and brags about last weekend's keg stand like it's the most impressive feat any human being has ever attempted. Luca is something else entirely, and I am intrigued.

"Wow, you really know your stuff," I comment, shaking my head in awe.

Luca shrugs. "It's my job to know it. Plus, now that I know this house belongs to a beautiful girl like you, I'm gonna work extra hard at it."

I open my mouth to respond, but no sound comes out. It's not even that suave of a pickup line, and yet I'm literally speechless. I look down at the ground, my heart racing.

"Come with me," Luca says suddenly, reaching out to take my hand. I glance back up, startled at this intrusion, and meet his vivid green eyes. He's smiling at me brilliantly and I realize there's not a cell in my body that can refuse him. It's stupid, but it's true. He's got me hooked, and even though I don't know a thing about him, I will follow him anywhere.

"Where are we going?" I ask as he pulls me along.

He looks back over his shoulder. "Shh. Just be cool. You finished off that water so fast, I'm just gonna get you something better to drink. It's a balmy summer evening."

I have to laugh a little at the ridiculous wording. What a weirdo. He leads me to the back of one of the utility vans, glances around surreptitiously for a moment, and then slides the side door open, gesturing for me to follow him inside.

"You know, I think this definitely feels like the start of some cautionary tale I read as a child. Something about not getting into a van with a stranger," I remark, lifting an eyebrow.

Luca chuckles. "Okay, I can see how this might be weird. But I swear, I'm not about to kidnap you or anything. Although judging from the house your dad is building, it looks like I could probably get a pretty sweet ransom for you."

"Yeah, that definitely makes me more likely to climb into this van with you," I joke, crossing my arms over my chest stubbornly.

Luca shrugs, still grinning. "Fine, fine. You can hang out there. I'm just going to mix a couple of drinks. Something to cool off with. Better than water."

He starts digging around in a couple of coolers, taking out different bottles of what looks to be liquor and mixers, concocting a drink he pours into two red Solo cups, handing one off to me.

"So now I've gone from following a stranger back to his van to now accepting a strange drink from the back of the stranger's van. Great. My mother would lose her shit," I say, rolling my eyes. "I don't drink, by the way. Not usually. I'm only sixteen."

"I'm seventeen," Luca says, casually taking a sip of the mystery drink. "But who cares? Nobody has to know but you and me, and I'm sure as hell not going to tell anybody."

"This better not have anything funky in it," I warn, sniffing the drink hesitantly. It smells vaguely sweet, but I don't know enough about alcohol to place any of the scents.

"Funky? *Merda*, you really don't trust me, do you?" he responds, sounding ever so slightly offended that I would suspect him at all.

"Well, I don't exactly know you. For all I know you could be a murderer or something."

"Yes, I'm a carpenter moonlighting as a murderer," Luca laughs. He takes another long sip of his drink. "I don't have time for a double life, Miss Serena. What you see is what you get."

Narrowing my eyes at him suspiciously, I finally taste the drink. It's actually rather delicious, and the liquor sends a warm wave right down through my body. Luca grins.

"What is this?" I ask.

"I like to call it a bastard Americano," he answers.

I snort. "A what what? I thought an Americano was a kind of coffee drink."

"Not this one," he says, shaking his head. "It's supposed to have vermouth, but I don't have that. It's Campari and soda water. An Americano for the pretty Americana," he adds, giving me a wink that makes me blush.

"So, if you've been drinking this stuff all day, does that mean you're drunkenly building my house?" I inquire, giving him a critical look. Luca scoffs.

"No, no. This is all for the end of the day. For me, at least. Some of the guys sip on beers throughout the day, but I like to keep a clear head while I'm handling heavy machinery, myself."

"Good, because if I fall through the floor because somebody was too drunk to properly assemble my back porch, there'll be hell to pay," I declare, trying not to sound too haughty.

"If you fall, I'll be there to catch you, *mia passerotta*," Luca says, and I catch onto the accent at last. It's Italian. Of course it is. I feel like an idiot for taking this long to figure it out. My mom's family has been in America long enough to have lost the accent decades ago, and my dad does his best to keep his accent under control, but most of his friends and colleagues sound a lot like Luca does. After all, this is New York.

"*Passerotta?*" I repeat, confused. My parents never spoke Italian with me growing up, so I unfortunately never learned it, even though everybody who hears my name assumes I speak it.

"Sparrow. Little bird," Luca defines, waving his hand.

"Never heard that one before."

"Good, then I'm the first," Luca says smoothly, downing the rest of his drink. "Your dad's not a cop or anything, is he?" he asks, half-jokingly.

I shake my head. "No, definitely not. But he would still be angry if he caught us doing... this. So we should probably get out of here."

"Get out of here?" Luca repeats, setting down his cup and climbing out of the van to stand in front of me. He's standing close. So close. I can feel the heat radiating off of his body, smell his masculine scent. He looks down at me with those green eyes and I almost feel my knees buckling.

"Where would you want to go with a guy like me?" he asks softly. A shiver of something new, something dangerous, tingles down my spine.

"Serena! Time to go, pumpkin!" I heard my dad's voice carry from across the property and I freeze instantly. The last thing I need is for him to come around back and discover me standing here with one of the construction guys, drinking alcohol from a van.

I swallow hard and look up into Luca's face. He doesn't waver in the slightest, completely unafraid and unabashed. "Tomorrow night. S-six o'clock. The park around the corner from here," I tell him quietly. "I'll see you there. Okay?"

Luca smiles and lifts a hand to take the cup from me. He nods. "See you then, Serena."

I back away slowly, not wanting to leave. Then I force myself to turn and hurry back around to the front of the house to grab my stuff and head home with my dad. On the way home I dutifully answer my dad's inane questions about my day, listen to him talk excitedly about plans for the house, and complain about extended deadlines the foreman keeps missing.

And all I can think about is Luca. Those green eyes.

I'm going to see him tomorrow. Tomorrow. *Tomorrow...*

⁓

The alarm goes off and I sit up violently in bed, my heart racing as I search blindly in the dark to turn off the sound. It's time to get up and go to work. It's time to shake off my dreams, shake off those years of waiting, and get back to my life.

Without Luca.

My chest aches as I drag myself out of bed and into the shower. I wish I could climb back into bed and resume my dream where it left off, go back in time to relive those first early days, when Luca first appeared in my life like a mirage. We were just kids then, and so stupid. We had no idea that there was a big, scary world waiting to close its jaws around us. We thought the only thing that mattered was setting the next date, waiting for the day when we could sneak out to be together again. God, I wish I could go back in time and live those days over and over again.

Things were so simple. Or at least we weren't yet aware of how complicated they could get.

It's been two years since they took my Luca away from me again, threw him behind metal bars, locking away my heart and soul. He's in prison, and even though I'm free to walk around outside and go about my life, I'm imprisoned, too. Because none of my freedom means anything without being able to share it with the man I love.

Everybody and everything conspires to keep us apart, and I don't know how to break through the chains and get to him. Every second we're apart, that bridge between us crumbles just a little bit more. I have his pictures everywhere and I stare at them every day. I refuse to forget a single detail of his face, even though I'm sure his time behind bars has changed his face, has changed his heart.

I can only hope that one thing won't change: his love for me.

wo years.

It's been two years today since I was put into this hell-hole, sentenced to ten full years at Sterling Correctional Facility. Two years since I breathed fresh air as a free man.

But my love for Serena, my one shining light, has only gotten stronger.

I feel my muscles burning as I push the heavy weights up. With each passing moment, I feel the cold metal grip against the palms of my hands. I feel the tension of the weights from my thick forearms to bulging biceps, all the way down to my shoulders and pecs. A thin sheen of sweat covers my bare chest as it slowly falls while I push the weights up. I let air out of my lungs while I push up, my body working in perfect sync to make the rep happen.

I reach the top of the rep, and I hold it there for a second, and I can feel every muscle that works to hold it up. Since coming to prison, I've had nothing but time, and in that time, I've devoted myself to working out. I never realized how inexperienced I really was before I had endless time to hone my body.

Now, though, no muscle moves in my body without my knowing it. Each move is deliberate, measured. I'm not just holding a set of weights up. I know which muscles to tense and relax, exactly how to breathe. I even know how to feel my heart rate going up and down with my workout.

The natural rhythms of my body have become my only friends in here. And I know them better than I ever have in my life.

My arms slowly bend to lower the weights down, and I feel that sweet, familiar burn ripple through new places in my upper body as it comes down and I breathe in. I don't let this position last as long, and it's on to another rep immediately after.

My body stopped aching and complaining during these exercises long ago. Exercise has become the one thing I can rely on in here. Without something to hang onto, despair swallows you in this bleak place. I've seen it happen to other men. Prison drains you. It breaks you. It flushes out your whole world and makes you see nothing but empty grayness.

From the first day, I decided not to let that happen to me.

I started working out in my cell. I did push-ups to keep the feeling of aching arms with me as much as I could bear it. When I couldn't do any more, I did sit-ups. Every time the guards marched us out, I would hit the exercise equipment and do that until I couldn't handle any more.

My body became my focus. It never disappointed. Each day, I found new parts of me to refine and perfect. More muscles to work out, new parts within me to exercise. Every time I thought I'd perfected something, I'd find new ways to make the best use of it.

When I was a boy, Uncle Carlo taught me how to fight. He knew more than you would guess from his humble look. He had served in the Special Forces, and he passed that training on to me, as much as he was willing and as long as he could hold my attention. I learned from him, and I could fight well. But now that I really know what the human body is capable of, I know what those lessons were for. I remember things he taught me that my body wasn't capable of then.

When I've worked out so much that I can't push any part of me any further, I go over old fights in my mind. With each day that I grow stronger, I think of things I did wrong. Things I could have done better. I remember my fights with Lorenzo, and I laugh at how easily I could have killed him if I'd known the things I know now, if I was able to do the things this machine of a body can do now. When I lift the weights, I see a scar on my forearm that I got from that last fight in the Abruzzi compound. It's been a reminder of Serena, something that's always in sight when she can't be.

After twelve reps, I let my spotter take the weights from me, and I take a breath before sitting up and swinging my leg over the bench. My spotter gives me a clap on the back, and I nod to him. When I stand up, I notice other men in the exercise yard glance at me. My gaze passes over them as they look away. Nobody holds eye contact for long. When I stand up and take a step away from the bench, it's like a statement. My presence is bigger than theirs here, not just in the way I'm built, but how I carry myself.

Nobody fucks with me.

The other prisoners took notice when I started getting stronger. Every prison has a hierarchy, a pecking order of men who rule each other, gangs who keep to themselves. When I first showed up here, I knew I had to find my place in that pecking order, and it would happen sooner rather than later.

The first time I got jumped, I made my place clear, and

the punk who tried to pick a fight with me has the scars to prove it from when I drove him into the hard concrete.

He wasn't the last, either. But after a few months, people knew not to send mooks to pick fights with me unless they wanted them to come back with bruises and a few less teeth.

Still, every now and then, some new kid sees my body's stature and how the other guys tend to stay out of my way, and they decide to do something stupid.

That's the feeling I'm getting from the blonde new guy eyeing me across the exercise yard. He's not a scrawny guy by any means, but he's got the look in his eye of someone reckless. You learn to spot that look fast in prison. Some asshole with a chip on his shoulder can be a real problem if you don't see him coming.

I pretend like I haven't noticed the guy eyeing me, though, and I carry on like I would any other day. I look to my spotter and jab a thumb to the bench, moving over to spot for him in turn. I might not get tangled up in prison politics, but I'm not an asshole.

"I'm good," the guy says. "Pushed something too far yesterday, don't want to risk tearing anything."

"Smart," I grunt, and we exchange a short nod before parting ways.

I head to the bathrooms, making my way past the clusters of my fellow prisoners getting what they can out of our short rec time. I've come to learn the different gangs around and how to keep myself out of trouble that doesn't come looking for me.

There are Russians from Brighton Beach who keep to themselves for the most part, even more than the others. There are other Italians here from groups I don't tangle with. And of course, the Cleaners are here too.

Not directly, for the most part. A few of them have passed through in my time, but they're good at keeping their kind out. Makes me wonder just how many palms are greased in the NYPD by Don Abruzzi. But they make their presence known in other ways. Word gets in from the outside, and prison politics do what they do naturally.

And when I notice the blonde kid out of the corner of my eye following me, I have a feeling I'm about to see some of that in action.

It's a quiet walk to the bathrooms, which is never a good sign. Like the calm before the storm, except the calm means there's no witnesses. And sometimes worse, no guards.

But I step inside, do my business, and as I'm heading to the sink and wash my hands, I hear a series of slow footsteps entering the bathroom, coming to a stop near the door.

He really wants to do this, doesn't he? I frown. We prisoners would be better off having each other's backs instead of watching them, but some kids learn the hard way.

"You should think hard," I say as I face the blonde guy standing in the doorway with his arms crossed, jaw set, "about whether you really want to lose some of those teeth on your first week in here."

The man's face twists into a scowl, and he cracks his knuckles. "Tough talk for a marked man."

I raise an eyebrow at him. "Look, kid, you're new. I'm giving you a chance most of these guys wouldn't think twice about. Turn around and let me wash my fucking hands, and we'll forget this happened."

With that, I step toward the sink to wash my hands, but I see his knee move out of the corner of my eye.

Well, can't say I didn't warn him.

I reach up and catch the first punch he throws. He's stopped mid-lunge, and my arm doesn't budge a hair. He brings his other fist in for a shot to my gut, but I twist his wrist around and thrust him back against the wall. He hits it hard, and I hear his head hit the back of the tile wall. He gives his head and wrist a shake, and I turn to face him as he recovers.

"Don Abruzzi's got a price on your head, *Luca Lomaglio*," the guy says, rolling his shoulders back like he's getting ready for the fight of his life. "Didja know that? And man, the Cleaners are payin' good for anyone who can fuck you up."

This is news to me. My brow furrows, but when he comes in again, I can see his moves coming from a mile away. He tries to tackle me, and I move in with a quick shot to his gut, then another, and I hurl him to the ground, but he manages to keep his footing. He's a big guy who clearly works out, but he's got no finesse. Probably an enforcer.

He comes in swinging, and I put up my fists to parry and dodge the onslaught before I give him a quick jab to the nose that surprises him for a second. That's all I need. I seize his wrist and twist it around him, shoving him up against the wall and holding him there.

"Tell me some more," I order him.

"Get fucked!" he barks.

"Wrong answer," I say, twisting his arm a little more, and he grunts in pain and throws his free arm back, getting a hold of my ear.

He wants to fight dirty.

I don't give him the chance to do any damage. I spin him around and slam his face into the white ceramic sink, *hard*, and there's red on it after he cries out in pain and crumples to the ground.

He doesn't get back up. I hear him groaning in pain, but it's muffled. He's holding his mouth as blood trickles out, and when he moves it, I hear the clatter of a few teeth falling to the ground.

As he starts coughing, I move to a different sink and

turn on the hot water, calmly washing my hands off with soap and drying them off on my clothes.

"Tell the guards you fell," I say as he writhes on the ground. "Ratting and getting thrown in the hole after a botched fight isn't a good look."

But I hear the sounds of boots running outside, and I give the kid on the ground an almost pitying look. "Tough luck, kid," I say, moments before guards burst into the bathroom, and I don't resist as I'm wrestled to the ground by two guards while two more handle the blonde.

I'm marching back to my cell with the rest of the inmates, and it's a thoughtful walk. I narrowly avoided getting put in seg, though I have no idea how. These guards are the kind to throw anyone in there, if they have any excuse. I got lucky.

Though how lucky can I feel? I knew the Cleaners had it out for me, and I've been waiting for one of their soldiers to try something on me, but if he's spreading the word to random thugs, Don Abruzzi must just want to make my life a living hell.

I was careful in that fight. I held back more than I would have when I first got in here. Push your opponent too far, and you both get thrown in the hole, no matter who starts the fight.

At least I'm not entirely alone in here. As I walk past the cells, I glance into those occupied by my fellow Costa soldiers and enforcers. We trade knowing looks, sometimes nods, but we keep a low profile behind bars. I'm not dragging old grudges in here if I can help it.

They have a way of finding me easily enough.

But I know that the Costas in here with me are why I haven't had even more trouble from our enemies. I was arrested right after the assault on the Abruzzi compound, but word spread like wildfire, and I got word that I was a hero to the mob.

I gave the Cleaners a bloody nose they wouldn't forget anytime soon. Don Abruzzi vanished off the face of the earth for a while, probably hiding in some manor upstate.

Load of good that did me now. Stolen from my girl, from the only thing that mattered at all. I put it all on the line for her, and though the Costas might think I held my tongue to protect them, it was to protect her. I accepted my punishment to keep her safe. That was the deal.

Nothing can ever happen to Serena. And if I have to do time, then I'm still going to do everything I can to make sure that remains true. If I'd drawn out the court proceedings, turned the Costas on me...

Well, it wouldn't have been a wise decision, and I'd still have gotten my ass locked up.

When I get back to my cell, I notice two things. First, my cellmate isn't here. I don't know the guy very well, so I don't think much of it, because the second thing is a lot more interesting: I have mail. I smile at the sight of the handwriting on it, because I recognize it.

It's from Serena.

Serena and her letters have been a ray of hope shining through to this bleak and dark place. The crushing isolation is something that nobody is ever prepared for. Writing letters to prisoners is something so many people on the outside never even think about, but reading the words of someone not in prison is like a breath of fresh air. They're reminders that we're still ourselves.

They remind us that the outside world hasn't forgotten us, and that we're still loved.

And Serena's love could keep me going for a lifetime.

Everything I've done in here to perfect my body, everything I've done to keep myself sane, to keep hope alive, to remember the outside world, it's all been for her. The sight of her face before getting thrown into the back of a police car is both my dearest memory and what haunts me.

But letters are one way we can stay in touch. She writes to me as much as she can, even though her schedule is so busy running the shop alone again. As I run my fingers along the paper that I know she's touched herself, as much hope as it gives me, I feel a pang of guilt in the back of my mind.

I stepped back into her life for a moment of joy, only to get snatched away, just when we thought we would be together. Just when things seemed to be going *right*.

Those are thoughts I have to keep down deep. They'll consume me if I'm not careful, and I've seen guilt and regret eat people alive in here, driving them truly mad. I can't blame myself for what's happened.

But I can blame someone.

Detective Price has been my shadow, even since being in here. He haunts me, dropping in from time to time to summon me to interrogation rooms, drilling me for more information about "my case." He uses it as an excuse to push my psychological limits.

Taking me down earned him a reputation, and since he's deep in Don Abruzzi's pocket, that means he's had more leeway to investigate mafia operations in the Bronx, which means putting pressure on us.

And since I'm both the highest-ranking Costa member behind bars and the living symbol of his success, he has a close eye on me. I have a feeling he's also the reason that most of my letters out to Serena get mysteriously lost in the mail.

All letters get screened by guards. If something is deemed worth censoring, the letter goes in the trash. End of story. A lot more of my letters get censored than Serena's, but I know not all of hers make it in, either.

I cherish the ones that do, though.

I unfold the paper and read her fine handwriting.

Dear Luca,

Things were great at the shop this week! I started a new promo based on an idea Rafaela had. I'm having people bring back a few old shampoo containers to recycle in exchange for a free hand-soap to advertise that new scent I told you I was working on. It's been a hit so far! Also, Rafaela says hi. She says Nico does too, but you still owe him a beer... or five.

So, I forgot to mention it in the last letter I sent, but we just passed the anniversary of that time we went down to the beach. I know, I know, it's dumb to keep date-anniversaries, shut up! But when I'm lonely in bed at night, sometimes I picture us back on those sands again. I feel you pulling my shirt up over my head and tossing my bra to the side. My heart starts racing, and I think of your strong hands feeling me up. God, your fingers are so thick, but they were gentle with my nipples... at least, as gentle as they should be. I remember the feeling of your teeth grazing them, and my whole body misses you even more. Do you remember how wet I was for you when you touched me that night? I could never forget how good you felt, and your thick shaft going into me made me feel more whole than I've ever felt.

I've treated myself a little since you've been gone—I'm writing this wearing a new... outfit. I spent a little extra on some lacey pink and black lingerie. I love it! I'm looking down at the way it hugs my thighs, so close to where my legs meet, and all I can think about is you running your rugged carpenter's hands along them, your stubble brushing up against it before you let that tongue of yours out.

I can't stop thinking about you, Luca. I tried to make this letter about the usual stuff that's going on from day to day, but just thinking about us has got me in a different headspace. As soon as I'm done writing this letter, I'm going to go take care of that, and I'm going to be thinking of you inside me. Then I'll try another letter and see how that goes! I keep thinking about how much stronger you've gotten since you've been working out in there, and I wish I could be with you so badly. I wish I could slip into your cell for just one night. I've thought about that, and I've thought about you doing everything you could ever dream of wanting to do with me. Think about me the next time you're feeling lonely in there, and remember that I'll be thinking of you.

Serena

She signs her name with a bunch of little hearts drawn next to it. I smile and read the letter over again, and I feel the beast between my legs stirring at the thought of her. Steamy letters do usually get through, and they're a blessing.

My mind is already swirling with the thoughts of the things I'd do with my Serena if I had her with me. We don't get the conjugal visits some married couples enjoy, so letters like these are the best we can do. I'm not much of a writer, at least not like Serena is, but I've been trying my hand at returning the favor as best as I can.

I read the letter over a third time before I stow the letter with the rest, under my bed. I've barely finished doing so when guards appear at my cell door, and I give them a puzzled look when they open the barred door.

"New cellmate," the guard says gruffly to me as I stand up, keeping my face stony. A new cellmate could mean any number of things, and after that new guy tried to jump me earlier, I don't think it bodes well.

"What happened to John?" I ask, but the guard just grunts.

"Transfer."

Arching an eyebrow, I look to the two guards behind him to see who they're leading into my cell, flexing my fist.

SEVEN YEARS AGO

I check my phone incessantly throughout the day, taking every excuse to leave class and run to the bathroom or go out to the courtyard for a "breath of fresh air." I know it's becoming an annoying habit, and all of my friends roll their eyes at me when I take out my phone and click the screen open during a face-to-face conversation, just to see if I have any messages from Luca. They don't understand. It's rude of me, I know. But I can't help it. I just can't stand the thought of accidentally missing one of his rare, almost cryptic messages.

It's a different number every other time or so, because he uses those disposable, pre-loaded crappy little phones from the supermarket. I don't know if it's just because he can't afford a regular cell phone like mine, or if he prefers the air of mystery those burner phones give him.

I don't ask questions like that.

It's not important, really. All that matters is that he stays in contact sometimes. I wish he talked to me more often, but I know he's a busy guy. We couldn't be living more different lives. Class is back in for me and I've started my junior year of high school, and my thoughts are filled with the prospect of prom and passing my exams and turning in term papers. I think about making sure my stupid school uniform is cleaned and ironed every evening before bed, about how I'm going to do my hair and makeup in the morning. I think about whether I'm going to try out for our school's production of *A Midsummer Night's Dream* to bolster my college applications with some performing arts credits. I worry about which colleges I should apply to and whether I will qualify for scholarships, even though with my dad's money I probably won't need them.

Or at least I *used* to think about those things. I should still be worrying about that kind of stuff now, too, but instead I'm just checking my phone and zoning out in AP U.S. History class, my mind circling around Luca and wondering when I'm going to finally see him again. Since the day we first met a couple months ago at the construction site — which has been almost totally finished up by now — we've only seen each other in person a handful of times. Three times, to be exact. We did end up meeting at the park around the corner from my house in Riverdale, but we only had about an hour to spend.

I convinced my mom that I was just going to my friend Gemma's house for dinner and to watch a movie, and then I took a cab to the park. By the time I got there, Luca had already been waiting for a while. I was late, having been forced to endure my mom's interrogations. But he didn't seem to mind at all. His face lit up when he saw me, and my heart skipped a beat at the sight of him. I nearly floated down the pathway to the little pond where Luca was sitting on a bench. He had a small bouquet of flowers, as well as a half-full bottle of Campari.

It was a magical hour, just sitting there slowly getting tipsy with my mysterious new beau. Of course, we didn't *do* anything. Just talked for a while, comparing our favorite books and movies, talking about everything and nothing at the same time. I honestly couldn't even recall what all we discussed, because I was so blissfully caught up in just being in his presence. It was intoxicating, even more so than the Campari we took turns sipping straight from the bottle. Every time our shoulders brushed together, every time he looked directly into my eyes, I felt like I could simply melt into the bench. A puddle of goopy infatuation on the ground.

I hadn't wanted to leave, but I knew the longer I took, the more likely my mom would suspect something was up. Despite the fact that she's never been super involved in what I do with my time and I definitely consider myself closer to my dad, she does seem to have a weird sixth sense about my actions.

Dad always says it's because she and I are so similar, she can anticipate what I'm going to do. But I think that's crazy. We're nothing alike!

The next two times I saw Luca, it went about the same. I lied to my mom about where I was going, and then I took a cab to see him. Our second date was a movie. Some over-the-top horror movie that normally would have given me nightmares, but since I spent the whole time obsessing over whether or not Luca was going to try and put his arm around me, I hardly noticed the movie. Even with all the blood and guts and screaming. Luca is infinitely more interesting.

And he did, in fact, put his arm around me. It was enough to make me all tingly and loopy for the rest of the flick. Thank god for the darkness of the movie theater, because I must have looked absolutely crazy, grinning giddily while watching a horror movie.

The third date was a few weeks ago. We went to dinner in Harlem, some tiny Italian place where he spoke Italian to all the staff. It was a romantic candlelit meal, complete with accordion music and sparkling grape juice. Afterward, he walked me to my cab and just before I climbed inside, he kissed me.

I sigh to myself thinking about it as I slump against my locker, closing my eyes for a moment. I can't believe how lucky I am. That kiss was amazing, like nothing I've ever experienced before. Yeah, I've been kissed in the past a couple times, but it was always sub-par. Just another boring teenage first to tick off the list. But this kiss with Luca... felt different. Like it was *truly* the first one. Like it meant more than I can even express.

But that was three weeks ago. I haven't seen him since then, and he's only sent me one text message in all that time, about a week after our date. It was short, just "I miss you. See you soon."

I replied, of course, with lightning speed. I've sent him message after message, asking when we can meet again, what's going on, where has he been all this time? But I haven't gotten a single reply. In fact, there's a little voice in the back of my head that has recently started speaking up, chiding me that maybe he doesn't want anything to do with me anymore. I've run through so many scenarios in my head. Maybe I was just a summer fling, and now that school has begun again, he's over me. He's a high school dropout, working full-time as a carpenter with his uncle. He's got his own life path and maybe it doesn't include me. Maybe I was such a bad kisser that he wants to just forget about me. Maybe he found someone else. Maybe he moved away.

All these thoughts plague me during my waking hours and make it very difficult to keep living my life. I've fallen behind on my assignments for the first time in my life, and I've been withdrawn from my friends, unable to really confide in them about what's going on. They're all obsessed with guys from our school— the football captain, the trust fund boy whose dad owns a yacht, the artsy guy whose band might just make it big. I know they wouldn't understand my feelings for Luca. They wouldn't understand the kind of life he lives. Money is everything to them, and they wouldn't get why I'm interested in someone who can't "provide" for me, which is code for "he's not the kind of guy who will make me his beautiful, spoiled trophy wife." If that's what my friends want, then all the power to them. Hell, I used to think that was what I wanted, too.

But not anymore. I know I'm young and we've only seen each other a few times, but I know this is something big. This is real. The way I feel about Luca is real, and it's more important than anything else.

I check my phone for the millionth time. Still nothing. My heart sinks even lower.

I jump at the sound of the school bell ringing to tell me it's time for my next class. I groan and roll my eyes, closing my locker as I start to make my way down the hall to calculus. But one of the ladies from the front office suddenly steps out in front of me and gives me a smile.

"Hi, Serena. We just got a call to say that you're being checked out early today, so you can go ahead out to the parking lot to get picked up, okay? I already took care of the paperwork up front so don't worry about that. And, um, if you need anything just... just call us at the front desk, alright? We can get you a meeting with a counselor or get you an extension on your term papers— whatever you might need," she says, her voice sickly sweet as she pats me sympathetically on the arm. I give her a confused frown.

"What's going on?" I ask suspiciously. "I don't think I'm supposed to be getting checked out today. I don't have a doctor's appointment or anything..."

"Ah, well," she says, her eyes darting around nervously

like she wants to do anything possible to avoid this conversation. "It's official. I don't have any details, but I'm sure everything is just fine. Okay? Have a good day, dear."

She hurries away, leaving me completely lost. My parents wouldn't just check me out of school without warning me first. In fact, they hardly ever pull me out of class for anything less than an emergency. They're really obsessed with my school attendance. And I don't have any messages on my phone. If something was wrong, surely they would text or call me.

Then it occurs to me: maybe this is one of Luca's tricks.

It sounds crazy, sure, but it wouldn't surprise me in the least if Luca somehow found a way to make himself sound official on the phone and get me checked out of school. He told me that back when he was still enrolled, he used to find all kinds of ways to get out of class. Once or twice he even called the front office from a burner phone pretending to be his uncle to check himself out of class for an imaginary dentist's appointment! If he could pull it off then, surely he can still pull it off now. He does have a pretty deep, authoritative voice. I could absolutely believe that he could make himself sound really impressive on the phone with the front desk ladies. He probably had them swooning just from one phone call!

A grin spreads across my face and I hurry out to the parking lot, feeling light on my feet. If this is Luca's work then I will *totally* forgive him for ghosting me these past few weeks. Maybe that was the whole point, letting me stew in silence to build up the surprise! Once I'm outside, I look around, thinking I'll spot Luca skulking around.

But he's nowhere to be seen. In fact, the parking lot is pretty much empty except for a big black sedan slowly snaking its way out of a parking spot and over to the pickup lane in front of me. My stomach turns as I realize that this car is clearly here for me. I try to lift my spirits by telling myself there's a chance Luca somehow wrangled a car for a date with me. Maybe it's a rental. Or just a fancy cab. Who knows?

The car slows to a stop and the passenger side back seat window rolls down. I lean forward a little hesitantly, and to my dismay, Luca is nowhere in sight. A middle-aged man is in the car, and he says simply, "Get in."

I hesitate, my heartbeat picking up. "Um, I-I don't know. I think you might have the wrong person, sir," I reply quietly. But the guy simply stares at me, unblinking.

I try to reason with myself quickly. If this isn't Luca's work, then it must involve my parents. I can't imagine any other scenario. Maybe my parents did, in fact, check me out of class, but there's some reason they're tied up and can't come get me themselves. Besides, some of my dad's associates drive big black company cars like this one. This guy probably knows my dad.

"You're Serena De Laurentis, yes?" the man verifies, one eyebrow raised.

I nod. "Y-Yeah, that's me."

"Then you are exactly who we're here for. Get in."

I hesitate. Nothing about this feels right.

"Your father has been in an accident and we've been sent to collect you. Your mother is already at the hospital with him."

My world goes dark for a moment. I'm helped inside the vehicle by a middle-aged man who is wearing all black.

I try to regain my composure, my control, but I fail and lean back against the seat. I just have to focus on the here and now. I have to take in my surroundings. I look to the man next to me. He's big and burly, with facial features that make him look permanently stern, like he's constantly on the verge of giving someone a serious talking-to. He has thick black eyebrows, a contrast to the thinning dark hair on his head.

Going over the mundane details helps bring me back to earth.

"Wh-what? What happened? Oh my god, is he okay? Is he alive? Oh my god," I ramble, my eyes wide. The man beside me slips an arm around me, which only makes me stiffen up even more.

"He is in critical condition, but we expect he will pull through. Don't worry," the man says to me, giving my shoulders a squeeze that fails to be reassuring. "I'm Claudio, by the way, and our driver is Dino."

"I-I'm so scared," I murmur, staring down at my hands in my lap.

"We're associates of your father, and we're going to take care of everything. We will take you to him. Just remain calm," Dino tells me emphatically.

I nod, falling silent. I can't even think straight. The thought of something terrible happening to my father never crossed my mind. My big, strong, capable, powerful dad. I never imagined anything could ever bring him down. He's always been subtly immortal in my mind, impervious to the dangers of this world. He's a constant. A rock in my life, keeping me tethered to reality. What the hell could have possibly happened to him?

I stare down at my hands in complete numbness for what could have been minutes or hours, as time seems to stop entirely. The world has faded away entirely. Nothing matters. My mind runs in circles and my heart hammers away violently in my chest. I can't wrap my mind around this. I want to ask more questions, demand further details. I want to know what exactly happened, what kind of force of nature could possibly bring my father down. It seems impossible. I never could have predicted this. Why hasn't my mother texted me or called or anything? What kind of horrible chaotic situation would possibly keep her so busy and distracted that she wouldn't think to fill me in on what's going on?

Is my father going to survive? The man said he's in critical condition. That's bad, right? That's really bad. But he's supposed to pull through... I hope. God, I can't lose my dad. Not like this. Not now. I'm too young. I still need him in my life. And the house is only just now getting finished. If my father dies before he has a chance to see his project completed...

Suddenly there's a massive, violent jolt as the car runs over a pothole, and I am ripped out of my thoughts and into the present. I look up from my lap, blinking confusedly, and immediately my stomach flip-flops. Looking out the windows, I can see that we're nowhere near a hospital. We're on the other side of Central Park. I assumed they would have taken my dad to Mount Sinai. That's where several of his well-connected doctor friends work, and he's always said that's where we would go if anything were to happen to us. But we're not going in the direction of Mount Sinai, even though the surroundings do look familiar.

That's when I realize we're heading into my neighborhood, where our Manhattan apartment is located. Why are we going home instead of to the hospital?

"Where are we going? I-I thought we were going to the hospital to see my dad," I protest, panic clear in my wavering voice. The guy beside me, Claudio, gives me another squeeze. I want so badly to wiggle out of his grip. I hate having strangers touch me. My family has never been particularly affectionate, so it's extra weird to have this random guy with his arm around me.

"No worries, *signorina*," Claudio says coolly. "We are just going to swing by your place so you can grab some stuff for your dad. An overnight bag. He's going to be in the hospital for some time, and I'm sure he will deeply appreciate his daughter bringing him some comforts of home."

I relax a little, but *only* a little. This sudden change of plans seems very suspicious to me. Why didn't they tell me we were going to my apartment first? I'm impatient to get to the hospital and be at my father's side right now. The last thing I want to do is take a detour.

But something about the heavy silence hanging over this black company car tells me I should just keep my mouth shut. This is not the time for me to throw a tantrum. My dad is in trouble, and I need to just do as I'm told. Whatever he needs. In fact, I reassure myself, my mom is probably the one who suggested to Dino and Claudio that we go by the house first to get stuff for my dad. She *would* be the type to think of such a thing in a crisis. If these guys are associates of my father's, then I should trust them.

Right?

Still, I really, really hope this detour is a short one. I just want to see my dad.

We pull up to the curb outside my apartment and before Dino starts the laborious process of parallel parking on the street, Claudio opens the side door and lets me out.

"Go ahead up and get started on packing a bag so we can save time. We'll be up in just a moment. Be sure to grab some things for you and your mother, too. I have a feeling you're all going to be hanging around the hospital for a while," he instructs. I nod quickly and rush around to the front of the building, my heart racing as I bolt past the doorman and down the hall to the elevator. I mash the button for the seventeenth floor and pace back and forth in the elevator as it lifts, biting my lip as the tears threaten to spill from my eyes. Now that I have a moment alone, the full gravity of the situation is hitting me. My dad is hurt. Badly. I don't know what happened, but it's serious. My life as I've known it might be changing… forever.

There's a cheerful ding as the elevator reaches my floor. "Come on, come on, hurry up," I murmur impatiently as the doors slowly slide open. I race down the short hallway to our apartment, my hands shaking as I fumble to fit the keys into the lock. Once it's opened, I nearly trip over the threshold in my rush to get inside. I toss the keys onto the coffee table and bolt for my parents' suite to start rummaging through the closet and armoire. I've never put a lot of thought into what kind of clothing my dad wears, and it feels really strange to be going through his stuff, but I try to push the weirdness out of my mind. It doesn't matter right now. Nothing matters except going as fast as I can so we can get out of here and get to the hospital.

I snatch up a black duffel bag from the hallway closet and start throwing a few pressed white shirts and black trousers into it along with a few of my mom's pants and blouses. I rush into their bathroom to grab deodorant, a hair brush, toothpaste, toothbrushes— anything that looks like it might be useful and fit into the bag. Then I remember that I'm supposed to be taking some stuff for myself, too. With a groan I heave the duffel bag onto my shoulder and run across the apartment to my room, tearing the closet doors open. I hear the sound of the entryway door opening and closing, then the jingle of keys in the lock, as though someone is locking the door.

Weird. But I can't let myself be distracted right now. I'm on a mission.

I pull a few t-shirts and pairs of jeans from my wardrobe along with some panties and bras before making my way into my own ensuite bathroom to grab the necessary toiletries. All this time, I can hear the faint sound of Dino and Claudio walking around in the apartment, waiting on me to finish up so we can go. I realize upon looking at the contents of the bag, I probably haven't been the most efficient packer, especially in regards to what my dad might need. So I run back to my parents' room, passing Claudio on the way.

"How many days should I pack for?" I ask him desperately. "I-I have no idea what I'm doing here."

Claudio slowly saunters into the room, looking very much not in any hurry.

"I would suggest packing his best suit. Whichever one you think is most appropriate for a funeral viewing, since he is going to die any second now," he says calmly, fiddling with the cuffs of his sleeves. My heart stops.

"Wh-what? What are you talking about? Don't joke about that," I shoot back, totally dumbfounded by his callous demeanor. "You said he's in critical condition. That means he's not dead yet. He could still make it. How the hell do you know if he's going to die or not?"

He smiles and steps up to me, taking my chin between his fingers as he gazes down into my face. I freeze up at this intrusion of my personal space.

"Because the Costa boys don't make mistakes, *signorina*. We excel at clean, tidy executions. If we say a man is to die, you can be certain he will die," he says cruelly. I jerk away from him, shaking my head.

"No. No, no, no," I mumble, realizing that I've been tricked. I don't know exactly what's going on, but I know I'm in big trouble here. I throw the duffel bag to the ground and make a run for it, darting around Claudio and racing for the bedroom door. But Dino steps through the doorway and closes it behind him just as I approach the threshold, and in one swift movement he grabs my arms and pins them behind me tightly.

"No! Let me go! What did you do to my dad? Where is he? Who the hell are you people?" I shout tearfully, fighting Dino's grip with every ounce of my strength. But I'm deeply outmatched. He's a strong, powerful man, and I'm just a skinny sixteen-year-old girl who's never been in so much as a scuffle. Dino keeps me held in place with almost no effort. It's like trying to fight with a brick wall. Claudio walks around the room, picking up vases and peering at framed photographs of my family on the wall, wrinkling his nose in distaste.

"All of this money he's taken from his brothers and *this* is how he spends it? I should have guessed Armando De Laurentis would have such poor taste. After all, he did marry that spoiled little Gaspari *puttana*," he sneers, knocking a portrait of my mother off the wall. The glass front shatters on the hardwood floor and he gingerly steps over it, crossing back to stand in front of me.

I take a deep breath and let out the loudest scream I can manage, but I'm promptly cut off by Dino's huge hand clapping over my mouth, strangling the sound in my throat. Claudio glares at me with disgust.

"Of course you would be a screamer," he sighs, rolling his black eyes. "Just as petulant and worthless as your mother. *Tale madre, tale figlia.*"

"Where do you want her?" Dino asks. The question sends a prickle of primal fear rippling down my spine. Are they going to kill me?

"Bedroom. Hers," Claudio indicates. Dino nods and drags me, his hand still over my mouth, out of my parents' room and across the apartment to my own quarters. Claudio follows slowly, closing the doors behind us as we go. Once we're in my room, he snaps his fingers to get my attention. When I look over at him, my eyes widen. He's holding a small dagger.

"I'm going to have my associate here take his hand off of your mouth. I trust that you will be quiet. If you do scream, I will have no qualms about cutting out that pretty little tongue. You won't need it anyway," he threatens. "Are you going to be obedient?"

I reluctantly nod as much as I can manage under Dino's grip.

"*Bene,*" Claudio says. He waves his hand and Dino takes his palm off my face.

I stay quiet for a moment, proving that I won't scream.

"*Brava ragazza,*" he croons. "You see? Things work much more smoothly if you just behave, *signorina*. We don't want to have to lay hands on you... well, actually that is a lie. I would *love* to touch you. But I would be gentle. Probably." A sick smile spreads across his ugly face.

"What do you want with me?" I ask softly, my voice breaking. There's no stopping the tears now. There's no point. I know I've lost this battle before I even got a proper chance to fight back. I'm helpless here. I'm useless.

"Oh, it's a pity you even have to be involved. But if you are looking for someone to blame, you would do best to blame the dead. This is all your father's doing," Claudio begins, obviously taking great delight in telling me that my father is dead. I don't want to believe him. I want to think he's lying to me, just trying to upset me. But something tells me he's telling the truth about this.

My father is dead. My father is dead.

"What do you mean?" I press on, gritting my teeth. The tears roll down my cheeks in hot lines. Claudio heaves a wistful sigh.

"Well, for many years we considered Armando a brother. A good man. He was loyal, trustworthy even. But something changed. He became too greedy. He married the Gaspari girl and had a daughter and suddenly his priorities shifted. He no longer worked for the good of the brotherhood. He put his own family above us, his original family. His *real* family. He earned good money for us in the beginning, and we all prospered. But then do you know what he did? He started to keep it for himself. Lying to the Costa family. Squirreling away money that was not rightfully his. He betrayed us. For years. We are not without compassion, *signorina*. We gave him many, many chances to redeem himself, to come clean and return to the fold. But he continued in his traitorous ways. He was foolish, complacent. He got too comfortable," Claudio spits angrily.

"He thought we would forgive him again and again," Dino adds. "Your father was nothing but a snake! Running illicit business right under our noses, using our turf, our rules, our backing to build his fortune without cutting his brothers in on the spoils. We don't operate that way."

"No. No, we do not," Claudio cuts back in, shaking his head. "He was a liability and a thief and he had to be eliminated. How do you kill a snake in your garden, Dino?"

"You cut him with a rake," Dino answers, almost gleefully.

"All those years and no back-pay," Claudio swears, making a fist. "We aren't bad men, *signorina*. But we are debt collectors. And this kind of debt cannot be paid with purely money. We claim a life. This debt is payable with blood."

"So, if you've already taken my father," I start, nearly sobbing through the words, "what the hell do you want from *me*? Are you going to kill me, too? If so, just go ahead. You've already taken everything from me. I don't have any money for you. I can't... I can't fix this."

Claudio laughs derisively. "Oh, maybe not. But you can certainly suck some of the poison out of the wound your traitorous father left in our side."

Dino bursts out laughing. "Oh yes, *that* you can definitely do."

"You'll pay for your father's mistakes by whatever means necessary. You may not have any money to pay the debt, but you certainly have something else to offer."

"That is one jewel we can repossess. One thing your father cannot keep hidden from us."

My blood runs cold. Maybe they aren't going to kill me. But what they're hinting at… well, it almost seems worse.

No, it *is* worse.

I would sooner die.

Claudio walks over to the closet and slides the doors open, digging through my clothing.

"I've never been much of a clotheshorse. Dino, release the girl so she can help me pick out an ensemble that will best show off her assets," Claudio instructs. Then, glaring at me with a sickening grin on his face, he adds, "You've got a big night tonight."

SEVEN YEARS AGO

I throw Giovanni to the ground and fall down after him, getting my arms through his as he thrashes and swears at me. The group around us cheers for me or urges Giovanni to get his shit together.

Giovanni's tough, though, and he works his way out of my grip in the dirt and tries to get the upper hand on me, and we grapple as dust gets kicked up. Our work shirts are already stained brown, and we've breathed as much sawdust as dirty air. This is nothing.

We're in the little yard-space behind Uncle Carlo's workshop, and by the way things look right now, you'd think it's a regular community picnic of Italians.

Some of the other guys around my age are watching us wrestle, waiting for their turn to take on the winner. They're alright guys. I got into my share of serious fights with them the first few months I was in this big new country, but sometimes a bloody lip and a good fight are all you need to make a solid friend.

And the girls aren't far away. Most of them are Italians, but some of them are more local, come to see how we have a good time in the old country. We boys like showing off for them, and they sure as hell seem to like watching. A few of them are cheering us on, especially Giovanni's sweetheart.

I hate to make her man disappoint her, but I've got something to prove to these second-generation kids!

Giovanni has his knee in my stomach for a moment, and I almost think he's about to get the better of me. Just as he starts to try and pull us over and pin me down, though, I remember a trick my uncle taught me, and I move *just so* in his arms, making Giovanni lose his grip and giving me just enough advantage to turn him over on his stomach and wrench his arm behind his back.

"Fuck!" he groans, and he taps the ground to the cheers of some of the crowd around us as I stand up, holding my arms out and strutting around with a big, stupid grin on my face. It's a strut that's gotten me in more fights than I'd like to admit, but Giovanni and I are on good terms, and he's a pretty easygoing guy when it's all said and done.

As I put my hands on my hips and let myself breathe, raising my eyebrows at some of the girls cheering and clapping for me, I see past them to the handful of tables, where some of the older adults are hanging out.

Teenagers aren't the only ones who spend afternoons behind Uncle Carlo's shop. With a few tables, some decks of cards, and some homemade limoncello, Uncle Carlo managed to turn this little yard into a regular community center.

It's not unlike back home. Back in Taranto, we're all just a bunch of workers and workers' kids, so it doesn't take much for us to figure out how to have a good time with what we've got. And days like this, I'm starting to see why Uncle Carlo likes this country as much as he does.

These wrestling matches happen pretty fast and loose. Anyone who wants a turn dives in, and every now and then we get some grudge matches going, but we're all pretty good-natured. If anything gets too heated, we laugh it off over a drinking match when the adults aren't around, or if they're nice enough to turn a blind eye.

My next opponent is a big guy named Ricky, but the fight with Giovanni hasn't come close to wearing me out.

The fight is a back-and-forth of him trying to get a hold of me and me being too quick to let him. Just when I think I've got a hold of him, he surprises me, and vice-versa. Even though I've been here a while, there's still some national pride that goes into these fights. We're all Italians, but I'm fresh off the boat, so to speak. I've got to show off how we do things in southern Italy, and they want to see if they measure up to a hot-blooded European like me.

Their parents all tell them stories about how tough people in the old country are, and I aim to prove them all right.

The fight ends with me getting up under Ricky and suplexing him into the dirt, and the crowd of teens loses their shit. Apparently wrestling is pretty popular on TV here, so theatrics like that are impressive.

Ricky groans on the ground, and I stand up with a confident smirk on my face. There's no way I'm not the clear winner after that.

"Jesus, Luca, glad I got outta the ring before you turned that shit up!" Giovanni laughs as I step to the side of our little circle of friends, and he claps me on the back.

"Your mug's already ugly enough, don't wanna mess it up more," I say with a grin, ribbing him in the side, and he punches me in the arm as our friends laugh.

"Fuck, you've gotta get your uncle to teach us some of that ex-military shit!" Ricky says as he gets himself to his feet and dusts himself off. Ricky's big, but he's a softie deep down. He's already working in his parents' bakery, and he'll be happy to stay there. "You got an unfair advantage!"

"Hell, Ricky, if you wanna get your ass thrown down

again, all you gotta do is ask," I say back as Ricky makes his way over to me, and in response, he grins and wraps a big arm around my neck and grinds his knuckles into my head. I jab my rib into his stomach, and we break apart, everyone laughing.

"I wouldn't mind seeing that!" calls one of the girls from the other side as the circle starts to break up, girlfriends reuniting with their boys and some of the boys passing out beers to us.

I pry off one of the caps with my hand while I shake my head laughing, but Giovanni calls back, "Oh no, our boy Luca's only got eyes for that hot thing from the nice part of town!"

I punch at Giovanni while some of the guys laugh, and the girl rolls her eyes.

Serena and I hardly ever see each other, but all it took was someone to get one glance at us talking before rumors started spreading like wildfire. If you asked half of them, they'd tell you I was planning to steal her daddy's car and run away with her upstate at a moment's notice.

And honestly? If that spoiled little rich girl asked me to, I don't know if I could say no.

Serena De Laurentis is the *definition* of off-limits. She comes from a totally different world, her family is miles above me in the social ranks of the Italian community, and best of all, I'm just a dirty worker getting paid under the table at her daddy's new house.

Maybe that's what makes it all the sweeter the few times we do get together.

I don't even know her that well, but I feel like there's something about her that I just can't stay away from. She's stuck in my mind, teasing me even when we're away from each other. Rich girls are trouble, everyone knows that... and maybe all that's what gets my blood going all the more.

"I gotta see this gal they keep talking about," Ricky says,

crossing his arms. "An American girl who can get our native Italian's attention? Damn, she must be something."

"You gotta teach her some Italian and bring her to one of these things, man!" Giovanni says, and I roll my eyes.

"And let you sons-of-bitches get a load of her? I don't think so," I say jokingly. "But nah, her dad's an asshole, there's no way I could get her away from her... shit, what do rich people do for fun? Galas?"

"Opera," says another guy with a knowing nod. "My brother's a cook at that opera house they got, says all the girls there are decked out in dresses more expensive than his car."

"Think our boy Luca's a baritone, or...?" Giovanni starts, but I make like I'm about to punch him and he trails off, laughing.

While we talk, I've noticed a black sedan rolling up out front out of the corner of my eye. I glance over to Uncle Carlo and the other adults, and I see that he's noticed too.

There's a frown on Uncle Carlo's face.

A few of the guys notice where I'm looking, and we watch the doors open, and a few big guys step out. Two of them aren't dressed too differently from us, with simple jeans and white sleeveless shirts that show off some big-ass muscles and tattoos. The third guy, on the other hand, looks fancy. Nice shoes, black slacks, and a gray button-down shirt with the sleeves rolled up to his forearms. That guy has a sharp look in his eyes that I don't like, set under thick brown eyebrows and thinning hair.

I look back to the adults, and I notice the mood has died. Some of them look uncomfortable in their chairs, card games have ended, and Uncle Carlo is getting up with a grim look on his face to go meet the men.

I don't have to be told what that could mean.

Mafia.

My jaw is set tight as they make their way up the dirt

driveway. If the mafia is bad here in America, it's way worse back home, especially in southern Italy. The mafia acts like their own government, running everyone's lives and dealing brutally with anyone who steps out of line. They're a cancer, and they're strangling the whole country. I was raised to hate them. I was raised to fear them, too, but I'm not afraid of anything.

Because these bastards live on fear.

"Must have missed my invitation to your little party," the man in the nice outfit says as he exchanges an awkward hug with Uncle Carlo. If he's involved, then it's my business too, I decide. I hand my beer to Giovanni, who gives me a concerned glance, but I shake my head and push past him to approach the group.

"Just winding down a little after work, boys," Uncle Carlo says with a weary smile to them. "I figured you bunch would be starting your busy days right about now, is all."

"Ain't that considerate," says the well-dressed man, who looks at me as I approach. He smiles, and Uncle Carlo follows his gaze, shooting me a look that says I should have stayed in the crowd.

"Well well, you're getting bigger every day, aren't you, Luca?" says the well-dressed man.

"There a problem here?" I say, and the two big guys with the well-dressed man crack smiles as he raises his eyebrows.

"Fuck me, Carlo, is that how you teach your nephew how to talk to guests?"

Uncle Carlo flexes his fist, then looks to me. "Luca, this is Claudio," he says, nodding to the well-dressed man. "I don't think you've had the pleasure of meeting."

"No, but I know you," Claudio says, grinning at me. I don't return the look. "Look at you, you've got your uncle's courage."

"Is there something I can help you with?" Uncle Carlo says with a weary look at Claudio.

"Actually, all I came here for was a word in private with your Luca here," he says, and both me and Uncle Carlo's eyes widen in surprise.

"What?"

"What?" I say in tandem.

"It's family business," Claudio says to Uncle Carlo, "I'm sure you can appreciate that."

"If it's family business, then I should-" he starts, but I interrupt him.

"It's alright," I say, glaring daggers at Claudio, "we'll talk in the shop. No big deal. I'll come back when we're finished." I know there'll be trouble if we don't play ball with these fuckers, and there are too many vulnerable people around for me to be okay with that.

"Good man," Claudio says, patting me on the shoulder, and it takes a lot of energy for me not to whip around and bust this asshole's lip open.

The shop is pretty simple inside. Carpentry equipment and wood are laying all over the place, but it's pretty well organized. Uncle Carlo has always been tight about keeping things presentable. I know, because I spent my first week and a half here cleaning up the shop with him while he talked me out of running away.

I ran anyway, but I came back.

I walk with the three guys into the shop, and I lead them to a counter that I lean on, facing them with crossed arms and a set jaw. "So?"

Claudio is looking around the shop, though. He has an annoying, amused smile on his face. "Wow, your uncle really put together something respectable here, you know?"

I don't say anything.

"Bet he's teaching you all the ropes, too," Claudio says,

finally making his way toward me, his goons flanking him obediently. "And just look at those hands of yours—you'll make a fine carpenter one day, kid."

"There a point to this?" I say curtly.

The kind expression fades from Claudio's face a little, and he puts his hands in his pockets, stepping a little further. "I see you've got your father's attitude, too. *That* might be something your uncle needs to work on a little harder, kid."

"How do you know dad?" I say, feeling my patience shorten by about half. I don't like where this is going already, and he's hardly said anything.

"Just through the family business," Claudio says, that crocodile grin spreading back over his face. "Which is what I want to talk to you about today."

"The hell you are," calls a voice from the back of the shop, and Claudio turns his head to see Uncle Carlo storming in, red-faced. "For fuck's sake, Claudio, he's only sixteen!"

Despite Uncle Carlo's entrance, Claudio is unfazed, and he looks back to me. "Well I'll be damned, your body's outgrowing your age. That doesn't change things, though," he says dismissively as Uncle Carlo approaches, but the goons give him a look that says he's not going to come any further.

"Look, Claudio," he says, breathing heavily and regaining his composure. "I don't know what you're here for, but if it's got to do with his father, you can take it up with me."

"My orders are clear, actually," Claudio says, "and it runs a little thicker than blood." Claudio pulls up a stool and sits down, resting his arms on his legs, hands clasped as he looks up at me. "Luca, I'm sure your father was very happy to be able to send you here to America," he says, and I narrow my eyes at him as he smiles. "Land of opportunity, you know? You're better off here, getting everything you need from your uncle and his shop here. Can't blame a man for doing that, the old country's no place for a bright boy like you."

"Get to the point," I say, and Claudio gives a laugh.

"You're as impatient as your father, too. See, plane tickets aren't free, Luca, nor is a passport and all the other nice things that just happened to fall into place to let you get over here."

I can see Uncle Carlo's eyes widening, and I have a bad feeling in my gut. Claudio continues.

"Your dad borrowed a nice little chunk of money from my friends back in Italy. All out of the love of his heart, of course, but he's fallen on some hard times, and well, he's having trouble making his payments."

"I've got money," I say quickly, standing up with a furrowed brow, but Claudio and his goons laugh.

"You don't have the kind of money he owes," he says simply, "and even if you did, this is a matter of reputation, you see."

I feel my muscles tensing as I look at all three men. "If you plan on shooting me, you'd better not miss."

"Don't be stupid," Claudio says, standing up. "My boss here in America has spoken up for you, Luca. We take care of our own. He has a solution that my friends back in Italy have agreed to—something that will remind your father to be timely with his payments *and* help me out, all without spilling a drop of your family's blood."

I stare him down, and neither of us breaks eye contact.

"Now, I know you don't like the idea of working for us, Luca," he says coolly, "but this offer isn't really negotiable. I have one job for you—just one. You'll do it, and I know you'll do it well, and then we can forget all about this little meeting and us big bad criminals," he says, making scare-quotes with his fingers.

I take a step forward so I can lean into Claudio's face when I pronounce slowly, "Fuck. You."

The smile leaves Claudio's face. He takes a deep breath, then gestures to one of his goons. In the blink of an eye, the goon whips out a gun and points it at Uncle Carlo, who freezes, eyes wide. "Claudio, don't do this," he warns, putting his hands up.

"Listen, Luca," Claudio says in a still tone to me, folding his hands behind his back. "I appreciate your spirit, I really do. But this is a done deal. And if I go back to my boss and let him know how rudely you've been treating us, he'll have to tell my friends in Italy that our deal's off. And that will be *very* embarrassing."

Every muscle in my body is tense, and I'm ready to fight. I'd throw myself at them all right now if there weren't a gun trained on Uncle Carlo.

"You have a lot to learn about patience, Luca," says Claudio, his dead gaze cold as ice. "So I'll put this in terms even a punk-ass teenager like you can understand. You're going to do a job for us, and if you don't, not only will you have to use this carpentry shop to make a coffin for your uncle here, but my associates in Italy will start mailing you your mom and dad's fingers."

His cold face splits into the most chilling grin I've ever seen. I exchange one tense look with Uncle Carlo before Claudio speaks again.

"So, what do you say?"

SERENA

SEVEN YEARS AGO

*I*t's cold.

I can hear the rain hammering against the cracked window pane, smell the foul odor of damp trash down in the street. Sirens wail in the distance, but I don't dare allow myself to believe they might be coming to save me. Nobody is coming to save me. There's nobody left who even could. My father... my hero, my rock, he's gone. And he's never coming back from where those evil *Mafiosi* sent him. I grit my teeth and feel my whole body tense up as I curl my hands into tight fists. I need to stay calm. I need to accept that this—whatever this is—is my life now.

I can't save myself. And none of my friends know where I am or what I'm about to do. I haven't had any chance to talk to anyone, not with Claudio and Dino shadowing my every step and monitoring my every breath. They took my cell phone. I have no idea where it is now. For all I know they've used it to tell everybody in my contacts list to fuck off and never speak to me again. Anything to isolate me further. I wonder if they did. If so, maybe they sent a message to the last number Luca was using. Not that it matters. He's probably moved on to a new number by now, and besides, he hasn't shown any interest in me for weeks. I shouldn't count on him or anyone else. I'm all alone in this, and I better get used to that.

I'm standing in a dimly lit motel room, the blinking neon vacancy sign sending faint strobe lights through the thin curtains in shades of sickly pale green. Across the room is a rickety-looking bed with a lumpy mattress and threadbare brown sheets. The light bulb in the bedside lamp flickers ominously every few minutes like it's ready to burn out any second. There are stains on the carpet I don't even want to think about, pools of rust red and dark gold. Who the hell knows what all has gone on in this room? Or in any room of this shitty motel? I don't want to know, but I have a feeling I'm about to find out. I'm going to get a taste of something horrible soon. It's coming.

My mouth is so dry. I wish I could get a glass of water or something, but I don't have any cups here, and even if I wanted to try and collect tap water in my hands to drink, something tells me the water here probably isn't quite up to drinking standards. So I just swallow hard and stare up at the ceiling tiles, trying to breathe slowly and calm my racing heart. The tears burn in my eyes but I can't let them fall. It won't help. And Claudio was very emphatic about keeping myself pretty. I need to prevent my eyeliner from running down my cheeks.

I blink rapidly to stem the tears and hurry into the creepy little ensuite bathroom, slamming my hand against the clicker light switch. One of the bulbs over the mirror pops, sending tiny shards of thin glass flying, and I let out a shriek as I fall backward into the tub, tearing the shower curtain down as I go. I sit there stunned for a moment, my bare legs sticking up out of the tub while my head pounds from the pain of knocking it against the porcelain. I heave a deep breath and reach back to make sure I'm not bleeding. Thankfully, I'm not.

"That's gonna bruise," I murmur to myself as I gingerly climb back out of the tub, trying not to step on any of the shattered glass. In this moment, I'm grateful for the ugly, oversized black platform heels Claudio forced me to wear. If I were barefoot right now, I'd probably have my feet all sliced up. I crunch across the glass to lean over the counter and survey my face in the filth-streaked mirror. My eyes are pink-rimmed from crying and even my designer mascara and eyeliner can't conceal how tired and broken I look. I use my pinkie finger to fix a slight smudge of the dark red Yves Saint Laurent coloring my lips. It feels so strange, wearing my expensive makeup and slinky La Perla lingerie under my little black Moschino dress in a disgusting, barely-functional roach motel like this. I bought these things to impress my classmates and fellow fledgling socialites, my high-end friends. Shopping on Fifth Avenue was just part of my persona, the reputation I built for myself. It was expected of me then. Just a given. The lingerie I bought a couple weeks ago in anticipation of the time I would inevitably find myself stripping down for Luca. It was a distant dream then, something I suspected would happen once we'd been together for a year or so. Once things smoothed out and we could see each other more regularly. I was already planning a life with him. Sixteen years old and in love and so, so stupid.

Now I just want to rip off the lacy bra and panties and toss them in the dumpster below the window of this horrible motel room. I can't believe how different I am now from the girl I was just a few days ago. I still had dreams then. I was so certain of how my life was going to play out. Even though it had been weeks since I last heard from Luca, I was still holding out hope that he would show up and sweep me off my feet. I was thinking about the future, not realizing that even my present was in jeopardy. Everything I had, everything I was, I took it for granted.

Not anymore. Maybe this is payback for how wonderful my life was up until a few days ago. I was so fortunate, with my loving parents and my fancy apartment and my designer clothes. I never wanted for anything. I can admit it now easily: I was spoiled.

I guess it makes sense that now I'm being punished. Good luck or good karma or whatever you want to call it… can't last forever, can it?

It used to be that my job was just to get good grades, make myself appealing to colleges, maintain my looks, and stay out of any major trouble. I used to think all of that was so boring, so mundane. Now I would give anything to go back in time and slide back into that comfortable, dull life.

Tonight I have a different responsibility. Claudio drilled it into my head.

I am here to seduce a client. Well, not so much a client, as a victim of the mafia. A man who owes them money and has a penchant for underage girls. In other words, a complete and total scum bag in every imaginable way. I'm posing as a sex worker tonight, pretending to be something I absolutely am not. For god's sake, I'm a virgin. I mean, I've seen movies. I've read books and magazines. I haven't been living under a rock or in a convent for my whole life. I get the idea, the general setup I'm in right now. But I'm not prepared for it.

Of course, Claudio told me that I won't have to actually go through with it. I'm just supposed to act as bait, lure the guy into a false sense of security. I'm supposed to distract him and make him think he's in for a treat.

I shudder involuntarily. Ugh. *Gross* doesn't even begin to cover it.

And once the guy is totally vulnerable, caught up in the game, Claudio said that's when the Costa boys, his associates, will swoop in to "take care" of the guy. I honestly don't want to know what exactly that entails. I just hope my part in this will have ended by that point. It's bad enough I have to pretend to seduce the guy. I know I don't have what it takes to actually hurt him or anything. I just hope to god he doesn't touch me.

But that's too much to hope for, I think. And I doubt that tonight will be the end of my servitude to the Costa family. It's too easy. They've caught me, killed my father, distanced me from my mother—I have no idea what's happened to her—and they have so much rage toward my family. I know they won't be finished with me after tonight. Who knows how many more nights I'll have to do this very same thing?

Or worse?

Claudio and Dino didn't explicitly tell me I'm going to have to work for them more after tonight, but I can put two and two together. If my dad really did take that much money away from them, then surely one night isn't enough to repay his debts. They probably just think they can trick me into thinking this is the only thing I'll have to do for them. I know they think I'm stupid. And maybe I am. For believing that my father was a good, clean guy, that our good fortune was well-earned and deserved. For thinking that my amazing life could go on forever that way.

Nope. Tonight is just the beginning.

That thought makes me feel weak. Lost. Full of despair. My life as I knew it is over. This new, horrible chapter is on page one, and I dread reading the rest of the book. Sure, I could try to make a run for it. Climb out the window and shimmy down to the street. Beg somebody to let me in their car and drive me to the police station. But I know I wouldn't make it that far. I can't see where they are, but I know Claudio and Dino are close by, watching and waiting for the moment to strike. They'd stop me before my shoes even touched the pavement. There is no escape.

A bright light flashes through the window and I rush over to look outside. There's a beat-up truck pulling into a parking spot below. A dark green truck. The driver steps out and my heart sinks as I recognize that he fits the description of the mark for tonight. A tallish man with a potbelly. Balding. A graying mustache on his paunchy face.

That's the guy.

My pulse quickens and I start to panic. It's happening. It's really happening. I feel my knees buckle beneath me and I stagger backward, grabbing hold of the chipped counter of the kitchenette, trying to steady myself. I close my eyes and count slowly to ten. It's something I read online once, that when you're having a panic attack you're supposed to try and clear your mind and just focus on counting. Focus on the numbers. Slow your breathing down. Find your center and push away your surroundings.

But there's no pushing away this world around me. I glance out the window again. The man is gone, clearly on his way through the building to get to me. "Oh god," I mumble, nervously tucking the loose tendrils of hair back behind my ears. My hair is pulled back into a messy half-updo, which Claudio suggested. I wonder how I'm supposed to act when the guy gets here. I know he's going to knock five times and then I let him in. I'm supposed to smile. Be coy, but available. Vulnerable, but not easy. I'm supposed to be the innocent young girl, but still be sexy.

I'm not sure I know how to do any of that. But there's a knock at the door, followed by four more crisp knocks, and I know I have to try. It's time.

With my blood rushing in my ears I walk over and undo the three locks, opening the door to allow the man inside. I plaster a smile on my face and greet him.

"Good evening," I say, willing my voice to stay strong. I have to act natural.

The man steps inside and immediately looks me up and down, his eyes drinking in my tight little body, my breasts squished together in my fancy bra, the glittery lotion on my skin, the way the straps of my black dress slip ever so seductively off my shoulders when I shrug.

"You're much prettier than what I'm used to," the guy says lewdly. "The agency did really good this time. All along I thought they was sending me their best, but it looks like they've been holdin' out on me. You new or somethin'?"

For a moment my voice seems to have disappeared. The guy stares at me expectantly.

"Oh, uh, yes. I-I'm brand new. Just started," I reply. "You're—you're the first."

A huge grin splits his face and he crosses his arms over his broad chest. "Oh, I am, am I?"

I nod and smile, taking a few steps backward. "Yep. Yes. So if I'm a little nervous, that's why. I-I'm sorry if you were expecting someone more experienced."

"No, no. The greener the better," he says, a predatory flash in his beady eyes. "I've been hopin' for an opportunity to break a girl in. It's an honor."

"Oh. Well, I'll do my best not to disappoint," I respond, desperately looking for some way to stall. It occurs to me how little I know of the plan tonight. How far am I supposed to let this go before Dino or Claudio or whoever is out there steps in to take over? I'm not prepared for this.

"Well? Let's get started then. I paid for an hour and I intend to make every second count," the guy remarks, rubbing his hands together. I freeze up, glancing around nervously. But I have to try to be calm. If this guy catches on and realizes something is up, who knows how badly this could turn out. If I let the mafia down… I hate to think what they'll do to me.

"Okay. Yeah, um, just m-make yourself comfortable," I suggest with a smile. I throw in a wink for good measure and gesture toward the bed. To my relief, he follows my instruction and walks over to sit down on the edge of the mattress, starting to take off his boots.

But when he begins to unzip his slacks, my stomach turns. I feel like I might vomit. This is all getting far too real now. I can't do this. I can't.

But I have to.

"Wait!" I interject, and the guy looks up at me with a confused, slightly put-off look on his ugly face. "Um, let me… let me dance for you first."

The guy sits up and fixes me with a suspicious look. Then he shrugs. "You're a little awkward. I can tell you're a beginner. But why not. Go on then."

With my heart racing, I take a deep breath and start to sway, shaking my hair down out of its updo to fall in loose waves around my shoulders. I turn around and move my hips slowly, shaking my ass for this complete stranger. I move this way for a minute or so, turning in circles, raising my arms up over my head, tousling my hair, blowing kisses. I feel incredibly stupid, like it's obvious how inexperienced I am. I know this isn't going to keep him entertained for long. After all, he didn't come here for an amateur burlesque show. He came here to fuck me.

I keep hoping that any second now, the Costa guys are going to burst through the door and end this charade before it goes much further. But the seconds tick by with no sign of the cavalry. I'm alone here with this guy, and I have to up the ante or he'll get suspicious. Or worse… angry.

So I bite the bullet and start sliding the straps of my Moschino dress down my shoulders, peering back at him coyly. I bite my lip and look down at the floor, trying to glance up at him through my eyelashes like a sexy girl in a movie. The guy is watching me with a hungry expression on his face, his jaw twitching slightly as though he's trying to rein himself in. I rotate back to face him, curling my fingertips over the bottom hem of my dress to slowly slide it up my thighs, exposing myself in tiny increments. I'm doing my best, even though I have no real idea what is supposed to happen here, but I can tell it's not enough.

He wants more. He's expecting *much* more than this.

"Take it off," the man says gruffly, waving his hand in a forbidding gesture.

"I-I, uh, I'm a little shy," I stammer quietly, feeling my face turning bright pink. His eyebrows furrow together and he narrows his eyes.

"Shy? In this business? You'll get over that fast," he comments. Then he stands up, a smile pulling at the corners of his mouth. "I can help you get over it."

As he takes a step toward me, I reflexively take a step back. A flash of anger flickers in his eyes and he walks toward me more aggressively. I fall back and shake my head, feeling my stomach turn with dread and anxiety.

"No. Please don't," I murmur helplessly. It's getting hard to breathe, my heart is pounding so fast and hard. "I-I'm a virgin."

The man stops in his tracks for a moment, staring at me blankly. Then he grins, a shark-like, ravenous smirk. "You know, I've had other girls feed me that line before, but I never believed any of 'em. But you... I believe you. I bet you really *are* a virgin, aren't you?"

Instantly I realize that was the wrong thing to say. It was a reflex, an instinct to plead for mercy. But it's had the opposite of the effect I hoped for. He doesn't pity me... he just wants me even more. He *wants* a virgin.

"I'm sorry. I can't do this," I whisper, my throat tightening so it's difficult to even get a word out. The guy shakes his head and quickly closes the space between us, his hands falling on my shoulders in a tight grip.

"I didn't pay for an hour of teasing and moping," he snarls, leaning in close to my face. "I paid to fuck a pretty girl for an hour. Do whatever I want with her. I don't give a shit if you're a virgin. I don't care who you are or what you want. For this hour, you belong to me."

He easily rips the straps of my dress and starts yanking it down my body as I whimper, tears springing to my eyes. This is it. I can't fight him. It occurs to me that maybe this was the plan all along. I'm not here as bait. Claudio and Dino brought me here to be punished, to be some gross, horrible man's sex toy. I bet they've got some candid camera set up somewhere in this shitty motel room so they can watch, get their sick, sadistic pleasure out of watching me suffer.

The john scoops me up and throws me over his shoulder, roughly carrying me across the room and tossing me onto the lumpy mattress. The tears fall heavily now, and I don't make any effort to stop them. It doesn't matter if I cry or not. This guy is going to fuck me anyway.

He starts to crawl over me, stripping off his jeans as he comes my way.

In this moment, I wish I were dead.

Bang!

I scream and scramble backward against the headboard in fear at the deafening sound from across the room. The man turns around, bewildered, and we both see it at the same time: someone has burst through the door, through the various deadlocks, and is barreling across the room toward the bed.

"What the hell," mutters my attacker, swiftly pulling his jeans back up and reaching down into one of the back pockets to pull out a small, shiny metal object. My heart does a somersault as I realize it's a gun. But before he can turn and aim, the dark figure quickly grabs the john by both arms and jerks him off the bed, wrestling him down onto the filthy carpet. The gun goes flying across the room, sliding across the linoleum of the kitchenette area. I flatten myself down on the bed, my instincts warning me that it might go off, like it does on television. Amazingly, it doesn't.

"What the fuck is this? Some kind of sting operation?" shouts the john. He protests furiously, flinging his legs and arms around in a vain attempt to throw off his assailant, changing his story every couple seconds. "I wasn't gonna do anythin' to her! That girl... she—she's my daughter. No harm, no foul. Okay, she's not my daughter, but we—we're on a date! It's all consensual, I met her at a bar. I ain't a pedophile, man! And she said she was eighteen!"

I'm so in shock that it takes me a full ten seconds to register what's happening. I went from being in fear of imminent sexual assault to complete and utter confusion. I don't know if this is following the script Claudio led me to expect. And the man who burst into the room isn't Claudio. It isn't Dino.

But he's not a stranger either.

I realize with a jolt that nearly knocks me backward.

It's Luca.

~

*L*uca has my disgusting john pinned to the floor, the guy's flabby arms twisted behind his back with his face pressed into the stained carpet. I quickly move closer to the end of the bed to see what's going on. Just in time to see Luca calmly, smoothly wrap his hands over each side of the guy's head and twist it violently, fatally to the left with a sickening crack.

"Oh my god!" I shriek, feeling bile rise in my throat as I clap a hand over my mouth. Luca looks up at me, his green eyes flashing aggressively. He doesn't look like the romantic, attentive guy I shared a candlelit dinner with weeks ago. He doesn't look like the sweet, smooth-talking boy who poured me an illegal drink in the back of a construction van over the summer. This Luca is a different one. A stranger. Someone I should never be involved with.

He looks... like a cold-blooded killer.

Who is this guy? Where is the Luca I fell for? Have I been wrong this whole time? Is he involved with all this... this crap? Is he a mobster, too?

But then, just as quickly as it arrived, the darkness in his eyes fades away and he blinks a few times, clearly confused. He cocks his head to one side, never looking away from my face.

"Serena...?" he murmurs, like he just can't seem to understand how he's seeing me in this context. Like he doesn't believe I'm really here. The feeling is mutual.

He stands up, brushing off his hands on his dark pants. He's wearing all black, with a hooded sweatshirt hugging his muscles. He slowly steps around the fresh corpse on the floor and walks over to the side of the bed, his eyes locked onto mine. But I'm still afraid. I just watched the boy I thought was my prince charming kill a man with his bare hands. Sure, the guy was a slimy scumbag and it's probably better that he's no longer a threat to the community, but... still. That's generally an issue for the justice system to handle, not some handsome teenaged vigilante.

"Serena, what are you doing here? How did you—? Is this—?" he asks, shaking his head in confusion but never able to finish a whole question. I can feel the tears wet and sticky on my cheeks as I scoot backward away from him.

"Is he—is he dead?" I whisper, my whole body shivering. It isn't cold. I'm just terrified.

Luca nods. "Yes. He's dead. Clean and easy. That fucker can't hurt you anymore. Did he—did he hurt you?"

"He tried to," I answer meekly.

"*Merda*, Serena. I wish I'd gotten here faster," he says bitterly. He reaches out to touch my face but I shy away. I can see the hurt in his eyes. "You're safe now. It's okay."

"I'm sorry, but you just described a murder as *clean and easy*," I snap, my voice muffled slightly by sobs. "I-I don't understand what is going on. How did you find me?" I question, feeling totally confused.

"Don't worry about that right now. You're shivering. Where are your clothes?"

I point wordlessly across the room to the ripped and torn Moschino dress crumpled up on the floor. Luca looks over at it and sighs, his jaw tightening with anger. "I'm so sorry he did that to you," he says softly. Turning back to me, he adds, "Take my hoodie."

He takes it off and gently hands it out for me to take, respecting my boundaries. I put it on and slide off the bed to stand up. The sweatshirt is huge on me, nearly falling to my knees. I zip it all the way up to my neck. Luca and I stare at each other for a long moment, him too afraid to frighten me further, and me trying to decide how I feel. I'm so confused and overwhelmed. Is he one of them? Everything is happening so quickly and I don't know who I can trust.

But right now, I know what I need.

I race around to the other side of the bed, flinging myself into Luca's arms. He holds me tightly as I sob, running his hands down my back, smoothing my hair. "It's okay. I'm never going to let those fuckers hurt you again. You're safe with me. I don't know how this happened, but I'm damn well going to fix it."

I push back to look up into his face. He's gazing down at me with immense pain in his green eyes. Those beautiful eyes. "I'm going to make this right," he says resolutely.

There's a soft patter of footsteps and I seize up with terror, leaning around to look toward the door. There are two men coming in, walking softly. They're also dressed in all black, but carrying duffel bags which they set down on the floor. They pull their sleeves back to reveal bright yellow gloves, like the kind our maid wears to clean the bathrooms.

"Luca," I murmur, frightened.

"It's okay. They're the sweepers. They're just here to clean up the scene, make all of this go away so nobody finds out what happened," he explains calmly.

I have so many questions. Why is he so calm? How does he know what's going on? Why is he involved with something this horrible? How many times has he done this before?

And most terrifyingly, what does this mean for us?

"Come on," Luca says, interrupting my dark train of thought. "Let's get you out of here."

He puts an arm around me protectively and leads me out of the room. As we walk out, one of the sweepers says, "You know what to do." Luca stops for a moment and nods, without looking back at the sweepers, who have already begun the unenviable task of cleaning up a murder scene. Luca and I walk out of the motel and into a big black company car not unlike the one that picked me up from school what seems like ages ago.

I slip into the passenger seat, pulling my knees up to my chest. Luca turns the heat on, noticing that I'm still trembling. "What did he mean by that?" I ask suddenly.

"What?"

"That guy—the sweeper—he said you know what to do. What is that? What are you supposed to do with me?" I press on, reluctantly looking over at him across the console. He heaves a deep breath. Then he looks back at me, with a weary look on his face.

"Serena, I never wanted to get into this shit. I mean it. I don't want you to have the wrong idea, okay? Let me explain," he begins. I wait patiently. When he realizes I have nothing to say, he goes on. "Things are not good back home. In Italy. My family is poor, very poor, and the mafia runs everything back home. All the guys my age are being sucked into some really dark shit. There's just no other way to go. There's no alternative. But my parents, they didn't want me to fall into all that, so they sent me here to America, to work for my uncle. To give me a chance at a clean life. Only, the problem is, it's expensive to come here. I needed a passport and a visa and a plane ticket. Those things cost so much money, Serena, and my parents didn't want me to know how much they were sacrificing for me to have this shot at a better life here in New York.

"I'm glad I came here. I have a job. There are so many opportunities. I met *you*. But as it turns out, my parents didn't have the money to send me here on their own, so they had to ask the mob for money. To save me from the mafia, they put themselves in debt to them, thinking they could just pay it off over time. If I had known what kind of risks they were taking to send me here I would never have agreed to leave Italy, but they kept it hidden from me. My parents didn't want me to worry, and besides, they expected they could take care of it without my ever needing to find out. But it didn't work out the way they planned. Things have gotten worse since I left, and now the mafia is calling in those debts all at once. My parents can't pay. My uncle can't pay. And the mafia came to me out of the blue, threatening to kill my uncle and my whole family back home if I don't pay them back myself," Luca says, gritting his teeth.

I reach over and set my hand on his arm. He takes my hand in his and squeezes it tight.

"Apparently, the Costa family sees something in me. They think they can turn me into some kind of mindless soldier or mercenary. I get it. They think I'm just some dumb kid who will do whatever they tell me to do. I'm the right age. I'm the right type. And they have leverage, Serena." He looks over at me meaningfully. "I can't let them hurt my family."

"Of course not," I murmur softly.

"So they came to me with a proposition, a way to clear my debts. I was told to come to this location. They gave me a room number and a time. They made me kill that guy tonight," he says.

"Well, then," I start slowly. "That means it's over. Right? You did it. You—you killed that guy. He's dead. It's all done now. Your debt is cleared. Maybe mine is, too."

The look on Luca's face breaks my heart. It clearly hasn't occurred to him until now that the mafia is the reason I was here tonight, too. I stare down at my lap, fighting back tears as I begin to explain. "Turns out I had a debt, as well. My father's debt. Apparently, all these years he's been stealing money from the mafia. All this time I thought my dad was just a great businessman, maybe with some sketchy associates, but still a businessman at the heart of it. But I was wrong, I guess. He's been keeping this from me my whole life. And now it's over. They killed him. My father. He's dead now. I never even got to say goodbye."

"Serena, I'm so sorry," Luca says, squeezing my hand. "I had no idea."

"Me neither," I reply bitterly. I take a deep breath and force myself to stop crying. I'm running out of tears at this point anyway. There's nothing else to be done about it. I have to be strong. "Anyway, I guess it's over now. I did what Claudio told me. I was… I was bait for that horrible guy. I was supposed to pretend to be a sex worker and make him think he was gonna get lucky, you know. And I did. I fulfilled my end of the bargain. Now both of us are free."

To my dismay, Luca shakes his head. "It's not over yet."

"What do you mean? We both followed orders. It's done."

"No, Serena. Killing that fucker was only half of my instructions. I was supposed to come here, kill the john, and take the… the girl to a drop point," he reveals.

I feel my skin go cold. "Wait. So, you're supposed to take me away… back to—"

"Back to the mafia. Yes," Luca says sorrowfully.

"They were never going to let me go, were they?" I ask quietly.

"I don't think so. You—what you represent—you're too valuable. I think they're planning to make you do this again and again. And the other times, you might not just be acting as bait. Serena. I think they want you to do what you were pretending to do tonight, but for real."

Suddenly I feel like I might vomit, and I grind my teeth hard until I regain my composure. I look over at Luca, resigning myself to whatever fate I have to embrace. It's out of my hands. It's out of Luca's hands, too. This is bigger than both of us.

"I understand. Do what you have to do," I tell him emphatically.

He blinks in confusion for a moment, narrowing his eyes. Then it dawns on him what I'm saying, and he shakes his head vigorously. "No. No, Serena. That's not how it's going to happen. I'm not going to just hand you back to the wolves like they want me to. Fuck that. I agreed to this before I knew… before I had any idea you were involved. I can't believe I accepted this fucking offer in the first place. They *used* me."

"They used both of us," I mutter sadly. "And I can't let you disobey them. They'll kill your family, Luca. They already killed my father. Hell, for all I know, they killed my mother, too. But you still have a family. People who care about you. Don't sacrifice them to save me. I'm not worth it, Luca."

He glares out the window for a minute or so, not replying. Then, suddenly, he jams the keys into the ignition and fires up the engine. The car peels out of the motel parking lot and down the street. My heart sinks. He's doing what he has to do, I tell myself. I can't hold this against him.

The car rumbles down the highway back into the city, leaving the motel far behind us as I fall silent, trying to keep myself from crying. I already told him I'll accept whatever punishment is coming my way. I won't go back on that promise. But after some time, it occurs to me that Luca doesn't seem to be driving me to some mysterious location. We take a turn toward Manhattan and I realize we're going toward my apartment. Why would the drop point be anywhere near my house? Aren't the police looking for me at this point? It seems too risky. Suddenly, Luca's deep voice punctures the silence.

"I'll be damned if I let those fuckers turn me into a monster. I can't hurt you, Serena. I refuse to. They can threaten my life and my family's lives, but I won't let them turn me against the only girl I care about," Luca says angrily.

"What? But you said I'm too valuable. They're not just going to give me up that easily," I protest. A crazy, impossible idea pops into my head. "But what if we just run away? We—we can go somewhere far off, where they'll never find us. We'll leave all of this behind and start over."

"Serena, I wish we could do that. I would do it in a

heartbeat if I thought it would work. But this is the mafia. They have people everywhere, in the least likely of places. We could run, but we could never hide from them. Even if we had all the money in the world, they would find us, and we're both broke now," he explains.

"Then what are we going to do?" I ask. Luca is silent again, thinking.

Finally, he answers. "They made me an offer I couldn't refuse, and now it's my turn to do the same. I think I know a way to make myself more valuable to them than you are. In fact, I have a feeling I might be the one they're after in the first place" he growls. He takes out one of his usual burner phones and dials a number quickly, putting the phone to his ear.

"Who are you calling?" I whisper, bewildered.

"I demand to speak to Claudio," Luca says into the receiver. "No, you don't need to ask who the fuck I am. Claudio will know. Let me speak to him. Now."

My heart races. Why the hell is he calling Claudio? What is he doing?

There's a pause and then I hear the faint crackle of a different male voice from the phone, even though I can't make out the words he's saying. Luca replies in Italian, "This is Luca Lomaglio, you fucking scab. You've been a big talker up until now, but this time it's your turn to shut the fuck up and let me talk. Listen to me! I know what game you're playing. I know what you really want, and it isn't Serena De Laurentis. I am an asset, and all of you Costa fuckers know that. So, I'm going to make you an offer. If you swear to leave Serena and her mother alone, you will get something so much better in return. Do you understand what I'm giving you? I will work for you. Full-time. I'll steal. I'll fight. I'll snap whatever neck you want snapped. I'll belong to you. I'm from the old country, and my actions tonight should be more than enough to prove how valuable I can be. You let Serena go, and you can have me instead. As if that wasn't exactly what the fuck you planned all along, you fucking snake."

The car slams to a stop at the curb outside of my apartment building, and I sit completely frozen in place, staring at Luca in shock. The voice on the other end of the line is speaking, but I can't make out the words. Luca closes his eyes and lets out a deep exhale. "*Si, bene. Per sempre. Lo giuro,*" he says resolutely.

I wish desperately I could understand what he said.

And then, he hangs up the call with a click. The phone slides out of his hand and down into the seat. "Luca… what did you just do?" I ask breathlessly. He turns to slowly face me, giving me a faint smile. His eyes are shining.

"It's over. You never have to worry about any of this again," he says.

"What do you mean? You didn't answer my question. What did you do?" I repeat, beginning to panic. Luca reaches over and touches my face softly, lovingly.

"Your mother is upstairs in your apartment. She is unharmed. Go up and see her. I'm sure she is worried sick about you," he says, still avoiding the question.

I shake my head. "No. No, you didn't…"

"Serena," he interjects firmly, "please don't argue with me. I did what needed to be done. It's what they wanted, what they expected anyway. You were just a pawn. This was never about you, understand? They just used you to get to me. And it worked."

"Luca! You can't!" I burst out. "I won't let you!"

"It's already done. I told you, it's over. It was my choice, and I made it. I chose you."

Tears burn in my eyes and this time I just let them fall. "It's not fair. They can't do this— we'll just go to the police. We'll fix this. We—"

"No, Serena. No police. Don't even think about it. This

arrangement is… delicate. The Costa family need to know that they can trust me. I'm brand new. I pulled a power play by making this call tonight, and I need to build back that trust before anything else can happen," Luca explains. "You're free now, *mia passerotta*. You're going to survive."

"Without you," I murmur, my voice cracking into a sob. "I will never be free, not without you. I can't. I won't."

Luca gives me a warm, pitying smile and smooths the hair back from my face.

"Serena, listen to me. I could never turn you over to them. And even if I did, they would never let me go. Don't you see? This was the whole point. To make me give in. To bring me to my knees. I was never going to get out of this. But I found a way to get *you* out, and that's what I need you to focus on. Please," he adds, tracing his finger down my cheek to land on my bottom lip. I gently kiss the tip of his finger, closing my eyes. I can feel my heart shattering into pieces, but I know he's right. There's nothing I can do to change this.

I open my eyes again and Luca pulls me close, pressing his lips against mine in a soft, passionate kiss. When he breaks away, he says softly, "The best thing you can do now is leave. Go. Live your life. Try to forget any of this ever happened. And if you can… forget me, too."

"I don't think I ever could," I reply, leaning my forehead against his.

"Serena, my world has been so bright since you came into it. You've given me exactly the kind of hope and happiness my parents wanted me to find here in America. But some things, dark things, have followed me all the way from across the ocean. I refuse to let those dark things overshadow your light like they have mine," Luca tells me.

"You can't do this," I protest weakly, shaking my head as the tears drip down onto the slick leather seats. Luca gets out of the car and comes around to open the passenger side door, pulling it open and holding out his hand for me. Reluctantly, I take it and let him pull me to my feet. The cool night air breezes around my legs and I shiver. The city feels so huge and dark, like a monster waiting to swallow me up as soon as Luca disappears.

"You escaped a terrible fate tonight, *mia passerotta*," he says. "But I would be an even worse fate for you than that."

"I don't want to forget you," I tell him tearfully. He kisses me on the forehead, then peers into my face with those green eyes nearly glowing in the dim light.

"Try," he says simply. And with that, he walks back to the driver's side, slides behind the wheel, and drives away, leaving me standing alone on the sidewalk in the darkness.

I crave her touch more than anything.

The energy pent up in my body with need for Serena spurs me on when I'm in the exercise yard. Today, my legs work back and forth on the machine, and I listen to the rhythmic clanging of the metal weights behind me.

On most days, I focus my mind entirely on the burn in my body, the strain on my muscles. It's the only way to truly know your body's strengths and weaknesses.

But today, all I can think about is Serena. Sometimes, even my mind gives into the temptation to escape to a fantasy outside these horrible walls and iron bars.

I picture myself coming back to my home to find her there, jumping into my arms as I press my lips to hers and walk her back into the room, shutting the door behind me and pushing her onto the couch. I think of the feel of her soft, fresh clothing, fabric I haven't touched in so very long, before I rip it off her with so little effort. I can hear her gasp in my ear as I expose her before me—my lover and my victim.

I think to myself about how I'll descend on her like an

animal, tearing off the lingerie she described so sweetly, revealing her soft skin to me, turning to show me everything I've missed in these long years away from her. My rough hands have grown stronger and tougher, but the one thing they crave more than anything is *her*. I'd run my hands over her breasts, feeling the hard buds of her nipples as I run over them with my thumbs and listen to the soft, desperate sighing of her voice. Her voice is sweeter than the notes of a symphony in my dreams.

I can nearly feel her legs when I pull her panties down along her thighs, her calves, over her ankles, and I toss them to the side to devour her exposed body with my eyes.

Prison food is awful, but the one taste I've missed more than anything in the world is the taste of Serena's sweet honey. It's one of the many things I use to keep myself stable, to remind myself of the pleasures of the outside world. When I'm free from here, I'll bury my face in her pussy, rest her on my jaw and devour her with all the passion she deserves. I'll satisfy all the needs that have been so painfully pent up inside me for so long.

There is no privacy in prison, except for the little bit of it that comes with solitary confinement. I got a taste of that my first few months in here. One of the old big-shots on my cell block decided to pick a fight with me, and I left him with broken bones. Solitary is hell, but the one thing that kept me going was the thought of Serena.

I saw myself sinking deep inside her to the hilt after I'd feast on her pussy. I remembered the feeling of my balls hitting her ass as I enter her. I picture my thick, pulsing cock grinding against every inch of her inner walls, every depth that I'm so familiar with, yet there is always something new to discover in being intimate with Serena. In my mind, I'm right there with her, groping her breasts, letting my hands rove down to her hips and angle her up as I buck deeper into her, filling her up with myself in every possible way, my cock harder and stronger than ever before with my new strength.

When I'm free, my girl will enjoy every bit of my newer, stronger body. My *principessa* deserves nothing but the very best.

As I work out, I feel my blood running hot with my thoughts, so I use that to fuel my body to work out even harder. Eventually, I'm able to re-focus myself and clear my head. Going for a jog sometimes helps too, but in the heat of things, I can't keep her out of my head.

From the time we were young, I never have.

I finish my workout and stand up slowly, rolling my shoulders back and feeling my heart's steady rhythm in my chest. A jog might not be a bad idea to cool down. The recreation yard hardly passes as a good space for that kind of thing, but we all make do with what we have. I jump up and down a few times to shake my body out, then head off.

Jogging gives me some of the most privacy I can carve out for myself. Even on the exercise equipment, someone's always hovering around, but I'm rarely messed with when I run.

But I hear the sounds of footsteps running up behind me, and I get the feeling today won't be one of those days.

The footsteps are gaining on me. There's a chance it's just some hotshot trying to look tough and pass me, but I've been around long enough to know better. It's no surprise to me when I see two men out of the corner of my eye.

Dark hair and swarthy. They're Italians. I've seen them before, but we don't talk. That means this won't be a pleasant time.

"Good workout, Lomaglio?" says one of them, and I shoot them a glare as I slow to a stop.

"Cut the shit," I say, in no mood to be taken out of my private thoughts. "What do you want?"

"Woah woah," says the other, furrowing his eyebrows. "Don't knock *my* teeth out, big guy. You don't want to spend more time in the hole, do you?"

I look between the two of them, making sure to control my body language carefully. If I look like I'm about to start shit, we'll draw the guards' eyes, and they're not afraid to act before anything even happens.

But these two don't look like they're about to start a fight. There are tells you come to recognize, tense postures that are like red flags. The look of these two tells me they're here to talk more than act, though. I want to leave them be and walk away, but you learn better than to turn your back on anyone in a place like this.

"Then don't give me a reason," I say evenly.

"Look, Lomaglio," says the first guy, talking to me as if I were at a job interview. My face is unmoved. "Everyone knows you're a fuckin' maniac. We just wanna be clear on where we stand. You can appreciate that, right?"

"I don't know who you are, and I don't care," I grunt, my face stony.

"We're people who look after our friends," he says, crossing his arms.

"So some new guy slips in the bathroom and knocks his own teeth out, and you want to come start a fight in the rec yard?" I scoff. I'm careful with my words, because I know there's a good chance one of them is wearing a wire in exchange for benefits from the guards. Every prison has rats, and I don't take chances. I won't incriminate myself.

"No, you beat the shit out of friends of our friends, and we take offense to that," the other guy says, just as careful as me not to start bowing up and posturing.

"You're Cleaners," I say, a grim smile on my face. "You think you're a real gang on the inside. How sweet."

"Tough talk from a guy who's got a sweet piece of ass on the outside, all alone by herself," says the first man.

Now he has my attention.

"What was that?" I say, my eyes turning to him with a spark of fire in them. "I must have heard that wrong."

"Nothing to worry about, big guy," he laughs, "We can keep an eye on her a lot better than you can."

In my mind, I'm already weighing the satisfaction of breaking this man's face versus spending a few months in the hole.

"Yeah," says the second man, "you really oughta think about that before you go busting up our friends in here. See, you've got all that muscle on you, but her? I hear she's pretty soft. And anything you do in here is gonna bounce back on her, and buddy, that's gonna hurt her a lot more than it can hurt you."

"Not if you're dead," I say, starting to see red as I approach the men. I've forgotten all care for my stance, and a few other men in the yard are starting to look toward us. I don't care. Nobody threatens my girl.

"Lorenzo crumpled like paper in my hands. I wonder if all you Cleaners are made of the same stuff."

But just as the men seem getting ready to fight, I hear the sounds of whistles around us as a handful of guards rush over to us. The two Cleaners put their hands up innocently as the guards wrestle us away from each other. I could throw the guards around like dolls, but I go with them as they pull me away, my eyes glaring daggers into the smug men.

As I'm led back to my cell, though, I'm seething, because I know they'll make good on their threat. I can protect myself just fine in a place like this. But Serena? She's tough, but nobody can take on an entire mob on their own.

The guards march me down the path to my cell, and I don't pay attention to their yammering on about me being on thin ice for the last incident. I enter my cell stoically and hear the familiar sound of it shutting behind me.

My new cellmate's tired eyes greet me.

"Tough workout?" he asks, not bothering to sit up from his bed.

"Bad spotters," I reply, and he cracks a smile as I move to my bed and sit down. There's a piece of mail addressed to me that I push to the side for the time being. I need to refocus my thoughts.

My quiet cellmate is Eduardo Trueba. He's an old man, and I can tell by the way he carries himself in here that he's been inside for a long time and doesn't plan to see the world as a free man again. Men who have nothing to lose can be very dangerous, but Trueba is the kind of man who's hard to read.

His hair is white, he's got some weight on him, and he doesn't leave his cell very much. He has a book that he often reads with a cover in Spanish, but I haven't spoken to him very much.

He hasn't shown himself to be trouble, and that's good enough for me.

"You're a big man," Trueba says, "so long as you look like you're the biggest fish around, you'll always have little ones nipping at you."

I glance at him. He looks peaceful, sitting there with his hands folded over his belly.

"Maybe I should spend some time in the library, take a lesson from you."

He gives a chuckling grin. "Been here ten years, just one shank-wound to show for it. It's not a bad gig, if you can keep your blood cool."

I crack a smile of my own at that. In my case, both of us can tell that that's never going to happen. I pick up the letter again and push myself back on my bed against the wall. The others aren't back from the rec yard yet, Trueba looks like he's in the mood for a conversation, and hell, I could use a distraction too. I figure there's no harm in indulging the old man.

"Ten years?" I say with raised eyebrows. "You don't strike me as the kind of man who'd do hard time."

"That's what everyone says," Trueba chuckles. "Maybe I should get a few prison tattoos on my face. What do you think about a snake with flames coming out its mouth?"

I grin and nod, giving his face an appraising look. "That could be good, or maybe a knife. You can say your mind's still sharp."

He laughs out loud at that, a hearty laugh from the gut. "I like that, good thinking." After he settles down a little, he looks thoughtful again before he speaks. "I don't think my crime was so bad, but the law didn't agree."

It's an unspoken law in prison that you don't ask what people are in for, so I just nod, but he goes on.

"It was a bank robbery," he says, looking up at the ceiling with a wistful look in his eye. "We were damn good at it, too. Heard of the Harrison Avenue job?"

I raise my eyebrows and give a nod. I have heard of that one, in fact. It's one of the most famous robberies in the city's history, nearly forty years ago. A small crew hit a bank where some billionaire had a fortune in jewels, and as soon as the robbers had it, they all just disappeared, melted away into the city, and the jewels vanished too. It was like they were never there.

"That was me," he says, but there's no pride in his voice, just the simple words. "I planned the whole thing, and I got a hold of those jewels with my own two hands." He looks at his gnarled fingers. "It's funny, the only thing I could think about in the heat of the moment was how crazy it was, some punk like me from Harlem holding more money than I'd seen over my whole life. Apartment, car, everything."

"Couldn't imagine," I say.

He gives a sad smile. "Well, you do what you have to when times get hard. And times were hard for me and my wife. I have a big family, and where I grew up, you don't just leave them when you get married. Everyone just gets closer together. My friends and I, we saw a chance, took the risk, and…" he shrugs, "got lucky, I guess."

"Takes a hell of a lot of luck to knock over a bank," I say, folding my arms over my chest.

"Takes a lot more to get away with it," he says with a wink. "Dunno if I'm proud of what I did, but nobody got hurt, and boy, my family didn't have no problems for a good thirty years. And man, those were a good thirty years," he says, looking up at the ceiling, and I can see true happiness in his eyes. "Didn't live in luxury or anything, that would have gotten too much attention. We just kind of… did our thing, you know? Made sure my kids got college taken care of, didn't worry about bills, health, nothing. It was… it was nice."

"What happened?" I ask, interested now.

He shrugs. "They got better at tracking down people like me. That DNA testing stuff got invented, and eventually someone dug up my case, tested some old evidence, and the next thing I know, I'm getting arrested at my granddaughter's *quinceanera*."

"Damn," I say, shaking my head.

"That's what I said," he says with a sad grin, but that soon fades. "They roasted me in court, too. Wanted to make a big show of locking me up. I'll die in here," he says, nodding to himself. "I wouldn't mind, if it were just me. I've had a good run. Nice, happy years. But I worry about my wife sometimes. Sure, she's got the rest of the family to take care of her, and they couldn't trace what's left of the money if they tried, but still."

"Leaving someone alone like that without being able to

do anything hits you hard," I say, and he looks over at me. I see tears in the old man's eyes as he gives a short nod, then looks away.

"You get that," he points out.

"Yeah," I say, flexing my fist. "I get that." He looks back at me.

"You're young though. I don't need to know you that well to know you don't deserve a place like this. You oughta have your whole life ahead of you. You love her?" he asks, seeing right through me.

I look at the scar on my forearm and think of Serena. "I deserve everything I get in here, but I love her more than anything."

He nods sadly. "I'm too old to blame the law for anything, but when I was in that courthouse..." he tightens his fist, and I see some muscle flex in his arm. He's tougher than the impression he gives. "To them, criminals like me are just stepping stones. The lawyer who put me away is probably drinking wine on a yacht somewhere right now."

The look on Detective Price's face when he arrested me appears in my mind, and I clench my jaw, nodding. "Men like that are no men at all. I know that too well."

"Yeah?"

While we have something close to privacy, I tell him my story, from how I ended up working for the Costa family to how I ended up shoved into the back of a police car by Price. By the time I finish, prisoners are starting to file back into their cells down the halls, and our privacy vanishes with it.

And by that time, Trueba is watching and listening to me with interest, and I can see him sharing my anger. "*Sangre de dios,*" he mutters. "You live a more exciting life than I'd ever care for, my friend."

"More than I care for anymore either," I say. "And now,

I've got another eight years to look forward to. As long as that fucker is around, I won't see parole."

"Careful with that kind of thinking," he says, giving me a serious look. "It's easy to lose hope in a place like this, and that kind of thinking will do it. I've seen that stack of letters you keep under your bed," he says, nodding to my mattress. "Those things are going to save your life. Stick to them. Don't let them slip away. Keeps you tied to the world outside, and that's something that vultures like your detective can't touch."

I give a nod, but his words remind me of the letter in my hands. I'd half-forgotten about it, talking with Trueba. I look at the front, and my eyes widen. It's not from Serena.

It's got a fake return address on it, one that I know belongs to Nico, my comrade.

I tear the letter open and look at the words jotted down in his neat handwriting. Nico has been a point of contact for me for all things that have to do with business. He writes in code, of course. To the censors, it reads like a normal letter from a friend, but he uses phrases and specific wording that I understand perfectly.

And what I read is not good. My hands tighten around the edges of the page, and I feel the urge to drive my fist into the wall.

According to Nico, Serena's place is being watched by the police.

Trueba sees the anger in my face, but he doesn't ask what the letter says. He's sharp enough to know better than that. "Everything okay, Luca?"

"No," I say through my teeth. My mind flashes back to what those two goons tried to threaten me with. *Anything I do in here will come back to hurt Serena. And now, the police are watching her, the same corrupt cops that helped the Cleaners get me thrown in this hell-hole in the first place, no doubt.*

There's nothing innocent about what those cops are

doing. Corruption runs deep in our part of the Bronx, and I know that this means trouble. And if they're already going after Serena, that means they really aren't going to leave us alone.

Even if I try to stay out of trouble in here, they're not going to leave *Serena* alone. Trueba's words ring in my ears truer than ever. If it were only me, it would be one thing... but this is more than just me. This is more than just the mafia. This is the one I love, the one good thing through all this misery.

This is Serena. And there's nothing I can do from inside this place.

I read over the letter one more time, and I crumple it in my hand. My jaw is set, and my eyes are resolute. Trueba looks at me with a concerned face. "You alright, man? What's on your mind?"

I look back at him, but I don't answer, because I know exactly what I need to do. I have no other option.

I have to break out. Soon.

LUCA

I got one letter out to Nico. One letter encoded with brief but specific instructions. A little time later, I got one back confirming that he got my message. Nothing more. A prison break has to be organized, detailed, coordinated, and needs a lot of planning.

Those aren't luxuries I have. All I can do is make sure I can come through on my end and hope that everything else falls into place.

And today is the day. But I have one hurdle to get over before then.

I'm being led down the dreary halls of the prison to an interrogation room that I've been to many times before. My face is stony. If you show any emotion going into these types of meetings, the people around you start to suspect you of talking to the police.

Not that it will matter after today. My biggest worry in this meeting will be resisting the urge to tear the interrogator apart.

My hands are cuffed in front of me. Two guards march me forward, and as we approach the door at the end of the hall, another guard opens it and lets us in. They sit me down at a simple table in the gray, depressing room with nothing but a light hanging from the ceiling and a one-way mirror on the wall in front of me. Once I'm seated, the guards leave, and I'm left alone.

Time passes. He's keeping me waiting, trying to let my thoughts eat at me before he takes his shots. It's never worked with me before, and it won't work with me now. I don't talk to police.

Least of all Will Price.

After what feels like an hour, the door swings open, and he strides in, hawkish eyes watching me with smug satisfaction.

"Good morning, Luca," he says candidly, as if we were good buddies meeting up for a beer. I glare at him.

He pulls a chair out and takes a seat, beaming at me, showing off lively energy. Price has seen a lot of me over the past couple of years. I haven't given him a word, but that doesn't stop him.

The worst thing about seeing this pig all this time, though, is that I've seen him doing better for himself, watched him grow happier, more confident, and more wealthy. When you're a child, you're told that the worst people in the world always get what they deserve.

I always knew that was a lie, but Price is living proof.

"It's been a bit since I saw you last," he says, opening a folder in front of him and thumbing through a few pages idly. "Sounds like you've had a busy week." His eyes flit up to me, watching me for a reaction. "Two fights for a guy who says he just wants to keep to himself tells me something's up."

My stony stare doesn't shift. I might as well be a statue. Anything I say would just be fuel for him. He lives for shit like this.

After a moment of silence, he gives a thin smile and says, "You don't need me to tell you this is one of the most violent prisons in the country, Lomaglio. And so I hope I don't have to tell you that when the inmates cooperate with us in getting that violence under control, we're a lot more willing to help them out in turn."

He's lying. The last prisoner Price got to start ratting to him got hauled off to solitary and locked away in there when the other prisoners caught on and stopped talking to him. Price is cold. He doesn't keep friends.

When I don't reply, Price leans forward, dropping some of the pretense of being polite. "Are you worried about them, Luca?" he asks. "This report says the men you attacked have gang connections outside the prison. You know this is my ballpark, Luca, I can help you out here. I just need you to help me first."

Prisoners get desperate, and this kind of talk sways many of them. But I can smell the threat through his words. I say nothing.

"You're kind of a puzzle, Luca," he says, sitting back in his seat and looking through his files again. "You do more for the Costa crime family than just about anyone I've seen in, god, ten years. But if what the warden's telling me is right, you're practically a ghost in here. What happened? Costa's been busy since you've been in here—why aren't you on speaking terms anymore?"

That much is true. Nico has been my only point of contact with my old comrades, save for the other Costas in here with me, and we hardly talk. When we do, it's never about business. I'm not in here to be a pawn for anyone. Price glares back into my eyes before he crosses the line he's been dying to cross this whole time.

"Is this about Serena?"

Just hearing him say her name makes me furious. He doesn't deserve to speak it.

"That's understandable," he says, leaning forward in his seat, "a lot of inmates worry about their loved ones while they're inside." He smiles an empty smile. "Well, I can promise you, she's fine. I saw her just the other day, in fact."

I can't control myself, not in the face of such a blatant threat.

"This is between us, you coward," I growl, even as his smile splits into a grin. "Keep it that way, if you can call yourself a man."

"I'm sorry, what exactly am I keeping between us?" he asks, a mocking tone to his voice. Speaking at all was a mistake. I clench my fist and sit back in my chair, narrowing my eyes at him. "I'm just doing my job, Luca, you need to understand that. You're a high-profile offender, and you obviously have some enemies around here," he says, taking out photos of the men I've fought over the past few days and setting them on the table.

"Then why don't you tell the cameras why you're stalking some woman?" I say, nodding up to the camera in the corner of the room, hanging from the ceiling. These meetings are always recorded, and I'm sure he has a recorder on him to capture our conversation in case I say anything incriminating.

"I'm not stalking anyone," he says, half-laughing. "Luca, I don't have to remind you that Miss De Laurentis has mafia connections of her own. Quite a complicated past, in fact," he says, crossing his legs and folding his hands. "That's all in the past, of course, but as you know better than anyone, the past can come back to bite you."

My fists are tight, but I say nothing.

"It's in the interests of her safety that I keep an eye on her," he says, dropping his tone to a still, chilling one. "Just like it's in your interests to help me. Look, Luca, if I'm flying blind here for too long..."

He takes back the photos and closes his folder, standing up from his chair. "... then I can't guarantee that the people who want to hurt you won't make life hard for her on the outside."

"Don't threaten me, Price," I say in a low tone. He smiles back at me, but my eyes bore into him, memorizing every detail of his face, as if it isn't already seared into my memory. I'm going to make him pay for this. And I'll make him remember me.

"I don't make threats, Luca," he says as he turns his back on me to leave the room, his voice dripping with smug satisfaction "I'm just doing my job."

$\sim$

*B*ack in my cell later that night, I'm reading over the letters Serena sent me one more time.

Trueba is over on his bed, hands folded on his stomach. His eyes are on me, but he knows to give me space right now. My hands go over some of the words that Serena scribbled out on her letters, places where she tested her pen with little squiggles of ink.

It's the imperfections that remind me most of all that she's still out there, the same Serena, the same face, the same person I fell in love with. And it's all for her that I'm doing this.

I might not make it out of this alive. And if I don't, I want her words to be the last things in my mind.

"You're sure you're willing to do this?" I ask Trueba once I've finished reading and I tuck all the letters back under the bed. I'm speaking quietly enough that nobody can hear us outside our cell, and I don't look over at him when I do speak.

We have a plan, and we can't look suspicious on camera for this to have any hope of working.

"I'm an old man, Luca," he says, and I can hear how tired his voice is. "I hardly leave my cell as it is. Some time in solitary will give me room to think. Maybe pray, I don't know yet."

"It has to look real," I say. We've gone over the plan before, but I'm not taking any chances.

"It'll *be* real," he says.

Sterling Correctional Facility is on a small island just off the coast, one long bridge connecting it to the mainland. There's some woodland on the island, then nothing but icy waters and a couple other smaller islands not far off, all of them uninhabited and off-limits to the public. This prison feels as remote as it can, despite being so close to the city.

Nobody could make it through those woods on the island without getting picked up by the patrols, and they sure as hell couldn't hide out there. That means there is only one way off the island: the bridge.

And the only way a prisoner can get taken over that bridge is in the back of a police car... or in an ambulance.

The prison has its own medical wing, but they can't handle anything more than basic injuries. The news has been criticizing the prison for years, but they haven't lifted a finger. Even the guy I fought in the bathroom had to be driven to Emerson Hospital on the mainland, just a block away from the other side of the bridge.

The matter of me getting a serious injury is where Trueba comes in.

"Alright," I say, flexing my fists as Trueba swings his legs over to stand up. "Showtime."

"You wanna say that again, you Italian son of a bitch?" Trueba says loudly, strutting in the cell in the way the young men do when they're about to start a fight.

"I said you East Harlem fuckers are a dime a dozen," I snap back, standing up myself. Despite his age, Trueba is a tall guy, and he's got muscle under that fat. It doesn't look too out of character for a guy like him to square up with me. "I've fought punching bags with more fight than you chickenshits—no wonder the Cleaners moved into our turf!"

"You wanna see a punching bag, my friend?" he snarls, and he starts forward at me, pushing me in the chest with a firm hand. I barely budge, swatting his arm away, but then he reaches behind his shirt.

He pulls out a shank.

For an old guy, he moves fast. He brings the shiv around, and I brace myself. The pointed tip cuts through my hardened muscles and sinks into me, deep.

We've both been around violence long enough to know what wounds will cause some damage without killing a man, but that doesn't make it any less tricky to pull off and make it look real. The pain is the least of my worries.

I act like I've been taken off-guard and let out a grunt of pain. When he pulls the shank out and stabs it in again, I can already hear the boots of guards on the ground. We don't have much time.

I move as if trying to defend myself, but Trueba pops me in the nose with a quick, solid jab before he grabs hold of my shirt and drives the shank in again, and again, and again. I lose track of the stab wounds I'm getting, but the pain is incredible.

The last thing I see before falling to the ground are the prisoners across from us staring wide-eyed while guards appear at the door, getting it open and shouting to each other to call an ambulance.

Trueba gets one last good stab into me before three guards wrestle him off, pepper-spraying him in the eyes as he cries out in pain and gets tackled to the ground.

I've let myself take more of a stabbing than I got in some of the real fights with the Cleaners. My torso is on fire, and as I cover my wounds with my hands, I feel warm blood pouring from them.

In the confusion, I can hardly tell what's happening around me through the pain of the stab wounds. More guards come in. I think Trueba gets taken out, and when paramedics arrive, I hear bits of them shouting to one another: multiple stab wounds. Losing blood fast. Needs attention, stat.

Then come the golden words: "Get him to Emerson, now!"

I feel a twinge of pain in my side, and I have to fight to stay conscious as I'm loaded onto a stretcher.

What happens over the next few minutes is a blur. I feel myself getting rushed down some hallways in the prison. I try to move my arm, and I feel a clink of resistance. I manage to turn my eyes down to my hand, and I see it both covered in blood and handcuffed to the stretcher. There's some first-aid bandaging applied to my torso for the trip.

Fuck, I have to stay awake.

For a moment, I feel fresh air on my skin, the cool night breeze on the hot blood staining my clothes when they roll me across asphalt. I see the top of the ambulance above me as I'm loaded up into it.

I feel my body contracting, pain almost unbearable. It's like fire in my stomach. Just as much as Trueba was taking a risk in doing something like this for me, I knew I was taking a risk. There's no really safe way to get stabbed in the gut.

But this is my one shot. No matter how much pain I go through, no matter how much blood I lose, it's worth it for Serena. The words of her letters are in my thoughts when I hear the ambulance doors close, and the engine starts.

I can make out the paramedics above me, saying things I can't quite make out to each other before hooking me up to machines. I feel a needle go into my wrist, and a few moments later, I feel warmth rushing up my arm and into my whole body.

It's morphine. The pain starts to subside, and I let out a deep breath in relief as it gets into every part of me. I hate drugs, but if Nico pulls through for me, that morphine is going to be the only thing that keeps me going for what comes next.

And with the way things are going, I can only hope that Nico *can* pull through for me.

I can't tell where we are or how close we are to the end of the bridge. Now that I have something keeping the pain at bay, though, I don't feel like I'm about to drift into blackness anymore. I look down at my wounds, or try to. I can't see my bare flesh, so I can't see whether any of the shanks missed their mark and hit something vital.

If they did, I'm in trouble. No time to worry now, though.

"Jesus, who'd this guy piss off?" one of the paramedics mutters to the other.

"Wouldn't wanna meet the guy who'd pick a fight with this beast," he muses, checking something on a machine before turning to me. "How you doin', buddy? Try to stay awake, you should be feeling the good stuff right about now."

I give him a weary smile and lift my thumb.

The next moment, the whole ambulance lurches forward, then to the side as the vehicle comes screeching to a halt.

"What the fuck?" one of the medics cries, turning to the window to the driver. "Hey, what's going on?!"

"Fucking Christ, they've got guns," the driver says, and I see him raising his hands over his head. There's shouting outside.

One of the voices is Nico's.

"Hey," I say to the medics, who look from the road to me, wide-eyed. "You two seem alright. Keep your heads down and do what they say."

"You've gotta be kidding me," one of them says, but the back of the ambulance opens, and I look up to see Nico flanked by two other Costa boys with guns raised.

"Alright!" he shouts, stepping forward as the medics put their hands up. "I want his cuffs off *now*! Make this easy on us, we'll make it easy on you, let's go!"

The medics comply, and in a matter of seconds, Nico is unhooking me from the machines and helping me down from the ambulance while the other men hold guns on them, moving up to get them to their knees and handcuff them there. The paramedics in prisons are trained to deal with violence, but they know when they're outgunned.

And none of them were expecting to be held up at the prison's doorstep by four cars full of mob enforcers armed to the teeth. Hell, I wasn't even expecting Nico to bring that kind of firepower.

"You good, man? Holy shit, what happened?" Nico says as we step onto the street. I can't describe the feeling the moment my feet touch the ground.

Free ground.

I breathe the night air in, and I smile at him. "Ran into a friend's knife... a few times. I'll be alright."

"Not if you don't get help," Nico says, "you look fucked up, man! Come on, forget the next part of the plan—let's get you into the car and go see one of our docs."

"No," I say firmly. "Someone will find me."

"But-"

"Nico, we've got about a minute before this block is crawling with feds. You need to move, and fast. We're going through with the plan, the whole way."

"There's no way, Luca," Nico says, looking at me like I'm insane. And maybe I am. I haven't tasted freedom in two years, and it's almost as strong a drug as the morphine in my veins. "You'll die out there."

"Nico," I say, clasping his hand and giving a cocky

smile. "I owe you more for this than I've ever owed anyone in my life. But now's not the time. Remember what we planned, and get your ass out of here, got it?"

Nico frowns, then shakes his head with a laugh. "Shit, man, you beefed up, but you haven't changed at all, have you?"

"I had something good to keep my mind on," I say as I part from him, walking away.

I'm walking toward the coast.

Back toward Sterling.

I cast one last look back at Nico, and the scene of what's going to be in the news tomorrow as the most daring prison break in the history of Sterling. "Tell her it'll be okay!"

I see Nico start to get the men back to their cars and peel out before I look away from them.

And the next moment, still bloody and bandaged, I get a running start and dive into the icy waters.

In the years since those cops dragged Luca away from me and threw him in prison, I have turned into a major workaholic. Sure, for the first few weeks after he was sentenced, it was all I could do to pull my ass out of bed. I shut down completely, refusing to speak to anyone for a while. Rafaela, Nico, and my mom all did their best to accommodate my wallowing in self-pity, at least for a week or so. They brought me meals in bed: chicken soup, poppy seed bagels with my favorite veggie cream cheese, tubs of low-fat ice cream. Rafaela sat in bed with me and watched soap operas, both of us silent except for the crunch of popcorn or sips of wine. But I don't think any of them expected me to be that heartbroken for so long. My life was on hold, and it felt wrong for me to try and keep living as though nothing had changed.

Because *everything* had changed.

How was I supposed to focus on work when the love of my life was wasting away behind bars, probably getting beat to hell by other inmates and probably even the prison guards. God knows the cops have an axe to grind against him, and I'm sure they took every opportunity to knock him down a peg, legally or illegally. So for those first few weeks, I was useless. I stopped living. I had to be coerced into the shower, encouraged to eat, persuaded to change out of my bathrobe. If a psychiatrist had come to see me, she would have definitely ticked off all the boxes under "depression" and probably given me some pill meant to perk me up and give me a false sense of purpose again. In fact, at one point late in my wallowing period, I overheard my mother in the hallway talking on the phone with someone in a hushed tone.

The tone of her voice made me curious enough to creep out of bed and press my ear against the bedroom door to listen. It sounded something like this:

"Yes. Oh, no, I'm not the patient. I'm calling on behalf of my daughter. No, she's not a minor. She's twenty-three. Yes, I am aware that she's an adult, but this is very serious and I know she isn't going to help herself. She's... she's too far gone, you see. I-I'm very worried about her. She's not herself anymore and I don't know what else to do. Yes. Thank you. Okay. I understand. I'll hold for the psychiatrist."

There was a long pause, and I could feel my heart sinking down to the floor. It didn't take a rocket scientist to figure out what was going on. My mom was trying to get me help the only way she knew how. And it may not seem like a big deal to most people, but my mother has always been staunchly anti-psychiatry. She's old-fashioned and stubborn and she thinks it's all a bunch of witch doctor stuff. I, of course, disagree. I think someone's mind can be sick just as much as someone's stomach can be sick. It's all the same. But for my mother to overcome her ridiculous prejudice and actually call a mental health clinic on my behalf... well, that was more than enough to convince me that I was truly frightening everyone around me. I had allowed myself to slip so deeply into my own darkness that I forgot about all the people around me who still cared, who had to keep on going even though they were worried about me.

Besides, I knew deep down it wasn't my mind that was sick, it was my heart.

So that day, I slipped out of my room and walked up to my mom with an apologetic look on my face. She looked shocked to see me out of bed by my own choice, and I mouthed at her, "You don't have to do that," pointing at the phone. She nodded and hung up before the psychiatrist could even get there and take her off hold.

"Serena, we're worried about you," my mother said softly. I could see tears shining in her eyes, which was a rare sight. My mom may have grown up a spoiled mafia princess, but when my father died she became even colder and tougher than anyone could have predicted. So when she cried, it was really serious. I gave her a hug.

"I know. I'm sorry. I'm going to try and be better from now on, okay?" I assured her.

"You don't have to go through this alone," she told me. I nodded and forced a smile.

"Yeah. I know," I replied quietly. Then I perked up, which took great effort, and added, "Okay, well, I'm sure I smell terrible. I'm going to take a shower and grab some lunch, then head down to the shop to do some damage control."

I arrived at Bathing Beauty to find my accounts in disarray, the floor and shelves needing to be cleaned, expired products needing to be moved out and replaced with fresher ones. I set to work immediately, throwing all the energy I'd been spending on sorrow into a new project: cleaning up my life. And I've been working nonstop ever since. In fact, I have to admit that focusing all my frustration into work has kind of become my new addiction, but at least it's a productive one. At least I'm no longer lying in bed, drowning in despair. It could be worse.

So I spend as much time as possible at Bathing Beauty during the weekdays, clocking in at dawn and staying overtime whenever possible. The shop is so clean it sparkles, and I've reorganized the books and logs a million times. With my newly-attuned attention to detail and superhuman work ethic, the shop is flourishing. I think my customers have all told everyone they know about my shop or something, because things are going great. The bestsellers are flying off the shelves as always, but now even the less-popular products are in high demand. I've even hired a second worker to help me out, a high school student named Naomi who works at the shop after school. By all accounts, I should be proud of myself. I've taken a failing business and turned it into a success.

People are buzzing about Bathing Beauty, and I'm finally doing way more than just breaking even.

But I can't be happy. Not really. Bathing Beauty is just the receptacle for my pent-up energy, where I go to dump all my sadness and frustration and loneliness. I spend hours in the back kitchen testing out new scents, new textures and colors. I'm bouncy and charismatic in the shop front, chatting with customers, making connections. But it's all a show. It keeps me from losing my mind during the week, but we're not quite at the point where we can handle being open all week long, so I still have Sunday and Monday every week left open to mope and fixate on the dire darkness of my situation. Of Luca's situation.

Today is Sunday, and I'm sitting at the vintage desk in my bedroom, my pen hovering over a letter I'm writing to Luca. I write him every day. Every single day, whether I've just worked a thirteen-hour shift or not, I come home and sit here to hammer out another letter to my long-lost love. I have no idea if he's even getting any of these. I never get a response. For all I know, the guards or cops have confiscated every one of my letters to him. They could be locked away in some filing cabinet, in a manila folder marked *EVIDENCE*. I've tried to visit him, but they won't let me see him. I have no idea what he looks like these days. Hell, in my darkest moments it occurs to me that he could be dead, and I would have no idea.

But something tells me I would know. I would feel it. Something in the air would smell different, feel different. The sun wouldn't shine as brightly. The birds wouldn't sing as sweetly. My heart would be even heavier than it already is.

I would know.

And so, despite the lack of a response, I keep dutifully writing letters. Sometimes it almost reminds me of how I felt years and years ago, when I first met Luca as a teenager. When I used to send him text messages to his burner phone, hoping against hope I would get an answer that never, ever came. I wonder how much of my life will be spent waiting on Luca, sending messages that get no response. It's a depressing fate, I know, but something keeps me from giving up. I can't give up. Luca may be far away, and there may be a gigantic brick wall between us, but I know in my heart he's still there, and as long as he's on this planet I will never give up.

A teardrop falls from my eye and dampens the page, swelling the inky words into an unreadable blob. I groan and push the letter away, swiping at my eye angrily. I'll have to start over.

But first I need to take a break. This is really starting to get to me. "God, I hate weekends," I whisper to myself. I should take a walk. That might clear my mind.

I get up and walk across the room to my closet, pulling a sweater out and slipping it over my head. It's been getting a little chilly in the afternoons lately, and I don't have time to catch a cold. Bathing Beauty needs me. And I need the work to keep me sane. On the way down the hallway I stop by my mother's room and knock on the door. She looks up from her iPad and gives me a smile. It's still so weird sometimes to see her trying to be more affectionate, but I think after watching me fall into that depression two years ago, she's realized it might be beneficial for both of us to be a little softer. After all, she has some idea what I'm feeling. She lost a husband when I lost my father.

"Going somewhere?" she asks, cocking her head to one side.

I nod. "Yeah, just out for a short walk to clear my head. What do you want for dinner tonight? We could get takeout. I've been craving orange chicken lately. What do you think?"

"Sounds fine to me, sweetheart," she replies. "Be careful out there, it's getting dark soon."

"Okay mom."

"Remember, text me X if you're in trouble."

"I will," I answer. "Bye."

"See you later," she says, going back to whatever she's doing on that iPad.

I jog down the stairs and out the front door, locking it behind me. The late afternoon air is crisp and cool, and I can feel autumn blowing in. It's the time of year that makes me feel sentimental. Nostalgic. I think about the jitters of classes starting back up, the anticipation of holidays like Halloween, Thanksgiving, and Christmas. But these days, it's an empty feeling. Those expectations of a warm, love-filled holiday season fall flat when I remember everything I've lost. My father. Luca. It's just my mom and me now. Sure, there's Rafaela and Nico, too, but they're a couple. They have their own hectic lives to deal with. And sometimes seeing them together, how happy they are, how much they love each other, it just makes me sadder.

I wish I still had all of that. Hope. Love. A future I could look forward to.

But my life is on hold for eight more long, lonely years.

I sigh and shove my hands into my pockets to stay warm as I walk down the long driveway and turn onto the street. The trees are in full bloom, all jade green and white flowers. It's beautiful here in Riverdale, and I'm grateful that I've been able to save the house. My father's legacy. Well, what's left of it, at least. I can rest assured that my dad would be proud of me for holding it all together here, for taking care of mom. When I walk around this neighborhood, I remember how badly he wanted to move us here, give me a more comfortable, safe place to live. It's easy to feel close to him again when I think about it.

But I have no way of feeling close to Luca. Sure, I met him for the first time in what is now my backyard, but our relationship has fallen apart and come back together so many times that it feels fractured now. And besides, it's too painful to relive our memories together even now. It's been two years since they took him away, and it still breaks my heart every day. He shouldn't be in there. It isn't right.

Just then, I hear the squeal of tires and smell burning rubber. I swivel around in surprise. This is such a quiet neighborhood that anything out of the ordinary sticks out like a sore thumb. I scarcely have a chance to react before a big black car jerks to a stop right next to me. My stomach flip-flops as I realize I'm in danger. I turn to run, but two broad-bodied people grab me by the arms and wrangle me into the car, slipping some kind of bag over my head.

I start to struggle, trying to scream, but no sound will come out. I can hear the engine roaring back to life as the car takes off from my abduction spot, moving quickly away from my home and safety. I finally manage to squeak out, "What is this? Who are you? Let me go!"

"This is for your own good," says a male voice to my

left. He has some kind of accent, but it's so faint I can't recognize it.

"Yeah, fucking right," I swear, lifting my hands to try and remove the bag from over my head. But my arms get pinned back down by powerful hands, then bound behind my back.

"Please. Calm down," says a second deep voice, this one on my right.

"Calm down? I'm being kidnapped! I'm not going to be calm! Who are you working for? Who sent you? Where the hell are you taking me?" I shout.

The first voice speaks again: "You're going somewhere safe. Nobody knows you've been taken. And it's better that you don't see where we're headed."

"I guess I don't have any other choice, do I?" I snarl, settling back against the seat.

"No. You don't," says the second voice calmly.

I decide it's better to save my energy. There's not a damn thing I can do about this right now, and the more I struggle, the more likely my captors will do something worse to me. I've been under duress enough times by now to know the importance of picking my battles wisely. Besides, there isn't much fight left in me these days anyway. Without Luca, nothing seems to matter all that much.

We ride in silence for a long time, possibly hours. With the bag over my head, I can't even tell if it's light or dark, but I assume it's dark. Finally, the car rolls to a stop and my heart starts to race. I can smell something... water. Salty, briny water. The doors open and someone grabs me, dragging me out of the car and forcing me to walk beside them. I can hear water sloshing, the distant cry of seabirds. Where the fuck are we? Is this some kind of sick execution?

Am I about to be pushed into the water to drown? Is

this some *sleeping with the fishes* cliché?

I start to turn and try and run away, but the arms holding me are strong, and I can't go anywhere. I cry out as loud as I can, but the bag muffles my voice, and something tells me there is nobody around to hear me scream anyway. We walk for a while, the cold, humid air sending shivers down my body. Then, someone scoops me up in their arms out of nowhere, and lowers me down into what feels like... a boat. A small boat of some kind.

"What the hell is this?" I murmur. There's no answer. "Tell me what is going on!" I scream.

Quickly, someone wraps an arm around my head, covering my mouth. Someone holds me still while another person jabs an arm up inside the bag, stuffing a wadded-up cloth into my mouth. I cough and gag, flailing as much as I can, but it doesn't change anything. These guys are stronger than me, and I don't know how many there are, but I am definitely outnumbered.

"Sorry about the gag. It's for your own good," the first voice says.

My shoulders sag as I just give up. I can't move. I can't scream. I might as well just wait for whatever cruel fate these guys have in store for me. There is the distinct sensation of the boat being pushed into deeper water, then the sound of oars chopping the waves. Are we rowing out to sea? What the hell is going on?

I sit there, freezing and stiff in the boat for god knows how long. The rocking of the boat makes me feel a little nauseous, and I focus all my energy on not throwing up, because I have a gag in my mouth. I don't know if that would kill me, but if so, it seems like a horrible way to die. So I just force myself to think about other things. Accounts at work. Whether or not to hire a third worker. New products I would like to try out in the test kitchen.

And I think about this for... a long time. Until finally

there is the nudge of the boat breaching the sand of another shore. Or at least I assume it's a different shore. For all I know, we could have been rowing in circles for hours, only to return to where we started. The men force me to get up, then they carefully lift me out of the boat and onto dry land. They walk me several steps forward, away from the water, and then to my immense shock they pull the bag off my head and take out the gag. I blink in the darkness, my eyes slowly adjusting. A dense forest begins to materialize in front of me and I stare into it in confusion. Then I look around to see the men who brought me here. Tall, broad-shouldered guys. They all look fairly young, around my age, and they have slightly apologetic looks on their faces.

"We've got a bit of a walk," one of them tells me, and I recognize his voice as the second one who spoke in the car. "Let's get started."

Wordlessly, I follow them through the woods, carefully climbing through scratchy underbrush and hoping I don't run into any spider webs in the dark. Finally, after several minutes of trekking, we come to a building— what seems to be an old, slightly dilapidated house. It looks abandoned, with nature beginning to reclaim it as vines grow over it.

"Come on," says another man, the owner of the first voice who spoke to me earlier. We walk around back to a cellar door in the ground. He flings it open to reveal a rickety staircase. I swallow hard. This looks very much like I'm walking into a horror movie or something. I have no idea what awaits me down there, but I have a strong feeling it isn't anything good.

The men prod me forward and I reluctantly sigh and start to climb down the stairs, deep down into this basement in the middle of nowhere. To my surprise, when I reach the bottom, I'm standing in a big room full of expensive-looking vintage furnishings, all lit by a bright standing floor lamp across the room. "What the hell…" I murmur, trying to take it all in.

Then I see him. A tall, dark figure walking out of the shadows to stand in the center of the basement. He looks a little haggard and rugged, with his muscles even bigger than before, his hair longer and scraggly. But it's him. I would know his face anywhere.

"Luca," I breathe, my heart pounding a million miles an hour.

"*Mia passerotta*," he replies, a slow smile warming his face.

"Is it really you?" I ask, scarcely able to breathe. I take a step forward, my thoughts spinning out in every direction. "This is impossible."

Luca smiles. "It's me. I swear, I'm real."

"No. I have got to be dreaming or something. I mean, how...? I don't understand. You—you were in prison. You *are* in prison. I-I watched them take you away. Luca, I sent you so many letters. Every single day I sent you one and I never got one back," I ramble, shaking my head in confusion.

A flicker of pain crosses his handsome face. I can see the exhaustion, the hidden agony tucked away somewhere behind his smile. I can see how hard he's had to work all this time to stay strong, to hold it together. He seems so real, so lifelike, but changed. There's no way it can really be him, though. There's no way. This is some kind of elaborate trick. But who would do that?

"The prison security must have intercepted most of your letters. And I figured they'd never let me send one out of those fucking walls. Serena, you have to understand...

these people were doing everything they could to isolate me from everything. Especially you," he says grimly.

I run my fingers back through my hair, closing my eyes for a second as I try to put words to my confusion. I don't understand how this is happening. How it could be true that Luca is right here in front of me. Yesterday I was alone in the world, running in circles trying to stay busy to keep my mind from wandering back to him, to keep my heart from breaking. And now he's here.

But how in the world did he get out? And why was I brought here in such a harsh manner?

"You don't have to think so hard about it," Luca says gently. "I can see the cogs turning in your head right now, Serena. Trying to make sense of this. How it could be possible. Don't question it. Not now. There will be plenty of time to explain later."

"Later...?" I ask, my voice trailing off. "You mean, you're not going back? You're going to stay with me?"

Luca takes a few broad steps toward me, opening his arms wide. "Serena, I'm never going to leave you again, if I can help it."

Tears burn in my eyes and I can barely breathe as my feet carry me, almost floating, across the room to all but collapse in Luca's arms. I press my face into his chest, inhaling that familiar, woodsy scent I would recognize anywhere. This is him. He *is* real and he's right here. With me.

"I can't believe this," I murmur, just letting the tears stream down my face.

"Believe it," Luca says, kissing the top of my head and embracing me tightly.

"But Luca, I don't get it. Why all the secrecy? Why did those guys have to kidnap me and drag me across the water in a rickety little boat if you're free? Don't get me wrong, I'm a sucker for a romantic reunion, too, but couldn't you have just showed up at my house? Why all this drama?" I question, laughing a little. Luca holds me back to look into my face, those green eyes pulsing over me, reading into my heart the way he's always been able to do.

"It's more complicated than that, *dolcezza*," he answers gravely. "But for now, I just want to be with you. God, I've missed you more than words can even explain. I thought about you every single waking moment, and every time I managed to fall asleep in that fucking cell, I dreamed of you."

"I never stopped thinking about you. I never stopped loving you, just waiting for when we could be together again. Sometimes it was really hard to imagine a world where we would be in the same room again, Luca. I thought I would never get to touch you again. Kiss you," I explain, choking back a sob.

"You don't have to just imagine it anymore," Luca says, holding my face gently in his huge hands. He pulls me close and presses his lips against mine, his arms folding around me as I melt into his touch. There's the click of a door shutting somewhere behind me, and I realize that the men who brought me here have climbed back out of the basement, leaving me alone with Luca to give us privacy.

And thank god that they did, because I can't wait another fucking second.

Luca kisses me hard, his fingers tangling in my hair as he pulls me in close. I sigh into the kiss, feeling my body loosen up, probably for the first time in two years. My shoulders relax, the tension in my jaw slackens, and a smile tugs at my lips even as we kiss. This, all of this right here, is my happy place. My safe place. I've spent these two years rigidly going through the motions of a regular life, moving robotically from one place to the next. I've been all knotted up inside, waiting fearfully for the next shoe to drop. But now I can breathe again. Luca has brought back the light, the oxygen, the hope that once glimmered overhead.

I don't know what the future will hold, but I am so glad to be here with him.

Luca's other arm slides around me to hold me close, his fingertips pressing into the arch of my back. There's a kind of desperation to the way he grabs onto me, like he's afraid I could evaporate at any second. He's holding me like I'm a life preserver floating out to him in the middle of the deep, dark sea as the sharks circle in on him. Like he never wants to let go. I hope he never does. I want to be that for him, the lifesaving breath of free air.

"I never want to lose you again," Luca says gruffly as we break apart for a moment. He rests his forehead against mine and cups my face, his thumbs tracing over my lips. He closes his eyes tightly as he touches my face, almost like he's trying to commit my features to memory.

"I'm not going anywhere," I murmur in response. "You said that to me once, years ago, when we met up and went for drinks at the Room With a View. Remember?"

Luca sighs, his eyes opening up again as he smooths the hair back from my face. He looks at me intently, that glowing green gaze boring into my soul. "I remember everything. Every moment. Those memories have been my only allies these two years. On the outside, I made sure I looked hard. Intimidating. I kept a scowl on my face and wiped away any trace of joy or love so that nobody could find a weak spot in me. If anybody had known about you, how I feel about you, they would have used it against me. So I had to hide it away. But every single second I was in there, standing in line in the cafeteria, walking in the yard just daring anyone to even brush shoulders with me, sitting alone in solitary confinement... I was thinking of you. Reliving those little moments. Being on the inside fucks you up, Serena. You start second-guessing everything you thought you knew. Your life before prison seems like a dream or a TV show plot that happened to someone else. But it was different with you. I never second-guessed my feelings for you, the reality of what we have, even for a second. I didn't let myself forget a single thing."

I can feel the tears burning in my eyes again and I'm starting to wonder how much one person can cry before they physically run out of tears. I've got to be hovering somewhere around that limit by now. I reach up and gently take Luca's hands in mine, lowering them down away from my face and onto my hips, staring up at him wordlessly. He gazes back with equal seriousness, neither of us daring break eye contact. I can tell we're both just as desperate as the other, each of us terrified that this reunion will suddenly shatter apart, that we'll wake up from a shared dream in our respective solitary worlds. It's so hard to believe that he's here for real.

"Luca, I love you," I tell him emphatically. It's the only thing I can think to say right now. Words are so useless in times like this. Our love is too big to fit in a sequence of letters and syllables. It's more than that, and I'm going to show him the best way I know how.

I stand up on my tiptoes to kiss him, reaching up to pull him down to meet me. He leans into the kiss, his hands sliding down backward from my hips to grab my ass. He groans appreciatively when I press up against him, my breasts pushing into his chest while I can feel his cock stiffening against my hip. Just the sensation of that hardness pushing into me is enough to send a tingle down through my core, and I feel a warmth spreading between my thighs. It's been so long. I've only touched myself a handful of times since they took Luca away, and every time was painful, almost impossible. It felt like a trespass, a betrayal, and besides, nothing could ever, ever feel anywhere near as blissfully good as fucking Luca anyway.

Everything I did, all my alone time could never come close to comparing. It's been a long time since I felt this good.

God knows I've had a long, long time to wait.

"Do you know how many times I've imagined you in my head? Fantasized about running my hands over your beautiful body?" Luca growls, squeezing my ass with one hand while his other wraps around my hair. He gently pulls it back and to the side, tilting my head backward slightly to expose my neck. He leans in slowly, his hot breath tickling my skin and making goosebumps prickle up on my arms and legs.

"I've been dreaming of this moment for so long, Serena," he continues. Every syllable is like a ticklish, delicious puff of warmth dancing down the slope of my neck. Then he bends to press a soft kiss into the skin there and I gasp involuntarily. I can feel him smiling against my skin. "Fuck, I never forgot how good it felt to make you gasp, make you sigh and scream. But my memories are never as good as the real thing, are they?"

His kisses become harder, less teasing as he nips and sucks at the soft flesh of my neck, and I shiver with the anticipation of seeing those blushing red marks on my skin, reminders of who I belong to and how good he makes me feel. That dull ache combined with the ticklishness is enough to make me wet. "Don't stop," I murmur.

"Don't worry, I have so many plans for you," Luca whispers. He lets go of my hair and uses both arms to hoist me up, my legs instinctively wrapping around his waist as he holds me up effortlessly. I run my fingers down his upper arms, feeling the swell of muscles which have definitely gotten bigger in the two years since we were last together.

"You've beefed up a little since you went away," I remark, biting my lip playfully.

Luca grins. "Not much else to do in prison. Besides, the

stronger I am, the easier I can move you around. Do whatever I want with you."

He kisses me deeply, spinning around as he holds me easily in his arms. He carries me across the room to a vintage-looking, luxurious chaise lounge chair, sitting down with me still perched on his lap, straddling him. His hands rove up and down my back, sliding down to grab my ass, then back up to tangle in my hair. I can feel the hard heat of his cock beneath me, straining to burst free of his pants, and I can't help but start to rock against it as we kiss. Luca groans, his hands slipping around to grope my breasts through my shirt. I've only got a thin sports bra on underneath the shirt, and I can feel every pass of his fingers over my stiffening nipples. I let out a moan, my head tipping backward as my eyes roll shut. It's been so long that every single miniscule touch feels like an electric jolt right down to my pussy.

"God, you feel even better than I remember," Luca says, his voice gravelly and rough with need. I know he's been craving this just as much as I have, and I can't wait for him to finally unleash the ravenous desire he's holding back. I want him to let go completely, give in to the wave of irresistible heat growing between us. I want him to fuck me mercilessly, use my body the way he needs to, fill me up and make me his own. He squeezes my breasts gently, his thumbs slipping over my erect nipples, making me whimper.

He reaches down and grabs the hem of my shirt, yanking it upward. I lift my arms and let him tear the shirt up over my head, tossing it across the room. My chest is heaving, my breasts plump and restrained by the tight sports bra. "I missed these," Luca says, a hint of a smirk on his lips. He massages my breasts through the thin material, my nipples clearly visible as he pushes my tits together. I can't stand it anymore, so I push his hands away just for a moment while I peel off the sports bra and throw it down to the floor, letting my breasts spill free.

Luca lets out a sigh of approval, his hands immediately going back to my tits as he gropes me, pinching my bare nipples between his fingers.

"Yes," I hiss, closing my eyes and giving in to the sensation. I nearly cry out loud when he tilts me backward, then pulls one of my nipples into his warm mouth. His tongue flicks over the stiffened peak while his lips gently suck and bite. Every movement sends a spiral of pleasure through my body. I can hardly stand it, my hips bucking involuntarily as I rock against his stiff cock beneath me. Luca moves to suck at my other nipple, kissing and biting my breasts until I'm whimpering and slack in his arms.

Luca stops for a moment to tear his own shirt off before cradling me onto my back on the chaise chair. He takes off his shoes and mine, then stands up and unzips his pants, letting them crumple in a pile on the floor before bending over me. He tugs at the waistband of my sporty leggings and I lift up my legs so he can pull them off. He lets out a guttural moan as he realizes I'm not wearing any panties— the leggings are so tight and form-fitting that it's just more comfortable without them when I go for a walk or jog. I'm bare-naked in front of him, vulnerable and exposed.

"You're so beautiful," he murmurs, shaking his head.

"You can look at me some more later. Get back down here," I reply, smiling. It doesn't take any more than that for him to comply. He bends down over me, kissing my lips as his hands explore my body. His fingers drag down from my breasts to my stomach and hips, then slide along my trembling thighs. He parts them with one swift movement, then begins kissing a slow path down my body. I watch him closely, holding my breath as his lips approach the warm, wet mound between my legs. He looks up at me hungrily before gently kissing my clit. I whine a little, feeling my whole body tense up in anticipation.

He pauses for a long, painful moment, just letting his hands rub up and down my inner thighs while my pussy waits for his touch. I'm nearly aching by this point, desperate for him to touch me there. "Please," I beg softly. "I need you so badly."

With that, Luca leans down and runs his tongue up and down the length of my slit, sending shockwaves of pleasure over me. I groan and instinctively reach down, my hands clasping around the back of his head, pushing his face into my cunt. He plunges his tongue inside my aching hole, then slips back up to softly toy with my clit, rubbing that tight little bud with his tongue. It feels so fucking good I can hardly bear it, but before I can catch my breath, Luca closes his lips over my clit, sucking and flicking his tongue over the bundle of nerves.

"Oh, fuck," I murmur, getting lost to the sensation. To my surprise, he then slips two fingers deep inside my dripping pussy, curling them ever so perfectly to stroke my g-spot deep inside while he sucks at my clit. The overwhelming combined sensations makes me scream out and roll my hips against him, grinding my pussy into his face. He doesn't relent, even for a second, his fingers slamming into me fast and hard. It doesn't take more than a few seconds of this for me to cry out as my first orgasm shatters over me, my honey gushing over his hand. Luca withdraws his fingers and licks hungrily at my cunt, soaking up my juices as my toes curl and my body twitches.

"That's my good girl," he growls from between my thighs. "I've wanted to do that for a long, long time. But I'm not done with you yet. Nowhere near."

He straightens back up and I scramble to sit up, getting to my knees in front of him even as I can feel my cunt still pulsing with the aftershocks of climax. Before he even gets a chance to, I grab the waistband of his boxers and pull it down, letting his cock spring free. He steps out of the boxers and I look up at him, licking lips. I've wanted this for so many months. I've dreamed of tasting his beautiful, massive cock again. I wrap my fingers around his thick shaft, feeling that warmth and hardness I've missed so much, and begin to slowly slide my hands up and down. His cock twitches and Luca closes his eyes, his lips falling open. His fingers press faintly at the back of my head and I feel a thrill of pleasure at how badly he wants this. He needs me to suck his cock just as badly as I want to do it.

I lean forward and softly lick the head of his shaft while my hands continue to pump him, letting my hot breath wash over. "*Si, bambina,*" he groans, rocking forward just a bit so that the head of his cock bumps against my lips. I look up at him and he opens his eyes at just that moment to watch me pull his cock into my mouth, taking him in as deeply as I can manage in one smooth movement. He groans and clutches the hair at the back of my head, pressing my face down on his cock so that I'm almost gagging. I flick my tongue along the underside of his shaft while I pump him with both hands.

"Oh, that's so good, Serena," Luca says roughly. I begin to suck him harder, sliding his shaft in and out of my mouth faster and faster. One of my hands slips down to caress his sac while I suck his cock and his entire body shudders. I bob up and down on his shaft, devouring him with abandon.

"Fuck, yes," he groans through gritted teeth.

"Mmm," I moan, sending vibrations through his body. I'm sucking him hard now, sliding my hands up and down his flesh. I can feel him tightening up, like he's almost ready to explode. I'm so caught up in the moment, in the rush of making him feel good, that I don't want to stop.

But just before I can make him come, he gently nudges me back, his cock sliding out of my mouth with a wet pop.

"Not yet, *mia passerotta*," he murmurs, grabbing me by the shoulders and spinning me around so that I'm on my hands and knees on the chaise lounge, my ass up in the air. "I need to feel that sweet cunt," he says, and I shiver at the sensation of his engorged shaft tantalizing my slick hole from behind. He's toying with me, rubbing the tip of his cock around my pussy. I'm aching with the need to be filled up, stuffed and fucked hard.

"Give it to me," I whimper. "Please. Fuck me, Luca."

Instead, I feel his fingers push inside of me while his cock rubs against my ass, teasing me, pushing me closer and closer to another breaking point. His fingers stroke at my g-spot again while he groans at the friction of his stiffness against my taut ass cheek. The sensation builds and builds until I'm bucking backwards against his hand, whimpering and clutching at the edge of the chair.

"Oh my god, oh my god," I gasp, and just before I come again, Luca pulls his fingers back out and slides his massive cock inside of my pussy, filling me up and stretching my wet hole until it almost hurts. "Yes! Yes!" I burst out, slamming my ass back against him, letting him fill me to the hilt as he grabs hold of my hips.

"You like that, *dolcezza*?" Luca grunts. "You want me to fuck your tight little pussy harder? Tell me how it feels, baby."

"It feels... so... fucking... good," I choke out between thrusts, feeling my whole body tensing up as he fucks me harder and faster. He picks up the tempo, slamming into me again and again. He reaches around underneath me to stroke at my clit with his fingers while he fucks me and I cry out, my second orgasm exploding inside of me. "Luca!" I scream.

He doesn't stop, even for a second, fucking me hard

even as my body shudders with waves of pleasure, totally overstimulated. "You're gonna make me come again," I mumble, clinging to the chaise for dear life.

But he grabs me and lifts me up, spinning me around and leaning back against the chair with his cock still inside of me so that I'm now straddling him again. His legs are hooked over each side of the chaise with me speared on his cock on top of him. He holds me up by the strength of his arms alone, holding me in air, in place, while he thrusts upward with his hips, his cock pounding into me harder and harder. It's all I can do to even remember to breathe while he's fucking me, his swollen head striking that deep, delicious spot inside of me again and again and again.

"I want you to come for me, Serena," he growls imperatively. "I want that sweet little pussy to gush all over my cock. I want to hear you scream, *mia bambina*."

He fucks me so fast and hard that my cunt aches, burns with the ferocity of it. That arching knot of pleasure tightens and tightens until I'm gasping, climaxing with a shriek. "Fuck! I'm coming!" I cry out, bouncing up and down on his cock.

"Good girl, good girl," Luca murmurs, but I can tell he's starting to lose control, too. His thrusts are getting more erratic, more violent as he fucks me. He sits up straighter, pulling my legs around his waist so that we're face to face while I bounce on his shaft. I'm so wet that we're both slick, sliding against each other fast and hard. Luca grabs my ass with one hand, and my left breast in the other, squeezing and pinching my nipple while his cock hits my g-spot. He moves faster and faster until I'm almost slack, my body exhausted and giving in to the overpowering sensations of pleasure.

"Fuck me," I whisper, my eyes rolling back in my head. "Fill me up, Luca. I want... I want to feel you come inside me. Please. Give it to me."

"I'm gonna come for you, *dolcezza*. Gonna pump you full of my seed, baby. Gonna make you mine forever and ever," he groans, leaning forward to kiss me hard, his tongue pushing into my mouth while I feel his cock tightening up inside of me.

Even though I'm barely able to think coherently, I use what little strength I have left to squeeze my pussy tight around Luca's shaft, kissing him back as he groans into my mouth. With a few rapid thrusts, he lets out a roar and shoots his sweet, thick seed deep inside of me, his hands groping me, clutching me close to his chest. He thrusts a few more times and I can feel his come starting to leak out of me as we sit there, entwined around each other and breathing raggedly. Luca kisses my forehead and lifts me up, setting me down beside him. He stands up and starts to get dressed again, and I quickly follow suit, realizing that it's actually rather cold in the basement and my naked skin is getting goosebumps.

"I can't believe this is happening," I murmur, looking up at him as I tug my leggings back on. Luca walks across the room to retrieve my shirt and bra, returning them to me. "I can't believe you're really here. After two years."

"It's been too long," he replies. "I never want to be apart from you for so long again."

"Luca… all this time has been hard. Worse than I even predicted," I begin, biting my lip. I don't want to ruin the beauty of the moment, but I can't pretend like nothing happened. I want to pick up right where we left off but I can't deny that things have changed, at least a little.

"I know," he says, pain etched across his face. "I wish I could have come back to you sooner. Every day on the inside was a fight for survival. For sanity. At first, when they threw me in solitary confinement, it was almost a welcome break from constantly defending myself and watching my back. But after a while, that emptiness, that silence, it all starts to close in on you and you start wishing you could be back out with the other inmates. As it turns out, the only thing worse than being surrounded by dangerous men is being alone with your thoughts."

"I'm so sorry you had to go through that," I tell him, reaching up to touch his face. He leans into my palm, pressing his cheek into my hand before turning to kiss my fingers.

"All of that was bearable, though. The thing that nearly killed me was being away from the woman I love," he adds, pulling me into an embrace. "Not knowing where you were or if you were okay. That's the thing that kept me awake at night."

I give him a weak smile. "I was okay. Well, at first I had some trouble. When they took you away, I kind of fell apart. It was so hard to convince myself life was still worth living. I would just lie in bed and think about how badly you were being treated in there, how unfair it all was. I didn't want to get out of bed or do anything. Nothing felt right. Nothing seemed to matter. It was like, why should I try to go back to the life I had before you?"

"But you did. I can see it. I could tell as soon as you came down that ladder, you've been surviving. You have that look about you. Like you've taken on the whole world and you're winning," Luca comments, a hint of pride in his voice.

"I'm glad you see that in me," I reply. "For a long time I didn't see it myself. It was a struggle, picking myself back up and getting back into the grind. But I figured it out eventually: working hard kept my mind off of more terrible things. So I worked my ass off."

"How is the shop doing?" he asks.

"Good. Great, actually," I correct myself. "I've hired this girl to help out and sales are up."

"I'm proud of you," Luca says, beaming at me. I can feel

my face heating up. It's crazy. I just had mind-blowing sex with the guy, he knows every inch of my body intimately, but he can still make me blush with just a few words of praise.

"Thank you," I mumble, looking away. Changing the subject, I pipe up, "So, what is this place? I know the prison guards didn't arrange this whole shebang just so we could have a conjugal visit. What's going on?"

Luca sighs. "This is an old bootleggers' nest, a place where they used to hide out from the authorities, lay low in between big operations. Italian, of course."

"That explains the classed-up decor," I joke, raising an eyebrow. Luca chuckles.

"Yeah, we can never resist beautiful things," he answers, looking at me meaningfully.

"How did you find out about this place?"

"A friend of mine, a cellmate called Trueba, he told me about it. This place is a well-guarded secret, one the NYPD doesn't know about even after all this time. I'm sure you noticed what a pain it is to get here. Not too hard to believe that those cops wouldn't want to drag their asses all the way out here anyway," he laughs.

"Trueba? So, this cellmate of yours... did he help you get here or something? How did you arrange it? Luca, did you... did you break out of prison?" I ask, my throat going dry suddenly.

He takes both my hands in his. "Serena, I did exactly what I had to do to get out of there and come back to you."

"So, what now?" I ask quietly. "I'm sure they're looking for you."

Luca raises my hands to his lips, kissing them sweetly. "What happens now is we go back to where we were before all this happened. We go to dinner. We go to the park. We wake up in the morning together and we fall asleep at night side by side. We go back to being *us* again."

I can feel that annoying, all-too-familiar prickle of tears in my eyes, but whether they're happy or frightened tears I'm not sure.

"I want that more than anything in the whole world. But Luca, how are we—"

There's a resounding thump-thump-thump from behind us and we both turn around quickly to see one of the men who brought me here climbing down the ladder, looking sweaty and distressed. He looks at Luca and says, "Sorry to interrupt, but we've got trouble."

"No... no, you've got to be kidding me," Serena breathes as we pull up to Bathing Beauty and see the big yellow sign posted on the front door. We don't even need to get out to see the big bold word *CLOSED* written at the top of it.

Coming here in the first place was a risk, but it was a calculated risk. I had some men scout around the area before us to make sure there were no police watching the area. But just to be cautious, I also had them draw the attention of any beat cops a couple blocks down.

There's still no word of my escape in the news. They likely don't want to draw attention to the fact that one of Detective Prince's prized inmates escaped and are keeping it hush-hush. Still, it's been eerily quiet, and I know it won't last. But I have to take it day by day.

When the guard had intruded on us back on the island, he said there had been sightings of police investigating Serena's shop. Looks like the reports were right.

As we come to a stop around the back of the building and Serena hops out of the car to run up to the sign, I pull my hood over my head and don my old aviators. It doesn't help make me look less suspicious, but it does make me a little harder to spot as anyone but just another shady figure.

There's no shortage of those, this time of night.

I step up next to Serena and put a big hand on her shoulder as she stares at the notice with a gaping mouth, and I can see anger rising in her cheeks.

It's a police notice. The sign is a bunch of jargon, but in short, it says the business is temporarily closed because of an ongoing police investigation, and that removing the sign is a punishable offense.

"How could they do this?" Serena stammers, looking up to me with panic in her eyes. "This place is-is my livelihood! They don't have anything tying me to... anything!"

"It's a threat," I say in a grave tone, reading the thing over again and glancing over my shoulder. My hand slides from her shoulder to her smaller hand, and I give her a tug to follow me around the back of the building. "Come on, we should get out of sight."

"Where?" she asks, following me.

"Inside," I say. "Looks like nobody's doing any investigating right now, it'll be better than hanging out on the street."

We go to the back door, and Serena unlocks it to allow us to step inside. We enter, and I can immediately tell things are off.

Serena flicks on a light, and there are signs of tampering everywhere. As I step through the shop with her, I can tell that inventory has been moved around roughly, the office has been nearly torn apart from someone searching through any files Serena happened to have around, and even the front of the store has been looked through.

"They even took some of my chemicals," Serena says in disbelief, looking around at the damage, and as she turns on the office light, I can see the tears shining in her eyes. "How did they get a warrant so fast?"

I move to the front of the shop and find an envelope that was pushed through the mail slot. It looks official, and it has the police department's return address on it. "Looks like this is their notice," I say, turning it over in my hands and handing it to her when she approaches. She tosses it to the counter, shaking her head.

"I can't read that thing right now. I... I feel sick, Luca."

I wrap my arms around her, and she buries her face into my chest, where I feel her tears staining my shirt.

"This is my fault," I whisper, holding her snugly in my embrace, making her feel secure. God, I've missed that feeling, but I can already see the damage my return is causing. "They don't care about you. Not really. They know we're together, and this is a threat to let us know they're still watching. Hounding us."

"No," says Serena, looking up at me. Tear-marks are still streaming down her face, but she looks resolute. "No, this is about both of us. You've been strong for so long, Luca, but we're in this together," she says, managing a smile, and I move my hands down to her hips and give her a squeeze.

"You don't want to get dragged into this any more than you already are," I say.

"Are you kidding? This is my business, and whether they're after you or not, they're fucking with *me* now, too. That's why you're here again. I'm already in," she says, tightening a fist full of my shirt in her hand. "I'll be damned if I let everything I worked for go to hell because some... some crooked cop with a stick up his ass has a chip on his shoulder!"

I grin, and I scoop her up in my arms suddenly. She yelps, kicking her legs as she instinctively wraps her arms around my neck. "That's my girl," I say proudly, and she blushes in my arms. "I've missed that fire in you more than anything."

She smiles, and I bend down to kiss her on the lips, then I pepper her whole face with kisses, and her teary face is soon blushing and giggling instead. I walk her back to the office and set her on the desk. My hands wrap around her waist, and we just look at each other for a moment, smiling.

In spite of all the hardship, being able to just have some privacy with Serena is worth more than anything in the world.

"I know this is a lot," I say, giving her a gentle squeeze to reassure her. "There's no easy way to live with the police breathing down your neck, I can tell you that. But I can tell you one more thing." I put my hands around her face, gently bringing her forehead forward to touch mine to hers. "I've tasted freedom, Serena, freedom with you. And nothing is going to tear me away from you again as long as my heart is beating."

I see her smile, and she slips her hands around my sides, feeling the muscles rippling under my shirt. "It was so hard without you, Luca. I mean, I could handle my business fine, I wasn't exaggerating that much in my letters. But just... going to bed alone every night, waking up and forgetting that you weren't going to be there beside me, thinking I wouldn't feel you holding me up for another eight years..."

She pulls her head back and looks at me with those warm, shining eyes that move me like nothing else on this earth. "If I can survive that," she says, "and you can hold up in prison for so long, then together, we can do anything." She puts her hand in mind and interlaces our fingers together.

"You've grown so much stronger since I saw you last," I whisper in a low tone.

"You're one to talk," she says with a grin, running her free hand up and down my muscular side, then sliding her fingers to my front. She lets out a contented sigh at what she feels, and I put a hand under her chin to make her look up to me.

We look at each other like we're meeting for the first time all over again. Every moment with Serena feels like that; the first skipping heartbeat that makes my hardened heart go soft for just a second. Just long enough to get a taste of her and lose all control.

I bring my lips to hers, and as soon as they touch, we're lost in each other.

I let my tongue explore her mouth, and she welcomes it, giving a soft moan into the kiss as her tongue plays with mine in turn. We share warmth as I come in closer, reveling in the feel of her mouth on mine. Her lips are softer than I remember, her blush redder, her voice sweeter.

We move slower than the furious waterfall of energy we felt when we were first reunited. We're even more private now. God, how I've missed having privacy. Really *feeling* alone with Serena, feeling like my time with her can't be intruded on by anyone. Like she can take her time enjoying my body.

Everything I've worked for and waited for is in Serena, and her satisfaction makes me happier and more fulfilled than even my first breath as a free man did.

She puts both hands on my pecs, and I lower my arms to squeeze her hips to let her explore my body. Her fingertips trace the muscles on my upper torso, then go down to my abs. They linger on each and every one while we kiss, then slide to my sides and travel down to my waist.

I rock my hips forward slowly, inviting her to feel more of me. She goes to my thighs and feel the hardness, my muscles so tight they don't have any give. It's pure power under there, just like the rest of me. Her left hand moves up my thigh to where my legs meet, and when she touches the equally hard outline of my stiff cock through my jeans, I feel her draw in a sharp breath.

"We fucked in the safe house," I say in a husky tone, breaking our kiss, "now I want to make love to you. In the place it all began again."

She nods softly, and I move back just enough to pull my shirt up over my head and toss it aside, letting her get a full look at my body. She feasts her eyes, her mouth falling open. Even with my wounds bandaged, so much of my carefully sculpted form is on display, my swarthy skin looking as healthy as ever over hard muscle.

I reach forward, and she lets me pull her shirt over her head too, and I take off her bra to really look at her.

Her form has always been beautiful, but it's all the more irresistible to me after so long away from her. Her olive skin sets off the dark blonde hair spilling down her shoulders like the sun against bronze. I put my warm, rough hands to her breasts and feel them softly, my strong grip gentle. It teases a gasp out of her. I'm like a towering bear pawing at her as she sits there on the desk, exposed to me.

The way her breasts feel is incredible to me. I move my hands under them, feeling their weight in my palms before I bring my thumbs to the brown buds and run them over them, feeling them hardening, getting stiffer and more needy for me. They're begging me to devour them, and I will, soon. I want to take my time with Serena and learn more about this gorgeous new body I'm rediscovering.

I push everything off the desk to give us a clear space, and I gently lower her down onto her back on it and look at her. She's so beautiful that I almost feel like I shouldn't see her, like this is a holy ground that my sinner's heart shouldn't defile.

But I'm going to defile her, whether it's holy or not.

I run my hands down her sides this time, so soft and giving compared to mine. Every inch of her is velvety and pure, from her breasts to her hips to her belly button.

I bend over and breathe on her navel, then rove up her torso to her breasts, letting my five o'clock shadow brush against the soft flesh.

"I've dreamed about this," she confesses, and I'm close enough to watch her chest rising and falling gently yet excitedly, desperate for my touch.

"Have you?" I say, a teasing edge to my voice. I put my hands on her hips and stick my fingers under her pants. "And where did this dream take you?"

"I can't remember," she says, but I can tell she's lying, and I grin. "It all kind of got fuzzy, but I remember waking up and feeling all warm, like you were really there with me."

"Why don't we fill in the blanks, then?" I say, and I pull her pants down. She gasps as I expose her, and it's my turn to feast her eyes on her bare hips, thighs, and best of all, that beautiful place where her thighs meet.

I put my hands to the sides of her ass and bring my face down to her sensitive inner thighs, listening to her gasp as my stubble brushes that most sensitive area. Her breathy voice is like the note of a harp in the air.

Turning my face in, I let my teeth graze her inner thigh, from almost to the knee all the way up to her outer lips. There, I let my breath wash over her, and she shudders. Her fingers grip the edge of the desk, and she pushes her hips up just a little, just enough to let me know just how desperate she is for my touch.

My hands move up and down her legs, groping them greedily and feeling their warmth. I let my breath wash over her pussy once more before I give her what she wants. A taste I've missed for so long and couldn't possibly get enough of now.

I let my tongue out, and it dips just far enough into her lips to make her tense up and gasp, and I drag it up the length of her slit, all the way to the top. I've had a long, long time to think about how to kiss the most sensitive parts of her body just so, and so it's with the utmost precision that I let the tip of my tongue just barely flick the swelling nub of her clit.

Warmth radiates from her, and everything just feels *right* as I taste her. I can't contain a deep, gravelly groan from my chest as the taste awakens my tongue. Like a great engine roaring to life, my body feels energized with power. My grip tightens as I grope her ass, and my gentleness gives way to passion as I open my mouth and revel in the feel of her pussy.

My tongue goes out again, this time going deeper into her. The deeper I go, the hotter it gets, and each time my tongue darts out, I taste more of her, more of that sweet well that I've been thirsty for after all this time. I start to get more generous with my tongue, letting it widen to play with the sensitive outermost parts of her pussy while the tip dives deeper into her.

I let her feel me just like I'm tasting her. I arch my neck with the next stroke, letting my stubble brush against her warm lips that are getting wetter and wetter each time I go down to draw more of her honey out of her.

Serena overflows with feeling for me, and my cock swells stiffer and stiffer with each passing second. As my tongue darts in and out, I let my hands revel in the feeling of her ass and her hips. The way her flesh gives way to my strong hands is something I can't get enough of. I love that I can squeeze her and feel no hardness, just her soft, giving skin that I can't wait to sink my shaft into soon.

I feel her thighs squeezing around my head, and the grip I have around her hips gives me total control to keep Serena wrapped around my face. I have to tame my passion as I feast on her pussy, savoring every moment that I can feel her heartbeat against my tongue.

Her sensitive nub is so swollen, so needy for me, and each time I let my tongue roll over it, I can hear Serena letting out gasps of need. Her knuckles start to get white on the table as I get more rhythmic and relentless with each stroke of my tongue, never slowing down for a moment. My strokes are careful yet strong, dipping down into her lips and coming up to the clit. Each time, I let the tip of my tongue stay there at the clit for just a little longer, tormenting it, letting it kiss the honey from her depths

Soon, I feel Serena's hips starting to twist, and she writhes against me. She needs release, and her body is going to reach it soon.

I keep letting my tongue dart in and out, and her legs wrap around me as she pushes her hips up into me. She isn't looking at what I'm doing, her head back and her golden hair spread out over the desk so carelessly, but she wants more of whatever I'm giving her.

She needs it. Her body needs it. Her heels dig into my sides as best they can as I hear the tiny squeak of her voice as she draws in a pained breath. My hot breath washes over her soaking pussy as my tongue drives her over the edge.

She lets out a beautifully long, high-pitched gasp that fills the whole room while my face gets soaked, and I grip her hips tighter, arching her up into me, and when her tension finally starts to relax, I let my stroking get slower again, nursing her through the end of her orgasm.

I can feel her pleasure pulsing all around me. I can smell her in the air. It's a sensory overload for both of us, but I've been denied it all too long to stop now. I lift my head up and look down at her gorgeous form on the desk. She glows, a smile on her face as her eyes flutter open to look at me.

"Can you sit up?" I ask, and she pushes herself up on her elbow to tilt her head at me.

"Yeah," she says between breaths, "why?"

Instead of answering, I just smile, backing up and pulling her shoes off, then pulling her pants the rest of the way off, leaving her completely naked on the desk.

I hoist her up by the hips and move her aside to give me space while I lay down on my back beside her, and her eyes flutter in confusion before I seize her by the hips again and lift her up over me.

"Luca, what are you-" she laughs, squirming in my grasp as I hold her up with thick arms and strong hands, and I grin up at her as I sit her down on my chest.

"I'm not done with you yet," I growl, and before she can reply, I bring her forward and let her rest on my jaw. Before she realizes what's happening, I let my tongue out and swipe it up her slit

She shudders, nearly losing her balance up on top of me, but I'm in complete control of her. I slide my rough hand up to the small of her back to let her know I've got her, and I start lapping up her pleasure all over again.

She's wet and hot, and looking up at the landscape of her body just makes me love being able to hold onto someone so beautiful all the more. I have such a sure grip on her that she could go limp and I'd still be able to hold her up.

And the way she looks up there, that might well be what I have to do.

She keeps trying to make little thrusts forward into me, but I control her, making her entirely at the mercy of my hands. She is like a doll to me, and I can move her any which way I please. But I only want the angle that will let me play with her swollen, needy clit best.

The more my tongue strokes, the wetter my face gets, until the scent of her lust fills my every breath. With each move of my jaw, my stubble brushes against her and sends tingles up her body.

But I had already gotten her going, so it isn't long before I start to feel her getting tense again. I feel her thighs clenching around my head, and her pitiful thrusts forward get more desperate, more needy. I lose track of how long it takes her to tense up, but the second time feels even more tightly-wound than the first before it all comes spilling out.

She gives a shuddering gasp, and I dig my fingers into her hips and pull her closer to me to let one long, deep stroke of my tongue run the length of her slit while I feel her pussy tremble around me, the orgasm wracking her body in my iron grip.

"Oh god, Luca," she gasps, her face blushing furiously as I help her slide back onto my chest, resting her on me as I look up at her and lick my lips. "I... I think I need a second," she says, and I help her down while I stand up and bend over her, looking her in the eyes. I cradle her head in my hand as she pants, looking up at me lovingly.

"How does it feel, *dolcezza*?" I ask in a husky voice.

"Everything I've been missing," she manages to say through desperate breaths, and she puts a hand on my chest to feel my deep breathing before I bring my lips to her. My whole face is wet with her, and she moans into my mouth at the taste of her own passion. Our tongues play with one another again as I curl my fingers in and take a fistful of her hair.

We break our kiss so that she can breathe again, and her eyes look dizzy with ecstasy. "I want to keep going," she says, words that fill me with pride. I bring my lips to hers again, putting one hand on her thigh and one on her breast to grope her, squeeze her, feel her like I've wanted to feel her nonstop for so long.

"Every night I fell asleep in that cold place thinking of

you," I say, my voice deep and rough in her ear, and she sighs contentedly. "It was the only thing that could keep me warm. Thinking of you, of each time we fell asleep in each other's arms."

"When I wrote that letter about the lingerie," she says, a playful smile coming across her lips, "I... wasn't exaggerating when I said I'd be thinking of you. I thought of you every time, Luca. Even during the day, I-I couldn't think about life without you."

"Those letters kept me going, Serena," I say, our eyes fixed on each other. I loved Serena dearly before I was put away, but you never know how thirsty you are for someone until you're taken away from them. Now, I'll let my eyes take in as much as I want of her. "I couldn't have kept going without them."

Our lips touch again, slowly, intimately. I can feel her heartbeat through her lips, and the heat of her body warms me. When our lips part, I stand up and run my hands over her legs. She can see the outline of my cock hard under my pant, and her eyes are locked on it.

"Ready for more?" I ask, my thumbs making small circles on her inner thighs. She shivers and nods, biting her lip in anticipation.

I reach forward and take her by the hips, then lift one of her legs up and drape it over my shoulder, holding her up with my other hand.

I unbutton my pants and let my cock spring free, and I see Serena watching it with hungry eyes. It makes me happy to see her take such pleasure in my body. She reaches forward, and I tilt my hips in just enough to let her touch my cock. She lets her fingers dance up and down the shaft, her palm brushing up against it before she gives it a gentle squeeze. Her thumb brushes over the crown, and I feel warmth up my body at her touch.

I can see that being able to get such a response from me

excites her. She runs her hands up and down a little more, from the base to the tip.

"I missed this," she says through a smile, and I laugh quietly, rubbing the leg on my shoulder.

"Let me show you how much it missed you," I growl.

I take her hips, and she has a second to remove her hand before I put the swollen, needy, dark crown of my cock to her lips and enter her.

I only put the tip in, and I rock back and forth to move it in slowly, because her mouth is already hanging open. She must be tingling all over just from the feeling of my tongue, so I'll be careful... but my passion can only be slowed so much.

Bit by bit, inch by inch, I slide myself into her, and she's so slick and ready that it feels like I'm gliding into her.

Biting her lip and clenching her eyes, I feel her tightening around me with every bit that I put into her, feeling her pulse around me. When I'm about halfway in, I give her thigh a loving squeeze before I start bucking.

My rhythm picks up fast. I rock back and forth, my balls heavy and full of virile seed that aches to be released. Serena is the only release worth having, and she's worth every moment of wait.

I drive myself into her, then back out, leaving almost nothing but my crown inside her before I go back in again. Each time, I feel her shake. Each time, she gasps, a loving, ecstatic moan in the air that's getting hot with our fucking. I go a little further in each time, and soon, I'm feeling my heavy balls hitting her ass.

I feel every inch of her insides as I get faster and faster, and my rhythm becomes more machine-like with every thrust. I feel her squirming, and I move with her to get closer and closer to those places inside her that drive her wild. I know so many of them, but rediscovering Serena is endlessly rewarding.

She gets more tense the more I go, and before long, I'm down to the hilt inside her, pumping in and out over and over again like a piston, nothing but love and raw power between us, charging the room. It's like electricity, and I feel it coiling up within me with all the passion and energy of our very first time.

With each thrust, I'm holding onto her hips and keeping her steady, watching her body laid out on her side, her mouth frozen open and her eyes looking up at me.

"Oh... oh... oh fuck, Luca," she gasps.

"This is for you, *dolcezza*," I growl, "I love you."

No sooner have the words left my mouth than I twist her hips just enough to start grinding up against her g-spot, and she arches her back as I feel her tense and start to shake, barreling closer and closer to the edge of ultimate pleasure. At the same time, I feel my balls start to tighten as fire fills my cock, running up into my torso and spreading to every limb.

At the same time, we both come, my fingers digging into her thighs while her nails claw at the desk. My seed shoots out in a hot, long, filling burst that floods her pussy and mixes with her honey. It's messy, hot, and our groans fill the room with noise, but it's our private love, something more intimate and wonderful than I could dream of in my wildest fantasies.

Pulse after pulse, I pour myself into her. My every muscle tenses and relaxes with that unmatched feeling of release. Her body goes limp, and I'm the only thing holding her up after a few moments. She's like a ragdoll in my hands, our fluids spilling out through the great shaft of my cock inside her.

When our orgasms relax, I'm still hard, and I grind inside her gently for a few wonderful, blissful moments. My cock twitches a few more times as the last pulses of my love for her empty out into Serena.

Finally, slowly, I carefully start to work myself out of her. I have to be careful with so much stimulation. Her pussy is on fire, I know, but I'm gentle with my girl. She whimpers as I take myself out of her, watching some of my seed run down her olive skin. One last bit of pearly fluid comes out of my cock's head, landing on her pussy's lips like a jewel.

I want to stand back and admire our work, but I can't bring myself to tear away from Serena just yet. I stroke her body, watching her bare chest rising and falling, and her eyes finally flutter open just enough to look at me. Her tired lips crack a smile, and I wink at her.

"Good practice for later," I say, my voice still husky, and her eyes widen.

"Practice? For what?"

"A proper bedroom tonight," I say, and I give her ass a slap that rings through the room, making her squeak. With a grin, I add, "we've got a long time to make up for, baby."

"It's been a long time since I was last out here," Luca says, looking around through the windshield, his hands gripping the steering wheel. There's a hint of nostalgia in his voice, a smile tugging at his lips. He reaches over the console to take my hand, giving it a squeeze. "Not since our one night here."

He glances over at me with a wink, which immediately makes me smile.

"I suppose the mafia isn't usually so concerned with suburbia. That makes sense. I definitely remember thinking Riverdale was a kind of step-down for my family, even though my dad was convinced it was the right choice. I just thought it would be so boring living so far away from the action in the middle of the city. I mean, after living in Manhattan I think any place would feel pretty dull by comparison. I remember being so scared that I would fall out of touch with my best friends who all still lived in the city."

"Did you?" Luca asks.

I chuckle, rolling my eyes.

"Yep. I mean, it's not like they cut me out intentionally or anything, but we definitely drifted apart. Turns out, nobody was particularly excited about the idea of driving all the way out here to hang out. And besides, after what happened with my dad and... you know... I kind of shut down for a while. My mom and I had lost everything — my dad, our money, our reputation — it was just a lot to deal with all at once. I found out really quickly that most of my so-called best friends were more like fair-weather friends. They didn't want to come all the way to Riverdale just to pat me on the back while I cried. And, you know, they were all rich kids. They couldn't relate to me anymore after my family lost our fortune."

"I don't know how you did it," Luca says, shaking his head.

"Well, at first I didn't do anything except cry. We both did. My mom is a tough lady, and the only time I have ever seen her cry was during those first few weeks after Dad died. It was scary, seeing her like that. Dad and I had always joked that she was like a fortress or something, that nothing could get to her. Tear-jerker movies, sad songs; nothing could break her. But during that time, she *was* broken. We both were. Broken *and* broke."

"I wish I had been around to help you," Luca tells me sadly. I lift his hand to my lips and kiss it gently.

"You did help. You saved me from... from having to *repay* my father's debt. You paid it for me," I assure him. "After I laid in bed crying and feeling hopeless for a while, I managed to scrape myself out of bed and get back to work. Thankfully, my dad had paid all my private school tuition ahead of time, so I didn't have to worry about being kicked out of school. So I jumped back into the flow of going to class and doing homework, preparing for college applications. All that normal stuff. Because of you, Luca. Everything I have, after my dad died... it's because you cared. Because you sacrificed everything to make sure I could keep... so I could keep living."

My fingers run over the back of his hand and I smile at him gently. He was the reason I was able to pull myself out of my self-pitying slump. I knew he didn't save me because he wanted me to be lost in grief. I lost my dad and him in the span of a week, and it broke my heart in pieces. But neither of them would have wanted me to throw away my future.

"And my mom finally got out of the house and went back to work. I use the word 'work' loosely because, truth be told, she didn't really know what she was doing. Bathing Beauty was more like a hobby for her back in the day. We employed real workers to keep the place running, and my mom would occasionally drop in to micromanage or just check to make sure things were still going okay. After Dad died, we didn't have the money to pay them anymore, so we had to let them go. That was hard. Hell, one of the ladies who worked there was an old babysitter of mine from when I was little. But they all understood the situation, you know. So my mom took over all the business of running Bathing Beauty. My mom, who was a mafia princess, who had never had to hold down a real job in her life."

"Sounds like a recipe for disaster," Luca comments.

"Oh, it was," I agree. "She really struggled to even manage the store front properly, much less balance the accounts or deal with shipments. Back then, the shop was just stocking artisanal soaps and stuff from other people who actually made them. The kitchen was just kind of sitting there, unused. My mom didn't know how to cook a meal at home, much less cook up all-natural bath oils and stuff. It was definitely disastrous, because we didn't have the funds to keep stocking other people's work, but we didn't know how to make that stuff on our own. The summer after junior year, I started working at Bathing Beauty with my mom to help out, because things were getting pretty desperate between trying to keep the business afloat and keep paying for the house."

"What a nightmare," he says, squeezing my hand. I love how he looks at me. How he listens to me. I feel like I'm talking so much, but he's just engrossed, fascinated by what he missed, all those years ago. All the things we never got to talk about when we got our second chance together.

"It felt like one, for sure. Trying to work with my mother, who was both an uptight micromanager and totally incompetent at the same time. It drove a wedge between us for a bit, because tensions were just so high at the shop and at home. We spent way too much time together, especially considering the fact that before all that, we were never super close. I was always more of a daddy's girl. Finally, though, she started letting me take more control over the shop. As it turned out, I kind of had a knack for business. I was a good salesperson, more approachable than my ice-queen mother. When she no longer had to focus on the storefront, she was actually fairly good at the bookkeeping aspect of the job. When I asked her about it, guess what she said?"

"What?"

"That she was actually a mathlete in high school," I answer, laughing. "Which was so weird to picture. My mom as a student in the eighties, rich and popular but secretly on the mathletes team. I never would've guessed."

"Well, the apple doesn't fall too far from the tree. Seems like every woman in your family probably has some secret strengths nobody knows about," Luca says pointedly, smiling.

"I discovered one of my own when I started working at the shop. One day, my mom got in a really nasty phone argument with one of our suppliers and he pulled out, refusing to work with her again. On a whim, and a little bit out of desperation, I decided to try my hand at making soaps and oils myself. We tricked out the kitchen with some extra tools and appliances and I got to work, reading dumb how-to articles on the internet to teach myself as I went. The first batch wasn't pretty, but it did smell nice. The second batch, though... it was pretty much perfect. So we started selling our own stuff that I made myself in the kitchen. That was a great feeling," I reminisce.

"And you were so young then, too," Luca remarks.

"Yeah, I was seventeen at that point. And I fell in love with the business. My mom and I, we were still hurting from what happened, both of us trying to recover. And Bathing Beauty was there for us, something we had to pour our hearts and souls into. Something to distract us from how scary the world had gotten. For a while we were a pretty good business partnership, and there were even times when we got along, laughing and joking around in the shop in between sales. I remember one weekend, I decided to take on making a huge batch of products, so my mom brought an old TV we had in my dad's study into the shop kitchen. We put on a classic movie marathon; you know, *Arsenic and Old Lace*, *Bringing Up Baby*, all that stuff. We worked side by side to get it all done."

"Never underestimate the power of two women in a desperate situation," Luca says, his words filled with pride. The car turns a corner and we start our way down my street.

"It was great. I mean, we were still struggling to get by, but we were finally treading water instead of just drowning. Things were really turning around," I explain. "Senior year started back up and I had to go to class during the day, but I worked at the shop after school and on weekends. My mom was starting to get a better handle on running the shop while I wasn't there, so after graduation I started college, thankfully on several scholarships."

"Smart cookie," Luca comments, grinning.

"College was awesome. I finally had a little more freedom, and for a while I even moved out of the house and got a roommate in the city."

"Rafaela."

"Yep," I answer. "Rafaela. Finally, I had a friend who was in the same boat as me. She wasn't a rich kid or even a former rich kid; she was working her ass off to get by the same as I was. It was refreshing to not have to hide how hard my life was. She was so understanding. She still is. I'm really glad I met her."

"She and Nico are good people. Certainly the kind of people you want on your side," Luca agrees. He pulls the car into the long driveway of my house, headed toward the garage.

"When my mom got hurt on the job — she burned her arm pretty badly mixing chemicals in the kitchen — I moved home to help look after her and the shop. I have no idea how I managed to run the shop and still graduate from college with my degree. Rafaela wanted me to stay, but I just knew in my heart I had to go home. It was probably an overreaction on my part, but I had already lost one parent, and I was terrified of losing my mom, too. I kept imagining her falling down in the shop one evening after closing and nobody being there to help her. I know it sounds crazy, but her little injury scared me to hell," I admit.

"It doesn't sound crazy at all," Luca says. "She's family."

"Wow, I'm sorry for talking your ear off," I laugh, a little embarrassed.

Luca parks the car and turns to look at me, an earnest look on his handsome face as his hand cups my jaw, staring into my eyes.

"Don't ever apologize for talking about yourself. For sharing your excitement with me. I love hearing about your history. Just proves to me again how tough and determined and capable you are."

He leans in, his mouth gently pressing into mine, and I feel my shoulders soften into the tender kiss. I've never met someone like him before. When we were young, he was so hot and cold. Of course, now I know what he was involved in to make him so distant.

I'm determined to make sure we never have that distance between us again. My dad and Luca protecting me from the Mafia has never saved me from heartache for long.

"I know it seems ridiculous to keep paying for this house even when my dad died. It would have been easier to try and sell it, just keep living in that apartment in Manhattan. But I just couldn't do it. This house, huge and unnecessary though it is, meant so much to Dad. He poured his heart and soul into this place, and I just can't bear to part with it. Not yet anyway."

"I understand," Luca says, getting out of the driver's seat and coming around to open the passenger side door for me. He gives me a hand, helping me out of the car. "People do crazy things for family. For the ones they love."

"Ain't that the truth," I agree, smiling at him. "Wow, it's crazy to be back here. With you."

Luca nods, looking around with a look of mild surprise on his face.

"Yeah, I never expected that I would get a chance to see the house in its finished state. It was still kind of a mess when I was last here."

"Can I ask you something?" I start suddenly, biting my lip.

"Of course. Anything."

"Why didn't you come back? I mean, after the first day

we met when you were working on the construction crew, I never saw you here again. We had to sneak around to other places, remember?" I ask, cocking my head to one side.

Luca smirks.

"Well, the contractor gave me some other assignments, other houses to work on at the time instead of your house. He claimed that my particular carpentry skill set would be better suited for other projects. But the short answer he never outright admitted to was that he saw you and me together and didn't want to run the risk of getting in trouble with your father."

My face flushes hot.

"Oh no. I'm so sorry. You mean I cost you a job?"

"No, no, it was fine. I had plenty of assignments on hand to keep me busy," Luca assures me, taking me by the hand as we walk up to the garage entrance to the house. "That was one thing my uncle was always adamant about: keeping me busy. I think he was worried that if I had too much free time, I'd end up going down the wrong path like so many other guys my age in the same position. He wanted to protect me, I guess."

"Okay. Good. I'll take your word for it. I could never forgive myself if that was all my fault," I tell him honestly.

He waves his hand dismissively as I fish out my keys and open the door to let us into the house.

"It's not like you forced yourself on me. I was pretty assertive with you, if I recall correctly."

I can't help but grin, remembering how suave and flir-tatious Luca was then as a cocky teenager who knew exactly how good-looking he was, how impossible it would be for even a straight-laced good girl like me to resist his charms.

"You certainly weren't lacking in confidence, that's for sure," I laugh.

"I was a little arrogant back then," he agrees, smiling.

"You had every reason to be. You still do," I tease, strolling into the kitchen. "Do you want something to drink? My mom thinks beer is gross so we don't have any of that but we do have wine."

"Sounds just like the Luisa Gaspari I remember hearing about from the guys back in the day. Classy woman."

"It's okay. You can say 'uptight.' I live with her, I know what she's like," I joke, taking out a pair of wine glasses and a bottle of Shiraz. I pour us each a glass as Luca chuckles.

"Your words, not mine. So, where is Mama De Laurentis today?" he asks. "I hope she wasn't too worried about your sudden disappearance."

I shrug, turning to hand him his wine. "She was definitely concerned. I had a bunch of missed calls and voicemails, of course, but she believed my story about going into the shop to do late-night paperwork. At least, I think she did. I mean, I'm an adult, so she can't exactly call the police just because I'm gone a little longer than expected. Either way, she's out of town today, visiting one of her cousins down in Newport."

"So we've got this giant house all to ourselves, then?" Luca inquires, raising an eyebrow. I nod, taking a sip of my wine to hide my smile.

"Yep. I don't think she's coming back until tomorrow."

"Well, I'm sorry to miss out on meeting your mother but... I'm not *that* sorry," he says.

"I guess now we just have to figure out what to do with all this free time and space we have to fill today," I tell him innocently, sipping my wine as I bat my eyelashes at him. He grins.

"Yes, whatever will we do to pass the time? I can't think of a single thing I want to do with you right now," he says, his voice low and deep. "Any ideas?"

"We could... play chess. Or watch daytime soap operas.

Oh! I know: we could dig that Monopoly box out of the attic. So many fun options," I remark. Luca downs his wine in one long draught and sets the glass down behind him on the counter, sauntering over to me. I can feel my heartbeat quickening instantly, my body warming in anticipation of his touch.

He backs me against the kitchen island, putting both hands on the counter on either side of me. He takes the wine glass out of my hands and places it on the counter behind me, leaning in close to my face. I can see the deep ivy green of his eyes, the tiny flecks of gold scattered around his irises. I can see now that there are a few tiny freckles across the bridge of his nose, and that his lips are so full and soft-looking. I can't help but lick my own lips.

"Huh. I just thought of something we could do together today," Luca growls softly.

"Oh?" I murmur, my breath catching in my throat. "And what is that?"

"What are your feelings on getting bound, blindfolded, bent over, and fucked from behind?" Luca suggests, his lips mere centimeters from mine.

I can scarcely remember to breathe. "Positive. I-I have positive feelings about that."

"Good," he murmurs, and captures my mouth in a deep kiss. His hands come up to cup my face, sliding back through my hair as he presses into me. I can feel his cock hard against my hip and it's all I can do to keep from reaching down to touch it. The space between my thighs feels so warm, tingling with desire already.

His tongue pushes into my mouth and I let out a groan, feeling my body go limp in his arms. He has the magic touch— the ability to make all my tension melt away, turn me into a lovesick ragdoll. He can do whatever he wants to me. Anything.

I instinctively reach up to touch his face, but he quickly

moves my hands behind my back, holding my wrists there with one huge hand. For a split second a thrill of true fear shocks through me, as though my body is remembering the times I've had my hands behind my back before... the *bad* times.

But I quickly remember that this isn't a bad time. I'm safe. I'm with Luca. And even if things get a little rough — and god, I hope they do — he will never actually hurt me or push too far. The trust between us, the knowledge that he will always listen to and respect my wants instantly calms us.

And I know that if I ever say our safe word — Crimson — that he would instantly stop. Knowing that allows me to relax and feel the thrill of arousal run through me.

He wedges his leg between my thighs, rubbing against the tingling heat of my crotch. I shiver at the rolling wave of pleasure even this small movement gives me. Luca chuckles, a low, guttural sound. Almost sinister, but not.

"You're so hot for me, *dolcezza*," he murmurs, gently biting my bottom lip. "Maybe I should help you cool down."

With that, he spins me around, pinning my arms behind my back again as he deftly slips off his leather belt. I hold my breath, glancing over my shoulder to watch as he binds the belt around my wrists. The sight of my hands tied with his own belt, still warm from his body heat, turns me on more than I could have ever predicted.

He spanks my ass with a resounding slap, then moves my hair over one shoulder and bends to kiss my neck. The combination of delicious stinging and ticklish kisses makes me tremble, and I back into him slightly, rubbing my ass against the hard cock straining in his pants.

"What a dirty girl," he hisses in my ear.

It occurs to me suddenly that I might actually be literally dirty at the moment. After all, I did go straight from jogging in my neighborhood to being rowed across a body of water, through the woods, and down into a dusty basement. And we fucked there. It's been a very hectic 24 hours.

"Well, maybe I should clean up a little bit, then," I remark suggestively, trying to make my plea for a shower sound somewhat sexy. Luca chuckles, kissing the side of my face as he frees my wrists from his leather belt. I'm a little disappointed at this, but I hope to god it's just a rain check and not a cancellation.

"That's not a bad idea, as long as I can come, too," he replies. My heart flutters.

"Oh, I hope you will," I answer mischievously. My plan is working!

He breaks away for a second and goes over to the refrigerator. He opens up the freezer drawer for some reason, looking for something.

"What are you looking for?" I ask.

He takes out an ice tray. "A-ha. You know, I'm a little surprised. I thought a fancy kitchen like this would certainly have an icemaker built into the fridge."

"Yeah, after Dad died and I took over the finishing touches on construction I decided to cut corners with some cheaper appliances. But why do we need ice?" I press on, totally lost.

Luca grins as he walks over and sets down the ice tray for a moment, then scoops me up in his arms easily, holding me with my legs around his waist while he picks the ice tray back up. I'm amazed again at his strength and control, although by this point I shouldn't be shocked by anything he does anymore. And besides, I'm sure two years with nothing better to do than lift weights and work out has definitely increased his physical abilities.

"Just wait and see," he answers simply. And with that, he carries me out of the kitchen and, more impressively, all the way up the staircase, and down the hallway. He carries me to my room, crossing my bedroom and setting me down in the bathroom.

"You know I *can* walk, right?" I joke.

"You work too hard already," he replies, shrugging. "The least I can do is get you off your feet every now and then." He turns on the shower, eyeing the detachable shower head as he adjusts the heat and closes the bathroom door. I start peeling off my clothes, thankful to be out of them since I've been wearing them for way longer than I would like to. Luca follows suit, revealing his powerful chest and arms, the rippling muscles of his stomach, his strong legs. Even though we've already fucked twice in the past 24 hours, I can't help but feel that same overwhelming wave of desire for him again. I wonder if it will ever wear off. I hope not. I doubt it.

"After you," he says, gesturing to the shower. There's a rather naughty glint in his eye, but I don't question it. I climb into the shower, sighing with relief as the hot water cascades over me, warming me up and washing away the grime and stress of the past day and night. Luca comes in after me and squeezes body wash into his palm to start washing first himself, then me. I inhale sharply as his huge hands slide up and down my body, sudsy and slippery. His fingers toy with my nipples, slipping over them and cupping my breasts as I close my eyes and lean into him. My hair falls in soaked tendrils down my back as I tilt my head back slightly, giving in to the combined sensations of soothing hot water and Luca's hands caressing me.

Suddenly, a new sensation explodes into my attention: icy-cold burning across my nipples. I open my eyes and look down to see Luca sliding a quickly-melting ice cube around the stiffened peaks of my breasts. The sensation is confusing at first: both slightly painful and uncomfortable as well as strangely arousing. My body responds with a warm dampening between my thighs, my heartbeat quickening. Just as my nipples start to go a little numb, Luca dives in and captures them in his hot mouth. I let out a little whimper at how amazing it feels. I never considered ice-play before; it just never seemed to make any sense to me.

But it *certainly* makes sense to me now.

"How's that feel, *mia passerotta*?" Luca asks as he moves from one nipple to the other.

"Fantastic," I sigh, closing my eyes again.

Luca lowers down to kneel in front of me, sliding another ice cube down the length of my body as he goes, making me shiver. He gently pushes my legs open further before slowly circling the ice cube around my pussy, getting close but never actually touching my clit. I tremble, my mouth falling open as I look down at him. Luca locks eyes with me, watching my face as he moves the ice over my clit. I cry out, almost recoiling from the strange burning on my most sensitive part. But he leaves it there only for a second before grabbing my leg and holding me steady as he hoists my thigh onto his shoulder and leans in to run his tongue along the length of my slick vulva, circling around my clit and finally closing his mouth over it.

"Oh fuck," I breathe, my arm reaching out to balance myself against the shower wall. Luca licks and sucks at my pussy ravenously, his tongue plunging in and out of my hole while his hands slide up my thighs and around to grab my ass. Without even turning away from my pussy to look, he reaches back suddenly and grabs another ice cube, then rubs it against my opening while he gently nibbles and sucks my clit. By now my legs are trembling, struggling to hold myself up in the throes of pleasure.

"Luca, oh my god, I-I'm gonna fall," I whisper, afraid of

my legs giving out but not wanting the amazing sensations to end.

"I won't let you fall," he says gruffly, releasing me so he can put my leg back down and prod me to turn around so I'm facing away from him, into the spray of water. There's a metal safety bar in front of me that I bend and reach down for. Quick as a flash, Luca opens the shower curtain and steps out dripping wet to grab his belt, then walks over to fasten it around my wrists and the safety bar, binding me there.

He gets back into the shower behind me, grabbing my ass and sliding an ice cube down to my slit. "You look so beautiful tied up here for me," he growls, giving my ass a hard smack.

My pussy tingles and aches from the cold and wanting.

"Fuck me, please," I moan.

"Is that what you want, baby? My cock inside your tight little pussy?" he teases.

"Oh god yes, please," I beg, shaking my ass against him. I look back over my shoulder and he smiles widely, a devilish look on his impossibly handsome face. He slides his cock against my ass, rubbing into me as I feel my pussy aching for him. I need it.

Finally, he shoves his cock deep inside me and I cry out with pleasure as the head of his thick shaft bumps into that sensitive little spot. He holds still for a moment, just letting my pussy clench around him. I can't stand it... I need him to move. I need him to fuck me.

"Can't believe I never tied you up like this before," he comments, his voice thick and low.

I rock my hips, sliding back against him, my body begging for him to thrust.

"Greedy little girl, aren't you?" Luca groans, and I can tell it's taking all his willpower not to just give in and fuck me.

"I need you so bad," I manage to mumble.

At last, he rears back, his cock nearly sliding all the way out of me before slamming back into my pussy hard, again and again. I have to bite my lip to keep from screaming out, my wrists aching from being bound while my body trembles at the overwhelming pleasure of his cock spearing into me.

"You feel so fucking good, *dolcezza*," Luca moans, slapping my ass. His hands fall to my hips, gripping me tight as he thrusts into me faster and harder, animalistic needs overcoming his willpower as he loses himself to how good it feels. I'm already gone, my thoughts totally scattered to the wind and replaced with nothing but blinding hot pleasure.

"Harder," I murmur, and Luca obliges eagerly, picking up the rhythm and striking deeper inside me. My orgasm appears out of nowhere, and I can feel my cunt pulsating around him, shuddering with wave after wave of bliss as I whimper incoherently.

"You just love being bent over and fucked, don't you, Serena?" he grunts through gritted teeth. "Dirty little angel."

"God, I love your cock," I pant, my words slurring as I close my eyes, riding the waves of pleasure. "Feels so… fucking… good."

"I've missed this so much, your filthy mouth, your perfect body, your tight little cunt," Luca groans, his fingers digging into my hips as he fucks me. His tempo is getting erratic and wild and I can tell he's getting close to the edge, so I start moving my hips a little bit to bounce against him, adding a little more tension to each powerful thrust.

"Show me how much you missed me," I demand between thrusts.

Luca fucks me faster, leaning over slightly and reaching

around underneath me to toy with my clit, rolling that sensitive little bud between his fingertips as I let out a shriek.

"Fuck! *Just* like that, Luca, yes!" I whine, feeling my second climax fast approaching.

He doesn't slow down for even a second, even when I cry out, coming again as my pussy shudders around his thickening cock. I can feel him tightening up behind me, his fingers rubbing at my clit almost too hard.

"Yes! Yes!" he grunts, and with a few more quick snaps of his hips I feel him explode his hot seed inside my pussy. He thrusts several more times, pumping me full of every last drop before withdrawing. I feel my legs trembling, my knees threatening to give out, but then Luca reaches around to undo the belt and free my hands. He tosses the belt back out of the shower and helps me stand up and turn around to kiss him passionately under the hot spray of the water. He takes the detachable shower head and sprays me down thoroughly, then to my surprise, he turns me back around and begins washing my hair with gentle hands. I can't help but sigh appreciatively at the soothing gesture.

"Ever since I was a little girl I loved having my hair played with," I mumble as he massages green apple-scented shampoo into my scalp.

"I love you," he says suddenly. "I dreamed of doing this the whole time I was in prison."

"What? Washing my hair?" I ask, half-joking.

Luca laughs. "No. Fucking you. Holding you. Just being with you."

"I never want to be without you again," I tell him earnestly as he uses the shower head to start rinsing my hair. After that, he rubs conditioner into my hair, paying close attention to every strand. Hell, he's doing a better job of it than I do.

"I don't plan on being apart from you ever again, Serena," he says seriously.

He rinses the conditioner out of my hair, combing his fingers gently through the tangles and snarls before setting the shower head back in its dock. I turn around to face him again, planting a kiss on his soft, perfect lips. "What are we gonna do?" I ask him quietly. "We can't stay here."

"I know," he agrees.

"My mom isn't here now, but she'll be back tomorrow, and Luca… you're still a fugitive. If she sees you, I don't know what will happen. I mean, she'll ask questions. She's never met you, but I know her. She's been waiting for me to find a guy and settle down for years now," I explain.

"I know," Luca repeats. "I will have to find somewhere to hide out, at least for now."

My heart sinks. "You mean 'we' will have to find somewhere to hide out."

Luca kisses my forehead. "You have a life here, Serena. I won't disappear on you, but I also can't let you just throw away everything you have for me. I refuse to derail your life yet again. It wouldn't be fair."

"Fair? How about I let you know when something isn't fair to me, huh?" I reply adamantly.

Luca smiles fondly. "You're a spitfire, you know that?"

I shrug. "Takes one to know one. Besides, if you think I could possibly live my life the way it was without you in it… well, you don't know me half as well as you think you do. Wherever you're going, I'm going with you."

"But what about Bathing Beauty?" he asks.

Sighing, I shake my head. "Well, it's shut down for now anyway, right? Not a whole lot I can do about that. Luckily, things were going really well for a year or so there and I've got money saved up. Enough to last me a good while. To last *us* a good while."

"I can't let you do that," Luca protests, gazing into my eyes meaningfully.

"Luca," I begin, raising an eyebrow, "no offense, but I'm a grown adult. I make my own decisions. I'll spend my money and my time however I see fit. And I want to be with you. Whatever that might mean."

A smile splits his face, pride shining in his green eyes.

"You never stop amazing me, Serena De Laurentis. But I don't know where I'm going to be. My contacts are still distant at the moment, and I don't have a blueprint for the next stage of my plan yet. Things will probably get a little hairy before they get better. Who knows where I'll end up until then."

Suddenly, an idea slides into the forefront of my mind. "Wait. Let me think for a second."

"What is it?" he asks, his thick brows furrowed.

I can't help but grin as a plan hatches in my head. "I know a place. Upstate, there's this cabin my parents rented for us a couple summers when I was a kid. We went up there for some 'peace and quiet' so my dad could fish and sit in a hot tub while my mom mostly just complained about the lack of restaurants and shopping. I used to play in the woods and go swimming in the pond. Build bonfires with my dad. Grill hotdogs and hamburgers. You know, all that stereotypical family time summer stuff."

"Wow. Talk about the American dream," Luca remarks. "But I don't know if that's a great idea, Serena. Any place your parents rented must be high-profile. Fancy. The opposite of a good hiding place."

I shake my head, turning off the shower faucet and reaching for a couple of dry towels from a shelf, handing one off to Luca. "No, no. It's perfect. I'm serious. It's out in the middle of nowhere. I mean, it's probably about an hour from Ithaca, but I promise it's remote and private as hell.

We didn't even have cell service the whole time we were there. Nothing. It's a dead zone."

Luca's expression changes from skeptical to considerate. "Well, I suppose we could look into it. But what about your mother? Won't she worry?"

"Pfft," I snort. "I'll just tell her I'm taking a little sabbatical. And the dead zone is a great excuse to not be in touch. It's perfect."

"And what about paying for the cabin? Don't those kinds of places usually require ID for checking in? I can't exactly show my face in public places at the moment," Luca says.

"Nah. From what I recall, the guy who runs the property isn't even there most of the time. I think he lives in a town far out of the woods. And he seems like a very laissez-faire type of guy. I don't think my dad even paid with a card. I remember him just handing over a wad of cash and getting a set of keys in exchange. Easy-peasy," I say, shrugging.

Luca nods, tying the towel around his waist. He's silent for a moment, clearly deliberating on my suggestion. Then he says, "Okay. We can try it. But I can't leave town yet. Not without taking a parting gift."

I'm still a wanted man. Every second I spend in this city is a risk, every night a threat of getting thrown back into that hell-hole I escaped.

I should disappear, smuggle myself back to Italy and vanish from the face of the earth for the rest of my life. But that would mean leaving Serena behind, in danger. That is no life I want to live.

My old friend Trueba comes to mind often. I worry for him, knowing he's spending time in isolation on the inside. But there was no hesitation in him when he agreed to do what he did. Old men want to live through the young, sometimes. The best thing I can do for his memory is not make the same mistakes as he did.

I won't get caught.

But I've given it more thought than that. When I realized I'd have to do something big to get the money I need to keep me and Serena safe, I couldn't help but think of Trueba's story. One big heist was all it took to make sure they were set.

But it caught up to him eventually.

Jewels are hard to trace. His mistake wasn't the heist.

It was who he stole from.

"Are you sure your man will come through for us?" I ask Nico, who sits in the passenger's seat of the car next to me. We're parked in the lot behind an old convenience store, waiting for a word from one of Nico's friends.

"I'll skin his ass if he doesn't," Nico mutters, watching his phone.

There's a jewel handoff going down tonight. While the Cleaners moving into our territory was harsh on the Costas' business, seeing which of our old contacts started working for the enemy told us who we could trust. When the Cleaners moved into the south side of the borough, a small ring of jewel smugglers we knew went silent.

That means they're working with the Cleaners now, who probably need the money, badly. Nico did some investigating and got a tip that a handoff is happening tonight. Before the sun rises, tens of thousands of dollars' worth of jewels smuggled into the country will be handed over to the Cleaners... but we have other plans.

All we're waiting on is Nico's informant to give us a location. Smugglers like this don't stick to the same sites.

I hate the jewel trade. It's a bloody business, and if there were any other way, I'd have nothing to do with it. But I'd rather the money not fall into the hands of the Cleaners, and I can use it to secure a better life for me and Serena.

As for Nico, my accomplice tonight, he's planning to use the cash to buy Rafaela a wedding ring. Since he'll be fencing the goods and putting the money in my account, I promised him I wouldn't tell.

I take a drink from the thermos of coffee in my hand when I see Nico's screen light up, and he smiles.

"Got it."

"Then it's show time," I say, and I pull out of the parking lot to start heading toward the coordinates Nico's man gave us. By the looks of things, it's just outside the city.

I drive down the highway, following the directions Nico gives me. I have to be careful out on the road. If I get pulled over, it's all over. Besides the fact that I'm a wanted fugitive, I'm carrying a lot of guns, and I don't exactly look like a harmless sportsman. It's late at night, though, and the police are watching for drunk drivers, not men on their way to a heist.

"You know this is insane, right?" Nico asks after taking a swig of the coffee and checking his guns. "We haven't cased wherever we're going, we don't know what kind of manpower we're up against, we can't call for backup since the rest of the boys don't know we're doing this tonight."

I open my mouth to answer, but Nico interrupts me, "You're gonna say 'love makes you do crazy things, my friend,' aren't you? Don't fuckin' do it, I swear to god I'll push you out of this moving car.

Words stolen from my mouth, I just smile smugly while Nico scoffs.

~

"He can't be serious," I say as we pull up to the wire fence near the coordinates. "Nico, I mean it, is he joking?"

Nico is biting his lip with his eyebrows raised as he looks up at the site the handoff is supposedly going down at. "This guy doesn't joke much."

We're looking up at an old, broken-down Ferris wheel, long since rusted and out of use. Not far from it is a booth advertising cotton candy and funnel cake, but the glass windows are long-since smashed in, and some of the lettering is missing. I see a rat scurry across the counter of a shooting booth that's had all the toy guns ripped out of it.

An abandoned fairground.

"Not a bad cover," I admit under my breath before I pull my ski-mask over my head. Nico does the same. We're outfitted in all black, and we have our guns strapped to us. I think about the way I looked last time I went out on a job like this, and it makes me feel like I was just a kid back then. Maybe what was left of the young buck in me died in prison. I still have the energy, but I know how to handle myself now.

Time to see if it was a change for the better.

Communicating through signs, Nico and I find an opening in the old fence and make our way inside, moving silently.

The shadows of the fairgrounds all around us seem to move out of the corner of my eye. Every now and then, I think I can hear the sound of something skittering. I know it's a rat or a bird, but I can't shake the feeling that old ghosts hang around this place.

I've never liked fairs.

Soon, I stop Nico as a more human sound reaches my ears: footsteps. I gesture for him to follow me, sticking to the shadows, and we creep closer after the sounds of several men and hushed voices up ahead.

We come around the corner of what looks like an old haunted house-type ride, complete with a badly painted giant bat looming over the entrance. We get low and stay put, because at the open space up ahead in front of it, I see our targets.

There are five men total. It's hard to tell who is who at first, but their body language gives them away. Two of them are Cleaners; one of them is receiving a large black bag from the others, and the other man stands close to him, tall and as imposing as I might be at a meeting like this. The other three look a little more nervous as they hand off the bags. They are right to be. The Cleaners aren't to be trusted. It must have been hard for them to set this meeting up in the first place.

I smile under my mask. Icing on the cake.

Hand on my silenced pistol, I wait until nobody's gaze is turned toward us, and I raise the weapon to take aim. My sights set on the big Cleaner, but when I get a better look at the other man handing off a bag full of jewels, my heart skips a beat.

That face. I know that face.

I lower my weapon as my eyes widen, and Nico looks at me, puzzled. Any other time, I would swear my eyes are playing tricks on me, but I'd recognize that face anywhere.

One of the smugglers is a cop who was at my arrest two years ago.

Nico looks confused, but I give his arm a warning squeeze and shake my head ever so slightly, so I don't draw attention. Things just got a lot more dangerous. We can't risk killing a cop. My head is buzzing with questions, most of all, why is he here?

I'll have to worry about that later, though. For now, I have to figure out how we leave here without a cop's blood on our hands, because I'm not leaving without the jewels.

I hold Nico's arm until the men finish their transaction. Nods are exchanged, and the groups part ways. Thankfully, the smugglers are in a hurry. They'll be out of the way soon enough. We're still as shadows as each one stalks off, and the moment it's safe, I nod for Nico to follow me.

We're going to have to take down the Cleaners separately.

Nico is giving me a "what the fuck are you doing" look, but I press on. We move as quietly as we can around the building to head off the Cleaners. I'm moving faster than I should, and I have to catch myself to slow down. My thoughts are all over the place, but I have to stay focused. I can figure the rest out later.

We round the corner, and we both freeze in our tracks.

At the far end of the haunted house's side stands a third Cleaner we hadn't noticed. A lookout. And he's looking straight at us.

I have no time to think. I raise my gun, aim, and fire, all in the span of less than a second. The man jolts and staggers back, a bleeding hole in his forehead, and he falls to the ground. We'd be in the clear... if the two men with the jewels weren't just about to pass by him, each of them carrying bags.

"Fuck!" one of them shouts, and they take off in opposite directions.

There's no hesitation in me. "You take the fast one, I've got the big guy," I say, and I take off sprinting. Nico takes off the next moment, and we're on our targets like bloodhounds.

My man goes back the way they came, toward the haunted house. I round the corner just as he rounds the one further down, bringing him around to the front of the house. I curse silently as I go after him, and when I reach the corner, he's gone. There are no hiding spots nearby that I can spot, except...

My eyes fall on the haunted house, and I grit my teeth. It's a tight space with many shadows, places to hide, and a service exit somewhere inside. He chose a smart place to hide. That's not going to stop me, though.

I take my weapon out and move in after him.

It's hard to stay quiet inside the creaky old building. Each step I take risks making the rusty metal floors groan, and I can hardly see anything. The only upside is that he's at the same disadvantage. But I don't underestimate him. He had the luxury of casing this joint. He might know it better than I expect, so I can't let my guard down.

Every other thought leaves my head. I don't worry

about Nico, or about what might happen outside. I'm focused on my sole task.

Keeping low, I move past the ticket stand inside. If there's a service exit, it's probably toward the back of the ride. I have no idea whether the entry or exit tunnel is the fastest to take, so I check the doorways of both before darting down the entryway.

Then I hear the sound of a shuffling footstep some ways ahead, and I know I made the right choice. If he moves too fast, he'll alert me to where he is. My eyes slowly begin to adjust to the dark, and I look in the direction of the sounds.

As if on cue, though, I hear the sounds of running footsteps down the winding hallway, and I take off after him. To my sides, I see the old deactivated skeletons and rusty monsters used to pop out at people on the ride. They're more unnerving when still and lifeless.

There's the sound of a gunshot, and I come to a halt and dive into cover, pressed up against an animatronic werewolf in a nook as I raise my weapon, ready to fire back. But there are no more shots. I peek out just long enough to look into the darkness. If he can't see me, I can't see him, but if he's blind-firing back at me, he's starting to panic. I have to use this to my advantage.

Moving as silently as I can, I hold my gun out and start to feel my way along the wall toward the source of the gunshot.

As my hand runs along a wall, I feel it brush against something cold and metallic. I feel it more and realize that it's a switch. An emergency power switch? Brakes? Security? I hesitate a moment, but I know I need some kind of distraction, anything, so I pull the lever.

The whole building seems to shudder as the last sparks of energy course through the place. Down the hallway ahead of me, loose wiring overhead pops loudly and rains sparks down, and it lights up the room enough to show me my man, white-faced at the end of the hall.

We raise our guns at the same time and fire off, and I feel the sting of the bullet grazing my shoulder. I sprint forward and start zig-zagging my way down, but when the wires spark again, the man is gone.

The sounds of his footsteps are muffled by the mechanical whirring I hear all around now. Some generator somewhere must have a little juice left in it. I curse my luck. The half-working haunted house is a lot creepier than a dead one.

I get to the end of the hallway and halt at the corner. Behind me, I hear a rolling sound, and I turn to see one of the empty ride cars clunking its way down on the metal tracks. I let it roll around the corner, cobwebs hanging overhead, and as soon as it appears in the next hallway, I hear two gunshots ricochet off the empty car, followed by a curse.

He's waiting for me. I have to think of something.

My eye catches something across the deadly hallway that's frankly, horrifying. The ride has sparked to life, which means the animatronic monsters within are trying to move like they did when the fair was running normally. Across from me is a robotic mummy, and every few seconds, it starts to jolt around awkwardly as if trying to pop forward and scare a guest, but a big loose cable running across its chest is holding it back. That gives me an idea.

Just before the next time it pops out, I aim my gun at the cable and fire. With a spark, it's cut in two, and a second later, the mummy pops out of its plastic sarcophagus, arms raised and jaw hanging open.

"Fuck!" comes a shout from down the hallway, and there's a gunshot, and part of the mummy's head comes off from the gunshot. I take the distraction and pop out of cover myself.

Just as I planned, the man's wide eyes are fixed on the mummy, and by the time his face turns to me, my gun is trained on him, and I squeeze the trigger.

Two quick shots, and the man falls to the ground, dead. I race forward with my gun pointed at him, and I make sure he's down for good before I take the bags and sling them over my shoulder.

That went well, but I don't have any time to celebrate: Nico's still out there.

I race out of the haunted house and listen for the sound of fighting. It doesn't take long before I hear the gunshots of the other man. Nico's using a silenced pistol like me, so I can't figure out his location by listening.

I reach the gravity-spinner ride and move carefully around it before I finally see movement. Nico is blind-firing, ironically pinned down in the shooting gallery booth. Judging by where he's shooting, I can get an idea of where the Cleaner is.

I should be able to flank him. I move around the opposite side of the gravity-spinner, and I can make out motion just beyond a merry-go-round. I clench my jaw. I can't deny that the big, badly painted plastic horses will make for good cover if I want to approach quickly. I can see the shooter crouching behind an overturned popcorn stand.

No time to think of alternatives. I rush forward, still close to the ground, and before I can give the other man a chance to react, I use one of the fake horses as both cover and a rest for my arms to take aim, and with the squeeze of the trigger, the man goes down, slumping over his bag.

Nico and I are both still for a moment, as if expecting something else to happen, but after a few beats, we both stand up, grinning at each other, and Nico shakes his head as we make our way to the corpse to get the bag.

"Shit, man, I'm glad we didn't tell the others about this after all," he says, taking the bag and slinging it over his shoulder while I check the dead man. "All this? Nobody would believe this bullshit."

We get the bags together and make our way back to the car as silently as we came in, and in a few minutes' time, we're driving back into town.

"Goddamn," Nico says as he looks over the insides of the bags. "Don't think I've ever seen this much money in one place. Even if it is in rock-form," he jokes, not daring to touch the glittering stones even now.

"Jewel thieves have the right idea," I chuckle, glancing at the payload. "You should just skip buying a ring and use one of these rocks for the engagement ring. Find a nice jeweler to do it for you on the down low."

"No shit," Nico laughs. "Nah, Rafaela would kill me." He glances at my arm and notices a dark patch in my black sweater where I'm bleeding. "Hey, you get hit, man?"

"Nothing serious," I say, shrugging my shoulder. "Got a little more muscle to absorb the sting there now. You all good?"

"He couldn't get a shot in on me," he says proudly, "but you still saved my ass back there. Reminds me why I keep helping your ass out."

We chuckle, and I jab him with my elbow. When he stops laughing, Nico looks over at me with a thoughtful look on his face.

"You've been pretty quiet about all this, though. Just what are you thinking about doing with all this cash? 'Keep Serena safe' is a little vague."

"I'll worry about that," I say, smiling. "I've got something special in mind for my share of the cash."

*I*t's a beautiful day, with the kind of crystalline blue skies and puffy white clouds that would look more natural on a painting than in reality. The sun shines down cheerfully over the winding road in front of us, and a delicious earthy breeze filters in through the rolled-down car windows.

Luca has his elbow resting on the window frame, gripping the steering wheel with one hand while the other reaches over to hold mine. He turns to smile at me, looking absolutely gorgeous in his shining aviator shades and just a hint of a prickly five o'clock shadow. He's wearing a white t-shirt with the sleeves slightly rolled, blue jeans, and brown boots. He looks like a rugged, sexy woodsman heading out for a day of tromping through the forest. And I guess that's not too far off from what we're about to do.

The drive up here from Riverdale has been amazing; perfect weather the whole time. Ever since I was a little kid I've loved road trips, and I always dreamed of going on a long drive like this with a handsome man who made my heart flutter. I smile and think, *wow, young Serena would be so happy if she could see us now.*

Of course, everything isn't roses and sunshine. Luca more or less disappeared for about a week after that day at my house in Riverdale. He kept in touch this time, sending me updates from a burner phone, just like old times. Only now he doesn't keep me waiting in such dreadful suspense.

I don't know what kinds of shenanigans he got into, and I didn't dare ask (honestly, I don't know if I even want to know), but when he turned up to collect me for this trip upstate, he did look a little worse for wear, like maybe he's been in some kind of fight. I know he leads a dangerous life, and now that he's a fugitive, danger lurks around every corner. But I have to swallow down my fear. After all, you can't love a dangerous man without expecting some rough patches, right?

Besides, he's with me safe and sound now, and that's what matters to me: collecting these precious little moments together when they come along. I used to think I wanted stability, calmness.

Now I know I just want Luca, regardless of what that might mean.

"God, it's a gorgeous day," I remark, gazing out the window at the trees and other vegetation starting to thicken around us as we drive.

"Perfect," Luca agrees. "I can see why your family used to vacation up here."

"It's been so long since I came here last, but it doesn't even look any different. Well, some of the trees look bigger, but otherwise it's all the same. It's weird to think about how much I've changed, how different my life is now, but it's like time didn't touch this part of the planet," I muse aloud, dangling my arm out the window for a moment to feel the breeze.

"Like stepping back in time," he says.

"Exactly."

The car rumbles over a rough spot and I notice the

paved road has given way to gravel now, the tires crunching as we roll along. "Sorry about your tires. I forgot about the gravel."

"This car has definitely seen worse times than this," Luca laughs. "Besides, I'm an excellent driver."

I raise an eyebrow and glance at him, amused. "Well, you're not lacking for confidence, are you, Mr. Tokyo Drift?"

"Trust me, when you've worked the kind of job I have, you quickly learn to be an expert with all the tools of the trade. Tactical driving is just part of the necessary skill set," Luca explains.

"Oh, up ahead! Look!" I exclaim, scooting forward in my seat and pointing toward a small wooden structure just barely peeking out from behind the trees down the path.

"Is that it?" he asks. "Where do we go to check in?"

"Oh, it's not that complicated. There's kind of a scout's honor type system up here. You just leave the money in an envelope in the mailbox when you leave," I tell him. "Come to think of it, I'm starting to understand why my dad liked this place so much. Privacy and convenience. A property owner who doesn't ask questions and couldn't be bothered to care anyway."

"A Mafioso's paradise," Luca agrees, grinning.

"So many things are starting to make sense looking back now," I sigh, shaking my head. "But whatever the purpose was, I have a lot of great memories here. It's so nice to be back. I can't wait to show you around and frolic in nature with you."

I squeeze his hand and he laughs. "This is definitely more your speed than mine, but it will be interesting to say the least."

"Oh, you'll love it, I promise."

Luca pulls the car up to a spot next to the cabin and as soon as he turns off the engine and the doors unlock, I burst out of the car and take off toward the dense woods, unable to keep a grin off of my face. Luca takes off after me, but when I look back I notice he still looks a little tense, glancing over his shoulder like he's afraid someone might randomly appear behind us. Like he's still worried that we might be watched or followed, even all the way out here in the middle of nowhere. I decide to make it my mission to distract him and get him to relax by whatever means necessary, and I already have a few ideas in mind.

"Come on!" I shout back at him, heading down a barely-there path in the forest. I'm navigating more by instinct than logic, hoping my memory will lead me in the right direction. Just as I stop short at a little babbling creek, Luca catches up to me and grabs me in his arms, swinging me around as I cry out in mock fear. He sets me back down and kisses me, cupping my face in his huge hands as we stand on the mushy bank of the creek.

"Are we going to cross this thing?" he asks, gesturing toward the water.

I take note of a few smooth, large boulders in the creek and nod. "Of course! We're just going to step across those rocks there." I break away from him and deftly hop across to the other side of the creek, beckoning for him to follow. Luca looks a little skeptical at first, but then he easily leaps across.

"Fun, right? Hopping around the streams was one of my favorite things to do here as a little kid. It's easy to do nowadays, but when I was small it was way more intimidating, I swear," I admit, laughing.

"I bet you were the cutest little girl," Luca says. "I can just picture you tiny and courageous, crossing a creek like some brave adventurer."

"I definitely felt like that's what I was," I say, smiling widely. "Well, let's keep going. I think we're on the right path."

"To where?"

"You'll see!" I exclaim, bolting through the trees again with Luca close behind. My heart is racing, my lungs filled with fresh forest air. The sun reaches down in golden-white streaks through the canopy, illuminating patches of earth. I feel happier than I've been in a very long time, like I'm finally free. Despite growing up as mostly a city girl, with my Manhattan apartment, designer clothes, and trust fund friends, I think I've always been a country girl at heart. Or something like that. I feel so at home here in the woods, running free and wild where nobody is around to judge me for my lack of composure. I can be myself here, and only the trees and lurking wildlife can watch.

Luca darts up behind me and scoops me into his arms, carrying me for a few minutes. We're both laughing openly, grinning from ear to ear as we race along down the narrow path. If you weren't looking for the trail, you wouldn't notice it, because the grass and weeds have begun to reclaim it. I imagine business must be pretty slow for the cabin owner lately. On the one hand, it makes me sad that this place seems to be largely forgotten, but on the other hand, it's nice to know that it's almost like my own personal private world. Like I alone know the secrets of this magical forest.

Luca sets me down and we start walking briskly, hand in hand, down the way as the sound of rushing water grows louder. He looks at me in confusion. "What is that?"

"Be patient. You'll see," I tease him, poking my tongue out at him.

A few more minutes of walking and we arrive at our destination: a small but beautiful waterfall tucked away behind a thick patch of trees we nearly have to squeeze through to reach. Luca's face changes from confusion to full of wonder, and I can't help but beam at how happy he looks. I can tell he never expected to come across something like this, and I'm overjoyed that I got the opportunity to put that look of awe on his face.

"You like it?" I pipe up, biting my lip.

Luca turns and kisses me passionately, holding me close. When he breaks away he says softly, "This is beautiful, Serena. Thank you for taking me here. I — we — needed this."

"Agreed. That's what I love so much about being out in nature. It's like hitting refresh on your whole life, like all your problems stay behind in the city and you can finally breathe again," I say, shaking my head in amazement at how lovely it all is. "I can't believe I waited so long to come back here. I could've really used a visit here during all those difficult years."

"I never got to do things like this growing up," Luca says, standing with his hands on his hips as he surveys the scene appreciatively. "Back home in Italy I ran around the countryside sometimes, just causing trouble with my equally delinquent friends. But it wasn't like this. And when I came to America, my childhood was over. I went from a scrappy little kid to a man overnight, becoming my uncle's apprentice, learning the carpentry trade. Sometimes I wonder how different I would be if I had stayed in Italy. Or if the mafia had never threatened my family."

"I'm sorry," I tell him earnestly, taking his hand. "I can't imagine what you've been through. I wish you'd had a chance to grow up like any other kid, instead of having those years stolen away from you."

Luca shrugs and gives me a peaceful smile. "It is what it is. And besides, the way I see it, all those shitty things only led me down the path to you. And that makes it all worth it."

He pulls me close and kisses me again, his hands stroking my hair, sliding down to grab my ass as he pushes against me. I feel that familiar flicker of tingling warmth pass down my body and makes me shiver. I know exactly what I want. Right here, right now.

Luca leads me over to a huge patch of soft moss on the dry rocks off to one side of the waterfall, where every now and then a stray fleck of water flies over to land on us. He guides me to the ground, his fingers tangling into my hair as he stares into my eyes. I'm transfixed, held captive in the perfect, blissful moment.

There's no sounds of the city, no fear in my heart, no sorrow. It feels like I've shed myself of all the baggage I've been carrying for so long.

For the first time, I feel totally reunited with my long lost lover, without all the worries and fear marring every emotion. Ever since he's returned, I keep having the feeling that it's fleeting. That soon, he'll be caught. That he'll be taken away from me once more, and I'll have to face life without him all over again.

But in the peace and serenity of the forest, no one can touch us.

Luca's fingers work along my skin, snaking up beneath my shirt as his lips press against mine. His tongue is soft but exploratory as it swipes across my lower lip, leaving his taste on me as he easily unhooks my bra.

He makes quick work of my jeans and panties, as well, folding all my clothing into a neat little stack beside us before he strips out of his own clothes. Goosebumps prickle up on my skin, our bodies both totally exposed to the cool, fresh air.

"You know, this is strangely similar to a dream I had one night while I was locked up," Luca says softly, kissing his way down to my breasts. "I dreamed that you and I were making love on the edge of a massive waterfall. Of course, in the dream there were also talking trees, but that's beside the point."

I giggle at that image but my laughter is interrupted by

a sigh as Luca gently bites and sucks at my nipples, his hand trailing down to cup my mound. "Well, I'm glad these trees don't talk because I'd hate for them to tell anyone about this. Two people fucking in the woods, surrounded by nothing but nature."

"Yeah, I would hate for them to tell anybody about how wet you are when I touch you, how you shiver when I stroke your sweet little clit," Luca growls, his fingertip swirling around that tight, sensitive bud while my hips rock back and forth involuntarily.

"Oh fuck," I moan as he slides down between my thighs to lick and suck at my pussy. I reach down and tangle my fingers in his dark hair, gently pushing him down into my cunt. The waterfall pounds away, the constant white noise of rushing water only adding to the symphony of sensations I'm feeling. Just before I come, Luca pulls away.

I whimper plaintively, disappointed.

But he quickly pulls me up and lies on his back, moving me to straddle him. I bite my lip, eager to ride his cock. I position the head of his shaft at my slick opening and slowly slide him inside of me, groaning with pleasure as I sheath him completely.

"Fuck, Serena. I want you to ride my cock hard. I want to fill you up and make you ache," Luca instructs, his voice husky and low. I begin rolling my hips, slowly and carefully at first, then more frantically as my climax approaches. It doesn't take long for me to explode, crying out as I start bouncing up and down on his cock, feeling him strike my g-spot over and over again.

"Ohh, it feels so fucking good," I murmur, closing my eyes as I ride him harder and faster. Luca's hands slide up to cup and massage my breasts, his fingertips passing over my nipples and making me tremble, starting to lose control. I don't want to go slow. I want to fuck him hard and fast, give in to my animalistic desires.

Luca sits up and pulls my legs around him so that we're facing, my knees hooked around his waist. He kisses me, reaching down between us to rub my clit while I ride his cock. I moan into his mouth as he takes control, bouncing me up and down and thrusting up into my pussy.

"Good girl, good girl. Come for me," Luca murmurs in my ear, his warm breath sending shivers down my neck. Almost as though by magic, I come immediately, my whole body shaking with the waves of intense pleasure. Luca leans me backward, holding me up with his free arm so that I'm nearly horizontal, still speared by his cock as he thrusts up into me and strokes my clit.

He picks up the pace, slamming into me with loud, wet smacks, and I can tell he's getting closer and closer. "Ready for me to come inside you, *dolcezza?*" he says, circling his thumb over my clit so that I'm almost overstimulated to the point of exhaustion.

"Yes! Oh God, yes!" I manage to choke out, my heart hammering away beneath my ribs.

"Fuck!" he bellows, seizing up and shooting his sweet seed deep inside of me as I come at the exact same time, my whole body going limp as my pussy clenches around him. He thrusts a few more times, his hands still on my back, holding me still. His gaze holds mine, both of us recovering from our orgasms.

He kisses me as he withdraws, both of us falling on our backs, panting and sweaty. The fine mist of the waterfall is welcome, cooling our skin as we lie there totally spent and happy. Luca grabs my hand and squeezes it.

"If I die and go to heaven and it isn't exactly like this, I'm going to feel so cheated," he says, laughing. "I genuinely cannot imagine anything better than this."

"Everywhere is paradise with you," I tell him, glancing over to meet his vivid green gaze with a smile. "What's that song? Heaven is a place on earth?"

"That's the one," he agrees, kissing my hand. We lie there in silence for a few more minutes, both coming down from our shared high.

Finally, I can't keep those questions at bay anymore and I ask hesitantly, "Luca, where were you this past week? You just kind of went off on your own. And when you came back, you had all that money. What happened? What did you do?"

He looks over at me with a pained expression. "I didn't want to worry you."

"I know. But I would rather have some idea of what's going on. That scares me way more: the unknown," I explain truthfully. I thought it would be easier not knowing, but it's clear to me now that the secrets scare me more than the truth possibly could.

"Okay. I was involved in a theft. A big time. A heist, you might even say."

"What?" I burst out, sitting up and looking at him with wide eyes. Luca sits up, too.

Calmly, he explains the whole operation, and I listen intently, my mind racing in a million directions.

"I can't believe you would take a huge risk like that just after breaking out of prison. Luca, you're a fugitive. That raises the stakes for everything."

"I know. But Serena, you have to understand that taking risks is part of my job. It's just the way I have to live my life. I promise that I'm as careful as can be. I take risks, but they're calculated risks," he says. "And I knew you would be afraid, so I kept it from you."

I bite my lip.

"Luca, listen to me. I know you think I'm some delicate little flower you have to protect from all the dangers of your world. But remember that I grew up around the mob, too. Even though I didn't know much about it then, and I didn't know any different, my dad was involved in some pretty illicit stuff. And after he died... " I shook my head. "Luca, not knowing what was going to happen to me, if I was going to... if that man was going to be able to touch me... I didn't know if that was my life. And not knowing, I imagined all the worst scenarios. That's what it's like when you leave me, without telling me. My imagination runs wild. Besides, I'm in love with you. Anything you have to deal with you should be able to share with me. Okay?"

Luca shakes his head in amazement, smiling at me warmly.

"Most women would shy away from a guy like me. How are you so brave?"

I shrug, leaning over to kiss him.

"Love makes you brave. From now on, I want to know what's going on. Even if it's dark. Even if it's dangerous. I want to have a say."

"I'll do my best to include you," he concedes, kissing me again. "I could never deny you anything, you know that? You've got some kind of crazy hold on me."

"It's my superpower," I joke, grinning. "But if we're going to be on the run, undercover and underground and all that, I think we need new aliases."

"Aliases?" Luca repeats, giving me a dubious look.

"Yeah! You know, like code names or something. Fake names."

"That's not usually how we operate, but I'm intrigued now. What name would you give me? Or yourself?" he asks, amused.

I squint at him, thinking hard for a moment.

"Hmm. We need a theme or something. Shakespeare, maybe. Like, you could be Horatio. Or Lysander."

"Oh, those are terrible," Luca laughs. "And what would you be called? Juliet?"

"Juliet? So mainstream! I take it you didn't study as much Shakespeare as I was forced to read," I giggle, pondering female character names. "I could be Rosaline or maybe Olivia."

"Your names are way better than mine," Luca points out. "I sense some unfairness here."

"Fine, you can be something normal like Alexander," I tease, nudging him with my shoulder. Then, I sober up and add, "But seriously, Luca, I don't want there to be any more secrets between us. If this is going to work, we need to be honest with each other. No surprises. No hiding things. You trust me, right?"

"Of course I do. Trust was never the problem," he answers seriously.

"Okay. Good. It's settled then," I declare, grinning. "You and me, we're a team."

Inwardly, I make a different promise: that I'm going to take life by the horns from now on. If I'm going to be on equal grounds with Luca, I need to be brave. Not reckless, but definitely courageous. I need to be strong and assertive. I need to take charge.

"No more trying to 'protect' me by keeping things from me. After all, I always find out sooner or later anyway," I say, shrugging.

"Sounds fair to me. If you think you can handle it, I won't hold back," he says. Then he adds, "Seems like as good a time as any to break out of my usual routine."

I look at him confused as he gets up and offers me his hand.

What the hell does he mean by that?

LUCA

*D*owntown Ithaca is not a world I'm familiar with in the least, even with Serena around my arm at my side. It was my idea to come out here, but with every passing second, I'm feeling more like a fish out of water.

There's none of the bustle of the city here, none of the rush and looming buildings that I was just getting used to calling *home* back in the Bronx. It's almost too quiet for my taste, but I have to admit, I feel like I can breathe here. There's plenty of green, and fewer people look anxious or stormy.

That doesn't help my situation, though. I'm clad in the same old clothes I had before we left, and while I'm not one to worry about fashion, I can tell I stick out here. As we walk down the wide brown sidewalk flanked by shops on all sides, Serena notices how often I'm adjusting the hood and sunglasses I'm wearing to hide my appearance. She finishes off the mint gelato I bought for us a few minutes ago and throws the napkin into a public trashcan, coming to a stop as she does.

"Relax," she says, stroking my arm as I smile down at

her. "We're miles away from, well, everything. NYC may as well be a whole different country up here."

"That's part of the problem," I say, looking around at the hipster couples with big hairstyles and sweaters. That gives me an idea, though. A thoughtful smile on my face, I look over at some of the outlet shops nearby, then down at Serena, who tilts her head to the side.

"Whatcha thinking?"

"That we didn't bring enough clothes," I say, smiling a little more broadly at Serena, whose eyebrows go up.

"I... never thought I'd hear you say that," she admits.

"No, but you've been through a lot. I don't get enough chances to spoil you like a proper Italian girl." That makes her blush and smile, and I take her hand to tug her along into the nearest designer clothing store to start spending some of that money I worked so hard to get.

Serena's eyes light up as soon as we enter the place. I can see her mind going back to when she was a teenager on her father's big budget, because I don't have to look at the price tags on some of the clothes in here to know they're above what she usually gets.

"Ohhhh, this is good. This is very good," she says, wandering in ahead of me and looking at the various odds and ends of the fall line of clothes. She looks back at me with glittering eyes and an eager smile.

"Are you sure about this? If you really turn me loose in here, I think I can put a dent in that paycheck of yours." She winks, half-joking, but even if she were dead-serious, I couldn't deny her anything.

"Don't think about the price," I assure her, stepping over to her and planting a kiss on her forehead. "I'll take care of that part."

That's all it takes to get her going on a tour of the store that seems to warm her soul. After about an hour of trying things on, getting new sizes, and even experimenting a little, Serena finally comes out of the dressing room with an ensemble she looks like a regular local in: an oversized, unreasonably cozy green sweater that still makes her body look irresistible. She picks out an equally oversized tan-brown scarf that goes with it and matching tall boots and black leggings.

Even though I've been getting odd looks the whole time I've been in here, my stony expression splits into a grin when I see her, partly because of how cute she looks in her outfit, partly because her happiness is so infectious.

"What do you think?" she asks, holding her arms out and twirling in place, and before she finishes, I wrap my arms around her and pick her up, to her delight, kissing her on the neck.

"Perfect," I say, setting her down and giving a smile to the dressing room attendant, who stands awkwardly nearby. "We'll take it. All of it."

That changes the attendant's mood quite a bit. A few minutes later, I've convinced the store owner to let Serena wear the new outfit out of the store with her old clothes in the bag. Something about the way Serena's eyes widen when I hand the cashier a big wad of cash fills me with pride. I like providing for her, even if it's on things that aren't totally essential.

When we walk out of the store, I can't help but laugh at the new spring in Serena's step.

"I never knew you had such a thing for new clothes."

"It's one of those things I kind of reward myself with when it's been a really good week at the shop," she says, wiggling a little when I hug her to my side. "I mean, nothing this nice or this much, but a little thing here and there is good." But it isn't long before her eyes get thoughtful as she looks my outfit up and down, smiling mischievously.

"What?" it's my turn to ask.

"Your turn, obviously," she says, and before I can protest through my chuckles, she's tugging my big arm toward the closest men's apparel store.

This is as much for Serena as it is for me.

My tastes are usually simple. I went through most of my life in the Bronx in jeans, a white t-shirt, and a leather jacket. Apparently, I need to get a little more creative than that to fit in up here in Ithaca. Fortunately, I don't have to leave my style behind too much to do that.

After a few minutes, I come out of the dressing room with an outfit that Serena seems to like very much. Even though the hand-knit tan sweater is the biggest size they have, my muscles are still visible underneath, making it a snug, warm fit. Over it, I get a big coat in a darker brown with a flared collar, and I finish the ensemble with a simple crimson beanie and a new set of aviator sunglasses. I get a new set of jeans and boots, too, just in case I wasn't fitting in with the outdoorsy style enough.

I like it mostly because it keeps my appearance a little less than obvious, but the smile from Serena and the big thumbs-up from the attendant tell me it's stylish enough that I won't stick out like a sore thumb anymore.

One big fat receipt later, we step out onto the street again like new people. I have to admit, it feels good to be wearing a new set of clothes. Serena can't stop looking up at me, either, which gives me a quiet sense of pride.

"See something you like?"

"A lot," she says, a silly grin on her face, but then she narrows her eyes, reaching up and touching my beard. "Just one more thing to freshen up, and you'll be a new man."

Another hour later, we step out of a hipster-y barber shop, and I've got a new haircut and trimmed beard. You'd never guess I spent the past two years locked away in prison. I started to protest the haircut since I'll be wearing the beanie anyway, but Serena insisted.

I can't argue with the results, either.

"So, I've never been this far north," I say as it starts to get closer to the time to get an evening bite to eat. "What does a perfectly normal, definitely-not-fugitive couple get to eat in upstate New York?"

"Good question," she giggles, playfully slapping me on the chest, "but maybe don't google 'what do fugitives eat,' ok?" We laugh and wander around a little more, but it isn't long before we spot a place that looks good to both of us. When price isn't an issue, those kinds of things get a lot easier.

We step through the doors of a local brewpub, a building with exposed brick and a cozy interior, complete with a roaring fireplace toward the back of the building and wooden tables all around. There's a good mood in the place I can't quite put my finger on. Maybe it's what Americans call *good vibes*.

A little while later, both of us are sitting side-by-side at a corner table, backs to the walls so I can see the whole place, and the waiter brings us the beer and cheese soup we ordered, complete with breadsticks and some rich, dark beers.

"Carbs on carbs on carbs," Serena says as I wet my lips and take the bread basket to start loading my plate. "You really know how to spoil a girl, huh? Good to know prison didn't change that."

"After prison food," I say after a long drink of the outstanding beer, "you learn to love the little pleasures in life like good food."

"You won't hear me complaining," she says with a smile, and she takes a drink of her beer and blushes after setting it down. "Wow, little stronger than I was expecting."

"It's not Italian, but I think I can appreciate American

drinking," I say, and we dig into our food. It's hearty and hot, exactly what you'd want on a fall day that's just starting to get cool enough for sweaters and boots. The cheese is rich, the beer helps us relax, and the atmosphere of other young people chatting and enjoying themselves makes us feel... comfortable. It's not something I'm used to, I realize.

Just *being* somewhere with Serena is a special pleasure I missed dearly.

"You look thoughtful," Serena says as she sets down her beer, going through it a little faster than I am. It's making her cheeks rosy, and the whole picture of her looking a little tipsy in that sweater against the brick wall makes my heart feel all the warmer.

"I just forgot how much luxury there is in the world," I say, looking around at the place with a smile on my face. "I know this place doesn't look like much, but it's these little things you forget when you're locked away."

"Like beer and cheese soup?" she asks with a playful smile on her face that I return.

"Yes, like beer and cheese soup," I say. "Really though. Little things. Walls and floors that aren't gray concrete. The feel of a warm fire. Clothes that aren't the same thing every day." I look back to her. "Spending time with you."

I kick her gently under the table, and she crosses her leg with mine, resting her chin on her hands and beaming at me.

"Those letters really did keep me going in there," I say to her, leaning forward. "I would have lost sight of the real world and all its pleasures. They were like... little breaths of fresh air before going back down under again. I can't believe how much I took for granted out here."

She nods thoughtfully, swirling her beer around. "I've thought about that too. There's so much I don't even think about in my day to day life."

"One thing I could never take for granted, though," I say in a low, husky tone, and I lean forward to kiss her on the lips which she meets with a soft, surprised moan, made all the warmer by the beer.

When we break apart, I pull out a few bills and set them on the table. I nod over to the couches by the fireplace as another group gets up to leave. "I've got the bill. Want to get a few more drinks?"

Serena hesitates a moment, biting her lip and squirming in her chair. I know that look: she's not used to spending that much, not for a long time. But I put a hand on her smaller ones and give her a reassuring smile, and that old excitement comes back to her eyes. "Oh, sure, why not?"

Serena goes to 'save' the seat while I go and get more drinks: a beer for me and a mixed drink for her, one of the fancy cocktails she picked out from the menu with cinnamon and whisky. When I walk back over to her, I can see she's already curled herself up by the fire, looking at me with the firelight dancing off her hair.

She looks radiant. Every time I see her, I'm reminded of how lucky I am to have her with me, and it reminds me what I'm fighting for. It's not just me anymore. A lot of young men forget that. I'm not so foolish.

I sit down, making the couch groan in protest under my bulk as I wrap my big arm around her and hug her to me while we clink our glasses together softly in the fire's warmth. We're almost too close to the fire that it burns, keeping just barely out of harm's way, still enjoying ourselves together. It's just like our everyday life, but so much richer.

"I think I could get used to a place like this," I say, running my hand up and down her arm as she sips her drink through the tiny straws they gave her.

"Are we turning into upstate hipsters now?" she giggles, wiggling her hips into me.

"Not quite," I chuckle, "but I have to admit, I missed the quiet life."

"Was your hometown quiet?" she asks.

"Kind of. Taranto isn't a quiet place. But my home was on the outskirts of town, and it's a lot more peaceful out there. Not nearly as rich as you are here, but there's something to be said for the... rustic charm," I say, smiling down at her before planting a kiss on her lips. I feel my manhood growing between my legs, and even though I can't act on it here, it makes me feel even closer to Serena.

"I could get into that," she says.

"You might like it around here more, I think," I say, "but I'd like to take you there sometime. Here, though," I say, pointing to the tables around the place, "I can tell some friend of the owners must be a carpenter. These are good tables. Chairs, too. They make some of these things in factories to look like they're handmade, but any real carpenter can tell the difference."

She nestles her head into my shoulder and gives a contented sigh. "I suppose I could see us up here. My shop could do alright in a place like this, and everyone needs carpenters."

"True," I say, squeezing her thigh, "I could go just about anywhere you think you'd like to set your business up. Not that the Bronx is too terrible."

"It's alright," she says, wistfully looking into the fire, "just... a lot of baggage, you know?"

"I do know," I say, staring into the fire with her. We're quiet for a few moments, but she looks back up at me and smiles.

"I'd rather make new memories with you."

I bring my face down to hers, and we lock lips, a deep, long kiss. I don't care that we're in public. I love the feel of her melting into me as our tongues explore each other briefly, and we break apart. I'm about to kiss her again when the sound of music reaches our ears, and I turn my head to see a band playing live music up on stage. It's folksy, and to my surprise, the singer is Italian, singing in my mother tongue. I have to admit, they're not bad, and I smile at them.

Serena nudges me.

"Hey, it's kinda like the old world music you and your friends used to listen to."

I blink and give her a confused look, laughing.

"Wait, do you think this is what that sounded like?"

"Shut up, it is!" Serena says, giggling yet blushing, self-conscious.

I laugh and hug her close to me, peppering her in kisses as I set my finished drink on the table and start to stand up. "Okay, now I *have* to bring you back home and show you the real music. But at least I can remind you how we dance back home."

"Luca, this is a restaurant!" she laughs as I pull her to her feet, but I don't care.

"Good, we can show them too," I say, and we start dancing to the lively tune in front of the fire. The band catches on and keeps the good vibes going, encouraging us to keep going as we move to the rhythm and Serena nearly falls over from laughing so much, the alcohol and the mood getting to her.

Works every time.

But soon, the song winds down, and I don't want to attract *too* much attention to ourselves. I admit, it was a little irresponsible to start dancing with my girl in a crowded restaurant, but nobody's going to recognize us here.

Besides, a life not taking risks for your loved ones isn't a life worth living.

I open my eyes to the sight of golden sunshine streaming in through the window, through the pale green privacy curtains Luca always keeps pulled shut. They're sheer enough to let the light in, but provide just enough coverage to be worth closing. I know for a fact there isn't going to be anyone all the way out here watching us, but Luca is still paranoid, understandably. He's a dangerous man on the run, and I know there are so many different factions of equally or more dangerous men looking for him. Still, I wish he would relax a little here at the cabin.

I check my cell phone tucked under the pillow charging and see that it's already after eleven. With a yawn, I hold my arms up over my head and stretch, reveling in the slight achiness of my body. I smile to myself, knowing exactly why I'm so sore today: last night we had some seriously acrobatic sex. Amazing acrobatic sex. Luca bent and positioned my body in ways I didn't even think I could manage.

I turn over in bed, instinctively reaching out for Luca,

but to my confusion, he's not there. The spot beside me in bed is empty and cold, and my heart sinks. Despite my desire for Luca to relax, in moments like this I can't help but panic a little myself. I quickly sit up, holding the sheets to my neck to cover myself, and look around the room. His stuff still appears to be in the same places: his jacket hanging over the corner chair, his bag on the floor by the bathroom entrance. So he couldn't have gone far. Unless he didn't go willingly.

I swallow hard, feeling the hairs prick up on the back of my neck.

"Luca?" I call out, my voice scratchy and rough as it always is first thing in the morning. There's no reply, and my pulse quickens as I gingerly, quietly scoot out of bed and pull a robe around my body to go search for him. Just as I start to walk across the bedroom, there's a soft *thunk* from the other side of the cabin and I freeze in place. Then I hear footsteps, rather heavy, like a man wearing boots. Someone is whistling cheerfully. I feel like I'm going to faint for a second, my heart is racing so quickly, but then it occurs to me that the intruder is whistling a familiar tune: Sinatra's "Strangers in the Night." Luca and I played that last night on the cabin's ancient entertainment center (the thing had to have been bought in the eighties) while we cooked dinner together.

"Luca?" I ask hopefully. The footsteps get louder as the intruder comes through the doorway and I let out a sigh of relief to see that it is, in fact, the man I love, and not some murderous hit man breaking in to kill me. Although, considering Luca's history, I suppose maybe I should reserve judgement on hit men from now on. He looks a good deal different from how he did when we first arrived here at the cabin a month or so ago, with his hair grown out and his beard full and bushy. He always looks so rugged and woodsy nowadays, and while it's a much different version of him than I'm used to, I can't say I don't love the lumberjack look on him.

"You're up," Luca says, smiling as he leans in to kiss me gently. "I thought after last night you would want to sleep in a little longer. Maybe I didn't work you as hard as I could have," he adds with a wink. My cheeks burn pink.

"It's after eleven. This is sleeping in for me. In fact, I can't remember the last time I woke up after nine. I think the sunlight woke me up. Or the birds singing outside," I guess.

"This place really is idyllic," he says. "Isn't it better to wake up to the sound of birds instead of an alarm clock?"

"Oh, definitely. I don't know how I'll ever go back to that stupid beeping after this," I agree. "What are you doing up so early, though?"

Luca looks away, a small gesture that most people wouldn't catch, but I know him better than anything. He's big on eye contact, always holding my gaze when we speak. So whenever he averts his eyes I know something is up. I notice that he does look a little weary, a little sleep-deprived. But then he just shrugs.

"I was just setting up a couple more cameras around the premises," he admits, taking off his coat and hanging it over the chair with his thicker jacket.

"Oh," I say simply. Then I can't help but step up to him and take his face in my hands, looking up into his gorgeous face. "Luca, don't get me wrong, I know the stakes are really high for us right now. Especially for you. And I get that you want to be cautious, but... I don't think you need to be this paranoid."

I feel a tiny bit hypocritical lecturing him on this directly after I mistook him for an intruder coming in to murder me, but still. It needs to be said.

Luca smiles warmly and turns to kiss each of my hands before pulling me in for a tight hug. His beard is scratchy against my forehead and I wrinkle my nose at the ticklish feeling.

"I will try my best to relax," he promises. "I just want to be as sure as possible that we're safe here. I could never forgive myself if you got hurt just because you're with me."

"I don't even remember you buying extra cameras," I laugh. "When did you do that? The last time we were in Ithaca—"

"You went to the frozen foods section and I just took a little meander through the electronics department," he answers, a little sheepishly.

"Damn. You're sneaky," I remark, raising an eyebrow.

He shrugs. "Well, considering the profession I've worked for the better part of a decade, that really shouldn't be much of a surprise."

"Speaking of surprises," I begin, "you did kinda scare me this morning when I woke up and you weren't here. I know I just got finished telling you to relax, but I was a little worried. I think we could all do with fewer surprises around here, don't you think?"

Luca kisses my forehead, a mischievous light in his eyes. "Well, how about just *one* more surprise? It's a good one, I swear."

"Uh, okay. What is it?" I ask, taken aback.

"Get dressed and I'll show you. It's outside."

I quickly put on jeans, a thick sweater, a coat, and my well-worn boots. Luca puts his jacket on and leads me out of the house into the brisk December air. The sun shines down, warming us even as the breeze makes me shiver. I'm not as accustomed to upstate New York winters, having only ever visited here during the warm summer months. The other day we actually had a flurry of snow, which was beautiful to watch from the warmth of the cabin.

"Where are you taking me?" I pipe up, crunching through the dead leaves on the ground.

"Just down the hill toward the pond."

We walk for several minutes until we arrive at the squelchy, muddy bank of the pond and Luca tells me to close my eyes. I oblige, standing there feeling a little bit foolish until he announces that I can look. I open my eyes and see him beaming at me, standing next to what looks to be a hand-built two-person canoe.

"What is that?" I ask, grinning.

"It's a canoe, obviously," he replies, gesturing to it. "Can't you *tell* what it is?"

I detect just the slightest note of concern in his voice, like he's second-guessing his ability to make an instantly recognizable boat-like structure, and I burst out laughing. "Yes, yes, I can tell it's a boat. I just mean, where did it come from?"

"I built it myself. For you. Well, and for me. Two people can ride in it."

"Again, when did you find the time to do this?" I inquire incredulously.

"Here and there. Mostly while you were cooking meals or taking naps. You know, for such an ambitious, detail-oriented woman, you are shockingly unobservant some-times," he chuckles.

"This is amazing, Luca. Seriously, I can't believe you just happen to know how to build a boat. Are you sure it's sea-worthy? Well, pond-worthy?" I ask, biting my lip.

"I'm sure. I am a carpenter, after all. I've been itching to try a project like this for a long time. And if it makes you feel any better, I did read about a hundred articles on how to build the perfect boat. So I have the great experts of the internet to back me up," he jokes. "So, how about it? Want to take this baby for a ride? Don't worry, I only bought one set of oars because I'm going to do all the work."

I hesitate, looking nervously at the little boat. It's not that I don't trust Luca's craftsmanship, I've just always been kind of wary of large bodies of water. I mean, I have spent most of my life living in New York City. It's not like I've encountered all that many opportunities to ride in a boat. Even when I used to go swimming and fishing with my dad here growing up, it would always take about half an hour of coaxing and reassurance before I would get over my fear. And that was with a professionally-made fiberglass boat rental, not a little wooden canoe made by an admittedly talented guy who usually builds house frames, not boats.

"Come on, I even packed us a picnic," Luca urges me, pointing to a little woven basket sitting at one end of the boat.

"This is so cute," I laugh. "You're so prepared."

"Always," he says, grinning. "I promise it'll be fine. I won't let you fall out of the boat or anything. I've got you."

"I know you do," I tell him, nodding. I heave a sigh. "Okay. Fine. I'll do it. But only because you worked your ass off to make this beautiful little boat. Plus, I'm starving."

Luca helps me settle into one end of the canoe, then takes the oars and pushes us off from the shore, sitting at the other end of the boat. I can feel my stomach turning a little as I look back and see the banks of the pond drifting back away from us as we move out into the open water. It's a small enough pond that you can see shore from all points, but just big enough to be passable for fishing and swimming.

"What are you thinking about right now?" Luca asks. I giggle.

"Just remembering how my mom used to get so angry when Dad and I came back to the cabin dripping wet and muddy after hanging out at the pond all day. She's always been such a clean freak, but back in the city we had a maid when I was growing up. Here at the cabin she had to do her own cleaning, though, and we definitely didn't make it any easier on her," I explain.

"A maid?" Luca repeats incredulously, raising his eyebrows. I nod, blushing.

"Yeah. Yeah, I know. It's embarrassing now. My mom didn't have a job or anything except for occasionally checking in at Bathing Beauty, but she still refused to do housework or cooking most of the time. It's how she grew up. The Gasparis always had house staff, too, so I guess she just never learned to do any of that stuff on her own," I go on, shrugging.

"Wow. Your childhood and mine couldn't have possibly been more different," he says.

Shivering in the cold air combined with wind across the water, I answer, "I know. So weird that fate brought us together from such different worlds."

"Are you cold?" he asks. I nod.

"A little bit. I should've put on leggings under these jeans."

Luca opens the picnic basket and hands me a bottle of Campari. "This will help you warm up, if you're interested. I swear there's actual food in there, too."

"Well, I'm sure it's five o'clock somewhere," I say, gladly taking a swig of the bottle and blanching a little at the bitterness. "And what about you? Are you going to drink and row? What if some pond cop pulls you over?"

Luca laughs. "I'm not too worried about that. Besides, I know how to hold my booze."

I take out the neat little prosciutto-and-mozzarella sandwiches and freshly-chopped pineapple out of the basket, distributing the food between us. Luca stops rowing, letting the boat float freely out in the middle of the pond while we have our little picnic. We laugh and joke about our respective childhoods, sharing memories, learning more and more about each other. I want to know everything there is to know about Luca: the good, the bad, and the dangerous. Even the ugly parts are beautiful, all part of the magnificent package that is the man I love.

Out here on the pond, surrounded by the stillness and silence of open water, Luca looks so happy. Those teeny-tiny little crinkles at the corners of his eyes appear when he laughs, when he smiles big. The cool air has whipped his face, making his cheeks ruddy and his hair ruffled. I can see that this is what he needs: a quiet place to unravel and forget about the horrors of his former life as a hitman and his current life as a fugitive. Underneath those awful labels, he's just a handsome man with a huge heart, the carpenter from southern Italy who came to this country to find a better, safer way to live.

I want to give him everything, fulfill that hope he had coming here.

As much as I try to get him to talk about his past, he still manages to steer the conversation back to me. As always. "So, Bathing Beauty. What are we going to do about it?" he asks.

"I've been thinking over it, trying to figure out how to keep it afloat with this massive setback. I need to get those cops off my back and reopen. I won't just roll over and let them take everything from me," I say vehemently, feeling warm and buzzed from the Campari.

"Well, I'll fight with you, tooth and nail. We're going to get the shop back open and running, I promise. I don't know how, but we'll make it happen," Luca promises.

"Sometimes I just look around this place and wonder what it would be like if I had a different life. Somewhere far away from the hectic environment of the city. It gets so tiring, fighting off attacks from every angle. I wonder if any of the towns outside of the forest here would welcome a shop like Bathing Beauty. Artisan goods. Humble craftsmanship," I muse aloud. "And not too far from a city, with Ithaca just an hour down the road."

"You really love this place, don't you?" Luca says. "I would've assumed you were the never-leave-the-city type back when we first met."

"Oh, back then I was just doing what all my high-society friends were doing. They were all obsessed with city life and looked down on anyone who didn't live in the five boroughs. Hell, when one of my friends moved to Staten Island, even that wasn't good enough. So I guess it had to be one of the *four* boroughs. Competition was steep and everybody was so neurotic and over-concerned with what everybody else was doing and thinking. My mom got caught up in that kind of style, always pushing for the next big status symbol. It's a vicious cycle," I explain.

"We are having a good time out here in the middle of nowhere," Luca agrees. Then, he adds wryly, "Way more fun than you would expect from two people hiding from the authorities."

I grin.

"Yeah, I mean, under normal circumstances this would be hell. But anything with you is heaven. I can't imagine being anywhere else, even with all the trouble following us."

Luca leans forward and kisses me, and I can taste Campari on his lips. The kiss deepens as his hands move down my body, sliding down to cup my breasts through the thick fabric of my sweater. I can feel my body responding warmly to his touch, the thrill of a buzz heightening all my senses. Luca gazes into my eyes, something like fire flickering in his eyes.

"What do you say we bring this boat to shore?" he

murmurs, and I think I know exactly what he's getting at. I nod, biting my lip.

"Yes, please."

Luca's powerful arms get to work, rowing us to the muddy banks off to one side of the pond quickly. He helps me out and carries me across the shore to the dry earth, leaves crunching under his boots. He sets me down and we kiss, his arms folding around me. Just as I'm melting into his embrace, we hear the distinctive sound of a twig snapping somewhere nearby. We break apart and freeze, both of us glancing around nervously.

Suddenly we hear a man's voice.

"Hey, you there."

A man dressed in what looks like a forest ranger's uniform comes out of the woods holding a clipboard and walking stick. He's an older guy, probably in his fifties, and he has a very suspicious look on his face. My heart races. I never expected to run into someone way out here. The cabin, the pond... it all feels so isolated, but I guess not!

"You kids doin' okay out here? Pretty far off the trail," the ranger says.

Luca smiles, jumping into character. "Yeah, just doing a little exploring."

"That your boat?" the ranger asks, pointing to the canoe.

"Yes, sir. We've been itching to take it out for a spin," Luca explains.

"It's a little cold out, but the sun is shining so we thought today would be a good opportunity to hit the water before the snow starts up again," I pipe up.

The ranger nods and smiles. "No worries. Just be careful out here, alright? Cell service isn't so good in the forest and I wouldn't want ya gettin' hurt."

"We'll be careful. Good to meet you," Luca says. The ranger tips his hat and carries on his way, leaving us standing there silently. Once the ranger is out of sight, I look up at Luca worriedly and he gives me a light squeeze.

"We'll be okay. But that was a close one," he whispers, but his face says everything his words don't: we need to leave. Soon.

SERENA

*S*now falls softly on the windshield as I drive the big black sedan back down the curving woodsy roads to the cabin. I'm on my way back from a quick shopping trip in Ithaca, getting some groceries we desperately needed. It's nice to be out in the middle of nowhere — feels a lot safer than being in the middle of a crowd, especially with my fugitive Mafioso boyfriend — but it's not the most convenient situation. Still, I don't mind it very much, having to make solo trips to Ithaca. I love driving on the lonely country back roads, as long as the weather isn't too terrible. I would much rather be making these little trips with Luca, but we've recently gotten more nervous about his being out in public. I'm always worried that someone will recognize him somehow, even way out here upstate, and turn him in.

Today I was especially glad he stayed behind at the cabin, because it's Christmas Eve, and the crowds were out in full force today in Ithaca. The grocery store was packed with families buying gigantic turkeys and tins of holiday cookies, parents racing down the toy aisles to buy last-minute gifts for their kids. I went in with a simple list of groceries, planning to have a low-key Christmas with Luca, hand-making pasta and antipasti tomorrow. It was difficult to resist going down the street to the cluster of specialty shops to look for a Christmas present to give him, but he made me promise not to get him anything. A low-key Christmas. No gifts, no fuss. Just quietly spending time together by the fire.

I mean, I can't complain. I love the holidays, but for so many years it's been just my mom and me, so I've gotten accustomed to *not* going all out for Christmas. I do miss my mom, and I worry about her being all alone for the holidays. Cell service is still virtually impossible out in the sticks, but on my drives into Ithaca I usually give her a call once I'm in range.

I'm worried one of these days she's going to swallow her pride and plead with me to come back, or worse, start asking questions I know I can't truthfully answer. But she's promised that she is doing just fine on her own, and even hinted that she might be spending the holiday with "someone special." I know how secretive she is about that kind of thing — I've never spent much time with any of her social circle — so I didn't press her for more information. Besides, if my mom has finally joined this decade and made herself a Tinder account or something, I *definitely* do not need to know about it.

On my own end, romance is truly in the air, floating around our little cabin hideaway just like the soft flurries of pure white snow. It's hard to believe that just months ago I was alone in the city, fully expecting to never see him again, and worrying that even if I did get to see him, he would be irrevocably changed by his time in the clink. And he has changed, of course. I see the faint worry lines on his face, the hint of sadness in those beautiful green eyes, the way he sometimes grinds his teeth at night when he's sleeping. It's a tension I hope someday he'll be able to release, but for now it's perfectly understandable.

Especially since he's now dealing with being on the run. Anyone would be tense and a little paranoid in this predicament. But apart from that edge, he's the same man. Maybe even more of a man than he was before. Granted, it makes sense that he's changed over time. After all, he was only a teenager when we first met. And so was I. It seems like both of us have changed, becoming both tougher and softer at the same time. The world has hardened us, but when we're alone together we're soft.

I think we're good for each other. In fact, I know we are.

I pull the car down the gravel road up to the cabin and park. Just as I'm turning off the engine, my stomach twists and I feel a little nauseous. I clap a hand over my mouth and catch a glimpse of myself in the rearview mirror. I look slightly green. I don't know why this keeps happening, but I must have caught some kind of icky bug. I'm not too surprised, since I'm notorious for getting sick over the holidays. My body just doesn't love cold weather.

I walk around to the back of the car and pop the trunk open, but before I can even pick anything up, I hear the front door of the cabin click open and in a few quick strides Luca is beside me. "You're back," he says, grinning as he easily loads up his arms with all the grocery bags.

"Yep," I answer. "You're awfully smiley. What's going on?"

Carrying what has to be at least twenty pounds of groceries, he gives me a wink. "What? I can't just be excited to see the love of my life returning safely home after her harrowing drive through a blizzard?"

I burst out laughing as I follow him up to the cabin. "A blizzard? Luca, it's barely snowing." As I step through the doorway, my eyes adjust to the dimmer light and I realize that the entire place is strung up with twinkling Christmas lights, white candles flickering on every surface, and there's a pervasive sweet smell in the air. Is it… eggnog?

"Oh my god," I breathe, looking around in awe. Luca sets all the groceries down in the kitchen and starts putting things away, looking over at me happily.

"I know we said 'low-key' Christmas, but I felt like the place needed a little bit of holiday ambiance. I was going to put on some music, but the guy who owns the cabin must have the worst taste in Christmas music imaginable. All I could find was an old *Feliz Navidad* record. You'd think someone with that much Frank Sinatra in their collection would have better taste, but apparently not," Luca laughs.

"Again, when did you possibly have the chance to buy all this stuff?" I ask, shaking my head. Luca saunters over and puts his arms around me, giving me a rather smug smile.

"Like I've said before, you aren't very observant. As soon as you set foot in the snack aisles I know your attention is completely taken up trying to choose between chocolate chip cookies or chocolate graham crackers, so I just quickly sneak away to electronics. You really have yourself to thank for this. You're very easy to surprise," he explains.

"Okay, okay, I get it, I'm oblivious," I laugh, rolling my eyes. "But in my defense, chocolate is *very* distracting."

"Hey, I'm not complaining. All the sneakiness is worth it just to see the look on your face when I get to surprise you with something," he says, kissing me on the forehead. "Plus, I do have an ulterior motive here. The fairy lights might be for Christmas cheer, but the candles are supposed to set a different kind of mood, if you get my drift."

I smile and lean in to kiss him, standing on my tiptoes. "Oh, you don't need to light a bunch of candles to get me in the mood for that."

Luca scoops me up in his arms and carries me down the hall to the bedroom, gently tossing me onto the gigantic bed. I can tell the sheets have been freshly washed and dried — another surprise he took care of while I was out — and there are more candles lit up around the room. I lie back and stretch out, watching greedily as Luca strips off his long-sleeved Henley and jeans, then his boxers. It's a delicious sight, his muscles rippling in the flickering candlelight as he climbs onto the bed beside me. He leans down to kiss me, his hands sliding down to grope my breasts as I feel warmth spreading between my thighs. Even his simplest touch sets me on fire, my body waking up instantly. He reaches down to pull my thick blue sweater up over my head, peeling away my undershirt, bra, jeans, and panties quickly. I can tell he's eager for it, his patience limited.

I love it when he's like this, when I can tell just how difficult it is for him to take his time with me. Slow and sensual is good, too, but there's just something so satisfying about seeing him unable to resist me for another second that really turns me on and makes me feel special. He bends to pull one of my nipples into his warm mouth, his tongue playing over the stiffened point. I groan and arch my back to meet his lips as his hand slips down between my legs to stroke my clit.

"Already so wet for me, *dolcezza*," he murmurs, moving to my other breast.

"You make me wet just by looking at me," I answer breathlessly, my eyes rolling back in my head as he expertly circles my clit with his forefinger, giving me spikes of pleasure. Then he moves his hand down, sliding two fingers inside my slick hole to stroke my g-spot slowly and teasingly. He backs down between my legs, leaning in to enclose my folds in his mouth, his tongue flicking over my clit while his fingers thrust into me faster and harder.

"Oh fuck," I murmur, rolling my hips to meet his touch. I reach out and grasp at the bed sheets with both hands, feeling my pleasure mounting higher and higher. "So—so good."

"Come for me, Serena," he says softly, his fingers curling ever so slightly to push harder against that heavenly spot deep inside me. He sucks at my clit, sending spirals of warmth and tingles up through my body and I clench at the sheets as I climax with a whimper.

My body goes limp as he quickly slides off the bed and picks me up so that I'm straddling him, my legs around his waist. With my pussy still shuddering with the after waves of my orgasm, he walks me over to pin me against the wall and slams his cock inside of me with one fluid shove. I cry out, immediately coming again. I can feel my honey gushing over his cock as he rears back and thrusts into me again and again, fucking me hard against the wall. He has one arm holding me up and the other holding my wrists together above my head as he fucks me, spearing me with his thick, hard cock.

"Yes! Oh god, fuck me," I moan, closing my eyes as I lose myself to the shocks of pure bliss radiating through me. I revel in Luca's ridiculous strength, his ability to hold me up and fuck me so hard with ease, like I weigh nothing at all.

"I know you love it like this," he growls through gritted teeth, leaning forward so that his lips brush against my ear. "You love it fast and hard, don't you, baby?"

"Yes, yes, yes," I murmur, feeling a third orgasm coming on. The head of his cock is slamming into my g-spot while the friction of our bodies pressed up together stimulates my clit, combining into an indescribable pleasure.

"I want to hear you come, *mia passerotta*. I want to hear you scream for me," he commands softly, sending ticklish shivers down my spine. "Tell me how good it feels."

He fucks me faster, the slick slap of his balls against my ass resounding in the quiet room as my pussy clenches tighter and tighter. "Oh my god, oh my god," I moan. "Luca, it feels so fucking good. You're so deep! Oh fuck."

"*Si, dolcezza*," he whispers. "Tell me more."

"Luca, you're gonna make me fucking come. Oh god, it's too much— I-I can't take it. It feels so good. I love it when you fuck me like this. Don't stop, don't stop, don't—" my words break off right as another orgasm shatters across my body and I shudder, my legs shaking uncontrollably as Luca keeps going, not slowing down even for a second. A moment later, he bellows my name and holds me close as his own orgasm explodes, shooting hot spunk deep inside my pussy.

He rests his forehead against mine, both of us breathing heavily as we struggle to recover from the overwhelming pleasure. Then, without a single word, Luca carries me into the bathroom and turns on the shower, setting me down.

"Fuck," I mumble, brushing the hair back out of my eyes.

"Indeed," Luca agrees, an exhilarated smile on his face.

"Merry Christmas," I tell him, laughing breathlessly. We both step into the shower and he starts washing us off, starting with me, as usual.

"That was the best Christmas gift I could ever ask for. Who needs anything else?" he says, lathering soap over my shoulders as he leans down to kiss me.

After we shower off, we eat a quick dinner and get ready to climb into bed, both dressed in warm pajamas. Luca looks ridiculously handsome in his plaid flannel pants, his shirtless chest powerful and glistening with post-shower dew. Just as I'm pulling the sheets up over myself and about to turn off the bedside lamp, Luca comes over with his hands behind his back.

"I know we said we weren't doing gifts, but I did get you something," he says.

I sit up in bed, confused. "Oh, but I didn't get you anything!" I lament.

He shakes his head. "Don't worry. This gift is as much for me as it is for you." He hands me a little golden box about the size of a standard book. I take off the lid to reveal two navy blue passport books. I frown at them in confusion, then look up at Luca, who's smiling warmly.

"What is this? I already have a passport," I ask.

"It's a chance at a brand new start," he begins. "Those passports contain new identities for us to take on. I've been in contact with some of my people, and they're arranging for us to be smuggled out of here. I've done some research and found a quiet, beautiful town just over the border in Canada where I think Bathing Beauty would do very well. We could finally be free and safe to live our lives, Serena. We could stop hiding here in the woods and be regular people again. We could be together without so much paranoia and fear. We can start over."

"Oh my god," I breathe, thumbing through the pages of the fake passport made for me. It looks completely authentic, identical to the one I already have except that it has a different name. I recognize the names as the Shakespearean character aliases I jokingly selected for the both of us weeks ago. "Are you serious about this?" I ask.

"Dead serious. All it takes is one phone call tomorrow morning and we'll be on our way to freedom and safety, Serena," he explains.

A million thoughts race through my head as my logical side argues with my romantic side. However, this time all the questions raised by fear are squashed back down with hope. My mother has a passport. She can visit us anytime. Rafaela and Nico can visit, too, and Raf always talks about wanting to see Niagara Falls anyway. The shop is doing well enough that I could probably afford to open a new location, maybe even keep the New York shop open, too. I can send money home to my mother, and the house should be paid off within the next few years anyway.

We could stop living under the shadow of fear. We could be free to walk down the streets hand-in-hand, knowing nobody could recognize us. Nobody would know our names.

My heart skips a beat. This dream… it could come true.

"What do you say?" Luca asks, and I detect a slight hint of nervousness in his voice. I give him a smile, climbing out of bed to hug him tightly, pressing my face against his chest.

"I say yes. I say let's do it. Tomorrow," I tell him earnestly.

~

On Christmas morning, I wake up to the smell of bacon frying in the kitchen. As my brain comes awake I remember our discussion the night before, the fake passports, the plan to escape to Canada. I can't help but smile as I bound out of bed and out into the living room. I see fluffy pancakes, maple syrup, a bowl of fruit, and a plate of bacon on the table waiting for me, but no Luca. I walk into the kitchen to find him standing by the pantry, but when I catch sight of the serious look on his face, my smile fades away. He's holding his phone to his ear, and I realize that's why he's hiding out over here by the pantry. Weirdly enough, through a lot of boredom and trial and error, we determined that the only spot in the cabin where we can get any hint of a signal is right by the pantry door. At first, I think that he must be making the call to his people to get us smuggled into Canada like we talked about, but when he hangs up, the pain on his face only intensifies. He looks over at me with baleful eyes.

"What's wrong?" I ask, worried.

He sighs, running a hand back through his hair. "Change of plans. Something awful has happened. I have to go back to the city."

LUCA

$\mathcal{I}$t's a risk to get so close to the crime scene, but I can't hold myself back. I have to see this with my own eyes. We pull up to the sidewalk around the corner and down the road, far enough that nobody would suspect us, and I pull out a pair of binoculars to look at the building down the road from us.

My heart sinks at what I see.

"Luca... I'm so sorry," Serena whispers, putting her hand on my arm.

Uncle Carlo's workshop has police tape wrapped around the whole perimeter and over some of the shattered windows. The walls are riddled with bullet holes, there's broken glass all over the ground, and I can see the door has been kicked down. I can even see shells on the sidewalk, and a few uniformed people are walking around the place. They're too busy with their work to look our way. I can just barely make out some of the inside of the shop, and I see splintered wood: signs of a fight.

And there's blood on some of that wood.

I lower my binoculars, and I can feel the color leaving my face. The message I got in the cabin was that Uncle

Carlo's place had been hit. I wasn't expecting something like this.

"And Nico didn't say…?"

I shake my head. "He just told me the shop had been hit. I... I don't remember anything else, it got hazy after that."

"Should we go up there and see…?"

"We can't," I say through a tight jaw, clenching the wheel so hard my knuckles turn white. "Even after those investigators leave, there will be someone watching this place. They'll be waiting for us. Disguises won't matter." We're both wearing sunglasses and hats now, but my frame is easy to recognize this close to where I'm being looked for.

"Those bastards," Serena says in a thin voice, and even as she does, I'm looking at the place and seeing glimpses of the past. I see myself running away from that shop my first few weeks here, only to end up back there shortly after. I see my friends and me wrestling in the back. I see Uncle Carlo teaching me how to defend myself, how to be an American, how to work to support myself. I see him being a father to me when my father couldn't be there.

Then the image of him getting shot alone in the darkness flashes into my head. I feel something hot on my face, and I realize a tear is running down my stony cheek. Serena must have noticed, because I feel her small arms wrapping around my bicep and resting her head on it.

We're quiet for a long moment.

Then there's a tap on the car window.

Instinctively, my hand goes to the gun at my side, and my eyes snap to the window, ready to fight whomever it is, but I only see Nico looking down at us, putting his hands up after seeing my gesture.

I let out a sigh, tension leaving my shoulders, and I roll the window down.

"Jesus, try to be here more than an hour before you get

arrested again," he says as I relax my hand, and I unlock the door, nodding for him to get in the back. He does, and I roll the windows back up once he's safely inside.

"Hey, Nico," Serena says, smiling apologetically back at him.

"Sorry to get the jump on you," he says, running his hand through his hair. "Wish I could have said more over the phone, but I don't know who's being listened to anymore. We're going through burner phones like water."

"What happened here, Nico?" I say, my voice gravelly. "Where is Carlo?"

"He's alive," Nico says first, and I see Serena visibly relieved. I am too, but my anger makes my emotions hard to read. "But Luca... he's not in a good way. He's comatose in the hospital. We've got our men keeping an eye on him, but the police aren't making it easy. They keep trying to question our guys."

"This was a setup," I growl.

"No doubt," Nico says grimly. "I heard about what happened here a few minutes after it went down. One of our guys happened to be at the gas station down the road and heard the shots. Weren't any cops around for a mile."

"Oh my god," Serena says, her eyes widening. "They were in on this?"

"Price," I say.

"The cops have been putting on more and more pressure ever since you got out, Luca," Nico explains. "They tried to be subtle at first when you got out: nobody wanted word spreading that someone broke out of Sterling. That's why your face hasn't been plastered on every TV and newspaper in the country. So instead, Price has been leading an investigation that's been twisting *our* arms."

"Have there been arrests because of me?" I ask, turning back to look at him for the first time.

"No," he says, "turns out that you keeping out of Costa

business while you were in prison really helped us out. They can't make the connections they need to start making arrests. But they can harass us so much we can hardly move, and that's what they've been doing since you got out. The Cleaners are getting bolder, and the cops are making it easy, since Price is in their pocket."

I rub my forehead, feeling a headache coming on. This is too much. How could everything have boiled over so much so quickly?

"We shouldn't stay here too long, speaking of," Nico says, glancing out the back window. "Let's get to the Room With a View."

~

Nico did good with his share of the heist money. He and Rafaela have fully rebuilt and renovated the Room With a View to look better than it ever had been before. While Serena and Rafaela throw their arms around each other and hug warmly, Nico and I take a seat by the bar.

"Cleaners were *beyond* mad about the heist we pulled off," Nico says in a low tone. "They needed that money bad. They can't prove we're involved, but they can throw a fit."

I clench my fist and feel my teeth grinding. "This is my fault. I should have planned better."

"None of that bullshit," Nico says, pouring us a couple glasses of limoncello. "You and I both know what those fuckers are capable of. If it hadn't been this, it would have been something else. You killed Lorenzo Abruzzi."

It feels like a lifetime ago that I killed that wretch. Mafia royalty in his own right. "Wonder how he's enjoying his little corner in hell."

"Not as much as we'll enjoy ours," Nico says, and we clink our glasses together and drink.

Serena and Rafaela come over to join us after their quick reunion, and we all sit together at the bar. For a moment, it feels like old times.

"Luca, one of the boys sent me a picture of your uncle from the hospital to let me know he's still hanging in there," Rafaela says gently. "If you want to see, for peace of mind…"

"No," I say, shaking my head. "I don't want to see him like that. *He* wouldn't want to be seen like that."

"No problem," she says with a quick wave of her hand. "Anyway, good to see you both. Life's treating you two alright, I see," she adds, looking our outfits up and down.

"Helps to blend in," Serena says.

"Not anymore, though," I say. "Someone found us up there. I took care of it, but we can't keep running like this. If we go further, more people will just keep getting hurt here."

Serena nods in agreement. "Now we just need to figure out where to start."

"We could try to mobilize some of the Costas," Nico says, leaning on the bar. "You've still got a lot of friends here, Luca, not just me and Rafaela."

If I'm honest, I want even less to do with the mafia now than ever. I want to leave that life behind me, and I plan on making that happen. But now isn't a good time to try and burn that bridge, not while we're recouping here with two good friends who still have close ties to the Costas.

Much like Italy, the mafia here is a complex web that isn't always so easy to work around.

"This is personal," I say simply, "and I don't want to fan the flames of another war. Enough blood is getting shed without my help. Besides, we know now that things are going the way they are because of Price and his lackeys in the NYPD."

The others nod in agreement. "The police are untouchable, though," Serena points out, "it's not like another gang where you can go in and just start fights until things go our way. How do you go up against a detective?"

A confident smile crosses my face. "I have a good idea of where to start."

"Are you sure about this?" I whisper to Luca as we walk up to the nightclub. The bass is booming, making the very pavement outside vibrate to the beat. I'm wearing a tight black dress, dark hosiery, heels, and a black leather jacket, and I'm shivering in the cold winter air. The city is wide awake and pulsing with life, from the neon signs to the honking horns and shrill laughter of a bachelorette party group filing clumsily into a bar across the street. It's strange to be back in New York after our stay in the cabin, to be surrounded by so much noise again. Back to the real world, where all our fears still live, waiting for us to walk back into focus.

I would be lying if I said I wasn't afraid. I'm definitely scared.

"I'm sure. This is the way we have to do this," Luca answers me in an undertone. The bouncer stands up as we approach, crossing his arms over his broad chest. He's a big guy, but still not as tall as Luca. However, he looks infinitely meaner, with his shaved head, scowling eyes, and face tattoos. He seems a little rough to be working the door at a nightclub like this, but I suppose the more exclusive the club, the more aggressive the door guy has to be.

He opens his mouth to inevitably tell us to fuck off, that the club is at full capacity, but then he stops short, his eyes falling on me. He gives me a quizzical look for a second, like he's trying to figure out who I am. My heart starts racing, worrying that maybe he recognizes us somehow, that maybe I'm known as an accomplice to Luca the fugitive. But then he smiles.

"S—Serena?" he asks haltingly. "That you?"

"Uh, yeah," I answer, confused. He nods slowly.

"Yeah, yeah. It's me, Damian. We took that comp sci class together in college, remember?"

It dawns on me that I have actually shared a classroom with this guy before. Maybe I can use this to our advantage. I give him a big grin. "Oh yeah! Hi! How—how are you?"

"Great! I'm graduating in the spring, but for now I'm doing this job to get by. Crossing my fingers I get picked up as a CPA somewhere. Just tossin' out a million resumes right now, ya know. Gotta follow the grind, man," he explains cheerily. I remember him as a scrawny computer nerd type, but I guess in the past few years he's either hit the gym five times a day or possibly gone through some miraculous second puberty.

"That's awesome, Damian. Good luck!" I tell him, amused by the spontaneity of this interaction. I mean, who would've guessed it? Sometimes even New York can feel like a small town. Damian moves aside, gesturing for us to go inside.

"Thanks! Well, it was good to see you, Serena. Go on in and have a great night!" he says brightly as we walk into the club. I can feel Luca's eyes boring into my head and I look up at him, stifling a laugh. He's shaking his head, eyebrows raised.

"That was lucky. Good thing you've got a memorable face," he says, grinning.

"Yeah, talk about kismet," I laugh. We make our way over to the bar and Luca orders a couple shots. I shake my head, and he doesn't push me, taking both of them in quick succession. The seriousness of what we're about to do tonight is flooding back into my mind. Luca obviously notices my tension, and takes me by the hand, leading me out onto the crowded dance floor. The last thing I want to do right now is dance, but he's insistent.

"We need to play it cool. Be convincing," he whispers in my ear. "We're just a young couple here for a casual evening of dancing. No big deal."

"How will we know when he gets here?" I ask quietly as Luca takes hold of my hips and starts to sway with me.

"I'm keeping an eye on the front entrance and the employee's entrance toward the back. He doesn't work here but he's a regular, so he might come in through there to go undetected. But he knows what I look like, and I know what he looks like. We'll find him, no problem," he explains.

"What if he doesn't show?" I ask, biting my lip.

Luca shakes his head. "He will. Trust me. This guy might be the only person on the planet who hates Price as much as I do."

We dance together for what feels like hours. I'm beginning to feel hopeless when finally Luca puts a hand on my arm and nods in the direction of the back of the club. Even though I didn't know what he looked like before tonight, I recognize him instantly by the world-weary look on his face. He's a relatively tall man, but he walks with a slight stoop, like he's perpetually ashamed of himself, trying to make himself look smaller. He has thinning salt-and-pepper hair and deep frown lines on his paunchy face. He looks over and locks eyes with Luca, both men nodding once in acknowledgement before the ex-cop walks over to a booth against the wall and sits down.

Luca orders a beer and we head over to the booth where our contact is waiting. I can feel my heart beating fast, but for some reason my mind is totally cool and collected. After spending all this time with Luca on the run, I think my tolerance for high-stakes situations has gotten a little higher.

We settle into the booth across from the ex-cop and Luca slides the beer across the table to him. The guy gladly accepts it and takes a long sip before speaking.

"Sorry, I wasn't expecting you to have company," he says quietly, his voice a little rough. I can tell he's probably been a lifelong smoker. Luca nods.

"This is Serena. And you already know who I am," Luca says.

"Hi Serena. I'm Hank. Ex-cop, ex-success story, ex-productive member of society. Nice to meet you," the guy says flatly, taking another drink of his beer.

"I'm sorry... can I just ask a question?" I begin, leaning forward and lowering my voice. "What made you quit the force?"

Hank sighs and answers, "An operation went foul at the fairgrounds a while back. Found my own neck on the chopping block. Could've made some serious waves if I spoke up, but Price would have my head before I even got the words out. So I decided it was best to just cut and run."

"So, you worked closely with Price?" I press on.

He nods, rolling his eyes. "Oh yeah, Price and I go way back. We were at the Academy together, rose up in the ranks side by side. He got accolades, I got accolades. He got promoted, I got promoted. We were on parallel tracks to greatness, you know. Colleagues working our asses off on the same team for the greater good. Or so I thought."

"Price used to be on the straight and narrow once upon a time, then?" Luca suggests.

Hank shrugs. "I don't know how far back his dirty business goes. He could've been scheming since day one at the Academy for all I know. I had no idea for the longest time. I guess that's part of why I wasn't cut out to be a cop after all: I just kind of assumed the best of everyone. You can't do that in my former line of work. Ain't nobody one-hundred-percent clean. Price was a good cop, don't get me wrong. He made arrest after arrest after arrest. He shut down gangs and crime syndicates, threw a bunch of small-time dealers in the clink. If the chief had been handing out gold stars, he would've been a goddamn constellation. But turns out, he was double-dipping. Got one hand on the badge and the other digging into places he got no business in. Jewel smuggling, gambling rings, even sex trafficking."

He shakes his head, his fists tightening on the table in front of him. "That fucker was moonlighting for both sides all along, but really it's not about good or bad. Price doesn't work for anybody but himself."

"Are you the only one who knows about this?" Luca asks.

Hank chuckles, but the laughter doesn't warm up his cold expression one bit. "Nah. I can think of a half dozen guys on the force who could give evidence about Price's shady business dealings. I got evidence of my own. But nobody's gonna speak up."

"Not even you?" I pipe up. "You're already off the force. What do you have to lose?"

He stares at me for a moment with narrowed eyes. "You don't get it, do you? This is bigger than just a stupid job. I got the hell out of dodge because that was the only way I could at least kind of hold onto what's left of my damn conscience. Price has friends in high places, but it's his friends in low places you really gotta watch out for. Everybody hates him, but he made damn sure they're afraid of him, too. We all know what that rat bastard is capable of, and nobody's willing to risk life or livelihood to take him down. He's too powerful."

"The bigger they are, the harder they fall," I interject. "And if you came out to meet us here tonight, that must mean you haven't totally given up all hope yet."

Hank gives me a weak, almost wistful smile. "Hope? Nah. I'm way past hope. Nowadays all I got left is desperation and spite."

"Well, then maybe you're just desperate enough to help us," Luca says. "You said you have evidence. Good enough to put him away?"

"I don't know. Maybe. But it wouldn't make a difference unless we got everybody on our side, and that'll never happen," Hank laments. "Look, I feel for you, man. I get it. Price has taken so much away from me, from you, from a lot of people who didn't deserve it. I admire what you're trying to do here, but it's never gonna work out."

"We can pay you," Luca says. "We can get your job back. We can take Price down."

"Man, it's not that I don't wanna help you. It's just that I can't. I already lost everything when I quit the force. That job was everything to me, all I ever wanted to do with my life since I was a little boy playing cops and robbers. But that department is all in Price's pocket nowadays. Ain't nothing you or anybody else can do about it. The stakes are too high."

He gulps down the rest of his beer and starts to slide out of the booth, trying to leave. Desperately, I blurt out, "What if we could promise you a new start? A do-over, somewhere far away. Y-You could get away from all this. Pretend it never even happened."

Hank turns back to look at me with his brows furrowed. Luca looks at me, too, confused at what I'm talking about. "A new identity. Untraceable," I go on, glancing at Luca meaningfully. "We can do that, can't we? We can get him out of the country."

Luca catches on, realizing that I'm talking about the fake passports he had made for us, the ones with the pictures missing. He nods, gesturing for Hank to sit back down.

"Yes. We can promise you safe passage out of here. Consider it a guerrilla-style witness protection service," he explains. Hank slowly slides back into the booth, looking apprehensive.

"In exchange for your evidence and your assistance, we can get you a new life. A new chance to make something of yourself, without all this baggage weighing you down," I tell him.

Hank looks back and forth between us, clearly torn. Luca and I wait silently, impatiently for him to say something.

feel like I can hear my heartbeat getting slower and steadier as I bring the car to a stop and turn off the engine. It's a skill I learned in prison. I forced my body to calm down and be ready for anything when having to deal with the police.

Most of all when dealing with Price.

Some close contacts and I set up a meeting with him under the pretenses that he's meeting his the ex-cop we met at the club. It's a run-down bar just off the highway on the outskirts of the city where bikers tend to pass through. Not the kind of place you'd expect to be finding a cop, but Price has an understanding with the owner, and from what I understand, the two have a tenuous alliance, of a sort.

That's going to be a problem. But this is the one shot I have at getting Price alone, maybe even off-guard. It's a risk I need to take.

But it isn't a risk I'm willing to put on anyone else. That's why I'm out here alone tonight.

I lied to Nico. I told him I'd meet him at the Room With a View to plan a proper setup with all the support I really need for a job like this. But to do that would be to ask too much of a man who's already given me too much. And besides, if this goes sour, I don't want him to get his name implicated in something as big as this. It's a miracle he's kept himself out of too much hot water so far.

As for Serena, she thinks I'm meeting Nico too. It pains me to keep her in the dark more than anything, but she's the one person above all I can't risk getting hurt. Right now, nobody knows she's been an accomplice to a wanted fugitive. I want to keep it that way.

I feel the little disk in my jacket pocket. It's one of many copies I made, of course. Our ex-cop friend really pulled through: there are more people willing to move against Price than I ever expected. Most of them are beat cops who are too young to get jaded, but there are a few mid-level people running desk jobs in the force who have been paid to cover up Price's paper trail of corruption. Just enough to knock him off his high horse.

I push the door to the bar open and step inside to the smell and thick haze of smoke. Old rock is playing while rough-looking bikers hang out around the pool tables or at the bar. I don't stop as I move in. I'm not planning to stop and chat with the bartender before heading upstairs.

Price's usual meeting place is the rooftop. The sign on top of the front of the bar makes sure anyone up there has a little privacy from the street view, even though the building is only a story high.

Unfortunately, I see the stairs leading up to the roof are past the bar. I'll be noticed heading upstairs. No matter. Price still can't get away.

I head toward the bar, and I'm about halfway there when a voice behind me makes me freeze.

"Hey, think I'd let you go in there alone?"

As I stop, I can't help the feeling of a smile tugging at the corners of my mouth. "You tailed me. Well done."

"Learned from the best," says Serena as she steps up

beside me and I look down at her. "Don't worry, I didn't snitch to Nico."

As I see her standing there beside me confidently, I don't feel any impulse to tell her this is too dangerous for her or too much for her to handle. She has her family's blood in her, after all. She's my girl. I should have known that any girl of mine wouldn't accept anything less.

"Be ready, then," I say in a low tone, barely audible over the sounds of the bar. "I don't expect this to go so good."

"I'd be disappointed if it did," she says with a wink.

I step up to the bar, and as I start to head to the stairs, the bartender's eyes snap over to me. He's a squirrelly little guy with a chin-strap beard and a shaved head.

"That's staff-only," he says with a suspicious look.

"I have business upstairs," I growl, moving past him and taking Serena's hand as I go.

I don't hear him shout after us, which tells me something's up.

"He was texting something on a burner phone last I saw him," Serena says as we hurry up the stairs. That confirms my suspicions.

"He must be in Price's pocket," I say, pulling out a gun and holding it at the ready. "We've lost some of the element of surprise, then."

"Not all of it," Serena points out.

"No, not all of it," I say with a smile as we reach the door to the roof. I stop, turn to Serena, and pull her into me to press my lips to hers briefly.

"I love you," I whisper.

"I love you," she says back with a smile. "Let's handle this, together."

I kick the door down.

My gun is out and ready, but instead of hearing the gunshots I was expecting, I hear the sound of someone blowing smoke.

Furrowing my brow, I look at the figure standing at the edge of the roof toward the rear of the building, his back to me, a glowing cigarette in his hand.

"You move fast, Luca," says Detective Price, not turning around to face me. He's staring out into the woods behind the bar, and I see him slip his phone back into his pocket. "Gotta say, I wasn't expecting my man to turn me out like this. Well done."

"What, were you hoping your winning personality would keep him in line?" I ask as Serena steps up beside me, her fist gripping her switchblade.

"Good point," he says with a quiet, humorless laugh, turning around to face us, "but when he's found dead in his apartment, I'll make sure the report says that he was a loyal friend of yours."

"If you were calling for backup, I'd call them off," Serena says, and Price raises his eyebrows, amused. "We've got something you don't want them seeing."

Showing my hand, I carefully remove the disk from my jacket pocket, holding it up for Price to see. A thin smile comes across his lips.

"Get a little dirt on me, did you?" he says, lighting up another cigarette. The smoke swirls around his face as he breathes in and out, cold eyes flitting between us. "Looks like I have some housecleaning to do when we leave here."

"There's enough info on this disk to put you away a lot longer than I would have been in prison," I say, twirling the disk around before putting it back in my pocket. "I would guess there are a lot of boyscout-types on the force who'd like to get their hands on this." Price is keeping his cool, but I can tell it's a thin veil. His eyes follow the disk as I put it away, and he isn't as calm as he was when he would talk to me in prison. We're getting to him.

Still, he keeps a poker face that would fool most people.

"Come on, you don't think I'd call the boys in blue to

back me up at a place like this," he says, gesturing down to the bar itself."

"No," I agree, "there's a lot of things here that would be embarrassing to explain."

"Y'know," he says, "I'm sure you're new to the whole 'whistleblowing' thing, but usually, you keep things a little more uh, subtle than this."

"I'm here because this is personal, Price," I say, stepping forward, my fist clenched. "This is more than just you chasing me down. You've made Serena's life hell. You went after my associates. You tried to kill my uncle!" I bark, and I have to fight the urge to fire my weapon into him right then and there. "We're past you just stroking your ego or building your spider's web of corruption in the NYPD. This has become between you and me. Why?"

"Are you serious?" he laughs, flicking his cigarette to the ground and snuffing it out. "Listen, Luca, you've been a lot more pain than you're worth, but you've got guts, so I'll level with you. Organized crime? That shit is *fantastic* for me. You mafia families have your factions and your blood feuds and your politics. You're like little governments flying under the radar. And it just so happens that some of us cops realize, 'hey, this can work out for us, if we open our minds up a little.' So I help some Mafioso out here, they help me back. When one family loses power, I shuffle my priorities around, and at the end of the day, I get a nice paycheck. It ain't pretty, but it *works*, get it? People like me are what keep the city running. The mafia keeps the streets cleaner than they would be, and I just help the right Mafioso do their jobs and stay in their place."

He takes a few steps forward, raising a finger and gesturing between the two of us with a hardening face.

"But you two? Some upstart rebel without a cause with a chip on his shoulder and the bratty daughter of a mafia don who should have been killed off with him a long time ago? You two are a threat to all the good stuff we've got going on. You outlived your usefulness a long time ago. The Abruzzi family, those guys you call Cleaners? *They're* the future of the Bronx."

He turns his eyes to me, narrowing them. "And if I've gotta kill some useless old man to make that point, nobody's gonna cry, and it'll be a lot cleaner than dragging out a bloody mob war."

"I never asked for any of this, you fucker," I growl, stepping forward and gripping my gun, but he just smiles.

"Ah-ah-ah, let's not add cop-killing to your track record now."

"I don't have to kill you," I say, controlling my temper, for Serena's sake, though each word is laced with anger. "As much as I want to. I want you to disappear, Price. Back off my family, and that includes the Costas. Get a transfer somewhere quiet, and I'll leave your reputation intact. It's cleaner that way, like you say. Cross me, and you'll rot in the prison cell you had set up for me," I say with finality.

Price stares into me for a moment, then licks his lips and scratches his head. "Hate to burst your bubble, but I already decided how this was gonna go down before you even got up here."

Before I can ask what he means, I hear the sounds of crashing glass and breaking wood from downstairs.

"Hear that?" Price says with a chipper smile. "That'll be the bikers downstairs. My bartender friend knows how to get a fight going, and man, some of these gangs get *violent*."

In the blink of an eye, Price draws a gun, and mine snaps up to him… but he aims his at Serena, and we both freeze.

"So when they find your bodies," he explains in a cold, even tone, "you'll just be two fugitives who were in the wrong place at the wrong time, and by the looks of things, there'll be nobody else to handle that blackmail of yours."

We're frozen for a moment before I hear a creak behind me. Pierce's eyes move to the door for half a second as the bartender emerges from the stairs with a lead pipe in hand, and I take my chance.

But I don't shoot. I can't risk that.

I dive for Serena, and just as my body wraps around her and pulls her to the ground, Pierce fires, and I feel my side burning.

"Kill them!" Pierce shouts, and he dives for cover behind an AC unit as I get off Serena and fire at him.

Adrenaline surges through my body as my bullets make sparks on the unit, and I realize Serena has rolled away from me, blade flashing.

"Serena!" I shout, but she's already rushing toward the bartender, who looks just as surprised as I am. But I don't have time to watch their fight: a bullet whizzes by my ear as Price blind-fires.

Gritting my teeth, I fire twice more at the unit he's hiding behind, and as I fire, I barrel toward it. Faster than I knew I could move, I leap up on top of the unit and fire down toward where he is, and I see his crouching form turn with wide, white eyes in surprise. He tries to raise his weapon to me, but I descend on him so fast that when he fires, his wrist is already on the ground under my hand, and the bullet ricochets off the sign.

I have him nearly pinned, and I bring my head down to his nose to disorient him. He grunts in pain as I make contact, but he lands a hard blow to my side where I was already bleeding from the gunshot wound, and I'm forced to release him.

He staggers to his feet, but I'm back up the next second. He squares up with me, fists raised, and we trade blows like boxers. Our guns have fallen to the side, and I don't think either of us notice until we're already swinging at each other, our hatred runs so deep. He lands a blow on my jaw, and it's got more force behind it than I knew he had in him, but soon I have the chance to move in close and grapple him.

I bring him down to the ground with all my weight, and as I wrestle him, I catch sight of Serena fighting with the bartender.

I can't avoid watching her for a moment, my heart leaping into my throat as I see him lunge, his brutish moves careless, but I swell with pride at the sight of Serena handling herself perfectly: she moves as nimbly as if we'd been training just yesterday, and I watch her dodge the heavy swing of the lead pipe and move up close to the bartender, grabbing him by the wrist with one hand before she brings her knife up under his arm.

At the same time I hear the blade go into his flesh and hear him scream, Price lands a solid punch across my face, then grabs it, trying to get his thumbs up to my eyes.

I roll with him, putting my knee to his stomach and wrenching him hard, and we're deadlocked, our pressure points putting each other in intense pain.

"I... I was there, you know," he snarls as we struggle, "at the shooting. I saw the whites in the old man's eyes when the bullets flew into his house."

I start to turn him around and wrench his arm behind him, but the knees me in the stomach and rolls away, and we're on our feet again, both breathing heavily. There's a wild look in his eyes as he gets ready for me again, and he wipes away a little blood from his lip.

"Don't worry," he says, "when you're dead, I'll make sure Serena isn't lonely this time."

It's then that I notice he's standing beside one of our guns, and he dives for it. I start to run forward, but as his fingers wrap around it and he lifts the weapon...

... There's a solid *whump* as Serena swings the lead pipe

across the side of his head, and Price falls to the ground, clutching his head as his mouth is fixed in a silent scream.

"Luca!" Serena calls as she tosses me the pipe, and I catch it solidly as I stride forward, flashing a smile at her, the bartender dying behind her.

"The gang fight isn't a bad cover," I say as I loom over him, knuckles white as his reddened eyes glare up at me, still dazed. "I think it'll do for you." I lift the pipe above my head and take aim.

"Say hello to Lorenzo for me."

I swing down.

"Serena!" rings out a clear, excited voice from down the hallway. Rafaela comes rushing toward me to give me a hug. Luca steps aside for a moment to let us reunite, watching with an amused smile. Rafaela looks at me with her big brown eyes twinkling and her cheeks flushed and I can tell she's already a couple drinks in. "I heard about what happened. Holy crap, *chica*, that's some seriously fucked-up shit."

She then turns to Luca and gives him a hug, too, surprising both of us. Rafaela is a huggy person, but she's usually a little more reserved than this. I laugh at the shock on Luca's face as he hesitantly pats her on the back. Raf looks up at him and says very gravely, "I can't thank you enough for keeping Serena safe. That's my best friend, you know. If anything happened to her I would fall apart."

"As long as I'm around, nothing will happen to her. I promise you that," Luca replies warmly. Rafaela nods and turns back to hook her arm through mine.

"How many drinks have you had tonight?" I ask her, stifling a snort. She flips her hair over her shoulder, trying her best to look offended, but she's still smiling.

"Not enough. *Vámonos!* We're celebrating tonight and you two are the guests of honor!" she declares, leading the way down the corridor.

We're on the top floor of a swanky corporate tower, one of the buildings I used to marvel at as a teenager, thinking that one day I was going to be a super-powered businesswoman in a pencil skirt, heels, and a white button-up starched and ironed by my home staff. It seems like a million lifetimes ago that I nursed that dream, and it couldn't be further away from what I dream about now. I used to long for fortune, notoriety, all the typical status symbols my parents taught me to lust after: fancy high-rise apartment, designer wardrobe, expensive car, maybe even a yacht. But now I just want the simple things: peace, freedom, stability, and most of all, love.

My heart flutters as I look over and lock eyes with Luca. He gives me a fond smile, warming the hard features of his handsome face as soon as he looks my way. I reach out and take his hand even as Rafaela leads me by the other arm. In a way, this is the best I could ever ask for. Walking side by side with my man and my best friend.

"So, who owns this building? I mean, this seems like an unlikely choice for this kind of crowd," I ask curiously. Luca chuckles.

"You would be surprised how far the strong arms of the Costa family reach. The top three floors of the building belong to a shell corporation. A front. Don't get me wrong, they do regular business, as well. Trades, marketing, all that. But it's also a Costa headquarters, owned by one of the highest-ranking guys in the family," Luca explains.

"Ah," I say, nodding. "Big-wig type. Should I be worried about meeting him? I mean, with my dad's history and everything?"

Rafaela interjects, "Everyone there is so friendly! Those

people know how to party. They got hors d'oeuvres, champagne, an open bar, good music—"

"Don't worry. The Costa family will welcome you back just as quickly as they'll ostracize you. They're a mercurial bunch, but for now, things should be settled smoothly. Besides, you were never really to blame for your father's actions. These people can hold a grudge like no other, but even they have to admit at some point that you weren't involved. You were taken advantage of and duped just like they were. I mean, you were still a kid," Luca explains reassuringly.

"I hope so. The idea of walking into a room full of dangerous people who despise me is enough to make me wanna turn around and run back down to the car," I lament. Rafaela gives my arm an encouraging squeeze.

"If it helps, remember that you were also the one to assist in the disposal of Officer Price. He was one of the Costa family's most hated enemies. And the mafia tends to follow the rule that the enemy of their enemy is their friend," Luca adds.

Sighing, I straighten up and prepare myself to walk into the room. We walk up to a set of double doors at the end of the corridor and Rafaela goes in ahead of us, cheering excitedly. Luca kisses the top of my head.

"Everything will be alright. These people are happy to see you. I promise," he whispers.

I nod and force myself to smile. "Okay. Let's do this."

We open the door and step into the spacious, airy room amid the cheers of a big crowd of well-dressed people holding champagne flutes. They all look genuinely overjoyed at the sight of us, and Luca raises our arms up together in a gesture of victory, making them all cheer louder.

"Welcome, friends!" calls a pot-bellied man at the front

of the crowd. He has thick dark hair, a bristly mustache, and he's wearing an expertly-tailored suit.

"Come in, come in! Get yourselves a drink!" says another man.

"Join the party!" says another. Luca looks at me grinning.

"Well, you heard them. Let's hit the open bar," he suggests. My stomach turns at the mere thought of a drink, but I follow him to the bar counter anyway, and order a ginger ale.

"Luca! *Mio amico!*" booms a deep voice from behind us. We both turn around to see a huge bear of a man stride up to us and pull Luca into a manly embrace. With a heavy accent he says, "You look good, *fratello*. And is this is the girl who helped you take down that *bastardo*, Price? She's a beauty! Well done!"

"Oh, thank you," I laugh nervously, but then the man hugs me, too, before heading off down the bar to mingle with some other people. Luca shrugs, looking amused.

"I knew him as a teenager back in Italy," he explains quietly. "Some of these guys I have not seen in a very long time. But mafia family is tight. They make it their business to recognize their fellow man."

"And what about you? I thought you had one foot out the door?" I ask, whispering.

Luca takes a long sip of his drink. "We'll play it by ear. Tonight, as far as anyone knows, nothing is amiss. Let's keep it that way. Besides, tonight we really should be celebrating. Are you sure you don't want something a little more… festive than ginger ale?"

I laugh. "Yes, I'm sure. Just, uh, not feeling very well. But I'm fine."

"Okay. We have a lot to celebrate tonight, *mia passerotta*. Let's join the party. Take my hand. It'll all be fine, just follow my lead," he says, kissing my hand before he leads me back into the fray so we can mingle with everyone else. Every single person we encounter seems over the moon to talk to us, everyone congratulating and thanking us for what we've done. I'm still feeling just a tad bit conflicted over my involvement in such a dirty mess, but it's a little easier to feel better about it when every single person in the room is thankful for it.

And we *do* have a lot to be thankful for. We're both alive and well, for one thing, and Price is not. That man can no longer terrorize the people of this city, mafia or civilian. I keep reminding myself that taking out Price is probably an example of extinguishing one life in order to save countless lives. Room With a View is almost completely rebuilt by now, using the money from the jewel heist, and the grand re-opening is scheduled for next week. Rafaela and Nico are safe and sound, and they seem happier than ever. With Price out of the way, the cops have released their chokehold on Bathing Beauty, and I've scheduled its reopening the same day as Rafaela's so we can have a combined celebratory drink that night. I just have to get some of the accounts back into order after falling into disrepair for so many weeks, and I need to re-hire my former employees.

My mom has met and started dating some mystery guy she hasn't let me meet yet, but either way I'm jumping for joy at this news. She's not going to be all alone in that old house anymore. She has someone to look after her and love her. So I'm moving out of the Riverdale house as soon as Luca and I find an apartment in the city that we both agree on. It'll be bittersweet, of course, leaving the house where I feel closest to my father's memory, but I can always visit anytime I like. And besides, I'm old enough now that it seems silly to live at home.

And the thought of moving in with Luca and having him all to myself with all the privacy in the world 24/7?

Well, that's motivation enough to get me all packed up and ready to go.

Luca and I move from group to group, mingling and chatting with different rough-looking men and bejeweled women, all of whom are happy to see us. Luca speaks Italian with a lot of them while I just sort of nod and smile, but it doesn't matter that I can't tell what they're saying. The celebratory vibe in the room is infectious, and soon I'm feeling downright giddy. Periodically, Rafaela and Nico pop over to talk to us, with Raf excitedly chattering away about how awesome it will be when our respective businesses open back up again. She's probably hugged me about twenty times in the past hour or so, and it's all Nico can do to keep her upright and walking straight, she's had so many cocktails.

Finally, someone announces that dinner is being served, and we all file into another adjoining room with a massive, long table set up for everybody. The table is laden with a ton of delicious-smelling foods and countless bottles of wine, both red and white. My stomach growls as we hurriedly take our seats, with Luca and I being directed to the head of the table, taking our places as the guests of honor. After a brief speech from the same paunchy dark-haired man who first greeted us upon entering the party, we all dig in. I heap my plate with pasta and salad and olives.

About ten minutes into the meal, Luca suddenly stands up and taps his glass with a spoon, calling us all to attention to make a speech. I look up at him, surprised. Everyone sets down their utensils and falls silent, looking at Luca expectantly.

He looks down at me and smiles, his whole face lighting up.

"Friends, brothers, everybody... I cannot thank you all enough for this fantastic evening. The Costa family knows better than anyone how to celebrate good news when it comes, and so it is my pleasure to deliver some more good news for us to toast," he begins. He pauses, and the room is dead silent. He turns to me, those green eyes vibrant in the dimming sunset behind us through the big glass pane of the windows.

"Serena. You are the love of my life. In fact, before I first met you as a teenager, I had no idea what love could even feel like. I assumed I would walk this world alone, following a solitary path. But from the very first moment I laid eyes on you, I knew there could be no greater dream to reach for than to make you mine. I would cross any ocean, climb a mountain, fight any enemy for you. I would change the world a thousand times over just to make you smile. *Mia passerotta*, you have always been the guiding light, the beacon that has led me back to shore when I thought I might be eternally lost at sea. Any success, any good fortune that I might achieve is all because of you, and nothing else can ever compare to the way I feel when I'm standing beside you. Serena, with your love I am invincible. Unbreakable. You make me stronger. You make me proud. You make me a better man. And I will do anything and everything in my power to keep you by my side for the rest of my life."

He kneels down next to my chair and I feel my heart skip several beats as the room erupts into gasps of surprise. "Oh my god," I murmur breathlessly, staring down at Luca. He smiles at me, eyes shining, and takes a little velvet box out of his coat pocket.

Luca opens the box to reveal a white gold band with a gorgeous, sparkling diamond. My jaw drops and I feel my lungs seizing up, like I've suddenly forgotten how to breathe at all.

"Serena De Laurentis, would you do me the ultimate honor of becoming my wife?"

Tears burn in my eyes and spill down my cheeks as I break into nervous, joyous laughter and throw my arms around him. "Yes! Of course! Absolutely!" I sob happily. Luca hugs me tight while everyone bursts into deafening cheers and applause all around us. My heart beat has gone from zero to a million in a moment, and I can't seem to wipe the smile off of my face as Luca kisses me again and again, his hands stroking the hair back out of my face as we embrace.

Suddenly, it becomes absolutely imperative that I share with him the secret I've been holding back from him for the last few weeks. He needs to know. Right now.

While the whole room continues to pour celebratory glasses of wine and chat happily about how amazing the night is, I lean in close to Luca's ear and whisper, "Luca… I-I'm pregnant."

He pulls back and looks into my face with wide eyes, shocked. Then he grins, laughing as he kisses me. "Are you sure? Really?"

I nod vigorously, a giggle escaping my mouth. My whole body is trembling, overwhelmed with the joy of the moment. "Yes. I'm totally sure. Luca... we're going to be parents."

"*Mia passerotta*," he breathes, shaking his head in awe and happiness, like he just can't believe his good luck. "This is all I've ever wanted. More than I ever could have hoped for."

"I love you so much," I tell him.

He slips the engagement ring onto my finger, and miraculously, it fits perfectly.

"I love you, Serena. Until the day I die," he replies.

As we stand up, Rafaela and Nico come rushing over, Raf throwing her arms around both of us. There are tears streaming down her face and she kisses both of my cheeks. The rest of the evening is spent in impossibly high spirits, everybody wine-drunk and joy-drunk as the hours fly by like mere minutes. Finally, around one in the morning, the party starts to wind down, and my pregnant body is begging for me to go home and get some sleep. We haven't found an apartment together yet, so we've been staying at Room With a View in one of the finished rooms. It's been pretty great, actually, since the place isn't officially open yet. We have perfect privacy to do whatever we want... which is usually just each other.

Luca and I take several minutes to say goodbye and thank you to everyone before heading down the elevator with Nico and a very, very intoxicated Rafaela. Luckily, Luca stopped drinking about three hours ago, so he's stone-cold sober by the time we reach the street outside. I offer to drive, since I'm pregnant and therefore absolutely sober, but he insists.

"I'll go get the car and drive it around to you. Just wait here with Nico and Raf," he tells me, giving me a kiss on the cheek.

"Fine, fine. But you know I'm not *that* pregnant yet. I can still walk just fine," I reply teasingly. He gives me a shrug, grinning widely as he heads off down the street to collect the car.

"Nope. No excuses. You're not going to lift a finger for the next nine months if I can help it," he calls out. "Might as well get used to it, *mia passerotta!*"

I shake my head and roll my eyes while Rafaela sings loudly beside me in Spanish. She's had way too much to drink and I know she'll be feeling it in the morning, but if there was ever a good reason to drink way too many cele-bratory toasts, tonight would certainly qualify.

Life is a dream. Nothing could ever be better than this.

Suddenly, there's a deafening crack and Nico yells, "Get down!"

He tackles Raf and me to the ground as a hail of smaller bangs crack through the air.

Bullets.

I roll over and stare down the street, my eyes going wide as I take in the bright explosion of flames licking upward toward the night sky. Down the road. Where Luca went to get the car.

"Luca!" I scream, scrambling to my feet and making a run for it. Nico grabs me by the arm and pulls me back.

"Serena, no! Don't go down there!" he shouts. By now, many of the other partygoers are down on the street, too, and the crowd becomes a mass of panicking, screaming people. Everyone is running, many people falling to the ground as another hail of bullets rain through the air.

I hear somebody shout, "Car bomb!"

No. No, no, no. This can't be happening. This is just a nightmare. I try to break out of Nico's grasp and run down the street. I have to know. I have to see which car exploded. I need to look at it with my own eyes, even though I already know.

It was Luca's car.

I know it in the deep, painful ache of my heart.

"Luca!" I scream, my voice cracking as Nico and Rafaela drag me back away down the street to their own car, forcing me into the back seat. "No! Let me go to him! Let me go!"

"We have to get out of here," Nico explains, throwing the car into gear and peeling out down the road in the direction of the explosion. "The Cleaners must have known we would all be here. Somebody leaked it. We're not safe, Serena."

Rafaela is crying hysterically, huddled in the front passenger seat while I turn and gaze wide-eyed out the back window of the car as we pass the explosion. The car is in flames, with hunks of metal and glass strewn all across the road. There is no sign of Luca.

My voice freezes and disappears in my throat as I press my hands to the back window, watching as we drive away from the smoke and flames. I hold my eyes open for as long as I can, not even daring to blink in case I miss the sight of Luca escaping the fire.

But he doesn't.

He's nowhere to be found. He's gone.

As Nico's car hurtles down the road, the flames shrink away into a mere blinking light in the distance, and I close my eyes just as the tears start to fall.

KILLER ON FIRE

He said he'd always keep me safe.

He told me everything would be okay in the end. He promised me that no matter what happened, we would face it together. Side by side. Hand in hand. Luca and Serena, us against the world. After everything we've been through, it was easy to think we could overcome all odds and emerge victorious together. Love conquers all, doesn't it?

He told me so. And I believed him.

Is this cruel world going to make a liar out of the love of my life?

Almost like an answer, the car jostles and thumps over a pothole in the road, causing the seatbelt to strain against my barely-pregnant belly. I instinctively lay my hands over my stomach. As though that might be enough to protect the child I'm carrying. As if I have any control over what happens to my baby and me anymore. A lump forms in my throat, aching as I force myself to swallow down another dry sob. I'm all cried out. In fact, I'm probably pretty dehydrated from crying for so long. How long, exactly, I'm not sure. Time stopped for me the moment that car bomb exploded. The hours stopped making sense when Nico threw Rafaela and me into his car and sped away from the scene of the crime.

All I know is that I've been in a car—various cars, actually—for what feels like an eternity. Hours and hours, probably. I've lost count of how many times I've switched off into a different car, with a different driver. I don't know where I am or where I'm going. The scenery outside my window, dimly lit by streetlights and the crescent moon, all blends together into nothingness. I can't make the world around me make sense, not without Luca by my side.

He's all I can think about. It feels like there's a massive, gaping hole in my heart, and I can't find the missing piece to make it complete again. I'm trying to figure out what led me to this moment. How the hell did I get here? Alone and afraid and broken-hearted? I've replayed the scene a thousand times in my head: the hail of bullets, the explosion, the flash of bright light, the smell of burning metal and rubber. Nico pushing me to the ground to shield me from attack. Rafaela sobbing. The screams of the crowd, the bodies dropping in the street.

The sight of what used to be Luca's car, now a mass of flame and smoke, shrinking smaller and smaller on the horizon in the rear view mirror as we drove away and left the man I love behind in the impossible wreckage. Not a single sign of life. Nothing at all to give me some tiny glittering bead of hope that Luca might have survived. I kept waiting for that sign, long after the burning car was out of sight. I expected Nico to assure me that Luca was just going to the hospital. That he was hurt, but alive.

But it didn't. Nothing happened. Nothing changed. That sign never came.

Nico drove for a long while. Rafaela finally stopped crying and we rode in silence. I was too shocked to even speak, just staring down at my hands. The ring sparkling on my finger. After an hour or so, Nico spoke up. He informed me solemnly that he was taking me to a drop point, where I would be transferred to another vehicle for the next leg of my getaway journey. I didn't even respond. There was nothing to say. Sure, I could have asked where they would take me, where I would end up, who was going to look after me, how long I would have to be gone. Was this going to be permanent? What would happen to the baby? Would we just start over? Begin a quiet new life somewhere far away, try to forget the horrors I've witnessed?

But honestly? I didn't care. Not then. Not right after watching the love of my life be devoured by greedy flames. Watching my whole heart, my future reduced to ash.

I have hardly noticed the faces of the many men who have driven me all this way. There were so many pass-overs, so many cars... They're trying to be secure, and every couple of hours, I have to shift from one vehicle to the next, in a daze.

I haven't even noticed which direction we're going. I couldn't tell you the make and model or even the color of the vehicles I've been traveling in for the past half-day or so. It doesn't matter anyway. Wherever I end up, it'll all be the same. Without Luca, there is no safe place to go. There is no hope anymore.

I've stayed pretty much silent all this time, except for when necessity made me speak up and ask the driver to pull over so I could throw up. I don't know if it's pregnancy nausea or just my body reacting to the horrific scene I keep replaying in my head, but my stomach just won't settle. I haven't eaten for hours, and I've barely touched a drop of the bottled water Nico shoved into my purse before passing me onto the next driver. I know, deep down, eventually I will have to give in and start acting like a person again. If not for my sake, then for the baby's sake. But right now, I just can't bring myself to care.

When these current drivers took me into their car, they made me turn my phone off just in case the Cleaners might somehow tap my phone or track it. But after a while, I surreptitiously turned it back on. The threat of being tracked down by the bad guys doesn't scare me like it probably should. It seems more important to have my phone on. Just in case. I keep thinking my phone will buzz with a text message.

Mia passerotta, not even death can take me from you.

I swallow hard and check my phone for the hundredth time. Nothing. Of course.

"Take this exit," says the stocky guy in the passenger seat. The driver nods. I finally look out the window and catch a glimpse of the sun rising through the clouds. The sky is streaked pink and orange, casting a beautiful peachy glow over the highway, the trees lining the pavement. We're crossing state lines, heading west, I think. Maybe south? Not that it matters.

My stomach lurches again and I clap a hand over my mouth as I feel the bile rising up my throat. Ugh. Not again. I struggle to gain some composure for a moment, and then lean forward to tap the guy in the passenger seat on his muscular shoulder.

"Sir," I murmur, my voice sounding rough from the hours of crying. He turns to look at me with mild surprise, almost like he's forgotten I've been back here the whole time. "Could you guys pull over somewhere? I think I'm gonna be sick again."

"You got food poisoning or somethin'?" he asks, raising an eyebrow. The driver reaches across the console to shove him on the arm.

"She's pregnant, you prick," says the driver, his voice low and gruff. "Remember?"

The stocky guy makes a face halfway between a grimace and a wince. "Oh. Well, what the hell do we want with a pregnant lady—"

The driver reaches over and punches him in the arm before he can finish the sentence. I roll my eyes and rest my forehead against the window, trying not to vomit all over the swanky leather interior of this getaway car. The trees flashing by are making me feel sicker, my head spinning. I close my eyes and just try to focus on breathing slowly. In and out. In and out.

After a few minutes of gradually slowing down, the vehicle pulls onto a shoulder and rolls to a stop. I hurriedly push open the door and run as fast as my cramped legs can carry me to the edge of where the woodsy brush begins to keel over and vomit. Once I'm done, I hobble weakly back to the car, finally use some of that bottled water to rinse my mouth out, and settle into my seat again. I click the seatbelt over my chest, a hand cradling my barely-there baby bump. As the car pulls back onto the road, the passenger-side guy turns around and offers me a stick of minty gum.

"Might help ya feel a little less gross," he says, shrugging. I take the gum thankfully.

As I'm chewing it, I happen to glance up at the rear view mirror and notice the driver staring at me. As soon as we make eye contact, his eyes flick back to the road. Weird, but then again, I suppose it's not every day these guys have to transport a random pregnant girl across state lines.

Especially if they know what kind of shit I'm running from.

It's not like these Costa guys know how to comfort a grieving, emotional, hormonal woman. Stuff like this is probably not high on their list of priorities, and I can't imagine their training prepares them for a situation like mine.

A stupid thought pops up in my head: *they're more afraid of you than you are of them.* If I wasn't so depressed and numb, I might have laughed. But no sooner does this amusing thought appear than it disappears, and the image of Luca's face, smiling down at me at the celebratory dinner table last night swims to the front of my mind.

That handsome, strong face. Those sharp cheekbones. Those sensuous lips. Those olive-green eyes lit up with flames of love, burning brightly for me alone.

Now a different kind of flame is burning. My eyes itch, wanting to cry but unable to pull any tears. There aren't any left. I feel my cheeks going red, my heart skipping a beat and that pit in my stomach as I remember that I will never get to see those beautiful eyes again. He's gone. Luca is gone, and I am all alone in the world.

Well, not quite alone. Luca may have left me, swallowed up by the fire, but I'm still here and this baby needs to have at least one parent alive. I know it's what Luca would want —for me to pull myself together for the sake of the child.

It would shatter his heart to think of me just giving up, throwing in the towel.

He would want me to be strong. This baby needs me to be strong. He or she is all that's left of Luca in the world, and if I were to just let my grief take over instead of keeping a brave face and doing what I have to do for our kid, what kind of wife would I be?

Sure, we never got to have a wedding. We were getting there. We thought we had time. Why in the world should we have expected things to fall apart so completely? Besides, even if we didn't make it official in time, I will always consider myself Luca's wife. I've been his all along.

My heart has belonged to Luca since I was sixteen years old, and that isn't going to change just because he's gone. No, I've got to hold it together somehow. For the baby. For Luca's memory.

Which means I need to drag myself out of this darkness bit by bit. I need to remember who the hell I am. I will never, ever get over losing Luca. This pain is going to stay with me for the rest of my life. But if I let it dominate me completely, how can I be a good mother to our baby?

Nope.

I need a break from this constant mourning. A distraction, at least for a little while. Rubbing my stomach absent-mindedly, I decide to distract myself and try to make conversation. The silence is getting a little awkward anyway.

"So where are you taking me?" I pipe up, barely able to even conjure enough energy to sound interested in the answer. But I'm trying.

The driver and passenger-seat guy look at each other for a moment without replying. I start to wonder if they even heard me. Then the stocky passenger says, "Uh, you know. South."

"South," I repeat flatly. That's not much of an answer. Suddenly, I *am* a little interested.

"Mhmm."

"Okay," I mumble, frowning. "Could you maybe be more specific?"

"You don't need to worry about the details," the driver interrupts. "We're handling everything. You just sit back and relax, alright?"

"Oh!" exclaims the passenger-seat guy suddenly. He opens the dash compartment and takes out a white medicine bottle, the pills rattling around inside. "You got a messed-up stomach, right? Well, I just remembered we got these pills here. You know. For motion sickness and shit."

I catch the driver smiling into the rear view mirror. It seems strange, somehow.

The stocky guy turns in his seat and offers me two oblong olive-colored pills. I cock my head to one side, a little confused. Something seems off. When I was a teenager, I used to have horrible motion sickness. Bad enough that our family doctor prescribed me clinical-strength meclizine for it so that I could ride the subway without turning green in the face.

And I have never seen motion sickness medicine that looks like that.

"Wh-what is it?" I ask, hesitantly reaching for the green pills.

"Uh, what's this shit called again, boss?" the stocky guy says.

"What's it—oh yeah, Dramamine. Yeah."

"Right, right. Dramamine. It's Dramamine."

The passenger-seat guy twists back to look at me over his shoulder, his eyes glancing down to see that I'm still just holding the pills in my hand. He waits expectantly for me to put them in my mouth, staring at me with beady black eyes.

"Whatcha waitin' for? Don't you wanna feel better?" he urges me.

Just as I'm second-guessing my paranoia, there's a series of deafening cracks splitting the air, and a rain of shattered glass flies toward me from the left-side window. I scream and duck down, bending over my stomach and covering my head with my hands. The car jerks left, then right, hits a bump in the road, and starts spinning rapidly.

"Jesus Christ!"

"What the fuck was that?"

"Get your gun, get your gun!"

I close my eyes tightly and try not to throw up, my head swimming with dizziness as the vehicle careens out of control. There's a horrible whooshing sound as the car slides off the road, over the rumble strip, and thuds across the grass. I open my eyes just as another staccato cluster of gunshots rings out and a spray of bright red blood stains the dashboard. The driver's been shot!

The car rolls straight into a tree with a powerful thump. I'm flung forward, my head knocking into the center console with a nauseating crack. I feel my vision go dark and my body fall limp, all sound fading out into nothing behind the rhythmic thud of my heart.

When the light starts to filter back in and my head tingles as I wake back up, the passenger door swings open and a pair of powerful arms reach inside to yank me out of the back seat. I scream, thrashing and flailing with what limited strength my body can conjure up, fighting with my assailant. My vision is still blurry, my head pounding painfully, and I have no idea whose hands are on me right now. There's another gunshot, so close to me that my ears sting with a high-pitched ringing, rendering me both stunned and deaf and completely helpless.

SERENA

"Let me go! Get your hands off me!" I screech, flinging knees and elbows in every direction, hoping I can somehow dislodge myself from my attacker's grasp. I don't have much of a plan beyond that.

I mean, I may be only barely starting to show, but I'm still pregnant. What am I going to do? Take off running into the woods? Still, the fact that it's not only my life in danger, but the life of my baby, makes me fight that much harder.

I'm fighting for two.

"Serena!" the guy says through gritted teeth. He knows my name? And not only that, he says it with some degree of familiarity. Like he knows me. It's so off-putting that I stop struggling for a moment and turn to look at him square in the face. He sighs, shaking his head. His eyes are wide, exhausted, with purplish bags under them. He looks like he hasn't slept for a long time.

I don't immediately recognize him. I squint, tilting my head to one side. Confusion and curiosity have overtaken my fear at this point. He doesn't seem malicious, at least towards me, despite the fact that he just shot my drivers and caused my getaway car to smash into a tree. Then it hits me. I've seen his face before, and recently.

"You were... you were at the party," I murmur, my words slurring. Wow, I must have really hit my head pretty hard. His face swims in front of me and I have to blink a few times to focus again. He nods and gently sets me aside, but with one hand still locked around my upper arm, as though I'm a wild animal he needs to keep on a leash.

"*Si*. Yeah, I was there, Serena. We met briefly," he admits, exhaling slowly. He stares at the ground for a second, then looks back up at me with mournful eyes. "I cannot even imagine what's going through your mind right now."

I can feel my bottom lip trembling, my cheeks burning, my eyes itching. This guy seems to know how crushed I am. And it starts to make some sense. If he was at that party, then he's got to be an old friend of Luca's or something. Maybe he's hurting, too. But then... why the hell would he have intercepted my escape?

My heart skips a beat and I feel nauseous again all of a sudden. I whip around to look at the carnage behind us in the car. Glass shattered all over. The engine smoking profusely under the hood. Two men shot dead. Blood everywhere.

Instinctively I try to rip out of the guy's grasp, clapping a hand over my mouth and turning away.

But he doesn't let me go.

I give him a furious glare and snap, "If you don't let me go right now I am going to vomit all over your shoes."

He immediately releases his grip, but stays close behind me as I break away, running deeper into woods to throw up again. When I stand back up and turn around, I nearly bump smack into him. To his credit, he doesn't seem at all fazed by my sickness. But if he's the kind of dude who goes around shooting men in cars then, yeah, he's probably got a stronger stomach than most.

"A little space would be nice," I grumble, elbowing past him. He takes my arm again and I stamp my foot in annoyance. I do not like being manhandled.

"Okay, what's up with this? You better tell me why you just assassinated my... my getaway!" I demand.

He runs his other hand back through his curly black hair.

"My apologies. I have not slept much since... since what happened after the party."

"Yeah, well, you're not the only one," I retort, putting my free hand on my hip.

He nods slowly.

"I know. I know. It has been more difficult for you, I'm sure."

"So, any particular reason why you decided to smash up my getaway car and murder two guys in front of me?" I ask, surprised at my own bluntness. I'm usually a little more reserved than this, but it's like that numbness I was feeling earlier has gone away and left pure, righteous anger in its place. I'm finding it hard to give a shit about anything beyond getting some straight answers.

"Those men weren't Costa. Somewhere along the way, the Cleaners intercepted your route. Those two used to work for the Costa family, but they left. Went to the Cleaners. Fairly recently, too. Recent enough that the Costa brothers who passed you off to them just saw familiar faces in the dark and trusted them. They made a mistake. They'll be punished for that transgression," the guy says calmly, as though he's merely discussing the weather.

I, on the other hand, am terrified by what he's telling me.

"What?" I hiss, my eyes going wide. "You mean those

guys—they weren't taking me to safety? They were going to hurt me? And-and my baby?"

"Kill you or ransom you both, most likely," he replies.

"Jesus," I mutter, wrapping an arm over my belly. I look up at him confusedly.

"Then how... how the hell did you find me?"

"Your phone," he says simply. "It was off for some time, but then it came back on. We followed the GPS tracker Lu —an associate installed a while back."

"You can say his name, you know," I tell him quietly. "You don't have to pretend like he never existed."

We stare at each in silence for a few intense moments, and I can feel the combined sadness between us. It hits me that the dark circles under his eyes probably have more to do with what happened to Luca than this multi-state car chase he's been on to catch me.

I break the silence. I have to, before it can swallow us both whole. "Speaking of names—you said we met at the party but I have to admit, I was a little overwhelmed there. I don't remember your name, I'm sorry."

"Giovanni," he says. "Luca and I are—were—very old friends."

There it is. The past tense. Out in the air, hanging there between us. I have to fight the urge to cry. Just break down, fall on my knees, and cry. But I can't. Not now. Not here. I have to stay strong. I just need to survive this day, and then...

Then what?

I honestly don't know. I just have to focus on one step at a time. I just have to focus on the present mess I find myself in.

"What are we going to do about... all that?" I ask, gesturing back toward the wreckage behind us. Giovanni shrugs.

"*We* don't do anything. Our tidying-up team will be out

here any second now to make this look more accidental than it was. You're very lucky," he adds as he leads me back to where his car is parked, a few hundred yards down the highway. "This time of early morning, there aren't many other cars around. And those guys were taking you down a very secluded route. Probably trying to avoid the cops. Kind of bit them in the ass in the end, though."

"Uh, yeah. I'd say so," I answer, raising an eyebrow.

Giovanni almost smiles for a moment, but it vanishes as quickly as it appeared. Once we get close to his car, the passenger-side door opens and a butch-looking woman comes hurrying over with a little white kit in her hand. There's a look of motherly concern on her face as she comes up to me.

"Serena, this is Orsina. She's a medic with the Costa family," Giovanni explains. Then to her, he adds, "Make it quick, if you can. The sun's up now and there will be traffic out here before too long. We need to get out of dodge."

Orsina nods at him and then gives me a kind, reassuring smile. "How are you feeling?" she asks. "Did you sustain any major injuries in the crash? How's the little one doing in there?"

I shake my head. "I-I don't think I'm hurt, really. I did hit my head a little bit."

A flash of worry crosses her face, but the smile comes back quickly. "Okay, sweetheart, let's get you into the car. I'll tend to you in the back seat while Giovanni drives. He's right, we do need to get going. Are you feeling nauseous at all?"

I almost have to laugh at this question. Instead, I just nod as she helps me into the back seat of the car.

"Yeah, lots of nausea. But I was having that long before the car crashed."

Giovanni slides behind the wheel and starts the engine. The car quickly peels out and does a sharp U-turn, cutting across the grassy median and speeding off down the highway in the opposite direction of how I got here.

Orsina touches my arm softly.

"Serena, when was the last time you ate something?"

I have to wrack my brain for an answer to that. Truthfully, I don't remember much beyond the past hour or so. It's like my mind is desperately trying to cut out all the painful pieces so I don't have to think about them. I know I had to have eaten something at the party, but I can't remember.

"I-I don't know," I tell her honestly. And now, with this woman gazing concernedly into my face, the tears reemerge. My eyes tingle and my chin trembles. Before long, I'm full-on sobbing, and Orsina wraps her arms around me in a maternal hug, patting my back.

"I know, sweetheart. Just let it all out. If anybody on the planet has the right to a good cry right now, it's definitely you," she assures me. I weep on her shoulder for several minutes, all my emotions rushing back to me in a swarm of overwhelming feeling. Images flash to the forefront of my mind. Rafaela dancing and singing drunkenly in Spanish on the sidewalk. The streetlights casting fuzzy light over the street. The smile Luca gave me just before he walked away to get the car. The sky-high flames destroying the car with the love of my life trapped inside the inferno.

It's too much to bear. It's all too much. But I let the tears fall without trying to stop them. I take Orsina's advice and let it all out, not caring about how my tears are staining her shirt, how ugly my sobs sound, how weak I must look to both of them. It doesn't matter. I need this.

And when the tears subside, Orsina gently starts to dab a clean rag dampened with hydrogen peroxide at my left temple, near my hairline. It stings, to my surprise, and I let out a little yelp of pain.

"Oh, I'm sorry, sweetie," Orsina says, clucking her

tongue. "You just have a little wound here from the impact. Nothing too awful, just a relatively shallow laceration. Could be much, much worse. I know you don't feel too lucky right now, but you are."

"People keep telling me that," I murmur, the dizziness rushing back and mingling with the pain in my head. A throbbing ache settles in and I close my eyes, leaning back against the seat. As soon as I do, my whole body relaxes, like one big sigh. It hits me how tense I've been all this time, how tired I feel underneath all the stress.

"Here," the medic says, "hold this rag to the spot for a minute while I get a bandage ready. Can you do that for me, Serena?"

I nod and obediently hold the rag to my temple. There's a plasticky sound of something being unwrapped, and then Orsina takes the rag away, replacing it with a big bandage. She presses it down carefully, obviously trying her best not to hurt me, but every little feather-light touch stings like hell. Still, I almost welcome the sting. Physical pain is a lot easier to understand, to handle, than the ache in my heart.

"There ya go," Orsina says. "Now just leave that alone and it should heal up okay. Probably won't even leave a scar, if your luck holds out."

"Thank you," I mumble, suddenly feeling very sleepy. It's like the tidal wave of emotions has crashed over me and exhausted every last little fiber of my strength. I'm worn out, down to the very bone, with fear and sadness and confusion.

Then Giovanni speaks up and I open my eyes one at a time. "We had planned on sending you to a safehouse in backwoods Virginia. Somewhere out of the way and secure. But if your getaway was already compromised so early in the game... well, it's probably best to scrap Plan A and just move on to Plan B."

I can feel myself dozing off. "What's... what's Plan B?" I manage to whisper.

But I drift off to sleep before I can hear the answer.

~

J wake up to the sensation of being jostled forward, and my eyes fly open and wide. I sit up with a start, blinking blearily in the bright light of day. I'm still in the back seat of the car, with Orsina the medic sitting next to me. But the car isn't moving anymore. We've stopped.

The driver's seat is empty, and then the door to my left opens up and Giovanni extends a hand for me to take. Orsina gets out of the car and comes around to help him help me. I squint around, trying to make sense of my environment. My body is so tired, and that familiar nausea is prickling back up again, warning me that any sudden movement might send me hurling.

We're in the middle of what looks like deep woods. I remember vaguely Giovanni mentioning something about the backwoods of Virginia, but then I put together what he said: Virginia was Plan A, and we weren't going to do Plan A anymore. Unless he changed his mind?

"Where... where the hell are we?" I ask, the words jumbling in my mouth.

There isn't an immediate answer. Orsina and Giovanni are helping me down a long wooded path through the trees. My paranoia kicks back in and I plant my feet hard in the ground, refusing to take another step.

"Where. The hell. Are we?" I repeat emphatically, looking back and forth between the two of them. They exchange a worrisome expression, and I know something is up. Something I am not going to like one bit. "Enough with the secrecy! What's going on? I thought you said we were ditching the Virginia plan!" I exclaim.

"Yes. You're right. We're on to Plan B," Giovanni relents.

"Okay. Cool. Great. So what *is* Plan B?" I ask, crossing my arms over my chest.

Orsina steps closer to me and puts a steadying hand on my shoulder. "Sweetheart, you're going to overexert yourself. It's okay. You can trust us. You know that, right? You're not with the Cleaners anymore. You're with us. You're with family."

"Family?" I repeat, a little indignant. After all, I don't really know these people. Maybe Luca knew them, but he's gone now, and it's up to me to stay level-headed and cautious for the sake of our baby. They don't want me asking questions, clearly, and that scares me.

Giovanni sighs.

"Yes, Serena. I know you have been through so much in the past day or so. It's a lot to take in. But you have to trust us. From the second Luca fell in love with you, we became your family. If he trusted you, if he swore to protect you, then so do we. There is no safer place in the world for you to be than with us. Especially now that Luca's... gone. We want nothing more than to continue the work Luca was doing, and that involves you. And the baby. You're safe with us. I can promise you that."

"Everything is up in the air right now. I know it's hard. This time has been difficult for all of us. Luca was well-loved," Orsina interjects, her voice soft and emotional compared to Giovanni's powerful baritone. "But Serena... you have to trust us. We have to move quickly. Plan B is very time-sensitive. There isn't time to explain at the moment, but I promise we're not going to send you into the lion's den unarmed, so to speak. You're going to be okay. Just come with us."

Finally, I give in. There's no point in fighting it. What

other choice do I have? Once again, I'm just a grieving pregnant woman with nowhere to go and no one to go to. My heart aches and my head is pounding. Not long ago, my life revolved around the Bathing Beauty and trying to help my mom through her sorrow.

How long has it been since I spoke with her? Not long, I remind myself. The party was only last night. But so much has happened since. I wish I could just return home, curl up in her lap, and lament my heartbreak. I think about how she was when she lost dad, and I almost start crying all over again.

But that's a luxury for later. I'll tell her where I am once I know it's safe. Until then, it'd be more dangerous for her —for anyone—to know where I am.

Giovanni and Orsina are offering a lifeline, whatever it may entail, and it would be stupid of me not to take it. So I follow them down the trail, listening to the insects chirping, the underbrush shaking with small animals just out of sight. Being surrounded by nature like this takes me back to those glorious, lazy days in the cabin with Luca, just the two of us with no distractions. Just loving each other in the calm woods, the outside world a distant memory.

It was all just a fantasy we'd concocted, though. We were hiding from the harsh reality, from the fact that he was a fugitive, from the fact that there were dangerous men hunting us down and wanting us dead.

I'd give anything to live that fantasy with him again, though.

With every thought of Luca, I can feel my heart breaking just a little more. But I can't help it. As much as it hurts me, I can't stop thinking about him. About how we were together. A perfect fit. I thought it was fate. Destiny. We overcame obstacles I never would have imagined possible. We've been through hell together, and we were finally on our way to the good part, the safe part.

Or so I thought.

I couldn't have been more wrong.

Who would have guessed it? Who could have ever seen this coming? Certainly not me. I was blinded by love, and I never expected the world to be so cruel as to snatch Luca away from me again. It's not fair. It's not right. We were supposed to be together forever, and we would have been. I know it. We were meant to be. I'll never love anyone the way I loved him. The way I *still* love him, and always will.

I'm so lost in my bittersweet memories that I zone out completely until we come to a stop suddenly, walking out of the shady woods and into a broad clearing. The sharp glare of sunlight on metal blinds me for a moment and I shade my eyes with my hand, blinking. There's a flurry of quick activity around me: Orsina taking my hand and pulling me toward the source of metallic light, Giovanni breaking away to speak in rapid Italian with another man, who is speaking Italian, too. I can only catch a word every now and then.

Biglietto.

Volo.

Prezzo.

And then Giovanni is helping me up a staircase. And my vision stops swimming, becomes clear and sharp. I finally realize what is happening. But by now, it's too late. I turn around, trying to run back down the stairs, but Giovanni is right behind me, keeping me there, stopping me from getting back down. My heart pounds, panic taking over my muddled mind.

"No! What are you doing? I'm not going! You can't do this!" I scream, slapping at Giovanni, trying to push past him. But he's like a brick wall. I glance down at the pavement below and see Orsina looking up at me with a pained expression.

"Orsina! Don't let them take me! I can't—I won't go!" I

cry out. She shakes her head and looks away, refusing to get involved. All the while, Giovanni is marching me backwards up the boarding ramp toward the open door of the jet plane.

"Calm down, calm down," he's telling me. "It's going to be okay. Serena! You're going somewhere safe, somewhere they can't get to you."

Tears course down my cheeks.

"I don't want to go—I can't leave. What if—what if Luca needs me? I can't leave him here."

I know I'm not making sense, but I can't stop crying. Being in a different state from everything I ever knew was one thing. Getting on a plane and flying to who knows where?

I can't. I can't leave. I can't be so far away from him.

Giovanni pulls me into his arms in a hug suddenly, and after a moment I stop struggling, my tears dampening the front of his black shirt.

"Serena, he's gone. Luca's gone. But he's with you—okay? He's with you, wherever you go. You're not abandoning him. He's in your heart. And he would want you—and the baby—to be safe. Do you understand me?"

I break away and look into his face, but my vision is completely obscured by thick, crocodile tears.

"Listen to me," he says more quietly. "You're stronger than you think you are. Luca knew it. I know it. Deep down, you know it, too. I need you to find that strength, *si?* Find that strength and use it to take care of yourself and the baby. We're going to do everything we can to help you, but we can only help if you're willing. Got it?"

I give him a nod.

"Okay," I manage to choke out between sobs.

Giovanni pushes the hair back from my face, pats me on both shoulders, and then gives me a brotherly kiss on the forehead. "Don't worry. You're going to get through this, I know it. And someday, I'm sure I'll see you again, Serena. Hopefully under better circumstances."

Over my shoulder, he tells the flight attendant, "Take good care of her. She's one of our own. And keep a barf bag nearby. She's pregnant."

Then Giovanni turns me around and walks me through the opening to the jet. A flight attendant with a sweet smile takes my arm and leads me down the aisle to a comfortable, massive sofa-like seat complete with fluffy pillows and a downy blanket. As I settle into the seat, still totally in shock but knowing there's no point in struggling now, I turn back to see Giovanni. He gives me a wave, a hopeful smile that doesn't quite reach his eyes, and then he disappears. The door closes, and I'm alone in this plane.

Completely alone, in fact, except for the flight attendant. I'm the only passenger in this private jet, and I get the feeling this is not going to follow the usual prescribed route... wherever it is I'm going. As the plane starts to shake and rumble with lift-off, the flight attendant comes by and gives me two items—a barf bag, and a backpack. I set the first one aside and start to idly go through the contents of the backpack. I pull out several printed tickets, a passport that looks exactly like the one I have at home, and a huge wad of cash—in euros.

No. No way.

I pick up one of the tickets with trembling hands.

The destination... Napoli, Italia.

"Holy shit," I murmur, and immediately reach for the barf bag.

$\mathcal{I}$ stare out the window of the airplane, my eyes glazing over as I watch the gray and lavender clouds drift lazily by. The moon just barely strains through, its light splintering through the sky while the dull hum and buzz of the engine almost lulls me to sleep. But I can't sleep. I've never been able to sleep on planes, even when I was little.

Of course, back then it was because I was too excited, too interested in gazing out the window and being in awe of how far up we were to feel sleepy at all.

My mom would fall asleep instantly, a silky pink eye mask over her face, her perfectly-lipsticked mouth hanging open and snoring. It made me laugh to see her looking like that, all undignified, especially since she was usually so prim and proper. My dad, on the other hand, would stay awake with me, playing card games or twenty-questions. We would make believe that we were the co-pilots of the plane, pretending we were soaring to some distant land like Malaysia.

I'm sure he would have liked to catch up on sleep like my mother did, but he never gave in. He always did his best to entertain me on long flights, and it made all the difference. Playing with him was a great distraction from my motion sickness, my nervousness at being stuck on a plane with a bunch of strangers. I never properly thanked him for doing all that.

I miss him. And I miss Luca.

Why do all the men I love have to leave me behind?

I turn around in the seat and look around the interior of the cabin. I've flown first-class before, of course, but I've never had a private flight. Being the only passenger on the plane is awkward. I feel like the stewardess has got to be watching me, wondering who the hell I am and why the hell I deserve such special treatment. And she would be right to wonder about that. After all, I'm nothing special, myself. I'm just a random pregnant lady to them, some stranger.

I can't help thinking that the only thing that made me special was the fact that Luca loved me. And now that he's gone? Well, who the hell *am* I?

I close my eyes and set my hands on my stomach, trying to send reassuring thoughts to the little baby inside, even though I can hardly reassure myself. I remember reading that the stress a mother feels during pregnancy can affect the child.

That worries me, and that worry stresses me out even more.

I mean, even under normal circumstances, being pregnant is rough. I thought it would be a breeze with Luca at my side, but now everything has changed. I'm a single mom now, and I don't even have my own mom around to help me.

If I tell her where I am, then the mob will go after her. Force her to tell them everything. I can't put her in danger like that. I have to figure everything out on my own. I have to be strong for myself. I have to do it all.

But all I want to do right now is cry. I curl up in the seat as best I can, tucking my legs underneath myself, trying to get comfortable. But nothing feels right, and why should it? My whole world has been dumped upside down. Nothing makes sense anymore. I just wish somebody could tell me what to do, how to feel. My brain keeps circling back to Luca, those last beautiful moments we had together before he was ripped away.

His smile. His twinkling green eyes. The feeling of his hand holding mine.

My hands feel so empty and useless without his.

Despite how hard I've tried to fight it, the tears start to fall again. My heart is broken, and it's impossible to imagine a time when that won't be the case. I know I'll never love like that again. Luca was my everything. He still is, even if he's not around to see it.

Suddenly, there's a gentle hand on my elbow. I turn quickly to see the flight attendant kneeling beside me with a worried expression.

"Miss, are you alright?" she asks softly.

I hastily wipe my eyes with my sleeve and give her a nod.

"Yeah, yeah. I'm fine."

She tilts her head to one side, looking unconvinced. "Are you sure? Is there anything I can get you? Soda? A glass of wine?"

"Oh, I-I can't," I murmur, sniffling. "I'm pregnant."

And saying that out loud, for some reason, releases the floodgates. I start to sob uncontrollably, the stewardess's eyes going wide at the sight of my sudden meltdown.

"Oh no, Miss, I'm sorry. That man did say you were pregnant, didn't he? I totally forgot. It's just such a habit to offer guests alcohol, I didn't mean to—"

I reach out and take her hand despite myself. I know I probably look like a complete weirdo, totally off my head. But I don't care right now. I just need a hand to hold.

"No, no, it's not the pregnancy. It's—it's just that m-my fiancé just died and I'm trying to hold it together but I'm pregnant and he's never going to get to meet his own child and I'm going to be all alone raising this baby and I'm so scared," I ramble all at once, the words stumbling over each other in between sobs. The flight attendant's face has gone totally red and I can tell I am absolutely the most distressing customer she has had, maybe ever.

To her credit, she doesn't recoil from the emotional hurricane that I've become. She sits down in the seat beside me and squeezes my hand.

"Oh, I am so sorry. That's terrible. I can't even imagine how hard this must be," she says genuinely, shaking her head.

"I miss him so much already and I don't know when this is going to stop hurting so bad," I confess tearfully. She pats my hand, nodding supportively.

"It may take some time," she says sagely.

"How long?" I ask, fully aware that I'm asking her questions she doesn't have an answer to, but unable to stop the flow of crazy emotions pouring out of me.

"Oh, I don't know the answer to that. But I can tell you that you're stronger than you think you are, and you're going to be okay," she adds, emphasizing every word to drive the point home. "You and that baby are going to make it out alright. I just know it."

"Thank you," I mumble, suddenly feeling very tired.

"Could I get you something to drink? And some tissues? What would you like?"

"Do you have ginger ale?" I ask, rubbing my stomach. The nausea is coming back.

She stands up quickly, releasing my hand. "Of course! I'll be back in just a minute."

She rushes down the aisle and comes back with a box of tissues and a little bottle of ginger ale, which she pours into a glass with a bendy straw. She sets it on the fold-down table in front of me and then asks, "Is there anything else I can do? Should I turn the lights down so you can relax a little better? You've got a long flight ahead of you. It might do you some good to try and sleep if you can manage it."

I take a sip of the ginger ale and try to fight down the urge to race to the bathroom and vomit. I'm finally just starting to feel comfortable and sleepy in my seat and the last thing I need is to get back up. I look up at the stewardess and say, "Okay. Yes. That would be nice. Thank you."

She brings me a bigger blanket and then turns down the lights, leaving me alone with my thoughts once again. I glance out the window to see the darkness settling in, the sky turning from light purple to dense navy blue. Every now and then I catch a glimpse of the moon, thin and hook-shaped between dark clouds. I force myself to close my eyes and try to relax, pushing every dark thought out of my mind. If I alone am responsible for this baby, then it's our best interest for me to get some sleep. Especially since I have no idea what awaits us when this plane lands.

Finally, slowly, I drift off to dream.

"Dolcezza! Could you get the camera?"

I come down the stairs with a pink diaper bag and a camera slung over my shoulder, walking into the nursery to see Luca looking amused and impressed. He's holding the baby in his lap, both dad and child staring at each other with lovely green eyes. Our daughter is barely old enough to hold her head up on her own and she's already trying to stand, pushing off Luca's lap with her pudgy little legs. On the crown of her head little curly sprigs of dark hair grow, and her cheeks are chubby and pink. She's giving her father a gummy, adoring smile.

"She's going to be an athlete. I just know it," Luca says. "Look at this!"

"I know," I tell him, shaking my head in awe at our little bad ass. "The other day in the living room I looked away for one second and when I looked back she was rolling over onto her stomach. I didn't even know that was possible at her age."

"I wish I'd been there for that," he says. "Did you get a picture of it?"

"Yeah, yeah, of course," I laugh. "Speaking of which..."

I flash a photo of Luca and the baby, her tiny legs struggling to straighten out and balance on his thighs. She blinks in surprise at the sound of the camera shutter, then giggles.

Luca chuckles. "She's perfect, you know that, right? A perfect kid."

"I'm sure we'll take it back once she gets to the terrible twos but... right now I totally agree with you on that," I answer, unable to stop grinning. Everything is going so well. The doctor yesterday at our checkup appointment said the baby is progressing even better than we hoped. She was born a few weeks earlier than we intended, so there had been some concern at first. But now she's blown all our expectations out of the water. She's got her father's strength, that's for sure.

She yawns and lets out a whimper. "Oh! Probably time for a nap, is it?" Luca coos, wrapping her in his arms with her little head on his shoulder. He stands up and walks over to the crib to gently lay her down. For a minute, she fusses, her sweet little face screwing up and turning pink like she might cry. But instead, she just yawns again and stretches out, her hands curling into tiny fists as she closes her eyes.

"What a good girl," Luca says, beaming down at her. I stand next to him watching our daughter fall asleep. My husband, my rock, my guardian angel, puts his arm around my shoulders and pulls me close. He kisses me on the cheek.

I turn to kiss him on the lips softly, then gaze into those

*glorious green eyes I adore so much. I smile. "I don't think I've
ever been this happy," I whisper.*

"Life just gets better and better," he murmurs back.

Thump.

"Luca!" I mumble, blearily opening my eyes.

I wake up with a sense of panic, the plane lurching to
one side suddenly. It takes me a moment to find my bear-
ings, looking around the cabin in confusion. The events of
the past day or so come rushing back to me.

The explosion. The cars. The gunshots. The plane.

I look out the window to see the sun streaking through
the clouds. It's morning. I've finally gotten some proper
sleep. But now I'm forced to remember everything. Luca is
gone. That dream… is only that. A dream.

Just then, my stomach turns and I hurriedly grab the
backpack and get up from my seat, hobbling down the
aisle to the bathroom to throw up. After I'm done, I look in
the tiny square mirror and take note of the bags under my
eyes, the paleness of my face. I look like the living dead.

I haven't eaten anything in a while and anything that
might have still been in my system is certainly gone now.
My stomach grumbles, as though it's agreeing with my
assessment.

I wash my hands, splash some water on my face, and
pull my hair back into a ponytail. Then I pull an oversized
sweatshirt, sleek black leggings, and some comfy sandals
out of the backpack and change into them, leaving my old
clothes on the floor. I don't want them anymore. They just
remind me of the last night Luca and I spent together, at
that party, surrounded by people who cared about us.

My stomach growls again, taking me back to the
present moment. I make the silent promise to myself that
I'll find something to eat when the plane lands, whatever it
takes.

When I come back out, the flight attendant gently informs me that we'll be landing in about half an hour. Nervousness overwhelms me instantly. It hits me that I don't know where exactly to go when we get there. I go back to my seat and start pulling more tickets out of the backpack Giovanni gave me. The first one is a ticket from Napoli to Taranto. A train ticket. I immediately feel sick again. I have never visited Naples before, but I've heard about how crowded and scary it can be for a not-so-savvy foreigner.

I must look green in the face because the stewardess comes back and says, "Sorry you're not feeling well. When I was pregnant with my son Tyler, I was the same way. Constantly sick. It got better around the fifth month, though. It'll get easier, I promise."

"I hope so," I tell her, forcing myself to smile weakly.

I spend the next thirty minutes clinging to the edge of my seat, closing my eyes and trying not to vomit again. I tell myself this is not the time for me to be fragile. I'm about to take on a solo journey in a foreign country. I don't speak Italian, even though my parents spoke it to each other occasionally when I was growing up. I dig through the backpack and find, to my relief, an English-to-Italian phrasebook. Paperwork, tickets, money, clothes, and now this? Apparently Giovanni thinks of everything.

I hardly have time to peruse the phrases, though, before the plane comes to a smooth landing. I gather up the backpack and its contents, get myself straightened out, and pool what little composure I have left. When I disembark, the flight attendant comes out with me. She takes me by the arm and gives me a confident smile.

"I'll help you with this next step, but then you're on your own, I'm afraid. But I have full faith in you. Napoli is busy and intimidating, but you can handle it," she says, walking me through the airport. We get to the busy street out front and my jaw drops. This place is packed with locals and tourists alike, everyone jabbering away in languages I don't understand. Lots of people give me death glares, dirty looks, scanning me up and down like they can tell instantly I'm not from around here. I feel very exposed, very vulnerable. Especially with my pregnant belly. Luckily, the oversized sweatshirt hides the teeny barely-there baby bump completely, but I still can't shake the feeling that people can just *tell* somehow.

The flight attendant hails a cab for me and helps me into the backseat with what little belongings I have, then turns to the driver and gives him instructions in Italian. The driver nods and looks back at me, saying, "I speak some English. I'm taking you to Napoli Centrale. *Si?*"

I nod, hoping that's correct. Just before the cab drives off, the flight attendant gives me a nod and a thumbs up. "Good luck!" she calls out as the window rolls back up.

It's about a fifteen-minute ride to the train station, and I spend nearly the whole time staring wide-eyed out the window at the bustling city passing by. Constant horn-honking, shouting, vendors racing after people going past their wares without looking. The cab driver weaves in and out of standstill traffic, only barely avoiding a collision over and over again. Finally, it starts to make me so nauseous that I give up and start perusing the backpack again, looking to see what else Giovanni left with me. To my infinite joy, I find a simple little cell phone, pre-programmed with all the necessary apps, a portable charger hooked up to it. This is a great discovery, since my American cell phone is long dead and I couldn't charge it overseas.

When we arrive at the train station, the cab driver helps me count out the euros to pay him, and then I get out and I'm alone again. Alone in this big, sprawling, teeming city full of strangers who don't speak the same language as me. I swallow back the bile creeping up my throat.

I need to be strong. For the baby. For Luca.

I hold my head up high and hoist the backpack over my shoulder, walking into the station as confidently as I can. Fake it 'til you make it, I remind myself. The girl that used to walk into a room, confident and wearing the season's hottest styles seems like a distant dream, but I try to conjure her up once more, even in the far less fashionable outfit I'm wearing now.

I check my ticket and find out which train to get on, looking up at a digital times-table hanging high in the lobby. Then I track down the proper platform and get there early, settling in on a bench to wait for my train. I keep my belongings close and my eyes peeled for potential pickpockets. If there's one thing I know about Naples, it's that you have to be careful. And so I am.

Now that the panic of figuring out where to go is over, I start focusing in on the people around me, the hurried conversations in Italian I can't understand. I feel so out of place without any real luggage and no one to travel with. Apart from taking the subway in the city back home, I don't usually take public transportation, and certainly not alone. I wish I knew what anyone was saying. It would feel much less isolating to know what was going on. I swear silently to myself that my baby will grow up speaking Italian and English if I have to hire someone to teach her.

Just as I'm getting lost in these thoughts, there's a commotion down the platform and I idly look over to see a big, burly guy arguing with a much smaller woman. She's gesticulating wildly, shouting in his face even as he towers over her with his hands balled into fists. It looks bad. Very bad. Like any second, true violence is going to erupt.

The train rolls up to the platform and I stand up to join the crowds ready to flood the train cars as soon as the doors open. But then I hear a scream and look over to see the big guy grabbing the young woman by her ponytail. I notice then that she has a baby bump that is much bigger than mine. And suddenly all I see is red.

Almost as though I have no control over my body, I start marching over to them, with no clue what the hell I'm going to do when I get there. By instinct, I catch a glimpse of an abandoned, broken umbrella lying under a bench. I snatch it up and walk up to the couple just as the big guy is winding his arm back to hit her in the face. My heart pounding so loud I can hear it in my ears, I swing the umbrella at full force, cracking the metal rod across the back of the guy's head.

He lets out a bellow of pain and surprise and reflexively lets go of the pregnant girl. In an instant, I grab hold of her arm and yell, "Come on!"

The guy regains his sense and yells something most definitely vulgar in Italian and comes after us, but the girl and I manage to leap through the doors of the train just before they close. Shoving past confused, irritated passengers, I tug the girl along behind me through the train cars, trying to put as much distance between us and the doors as possible just in case her assailant managed to get in after us. But then I look to my left, out the window, and notice that the train is moving, leaving the station, and the big guy is still left on the platform. He's running after the train like an idiot, shaking his fist and swearing.

But we're safe inside, and I turn to the girl. She's pale and shaken, her eyes round and huge as she mutters breathlessly, "*Accidenti*, lady!"

DON ABRUZZI

y calm gaze rests on the Van Gogh painting hanging over the fireplace in my office as I listen to the soft sound of a pathetic excuse for a man sobbing in a chair behind me.

The painting is of a coastline, seen from the land, the perspective slightly raised up, as if the painter was standing on a hill. A small ship with a single rolled-up sail bobs in the water in the painting, and closer to the shore, a loose group of seven or so people stagger toward the sandy shoreline out of the water. Their faces are just blotches of color. The sky behind them is cloudy and gray, but there is light shining from behind the viewer, as if the shore is sunny.

Behind me, the man—as much as my mouth curls into a frown to call him that—blubbers a few words at me.

"Don Abruzzi, I...I don't know what I can say. My son, he's a good boy, he really is. He just lost his temper. He's young, he's hot-blooded, they're all like that."

"Your boy was rash," I say calmly, my gaze not moving from the painting on the wall. I'm seated still as a statue in my grand leather chair. "He picked a fight with one of my soldiers."

"He didn't know, Don Abruzzi," the man says, exasperated. "And he paid for it. Your man knocked out some of his teeth, he-"

"He's lucky he wasn't killed," I say matter-of-factly, slowly rising to my feet and folding my hands as I turn to look at him. The man is thin and middle-aged with graying hair, his eyes rimmed with red.

What a pathetic husk of a man.

"He understands that," the man says, nodding his head quickly. "Please, Don Abruzzi, I will take responsibility for anything we owe you because of this."

"I know you will," I say. "My soldier your boy fought with says it was over your daughter. I expect you'll tell her to show a little more respect to my men as well."

"Of course, I-"

"Moreover," I interrupt him, gesturing for one of the guards in the room to pour me a glass of wine, "Since it seems your boy has enough money to piss away in the bars picking fights with dangerous men, I expect you can manage a fifty-percent increase in your monthly payments."

His eyes go wide, and his face goes pale. "What? Don Abruzzi, please, I've just sold my car to make my back-payments already, and-"

"Your protection is clearly more expensive than we realized," I continue, unfazed. "If your boy is so liable to get into trouble, it's only fair to charge more."

"Don Abruzzi, I won't be able to stay in business if-"

I stop listening to the man's squawling, and I glance to one of my guards. With the slightest nod of my head, two of them move toward the man and haul him to his feet. He continues to make any excuse he can come up with as my men drag him out of my office.

I glance at them going while I take a drink of the black wine offered to me.

Pathetic.

As he's dragged out, my consigliere passes him on the way into my office. He takes his hat off to me out of respect, and I give him a nod to allow him inside.

"Come in, Enrico."

Enrico enters, and my guards close the doors behind him while I invite him to have a seat and have them pour him some wine to join me.

"Him again?" Enrico asks with a wry smile, nodding back to the door where I can still faintly hear the man crying out pleas for mercy. "You're a more patient man than me, Don Abruzzi."

I give a soft smile, then look back up to my painting.

"You see the people in this painting, Enrico? Every time I deal with men like that blubbering idiot, I look at this painting. Lost, weary parasites staggering into our territory, wanting just a taste of all the riches we've built up for ourselves here in New York. You give them just a taste, and they want more and more until they've drained you of everything. Push them too far, and they turn violent. It's all about knowing their breaking point—then you can keep them just where you want them. It's only fair."

"I'll drink to that," Enrico says with a broad smile, getting comfortable in his mahogany chair in what looks like a brand-new Armani suit.

We raise our wine glasses to one another. "*Salute,*" I toast before we take a drink and I sit back down behind my desk to face him. "Enough pleasantries, though. Tell me, have you found what I've asked for?"

Enrico takes a moment longer than usual to enjoy the taste of his wine, and I have my answer before he's even spoken.

"We haven't been able to find the De Laurentis girl, no."

"Is she still in New York?"

"We should assume 'no.' Lomaglio still has close allies in the Costas, and they got her away from the car bomb fast."

Now it's my turn to give him an even, silent stare before I speak again. "You don't sound optimistic about it, Enrico. Care to share your thoughts?"

Enrico clenches his jaw a moment, and I can feel his nervousness like a stink on him.

"The Lomaglio guy...Luca. He isn't-"

"Wasn't," I correct him.

"*Wasn't* like the other Costas. He commanded their respect in a way the other capos can't. That kind of loyalty extended to Serena De Laurentis. Luca's friends are going to make sure she's far out of the way. They'll know it's no use stashing her in some safehouse around town."

"And you don't know how far they've taken her...why, exactly?"

"Her trail just vanishes, Don Abruzzi. Whoever got her away from the hit on Luca did it fast and quiet, and nobody's talking. We don't have the means to-"

"*Find* the means, Enrico," I say, letting the slightest impatient edge come to my voice. A calm demeanor means that it only takes a light touch to get my point across, when I want something done. I look him dead in the eye, my gaze steely. "I'm giving you freedom to use whatever funds necessary, and I want you to hire a professional to get this done. I want the De Laurentis line to end with that girl, and I want it to end sooner rather than later."

"I understand, Don Abruzzi," he says, bowing his head, but he hesitates a moment. "Finding someone for this job might be...costly. There is one more thing we've picked up on."

I raise an eyebrow at him.

"There are rumors going around about an announcement she made before the hit. Serena De Laurentis might be pregnant."

I don't let any reaction cross my features. Inside, I feel frustration brewing up like a storm. Every day either Serena De Laurentis or Luca Lomaglio is alive, it's an insult to the Abruzzi name. It's a testament to my own son's murder and a challenge to my authority. But some bastard spawn of the two of them...?

"Very well then," I say candidly. "Whoever you find can deal with the problem before she gives birth and it becomes two problems."

Enrico stares at me a moment, and the look in his eyes makes me tempted to replace him. He still clings to useless, outdated values that do nothing but cripple you in this city. I set my wine glass down and fold my hands.

"Enrico, my friend," I speak to him with the kindliness of a grandfather. "I shouldn't have to remind you how this works, you know. Luca Lomaglio is dead. We killed him. If the De Laurentis girl has a child, and that child is allowed to grow up, that's one more rival, one more person who will grow up bloodthirsty for *vendetta* against us, against everything we've built."

Enrico shifts ever so slightly in his chair, but he nods. I lean forward.

"Blood for blood. This is for Lorenzo, don't forget that. And if this 'pregnancy' thing is a rumor, then let's keep it as a rumor, nothing more. Do you understand me?"

"Of course, Don Abruzzi," Enrico says, apparently finding his manhood again and acting with some dignity. "It will be done."

"Good," I say, and I gesture for my guards to open the door as Enrico begins to stand up. "See to it. And while we're on the subject of rumors..."

"Right, about Luca," Enrico says as he stands up and I

open my desk, taking out a small envelope. "Some of the men have been talking about how the hit went down. The soldiers talk—it's what they do. Nothing to be worried about."

"I know they talk," I say as I open the envelope and take out its contents. "Talk isn't good for business. Which is why I have these," I say, sliding a few photographs across the table. Enrico steps forward and looks at them, his eyes widening as he picks them up.

They show a large, burly, musclebound body lying on fire-scorched asphalt...and a bloody stump where its head should be.

"This is all that remains of Luca Lomaglio," I say evenly, giving him a meaningful look as he glances up at me.

He opens his mouth to say something, but I talk again before he can. "Make sure these circulate among the men. Understood?"

He takes the envelope and sticks the photos back into it, swallowing hard. "Yes, Don Abruzzi."

I smile.

"Good man. Now go."

I watch my consigliere stalk off, and I gesture for my guards to go too, which they do, silently—the way I like it. The door finally closes behind them, leaving me in peace.

I let out a breath, feeling tired already. If I still had my youth, I'd be out taking care of this myself.

My eyes drift back to the painting on the wall as I finish off my wine in a single swig. I look at the faceless figures staggering onto the shore, and I know that not long ago, we were those people. *Cleaners*, they called us. It's only thanks to me that we can one day be called the Abruzzi Family and command the respect we deserve. And I'm not about to let some bitch and her unborn brat ruin our war for the Bronx for me.

Not her, not the Costas...

And certainly not the fact that I never was presented with Luca Lomaglio's corpse.

"*Grazie per l'aiuto*," says the girl softly. She's sitting across from me in the train car, the two of us having settled down into some seats with a table in between. She looks understandably nervous, picking at her pinkie nail and biting her lip as she looks up at me through thick eyelashes.

This girl doesn't look a day over twenty and my heart immediately goes out to her, my maternal or maybe sisterly instincts kicking in. I've never had a sister, as I grew up an only child, but already I feel like I want to rescue and protect this complete stranger. I have this urge to go back to that Napoli train platform and beat her assailant mercilessly with that umbrella I picked up.

I don't know where this aggressive mama-bear instinct is coming from. Maybe it's just the pregnancy hormones. Either way, I know I can't abandon this young lady now, even if I can't understand a word she's saying to me.

"*Non dovevi farlo,*" she adds emphatically, looking at me with mingled fear and gratitude. I realize suddenly how crazy I must look to her—a random woman who swept in to help her and is now sitting in front of her totally silent. My face starts to burn pink and I give her a smile.

"I-I'm sorry, I don't speak Italian," I tell her quietly, glancing around. Nobody else in the train seems even slightly interested in us, which is a relief. Everybody is staring down at their books or iPads or phones, earbuds in, totally in their own little worlds. I start to let my guard down just a little bit. At least for now we should be relatively safe.

Meanwhile, the girl across from me has lit up, a big smile brightening up her pretty but solemn face. She looks completely different when she smiles, I notice. She leans forward as though to tell me a secret or something and says, "You speak English? I speak English!"

"Oh," I reply, surprised. "Well then, hi. Nice to meet you! I'm Serena—Serena Smith," I tell her, only barely stopping myself from giving her my real last name. I know I'm probably being way overly cautious, but after the events of the past couple days, I'm not feeling particularly safe sharing details with anyone, even someone who seems so vulnerable and innocent as this girl.

She giggles and holds out her hand for me to shake. "My name is Francesca Valenti," she introduces herself. "Are you American?" she asks, barely able to hide her curiosity.

I laugh. "Yeah, what gave me away? The accent?"

Francesca nods, sitting back against the seat. She looks more relaxed now, and I'm starting to calm down a little bit myself. "What brings you to Napoli?" she asks.

"Just doing some traveling," I lie quickly, but then when I remember I don't have any luggage with me and I don't have a backstory all plotted out in my head, I correct myself. "Actually, if I'm being honest, I-I'm kind of running away from… something."

Francesca's dark brown eyes go wide. She leans

forward again, glancing around before whispering, "Like… the police? Did you rob a bank or something?"

I snort and shake my head. "Oh god, no. Nothing like that. I'm not a criminal," I assure her, although when I consider my association with the Costa crime family, I think I might actually qualify as a criminal myself. Or at least an accomplice. And with the cops in the Cleaner's pocket, is that really even a distinction for them? "Just had some kind of bad stuff happen recently back home and I needed to get away for a while. Clear my head. Start over, maybe."

As I'm saying all this out loud, it's almost more like I'm telling myself than Francesca. It's hitting me just how little I know about what the future holds for me. My stomach turns and I have to sit very still and focus on not getting sick again. I close my eyes for a second and grit my teeth. When I open my eyes again, Francesca's face looks solemn and sad again.

"You are pregnant, too," she says, her voice barely above a whisper.

"How'd you guess?" I ask, frowning. I'm not really showing yet, my stomach still relatively flat unless you're looking really hard.

"You just turned green as pea soup," she replies, shrugging. "I know the look. I feel the same way. It's strange—people call it 'morning sickness' but I've been feeling sick all day, not just in the morning. Is it the same for you?"

I give her a nod. Of course, I still don't quite know if my nausea is due to pregnancy or just a side effect of all the horrible events that have happened to me lately, but I'll go ahead and blame it on the pregnancy. Might as well. It's easier to think about being pregnant than it is to think about losing Luca and the life I thought I was going to lead.

"Your husband… is he meeting you in Taranto?" Francesca inquires, gently patting her pregnant belly as she glances at the engagement ring on my finger. I have to bite my lip and clench my fists under the table to keep from crying. Oh, how I wish that were the truth. If only Luca would be waiting for me on the platform when I arrive down south. If only I could end this day in his arms, happy and safe at last.

But that's just not my reality anymore, and there's no point in pretending it still is.

"No," I answer, staring down at the polished-wood table between us. "He's… not with me anymore. He's gone."

"He left you? While you're pregnant?" she retorts, looking downright scandalized. "Men!"

I have to smile a little bit, despite the ache in my heart. If only that were the problem here.

"No, he didn't leave me by choice," I explain slowly. "I… lost him."

It takes a moment for Francesca to catch my meaning. Her frown gradually softens into an expression of extreme pity, and that look on her face almost breaks my heart for the thousandth time. She reaches across the table to place her hands on my forearm, looking terribly sad.

"Oh no. I am so sorry," she says, those big brown eyes going shiny with tears. "I can't imagine how you must feel. You poor thing."

I take her hands in mine and give them a squeeze. It was so weird, having a woman so much younger than me, someone I just saved from an abusive man, become so maternal to me in turn. But it feels nice to have someone show me some softness. The past couple days have been so sharp, so painful, that it's almost a relief to not have to be strong right now. I can just be honest, even if I can't tell her every detail.

"I'll be okay. I think," I assure her, hoping desperately that I'm right about that.

"You will be," she says, nodding vigorously. "You can

handle it. Look at you, traveling all by yourself in a foreign country. You will be okay."

I smile even as I can feel my eyes burning with tears. Somehow, hearing this young girl say it, I can almost believe that it's true. That I *will* be alright. But I don't want to think about it much more right now. We've got a long ride ahead of us, and I need a distraction. So I decide to turn the spotlight back on Francesca. After all, I'm obviously not the only one here with a tragic backstory.

"Enough about me," I say, "what about you? Who was that guy messing with you on the platform? And was I right to step in and intervene? I didn't even think about it —I just did it."

Francesca tosses her thick, golden-brown curls over her shoulder and her pretty face turns sour at the mention of the guy on the platform. She crosses her arms over her chest, narrowing her eyes. "That was the father of this baby, if you can believe it."

"What happened?" I push on, leaning forward to show my interest. And I am truly interested—I need to think about someone else's story for a change.

"He's a big, stinking *stronzo* is what happened," she proclaims. "That bastard has ruined my life for too long. He wasn't like that at first, you know. We went to school together, Pietro and me. We have known each other since we were very small. He used to pull my hair when he sat behind me in class, but everyone said he only did it because he liked me. Of course, my mama said to watch out for him, that he doesn't respect his mother and so he cannot be expected to respect me either, but I was stupid. And in love. I trusted him, you know? I thought he could be the one. Childhood friends! Everybody said we were so cute together. We've been dating since we were fourteen years old. I thought we were going to be together forever and everything would be perfect. How could it go wrong, you know?"

Her cheeks flush red and I can see that she's on the verge of tears. I give her a sympathetic look and shake my head. "It sounds so perfect, doesn't it?"

"*Si!* Exactly! I had no idea he would turn out to be so… so… *orrendo*. For a few years, it was all okay. He went out too much, he stayed out too late. He talked to other girls, sometimes right in front of me, just to cause a scene and make me cry. But he never laid a hand on me. I told myself that as long as the worst he did was make me jealous, I could deal with it. Some people have it so much worse, you know? That's what I told myself. He never laid a hand on me until about a year ago. And it came out of nowhere. One night I was cooking dinner and he came home from work looking so angry. I asked him what was wrong and he yelled at me, said he got fired and now he had to come home and be interrogated by his own girlfriend. I wasn't interrogating him, though. I just asked him what was wrong. I thought maybe I could make him feel better. But then he hit me. Just slapped me right across my face," Francesca says tearfully, pointing to her left cheek. She sniffles.

"Oh my god," I breathe, shaking my head angrily. "I can't believe he did that."

"It was bad," she agrees, wiping her eyes. "That was only the first time, and I thought it was only going to be the one time. I thought it would never happen again. But he never apologized, and it only got worse from that day on. He couldn't find a new job and every day he gave up a little more and a little more until finally he just stopped even looking for work. He just stayed home all day while I went to work. I am—*was*—a waitress at a cafe in our neighborhood. At night, he would go out with his friends to drink and party. And then he would come home after midnight and wake me up. He was always angry when he came home. Sometimes he would just go to sleep on the sofa. But other times he would get me out of bed and pick a fight with me. I was so tired, working all the time, but he would drag me out of bed and hit me."

"Francesca, that's horrible," I tell her, my heart racing with fury. I feel like this girl is my sister, my responsibility. Like I need to protect her. Hunt down that awful man and make him pay.

She nods, clearly struggling to regain her composure. I can relate. It's hard to keep all that pain tucked away. It's always trying to break free, burst through and break your heart again.

"And then," she adds, lowering her voice, "five months ago, I found out I was pregnant. I don't know how it happened. I was so careful. I've always wanted a baby, but I knew it wasn't safe to have a family with Pietro. If he hurt me so badly and I am a grown woman, how much damage could he do to a little child? I couldn't put them through it."

"Of course. That makes sense," I assure her.

She continues. "I had to hide it from him. And I wanted to escape, but I couldn't just leave. I know it sounds crazy, but I still loved him, and I kept thinking if he could just find a job and feel like a man again, he would stop hurting me. I've been with Pietro for six years. I didn't want to give up on our dream. I still thought maybe he would come around, that I had nine months to figure it out and make him love me again."

"How did you keep it a secret from him?" I ask her, confused. She stares down at the table, looking sorrowful again. Then she looks back up at me and shrugs.

"He just thought I was getting fat. He called me names, made fun of me for gaining weight. He even tried to make me skip meals, saying he wouldn't be caught dead with a fat girlfriend."

"What an asshole!" I burst out.

"It didn't even cross his mind that I might be pregnant, and I didn't want him to know, so I just let him think I was gaining weight instead. The insults were still better than him finding out I was pregnant," she reasons. "I thought once he started working again, he would stop mistreating me, and then I could come clean and tell him. So at first, I just looked around, trying to find work for him in secret. I asked everyone I knew. I tried everything. But whenever I suggested anything, whenever I told him there was a job opening, he would only get angry with me. He said I was just like his mother, bothering him instead of treating him like a man."

"That's not fair," I tell her. She nods.

"I know. I was only trying to help. But the longer he was out of work, the worse he got. I began to realize that there was no hope for us. No hope for the baby if I stayed with him. It was time to move on, to escape with my child before Pietro could find out I was pregnant. So I started hiding money from him. I was building a little escape fund so I could buy a ticket and leave. I was going to start over somewhere else, find a place to live and a new job and support the baby all on my own. I don't know anyone who has done that. But for me, it seemed like the only option. Finally, I saved up enough money to get out. I was going to buy train tickets and put a deposit on an apartment in Salerno, get a museum job. I was all ready to go," she says.

"What happened?" I ask.

"Well, about a month ago when I came home from work, Pietro was still at home," she says, taking a deep breath. "I was surprised to see him there, because he was usually out with his friends when I got off work. But he was there, and he was waiting for me. At first, I thought maybe he was going to apologize to me, stop his routine of spending all my money and disappearing during the night.

But then I realized he was holding the little box where I was keeping my escape money. He found it. He found all of it."

"Oh no," I gasp, feeling sick.

"He was so mad at me. He screamed at me, called me horrible names. He said I was a snake, a lying whore, for keeping all that money away from him. He dumped it all on the floor and told me to pick it up and hand it back to him. I did what he told me to do, but then I begged him to please just let me take the money so I could leave. I asked him to please just let me go."

"What did he do?" I almost hesitate to ask.

Francesca sighs. "He spent it all. Everything I had in that box. He took it with him when he went out that night and spent every last euro. And when he came back in the morning, he kicked me out, made me go stay on a friend's couch. Even though I pay for the apartment. Of course, my friend was angry. She called Pietro on the phone and yelled at him for treating me so badly, but when she was scolding him she accidentally let it slip that I'm pregnant. She said *'Pietro, you're a bastard for mistreating the woman you love, especially when she's carrying your baby.'* And then it was out."

"What did he do?"

She rolls her eyes. "I don't think he even knew what to do. One minute, he would yell at me, saying he would never be a father to our child. The next minute, he would curse me for keeping it a secret from him. He told me to get the hell away from him, but then he said that if I ever tried to leave him, he would kill me. I didn't know where to go. I was so afraid to leave the house that I couldn't go to work. I lost my job. All my money went to paying for the apartment even though I wasn't living there anymore. Then, last night, he showed up at my friend's house. He screamed and banged on the door until I came out. He had a baseball bat. He said he was going to beat me until I wasn't pregnant anymore."

"Holy shit," I mutter.

"I was lucky. My friend called the police and they took him away for the night. But I knew I couldn't stay in town. Not anymore. So this morning my friend drove me to the train station and I bought a ticket to Taranto. I knew he probably wouldn't follow me there. He's a born-and-raised Napolitano. He wouldn't leave Napoli for me," she explains. "But somehow, he found out I was leaving. He showed up at the station. He bought a ticket to get through the security and followed me to the platform. He grabbed me, said whether I lived or died, it was all up to him. Not me. He said he was going to throw me in front of a train. That's where you came in."

"I had no idea it was that bad," I murmur, totally shaken.

Francesca nods, a sad smile crossing her face. "You saved me, Serena. I don't know what to do when I get to Taranto, but at least I'll be away from Pietro. I'll be alive. Because of you."

I reach across the table and take her hands. "I don't know what I'm going to do when we get there either, but I know one thing for sure—we'll do better if we stick together."

Her smile widens, her big brown eyes glittering. "Okay."

~

*I*t's late afternoon when we arrive in Taranto, the two of us achy and exhausted from traveling while pregnant. When we step off the train into the tiny, dimly-lit station, a wave of panic seizes me. I realize that I have no clue where we are and no clue where to go.

"Have you ever been here before?" I ask Francesca.

She shrugs. "Once, when I was a kid. I don't remember much, though."

"Well, first things first: we need to find somewhere to stay for the night," I say.

Francesca nods. "*Si*. It's not safe to be out after dark. Not for… girls like us. But I don't have much money left. Pietro—he took my purse as soon as he found me."

I turn to her and take her hand. "Don't worry. I can pay."

She shakes her head, those curls bouncing around. "No, no. I couldn't possibly accept your money, Serena."

"Don't be silly. I'm not going to let you sleep in the street. We can find a hotel somewhere, get a room for a couple nights until we figure out what to do," I tell her firmly, not taking no for an answer. I've already kind of adopted her as my sister, my responsibility.

"Are you sure?" she asks, looking genuinely torn-up over the idea of my paying for her.

I smile. "Of course. We're in this together."

We walk out of the train station and immediately Francesca hails us a cab. We ask the driver to take us to a hotel, any hotel, and he drives us into the city center. We get out in front of a place that looks a little ritzy for our taste. I have money, but I don't know what lies ahead for me in the future. I don't know how long this money is supposed to last me. So we walk a couple streets over and find a hotel that looks considerably less fancy. We go inside and Francesca talks to the concierge desk clerk, booking us a room for the night.

The sun is sinking down over the horizon when we go up to our room, both of us dog-tired and overwhelmed. It's hitting me just how strange our predicament is—two young pregnant women in a foreign city, with no luggage and no plans. We order some food for delivery and settle down to eat, turning on the television to distract from how awkward and bleak our situation seems.

After dinner, Francesca says, "Ugh, I've got a craving for ice."

"Pregnancy craving?" I ask, lying back on one of the beds.

She nods. "I don't know why, but every time I eat now I want ice after."

I laugh. "I suppose there are worse cravings to have."

"That's true," she agrees. "I think there's an ice machine on the floor below us. I'm going to see if I can get some. I have some change in my pocket Pietro didn't find."

"Okay. Be careful," I tell her, feeling like a mother hen. She smiles and heads out, wobbling just a little bit with her hands on her belly.

I hoist myself up from the bed, thinking of taking a shower before bed. I walk into the bathroom and turn on the water, but just before I start taking off my clothes, I hear a knock at the hotel room door. I frown, confused for a moment, and then I realize it's probably just Francesca having forgotten to grab her room key. I walk over to the door and open it.

Immediately, I'm shoved backward, someone bursting through the door and slapping a hand over my mouth before I can scream. He pushes me against the wall and shuts the door behind him, his eyes black and shiny in the dim light.

"Quiet," he hisses. "I don't hurt you. You Serena De Laurentis, *si?*" His English is broken, but I understand well enough.

I just barely nod, hoping that this guy isn't about to kill me.

"*Bene.* They send me to help. I am Costa *fratello.* We supposed to meet at train station, but you not alone. I follow and wait. Who is the other girl?" he asks gruffly.

He takes his hand off my mouth.

"That's just a girl I met on the train. She—she's in trouble. Like I am," I explain.

"We must go. Before she come back."

"No," I protest. "I'm not going to just leave her behind."

"Cannot trust her. Could be enemy *informatore*."

"Francesca? No. She's not an enemy. She's just a girl who needs help. I'm not going anywhere without her," I tell him emphatically.

"We go now. Quick."

"No!" I shout, and he cups his hand over my mouth again. I glare at him, balling my hands into fists. He searches my face with his eyes for a minute. Then he sighs.

"You trust her?"

I nod, still staring him down. The man groans and releases me. I back away from him and fall back onto the bed, my heart racing. He looks over at me. "When she come back, we go."

"Okay."

A few minutes later, Francesca comes back in carrying a little bucket of ice chips. She's humming to herself, a smile on her face—until she notices the man in the room with us. Her eyes go wide and she stops in place, like she's paralyzed at the sight of him.

"Who—who is this?" she asks softly.

The man looks her up and down, then gives me a nod. My shoulders slump, relief taking over. "He's here to help us, Francesca. He knows my... my people back home. He's going to take us somewhere safe."

"Are you sure?" she asks, looking at the man sidelong with suspicious eyes.

I get up and walk over to link my arm with hers. "Yes. We can trust him."

She turns to me and shrugs. "Okay. But I'm taking the ice with me."

I smile. The man leads us both out of the room, down the stairs, and into the lobby. We leave the room keys by the front desk and walk down the street. The man helps us into an old-fashioned, classic black car, and drives us off into the night.

SERENA

TWO MONTHS LATER

I wake up to the sound of a rooster crowing, as I often do, just before dawn. I open my eyes, letting them slowly adjust to the near-darkness of the bunk room. Across the property, the rooster cries again, and I smile to myself. He's getting a little overly excited about his job as alarm clock for the women's shelter commune, but that's okay. We keep him around because the lady chickens like him, and the lady chickens give us eggs. Most of the eggs, we sell at the local weekly open-air market along with produce we grow and breads we bake, but we keep a good portion of the eggs we collect and the plants we grow for our own kitchen, as well.

It was nearly two months ago that the mysterious Costa contact showed up in my hotel room and whisked Francesca and I away to this place. At first, we were both overwhelmed, in shock at how drastically our lives changed in such a short amount of time.

Francesca, of course, fit in quickly. She speaks Italian fluently, and she's so young and bubbly that everyone adores her.

573

I, however, struggled to get by. In the space of several months, I've gone from a New Yorker with a bright future and my own business to an essentially homeless, friendless foreigner in a country I've never lived in before. The guy who brought us here assured me that he would get word to my mother back in the States, tell her that I'm okay and that she should not go looking for me under any circumstances. I'm sure that conversation, if it did indeed happen, was not a particularly enjoyable one. But whatever he told her must have been pretty convincing, because she hasn't shown up on our doorstep to take me back to New York yet.

And the more time that passes, the less I feel like an outsider here. At first, I was quiet. I was still grieving—and honestly, I still am—and without being able to speak Italian, there wasn't much by way of social interaction for me. I clung to Francesca for a couple of weeks. It's not that the other women here aren't friendly. They've been welcoming and kind to me since the start. But it wasn't until I started picking up Italian that I began to branch out and open up to them.

Francesca helped translate what I couldn't understand, and we made flash cards. She quizzed me on Italian and I taught her what I know about running a business. She says that once the baby is born and she gets back on her feet, she wants to open her own version of Bathing Beauty here. It will be difficult, but she's plucky and determined enough to do it, I think.

Nowadays, I can just about hold a fluent conversation with the other women here, and I've taken on some responsibilities on the property. I help with the cleaning and the cooking of meals. A few days a week I have garden duties, and on the other days I bake bread. There's a lot to do in order to keep this place running smoothly, and even though I'm pregnant, so are many of the others. We all help out and do our part. We support each other. We listen to each other's stories and lend a shoulder to cry on. I've always been kind of a loner, even when I was at the height of my high school popularity food chain. I just relied on myself, until I found Luca again, and then I relied on him.

But now? I am part of a community. The women here are my friends and family and coworkers all rolled into one. Sometimes it does feel crowded here. It's hard to find much time to myself, since we all share bedrooms and bathrooms and living spaces.

But honestly, it's probably for the best that I don't get much alone time. This place keeps me busy and distracted so I'm not constantly thinking about the horrific events which led me here. At night… that's when those thoughts creep back in. I toss and turn most nights, reliving the good moments I had with Luca as well as the bad—the day I lost him forever. And every day, my stomach gets a little tiny bit rounder, reminding me over and over again that Luca will never get to meet his own child.

I roll out of bed and stretch, turning on the lamp on the little table between my bed and Francesca's. She groans and squints in the light, turning onto her side and pulling the pillow over her face to block it out. I laugh and walk over, taking the pillow and tossing it aside. It's a routine we do almost every morning. The more pregnant she gets, the less of a morning person she is.

"How is it already morning?" she asks in Italian.

"Well, let's see: it was night, and now that's over, so it's morning," I reply, smirking.

She opens her eyes and gives me a look of mild annoyance. "Smart-ass," she says in English. I nudge her shoulder.

"Come on. Time to get up. Let's go feed the chickens," I tell her.

"Ugh," she moans, sitting up in bed and rubbing her

eyes. "Why are you always so happy in the morning? It's too early to be happy."

"Staying busy keeps me sane," I answer with a shrug. "As long as I keep moving, my brain can't catch up to me and make me think of stuff I don't wanna think about."

"Makes sense," she says, yawning. "Still would rather stay in bed, though."

"I'll meet you in the courtyard in fifteen minutes," I tell her with a wink. Then I get up and head down the hallway to the big communal bathroom. I slip into one of the shower stalls and hang my clothes up over the door. There are already a couple of other women in here, singing and humming in the stalls. There's a lot of singing here.

I think we all like to keep our minds busy, and thinking about lyrics and melodies is just another way of keeping bad thoughts at bay. Everyone here has a sad story. Everyone here has seen hard times. In a way, it's kind of helpful to know I'm not alone. By comparison, some of them have been through way worse stuff than I have.

Still, it doesn't make the pain any less awful. I still think about Luca every day. Every hour of every day, actually. He's always there, in the back of my mind, and there's still a tiny part of me that hopes he will one day come strolling through the front entrance of the shelter to rescue me and make me his bride like we planned. I still dream of the day when we can miraculously be a family together. I know it's probably hurting me more, prolonging the pain, to think about stuff like that. But I can't help it. It's like my heart doesn't understand that he's gone and he isn't coming back. No matter how hard my brain tries to convince me, my heart just keeps on believing.

After my shower, I dry off and get dressed. Most of the clothes we wear here are hand-me-downs, donations from thrift shops and such. I don't mind. It's not like I'm trying to impress anybody these days. My jeans and oversized sweater are comfortable enough to get work done while wearing them, and that suits me just fine.

Sometimes it does get a little claustrophobic, though, just hanging around the commune all the time. Some of the other women get to go out, get part-time jobs, volunteer in the community. The best I can hope for is to go to the weekly open-air market and help run the vendor stand. It's nice to get out and see different things every now and then, so I'm grateful for that. I would love to go out and wander around town, do some exploring with Francesca at my side. Go to a restaurant and order in Italian, since I could actually do that now.

But the man who brought me here was very emphatic about the security risks involved with my residence here.

He made the woman who runs this place, Daniela Russo, swear that she would keep me under lock and key. And she has. I understand that it's all for my safety, but it's still hard to be cooped up here all the time.

Daniela has recently put me in charge of feeding the chickens, even though I'm not allowed to touch them, collect the eggs, or clean the coops since I'm pregnant. Francesca helps me feed them, and a couple other women who aren't pregnant do the other parts.

My favorite part of the morning is now—when I walk out into the courtyard and all the chickens come running up to me because they associate me with food. I jokingly told Francesca once that it's nice to feel loved, even if it's only by a group of hungry birds. And it's true. Despite all the warmth and camaraderie I feel surrounded by the women here, I'm still starving for love. Specifically, Luca's love.

I keep wondering if maybe someday I'll stop searching for him in every shadow, listening for his voice in every silence. Somehow, I doubt it. I think my heart is going to keep looking for his heart for the rest of my life. And if I have to be content with that, I guess I'll make my peace.

I spend the day going about my usual chores. I clean our bedroom and help clean the bathroom. I make coffee and set out baked goods for breakfast. I help tend to the garden, pulling weeds and picking ripe heirloom tomatoes. In the afternoon, Francesca and I sit down to watch an Italian soap opera I've gotten embarrassingly addicted to, and after that we head to the kitchen to start working on dinner for everybody.

I'm boiling a massive pot of water on the stove when suddenly there's an ear-piercing scream from across the compound. My heart stops for a moment and I immediately turn off the stove and start running toward the sound, thinking that one of the older women has probably fallen and hurt herself.

But before I even make it out of the kitchen, someone pulls me into the pantry and shuts the door, putting a hand over my mouth.

It's a strangely familiar sensation, and I quickly realize that it's the man who brought me here six weeks ago. I stare at him wide-eyed and confused, wondering why the hell he would do this. I need to go see what's going on out there. I need to help my fallen friend.

I point toward the door, hinting that I need to leave, but the man shakes his head. Then I hear a few more screams, clearly from my fellow shelter women, and then *male* voices. They shout out in Italian, "Where is she? Where is Serena De Laurentis?"

My heart sinks.

"We will not hurt you. We have no interest in you. Bring Serena De Laurentis to us. Now."

My eyes well up with tears. How did this happen? How did they find me? How did the Cleaners come all the way from America to track me down here, in this most modest and unexpected of places?

Then I remember something slightly strange that happened last week at the open-air market. A young man with heavy, black brows came up. I cheerily explained our wares—tomatoes, zucchini, onions, garlic, peas, beans—but he wasn't interested. He simply stared at me, those black eyes boring into my face until finally I stopped talking. He disappeared into the crowd soon after, and I just chalked it up to a random weird occurrence. Maybe he thought he recognized me or something. Or maybe he was just an oddball.

But now it dawns on me that he probably did recognize me, and he had been hunting for me all this time, only to find me selling produce in the south of Italy with hardly a care in the world. I swallow hard. There's only one choice for me, isn't there? I certainly can't let the Cleaners hurt my friends here. No. I have to walk out of this pantry and hand myself over before anyone gets seriously injured. That's what I have to do. It's the right choice.

"Let me go," I manage to whisper behind the man's hand. He shakes his head again.

"No," he mouths at me. Then, still holding onto me, he edges toward the back of the pantry and scoots aside a barrel of canned goods to reveal a trap door in the floor. I stare at it in confusion. Has that really been here all this time? Just waiting for me in case I need to break away?

I guess I underestimated the severity of my situation. These Cleaners aren't like Pietro—they didn't give up on hunting me after I left town. They followed me here, like bloodhounds to a scent. And suddenly, it's like the past six weeks don't even matter. I was a ticking time bomb all along, a liability to all the wonderful women here who have become almost like family.

"You go. Downstairs. Find the door. Run the tunnel.

Don't stop," the man explains in broken English, his voice scarcely audible. "Come to a field. Keep running. Find the villa. Old. Ruins. Hide there and wait."

"What about my friends?" I ask, my eyes filling with tears.

"I protect them," he says simply. And I know there's nothing I can do. I have to believe him. I have to believe that he can save them. Still, I hesitate.

"Worse for them if you stay," the man adds, sensing my reluctance.

I can feel another piece of my heart shattering. This is the way it has to be.

So without wasting another second, I climb down through the trap door, down a rickety ladder, and find myself standing behind a shelf of odds and ends. When I step out around the shelf, I realize I'm in a basement.

I knew about the basement, of course. It's where we keep old clothes, preserved produce, and other stuff we don't have a place for. I've been in here before, but never through a trap door in the ceiling. I look around, floundering in the low light as I run my hands up and down the grimy walls until I find a door handle. With my heart fluttering, I turn the handle and step through the door into a cold, dark tunnel. I take a deep breath, close the door behind me, and start running with only the light of my cell phone screen to guide me. I run nearly blind, tears blurring my vision as I try not to sob, my footsteps soft on the muddy ground. I keep running until my legs feel weak, until my chest feels tight. I walk for a little while to regain my breath, and then I start running again.

I don't know how long I'm underground, but when I finally come to a round wooden door and push it open to expose myself to the cool air, the sky is dark overhead. I climb out of the ground and close the hatch behind me, covering it with dirt before I keep going. Just as the man described, I'm in a field. It looks to be the middle of nowhere. I can't hear anything but the wind.

I force myself not to think about Francesca. I force myself not to think about Daniela and the other women I left behind, the new family I've already lost and possibly endangered. I trudge onward, my feet feeling heavy and my heart racing. My lungs hurt. I'm out of breath, feeling dizzy and weak. But I have to keep going. For all I know, the Cleaners are hot on my trail, and I have no idea what my next move is. Where the hell can I go? Where can I hide?

These guys will always find me, won't they?

I keep walking through the dark, my phone battery quickly draining. I turn it off to save battery power and just walk blindly in the night, hoping the Cleaners don't find me before I can reach the next checkpoint. After what feels like hours and hours of walking, the massive shape of a white building looms in front of me. I squint in the moonlight, trying to make sense of the shape I'm seeing. I take in pillars, piles of rubble. A marble archway.

My heart skips a beat. There it is. That has to be it. The old ruined villa.

I race forward, hurrying to climb over the broken-down walls and slip through a busted window, tearing my sweater on a piece of jagged glass, but feeling grateful it wasn't my skin that got slashed. I stumble into what looks to have once been a grand living room of some kind, and I all but collapse on the concrete beneath me, out of breath and overwhelmed.

As soon as I'm sitting down, my body aches with relief. I lean back against a marble column and try to catch my breath, closing my eyes as the tears trickle down my cheeks. And now that I'm still, it's like all those horrible thoughts catch up to me.

Is this the way it's always going to be?

Temporary lodging? Temporary friends?

The constant threat of being discovered and chased out of hiding, only to find another little hole in the ground to cower inside? Am I going to spend the rest of my life on the run? And what about when my baby is born? How the hell can I raise a child like this—always running from one place to the next with no stability, no safety, no place to call home?

Am I going to end up this way over and over again? Alone and afraid?

Luca's face swims to the front of my mind. Smiling at me as he knelt down to ask me to be his wife. I said yes. I said yes, but it doesn't matter because he's gone and he's never coming back and I'm never going to be anybody's wife.

I'm so damn tired. I need to sleep. My whole body is giving up. I pull my knees up inside the oversized sweater and lie down on my side, the cold concrete instantly giving my body hell. It's not comfortable, and it's almost certainly not safe, but that's just the way my life is going to be from now on. The sooner I get used to it, the easier it will be.

I hope.

So I lie here quietly, breathing in the dusty air of the crumbling old villa, slowly drifting off into the closest thing to sleep I can hope for. I don't know how much time passes, and I don't know if I ever actually fall asleep for real, but out of the darkness and the silence comes the unmistakable sound of footsteps echoing in my broken-down fortress. I sit up, sleepy and defeated, to await my assailant. Will he take me captive? Torture me? Kill me?

It doesn't matter anymore. Not really. In a way, I almost welcome it. I'm tired of being on the run. Maybe it's time to just face up to the monster, let fate do what it will with me.

A voice splits the silence, deep and questioning.
"Passerotta mia?"

LUCA

This strong heart of mine has held up through beatings, gunfights I never thought I'd survive, and being baptized in fire. All the while, it's been steady, fierce, and unstoppable. It's a heart that refused to stop beating, all for the sake of Serena.

And the sight of my Serena shakes it like never before.

I rush forward to her, the love of my life, as her eyes go wider than I've ever seen them. I worry that she's about to pass out, so before she can even start to scramble to her feet, I stoop down and wrap my arms around her, cradling her as gently as the most precious treasure on the earth. On pure instinct, her arms go around the rippling muscles of my neck, and she melts into me, hot tears wetting my shoulders as her whole body shakes with her sobs.

We say nothing more to each other for what feels like an eternity. It's been so long, so painfully long since I've felt her touch, held her in my arms, enjoyed the very warmth of her body on my skin. I savor it, and I feel my own tear roll down my stony face as I breathe in the scent of her hair that I've missed so badly.

"Luca?" she manages through sobs at last, and the sound of her voice melts my heart.

I can hear so much pain in her.

"I'm here," my deep voice rumbles, holding back my own tears as I feel her body—delicate yet strong as steel all at once—trembling in my arms. My hand moves up to the back of her head, and I stroke her hair gently, kneeling down to sit down fully beside her.

It feels like we've been together for hours already, just riding out another of life's storms together, emotion flowing freely between us. I feel her heart beating against mine as I hold her, and I turn my face to kiss her on the head as her whole body shakes again with her sobs.

Finally, I feel her gently pushing back, and I realize how tightly I've been holding her. I let her look up at me, and I see her face swollen and red with sobbing. Her eyes are bloodshot, and she's looking at me as if she doesn't believe what she's seeing, like this is some kind of dream that she'll wake up from soon.

My face can't help but comfort her with a smile, and I brush some of her stray locks out of the way to see her better. When I broke out of prison a lifetime ago, I felt like the sight of her again was sweeter than anything I'd ever experience again.

The sight of her now proves me wrong.

"Luca," her thick voice manages. "You're...I...oh my god, you're alive!"

"Did you think a little thing like death could keep me from you?"

That earns me a smile from that gorgeous face of hers, ever so faint, still so tired, and she shakes her head, unable to hold back a laugh before she lets her forehead rest against my chest.

"Oh my god, Luca, this is...you're real, aren't you?"

"Real as you," I say, a few happy tears rolling down my

face now as well. I let my arms go down to her arms, and I give her a gentle squeeze. "But it's sweeter than any dream I've ever had."

She sniffs and looks back up at me with shining eyes and a smile that's tired, so very tired, yet so happy. But then my smile drops and gives way to a look of concern. I take a step back, still holding her arms, and I look her up and down.

"Are you okay? Are you hurt? Did those *stronzi* lay a finger on you?" My blood is suddenly boiling all over again at the thought as my eyes rove over Serena for signs of wounds. The thought of any of those fucking monsters so much as looking at the love of my life, of them harming my child.

On instinct, my hand goes to her stomach to feel her, and I look up at Serena to meet her eyes as she lays one of her small, soft hands over my big one.

"I...I think I'm okay," she says with a soft nod. "We're okay, I mean," she adds, giving the hand over her belly a light squeeze to mean the baby.

"What happened at the shelter?" I ask, my tone soft yet serious. I need to know what the situation is with us right here, right now. I'm prepared to run immediately if we need to. Anything to keep Serena safe. "Were you followed?"

It takes her a moment to think about what I asked her, her eyes fluttering as she gives her head a little shake of confusion.

"We...we were attacked," she says, "I'm not sure what happened. The guy who was helping us out, he took me into some side room and told me to come here. I mean, I think it was here—it's dark, and I was scared and confused, and I-I-" she starts stammering, so I simply nod, running my hands through her hair with an understanding face.

"It's okay, you're safe now," I say as I hug her tight to me again. I can feel her fighting sobs as the recent memories come back to the surface.

"I don't think I was followed," she says into my shoulder, and I nod. "Oh my god, I the other women there, I…"

"They can handle things," I say. "This old ruin isn't the only contingency plan they have. That shelter has been here for a long time. Some punk-ass kids from the Bronx aren't going to shake them, but those punks couldn't be allowed to know exactly where you are or get a shot at harming you."

"So they *were* after me," she says, pulling back and looking up at my face. "This was all because of me?" She gives her head a little shake and asks, "For that matter, how on earth did *you* find me? How do you even know all this?"

"I have many skills," I say with a cocky smile, and her near-tears break down into a laugh as she slaps my chest.

"Jesus, it really is you," she says before sniffing. "But seriously."

God, it feels good to laugh with her again.

"A lot of people helped you get here," I say simply. "Many of them are my friends—and I might have been dead, but that didn't mean I couldn't keep an ear out when I needed to," I say with a wink. She doesn't look satisfied, but I give her a squeeze. "I'll explain more, but first, I think your nerves need a break. I can't imagine how much you've been through today." I glance around the room we're standing in. "How long have you been here?"

"I…" she starts, following my gaze. "Not long. I just staggered in here and kind of…collapsed," she says with a blushing face. I nod.

"That's fine, I wouldn't expect any more from anyone in your place." I give her a reassuring smile. "This place is a shit-hole, but there's a little more to it than meets the eye. Come on," I say, and before she can say anything, I stoop down and scoop her up off her feet, cradling her gently in my arms.

"Woah!" she says, surprised, but she laughs the next moment, putting her arms around my neck again. It's good to hold her again. "If you're sure," she says, swallowing. "What *is* this place, anyway?"

I start walking her toward a small set of stairs leading up. They've seen better days, and there's dust everywhere, but it'll do in a pinch.

"In New York, we have proper safehouses buried in the urban jungle," I explain. "This is Puglia—Apulia, as they call it in English—we don't have that kind of luxury. This is the next best thing to a safehouse."

"Hiding out in ruined villas in the countryside?"

"More or less. This part of the country has seen better days. There are ruins like this all over the place, and you have to be a local to know where most of them are—they don't show up on internet maps."

"So...we're really safe here?"

I frown. "Depends on whether the local mafia is working with the men hunting us. I don't plan on staying here long, but we can take a moment to breathe."

"Sounds about right," she says, and I smile at her.

"In any case, this place isn't exactly a vacation home, but it does have a few amenities you'll appreciate."

A few minutes later, we're standing in a roomy bathroom with black and white tiled floors. The tub looks antique, but it's in good enough shape to use.

"Don't worry, there *is* hot water," I say as I turn the shower on to start running water. Serena is standing behind me, and I can feel her gaze on me. I would bet I know what she's thinking, too.

So, as steam starts to rise from the water, I turn around and smile at her before lifting my tight shirt off my body. "I know you have questions. But we should get a little more comfortable while we talk about it, don't you think?"

Her eyes go up and down my hardened body, and I can almost see the tension melting from her as she looks at the familiar scars, the familiar contours of my form...everything she remembers. It's as if she weren't really sure it were me until she saw the roadmap of wounds left on me.

She smiles.

"I'd like that."

I step forward and take her hand gently, putting it to one of the scars on my side and letting her feel it. I want her to know that I'm here, for it to really sink in—and I know that isn't going to happen immediately.

"I...I'm sorry," she says, laughing at herself a little as she shakes her head. "I know it's silly, I just...I can't believe you're really here. I saw you get-"

I gently lift her chin up to look at my still face before I lean in and press my lips to hers. Instantly, my cock twitches and swells at the familiar warmth that I've craved so badly. It feels so *right*. Every second, every single moment the two of us are touching, it feels like we were made for each other. I can hear her breath get quick for a moment before she lets out a soft moan into the kiss.

When the kiss finally ends, I nod.

"I know. Let me help you with this," I say, putting my hands to her shirt. She moves her arms to let me lift it up and over her head. I toss it to the floor while my eyes fixate on her belly. She's showing, and she looks more beautiful than I could have dreamed of—and I did dream of her. Every single night, I dreamed of her.

My hand strokes her stomach, and a wide smile spreads across my face. "I can't believe it," I whisper.

"Me neither," she admits, looking down at the bump with me.

"I should have been with you," I say, an edge to my

voice as I think about all the time I've spent away from my girl, away from my child. My hands reach around her back to undo her bra, and soon, it falls to the ground too. The sight of her whole bare torso, breasts and belly exposed, kindles something new in me.

There's a kind of beauty to my pregnant Serena that I can't explain. I feel the same desire for her, fanned stronger and hotter than ever, but there's a primal attraction to the sight of her that reaches some deep part of me I've never glimpsed before. It's intoxicating and fresh all at once.

"I've missed you so badly, Luca," she says as I unbutton her pants and let them slide down her legs, leaving her completely bare once she steps out of them. It doesn't take me long to get the rest of my clothes off, revealing the thick shaft between my legs, hanging half-swollen for her already.

I help her into the bathtub, and she sighs softly as the hot water runs down her body, washing away the whole painful day.

"We don't have any soap," I say, stepping close to her as she turns and looks up at me, "but water will do for now."

"I'm okay with that," she says softly as mist starts to hang in the room like a cloud. I smile, and my hands go to her shoulders, feeling the water pattering against our skin as I turn Serena around and run my hands down her sides.

My cock rests between her asscheeks as I explore her form, helping the water do its work as she leans back into me, resting her head against my chest.

"What happened back there, Luca?" she asks, and I know it's time to give her an explanation.

"I only remember patches of the night itself," I confess, my mind flashing back to it all. "I went to the car with one of the men. Fabio. He caught up with me and told me he's dinged my car a little when he was parking next to me—the poor man was a nervous wreck about telling me. But we'd both come in company cars, and he said he'd just had new speakers put into the one he drove, so he offered to swap cars so he could take mine to the shop to get touched up."

Serena puts her hands over mine, which have stopped at her hips. I stare at the wet tile walls as I remember that hellish night.

"Fabio was parked on the left of my car. We both went to our doors, and...it's patchy after that. Some car bombs go off when you open the door. That must have been what happened, because the next thing I remember, I was on the ground, my ears were ringing, and everything stung bitterly. I had glass and metal in me. The pain was so intense I felt myself slipping in and out from the very start. The bullets flying overhead sounded dull, I was so deafened. Our cars are reinforced to resist bullets—if there hadn't been that armored car between us..."

I pause for a moment. I had remembered enough to look over to where Fabio had been standing. He had just...ceased to exist.

"How did you get out of there?" she asks.

"The Cleaners weren't expecting resistance," I say. "My men were on me in a few seconds. I remember seeing a friendly face. It might have been Nico, but I can't remember. The last thing I said was to get you out of there, far, far away. Whoever I said that to knew what I meant."

"You had me sent here," she says. I give her a light squeeze and kiss her neck softly.

"America wasn't safe for you, Serena," I say. "This is the only place I know far enough away that it would at least buy me time."

"I thought you were dead... all these months," she says with a pain straining her throat.

"If I'd had a say in it, I would have been with you the whole time," I say, and it's the truth. I bring her hand to my scars again…the new ones as well as the old. "I woke up with one of the family's surgeons. He had me medicated while he treated me for…I don't know how long. Too long. I must have had more shrapnel in me than I realized. Broken ribs. All I could do was dream of you."

"Luca…"

"The first time I was fully conscious, I woke up to more stitches in me than I'd ever had before. But the Cleaners must have caught up to my trail by then, because that same day, one of their men showed up. Killed the doctor before I could get the IVs out of me and tear him apart." I look to some of the fresher wounds on my upper arm. "I knew it was going to be a rough recovery, but I couldn't stay there any longer. I got in touch with Raf and headed off to catch up with you. I still know the layout out here, and the contingency plans like this villa. I had to be careful to look for you quietly, but I couldn't leave you alone."

Serena turns around and looks up at me with big eyes. The water starts dousing her hair, getting it soaking wet and letting it hang on her shoulders like vines. I put my hands around her face, running my thumb over her lower lip as water patters off her and onto my face.

"The whole time I thought you were gone, I didn't know how I was going to keep going," she says, but her hand goes to her stomach as she looks down briefly. "Having some of you with me helped." She smiles as she looks down at what's going to be our child, looking absolutely radiant. "The baby is going to be as strong as you, Luca. I know it."

I put my forehead to hers, my heart swelling with pride.

"*Si, passerotta mia*, but it will get its strength from you."

She looks up at me and locks her lips with mine, and I feel myself swell so stiff that my cock touches her, pressing in, desperate to feel her warmth again. She draws in a sharp breath at the mere feeling of it, and I can tell that her body craves me every bit as much.

"I have a lot of time to make up for," I say as my hands go to her breasts, thumbs stroking over her hardening nipples. Water runs between us softly, warming us to each other even more.

"Yes you do," she practically purrs, pressing herself up against me. "Fuck, I've wanted you so badly, Luca."

"You've been through a lot," my voice rumbles, but even as I say so, we walk backward until she's pressed against the cool tile. "I can hardly keep my hands off you, but if you need to rest-"

I feel Serena's hand grip my cock firmly, and the mere feeling of her hand running up its length to the crown and lingering on my tip makes it rock-hard, desperate for her, the pressure in my groin so full and ready for her that it's almost painful.

Those playful eyes of hers are alive again with the very red-hot energy I fell in love with so long ago, lidded by long lashes.

"The only thing I need right now, Luca," she whispers, putting a hand on my chest and running her fingernails down it, "is you. Inside me. Now."

Feeling him grip me is like being in a giant's arms, and the easy strength he uses to pull me in and bring his lips to mine makes me feel safe for the first time in what feels like a lifetime.

It's strange, a grip like that, firm and powerful, should make me feel like he's taking control of me, taking everything into his hands. But I've spent so long on the run in other people's hands, hiding from place to place. I don't want that feeling anymore. And with Luca, somehow, being in his embrace helps me feel like I'm standing on my own two feet for the first time.

He's not another set of arms to hold me. He's my shelter in this storm.

I sigh into his kiss as the hot water rolls over my shoulder. It's so hot it almost scalds me, but his hands still feel warmer. And I'm feeling even warmer between my legs. That groan that rumbles in his chest, full of desire and strength...it's everything I've dreamed of. It's that sound, that feeling that's stayed alive in the back of my mind.

I still can't believe it's him. Seeing him at all after what happens defies all odds, all my expectations.

But really, that's what our whole relationship has been: against all odds.

I let Luca walk me backward in the shower, gently, until I'm pressed up against the cool tile wall. The room is so steamy that it's not icy, but it sends a thrilling shiver down my back. My heart is pounding, and I feel excitement welling up in me so hard that I'd be shaking if it weren't like a sauna in here.

My eyes slowly shut as I feel Luca start to explore my body. It feels like he's discovering everything all over again. His hands slide around my hips to my ass first, squeezing it gently at first. I give him a little thrust of my hips to ask for more, and wordlessly, he understands. The next moment, he pushes back into me and pinches me on my ass enough that I gasp into his kiss.

He silences me with his tongue. I feel it delve into my mouth, his rough stubble brushing against my face slightly. Fuck, I already feel so tense inside, ready to explode at a moment's notice. I can't hold myself back any longer.

My hands go up to his chest, and my nails dig into his flesh, running down those rippling, tight pectoral muscles, down to his abs. I'd count them if my head weren't so dizzy with need. Another shiver runs up my body, but not from the cold—this time, it's like old sensations I thought dead forever coming back to life. My body remembers everything about him, everything about the passionate seconds we passed together.

And it's desperate for more.

I crave him, every inch of him. My fingers run down his dark skin until they reach the V leading to his groin, and soon, my hands have found that thick, wet shaft that's as hot and ready as I am. It's pointed up toward me, resting against me, grinding against me every time one of us moves. I feel it harden and pulse at the same time that I feel my pussy wetten and warm in anticipation.

"I've missed you so fucking much," I gasp when our kiss breaks, and I tilt my head back to rest against the tile as his mouth goes to my exposed neck. We started gentle, but we're realizing that after so long apart...neither of us knows how long we can hold ourselves back before this turns into something more savage.

And that's something I think we're both eager for.

His teeth graze my neck at first, brushing against it with the stubble of his cheeks. Then I feel a nip, and I gasp. He presses himself in closer, and his hands grip my hips tighter as he starts to rub himself against me. The feeling of his teeth gently on my neck gets more aggressive, and I can feel that huge, strong heart of his thumping in his chest as he hugs me against his pecs.

He grips me possessively because he knows I'm his, even though we've been apart so long. My breathing is hot and fast as my lips hang open, water running in little streams down my face as I feel my whole body twitch with need for him.

He moves his hands to my back and claws me, running those rough carpenter's hands down my spine, feeling every inch of my smooth skin. His hands run down to my ass, where he rubs his palms into my cheeks, massaging me and groping me. His cock pulses with every new part of me he touches.

His body is powerful and built better than anyone I've met in my life. It's incredible to know that all that strength can get excited just by the touch of me—just by the *thought* of me.

"Serena," he groans in a husky voice, lips by my ear as he leaves my poor neck alone at last. "I told you I'd never leave you. Did you think I'd make a liar of myself?"

I'm too breathy to respond, and he nips my ear, making me whimper and squirm in his grip.

I can't take it any longer.

My hands go to his cock again and start running up and down its length. My eyes flutter open to meet his. The sight of his face there—steam all around us, his dark eyes piercing into my soul, water running down his short hair and those features that look like they were cut from the finest marble—makes my heart flutter. He could hold me paralyzed with that look.

His face cracks that boyish smile. My Luca. My own Luca.

He clenches his teeth a moment as my fingers run up his cock and my thumb brushes the tip. I can electrify him with just a touch of my hand, and that knowledge makes my heart soar.

"You're always playing with fire, *passerotta mia,*" he whispers as his hand runs from my hip to my thigh, still strong and firm as ever, and I have barely enough time to brace myself before he hoists me up just enough to impale me on his cock.

I let out a scream that he silences with a kiss. Neither of us want to be slow anymore. We can't take it, and the steam between us is only making us more and more worked up. We finally have all the time in the world, and damn it, I'm going to take advantage of that.

The feeling of that huge, familiar shaft entering me is unbelievable. It's as if my whole body were stretching out and feeling a swirl of relief all concentrated between my legs. It's hot and intense, stretching me taut and wringing me out all in the same feeling.

The water is hot, but I feel hot tears running from my face too. It's not pain—my pussy is so needy and so ready for him that he feels nothing but incredible in me—it's the overwhelming feeling of knowing that we're together again.

My inner depths pulse with ecstasy as his cock gets flooded with my honey. His tongue plunges into my mouth, and while one hand helps hold me up, his free hand goes to my left breast, groping me and rolling his thumb over the hard, stiff nub. I'm aching for him, and he holds nothing back.

Immediately, he starts thrusting up into me. We're in sync as if we'd never spent a single night apart. His hips move back and forth as I let my head roll back, his mouth going to my neck and ravishing the exposed flesh, then moving down to the nape.

I'm like a doll in his hands. My hair is soaking wet, and after he's had his fun toying with my nipple and getting it stiffer than ever, his hand goes to my back and takes a handful of it. The grip he has on me just makes me feel all the tighter, blissfully strung out in Luca's hands.

Each time he thrusts, his cock solid as a rock and pulsing with desire, I feel electricity run from the walls of my pussy up into the rest of my groin, then further up to tighten in my lower abdomen. From there, I feel every nerve in my body begging me not to let this stop.

I rock my hips in time with him, but even if I wanted to just lay back and enjoy it, Luca could have handled it. He bucks back and forth at a steady rhythm, not going too deep to hurt me but filling up every inch of what he explores of me.

"Serena," he breathes into my ears. He's practically panting, growling my name. "Serena, fuck, I want to feel you come on my cock. I want you to do that for me, baby."

"Oh god," I gasp, needing no encouragement. "Luca, I...I'm so close, please don't stop!"

He's a machine. I don't know how he's holding me up this way or how he can keep himself moving like this after whatever he must have gone through to find me all the way out here, but I would rather die than let it stop now.

Something wells up inside me, and I scramble to get my hands on his biceps to hold myself up. I feel so tight inside that I'm afraid I might lose control of myself and start convulsing, so I need something, anything to hold onto. I feel his biceps, but they're too thick and hard to get a good grip on. I whimper in desperation as I feel Luca hurdling me toward the point of no return, and just when I think I'm about to lose myself, Luca pushes me back and up against the wall just as I can't contain myself anymore.

He thrusts up deeper than ever as I come, and I let out a sharp, short squeak that melts into a long, ragged sigh while my body is pinned between the tile and Luca's hot body. After my limbs twitch and I feel my honey warming his cock and mixing with his precome, his cock pulsing inside me, I realize he's holding me up entirely. I've lost control of my body, and Luca is holding my limp form up with his strong arms and that solid dick that's just as desperate for release.

"I want you to come in me, Luca," I manage, afterglow radiating around me like a halo. "Please, I want to feel you fill me up, it's been so long!"

"Soon, *carissima*," he teases me, putting a finger to my chin and lifting my face up for him to kiss. It's sweet and short, and right now, it's the sweetest thing I could possibly taste. His tone turns dark when he leans in to whisper into my ear, "I'm not done making up for lost time yet."

Slowly, he draws his cock out of me, and I immediately try to push my hips back into it. I feel like I'm missing something without it in me, and I whimper in protest, gripping his biceps pleadingly. Luca must have noticed, because he chuckles, brushing a little strand of wet hair out of my eyes and kissing me again to pacify me while he slides out. "Patience," he urges me through that wicked grin of his.

"I need you in me," I say, feeling relaxation from head to toe already, a relaxation that's almost *heavy* on me like an aura. I sound stupid, but god, it's the truest thing I can say right now.

"I can't deny you anything, you know that," he growls just before he turns me around. I catch myself with my hands against the tile. He takes hold of my hips, perching his cock on the surface of my pussy as he takes his time groping my ass, his chest giving a low rumble as he savors the feeling of it.

"This, Serena," he says with a quick, wet slap of my ass that makes me whimper and wiggle my hips, begging him to spear me. "This could bring me back from the dead."

I don't have time to answer before he thrusts up into me. My fingers try to clench, but the tile keeps me pinned against the wall, my mouth hanging open as I feel warmth roil through my body in an entirely new way. His cock his long and thick, but just changing positions electrifies new parts of my body, reminds me of so much of what I've been missing.

Both of his massive hands reach around to grope my front, first cupping my breasts and squeezing, toying with them, flicking the hardening nipples with his thumbs and running his fingers teasingly over my areolas. I can feel every ridge of his cock inside me, ribbed with veins, pulsing with every motion.

He starts rocking steadily again, letting me take a breath so as not to overwhelm me with the sensation. But I can tell he isn't going to go easy on me—not by a long shot.

Even when I think back to all the passionate nights we've spent together, I don't know if I've ever felt him this taut and ready, so swollen, so...*huge*. His balls don't hit me in this position, but I can still feel their weight as they swing under us in the shower. He's swollen with need for me, and the thought of him unleashing himself inside of me is enough to warm me up inside all over again.

The way the past few weeks have been going, sex has

been the last thing on my mind. So this overwhelming presence of Luca all around me, inside me, filling me up, it all hits me like a truck out of nowhere. It's thrilling and relaxing all at once, like a medicine I didn't even realize I needed.

I feel the bulging crown of his cock inside of me grinding against me as he moves in and out, and soon, I feel my body electrifying as he reaches my g-spot. My whole body starts to tense, and I know he can feel it—I clench around him to make sure he feels, because I want Luca to share every second of this ecstasy I'm feeling.

His cock feels like it's white-hot against my insides, and I put my forehead against the wet tile wall so it doesn't fall over. I feel like jelly in his hands. Just as I'm starting to lose myself entirely in his steady, rhythmic pace that's picking right up to what it was a few moments ago, I feel one of his hands start to wander further down, away from my breast.

My pussy tightens in anticipation as Luca's strong, gentle fingers make their way to my clit. As soon as I feel his rough fingertip on my sensitive, swollen nub, he has to hold me up again as my legs shake, another orgasm crashing through me.

My body has been totally awakened to him, and the orgasms come more freely now. My panting breaths go in time with his thrusts. His tip strikes my g-spot while his fingers swirl around my clit, and I lose track of time in the rush of it all. I'm hardly aware that there's even water falling on us anymore. All I can feel is the swelling rhythm of my orgasms as his steady, pounding rhythm drives me home over and over again.

My body tensing up gradually and then relaxing with a beautiful, wonderful shudder is the only thing I use to measure time anymore. Just the feeling of Luca's hands around me again is almost as wonderful as the over-whelming feeling I have in every inch of my body.

I start to get a better footing in the tub, and Luca starts rubbing his hands up and down my body, really exploring me as if it's for the first time again. It hits me why I feel so unbelievably safe with Luca, despite all the danger that seems to follow us around. He loves me in a way that makes every second touching me worthwhile. I can feel it in his hands on my hips, on my stomach, on my breasts. He loves me, body and soul, the same way I love him.

Tears are running down my face again, and my eyes pop open when he slides out of me suddenly. I turn my head to look at him, but he's already grabbing my face and bringing me into a deep, hungry kiss at the same time he drives his cock into me.

We're locked in a long, deep kiss as he starts thrusting faster, and this time, I recognize the way he's losing his rhythm, the way he's starting to grab me like he's holding me to him. There's something brutal and animalistic to it, every bit as fierce as he is sweet, all in the same storm of feelings that he fans up in me.

I'm hopelessly, deeply in love with him, and my whole body roars up as one to join him when I feel his cock starting to tense up harder, balls tightening, bucking getting wild—never careless, but wild.

He spreads my arms out outstretched on the tile and holds me by the wrists as he pounds. He's leaving me totally exposed to him, unable to stop him as he tilts his head back and lets out a deep, ragged groan…

The feeling of his seed bursting into me is the most exciting and comforting feeling I've felt since…since…I can't even remember. It's all just a golden, dizzy blur as shot after shot of hot come washes my insides with Luca. He pours himself out into me entirely, and I feel filled with life all over again. I realize I'm smiling in the shower, hot water getting in my mouth as I almost want to laugh. My head is getting giddy, sensations so jumbled up and wonderful as we come together that I feel out of control of myself.

All I know is that I'm happy. Luca has me, he's coming in me, and we belong to each other. In my wildest dreams, I never could have thought that would be how tonight would end up. When I open my eyes once we've stopped moving, I'm half-expecting him to not be there. That this was all just a dream, or even the afterlife.

But Luca's still there, glowing as much as I am with that damned cocky smile on his face.

"Is this for real?" I let spill from my mouth. "I mean, are you a dream or something?"

"*Dolcezza*," he says, putting a hand to my cheek, "I've been asking myself that this whole time."

A few minutes later, Luca has dried me off with a towel that's a little too stiff for my liking, but beggars can't be choosers. We start to walk out of the bathroom, but I realize my legs are shaking too much from the...well, the everything.

Giggling, I'm swept off my feet by Luca before he carries me out the door and up to a modest little bedroom on the same floor.

"This place must have been nice when it was still lived in," I say as he sets me down beside a bed that isn't too gnarly, but it's seen better days, and the sheets smell a little like dust.

"Some of them are still in use," he says as he fluffs the pillows a little. "I'll have to show you one someday. For now, though, you'll have to take my word for it," he adds with a wink. "I've got some supplies I brought with me—I have a vehicle. We can eat light in the morning and get a move on. For now, though," he says, walking over to me and helping me get into the sheets. My eyelids got heavy all of the sudden.

Not that I should be surprised. All that adrenaline was bound to crash sometime soon.

"You need some rest," Luca says, sitting on the bed next to me with a warm smile as I beam up at him, bundling sheets around myself. I don't even care that the bed is stiff —I would sleep on a pile of hay at this point.

"That sounds..." I try to say before I yawn, and I feel sleep overtaking me like a warm bath.

Luca's smile splits into a grin, and he says something that makes my heart flutter, but I'm already falling deep into sleep.

...And the next thing I'm aware of, god knows how many hours later, is his hand on my shoulder and his deep voice in my ear. But it's not the warm and comforting sound I was expecting—it sounds urgent. I fight off the sleep all around me and look at his blurry face and his moving mouth. The look in his eyes tells me everything I need to know.

"We have to go. Now."

I heard them coming from a long way away. Sound travels farther in this landscape than many foreigners realize. And I heard cars. Several of them.

When Serena dozed off to sleep, I had been keeping watch. It was hard to tear my eyes away from that peaceful form, watching her chest rise and fall as her small hand rests on the tiny bump of her belly. Even in the midst of a storm, she's as peaceful as can be.

Exhaustion will do that.

I only had two guns on me when I came into the villa to meet her in case she'd been followed or worse, so as soon as she'd dozed off, I went back to my vehicle to get a little more gear: spare guns and a knife, as well as a set of clothes in case we made it to the morning undisturbed. I have a set of binoculars, but out here in the near pitch-black of the Apulian night, you can see a set of headlights from a long, long way away, and nobody would dare try to handle these roads with the lights out.

And when I spotted the headlights, it was about half an hour before sunrise. I wasted no time.

Serena gets out of bed quickly, snapping awake almost

instantly despite how deeply she'd been down. Within less than a minute, she's gotten up and pulled enough clothes on to move while I watch the window.

"How close are they?" she asks, concern in her voice. It makes my heart sink to know she's had to harden herself this much. No woman like her deserves to have to get used to such violence.

"There's nobody else on the roads this early," I say. "They're closer than I'd like, let's leave it at that."

"Right."

We rush down the stairs, and I already have one gun out while my other hand holds Serena's. I'm not going to let anything separate us while we're getting out of here. Not when we've just been brought back together.

By the time I throw the door open, I can already see headlights on the road as the vehicles hurdle closer toward us. I feel Serena's hand clench mine, and on instinct, I draw her under my arm as I help her run with me.

"Keep your head low," I command, and I ready my pistol as we rush toward my own vehicle.

It's a rough-and-tumble SUV that looks like it could withstand its fair share of action, because I came here planning for that. It's big and it's tough: two things that can be rare and valuable in a car for Southern Italian driving.

It's also a rental. Despite the insurance, I don't have much hope I'll be able to return it.

But even as we dart to the SUV, several sedans roar into view, all black, all tinted windows, and some of those windows rolling down.

We have a matter of seconds before hell breaks loose.

I turn so that Serena is hidden by my bulk, and I raise my weapon. My only armor consists of a tight white t-shirt and black jeans, meaning we need to get to the car *now*. I fire a few rounds that spark off the cars, and they start veering off to the side, both to get out of the line of fire and to get better shots at me. Serena doesn't scream, she just tries to make herself small as we race to the car. She's been through enough by now that she's started to harden herself against fear.

Gunshots start ringing out into the humid night air. I *feel* them whizzing too close to us for comfort. I duck down with Serena as we cross the rocky way to the door as I hear the shots ricocheting off the villa behind us, bits of decades-old stone chipping away.

I return fire, and my aim is deadly. I'm not interested in just causing a distraction. These men dare try to harm my Serena and my child, so I shoot to kill.

Glass from the tinted windows shatters as I fire at them with one hand while using the other to move Serena behind me once we reach the car. With me covering her, she opens the car and crawls into the passenger's seat. Once she's in and crouched down, I duck under the front of the car and hurry to the other side, blind-firing a couple of rounds from the corner before popping out and getting into the driver's seat.

We hear bullets ping off the edge of the car as I turn the engine on, throw the SUV into gear, and peel around harder than I've ever taken this thing. Dirt gets kicked up as I do a half-circle around the unpaved space that passes for a driveway in front of the villa before I roar toward the exit.

Two of the sedans had parked in front of the entryway to keep me from doing just that, but I head for the outer edge of the left one and throw my brights on to let him know he has about five seconds to decide to move.

I can see a pair of widening white eyes in the driver's seat as the man drops his gun and makes the wise choice to throw his car into reverse. I still scrape the front of his car as I tear out of there and onto the road, and I can already hear the engines roaring after us.

And I keep going past it, right off the road on the other side, into the brush.

"Oh my god what are you doing!" Serena gasps all in one breath, bracing herself with all four limbs in the passenger's seat with equally wide eyes.

"Hang tight," I say, checking the rear-view mirror as I change gears to get my vehicle *really* moving. "If these boys want us so badly, they can try to come after us."

"It's all rocks and trees out there though!"

"Exactly."

I don't have to look over to know Serena's looking at me like I'm crazy. I just cock an eyebrow and dart my eyes in her direction for a half-second to add, "Buckle up."

Serena scrambles to get the strap over her chest as I weave through a small grove of olive trees that have long since been abandoned and started to grow wild. Behind me, I see lights starting to come back into view.

I crack a smile. So they really do have a backbone.

"Why not just take the road?!" Serena asks as she steals a glance behind us. But the next moment, we can both hear the gunshots, so she ducks back down to where she was a moment ago.

"I counted five cars back there," I say, taking a sharp turn around a large boulder jutting out of the ground, dust flying up behind us. The ground is getting drier as we get further out. This part of Italy isn't that different from the landscape of the American West. "If we were on the open road with this monster of an SUV, it would be the easiest thing in the world for them to get us boxed in and pepper us with bullets."

Serena winces as we hear another bullet hit the back of the car, so I start veering right through some rocky terrain that would be hell on the tires of any other car.

"I know this landscape," I explain. "These boys that are after us? My bet is they're kids from the Bronx. Hardened killers, maybe, but not even the best of the best from New York know how to handle off-road driving like this."

Serena opens her mouth to speak again, but the loud sound of a car crashing against one of the trees behind us distracts her. I reach over and put my hand on her knee, giving it a gentle squeeze.

"Don't you worry—I haven't let myself forget the terrain out here."

Serena gives me a nervous smile, and that's enough for me.

I veer into some hills, and a quick glance behind me tells me there are still three of them. I heard one crash, and the other must have chickened out or lost a tire trying to come after us.

Barreling through the darkness, I wind through dried-out shrubs, twisted and dead trees, piles of rocks, and craggy, low cliffs. Turning around the corner of another ruined villa that's in worse shape than the safehouse, another one of the sedans chasing us doesn't clear the turn and tumbles over in a storm of dust.

That doesn't give us a moment to rest, though.

"Shit," I grunt as I look ahead of us. We're headed for a wide-open field. Judging from the rows of dirt and over-grown weeds, this used to be someone's homestead farm, long ago. And there's no cover anywhere to be seen.

"There's two more of them," Serena says, an anxious edge in her voice.

"Don't worry," I assure her. "But do hang on. I mean it this time," I add as I roll the window down.

"What?"

The next moment, I slam the brakes and turn the car sharply to face the oncoming cars, which veer to each side to try to avoid me. But my gun is already out, and I fire at the one on my left four times, right at the driver's side.

Its car horn starts blaring as the driver's body slumps forward and the car keeps spinning in a circle in the field.

I take advantage of the confusion—the other car tries to spin back around, but the car I shot at blocks its way while the passengers try to get the dead driver off the gas. It gives me all the time I need to rocket into the opposite direction, clearing the field.

"*Holy shit, Luca!*" Serena breathes.

"Are you okay?" I ask, looking at her seriously for a moment. She gives me an incredulous look, and it takes her a moment to just nod. "Y-yeah, fine. Where did you learn how to drive like this?"

"Look, there's not a lot to do out here," I say with a smug grin on my face as I glance into the rear-view mirror and see the other cars just now managing to get back on my tail. "When you're a boy with a bunch of friends and one of them has a beat-up car and some time to kill, well...it's a better way to pass the time than bare-knuckle boxing, right?"

"I mean…"

"We did that too, though," I admit before I veer off toward some dunes, and Serena yelps as the car takes a sudden dip.

Behind us, I can see the sun peaking up over the horizon, just starting to cast light over the landscape. We must have been driving out here for nearly an hour already.

My car can handle the small ditches and dunes the rough landscape has with ease that the shiny sedans behind us couldn't hope to match. For once, having the sleekest and fastest cars isn't an advantage. Still, I know it's only a matter of time before they decide to try something else, so I need to get creative.

I drive us past the dunes toward what looks like a ruinous pile of rocks to the west of us.

"What *is* all that?" Serena asks, leaning forward and squinting.

"Many, many years ago, it was a village," I say as we get closer. There are strange, round buildings with roofs that look like pointy pyramid cones and piles of stones all around them, along with scrap metal, broken-down cars, and even the odd rusty washing machine here and there. "Now, it's a scrap yard for some other village nearby. Those buildings are called *trulli*."

"Why are we driving toward them?"

"They're sturdier than they look," I say with a smile. Serena knows what that means by now, so she braces herself as I whip the car into the run-down ghost town and use the hand brake to help me around one of the little round buildings.

Before they even enter the village proper, the car whose driver I shot hits a ditch on the way in and gets stuck, pinned between a mound of dirt and someone's broken washing machine, spinning wheels sending a cloud of dirt flying up around it.

The final car makes it a little further, barreling after us as someone leans out the passenger window with a gun in hand to try to take aim at us.

But *trulli* are a little unusual in their layout, and it takes them by surprise to try to drive around a clump of them, only to find the row of houses extending farther than one would expect. The car slams on the brakes, but it careens into the stone buildings, endless stones from the roof collapsing over the car while the vehicle crumples against the stone wall.

We drive off, zipping through an old hazelnut grove to the blissful sound of nobody roaring after us. All I can hear besides the hum of the engine is Serena breathing for a few minutes, looking into the rear-view mirrors every few seconds to make sure there aren't any of them left.

When it's safe enough not to tempt fate anymore, she says, "Are...are they gone?"

"If any of them can catch up to us after the ride I took them on," I say, taking a deep breath and leaning back in my seat, "then they've earned a proper fight."

Serena looks like she's tense at that, and I chuckle, taking out my aviator sunglasses from the glove box and popping them on. "I'm kidding, *dolcezza*."

"Fuck you," she laughs, a nervous yet relieved laugh that lets her lean back in her seat too as we ride into the sunrise.

After a little ways further on the rocky off-road terrain, I bring us back onto the road. The highways out here are dirty and half-falling apart, but after the ride we've been on, even a rough road is a welcome feeling.

Ten minutes later, we're heading southward on the road, and it's taken us up onto a high hill that gives us a far and wide view of the area. With the sunrise peaking over the horizon, it's a gorgeous view, and my heart swells with pride to see Serena looking out the window.

Golden rays of sunlight touch groves and farmland for miles, cypress trees swaying in the distance as a gentle breeze blesses the landscape. The smell of early springtime flowers is in the air that whips around us.

"It might not be upstate New York," I say with a little fake humility, "but it's something, isn't it?"

"Yeah..." she says wistfully, a smile on her face. "I never knew all this was out here. It makes me..." She pauses, and her smile fades. "Nauseous."

I blink. "What?"

"No, I mean I need to throw up. Can you pull over?" She puts a hand to her chest and bites her lip, and immediately, I bring us to the side of the road and stop the car so Serena can hurry out and retch. I get out of my side immediately, my heart pounding—had she been hit? Was the strain too much? Is it just motion sickness?

Oh, wait, shit—morning sickness.

I come around the side of the car to Serena and put my hand on her back. "Take your time," I say, not sure how to comfort her but doing my best. "Nobody's out here this early."

"Oh god, don't look at me like this!" she half-laughs before being sick again.

"You've seen me in worse ways," I say with a grin, and when she finishes and turns to give me a weak smile, she sees me holding a towel, a bottle of water, and a little mouthwash for her.

"Wow, you came prepared, huh?"

"Traveling light doesn't mean forgetting the essentials," I say with a wink.

Serena cleans herself up while I help her, and after she spits the mouthwash out onto the ground, she takes a breath and gets back into the car.

As we pull off again, I'm quiet for a moment before I speak.

"I wish I could have been with you for more of this," I say, nodding to her. "The sickness, I mean. It's not easy to go through alone, let alone on the run like this."

"Me too," she says softly.

"How much longer do you have with that? Does it last the whole pregnancy?"

"I'm not sure—but no, they say it ends after about two and a half months," she says, furrowing her eyebrows. "But if I'm doing math in my head right, it shouldn't be too much longer? I'm not sure."

"Well, let's not worry about it right this second," I say, taking a turn onto a long road into a residential area. "We'll have time for that later."

We drive past a few modest houses and back onto a strip of mostly uninhabited road that takes us past some wild trees and rocks before a short bend. Past that, up on a small hill that looks so much smaller now than when I first left it, I see the sight that I've been waiting years to lay eyes on again.

Serena leans forward in her seat to look at it as I pull the SUV to a stop. It's a modest villa, large enough for a single family, mostly made of white stone with a little terraced garden out the side by a porch with laundry strung up to dry. There are a few palm trees swaying in the breeze outside it, and there's a single car out front.

"Um…" Serena says as I turn the engine off and step out of the car, gesturing for her to follow with a smile. She does, but she looks up at the villa with confusion on her face before I come to slip my arm around her and hug her to my side.

"Why are we stopping here? What is this place, Luca?" she asks, smiling as I give her a gentle squeeze. When I reply, I can feel a lump in my throat.

"Home."

As we walk up the steps to the clean white villa, my stomach turns again and again. I will my body to chill the hell out, let me have a calm moment for once. But between the pregnancy hormones, the car chase, and of course the rush of being reunited with Luca, I'm not feeling very well at all. Luca takes my hand, giving me a look of reassurance before knocking on the door. The porch lamp flickers on above our heads, washing us in pale golden light. I look sideways at Luca, still in shock that he's alive. I can't believe it. He's really here. With me.

I still keep expecting to wake up and realize with a pit in my stomach that it was all just a happy dream, another fantasy to confuse my brain and make me wish for things that aren't true. But he squeezes my hand and smiles and I tell myself that this *is* real. This is really happening.

Luca said this place was home, but I'm not entirely sure what he means by that.

Until the door opens to reveal a teenage girl, probably about seventeen, sitting in a wheelchair looking very sleepy. It *is* early in the morning, after all. Then her big green eyes light up and a look of revelation appears on her face. The color drains from her cheeks and her mouth falls open, gaping at us—but more specifically, at Luca. She mutters something to herself, shaking her head slowly as she stares at him. Luca, meanwhile, is beaming brilliantly. There might even be just the slightest sheen of tears in his eyes.

The teenage girl murmurs, "B-Luca? *Sei tu?*"

He nods. "*Si. Ciao*, Domenica."

She shouts over her shoulder, down the hallway behind her, "Papa! Mama! *Vieni!*"

She quickly waves for us to come in, rolling her wheelchair back out of the way so we can close the door behind us. The girl reaches up to take Luca's hand, tugging him down to give him a tight hug. There's a big grin on her pretty face, and it looks very much like Luca's smile.

He kisses her on the forehead and mutters, "*La mia bella sorella.*"

Just then, a middle-aged couple comes trudging down the hallway. There's a tall, broad-shouldered man with a proud, handsome face and thick salt-and-pepper hair, and at his side is a much shorter woman with chin-length, smooth black hair, luminous green eyes, and frown lines etched into her face. But at the sight of Luca, both of them stop in place. They stare at him with the same wide-eyed, slack-jawed surprise the teenage girl did.

"*Luca, è possibile?*" asks the woman, raising a hand to her cheek in awe.

Beside me, Luca nods. The older man steps forward, shaking his head. He reaches out to touch Luca's chin, then his jaw and cheek, almost like he can't believe his own eyes. Like Luca might just disappear into thin air at any moment. I know the feeling. It's the same way I feel when I look at him, touch him. That's just the effect he has on people. Once you meet him and really get to know him, you're constantly worried that you might lose him.

"*Papa, sono io,*" he says, nodding. "*Veramente.*"

"*Mio figlio!*" the older man exclaims, throwing his arms around Luca in a hug. The woman comes shuffling over to hug them both, her beautiful face crumpling into happy tears.

So this is Luca's family, the ones I've heard bits and pieces about, the ones who sent him away to America in hopes of giving him a better life, a chance at escaping the temptation of joining a criminal gang here in Apulia.

I stand aside, overwhelmed but content to watch the heartwarming scene unfold. The time will come to introduce me, but I'm not about to intrude on this golden moment.

The teenage girl looks at me suddenly, an expression of surprise on her face, like she's just noticing me for the very first time. She cocks her head to one side and says, "*Chi sei?*"

I answer her in Italian, hoping I can keep up with these fluent native speakers. "My name is Serena. I'm Luca's... um..."

"My fiancée," Luca intercepts in Italian. "Mama, Papa, Domenica—this is Serena De Laurentis. We met in New York when we were teenagers. I have loved her since the first day I saw her. She's come a long, long way to be here with me. With you."

I give them all a sheepish smile. It's been a long time since I've been introduced to someone's family, and never in a foreign language I can only speak with some small degree of fluency. I can get by, but I have a feeling I might fall behind if they start talking rapidly.

And of course, as soon as that thought crosses my mind, they all launch into one big hailstorm of rapid-fire questions and comments. They ask about how we met, how long I've been in Italy, who my parents are, where I come from. Am I hungry? Thirsty? Tired?

Once they take notice of my hand resting on my stomach, the topic switches gear and gains even more intensity. Am I pregnant? Are they going to have a grandchild? How far along am I? How do I feel? Have I been drinking enough milk? Is it a boy or a girl?

"Slow down," Luca interrupts, laughing. "There will be plenty of time to ask all the questions you want, but for now I think Serena might like to sit down and get comfortable. We have had a rough time getting here. Lots of travel."

Luca's mother rushes over to take my arm. I'm not an incredibly tall person, but next to her I feel like a giant. She's barely over five feet tall, and I find myself wondering how funny it would be if Luca had inherited his mother's height rather than his father's. Mrs. Lomaglio leads me into a little sitting room down the hallway, plopping me down on a cushy red couch before hurrying off to the kitchen. Luca, Domenica, and Mr. Lomaglio come in after us.

Mrs. Lomaglio comes back quickly with a cup of something warm and vaguely sweet. Maybe some kind of tea. I've never been much of a tea-drinker, but I'm not about to refuse anything this sweet woman offers me, so I gladly take a sip. She smiles broadly, pleased.

"Is there anything else you'd like? Fruit? Cheese?" she asks.

"Hard cheeses only, Mama!" Domenica interjects meaningfully. She looks back at me, blushing. "I'm studying to be a doctor. I take online classes."

"Oh, that's wonderful," I tell her. She looks positively joyful.

"Domenica has always been the smart one, even when she was little," Luca says.

"Both my children are brilliant," boasts Mrs. Lomaglio,

getting up to get me some hard cheese and fruit from the kitchen. "Coffee, Luca?" she adds.

"*Si*, Mama. *Grazie.*"

"I cannot believe it," says Mr. Lomaglio in his gruff, deep voice. I can tell he's a man of few words, keeping his thoughts to himself while his wife and daughter chatter away. "My son, come back to me after all this time."

"Of course, Papa. I couldn't stay away forever," Luca answers gently. "I would have come back sooner if I could. You know that."

His father nods very slowly, his jaw tightening as though he's trying desperately to keep from showing too much emotion. "What a fantastic surprise to see you again."

Mrs. Lomaglio comes back with a little silver tray of olives, grapes, diced pears, and what looks like long, triangular slices of either parmigiano or asiago. She sets the tray down on the little coffee table in front of Luca and me, and as much as I want to be a courteous, dainty houseguest, my pregnant stomach growls impatiently. I quickly start eating, munching happily while Luca catches up with his family. All the while, Mrs. Lomaglio glances at me with approval, like it gives her immense joy to watch me stuff my face.

"I'm surprised you remembered me so quickly," Luca says to his little sister, who is sitting with her hands folded in her lap. She shrugs and smiles.

"I may have been a little girl when you left, but I could never forget my big brother," she says warmly. "I cried so much when you went away. Once I stopped feeling so sad, I started feeling angry. I know now it wasn't your fault, but I was so mad at you for leaving."

"I never would have gone if I'd had any other choice," Luca answers, a note of intense sorrow in his voice. I pause my pig-out session to take his hand and give it a squeeze.

Mr. Lomaglio sighs. "It was never your fault, my son.

Sending you away was the most difficult thing we have ever had to do. Like tearing out your heart and sending it on an airplane across the ocean. We never wanted to see you go, Luca."

"Domenica wasn't the only one who cried for you," Mrs. Lomaglio speaks up, those gorgeous green eyes so similar to Luca's shimmering with tears.

"You were born at the wrong time, in the wrong place," her husband continues. "We had no idea that the mafia was closing in on our little neighborhood. We were not wealthy, and we were not well-known, but we had everything we needed to get by. A house, a garden, and lots of love. We were just happy to have our children—our strong, handsome son, and our sweet, beautiful daughter. If not for the mafia, we would have stayed happy. And we would have stayed together, all in one place, like a family should be."

"We shielded you from those bad men for as long as we could, my love," Luca's mother takes over. "All the years of your childhood, we tried to keep you safe from those who might exploit your strength and bravery, take advantage of your good heart. We wanted you to stay young, carefree, be a child for as long as you could before the world could pick you up and spin you around. But you grew so tall and strong, and the mafia took notice."

"They were always looking for young men to recruit for their grunt work," Mr. Lomaglio says, his face darkening. "Always on the hunt for another good soul to corrupt. They would offer the young boys money, fame, glamorous cars, beautiful women—anything to convince them to join the mafia. Luca, they were circling in on you. We saw them, following you home from school in their big black cars. Watching you play soccer with your friends."

"Do you remember your childhood friend, Alessandro?" Mrs. Lomaglio asks suddenly.

Luca nods. "Yes, of course. We used to climb trees together and go to the park."

"Do you remember when he stopped coming by? When he disappeared?"

Luca looks down at his hands, sadness creeping into his expression.

"Yes."

"They took him. Recruited him right off the street. I can still recall his mother weeping on my shoulder, begging me to help her get him back," she laments. "But there was nothing to be done about it. Once the mafia got its claws on someone, they were forever lost. And after what happened to Alessandro, your father and I had to make a very difficult decision."

"You sent me to live with Uncle Carlo in New York," Luca says softly.

Mr. Lomaglio looks so exhausted. "Yes. We gave you up when you were a teenager. We thought, we hoped, that if you could just stay out of the mafia's reach, they wouldn't be able to catch you. We knew that if you stayed here, they would snatch you up."

"They were threatening us already. Watching our house. Following us to the grocery store. We thought we were giving you a better chance of escaping."

"I know. I don't blame you for what you did," Luca assures them both. "I probably would have done the same thing."

"And then you went away, and I lost my guardian. My playmate," Domenica says, tears tracking down her cheeks. "I missed you so much, Luca. I couldn't understand why you left."

"It was very hard for everyone at first. The house felt so empty without you in it," Mrs. Lomaglio explains, wiping at her eyes. "But we made ourselves go back to our old routines. We had to keep living, because of Domenica."

"And then," Mr. Lomaglio says gravely, "she became so ill. Suddenly. Our joyful little girl was sick all the time, getting weaker by the day. We took her to the doctor again and again, and they could not find out the cause of her illness."

"I don't remember much from those days," Domenica says softly.

"You were fragile. We didn't know what to do. Finally, we got a diagnosis: it was multiple sclerosis. That was devastating to hear. We had already lost our son, and now we were afraid that we might lose our daughter, too," says Mrs. Lomaglio. "We decided that we would do whatever was necessary to help her. No matter the risk."

"The medicine, the equipment, the wheelchair, the private doctors—it was all so expensive. We fought and fought for the government to help us, but it was hard. Nothing was ever enough. One day, things got so bad that I did something I had sworn never to do: I went to the mafia to ask for help," Mr. Lomaglio admits, and I can tell this is his deepest shame.

"No," Luca breathes.

"Yes. We had to. We needed money, and there was nowhere else to turn. They did help us, once I begged them not to let Domenica fade away. And for a while, everything got a little better. Easier, at least. But then, as we feared, the mafia came to collect their debts," says Luca's mother.

"But we could not pay. The money simply was not there. And so they took what they could from me—my labor. They forced me to do work for them. Grueling, backbreaking work. But that was fine. It was bearable. Until they decided that was not enough. They wanted to make me truly suffer. And so they forced me to be involved in illegal activities. Driving stolen cars. Cleaning crime scenes to throw off the authorities. Working as a guard. I was so exhausted, Luca, between working at the factory, caring for Domenica, and doing this work for the mafia. They were breaking my body, stealing my strength. Finally, they pushed me to take part in the murder of a local baker, an innocent man who refused to pay protection fees to the mafia."

"Papa," Luca says, getting worked up. "Please tell me that isn't true."

Mr. Lomaglio's face is stony, even as the tears fall from his gray eyes.

"I am afraid it is the truth, my son. It is an atrocity I cannot be forgiven for. They told me if I did not take part, they would kill your mother and Domenica. I could not take the risk. But after it was done, I could no longer look at myself in the mirror. I wanted out, by whatever means necessary. I threatened to go to the police if they did not release me from contract. And by that point, I was already weakened. They had sapped my strength until there was almost nothing left. I was becoming useless to the mafia— more of a liability than an asset."

He pauses and sighs, staring down at the glossy tile floor.

"And so they shifted the debt I owed them. They knew I could never pay them back. I had no money, no power, no strength left in me. But they knew about you. Away in New York, working for your uncle, getting stronger and more impressive every day. They passed the debt from father to son, and suddenly, the terrible fate we worked so hard to keep you from came true. They had found a way to claim you, even after all that time, all that work, all our careful planning."

"And that's why I disappeared, Serena," Luca says, turning to me. "That's why I had to leave when we were teenagers. My life changed. I was no longer living freely." He looks back at his parents, then launches into an explanation of the past decade of his life. He leaves out some of the grittier details, I notice, but he gives them the essentials. Working for the mafia. Being framed. Prison. Escaping. The explosion. The long road to reunite with me.

"I am so sorry, son," Mr. Lomaglio says, cradling his face in his hands. "I can never forgive myself for what my actions have done to my family."

Luca stands up to walk over and crouch down between his parents' chairs, putting an arm around each of them.

"It isn't your fault. There might have been a time when I blamed you. But not anymore. I know you didn't mean for any of this to happen. It was out of your control, Papa. I don't blame you."

"No," Domenica says suddenly, her pretty face flushed with emotion. "It's my fault. If I hadn't gotten sick, none of that would have happened."

I interject suddenly, "You can't blame yourself. You were just a child, and you didn't choose to fall ill. It's just the way things are sometimes."

Domenica gives me a weak smile.

"Thank you. I feel so guilty when I think about these things. I just wish it had all gone so differently."

"Oh, my sweet sister. If I had known how you were suffering, I would have come back. I would have found a way to help," Luca says sadly.

"Well, now we're all back together," Mrs. Lomaglio says, standing up and putting her hands on her hips. "And I'm going to make the most of it. But for now, I'm sure Serena and Luca would like to rest, after traveling all night to get here."

"That would be wonderful, thank you," I tell her.

"Thank you, Mama," Luca says, kissing her on the cheek.

"I look forward to dinner tonight with my family all together again," Mr. Lomaglio says proudly as his wife leads us out of the room. She takes us out of the main house and across the property to a smaller building, what looks to be a guest house.

"Your father built this by hand," she explains. "We hope that Domenica will live here soon, to give her a little taste of independence before she takes the plunge and moves out on her own. If it were up to me, we could keep her here with us forever, to take care of her. But what she lacks in physical strength, she makes up for in spirit. Your sister is determined to make it on her own and live independently, even in her wheelchair."

"I have no doubt that she will. She's inherited her mother's stubbornness," Luca says, giving his mother a wink and a hug. She laughs.

"Settle in and relax, my loves. Tonight I will make dinner and we can talk some more, but I know you must be so tired," she says.

And with another hug for Luca and for me, she heads back to the main building, leaving Luca and I alone in this adorable, rustic guest house with a gorgeous view of the Apulian hillsides, dotted with olive trees. Luca turns to me and says, "Well, here it is: the place that made me who I am."

"It's just as impressive as you are," I tell him, grinning.

He leans in to kiss me, and instantly any idea of 'relaxing' goes straight out the window.

LUCA

*E*verything about her, the way she feels, smells, looks, it makes my heart warm, and I want the kiss to last forever. For one stupid, boyish moment, I feel like I *can* make it last forever, just me and her, away from everything. But finally, the kiss has to break, and even the sound of our lips moving apart makes my heart beat harder for her.

"No matter what light I see you in," I say, my voice thick and husky, "it always seems to come from inside you."

I watch Serena's soft lips smile slowly, and her eyes rove over my body with hunger in them. In this little room, I can feel that energy building again between us, an energy that neither of us can contain once we realize that we have a moment of privacy together. Even in public, I feel like I can hardly keep my hands off her, but now, there's nothing holding us back.

When she puts her hands on my broad chest and I grip her hips with my powerful, gentle grip, I feel that very feeling welling up inside me. But now, we have a moment to *breathe*. We can enjoy each other's presence, revel in the tense energy between us for a few moments. It's like drinking a fine wine slowly.

I kept the Costa's happy, and no one will ever breathe the location of my family home. Not that many know where that was in the first place. The Cleaners will never find us here, and I feel even safer than being in a safehouse. Here, I can protect all those I love.

But in this beautiful, perfect moment, I'm with my fiancé. Safe. In love.

And with several months to make up for.

I look into her eyes, and I see the beauty written in those nearly glowing irises that grow and shrink to focus on me. The light in the room is dim, but I can see every part of her clearly. It's so familiar, but so new. Her brow, her nose, her cheeks, her chin, her lips, all of her is the most beautiful sight I've ever looked at. I could stay here forever, just gazing at her, feeling like a teenager all over again.

They say you settle down as you get older, but with Serena, I've felt nothing but growing energy, more love for her, and more lust for her body.

"Every day we've been apart, I've wanted to ravage you," I whisper as her fingers tighten around my shirt, a soft, silent plea for me to take it off. "I've wanted to feel this. To feel you in my hands, *carissima*."

"I know," she says, her voice a harp's note to my ears. "Luca, I've dreamed about you so many times. I've woken up in the middle of the night so many times thinking you'd be right there beside me." My grip slides around to the small of her back, and I bring her into my embrace as she slides her hands around my torso and rests her head against my chest, listening to the strong, steady sound of my heartbeat.

I rest my chin on her head. "A life without you is not one worth living, Serena," I say. "For that time, I was dead."

She looks up at me, and I smile down at her. "But you give me life."

I bring my lips down to hers, and I can feel her sigh with need into the kiss. It starts slow, thoughtful. It's different than it was when we first reunited in that old safehouse, and I let Serena take her time in enjoying my body.

Tonight has meant so much. I feel more filled with love for Serena than ever before, and it's helped to ground us together in something that we can share besides struggle. Struggle has been so much of our relationship. We've fought together. We've run together. We've had to hide together.

So having a moment to step back and enjoy a moment of reality, a reality that's good and whole...it's a drink of cool water in the desert.

"I want to have more nights like tonight with you, Luca," she says after the kiss breaks and she grinds herself against me, hands roving up and down my body while her front presses into me. Her leg wraps around mine, and her hands go into my back pockets so she can look up at me with lidded eyes. "I want something stable. Family. *Our* family. I want it to grow and be something to be proud of."

"I want to give you all that and more," I say, "and I want every night filled with *this.*"

I walk her back to the bed, and she climbs back onto it, sitting on folded legs and looking up at me. She reaches up and gives my shirt a tug, and I smile. The fact that she gets so much pleasure out of my body never stops giving me pride. It's all the more motivation to keep my body as fit as I can, even when all this rough and tumble living settles down. I want to make myself perfect for those soft eyes every day.

She sits there like an angel, a single lamp's light behind her lighting the room, making her look like a true angel with a crown of golden hair spilling down her shoulders. In contrast, I loom over her with my broad shoulders and imposing, dark form, like a shadow.

I reach down to my shirt and pull it up over my body, drawing the move out slowly so she can take in every inch of my torso, every ripple, every muscle. She puts her slender hands to my stomach and brings her face to it to kiss it softly, nearly worshipping my body. Her hands run up my sides, and she turns her face to let her cheek rub up against my abs, feeling their warmth, nails tracing along my sides.

"Let me taste you," she begs me in a pleading tone I can't resist, "there's so much of you I want to feel inside me again."

"You can have it," I say, reaching down and running my hand through her golden hair, feeling how soft and thick her locks are, resisting the urge to take a fistful of it tight and fuck her senseless right then and there without hesitation, without restraint. "But I want to *see* you first."

She starts to take her shirt off hurriedly, but I kneel down onto the bed with her to stop her. My hands push hers aside, and I take hold of the soft fabric to lift it off. I let my warm hands brush against her skin as they go, and we move as if we're in a dream together, exploring each other's bodies like we have all the time in the world.

Because for just one night, we do.

I push her to her back after I've lifted the shirt off her, exposing that unbelievable body of hers, and I bend over her to start kissing her. I kiss her from her waist to her belly, then up to her breasts, still covered by her bra.

I let my hands grope them through the thick fabric, but it isn't long before I can't take it anymore. While I lean forward and tickle her neck with kisses, my hands reach behind her and unhook the thing and pull it off her. When I'm getting too excited and I'm starting to bite at her neck,

I push myself up to loom over her exposed form, drinking her with my eyes.

I hadn't noticed it before, but her breasts have started to swell from her pregnancy. That, or they're fuller and more ripe than ever before, and my cock swells tight in my pants.

I bring my mouth down to her nipples and let my breath wash over them. The sound of her excited gasp is music to my ears. I breathe on the other, holding my mouth so perilously close to her, teasing her painfully. She arches her back to push herself up to me, but I don't let her reach—I keep myself just out of reach, my hot breath the only thing stimulating those sensitive nipples.

They're stiff and begging to be toyed with, though, and soon, I give into the urge to devour them. I descend, first letting my tongue flick them while my hands grip her hips, holding her under my control as she lets out a desperate gasp. I take one of the swollen nubs between my teeth, letting the hard edges tease it harder and needier. She starts to pump her hips gently, hands scrambling for anywhere to hold onto, and I can swear she's about to come right then, her pants still on.

I let my tongue taste the soft skin of her breasts until I'm ready to reward her for her patience. I trail down her belly again, gently caressing her before I get to the button of her pants. With my teeth, I pop it open and grip the waist of her pants. She wiggles in a desperate effort to get out of them and help me pull them down, panties and all.

The sight of her hips stirs that animalistic energy within me. Their curve, the tone of her skin, that beautiful sanctuary where her legs meet, it's enough to drive me wild. But I know she's desperate to taste me as I am for her, and I won't deny my princess anything.

I stand up and look down at her as she squirms on the

bed completely naked, her olive skin beyond beautiful on the sheets in the dim light.

Once I'm up, her eyes flutter open, and she looks at me with anticipation, biting her lip as I open my own pants and slide them off. Normally, I'd just let the monstrous shaft of my cock spring free alone, but I want her to see every inch of my body in the same way I see hers. Nothing between us, nothing hiding from each other.

I want Serena, and Serena wants me.

So I kick my denim pants off my legs, revealing my pillar-like, muscular legs, and she crawls forward on the bed to my stiff, bulging cock. It's standing straight upright, extended toward her like a spear that she wraps her hand around, looking hungrily at the tip.

Her other hand goes to my balls, feeling their weight, holding them in her palm, letting out a soft sigh at how heavy and full of need they are.

She works her hands up and down my shaft slowly, and it's like an engine rumbling to life within me. I tilt my head back, closing my eyes and shutting out everything else but her touch. It's that much more intense of a feeling when I feel her tongue taste the tip of my dark, bulging crown.

Her hand slides up and down my shaft while her mouth plays with my crown. She runs her tongue around and over the tip, making my balls tense and my whole body feel warm. I reach forward and caress her hair in my hands, stroking it almost in a steady rhythm as she tastes me.

"I've missed this so much," she breathes over my manhood, and I can feel the desire to let loose and go wild in her every touch. She wants to work me until I release myself onto her, and it takes enormous willpower not to encourage her to do just that right now.

A few minutes more of this, though, and I don't know if I'll be so willing to hold back.

Finally, I feel her warm, soft lips kiss the tip of my cock while her hands lavish the shaft with attention. I hear her moaning softly into it as her lips part and she flicks the tip with her tongue. She takes the crown into her mouth and starts running the very tip of her tongue around the edges of my swollen crown. Even though it's my most sensitive part of my body, my cock is tough, and the faster the motions of her hand get, the more her teeth graze my tip, the more it excites me. I feel like my body's tension is unlocking itself bit by bit, and it's wild to me that this tiny woman in front of me can have such an effect on my massive body.

She starts to lick the bottom of my crown on the underside of my cock, right where it meets the beginning of my shaft. I smile as I realize she's been learning from how I tease her when my tongue is deep in her pussy, trailing up until it can toy with her clit.

I've taught this woman terrible things, and I'll teach her more and more, if I have my way.

Her tongue gets more adventurous, and she starts taking more of my shaft into her mouth, making sure to wrap her lips around my whole cock. It's not easy to take everything into her mouth, but the more of my cock's weight she feels resting on her tongue, the more she desires me. The more she wants to take in. The more she's willing to try.

"Your eyes are bigger than your mouth, Serena," I chuckle before a quick jolt of heat rushes up my cock. Serena answers me with a hungry sigh. She's not going to be turned away that easily.

She starts moving her tongue like a ripple, putting pressure as far back down my cock as she can reach and slowly dragging it up the underside of my cock. My crown is at the back of her mouth, kissing the soft, hot roof of her mouth so far back. With her free hand, Serena massages my balls, and I know she's coaxing me, begging me, desperately wanting to taste me.

I often take my cock out of her mouth at this point and thrust it deep into her pussy to finish. But tonight, Serena is working hard, and the hot feeling running through my whole body tells me it's paying off. I'll make it pay off for her.

Hell, I'll give her that and so, so much more.

I let myself lose my concentration and look down at Serena. The mere sight of her is enough to push me over the edge. Her golden hair sits beautifully on her shoulders, getting messy as she relentlessly worships my cock. Her eyes aren't closed—she's looking up at me, love in her eyes as she sucks my dark pillar. This is the love of my life, the most beautiful woman I've ever laid eyes on...and she's getting as much out of this as I am.

Soon, her free hand leaves my balls and slides down to her legs, where she starts to run it up and down her lower lips, and her eyes close again. Her lips tighten, and she gives a soft little yelp into my cock. I can hear the wet sound of her touching herself, and knowing that being on her knees at my cock has put her in this dizzy, lustful state makes me release.

My balls tighten, and my cock gets tenser than ever. Serena can tell what's happening, and she gets a firm grip on me for fear that I should pull away. I could give her hair a squeeze to make her back off and let me ruin her face, her perfect body, all with my seed, but I want her to follow through with what she's gotten herself into.

White-hot bliss wells up inside me, a tension that's almost painful and swelling with every half-second. Finally, my mouth hangs open, and I release a shot of hot seed into Serena's mouth, and the groan I let out is almost in harmony with the sigh of delight she gasps. My cock throbs, releasing more of me into her, but Serena doesn't pull herself away, nor does she let up—her hands keep working my shaft while she keeps my crown in her lips, taking in every bit of me I have to give.

She sighs in deep, blissful satisfaction as my cock throbs, and she runs her tongue up my shaft one last time before taking her lips from me. As she lets her fingers play up my cock one last time, a final spurt of my seed empties itself onto her chest, and she sits back, letting her head fall back while she props herself up on her elbows and smiling contentedly.

She's proud of herself.

I feel heat glowing around me as I breathe raggedly. My knees are weak, but not so weak that I can't give her what she's got coming next.

"You're smug," I say with a smile, kneeling over her and massaging my cock with my own hand.

"Maybe a little," she says with a wink. "I missed...every-thing about that."

I grab her hips and push her forward while I crawl onto the bed, and she gasps as I put my hands on her sensitive inner thighs. I grip her carefully, brushing the flesh with my thumbs while gazing down at her.

"Enjoy it while it lasts," I growl, and she starts to breathe a little faster as I part her legs. "Because if you think I'm done with you, you've got another thing coming."

With that, I bring my face down to her pussy and breathe in the scent, and I feel my cock twitch again, despite having just released itself. Serena is enough to get me going all over again in hardly any time at all.

I let my tongue out, and licks the honey off Serena's lips. It's the same sweet taste as I remember, made all the sweeter for how long I've been away from her, away from her honey. The strongest liquor in the world can't compare to her and what she does to me.

My tongue tastes her again, and again going deeper

each time, and each swipe earns a gasp from Serena—her hands push into my hair and grip my head, her hips thrust up into my face, and she throws her head back.

Tasting me has made her so ready, so needy, that she's already gotten my face doused in her wetness. My hands take hold of her hips and keep them down while I go to work on her poor lips. I kiss her, pressing my lips to her pussy while my tongue ventures deep into her, drawing up more honey that she pours out for me and using it to torment her clit with each stroke.

The taste makes my whole mouth water for more. Between the come on her chest and her come on my face, we're a mess, and the room feels hot, but we're lost in each other. Dizzy, drunk, whatever you want to call it, we can't keep ourselves off one another any longer. My hands take in every curve of her hips and her legs while I feast on her.

She squirms under me, desperately trying to move around and thrust harder as if that would help her finish any faster, but I control the situation perfectly. My grip on her is tight, and I show her that she's mine by keeping her down on the bed, subjecting her to my mouth on her pussy. I can feel her starting to tighten already, her pussy starting to wetten further and further in anticipation.

My rhythm gets steady. I dart out to her clit, stroke, and retreat, then over again, teasing her on her clit for just a split second before leaving her, and soon, that builds up little by little until she thrusts her hips up harder than ever before, and I release her to hold her up by her ass.

She lets out a silent scream of pleasure, holding my hair tight as she comes, and I bury my mouth and my face in her folds while they pulse and tighten around me, her whole body coming beautifully in my hands and all over my face.

"Oh Luca!" she breathes out, panting with desire, but I

don't respond. Instead, I start stroking her again as if I'd never stopped.

I go faster this time, sometimes deeper, exploring more of her that I'd dreamt of so many nights while wishing I was at her side, protecting her. I keep going until I feel that tension building up again, and I follow it through to release. With one orgasm having come through in careless bliss, more come more easily, and I drive them all with my tongue until I can hardly feel my face.

My mouth works her so long that I'm stiff and ready again.

Even though I've lost track of the orgasms wracking her body, I hear her give a whimper of complaint when I take my face from her lips and crawl up her body to pin her down by the wrists. Just as she opens her mouth to protest, I silence her with a wet, hot kiss at the same time that I drive my cock into her pussy.

She sucks in a breath when I enter her, and we kiss sloppily while I start bucking into her. We're both so overwhelmed with stimulation that we can hardly tell up from down anymore. All I know is that my hard cock is inside her pussy where it feels best, and her hot insides are wet and welcoming to me.

Our bodies pressed up against each other, I pick up a steady rhythm, ramming into her and grinding up against every spot I know to drive her wild. I pull back to loom over her, and my hands go to her breasts, thumbs toying with those nipples I bit at when we first got started. That feels like ages ago, we've gotten so lost in the moment, and my heart pounds furiously.

She looks up at me like she can't believe how soon I'm ready for her again, and the mix of excitement and worry on her face tells me everything I need to give her another night she'll never forget. I hold nothing back, savoring the feeling of her breasts while I take her, freely letting my own pleasure roil up into an unstoppable wave that soon starts shaking me from the groin up to my chest.

"Serena," I moan, and I try to bring more words to my mouth, but my mind is just a mess of lust and desire, and that's all I can say, over and over again until I feel my balls start to grow tight again.

I pour myself into her, letting out a ragged groan with my second orgasm as my whole body shudders. I've been through fights that put my life at risk, but nothing is as intense and fierce a rush as coming into my woman.

I hear her delighted sigh through the haze of my orgasm, and finally, still hard inside her, I feel the last of my seed emptying into her.

Slowly, gently, I lower myself to her, and we stare into each other's eyes for a few moments. Finally, I pull out of her slowly, slow enough that it doesn't hurt her, and I turn her so that she can spoon into me comfortably.

I slip my hand between her legs and massage her, feeling her whole body tingle while I gently bring her down from the rush, and I kiss her neck.

"I meant what I said," I whisper into her ear as I feel her breathing slowly, glowing.

"Meant what?"

"I want to give you nights like this every day," I say, my voice deep and rough. "And I'll stop at nothing to make that happen."

While I feel Serena wiggling into me and getting ready to doze off into sleep, messy and hot as we are, I know my words to be a truer desire than anything I've felt in my life.

The only question is just how much will get in our way.

"You look beautiful," Luca assures me for probably the hundredth time this morning. I'm standing in the middle of the tiny combined kitchen and living room space of the guest house, looking down worriedly at my outfit. It's just starting to get hot here in Italy, and considering I arrived here at the Lomaglio residence wearing my filthy sweatshirt and jeans, it was high time for a change of wardrobe. Unfortunately, I can't even dream of fitting into Mrs. Lomaglio's clothing—she is both much shorter and considerably rounder than I am. So Domenica, being the ever-helpful and generous girl she is, offered me some of her clothes for now, until I have time to pick out some new stuff for myself.

But Domenica is a seventeen-year-old girl who is very, very slender and not at all pregnant, so her clothing is a little bit tight and youthful for my body. I'm currently wearing one of her dresses, a knee-length blue frock with white flowers and spaghetti straps, along with a pair of Mrs. Lomaglio's sandals. Everything fits to some degree, but I still feel pretty weird. It's strange, you'd think after wearing a ton of hand-me-down donated clothes at the women's shelter, this would be second nature. But somehow, it's weirder when you know the people whose clothing it is. Or maybe it's just weird because I only barely know them. We just met, and now I'm living in their guest house and wearing their clothes.

Oh, and I'm pregnant with their long-lost son's baby.

Just a recipe for awkwardness, all around. But in their defense, the Lomaglios have been overwhelmingly kind and generous, constantly offering me more food, more drinks, asking if I'm comfortable, if there's anything else I need. It's very, very nice of them, but after spending so much time with my own uptight, closed-off mother for so long, it's a shock to my system to spend time with such a warm, loving family. It's not that my own mother doesn't love me, of course, she just has a very different way of showing it—and by that I mean she rarely shows it at all.

Luca's family, on the other hand, is almost over the top. They hug each other, they touch each other's faces, they profess their love like it's the most natural thing in the world. It's something I never would have pictured for Luca when I first met him. He seemed so tough and cool. *Too* cool to have come from such a cuddly family. But the more I get to know him, the clearer it is to me that this is how he grew up. He may be a powerful, imposing, even dangerous man, but underneath that jagged exterior, love and loyalty come before all else.

"I'm not sure my boobs quite fit in this dress," I mutter, looking down at my unusually impressive cleavage in this tiny dress. Luca walks over and puts his arms around me, smiling.

"Looks pretty good to me," he remarks cheekily.

I roll my eyes. "Well, of course you'd say that. I just don't want to look scandalous. Especially not with your family around. I'm trying to make a good impression here."

"Oh, don't worry about that. They already love you," he says, kissing me on the cheek. "Now, come on. I want to get to Alberobello before the gelato stands start closing for the afternoon. Don't you?"

"Oh yes, please," I laugh, letting him sweep me away out into the Italian sunshine. His father is away at work—he has a job in an office nowadays. Mrs. Lomaglio is busy cleaning, cooking, and fussing over Domenica, as usual, and Domenica is wrapped up in studying for her online classes. This leaves Luca and I all day to ourselves to explore and relax, finally spend some quality time together. We climb into the car and ride off through the rolling golden hills, holding hands over the center console.

The scenery outside is absolutely stunning. I can see why Luca remembers this place so fondly. It looks like a postcard, but not exactly the kind of landscape I would normally think of when someone brings up Italy.

It's less green than Tuscany, less mountainous than the northern regions. But it has its own wild, humble beauty. Birds flutter from one massive clump of thorny under-brush to the next, chirping and singing. Golden-greenish fields full of brown-and-white cows. Endless blue skies without a cloud in sight. Piled stone walls about knee-height frame the roads on either side.

I can perfectly imagine young Luca running free in these fields, climbing trees, kicking a soccer ball around, getting into trouble. The thought makes me smile.

It's a lovely drive out to the little town of Alberobello, which first appears on the horizon as a pearly-white spot in the distance beneath an incredibly lush blue sky.

Luca explains that this little town is home to several examples of historical architecture called *trulli* like what we saw when we were escaping in our latest high speed chase.

Once we park and start walking around, I can see why

he brought me here. The houses are bright white, made of rock and built straight into the limestone, with cone-shaped gray roofs. The streets are lined with them, and many of the *trulli* have been transformed into little pottery shops and art galleries, while other buildings are still in use as residences.

Colorful shelves jut out from beneath round windows, holding pots of flowers, number plaques, sometimes surnames. Tourists are around every corner, professional photographers traveling from all over the world to snap photos of the interesting architecture and gorgeous colors. It's nice to be able to enjoy the interesting architecture, this time around.

As we wander down the tiny cobblestone streets, Luca turns to me with a grin.

"What do you think?" he asks, as if there's any other answer to give.

"It's amazing," I tell him, shaking my head in awe. "I've never seen anything like this."

"Crazy to think I grew up just down the road from this."

"Yeah! When I think about where I grew up, this seems like some kind of fantasy land."

"New York has its charms, too. There are certainly much worse places to live," he says, shrugging. "But for me, this will always be home."

"I'm happy that you grew up somewhere like this. Everything you've seen, everything you've been through—all of that has made you into the amazing man you are today," I say, kissing the back of his hand.

"Come on, you sweet, sentimental woman, let's get you some gelato," he says.

We head down the street to a village square which looks to be meticulously maintained, full of tourists oohing and ahhing over the picturesque surroundings. We sit down at a little cafe, taking an outdoors table so we can people-watch and enjoy the sunshine.

Luca gets pistachio ice cream and I get hazelnut, and after that we order coffee and pastries. We sit there, just talking and soaking up the sun, being lazy and happy together, for what must be hours.

Finally, when the little woman running the cafe comes out to gently warn us that they're closing up shop soon, we thank her and head back to the car.

We take our time driving back to the Lomaglio property, stopping on the side of the road to explore an open field, to snap a picture together in front of an especially photogenic olive tree. We're acting like embarrassing, goofy tourists in love, even though Luca knows this place by heart, and it's wonderful.

By the time we make it back home, we're both sunkissed and tired and unable to stop smiling.

I don't know what the future holds for us, and I know this lovely dream has to end at some point, but for now, I'm just drinking in every last drop of happiness I can get. Luca is alive, he's in my arms, and I can't imagine anything better than this.

We wash up and get changed for dinner, heading over to the main house. As soon as we step through the door, we're greeted by the smells of delicious cheeses, meats, fish, and pasta Luca's mother has been preparing all day.

I have to wonder if she really goes all out like this every evening, or if she's just amping up the menu because Luca is here. Either way, I am sure as hell not going to complain. Especially since I'm eating for two.

At the dinner table, we tell Luca's family about the amazing day we've had, and I gush about how beautiful the countryside is, how friendly all the people are—including them.

I'm feeling so relaxed that I even let Domenica pour me

the tiniest glass of red wine, which I sip contentedly. I've never been a huge drinker, but being pregnant, I've really missed having some wine or a cocktail every now and then.

And of course, since they're Italian, they know exactly what wine to pair with what kind of meal. If there's one thing I have learned from my brief time here in Italy, it's that even when money is tight, Italians don't skimp on the quality of their diet.

They might skip buying a new dress or a new car, but they always eat like kings.

And I can *certainly* appreciate that.

As I'm digging into a plate of pasta, the family starts sharing stories about what Luca was like as a young boy. Apparently, he got into trouble in school—a lot. Not for anything too criminal, but he was very energetic and prone to pranking people.

"One time, he put a cricket in his teacher's purse," Mrs. Lomaglio says, clucking her tongue. "The poor woman almost had a heart attack right there in the middle of class."

"Oh, that's awful," I laugh, playfully hitting Luca on the arm. He shrugs, looking a little sheepish as he reaches for another scoop of pasta.

"*She* was awful. She used to make me write with my right hand even though I'm left-handed. Anytime I would go back to using my left hand, she would slap my wrist with a ruler!" he says defensively. "She was my least favorite teacher."

"Oh, was that Maestra Mancini?" Domenica asks, wrinkling her nose.

"Yes!" Luca exclaims. "Don't tell me you had to deal with her, too. How old is that woman? Is she still teaching?"

"Ugh, she was my least favorite teacher, too. And yes,

she's probably still teaching now. I don't think that woman will ever die. She's immortal," Domenica giggles.

"That's not nice," her mother scolds, though I can tell she's fighting a smile.

"Luca was such a troublemaker. So much energy. Always falling out of trees and catching little animals. Do you remember when you brought home that turtle?" Mr. Lomaglio says.

Luca chuckles. "Yeah, of course. I loved that little guy."

"What was his name again?" his mother asks.

"Baffo," Luca answers, laughing. "I kept him in a cardboard box with plants I picked inside it. I had the hardest time trying to figure out what to feed him without asking you and having you find out I was hiding a turtle in my room."

"I don't remember that," Domenica says, frowning.

"You were just a baby back then," Luca says. "I think that might have been why I thought I could get away with it—Mama and Papa were too busy taking care of you to notice me sneaking food out of the pantry to feed to Baffo."

"Oh, but I did find him," Mrs. Lomaglio says, rolling her eyes. "By accident. I was cleaning your room one day, looking for your soccer jersey while you were at school, when I tripped over that cardboard box and out came Baffo. I screamed so loud the neighbors called the police, remember?"

"They called me, too. They thought someone had broken into the house," Mr. Lomaglio says, shaking his head and grinning. "I rushed home from work only to find my wife, baby, two policemen, and a turtle in my living room. I have never been so relieved and confused in my life."

"Oh, I bet you were in big trouble when you got home from school," I remark to Luca.

"I don't think I was allowed to play outside for a week," he says.

"Served you right for scaring me so much," his mother chuckles.

"I think Baffo was probably much happier as a free turtle than living in a cardboard box in my bedroom, anyway," Luca admits, grinning.

"Oh!" I exclaim suddenly, putting my hands on my stomach. There's a weird sensation in my belly, something bigger than just butterflies, bigger than just nausea. I look over at Luca, who's looking at me with concern. A smile jumps to my face. "I think the baby just kicked!"

Mrs. Lomaglio gasps and comes rushing over, with her husband and daughter trailing after her, all of them eager to put their hands on my stomach in case it happens again.

"Maybe it's a sign that the baby wants to be called Baffo," Domenica giggles.

"I don't think that's on our shortlist of names," Luca says, laughing.

We wait quietly, patiently for a few minutes. Every one of them has a hand on my barely-protruding stomach. At first, I think it might have been a fluke, just indigestion or something. But then—it happens again! Everyone gasps, and Mrs. Lomaglio almost starts to cry with happiness.

"This is a cause for celebration!" she declares, rushing off to the kitchen and emerging again with a plate of sweet pastries.

I have no idea how this woman cooks and bakes so much all the time. She's like a machine. But we all gladly partake of the sweets, gushing to each other about how excited we are for the baby.

I know it will be awhile, but I'm already so excited to meet this kid, no matter how crazy the world around us may be.

After dinner, we help Mrs. Lomaglio tidy up, and then

head off to bed. I fall asleep smiling, lying next to the man I love, the man I thought I lost, who came back to me by a miracle.

I dream the same dreams I've been having for the past few months—Luca, the baby, and me, living happily together in a cozy house. Just doing the dishes together, cooking dinner together, spending time in each other's company like we should be.

And when I wake up early the next morning, I trot out to the porch to watch the bees and butterflies flitting around in the garden. The plants are all growing high and healthy, ready for the harvest. It's a modest life the Lomaglios lead out here, but they're comfortable. They're happy.

They don't have much beyond the necessities, but they eat well, they're as healthy as can be considering the parents' ages and Domenica's illness. They love each other unabashedly, and they spend their days in quiet joy, especially now that Luca is here.

I can't help but think about how much I envy them. This simple, humble, beautiful life they lead out here in the Apulian countryside—it's like a dream.

I imagine what it would be like for Luca and I to live this way. To find a little house of our own in the golden hills, plant a garden, grow some of our own food and go to the farmer's market or the grocery store for the rest. Eat wholesome, delicious, lovingly-cooked food. Watch the sunrises and sunsets together. Drink wine. Eat cheese and fruit. Drive down the winding roads and find new places to kiss each other under the bright blue sky.

It's everything I never knew I wanted. Maybe it's not the most exciting way to live, but when I really think about it, I've probably had enough excitement to last me a lifetime.

I just want to be comfortable and happy and

surrounded by love—and I can't imagine a better place for our little baby to grow up. Especially with Luca's family so close by. It just seems perfect.

After the sun rises, Luca joins me on the porch, kissing me on the cheek and wishing me a good morning. I'm just about to tell him about my dream, about how wonderful it would be to stay here and build a life together—when my phone suddenly buzzes in my lap. I pick it up and read the text message I've just received.

And immediately, an alarm bell starts sounding off in my head.

Something is wrong. Very, very wrong.

"What's the matter?" I ask, stepping forward to her, reading the concern and confusion written on her face. "Did you get some news from back home?"

"I...I don't know," she says, glancing up at me. "It's a message from my mom. But it's just an X." She shakes her head, forcing a smile. "Never mind. It was probably just an accident. I'm jumping at shadows. It's just kind of weird to hear from her. Feels like we're in a whole different world all the way out here, and the past few weeks have been so crazy that it feels a lot longer than it has been."

I'm not entirely convinced that's all that bothers Serena, but I don't want to push her, so with a raised eyebrow I nod, then soften my expression into a smile and come to give her a hug as she puts her phone away.

"That's understandable. You've been through a lot. Give it some time, and everything will settle down in your mind —a clear head is important in times like this."

She nods, taking those words to reassure herself as much as I try to reassure her. "Right." Brushing a strand of hair out of her face, she flutters her eyes up at me. "So, what's the plan for today?"

"Besides the massive breakfast that's about to start smelling heavenly inside?" I say, nodding back to the house, where I can see the silhouettes of my parents through the reflective glass moving around in the kitchen.

"Right, assuming I survive another feast," she says with a laugh, and I help her up to her feet, even though she doesn't need it.

"I convinced them to hold back from cooking dinner for us again so we could get out for a little time to ourselves," I say, holding her around the waist and beaming down at her. "I found out that an old friend of mine opened a restaurant in town, so we need to get down there and see whether it's bad enough that I can give him a hard time."

"*Don't!*" she laughs, slapping me on the chest before I scoop her into a hug, chuckling and peppering her cheek with kisses. "Seriously, be nice! Let's not accidentally make any rivals while we're here."

"I'm kidding—he was this big musclebound oaf back in the day, so it's funny to see him running a little restaurant now. But he's a good man," I say, giving her a light squeeze.

"Sounds like you," she says with a teasing quirk of an eyebrow.

"Exactly, which is why I'm sure it will be the best pasta you've ever had. But that doesn't mean I won't make fun of him while I have the chance."

～

*L*ater that day, my old friend doesn't prove me wrong.

The little restaurant he inherited from his father is on a plaza in one of the villages nearby, and it's a cozy hole in the wall that tourists usually wouldn't notice unless they knew what to look for. There are about ten tables in the place—not too shabby for this area. The floors are old, dark wood, and there are pictures from local history and important people all around the walls, along with a fireplace toward the back.

"This place is cozy," Serena remarks as we sit at one of the little tables, watching a few more people trickle in for dinnertime. It's a mix of younger people like us on romantic dates and older couples who are probably regulars or friends of the family—that's how places like this stay open.

"The family always did have an eye for interior design, as much as you can call it that around here," I say, beaming around the place.

She casts a look toward the kitchen, then whispers to me, "You don't think we're crowding the place, do you?" She tears off a piece of the tough bread that's been laid in front of us. "We ordered our food more than half an hour ago."

"That's normal, I promise," I say after taking a drink of the soda in front of me. If Serena isn't drinking, I'd rather not either, despite my friend's insistence that he give us a bottle of some of his oldest wine. "Service times in Italy are nothing like they are back in the USA. It's something you just...get used to. Kind of like how lunch and dinner can be all-day events, you usually go to a restaurant expecting to just sit around and talk for a long time before anything else happens."

She looks thoughtful for a few moments, then nods slowly. "Okay, I get it. I don't know if I like it yet, but I get it," she adds with a playful smile, and I grin, crossing my legs with hers under the table.

"I think it's more relaxed," I say with a shrug of my shoulders. "I always felt rushed in places in America, but you know, the country's changing. Who knows what it'll be like a few years from now."

"Maybe more than that, down here," she points out.

I nod, looking around at the old building. "A great deal more than that, true."

Before much longer, though, our food arrives, and we start eating—and I'm proud to see that my friend hasn't made a liar of me. Serena eats the food ravenously, giving me a thumbs-up between mouthfuls of pasta.

She's having *orecchiette alle cime di rapa*, to be precise. It's a traditional southern dish made with pan-fried broccoli, anchovies, chili, and garlic. A little unusual for the American tastes, but Serena seems to be appreciating it without hesitation.

It makes me happy to see her taken care of like this. I worry sometimes that all the stress of running around so much will wear on her, but she seems to have more energy than ever. And as my old friend cleans the bar up at the counter, he gives me a knowing grin with a glance to Serena when she's not looking.

I smirk and wave him off, and Serena looks up at me, wiping her mouth with her napkin.

"What?"

"Nothing," I say with a chuckle, "just old friends teasing me." I give her a once-over and add, "You make a good impression around here."

That makes her blush, and she shoves more food into her mouth to avoid acknowledging the fact that she's the most beautiful woman in the whole village.

But as the dinner goes on and we get closer to the end of our plates, Serena takes her phone out and sets it on the side of the table, periodically checking it.

I ignore it at first, but once it's out and on the table, I notice that Serena's demeanor seems to have taken an anxious turn. In fact, she's seemed a little tense all day—the easy going, loving energy between us so far has seemed muted ever since she got that message in the morning.

"You're looking at the message again, aren't you?" I say as I finish my dinner, setting my fork down and crossing my arms to rest on the table.

"Sorry, I know it's rude, I-"

I wave it off, shaking my head. "Oh come on, I don't care about that, Serena—I can tell something's bothering you. Did your mother have bad news to give you? Is she okay?"

She looks up at me with a little relief, as though she's glad to know that I'm only worried about her wellbeing first and foremost. Done with her food, she pushes it aside while I scoot my chair to sit beside her and look at the message she shows me.

"Here, look at this." She holds out her phone to me, and I take the little thing in my hand. She has an app pulled up —a secure, encrypted messaging app that makes it difficult to trace without the kind of resources only a government agency might have.

The little glowing screen displays a message that looks like it's from Serena's mother Luisa. But it's nothing. It's just one, simple little letter. An X. Probably accidentally hit it while she was getting dressed or something.

"Am I missing something?" I ask, handing the phone back to her. "I don't understand, it looks like an accidental text from Luisa."

Serena looks at me with increasingly worried eyes. "Mom outright *refuses* to use texting, she always has. She's like, you know, old-fashioned. She's always just called me and kept me talking for an hour or even hand-written a letter. The few times I've ever gotten a text from her, it's just been something quick like 'call me.' I've been trying to get her to get better at texting for years, but she never budges."

I furrow my brow. Any other time, I wouldn't worry about something like this, but now of all times, I have to admit that just about anything could make me suspicious.

"Then why just an X? Why not send you just a normal greeting?" I ask, crossing my arms.

Serena shakes her head, still looking at the screen. "No... It's that... When I was younger, and I first got a cell-phone, she hated the idea. She thought I was going to spend all my days on it and get bad self-esteem. The only reason she let me get it, is in case of emergencies. I guess because of dad's job. So when we agreed to get a family package, she made me promise to text her with one letter if I was in trouble." She trails off, looking to me with worried eyes.

I frown, rubbing my chin with a hand for a moment before I reply.

"An X," I guess, and Serena nods.

"But that was for you texting her, and that was a long time ago. Do you really think it's not just coincidence?"

Serena frowns, looking at the phone again.

"I want to think it's a coincidence, but she hasn't gotten back to me since. Do you think this is her secret SOS?"

"Luisa isn't totally in the dark. Through some of my friends back home, I had her updated on some very basic details about what's going on—she knows she can't reach you by letter-mail right now or make international calls." I smile warmly and add, "We have eyes on her, too, remember. She's probably safe and sound, and like you said, probably got frustrated trying to type up a text."

"True, that's possible," she admits, not looking totally convinced. "But that still doesn't explain why she hasn't gotten back to me. Gosh, that sounds overly paranoid, doesn't it?" She leans an elbow on the table, resting her head on her hand and rubbing her forehead.

"Not at all," I assure her, giving her shoulder a squeeze

and massaging her neck with one hand a little. "You have every right to be worried for your mother. This is why we take precautions. Tomorrow, I'll get in touch with my men and have someone check up on her to make sure everything is okay."

She smiles at me, looking appreciative. "I'd like that. Thanks, Luca." She looks back down to the phone, pursing her lips a little. "I'll just try texting her again, and let her know that I am going to die in pasta heaven."

"*Bene*," I say and wave down the server to beckon them over to us. "In the meantime, though, don't think you're getting out of here without dessert," I say, a smile on my face, but when I look back to Serena, I see her looking at her phone with worry.

I listen to my lover when I see that kind of worry on her face.

And whatever the real situation is with that message from her mother, I don't have a good feeling about it.

"Oh god, I'm stuffed," I groan, sitting back in the chair. Across the table, Luca laughs, setting his fork down and taking a sip of his red wine.

"I'm a little jealous," he says, looking back to me and grinning. "I wish I had the excuse to eat for two."

I pat my belly. "Well, don't be too jealous. I think the whole getting-to-eat-a-lot thing is really only a fair trade-off for the constant exhaustion and nausea."

"How has that been lately, by the way?" he asks, leaning forward and furrowing his brow. I love the way he does this—effortlessly transitions from goofing around to taking me very seriously. I can tell that underneath his jokes, he's often worried about me. Worried about the baby.

He keeps his concerns to himself most of the time, probably because he doesn't want to give me anything else to fret about, but I know him better than anyone. I can see when something is bothering him.

I can feel it.

"Much better, actually. I think being around your

family and… well, you, has helped a lot with the sickness," I assure him, reaching across to take his hand.

He nods slowly, and I can see the cogs turning in his mind.

"I'm sorry, Serena," he says suddenly, his face going solemn, his voice lowering.

I tilt my head to one side, confused at this sudden apology.

"Sorry? For what?"

He looks back up at me, those bright green eyes full of feeling.

"It's my fault. How rough the past few months have been for you. I should have been here, by your side, helping you all along. I feel like I abandoned you at the worst possible time. You're carrying my baby—our baby—and for all that time you had to do it alone. I can't help but think that's the reason you were so sick. You were stressed out and scared and lonely, just like anyone would be in that situation. I should have been there, Serena. I'm so sorry."

I give him a smile, shaking my head.

"Luca, I don't blame you for anything. You know that, right? None of this is your fault."

"If you hadn't met me, gotten tangled up in this mess—"

"Then I wouldn't be carrying this baby," I interject. "I wouldn't be in love with the most amazing man in the world. I wouldn't be here right now, sitting in a genuine Italian restaurant eating genuine Italian pasta and drinking a very small, very cautious glass of red wine."

I shrug and squeeze his hand.

"Luca. You have to understand: I don't regret anything. I don't regret any single thing of what has happened since you came back into my life that day at Bathing Beauty. Hell yeah, it's been difficult. Of course, it has. But it's worth it. Everything—every hardship, every moment of fear, every misstep, it's led me here. With you. And I can't think of anywhere else I would rather be right now."

He stands up and walks over to help me up, kissing my hand like a true gentleman. Gazing into my eyes with pure devotion, he says, "I've never met anyone quite like you. So strong. So brave. Our child is lucky to have you as a mother. And I am lucky to call you my fiancée."

We pay the bill and stroll back out onto the cobblestone streets of this quaint little countryside village. The sun is setting over the golden hills, casting pink and orange streaks through the sky. There's a pleasant breeze keeping us from getting too hot in the balmy, early summer evening.

Hand in hand, we walk down the street toward the sound of live music playing, both of us wondering what the commotion is all about. We turn a corner into a village square ringed with vendors selling gelato, wine, spritzers, *sgagliozze*, and *cannoli*. There's a band of lively musicians playing folk music while in the center of the square, a big gathering of people are dancing, some in couples, others in groups of young women.

There are many more people sitting at little tables arranged on the perimeter, watching the dance while they sip wine and chat. It's an almost magical scene: the music, the laughter, the smells of salt and sweetness mingling in the air.

Luca turns to me with an adventurous, mischievous look on his handsome face.

"What?" I ask warily. He grins and pulls me along behind him as we join the dancers. "Oh no, Luca, I'm not much of a dancer!"

"Don't worry," he says, grinning, "I am."

He takes the lead, spinning me around through the village square, teaching me how to find the beat and move fluidly with the music, without ever saying a word of instruction.

At first, I'm awkward, my face burning bright pink with embarrassment. Everyone around me seems to have taken dance lessons their entire lives or something. They all move freely and smoothly, never missing a single beat, whereas I feel like someone's weird grandpa at a family barbeque.

But gradually, between the little bit of wine I drank and Luca's patient faith in me, I begin to loosen up. And as soon as I turn off my brain and just go with the flow, it's like the music takes over my body, and suddenly I can dance. Maybe not like a professional, but at least nobody is laughing at my awkward moves.

Before long, I'm grinning and laughing, not giving a single damn about who may be watching or judging me.

After all, when I take into stock what's really going on here, how can I be self-conscious?

I'm dancing in a picturesque Italian village with the man of my dreams!

When the song ends, we walk over to a vendor to buy a *cannolo* to share, and on the way to find ourselves a table to sit at, a few men suddenly swarm over to us, laughing and shouting. For a split second, I'm afraid, until I see them all smiling and calling Luca by name. Luca's face lights up when he sees them, opening his arms to embrace each one of them. They begin to speak very quickly in Italian, but I can sort of follow along if I pay attention.

"Luca! Is that really you, my brother?"

"Holy shit, man! You used to be shorter than me, what happened?"

"What are you doing back in Apulia?"

"How long has it been? Ten years?"

Luca answers each of them happily, laughing and clapping them on the shoulder as he reacquaints himself with old friends. If there's one thing I'm figuring out very quickly, it's that Luca was very well-known in these little villages.

When I think about how much of a ballsy troublemaker he was when he was a kid, it makes sense. He's always been so charismatic and fun to be around, of course everyone back home would adore him.

He spends a few minutes chatting with them, introducing me as his fiancée, giving them a very sanitized version of the events which led us here.

Luckily, all his old friends appear to have been drinking, so they don't ask any questions. They just seem happy enough to see Luca again. They don't need all the gritty details.

After a while, they head off, presumably to keep drinking and meet up with some women.

Luca and I eat our dessert, listening to the music while he explains to me how he knows each one of the men who just came up to us. It turns out that most of them were schoolboys together, and they took part in many of Luca's pranks on teachers and other students. He assures me that they never did anything too destructive, but they were definitely not teacher's pets, either.

It's so strange to me, hearing how silly he used to be as a kid. By the time I met him, he was already so mature by comparison to all the guys I had classes with. He seemed like an adult, like he was world-weary and knowledgeable about everything there was to know.

But I guess the life he led, leaving home to work hard for his Uncle Carlo in America, must have changed him. Roughed up those soft edges he used to have. Now that we're so comfortable together, I can see little pieces of that old silliness and lightheartedness shining through sometimes. But it does break my heart to think of how quickly he had to grow up as a teenager. None of it was his fault, but he was the one who paid the price.

The band strikes up another song, this one slower and more romantic. Luca takes my hand and leads me out onto the dance floor again, pulling me close.

We spin slowly together, cheek to cheek, his hand on the small of my back. With the tempo change, most of the single dancers have gone to sit down, leaving just the two of us and a few other couples.

The singer croons about old lovers rediscovering one another, about old vows being renewed, about being together forever and ever in love. It's enough to make my hormonal heart beat a little faster, and I find myself fighting off the tears in my eyes. At the end of the song, Luca kisses me softly on the lips, his hand cradling the back of my head like I'm something delicate, something precious.

He rests his forehead against mine and whispers, "I love you, Serena."

"I love you, too," I answer, smiling.

As we walk off the dance floor, I see several people seated at the tables looking at their partners with lovesick eyes. They scoot closer to each other, hold hands. There's definitely been a shift in mood. Where before the square was filled with high-spirited laughter, now there's a seriousness, a sense of heavy romance in the air. And the two of us are affected the same way.

Luca leads me down the winding streets, away from the bright lights strung up from lamppost to lamppost, away from the music and the smells and the crowds of people. The further we walk, the more alone we are.

We arrive at a lovely, perfectly-manicured little park on the edge of the village. It overlooks the cliffside below, the hilly fields dotted with grazing animals and flowering bushes. The moon now hangs high in the velvety dark sky, only barely illuminating the face of the man I love, his flawless features nearly glowing before me.

He leans in to kiss me, softly at first, then more passionately. He pulls me in tight, our bodies pressed together so I can feel every rippling muscle. His hands slide down over my hips and around to cup my ass.

His tongue pushes gently into my mouth and I moan, feeling my body warm with excitement at his every touch. His hand roves up my body to grope my breasts, his thumb circling over my nipples, poking through the thin fabric of my dress. I shudder, feeling somehow both weak and powerful in his arms. I don't know how he does what he does to me, but god, I hope he never, ever stops.

He breaks the kiss for a moment, his eyes sparkling as he looks down at me.

There's a question there. My heart starts racing.

I murmur, "Go ahead."

He grins mischievously and scoops me up, carrying me over to the thigh-high stone wall that circle the park and keeps people from falling over the edge and down the cliff-side. He sets me down there, wrenching my thighs open with his leg as he kneels down in front of me. I can scarcely breathe, my whole body is on fire, anticipating whatever he's going to do to me.

Some part of me is acutely aware that this is dangerous. I'm literally sitting on the precipice of a painful, terrible fall. And at any moment, someone else could come strolling by and catch us out here, two lovers in the park. But I don't care. The only thing I care about is Luca.

He slides the hem of my dress up my thighs and hooks a finger under the band of my panties, tugging them down, exposing my sex to the night air. I shudder at the coolness of the breeze, my hands gripping the stone on either side of me. Luca looks up at me with a hungry stare, green eyes shining in the moonlight.

And then he leans in, his tongue flicking over my clit, enveloping my dripping pussy in his warm mouth. I toss my head back and groan, goosebumps prickling up on my arms and legs as he devours me. His tongue pulses in and out of my aching hole, sliding up and down the length of my sex, drinking me in. He plays with my clit, suckling at the tiny bundle of intense nerves until I'm bucking my hips, my hand on the back of his head, holding him there.

"Fuck," I murmur breathlessly, "don't stop, don't stop!"

He nibbles gently at my clit, then sucks it into his mouth, his tongue swirling around it expertly. I whimper, feeling my whole body start to tense up. He always knows just what to do, like he knows my body better than I do. Like I was built for him alone.

Luca spreads my thighs wider and slides one finger inside me, curling it ever so slightly to stroke my g-spot deep inside while his tongue works my clit. The sensation is almost overwhelming, almost enough to make me recoil. But if I withdraw, if I pull back from him, I could fall—down, down the cliff behind me. There's no place else to go. I have to just suck it up and deal with the powerful, intense waves of pleasure radiating through my body.

"Oh my god, oh my god, Luca!" I gasp, closing my eyes as my orgasm mounts. He groans into my pussy, and I can tell he's enjoying this. He loves it: sending me into near-hysterics with that amazing mouth of his. His finger slides in and out of me faster and faster, his tongue circling my clit until I'm almost in tears.

Finally, I erupt into shivers of exquisite bliss, climaxing and gushing sweet honey all over his finger. Luca eagerly licks up every last drop, not even letting up for a moment while my thighs tremble and I whimper incoherently.

He looks up at me, those green eyes fierce, almost frightening in their intensity. He stands up quickly, turns me so that I'm almost lying down on the stone ledge, one foot safely planted on the ground, the other leg dangling off the edge. He unbuckles his jeans, tugs them down along with his boxers.

His cock springs free, long and hard, and I can't help but gasp as he reaches down to rub my clit with his fingers, keeping me slick and wet. He's really going to fuck me right here on the edge of a cliff, in a public park, with a village gathering just streets away from us!

I moan, wriggling toward him, my body aching for him. My heart is pounding, all my senses heightened by the pure danger and thrill of what we're about to do. "Please," I whisper, "do it. Fuck me right here in the open. I need it, Luca. I need you."

He positions the head of his cock at my dripping pussy, sliding it around, teasing me, making me tremble and shake with desire. Leaning over me, he pushes my dress further up to expose my breasts. I've gone without a bra tonight, and at the rush of cool air, my nipples perk up. Still teasing my pussy with the tip of his shaft, he leans down to suck my nipple into his mouth. I groan as his tongue flicks over the stiffened peak, sending spirals of pleasure down between my legs. I roll my hips up against him, begging him to fuck me.

Luca straightens back up, looks me dead in the eye, and slides his cock deep inside me in one smooth thrust. I cry out, and he quickly covers my mouth with his hand as he starts to pump in and down out of my pussy, not even taking the time to go slowly at first. He fucks me fast and hard, slamming into my g-spot again and again as the two of us balance on the edge of the cliff. It almost hurts, but I can't get enough of it. I love the way he's using my body, filling my tight little hole with his engorged shaft like I'm some irresistible fuck-toy.

"Fill me up, Luca. Fuck me. Make me yours," I whisper, feeling the rough stone grinding almost painfully underneath me, chafing my bare skin. But the slight pain almost adds to the pleasure of the moment, and I grit my teeth.

"So good for me, baby," he groans. "Such a tight little pussy. You feel so fucking good."

"Oh god, I love it when you pound into me like this," I murmur, my eyes rolling back in my head. He picks up the pace, fucking me harder and faster, his hips snapping back and forth as he uses my pussy. I'm aching, nearly twitching with bliss, and I cry out again as another climax washes over me. I can feel my pussy pulsing around his cock, squeezing him, bringing him closer and closer to the same edge.

He slams into me with such force I can feel my body scooting closer and closer to the end of the stone ledge, but I don't even care. Fuck, if this is the way I have to go, then it's worth it. I've never felt this exhilarated before, filled with Luca's cock, my pussy aching for him to come inside me and stuff me with his sweet seed. Finally, he rears back and shoves into me with such force he has to grab me and pull me back before I can topple over the edge, and he groans, spilling his thick spunk deep inside my trembling sex.

He holds me close for a moment, letting every last drop of his seed fill me up. He leans down to kiss me fiercely, his tongue shoving into my mouth as his hands grope my breasts, my hips, my ass. After a few moments of this, we hear the distant echo of footsteps approaching. Suddenly remembering where we are and how sticky a predicament we're in, we quickly make ourselves decent and start rushing away from the park, hand-in-hand as we race back to the car.

Laughing with exhilaration, we get in the car and drive home, the car speeding along down the hilly roads. I can still feel his come leaking out of me, staining the brand-new dress I just bought, and it makes me feel satisfied. Complete.

But I'm not quite done with him yet.

We've got a little bit of a drive home to go, and there are almost no streetlights, and no other vehicles in sight. I reach over across the console, rubbing my hand over Luca's softening cock.

He glances at me, confused for half a second, and then realizing what I'm up to. With a devilish grin, I lean over, under his arms, to unzip his jeans and get to his shaft. At my warm breath on his bare skin, his cock starts to stiffen again. I take my time, teasing him with my tongue, sliding my hand up and down his shaft softly until he's completely erect again.

He moans, his hand coming down to rest on the top of my head, gently pushing me down, urging me to suck his cock.

And I gladly oblige.

I pull the head of his stiffened cock into my mouth, letting my tongue flick over the tip before I take him in completely. I almost cough when the head of his cock brushes against the back of my throat, but instead I just start bobbing up and down, fondling the base of his shaft with my hand while I work his hard length.

"Fuck, you're such a dirty, sexy woman," Luca says, just barely thrusting up into my mouth. I tease the head of his cock, licking my lips. I can still taste myself on him.

"I just can't get enough," I whisper, reaching down between my legs to stroke my clit, still dripping with his come. We ride down the highway this way for a while, my mouth sucking his cock, my fingers rubbing my pussy. Every time we go over a bump in the road, his cock slams into the back of my throat—and I love it as much as he does.

I bounce up and down, sucking him off, swirling my tongue around the head, pumping his shaft with my hand. It's not long before I'm climaxing again, moaning as I take Luca's cock deep into my mouth.

"*Brava ragazza,*" he murmurs, pushing my head down on his cock. "So good, *dolcezza.*"

Just before we pull up to the darkened Lomaglio residence, I suck him harder, bobbing up and down faster and faster until I can feel him tensing up. The car rolls to a stop just as he explodes in my mouth, and I swallow down his come hungrily, licking the tip of his cock. I sit back up, proud of myself, and Luca kisses me, not even caring about the taste of his own come on my lips.

We tumble into bed together, still kissing, ripping off each other's clothes. We explore each other's bodies like it's the very first time, touching and stroking. Before long, he's down between my legs again, licking my pussy and fingering me. Finally, exhausted and spent, we start to drift off in each other's arms, totally happy and blissful.

Just as I'm closing my eyes, a smile still on my lips, my phone buzzes on the bedside table. At first, I decide to just let it go. Let it wait until morning. But something, some instinct without a name, urges me to check it. I reach over in the dark and grab my phone, blinking in the bright light as I read the text message on the screen.

My stomach turns and I start to feel dizzy.

Another message from my mother, finally a reply! But the words make my blood go cold.

Hope you're well. I went out to dinner tonight. Walnuts in the salad.

To most people, this would mean nothing at all. But to me, it's a time machine back to when I was a little kid, to the first time my mother first sent back a plate of food to the kitchen at a fancy restaurant, complaining that there were walnuts in the salad. I was seven years old, and I asked her what the problem was. She explained that she is allergic to walnuts, and so she can't eat them. For some reason, in my child's mind, I took this as some kind of code word for when I didn't like something or didn't want to go through with something.

From then on, whenever I was scared, whenever I was in trouble, I would use "walnuts" as a code word, a clue to my mother that something was wrong. One time, when I was at a sleepover and I got scared and wanted to go home, I used my friend's parents' phone to call home and whisper, "Walnuts," to my mother. She immediately understood what I meant. She came and picked me up, took me home, giving some believable excuse to my friend's parents about why. My mother and I were never as close as I was with my father, but this was our *thing*.

The day that my first crush was mean to me in eighth grade during gym class, I sent my mom the text message: *Walnuts*. She checked me out for the day, took me shopping, taught me about how boys can be awful sometimes, but I shouldn't let them control how I feel about myself.

Even when I was in high school, trying to get through classes without crying because I was still reeling from the death of my father, I would send my mom the "walnuts" code word to tell her how the day was going, how much I was struggling. When I got older, I used the word less and less often, needing my mother to take care of me less and less.

X was the code word we'd agreed on.

Walnuts was the code word we'd always used.

I know something is wrong. She's in trouble, and she wouldn't use that word without knowing exactly what it would signify to me. I jump out of bed and start getting dressed, not even sure what I'm planning to do. Luca wakes up and looks over at me, confused.

"What's going on, *dolcezza*? Are you okay?"

With tears in my eyes, I look back at him and answer, "We have to leave. My mother is in trouble, and I have to help her. *Now*."

LUCA

I should have been ready. I should have known better. I should have acted sooner. I shouldn't have ignored my instincts.

I will not make such mistakes again.

The SUV races down the highway as fast as I can make the beat-up hunk of metal move. We have no time to waste, and there are few enough police out in the area that I'm not going to worry about going 40-50 miles over the speed limit. A trail of dust runs behind us like a cloud in our wake. I grip the steering wheel so tight that even I notice it.

Serena is in the seat next to me, watching out the window as we barrel down the road.

"Are you sure your friend will have everything ready for us when we get to the air strip?" she asks for the third time, looking over to me with worried eyes.

"If he doesn't, I'll kill him," I say matter-of-factly. Her eyes go wide, but I crack a smile at her to let her know I'm joking. If I don't ease the tension at least a little, we'll both get too strung out to focus, and focus is the one thing we need right now.

"I hope your parents aren't upset we had to leave so fast," Serena says, running her hands through her hair. "I'm so sorry, Luca, we-"

"Don't be sorry," I say, shaking my head, "this is an emergency. We'll be back to see them, and they know my life is...the kind of life that involves sudden changes in plans. It isn't as unusual as you'd think."

She nods, swallowing.

"The plane I have ready for us will get us back to the States faster than any airliner could," I say, watching the strong wind whip sand across the road ahead of us as we make our way toward the air strip. "Once we're onboard, it will be about seven hours straight to New York. I've already reached out to my contacts to have a company car ready for us when we get back."

"The Costas are still looking out for you?"

"I have friends," I say simply. "Friends look out for each other. Besides, I'm a walking symbol by now. It looks good for the Costas for me to stay in good shape, especially when I show up in New York again alive, back from the dead."

I see goosebumps on Serena's arm, and I take my hand off the stick shift a moment to lay it on hers, giving it a light squeeze.

"Is the family going to be okay here, though?" she asks, her eyes going wide yet again. "If anything were to happen to them because of us..."

"Not gonna happen," I say with a shake of my head. "Now that they have our scent, the only thing these dogs will be interested in is us. Besides, I've warned the village about these outsiders, and the local crime rings are on high alert. The Cleaners have connections in the region, but that's a different matter than a bunch of Americans rolling around causing trouble. And I've had some of my cousins come in to stay with my parents for a week or so, until things cool down. We don't have anything to worry about here."

She nods, looking thoughtful for a few moments. "I want to come back," she says with a determination that I can't help but admire in her. "One day, I mean, when we've gotten through all this. I want to come back and make sure the women's shelter is okay, that they're taken care of. Those women gave me a safe place for as long as they could—I don't know how, but I want to return that kindness."

"I'll make it so," I say with finality, and we exchange a short smile before we turn the corner to the last road we'll take in Italy.

A few minutes later, we pull up the long, open road to where a small private jet is sitting. The tarmac is a small one, really too small for anything to take off from, but it'll have to do for now. I can just barely make out the pilot sitting in the cockpit looking at us approaching through a set of binoculars, and he hails us as we approach.

"Another friend of yours?" Serena asks.

"You don't have anything to do but make friends in this part of the country," I say with a grin. "Well, that and ride cars wildly around the wilderness."

"Right."

The wind is picking up, but the direction it's blowing will only help the plane take off. I drive us not far from the boarding ramp, but my eyes are scanning the area around us.

Something feels wrong.

"I'll get out first," I say calmly, but Serena can pick up on my bad feelings more easily than anyone else. Still, she doesn't question it—she just nods and picks up her bag over her shoulder. "Get out after me. As soon as you're out, stay low and hurry into that plane, understand?"

"Got it," she says. Her eyes look into mine, strong and

resolute. I take her hand in mine, bring it to my lips, and kiss it.

I pull the car to a stop, and immediately, I get out of the car, my bag over my shoulder.

I take off my aviators to scan the horizon, eyes moving quickly. There are a lot of cliffs and vantage points from here. No signs of cars rolling our way full of Cleaners, though.

A moment later, I hear Serena's door open, and within a matter of seconds, I see her little form dart from the car up the stairs of the ramp, keeping low, just like I instructed her. My muscles relax a moment later once she's inside the plane.

Then I see it.

Out of the corner of my eye, for barely a fraction of a second, I see the sun glint off something in the cliffs to the south. I'd know a glint like that anywhere.

There's a gunman up there, watching us.

My jaw sets. I should duck and run, make a beeline for the plane, but instead, I step around to the front of the car.

My eyes are set dead-on where I saw the glint. And even from nearly a mile away, I know that I'm staring right back at the barrel of a sniper rifle.

There's no way the Cleaners had enough notice to set up a proper sniper nest this quickly. And I doubt they have many trained sharpshooters in their pocket. That leaves two options in my mind: either someone got lucky and is using that scope to watch us and let his bosses know we're leaving the country, or some young buck is going to try to take the shot.

So I step forward into the open, glaring right back at him.

If you want it so bad, go ahead, try and make the shot.

The wind is bad right now. It doesn't take a marksman to know that a shot at that range with this wind would be a tough one, to say the least. If the man behind that scope has enough skill, though, we're already dead, regardless of whether I run or stand still.

I stand there for a solid ten seconds, my face still as stone, daring him to make the shot. The sun catches the scope again. A quick glint.

Nothing.

My face twists into a frown, and I put my aviators back on. "Coward," I mutter, and I turn my back on the sniper, strutting to the plane and boarding without worry.

"Everything okay?" says my friend in Italian from the cockpit as I enter the plane. Serena is already sitting in one of the comfy seats, looking relieved to see me again.

"All good," I reply, smiling to him warmly. "Hope you can fly in this wind."

"Told you, I was air force," he says with a cocky grin. "And you won't be the first Mafioso I've smuggled out of the country on short notice. Just make sure the cash is in my account, or I'll kick you out over the Atlantic."

We laugh, and I take my seat across from Serena. "Get comfortable," I say, casting one more glance out the window to my homeland. "Before you know it, we'll be back in the Bronx. And we just lost the element of surprise."

~

*I*t turns out that getting comfortable is easier said than done on this flight. Seven hours feels like seven days, and passing the time has proven hard. We don't have much to talk about that doesn't go back to the danger Serena's mother is in, and because of that, it feels a little irreverent to try to focus on the brief good times we've had with my family.

So, three-quarters of the way into the flight, I'm doing

push-ups on one hand on the floor of the cabin. Serena watches me, if only to distract herself from the stress.

It isn't working so well.

As for me, I have to stay in peak physical condition, no matter what. This isn't a serious workout for me, just something to keep me warmed up, because for all I know, we could be landing in the middle of a firefight.

Until this is finished, I need to be beyond my A-game, and lying on my ass in a hospital bed didn't help my strength.

"But what if it's too late?" Serena says anxiously, and it's not the first time she's expressed that fear. I can't blame her. The situation isn't good. "What if something's happened to her already? Oh my god, I've just been goofing off like I'm on some vacation all this time and I'm the worst daughter ever. Or what if *nothing* bad has happened to her and someone stole her phone and is luring us into a trap and-"

"Then I will kill them," I say simply, lowering myself to the ground before putting both hands down to push myself up. I stride over to her, crouching beside her seat and taking her hand reassuringly. I'm bare-chested, having taken my shirt off to exercise more easily.

"Serena," I say in a low tone, looking into those anxious eyes, on the verge of tears for hours now. "You can't be everywhere at once. You had to run for your life. You ran for the child's life. You did the right thing—you kept your-self alive. If your mother isn't the kind of person who can recognize how important that is, then she's no mother at all."

Her face just watches me, trembling, and I know the great beast of fear within her is trying to push out any hope of comfort. I rise up and sit in the seat next to her, raising the armrest to pull her close to my chest, letting her head rest there.

"I don't know if I could forgive myself if something happened, though," she whispers.

"I know, *passerotta*," I say, stroking her hair gently with my thick fingers. "But we've gone through a trial of fire, both of us—and you're not used to this. What you've accomplished, what you've *survived* in Italy is a greater feat of strength than I could ever come close to."

"I don't know about that," she says with a soft smile.

"We're coming back from the dead, you and me," I say, looking down to that face I love so strongly. "You're doing all this for your family, nothing else. It would be enough for your mother for you to keep yourself and your future child safe, but going back to look after family? If that doesn't make you a good daughter, I don't know what does."

After a moment, she looks up at me with a struggling smile on her face, and she gets closer to me. My arms, warm from exercise, wrap around her comfortingly, and we hug with nothing but the droning of the plane all around us for a few moments.

"You are my strength, Serena," I say, squeezing her gently. "I mean that. We have each other, and that makes us strong enough to move mountains for what we love."

Just then, I hear the pilot's voice over the speaker.

"Luca, just to let you know, we just crossed into radius of American phone signals. If you have any calls to make, now's the time."

"Thanks," I call to the cockpit, and I nod to Serena, standing up and getting a phone from my bag.

A few moments later, the phone is ringing, and I'm pacing the cabin with a hand on my hip.

"...hello?" an uncertain voice answers from the other end.

"Hello, Giovanni," I say with a grin. "Nice to hear you again."

"Holy shit, Luca," Giovanni gushes, laughing at the other end of the line. "Don't give me a heart attack like that! Fuck, it's good to hear from you. You really didn't waste any time stirring up the goddamn wasp's nest coming back to life, huh? Rising on the third day too good for you?"

"It's a bad habit," I say, winking at Serena.

"Where are you?" he asks. "Can you even answer that? What's going on?"

"We're heading back to America," I say. "We'll be in the Bronx before the end of the day. I need you to make sure pickup arrangements are settled at the air strip. You know the one. I've already got some guys on it, but I want someone I trust there with them. Talk to Nico."

"You got it," Giovanni says, and I can still hear the disbelief through the phone. "I gotta say, Luca, it's fuckin' weird hearing your voice again. I mean, I'd heard rumors, but..."

"This is on a need-to-know basis," I say. "Trust me, if I'd wanted to go public with this, you'd be one of the first men I contacted. But what's this about rumors? What's the situation in the Bronx?"

"Shit, you don't know anything, do you?" Giovanni says in wonder.

"I've had a bad case of the 'dead,' Giovanni."

"Right, right. Well, things are uh, not good. We're in an all-out mob war, Luca."

I clench my jaw. "The Cleaners don't know when to die, do they?"

"They were backed into a corner for a while there, but anything backed into a corner fights hard. When everyone thought you'd been killed, they fought twice as hard to get back lost territory. Lot of good men are dead. It's been a bloody winter and a bloodier spring. Nobody even knows what the turf borders are anymore, it feels like every week some block is ours, then it's the Cleaners, you get the idea. Don Abruzzi dug his heels in hard, and he's holding the vendetta for his son's death against the whole Costa family. He circulated a bunch of news about your death, too, saying he had your body, photos, all kinds of shit."

I listen to all this with a still expression, taking it all in. When he's finished, I take a breath.

"Alright. Giovanni, I want you to get the boys back together. Only the men I've been on jobs with, you know the ones. Men we can trust. I'll explain more when we land, but the Cleaners probably know by now that I'm going to be back in town soon. I'm going to lead us on a job."

"A job? Shouldn't we touch base with Don Costa?"

"Fuck the Don," I grunt. "Has he given a shit when I've been busting my ass across the world on their account? No. You know who has stuck up for us? *Us*, Giovanni. If we want something done right, we do it ourselves. This is our neighborhood. Not the Cleaners', and not the Don's. I'll deal with the blowback later, if anyone wants to cross that bridge. You with me or not?"

There's a long sigh from the other end of the line before Giovanni says, "Shit, yeah, you know I'm with you, Luca. Alright, let's do this. I'll see you in a few."

I end the call, and I look down to Serena, who looks shocked at me.

"Did I just hear all that right?"

"I didn't survive a car bomb to go back to following orders like a grunt," I say.

"Well, yeah," she says with a smile, but it fades as she goes on, "I mean, what did you mean, 'job'? What are you planning?"

A cocky smile crosses my face. "We're going to find

your mother by drawing the bastards out of hiding first. And we're going to do that by finishing this where it started."

The car rolls to a stop just down the block, and it hits me how strange it is to be surrounded by these familiar sights again. Italy feels like a world away, like a dream I wish I could get back to. Those sweet, happy memories are fading away, almost like it never happened at all. It's heartbreaking, but at the same time, I know there's a lot I need to get done here. I can't just live in denial forever while the world keeps burning down everything I've built around me.

Maybe someday things will be soft and easy again, but now is not that time.

Now, it's time for action.

I hop out of the car before Luca can even turn off the engine, and I start marching my pregnant self down the street, my stomach churning and my heart racing. As I approach the building where Bathing Beauty is located, I nearly double over to throw up at the sight of it.

My beautiful store, the shop I have worked so hard for, is in shambles.

There are streamers of yellow caution tape all over the

entrance, the windows busted up and cracked, tiny splinters of glass littering the sidewalk. I cover my mouth with my hands in shock, stepping gingerly through the broken glass to the front door. With a shaking hand, I take the key out of my pocket and fit it in the door. I have to jostle it to try and get it open, since the door is hanging slightly crooked on its hinges, like it's been knocked off-angle. Like somebody kicked the door in to break inside the shop. To my surprise and panic, the key doesn't quite fit like it used to. I thought it was opening up, but apparently the door is just so messed up that it can't open anymore like it used to. Luca comes up behind me and takes my hand.

"Come on, *mia passerotta*. I'll get us in somehow," he tells me gently. He leads me around the back of the building, to the rear employees' entrance. As expected, my key doesn't fit here either, but luckily Luca has enough brute strength to break through the door, shattering the lock in the process. I rush inside and start turning on the lights—half of which don't turn on, and the other half only flicker pathetically, like they've been smashed to bits.

As I walk through the kitchen and storage rooms, I can feel a lump rising in my throat.

The shelves are all knocked over, chemicals and equipment scattered all over the floor. Luca grabs me by the arm and says, "Be careful, Serena. I don't think you should be here, breathing in these chemicals. It's not safe for you or the baby."

"Just... just let me look around a little bit. I-I need to take stock of things," I say, my voice already shaky. Leaning on Luca for support, I walk through to the main shop front, my breath catching in my lungs as I take in the horrific scene. The state of things is even worse in here. All the cabinets and shelves have been ripped out of the walls. All the products are smashed and poured on the floor. The files are spread out everywhere, some of them ripped to pieces. All my hard work is lying here in bits on the ground, unceremoniously dumped out and trampled on.

I immediately start to cry, unable to hold back the waterworks. The waves of devastated emotion crash over me and I crumple to the floor, burying my face in my hands. I sob openly, feeling my heart shatter into a million pieces. First, I learned that my mother is missing and most certainly in danger, and now my beloved shop, the business I've worked so hard to keep going, is destroyed. My family's last asset, our last hope, dashed to pieces by the enemy.

Luca rushes over to comfort me, tugging me into his arms and kissing my forehead.

"I'm so sorry, Serena," he murmurs. "Those bastards are going to pay for this. I promise."

"Everything I had here is ruined. My old life—I'm so stupid. I abandoned it all. I was having such a wonderful time in Italy with you, and I was so selfish to think I could just leave it all behind and it would be okay. I'm an idiot. I shouldn't have just let it all go so easily. I should have been here to make things right," I sob angrily, shaking my head. "I'm so mad at myself. I can't believe I let this happen."

"Serena, stop. This isn't your fault. You didn't choose to leave, *dolcezza*. Remember? You had to go. It was the only way to save you and the baby. You did what you had to do to survive."

"Yeah? And now what? My mother is in trouble, the shop is ruined, and I can't do anything to fix it. I've made such a mess of everything, Luca, and I don't know what to do!"

He helps me stand up and leads me over to sit down on a stool miraculously left standing behind the beaten-up cashier counter. He kisses me on the cheek. "Just sit here for a minute. Breathe slowly. It's going to be okay. I'm going to *make* this okay. Just trust me."

I sit there, breathing deeply, doing what I'm told, because… well, what the hell else can I do anyway? The tears slowly begin to subside and I calm down a little bit, coming out of the darkness to notice that Luca is going around the room with a garbage bag, cleaning up as he goes.

"What are you doing?" I ask, frowning.

"Cleaning up. Just like old times," he says, giving me a reassuring smile.

Despite how awful everything is, I can't help but smile back weakly. "What's the point, Luca? This place is a mess. It's shut down. There's no hope for Bathing Beauty. This shop has been beaten down and vandalized and destroyed so many times by now, what's the use?"

"Well, I'm not giving up. Not yet. We've rebuilt this place before, and we can sure as hell do it again, Serena," he says. He walks over to me and takes my hands, kneeling in front of me. "Listen to me, okay? This is important. You can't stay here. It's not safe. All these crazy chemicals in the air have got to be dangerous for you and the baby. I have a plan, but you have to trust me and do what I say. Alright?"

I look at him suspiciously.

"What exactly am I agreeing to?"

He sighs.

"Serena. I have a lot to get done here."

"What is your plan? You have to tell me, Luca."

He hesitates for a moment and I add, "I'm the mother of your child. I'm your fiancée. You and me? We're a team. That means you have to keep me in the loop."

Luca smiles again, shaking his head.

"God, you're stubborn. But you're right. Okay." He takes a deep breath and continues, "Here's what's going to happen. I'm going to clean this place up, get the lights back on, make it look like it's up and running again."

"But why? Won't that just make the Cleaners suspicious?" I ask.

He nods.

"Exactly. But it won't just make them suspicious, it will make them angry. It will draw them out, get them to come here and try and put us back in our place."

"Luca…" I breathe, my eyes going wide. "Are you really setting a trap? That isn't a good idea. It isn't safe."

He kisses my hand.

"Yes. But the time for playing it safe has passed. And besides, I won't be alone here. The Cleaners think we're alone, you and me. They think we're free agents. I made sure to spread word around town, get the rumor mill started on telling everybody that I quit. Broke away from the Costa family for good. The Cleaners will think I'm severely outmanned here. But what they won't know is that there will be Costa members hiding in wait all around here. The Cleaners won't send the big guns in to get me— they won't see any reason to. So when they show up, *they'll* be the ones outnumbered, outgunned."

"That's crazy, Luca. You can't do this," I tell him firmly, shaking my head. "It's too risky. You know that. I-I can't let you do this."

"Serena, it's the only way. If you've got a better plan, let's hear it."

I sit silently, my mouth closing as I realize he's right. I don't have any other ideas.

He cups my face in his hands.

"*Dolcezza*, I can do this. I've faced worse enemies than these before. Do you trust me?"

I nod.

"You know trust isn't the problem. I trust you with my life."

"You're just going to have to let me do this, even if it scares you. I promise it will work. It will all be just fine in the end," he assures me. "But you can't stay here. I won't let you become a casualty of this war. It's my fight, Serena, not yours."

"What do you mean? I'm not leaving you here. Bathing Beauty is my responsibility. And you—you're my fiancé. I can't just abandon you when you need me!" I exclaim.

Luca pulls me into a tight hug. "I can only do this if I know you're somewhere else—somewhere safe. I will not let them anywhere near you. I'm the prize in this honeypot, not you."

"Where will I go?" I ask, shaking my head as my eyes fill with tears again.

"Rafaela's. She's coming to get you any minute now."

Just as the words leave his mouth, there's the honk of a car horn outside. I look back over my shoulder and see Rafaela in Nico's car, looking very solemn and pale.

"Luca, don't do this," I beg, clinging to him desperately.

"It will all be okay," he says, nearly dragging me out the door. I continue to cry and protest as he pulls me around to the front of the building, taking out his phone to make a quick call. "Giovanni. *Si.* Tonight. Go ahead and send them. It'll all be in place by then."

He gently pushes me into the passenger seat, then looks up at Rafaela and says, "Take care of her. Make sure she eats. And drinks water. And make sure she relaxes—"

"Got it," Rafaela says curtly, nodding. "You do what you have to do."

"Luca!" I cry out tearfully. "Don't you dare."

"*Mia passerotta*, I will see you when the smoke clears. I love you," he says, leaning through the window to kiss me even as the tears streak down my cheeks.

Rafaela throws the car into gear and we take off down the street. I glance back, seeing Luca's shape getting smaller and smaller until he disappears. I turn to Rafaela, who is staring stony-faced at the road.

"Take me back!" I shout at her. She shakes her head. I can tell this is incredibly hard for her. She doesn't like having to drag me away against my will. "Rafaela, turn this car around."

"No!" she barks back. "No. I can't do that, Serena. You're my best friend and I love you and I'd do anything for you, but this? This is out of our hands."

"Please, Raf. I can't just leave him back there. Not—not again," I whisper, thinking back to riding in this car as it sped away from the explosion, leaving the love of my life behind.

There are tears in her big brown eyes. "*Hermana*, no. This is my part in the fight, okay? There isn't much I can do. Nico and all the others—they can fight. But I'm no fighter, Serena. This—taking care of you—this is the only way I can contribute. I have to do what I'm told."

"You don't understand," I whimper.

She stops the car suddenly, turning to me with flashing, angry eyes.

"*I* don't understand? *Amiga*, I know exactly what you feel! Do you think I don't break down and cry every time Nico goes out to do god-knows-what for the mafia? Do you think I haven't been worried sick with panic the whole time you've been off in Italy? I had no idea whether you were alive or dead all that time! Do you really think I don't know what you're going through? I was there, too! I saw that explosion! And the whole time I just kept thinking, 'That could have been Nico. That could have been Serena. Hell, that could have been me.' Don't you understand that I've been terrified, too? Serena, you know me better than that. You're like a sister to me, and this is the one way I can do my part. Just let me do my part," she says, her lip trembling as she bursts into tears, too.

"Oh god, I'm so sorry, Raf," I mutter, reaching over to hug her.

"I've been so scared, Serena. I thought my best friend was gone forever," she cries.

"If I had been able to reach out to you, I would have. You know that, right?" I assure her.

"I know, I know."

"I can't imagine how scary it was for you, being stuck here, not knowing what was going on," I tell her, and I mean it. Guilt floods into my heart. I hadn't even thought about it. Poor Rafaela, worried half to death all this time.

"All along, I've just been quiet, doing what they tell me to do. I used to think I was pretty tough, you know? I thought I was strong. But this stuff? It's way over my head," she sniffles.

"Rafaela, you are strong. You always have been. It's scary, but you're still here. Right? You're surviving! And thank god, too, because I don't know what I'd do if anything happened to you," I confess. She wipes her eyes.

"I'm sorry for blowing up at you like that, but I've just been so wound up, so tense all the time waiting for the next shoe to drop," she says, trying to calm herself down.

"I know the feeling. It's okay. You have every right to feel that way."

"Dios mio, I just hate standing on the sidelines, knowing I can't do anything to help. You know? It's awful. I want to do more, but there's nothing I can do," she laments, frustrated.

"You know, we don't have to just go sit and wait like the guys tell us to," I begin cautiously, not wanting to upset her further. "We don't have to just watch while the men we love go charging half-cocked into battle. We can help."

"How? How the hell can we do anything?" she asks, looking at me sideways.

"We refuse to sit on our hands and wait for everything

to be okay. We join the ranks and we *make* it okay. We fight," I suggest.

"What are you saying?" she says, frowning at me.

I take a deep breath.

"We go back."

"**B**e straight with me, Luca," says Giovanni, peering out the open door with a cigarette hanging out of his mouth while he loads his pistols. "Think they'll take the bait?"

"Have you seen any cops roll by in the past two hours?" I reply, my arms crossed as I watch with him.

"Nah."

"There's your answer. This is a challenge, and they've accepted it."

"Fuck me," he says, flicking his cigarette out onto the street and flashing a half-grin at me, "I forgot how dramatic things could get with you around."

Bathing Beauty looks like it's back in business. We've torn down all the boards from the windows, dusted off everything, gotten the power back on, and even turned some of the lights on. It's late by now, and most of the other shops on the block have shut down. The fact that this place is a glowing beacon of light makes it look conspicuous already.

When I said it was a challenge, I meant it. There aren't many people tied to the mafia who don't know about this place by now. First it was the place Serena, last of the De Laurentis mob royalty, was supposed to live out a quiet life, an old front turned legit. Then it became known as the beginning of the end for Lorenzo Abruzzi after he tried to get Serena to pay protection and I showed up. When I was in jail, the Cleaners didn't forget about this place. Seeing it all but shut down must have been like a monument to their victory after they thought they killed me.

I couldn't have sent a stronger message if I'd thrown a glass of wine in Don Abruzzi's face.

Giovanni and I walk away from the windows and move back to the main floor of the shop, where we've got my own little army with us. Eleven men in total, not counting me. We've got a scout watching the roads for us to give us the heads up.

Most of these men are low-ranking guys. Guys I've done jobs with, some of them who still can't believe their eyes when they look at me walking and breathing, still alive. One of them even saw the car bomb go off.

And they're my people, as far as I'm concerned. A few of them have girlfriends of their own back home who don't know whether they're going to come home tonight. Some of them won't, but it'll get even worse if we don't take a stand now. The bosses don't care about that. They only care about their money.

Me, I'm interested in protecting the neighborhood.

My phone buzzes, and I put it to my ear.

"Three cars on their way. Get ready."

"Good," I grunt, and no sooner have I hung up the phone than I realize the whole room is looking at me, waiting for a word. I'm not one to give speeches.

"Three tin cans full of dead men are rolling our way," I announce, taking out my guns and casting a hard gaze over all of them. "They're on their way to try to fill this place with bullet holes and make this neighborhood their own, and they're not gonna stop until all of you are dead. But I just dragged my ass across five thousand miles of ocean with them on my heels, and believe me when I tell you they're not half the hot shit they think they are."

A few of the men give resolute nods.

"I know you all. Lucca, I still got the smell of your uncle's barbecue in my jacket. Frankie, I've still got the scar from when we worked on our first car in the junkyard. Mario, you still owe me a beer, and hell is a dry county, so we're not going down without it."

They laugh, and I glance over my shoulder as the sound of rolling tires on asphalt reaches my ear. I look back to all of them with a serious expression.

"And I sure as hell didn't come back from the goddamn dead to get shot up by these punks again. Showtime, men, let's give 'em hell!"

Dressed in a dusty leather jacket, black shirt that won't show blood as easily, dirty blue jeans, and black boots, I move behind an island counter in the middle of the shop, feeling like I'm holding the center in a battlefield. Some of the men are behind the checkout counter. Others are behind walls, crouching or standing, all toting guns and all ready for action.

The door is open. It looks like an invitation, but I had something else in mind.

With headlights off, the three black sedans roll into view, windows down, men packed into them. They roll up toward the building, and before one of them can even think to lean out and start taking shots, I take action.

I pop up from hiding and fire a round straight into a tire of the front car.

Immediately, it skids, taking the passengers by surprise, and the men take that as cue to start firing. We won't be sitting ducks for this one.

As bullet holes start appearing in the cars and ricocheting off, Cleaners start pouring out of the opposite doors and taking positions behind their cars. They know they can't stay there for long, though. It's only a matter of time before someone hits a gas tank, and while the police might be paid off to keep clear, an explosion like that won't be one they can ignore.

My men are good shots. As the Cleaners dart for cover, firing rounds into the shop and shattering the glass of the windows, Giovanni downs one of them with a shot to the throat while another of my men lands a clean shot through the heart of another.

The bullet holes appearing in the shop tell me they're packing some heavy heat. Still, the men are managing to hold them down, and they're not about to gain ground on us anytime soon. The only question will be whether or not they're able to make a push inward once—

"Luca!" Giovanni yells, interrupting my thoughts. I look over at him as I get back down to cover, and he points to the third car.

It's still moving. And it's headed around to the back of the shop.

"Are they trying to fucking flank us?" he shouts, and I waste no time in taking aim at the moving car. Its tires are shot to hell, but it's still heading around. Whoever's in there is determined to get the drop on us if it's the last thing that car does.

Two of my rounds fire into the backseat before a bullet grazes my forearm and I'm forced to withdraw, gritting my teeth.

"You got one, maybe two," Giovanni shouts, "let's get some men back there!"

"No!" I grunt in reply. "Give any ground here, and they'll overwhelm us. I'll handle this one myself. Cover me!"

I don't give Giovanni time to reply, but the men overheard me. They start concentrating fire to give me cover as I roll out from behind the counter. When I get back to my feet, both guns are out, and I unload into the other cars, watching men taking cover behind dumpsters as the cars take heavy hits.

It looks like I'm firing wildly, but every shot is measured. I've gotten skilled at this over the years, and my exercise hasn't failed me. I watch no less than three men go down before I force myself to focus on my objective again.

I head to the back room.

If the third car was heading around back, they'll be coming in from the rear entrance. I have a man back there just in case, but he won't be enough to handle a car full of men.

When I appear in the back room, my guard looks at me with anticipation. "I heard shit going down out front, where do you want me?"

"Up there with them," I say, clapping him on the back. "I've got this."

"You sure, Luca?"

"I'm always sure."

He nods and follows my orders, leaving me alone in the room. I know I have all of about ten seconds to prepare.

That's enough time to reload my guns.

I can hear feet running outside, and my eyes dart around the room. I have no time for intricate traps. What I *do* have is a rack full of old cleaning and soap making supplies near the door. It's not elegant, but it'll do. I can push it onto whoever piles inside and at least get the element of surprise on my side. I pull it away from the wall and position it to face the door from the side.

But before I can get it just the way I want it, the door gets yanked open, and I see the arms of a man holding a gun appear in the doorway from my angle.

Fuck it.

I simply raise my gun and blow his hands off at the wrist.

Through the howl of pain, I shove a large jug of lye off the shelf and into the doorway just as bullets start peppering it.

The caustic liquid pours out, and I hear a few yelps of pain as the men scramble back, giving me just enough of an in to make my move.

I appear in the doorway the next moment, and three shots later, the two gunmen and the one on the ground slump against the wall of the alley behind the store, blood running from shots to the head.

Three dead here, one killed in the car...

I'm missing one.

And that instinct tells me to dive half a second before the fifth man springs out of hiding behind a dumpster to fire at me as he rolls, just as I did less than a minute ago.

He's tall, heavily built, and he knows how to move. This is no ordinary mafia soldier.

When I get back to my feet, he's doing the same, but we're at too close range to shoot at each other. He tries to whip me across the head with the butt of his weapon, but I drop my guns and catch him by the wrist and deliver a hard hit to his stomach.

He's hard as a rock, and he brings his head crashing down to mine. It stuns me, to my surprise, but I squeeze his wrist until he drops the gun with a grunt of pain.

He tries to bring his head down to hit mine again, but this time, I release him and back up, kicking his gun across the alley. We freeze for a moment, staring at one another with bloodlust in our eyes, arms out and ready.

Then his face twists into a sneer.

"Never thought I'd get to look you in the eyes, Luca Lomaglio," he says.

"I look everyone I kill in the eyes," I say as I wipe a trickle of blood away from my forehead. "Have we met?"

"Nah," he says with a casual laugh, "but you made me a rich man. Remember that raid on the junkyard fight all those years ago that was supposed to get your ass killed?" He winks at me. "I was the Costa insider that helped set you up. The Abruzzi family pays a hell of a lot better, you know. Not that it matters now."

My jaw clenches.

"So, when I kill you, it'll be for each of the men who died that night." I lunge at him, and he rolls out of the way and catches me under my ribs. I grunt, but I strike back with my elbow and catch him on the chin.

He stumbles back, then lunges at me with both hands, and we grapple. He thrusts me against the wall behind us, and he tries to land a punch on my face, but I bring my whole head forward to connect my forehead to his nose. He howls in pain and staggers back, and I take my chance.

I rush forward and catch him around the waist, bringing him to the ground with a hard thump. But this guy's more nimble than he looks. I try to get up on him to start pounding his face into the ground, but he twists and throws a punch right at my nose that I have to roll off him to dodge. Both of us on the ground, he swings his leg around to bring it down like an axe on me, but I catch it, holding up an immense amount of force that went into the blow, gritting my teeth.

I twist his leg until he howls, but he lifts his other leg and lands a blow in my chest that pushes me back and off him.

That's when I feel something cool against my hand. It's of the guns that I dropped when we started this fistfight.

Moving as fast as I can force my body to, I snatch the pistol up and get to my feet, pointing the gun directly at my opponent…

...and I find myself looking straight back at the barrel of my other gun, held in his hands, trained on me.

Both of us freeze. He's on the ground, aiming up at me, and I'm not budging an inch from him. We're locked in a standoff.

There's no sound in the alleyway besides our heavy panting and the ringing in our ears.

And at the same time, both of us realize why that's odd.

"The fighting's over out front," he growls.

"Sure is," I grunt back, my finger on the trigger. "That means this standoff will be pointless in a few seconds."

"Yeah," he says, eyes narrowing and a smirk growing on his face. "That leaves us one question: which side won?"

On cue, a voice barks from the other end of the alley behind me.

"Drop the gun, asshole!"

My muscles tense for a moment.

Then a stupid grin crosses my face while his vanishes. Slowly, he sets his gun on the ground and raises his hands as footsteps behind me approach.

And Serena appears at my side, a gun held out in front of her in shaky hands.

"I thought I told you to stay away," I say, but it's in an almost playful tone. I should have known better than to think she'd stay put. And fuck, I'm glad she didn't.

Still, she gives me a deserved kick in the shin. "Get your finger off the trigger too, hun."

"What? Why?"

Serena takes aim at the man, fire in her eyes. "Because I don't want you to kill him before he tells us where the fuck my mom is."

I can't believe I did that.

I cannot. Believe. I did that.

Looking down at the shiny weapon in my lap, I gulp down my panic. I, Serena De Laurentis, a girl who used to get woozy at the sight of blood, who used to not even be able to handle watching action movies if they got too intense—I just held a man at gunpoint.

Who the hell am I anymore?

I look up and out the window of the back seat of the stolen car, watching the city pass by, the buildings getting smaller and farther apart until we're way down the highway, leaving the skyscrapers behind. Leaving the shop, the one I've sweated and cried over, behind. Leaving the scene of a bloodbath. A battlefield.

The words stumble out of my mouth out loud this time: "I can't believe I did that."

"Serena," says Luca softly. "Serena, look at me."

I slowly drag my eyes away from the window, turning to gaze at Luca's face in the rearview mirror. It's still jarring to see him wearing the clothes of the man I held at gunpoint. After I finished interrogating the guy, Luca made him switch jackets and give up his hat. He's got the collar up and the hat pulled low, almost over his green eyes, to disguise himself.

He looks concerned as he stares at me in the mirror, but still gleaming with something like pride. I can't believe what I'm seeing. He's actually proud of me for what I did back there.

"Hmm?" I manage to mumble through my stupor of shock.

"Are you okay? *Dolcezza*, talk to me."

"I just pointed a gun… this gun," I begin, nodding at the weapon in my lap, "at a person. Like, a living person. I just threatened a man with a gun."

"Yes. You did."

"While I'm pregnant."

"Yes. That's… that's true."

"I-I can't help feeling like that's going to have some kind of, I don't know, effect on the baby. Like, it's going to be born with this inherent bloodlust or something," I confess.

Luca looks at me sideways, clearly trying not to smirk.

"Serena, you did what you had to do. And it worked. Because of you, we now know where they're keeping your mother. We know where we have to go to rescue her. You did that. You made that happen," he says, shaking his head in awe. "Now, do I want you to ever do that shit again? No. Hell, no. After all this is over, I never want that kind of violence anywhere near you or the baby. But Serena, listen to me. You did the right thing. You got the information we need. And you didn't shoot the guy."

"Yeah, but he didn't know I wouldn't," I say, trembling a little. "Shit. *I* didn't even know if I wouldn't. What does that say about me?"

"It says you're one tough lady, and you're loyal and brave as anyone I've ever known. It says that when shit gets hard, you pull yourself together and you make things happen. It means that you'd do anything for family. For love. And that, *mia passerotta*, is what I love most about you."

He looks over at me, just the hint of a smile playing on his lips.

"Now, what I need you to do for me is stay angry. Don't let fear or guilt overcome you right now. There will be time to reflect on your decisions later. Right now, I need for you to get really, really pissed off. These people have fucked with the wrong woman, right?" he says, trying his best to amp me up. But truthfully, he doesn't need to. Because underneath my shaky hands and my nervousness, I *am* pissed. I'm furious.

Those bastards not only destroyed my store, unhinged my life, tried to kill the man I love, terrified my friends, and put my baby in danger, but now… they've messed with my *mom?* Trading her around like some pawn, like she's a prisoner of war, just a commodity to be tossed back and forth between both sides?

Hell no.

Not *my* mom. We may not have the closest mother-daughter relationship in the world, but we're still family.

Back at the women's shelter, I saw all kinds of girls down on their luck, pushed aside, battered, whittled down, forgotten about. Nobody was going to look out for them but us. Nobody looked out for me there but my fellow women.

I know if Luca had been there, he would have protected me—but he hardly needed to. Those women saved me, built me back up after I thought I lost everything. If there's one thing my time at the shelter taught me, it's that women have to stick together, regardless of our differences.

And that includes my mom.

She's still the one who raised me, who helped me

become the woman I am today. She loves me, and I love her, and I'll be damned if I let the Cleaners hurt her.

Especially because they know exactly who she is. They know exactly where she came from.

Her family name used to mean something to these people.

They used to fear the Gaspari name. Her father—my grandfather—was a revered member of the community. Those same guys who are holding her captive now used to whisper among each other about how my mom was uptight. Frigid. Snobby. They thought she needed to be brought down a peg, taught a lesson.

Well, not today. For all her faults, my mother is not the cold bitch they think she is, and even if she was, who could blame her? Living in a man's world, surrounded by all these men, including her only family members, who treated her like a pet or a trading asset. I remember the way my dad used to talk about how all his buddies back in the day said he was crazy for marrying her, that she was too full of herself. Too uppity.

I remember what my dad said to me: "Show me a man who says he won't marry a strong-willed woman, and I'll show you a man who is too weak to deserve her in the first damn place."

She went on living and doing her thing long after my father died, after his debts came to light, after everything fell apart. She could have run away and hid, licked her wounds in the shadows.

But no.

She was too strong, too proud to give up that easily. My mother knew as well as I did what kinds of awful things they all said about her, about us. And she didn't let any of them drag her down. I will defend her until the end, because maybe the reason we don't get along very well is that we're just too alike. Two strong-willed women who fall in love with the only men who are strong enough to handle us.

I smile to myself.

"Don't worry, Mom. I'm on my way," I murmur.

After a while, we pull up to a truck stop wait out in the middle of nowhere. The street lights only flicker dimly, as though nobody really cares enough to fix them out here. As we turn down the gravel way, Luca flashes the headlights in the direction of a big truck waiting there. It flashes back at us. Go time.

"Here we go," Luca says quietly. He tugs the hat a little further down on his head. Two Cleaners in similar dark jackets and hats get out of the other truck and start walking our way. I slink down in the back seat, hiding myself from sight in the darkness. The last thing we need is for the Cleaners to recognize me and catch on to our ruse. I can hear their footsteps splashing through the puddles on the ground. My heart starts racing.

"Are you sure about this?" I ask, barely even loud enough to hear.

"Too late to back out now," Luca answers at the same volume.

"What are you going to do?"

"This will require... a delicate touch."

"What does that mean—"

Just then, the car door flings open and I hear two shots ring out with an earsplitting crack. Against my better judgment, I sit straight up and look around, desperately hoping the shots came from Luca and not from the Cleaners. Relief floods over me as I see Luca pointing his gun at a guy on the ground, cowering next to the man bleeding out beside him. Neither of them look mortally wounded, just shot in the legs to keep them still.

Without another moment of hesitation, I burst out of the car and start bolting toward the Cleaners' truck, hardly thinking about the concern that there might be more of them lying in wait just in case something goes wrong. I don't see anyone else around, so I quickly throw open the front cabin of the truck, take the keys from the ignition, and run to the back. With one hand still gripping the gun, I use my other hand to shakily put the key in the lock, throwing open the back of the truck. I point the gun into the darkness, just in case there might be another man waiting there to shoot me first.

Then I hear it—a scream from the darkness.

A woman's scream.

"Serena?!"

A human shape comes fumbling out of the dark cargo bed—the shape of my mother. She looks bedraggled and angry and a little shocked, but it's definitely her.

"Serena, is that a *gun?*" she gasps.

I can't help but burst out laughing, both relieved and amused by the ridiculousness of my mother's question. "Oh my god. Yes, Mom. This is a gun."

I help her out of the truck and, setting the gun down on the ground, throw my arms around her in the tightest, most genuine hug I've ever given her. "Mom, I'm so glad you're okay!" I cry.

"Oh, I'm okay. I could definitely use a bath, though. These filthy men have never seen a bar of soap in their lives, I bet," she scoffs, already back to her old self.

I kiss her on the cheek.

"Yeah, I think cleanliness is pretty low on their list of priorities, despite their name," I agree, laughing as I take her hand and lead her back around. She gasps again at the sight of the Cleaners on the ground, now being tied up together with rope, courtesy of Luca. He comes over and offers my mother his arm, which she hesitantly takes to lean on.

As we walk back to the car and get inside, she looks him up and down.

"So you're the man who's responsible for all this," she says coyly, gesturing toward my pregnant belly.

"Mom! He's also the man responsible for saving your ass," I retort.

She turns on me, her eyes flashing.

"You think I don't know what kind of man this is? I was married to the mafia! Hell, I was born into it just as you were! Serena, do you remember how often your father was away? How long we would wait for him to come home? How many days he would go out and not call? Maybe you don't remember—you were just a child. But I remember everything. I remember waiting up all night for him to come home, to call and let me know he was alive, at the very least."

She takes a deep breath, smoothing her hair back from her face.

"The point is, my dear, you must be careful. Both of you. I will not watch you struggle the way I have," she says to me emphatically. I step forward and take her arm gently.

"I know. And trust me, I have an entirely different life planned for us. For me and for the baby. Your grandchild isn't going to live in that world. I promise," I assure her.

Seemingly satisfied with my response, she turns back to Luca.

"And you! I can tell you're a capable man. But you have that look of danger about you. I know that look. Listen to me very carefully: this girl, my daughter, is my heart and soul. If you ever put her life in danger again, I will make sure you regret it for the rest of your life," she says, her prim and proper tone in direct opposition to the ferocity of her words. My jaw drops. I have never heard my mother speak that way.

Luca smiles good-naturedly.

"Yes, ma'am. I understand. Your daughter has changed my life. She's made me a far better man than I ever was before. I intend to spend the rest of my days protecting her and making her happy. Serena is my fiancée. And we would be married by now if not for… extenuating circumstances. I can assure you that is my top priority once everything gets sorted out," he says, the very pinnacle of courtesy and patience.

She stares at him with her eyes narrowed for a moment, then smiles approvingly. I release a breath I had no idea I was even holding.

"I like this one, Serena," she tells me with a wink. "However! I do not like the fact that you have come charging in here with a gun while you're carrying my grandchild! Serena, you should know better than that! What if something had happened? What if the gun misfired? What if you fell down and injured yourself? What if—"

"Yes, I know, I know. Trust me, I don't plan on making a habit of it," I assure her, helping her into the back seat of the car. She crosses her legs and folds her hands in her lap, looking every bit as dignified and ladylike as she always does, even considering her ragged, dirty clothes and tangled hair. She's missing one shoe, too, I notice. But I figure that is absolutely not the best thing to mention at the moment.

As we drive back onto the highway, Luca looks at her in the rearview mirror, like he did to me not even twenty minutes ago.

"Mrs. De Laurentis, I know this may seem like an odd question, but I have to ask: I don't suppose there's any chance you might know where we could find Don Abruzzi, is there?"

I turn and look at her, waiting for some kind of snappy response.

Instead, she sighs heavily and rolls her eyes. "Ricky

Abruzzi? I've known that little bastard since we were in grade school. I can tell you exactly where he lives. Hell, I can tell you things about that man you wouldn't believe."

Luca and I look at each other, smiling, as my mother tells us everything she knows.

DON ABRUZZI

"I assure you, it's real," I say, gesturing up to the lion's head mounted on my wall in one of the smoking rooms where some of my guests are lounging and drinking. "This one was from a hunt in Zimbabwe back in...I want to say '85? I was a younger man back then," I add with a laugh, and the handful of men looking at the trophy with me laugh politely with me.

We're about two hours into this little house party at one of my private homes outside the city, and it couldn't have come at a worse time.

The men standing around me, along with most of the guests, are some very important men of the Bronx. And in the next few weeks, they're going to become *the* most important men in the Bronx.

Most of them are men like me. Some of them come from other lesser mafia families that have been very reasonable in realizing that the Abruzzi family is the future of the Bronx. Some of them come from less organized parts of the city's underworld—there are the drug traffickers with their South American connections and taste for luxury and decadence, there are the smugglers who *deal with women,* and there are security contractors who provide mercenaries to men who need them.

Not everyone comes from that unsavory part of life, though. There are more than a few lawyers here, along with a few small-time local politicians, most of them already having mafia connections. Some of them are new faces, though.

There's an air of promise and a new future for my family in this house. It's a party I've been setting up for several months now, and it's going splendidly—which is why I *should* be having the time of my life.

Instead, an old thorn in my side is aggravating me.

Luca Lomaglio couldn't wait *one more week* to come back from the dead, could he? By the time I got word from my incompetent men that he was on his way back to New York, he must have already been halfway across the Atlantic. I hardly had time to get men looking for him before I got word the Costas had holed up in the fucking soap shop.

Once they're all dead, I'm going to have the place burned to the ground.

But business like that waits for no one, so I'm having to wait for status updates on a fucking firefight in the streets while entertaining the men who are going to rule the Bronx under me in the next few years.

"Come on, Don Abruzzi," says Mr. Giudici, one of the biggest meth kingpins in the neighborhood, "I'm sure hunting lions wasn't the only thing you spent time doing down in Zimbabwe."

"Certainly not," I say, flashing him a smile. "There's an ivory statuette I need to show you in the gallery, if you remind me—and of course, there are some other exquisite things Africa has to offer." I lower my voice, even though my wife is long dead and not around to hear me say, "And the women you can acquire are like nothing you've ever experienced." Amid the chuckles from the men, I add, "Except, of course, what our friend Mr. Ghardesca can offer." I give a polite gesture to the man himself, one of the last major human traffickers in New York.

"I hope not to prove you wrong, Don Abruzzi," says Mr. Ghardesca, raising his glass of wine to me, and the rest of us raise our glasses briefly.

"Quite so, quite so," I chuckle.

Then I hear someone clear his throat behind me, and somehow, I know it's going to be bad news.

"Yes?" I ask, peering over my shoulder to see one of my capos standing there, phone in hand. "Is this important, Tom?"

"Valentino needs you to give him a call," he leans in to say in a low enough tone that only I can hear him. "It's about the soap shop."

His face is glassy.

But I'm used to keeping myself composed, so I just turn to my guests and smile affably.

"Gentlemen, if you'll excuse me, I need to get some fresh air. In the meantime, Tom—get these good gentlemen a little food, it's been a bit since we've eaten. Some of the cigars too, and one for me when I get back."

"Yes, Don Abruzzi."

I take the burner phone from his hand and make my way out of the house into the back yard, and as soon as I'm out of sight of the other men, my jaw clenches.

I trudge down a little cobblestone path I had laid in my backyard leading down to a spacious gazebo that over-looks a large pond. It was one of the first things I had built when I bought this place, and it's become the place I go to when I need to make business calls. It's far enough from the house that nobody can hear me, and it's elegant enough that I don't look impolite as I would walking down the road out of sight.

I call Valentino, another one of my capos, and glare out onto the pond while I listen to the rings. He picks up almost immediately.

"Need this to be important, Val," I growl into the phone. "What's the situation at the soap shop?"

"That's the problem," his gruff voice says immediately. "Haven't gotten an update yet. Should be over by now."

My grip tightens on the phone, and I have to hold back the urge to hurl it into the pond and scream. I take a deep breath and try to focus myself.

"Do we have eyes on the ground over there?" I say, trying to get *some* intel out of him.

"Can't get a hold of anyone who hit the place," he says. "I've got men headed down there now to try to scope it out."

"They'd better have a fucking good reason for not checking in," I say pointedly, "and who the fuck was leading them? Jack, the Costa turncoat? Make sure that chickenshit isn't pulling anything stupid or I'll have his liver cut out, understand?"

There's silence for a few moments between us as I take a few breaths, pacing back and forth in the gazebo and wishing I had a cigarette in hand. Better yet, a little morphine.

"Luca Lomaglio was going to be at that soap shop, Val."

"Yes, boss."

"I need him dead, Val."

"Yes, boss."

"I'm done playing goddamn games with this," I say, rubbing my temple. "If they want to try to jerk us around, we jerk back. Execute Luisa De Laurentis, we don't need her anymore. I was gonna put a fucking bastard in her belly, but the bitch is probably too dried up down there to be of any use anyway."

Valentino doesn't reply.

"Val, don't you fucking get cold feet on me now," I say in a low hiss, careful not to look half as furious as I am from a distance, in case anyone's watching from the house. "If you don't do it, I'll come down there myself and personally put a bullet in the poor widow's goddamn heart right before I put one in yours."

"I can't get a hold of the men who have her, either," Valentino says in a muted tone.

My face goes pale.

One group not checking in is bad and could mean something *very* bad. But two groups going silent…

"Run that by me again, Val, I must be hard of hearing."

I hear a sigh from Val's end of the line, and I can almost see him running his hands through his hair nervously.

"We can't get a hold of anyone who's on the ground out there. I've already got men on the way to find out what's up with the De Laurentis widow, and-"

I hardly listen to everything else my capo rattles off to me. I'm leaning against the gazebo, rubbing my head as a throbbing headache starts blooming.

"Val?" I interrupt him after a few moments. "Listen very carefully. A hell of a lot depends on Luca Lomaglio being dead and Luisa De Laurentis on her way to being dead. You've made it very clear that things are not ideal right now," I say tersely, "but you're a competent man. I have my hands full with these other…gentlemen…at this party. So I'm giving you free reign to spend whatever you need to make this problem go away. You do this for me, maybe I'll let you have a turn with Serena De Laurentis before we ship her off to the Russians, or wherever the fuck Ghardesca sends his women."

"Understood, Don Abruzzi," Valentino says, swallowing hard. Before he can say anything else, I end the call.

Just a few more hours, and I can clear the house out and give this the attention it deserves, I think to myself as I march back up to the house.

When I open the back door and step inside, the smell of Sicilian black wine being poured greets me, and I feel just a little of the stress melt away. I greet a few more people on my way through the kitchen, all smiles and handshakes, like we're all old friends just watching out for each other, like none of the ugly business we carry out is right under the surface.

It's the game we play in the mafia. We hug, we kiss each other on the cheek, and my subordinates kiss my hand before doing what I want them to do to keep our pockets lined with money. I was born into it, and it's been going on for hundreds of years before me.

I'll be damned if some punk-ass carpenter from Taranto fucks that all up for me.

But first, I could use a few of the oxy pills I have in the bathroom upstairs. As I navigate the party guests, I smile and politely excuse myself on my way to the fine wooden stairs to the second floor.

None of the guests are up here, so it gives me a little quiet comfort. No sounds but my footsteps and the ticking grandfather clock in the hallway leading to the master bedroom.

I run my hand through my hair as I enter it, crossing the massive bedroom with its four-poster bed and entering the grand bathroom, tiled with white marble and big enough to be a spare room of its own.

At the mirror, I glance at my face before reaching for the orange bottle of pills on the shelf. I pop a few of them into my hand...and I pause.

The hairs on the back of my neck stand on end.

I slowly lift my eyes back to the mirror, and my whole body goes still.

In the reflection, I see the doorframe behind me leading back to the bedroom.

Standing in the doorway is Luca Lomaglio.

"Hello, Ricky," his deep voice rumbles. He looks like he just came from a fight, yet he's calm as a statue. And there's a silenced pistol in his hand.

Fuck.

Staring him in the eye through the mirror, I take the pills dry before setting my hands on the sink to hold myself up. I stare at him for a few long, hard moments before speaking.

"So sorry, Luca," I say, keeping my voice calm but not hiding my hatred for him. "Your invitation must have gotten lost in the mail."

"Actually, I'm Lusia De Laurentis's plus-one," he says, tilting his head to the side with a cocky smile. "Might've gotten lost getting here without her help. She and her daughter say hello."

My mouth twists into a grimace.

A hundred thoughts go through my head at once, and then they all settle. Everything feels still, except for a singular hatred in my heart for the man in the doorway and everything he's done to my beautiful empire. I'm still looking at him through the mirror, and I don't know if I could tear my eyes away if I tried.

"Not a bad play," I admit at last. "You made yourself a legend, snuffed out my lineage, got yourself fucking a fertile piece of old mafia royalty, and got me in the one place where the Abruzzi family will never recover from. Shit, what are you, thirty? Not even that old? You don't even know who half the fuckers downstairs are, do you?"

A sick laugh comes from my chest.

"You might not have finesse, but I know skill when I see it. You'll do well as don of your own family, Luca Lomaglio."

His face goes hard, and he narrows his eyes.

"Really? That's what you think this is about? You think I'm here to take your place and keep running this shit-show?" He shakes his head slowly. "I was raised by a carpenter. I grew up between one of the poorest towns in Italy and the poorest neighborhoods in NYC. I don't make *contacts*, Abruzzi, I make friends. I've made bonds that last. And we're all sick of this bullshit you're running. But most of all, you hurt the people I love, and you've hurt a lot more than that."

"You've gotta be kidding me," I laugh, turning around to face Luca. "Am I really about to get killed by someone who thinks he's doing good for the world? This isn't how we do things, you fucking boyscout. We do this because those of us who are better than the rest know how to handle ourselves. That could be you, but you're too fucking dense to see it. You think you're some kind of saint?"

"No," he says, cracking a smile, and he raises his pistol to my head. "A saint would let you live."

*B*oom!

The cork of the champagne bottle shoots up toward the ceiling, and Giovanni swears as he runs across the room to catch it, not spilling a drop of the bubbly liquid he just opened. Well, unless the foam gushing out the top counts.

"*Accidenti*, Giovanni, can't save it for the reception?" I shout at Giovanni in Italian as he catches the cork triumphantly, holding it up for the other groomsmen to see. "If you don't keep steady during the vows, I'll kick your ass."

We laugh, but honestly, I couldn't care less if he was trashed—this is the happiest day of my life, and nothing could change that.

I'm wearing a jet-black fitted tuxedo, minus the coat, and all the men are helping me get ready. Nico, my best man, is helping me with the bowtie in front of a large mirror.

"It's not for me," says Giovanni, "I've got a few bottles I'm gonna give out in glasses to the guests when they get here. Real fancy, I saw someone do it on TV."

Nico and I exchange a grin, and I catch sight of my dad chuckling behind me in the mirror.

"Well, what's one bottle among a few groomsmen? None for the groom, though—I've got a bottle of your mother's limoncello we're going to get into at the reception," he says, wagging a finger, and I grin at him.

My own wedding. I never thought I'd see this day in a million years, and I'm even more stunned that my parents are able to see it. My mom is off with Luisa fussing over Serena and helping her get ready.

The past few months have been a storm, though, and this may technically be the calm *after* the storm, the energy definitely hasn't settled down.

I killed Don Abruzzi that night. He wasn't the only monster in that household I dealt with that night, either. The whole of the Bronx's underworld took a massive hit thanks to me, and since then, the remnants of the Cleaners and their allies have been broken, weak, and driven into hiding.

Finally, definitively, the Cleaners are finished, and the last nail is in the Abruzzi coffin.

Abruzzi was right, too—if I wanted to, I could step into this power vacuum and become the most feared man in this side of New York.

But that's not me. It never has been, and it never will be. I've gotten a taste of what it means to have family, to risk losing it, the joy of building it. It won't be too long before I'll know what it's like to raise one with Serena.

The thought makes my heart swell.

"Careful, Dad, these Americans might not have as much restraint as you," I say as Nico finishes with my bowtie and pats me on the shoulder.

"Damn, Luca, you clean up alright," Nico admits, admiring the outfit as I do the same.

"Yeah yeah, you had your chance with me," I joke with

him, ribbing him in the side while he play-punches at me like we're a couple of boys fighting in the yard again.

My phone buzzes, and while I check it, my dad glances around at all the assembled men, some of them still getting their outfits ready while others like Giovanni...well, wander around making trouble.

I wouldn't have it any other way.

"Almost," I answer my dad after looking at my phone, grinning broadly. "Last one just showed up."

"Oh, another one of your friends?" he asks, and I nod for him to follow me.

"Someone you'll want to meet," I say, leading him to the door of the chapel. He follows me with a happy but confused face until I push the door open. When he looks down the steps of the chapel, he looks like he's about to faint.

Uncle Carlo climbs out of a cab, leaning on a cane and giving a mile-wide grin up to my father.

"...Carlo," my father breathes, his voice weak. "Carlo!" Hurrying as much as an older man can, he hobbles down the stairs as my uncle's grin breaks into warm laughter, and as soon as the two men are together, they throw their arms around each other in a warm hug, their voices breaking as they laugh.

"*Mio fratello!*" Carlo nearly sobs into his brother's arms, and the two begin talking to each other in rapid Italian in low tones, their eyes as full of tears as of emotions.

News of Carlo's recovery had been a huge relief to all of us, but when I heard my parents could make it, I wanted to make sure the reunion was worthwhile and I managed to avoid the subject of Carlo and keep the surprise.

I was a little worried the surprise would give my dad a heart attack, but the two of them are more hardy than I was worried. They almost look young again.

Nico appears at my side. "Damn, you don't see the resemblance until they're together again, huh?"

"I know. They've lived worlds apart for a long time. They'll have...a great deal to catch up on," I say, putting it lightly and flashing Nico a smile. "Come on, let's leave them to it. We've got a wedding to finish setting up."

~

*E*ven though it's barely a couple hours later, it feels like an eternity of waiting, but at last, everyone is gathered together and ready for the ceremony as the music starts.

All across the room, faces are glowing with anticipation. The sides could hardly look more different, too. On the one side are Serena's family and friends. Of course, because of everything that happened with her father, it's only her mother's family that's represented, but they're all there and looking beautiful. Dark skin and light hair seems to run in the family, and they could practically be cousins to the other side of the family. My southern Italian family is on the swarthy side, and good god, are there a lot of them.

There are cousins and second cousins and third cousins, many with their families, thanks to me being able to help some of them over. Turns out I even have a few distant relatives already in America who immigrated separately. The whole chapel is as Italian-American as it could be.

Then the doors open, and I'm genuinely struck dumb as the music starts.

Serena looks downright angelic. Her dress is a lovingly intricate pattern of lace at the top, and from the hips down the center of her legs, the pure-white fabric is smooth as fresh snow on a mountainside with two tresses of fluffier fabric down the sides of her legs like wispy clouds. Her beauty is ethereal, and the long golden hair curling down her shoulders is like a crown to it all.

But her face is what draws my attention. I've seen Serena's face through good times and bad times, lying beside her in bed and running from life-threatening danger. I've seen it weeping bitter tears, and I've seen it beaming with real, true happiness.

But when I look at it now, I see all that glowing bright in that one expression, bound up together. Of course, I can't help the stupid grin that crosses my face, and as she sees me, her face does the same.

Rafaela is her maid of honor, watching her approach proudly, and Nico on my side is nearly in tears. Luisa stands nearby, holding our newborn baby son, healthy and strong, who'll one day have the strength of his father and the courage and heart of his mother. Luisa's tears flow much more freely down her beaming smile.

I've heard some people say that watching your bride come down the aisle toward you is like seeing a new person, starting a new life with them as a new pair of people, building something from the ground up together.

With Serena coming toward me, I feel nothing like that.

I see the girl I fell in love with on that old construction site. I see the woman I reconnected with after what felt like a lifetime. I see the face that greeted me when I broke out of prison and endured so much without me. I see my lover, who fought to make it through a world that's been lined up against both of us since we were teenagers.

Soon, Serena is standing in front of me, her eyes wet with tears, and when I blink, I realize mine are too.

The minister doesn't even have to start speaking for us to know that we're already in this together forever—we always have been, through the good times and the easy times, and with all the worry and danger behind us at long last, nothing can shake that ever again.

We'll always be bound for life.

EPILOGUE - SERENA

TWO YEARS LATER

"Voglio giocare all'esterno," I say very slowly, sitting on the porch with my two-year-old standing wobbly on my lap. I've been trying to teach him Italian alongside English, to surprise Luca's family when they come to visit in the summer.

"Voglio... gio... Daddy!" Matteo sounds out, exploding into giggles at the end of his 'sentence' when Luca comes walking up the driveway, returning from delivering one of his latest carpentry creations. Matteo starts bouncing and wiggling, waving his arms excitedly as he always does when Luca comes home.

My husband looks exhausted but happy, his muscles showing through his white T-shirt, smudges of oil and grime on his clothing.

He's been working as a carpenter from home, building custom cabinets, armoires, sheds, even taking on jobs working on houses like he used to as a teenager. It's the kind of work he was made for—solitary, precise, intense. He knows how to take a customer's list of wants and needs and transform their dream into reality.

Luca is amazing at his job, getting customers from far

and wide to drive all the way out to our teeny tiny little town on the outskirts of Ithaca, New York, not too far from the cabin where we once hid out together. It seems so long ago that our lives were that way—scary, uncertain, always changing.

Nowadays, things are simple. We work with our hands —Luca builds things, I've turned Bathing Beauty into a lucrative online bath goods shop, shipping my luxurious creations all over the country. We grow things in our garden, using knowledge I picked up during my time at the women's shelter in Italy. Luca even built our house, almost entirely by himself, by hand.

Shortly before the baby was born, the house was finished, and we moved in just in time.

A week later, before all our boxes were even fully unpacked, Matteo was born healthy and huge. On the phone, Luca's mother did warn me that Luca was a heavy baby, but I guess I just never expected Matteo to turn out to be as big and strong as his father.

I'm grateful, though.

Matteo has his father's size and his beautiful green eyes, and he has my dark-blond hair and button nose. He's in his terrible twos right now, but if I'm being perfectly honest, he's about as far from terrible as it gets. He's a little rowdy sometimes, but when I think about how Luca apparently was as a young kid, it's no surprise that he would inherit those genes. I'm ready for it, though. All of it.

"How is my beautiful wife this afternoon?" Luca asks as he walks up and bends down to kiss me. Matteo blows raspberries, shaking his head at how gross his parents are.

"I'm wonderful. What did we do while you were gone… oh, yeah. We picked some tomatoes and we read a couple of books, didn't we, Matteo?"

Our son nods and reaches for Luca, who scoops him up and swings him around, making him laugh.

"Sounds like a great time," Luca says, kissing Matteo on the cheek.

"How did the delivery go? Did they love their new coffee table?" I ask, getting up to follow Luca into the house. He sets Matteo down in the living room and immediately the two-year-old goes running off down the hallway, yelling about how he's going to show us his favorite toy car. Never mind the fact that he's shown us this car every day for the past week.

Luca grins.

"They loved it. Mrs. Harris, you know the older lady who ordered it, she actually cried when she saw it. Can you believe that?"

"Well, you're very good."

"It's a coffee table," he says, laughing. "But as long as they're happy tears, I'm fine."

Just then, my phone buzzes in my pocket and I pull it out to read a message from Rafaela. I grin and type out a response.

"That Rafaela?" Luca asks.

"Yep. She said she switched some shifts around and got her patients covered, so she is for sure going to be available the whole week to come up and watch Matteo for us," I announce happily.

"Phew. Crisis averted. I doubt your mom would survive a week up here in the woods to watch him," Luca jokes. And he's right. I mean, she would suck it up and deal with it, but my mother is absolutely not the outdoorsy type. She'd be missing her bi-weekly manicure and constant French cuisine delivery very quickly.

"Aunt Raf?" Matteo chirps, suddenly toddling back into the kitchen.

I stifle a giggle. Matteo is honestly a little obsessed with his Aunt Raf. At first I was a little worried when Luca and I started planning this road trip across America, thinking

Matteo would feel left out. But I know once Rafaela gets here, he'll be so distracted playing with her and Nico that he'll hardly even notice we're gone.

And with all the hectic life changes of the past couple years—getting married, moving up to Ithaca, having Matteo, settling into our new jobs—we haven't had a chance to have a real romantic getaway, just the two of us. The timing is perfect, landing right around our anniversary, and even though it will be difficult being away from Matteo for a whole week, we're looking forward to it.

Besides, Rafaela has been begging us to let her babysit for longer than a day or two. She and Nico are trying to get pregnant, and they could use all the childcare practice they can get.

"Did you get the confirmation for our reservation at that fancy hotel in San Francisco?" I ask Luca, scooping Matteo up into my arms and booping him on the nose.

"Yes. They want to know what time we'll be checking in, but I'll email them with the details later," Luca says, opening the refrigerator and pulling out a bottle of wine. "So, what are we thinking for dinner? You feel like cooking or do you want me to pick up some pizza?"

"Hmm. I'll cook if you want to keep Matteo busy," I tell him, eyeing the bottle of wine. "Oh! I almost forgot: you'll never guess who I heard from today."

"Who?"

"Francesca!" I exclaim, still giddy with the news. "She said she's been doing really well. She finally moved out of that awful apartment and got a place down by the beach."

"Whoa, *e fantastico*," he says, genuinely impressed. Francesca's had some rough times trying to get settled, balancing being a single mother to her daughter, Luciana, and finding full-time work. But recently, she met a guy who's been treating her very well. I'm so happy for her.

"Yeah, she's still helping out with the shelter, of course.

She said everyone there is doing well, too, but they miss me," I add.

"Well, as soon as Matteo is big enough to handle such a major trip, we'll go visit. My parents are dying to have us stay with them again. I think they really just want my opinion on the new guy Domenica's been seeing, though," Luca says, chuckling. "One of these days, they'll understand that whatever Domenica wants, Domenica gets. She's just as stubborn as I am."

"Yeah, there's a lot of that going on in this family," I remark cheekily.

"Hmm. I'll never get tired of hearing that," he says.

"What?" I ask, reaching for the bottle to pour myself a glass of wine.

"*Family*. Sometimes I still can't believe how lucky I am," Luca explains. I set Matteo back down and walk over. Luca folds me in his arms and kisses me. Softly, but with passion.

"Me neither. It feels like a dream," I tell him, grinning.

"But better than a dream," he says. "Because it's real."

~

Thank you so much for reading! I hope you enjoyed this trilogy <3 If you have a moment, please leave a review. Other readers are dying to know what you thought.

I have plenty more bad boy romance for you, so make sure you check out my other books on the next couple of pages, and sign up for my newsletter to be notified when I have a new release on the way!

~Alexis Abbott

Romantic Suspense:

HITMEN SERIES:

Owned by the Hitman

Sold to the Hitman

Saved by the Hitman

Captive of the Hitman

Stolen from the Hitman

Hostage of the Hitman

Taken by the Hitman

The Hitman's Masquerade (Short Story)

HEARTBREAKERES MC (COMING 2019)

Breaker

Ironsides

Bones

Big Daddy

THE KILLER TRILOGY:

Book 1: Killer for Hire

Book 2: Killer Desire

Book 3: Killer on Fire

HOSTAGES:

Trafficked

Stealing Her

The Assassin's Heart

Killing For Her

Abducted

ABOUT THE AUTHOR

Alexis Abbott is a Wall Street Journal & USA Today best-selling author who writes about bad boys protecting their girls! Pick up her books today if you can't resist a bad boy who is a good man, and find yourself transported with super steamy sex, gritty suspense, and lots of romance.

She lives in beautiful St. John's, NL, Canada with her amazing husband.

facebook.com/abbottauthor

twitter.com/abbottauthor

instagram.com/alexisabbottauthor

bookbub.com/authors/alexis-abbott

pinterest.com/badboyromance

youtube.com/AlexisAbbott

ACKNOWLEDGMENTS

Thank you to my amazing Patrons. I'm constantly humbled and grateful for your support.

Ramona Cabrera
Melissa Hedrick
Virginia Swanson
Dawn Daughenbaugh
Don Doss
Stacie Currie

If you'd like to join them — and get my ebooks or paperbacks — you can find me here on Patreon.
https://www.patreon.com/alexisabbott